Judas, My Brother

Judas, My Brother

The Story of the Thirteenth Disciple

An Historical Novel
by

Frank Yerby

The Dial Press, Inc. New York

The following four quotations, two ancient, two modern, have been included only to serve as fair warning to the prospective reader. The author humbly beseeches anyone who is emotionally* dependent upon myth, legend, dogma, and creedal preconceptions, to close this novel quietly but firmly at this point. He also asks that no bookseller accept a buyer's money for *Judas, My Brother*, without having previously allowed him to read this page.

"Primus in orbe deus fecit timor."

PETRONIUS

"Tantum religio potuit suadere malorum."

LUCRETIUS

"My final reflection, I'm afraid, was that if hypocrisy can be said to be the homage vice pays to virtue, theology could be said to be a homage nonsense tries to pay to sense."

JAMES GOULD COZZENS

"I believe that man must learn to live without those consolations called religious, which his own intelligence must by now have told him belong to the childhood of race. . . . Man has only his own two feet to stand on, his human trinity to see him through: Reason, Courage, and Grace. And the first plus the second equals the third."

DON WANDERHOPE

---

* That anyone could be intellectually dependent upon them is, the writer confesses, beyond his capacity for credulity.—F.G.Y.

A Word to the Reader

This novel is a demythologized account of the beginnings of Christianity; and, therefore, I am sadly aware, sure to be labeled controversial. Actually, there is nothing controversial about it. The vast majority of scholars, especially those counting themselves among the Protestant branches of Christianity, have known for centuries that the origins of the Christian religion must have been very like the processes depicted in this book. Today, as the rumbles from Holland show, even enlightened Catholics are beginning to reexamine the issues, to free themselves from the mindcrushing weight of churchly dogma.

The research for this novel has occupied me for fully thirty years. It has twice taken me to Italy, Greece, Egypt, Jordan, and Israel. I have visited every place herein described, including the ruins of the caves where the Dead Sea Scrolls were found, and those of the Essene Monastery at Khirbet Qumrân. I have walked through the wilderness of Judea, passed over roads where, two hours before my arrival, Jordanian mines blew to bits a jeep carrying four Israeli soldiers; I have come under the muzzles of the guns pointing down from Mount Sinai, and across the Mandelbaum Gate, when the Israeli retaliatory raid on the Jordanian town of Samu, on November 13th, 1966 almost caused a preliminary to the June 1967 Arab/Israeli War. I mention this not to boast (I was as frightened as any normal human being would be under those circumstances) but to remind the reader that this work was written at considerable cost, and to ask him to take it as seriously as it is intended.

This novel touches upon only two issues which, in a certain sense, might be called controversial: Whether any man truly has the right to believe fanciful and childish nonsense; and whether any organization has the right to impose, by almost imperial fiat, belief in things that simply are not so. To me, irrationality is dangerous; perhaps *the* most dangerous force stalking through the world today. This novel, then, is one man's plea for an ecumenicism broad enough to include reasonable men; and his effort to defend his modest intellect from intolerable insult.

Beyond that, I hope that you, Reader, will find it also the rattling good tale I intended it to be; for, if you can put it down, whatever the value of its dialectics, I have failed the novelist's primary task.

FRANK G. YERBY

Madrid, Spain   *September 2nd, 1967*

Prologue

I   *"The Author to Theophilos:** Many writers have undertaken to draw up an account of the events that have happened among us, following the traditions handed down to us by the original eyewitnesses and servants of the Gospel. And so I, in my turn, your Excellency, as one who has gone over the whole course of these events in detail, have decided to write a connected narrative for you, so as to give you authentic knowledge about the matters of which you have been informed."

—THE GOSPEL ACCORDING TO SAINT LUKE,
CHAPTER I, VERSES 1–4.

II   Nathan bar Yehudah, to His Imaginary Excellency, Theophilos, Greetings! Or did you live perhaps, after all, despite that solemn pseudonym that the Saintly Physician Loukas gave you? *Theophilos*, by interpretation, *God Lover!* There are not many men that name would fit. . . .

"Yet almost I persuade myself that I knew you once, God Lover. Was it in Athens, where we listened to Sophist and Singer, heard the hypokritoi chant immortal lines, frequented flute girls and hetairai, drank deep of life, gamed our youth away? Or was it at Lesbos beside the wine-dark sea? Or at Ephesos where—

"I grow old. My mind wanders. Surely I only invented you, God Lover, as I've invented so many things: New myths for old, shining legends, grander lies—I know not. I do not know. . . .

"Still, the device is useful. I will copy the great fictioneer, mythmaker Loukas (Did he, himself, believe the fables that he wrote? Or did he merely intend that others should believe?) and call you Theophilos, Lover of God, imagine you a Christianos, address to you this narrative

---

* Theophilos (and not Theophilus, as most editions of the New Testament have it, since Loukas, a Greek-speaking Syrian, wrote in Greek, not in Latin) was almost surely imaginary. The name itself θ←ος, *God*, plus Φιλος, *friend, lover*, is suspect. By using it Loukas, Saint Luke, clearly intended to let his readers know that his dedication was a mere device whose real purpose was to explain to the general reader the author's subject matter.

written in your lovely, all but universal tongue. For herein, my imaginary friend, is truth unblemished, from one who witnessed your Lord Iesous' life, who called him not Master, but friend. I have lived too long to permit lies or to write them. I fear me it will distress you: To dreamers, Truth is an unlovely thing. . . .

"But who loves Truth loves God. For God is Truth—or nothing. Therefore to you, Theophilos, God Lover, Imaginary Friend, I dedicate this: my life, my book. . . .

Farewell, NATHAN."

Table of Contents

Book I

In which I belatedly learn the history of my family, the mystery surrounding my birth, become friend of a strange Galilean boy called Yeshu'a ha Notzri, and run away with a Roman centurion's daughter

Book II

In which I lose forever my beloved, return to Judea, take refuge among the Essenes, meet Yeshu'a again, and have my second encounter with Lucius Pontius Pilate, Procurator of Judea

Book III

In which I become entangled with the harlot Shelomith, and what was even less pardonable, Claudia Procula, the Procurator's wife, build an aqueduct, run afoul of the Zealots and witness a baptism

Book IV

In which I become more deeply involved in the affairs of Yeshu'a the Nazarene, witness some miracles, work two myself; and, at the cost of considerable hurt to my poor flesh, acquire myself a bride

Book V

In which I follow Yeshu'a ha Notzri up to Jerusalem

Book VI

In which I witness two trials, a crucifixion, and a resurrection

Notes

Book I

In which I belatedly learn the history of my family, the mystery surrounding my birth, become a friend of a strange Galilean boy called Yeshu'a ha Notzri, and run away with a Roman centurion's daughter.

Chapter I

MY UNCLE HEZRON's farm near Nazareth in Galilee is part of my childhood, in spite of the fact that I was born in Judea. You see, my uncle went up to Jerusalem to attend the wedding of his brother, Yehudah, to Eli-Sheba bath Boethus, a daughter of our greatest priestly house. And the impression that my uncle, Hezron ben Mattathiah, made upon the tiny, birdlike aristocratic maiden who two years later became my mother, was so great that had it not been surrounded by the religious aspects of awe and reverence, it might have troubled my father's sleep.

Anyhow, starting when I was eight years old, she sent me every blessed summer north to Galilee to bring me under the direct influence of so pious a man. Which, as I shall relate, had most disquieting consequences.

On the day that my history begins—for life commences not with birth, but with the onslaught of awareness—I remember climbing for hours away from the flatlands of my uncle's estate, up among the hills that encompassed it round about, coming breathless at last to the top of a slope, and sitting there lost and dreaming as the sun slanted across the camel humps of the little hills to the westward, and turned the waters of the *Mare Internum*,[1] the Great Sea, burnished silver like a shield, so bright I had to turn my eyes from them and cool my smarting gaze upon the soft green Valley of Jezreel to the south, crowned and surrounded by stark naked mountains, among them Moreh where our great Gideon fought, and those of Gilboa, where mighty and piteous Shaul was slain. To the east, I could see Mount Tabor, rounded, burnt brownish green with its scant forests; further east, in Transjordania, the mountains of Gilead, from which no balm ever came, jagged, tortured by the endless wind-driven scourings of desert sands; then south and west, angling my gaze behind a cupped hand across the sight-murdering glare of sun. I could see Mount Carmel falling wooded and green in long slopes to the Great Sea. A land, this, for prophets, for

dreamers; for, peering northward through pale violet haze to where
range after range followed one another, jagged, saw-toothed—the
mountains of Napthali, Harmon's white fang gnawing blue heaven,
and even, far off and unclear, the snow-glistened peaks of Lebanon
—the critical, questioning mind lay dormant, the faculty for doubt was
stilled.

But I couldn't see the low-lying Sea of Galilee—which isn't really a
sea at all, but only a lake—from there. The Tetrarch Philip, who, of all
Herod's sons, seemed most anxious to please the Romans, going so far
as to put the Imperator's image upon his coins (among us Idolatry, and
a terrible crime), called it Lake Tiberias. Despite him, in my childhood
we continued to call it Lake Gennesareth, which is its Aramaic name.
But, by whatever name you call it, surely it is the loveliest lake in
all the world.

Sitting there that fateful morning, gazing in the direction of the
lake I couldn't see, the feeling of being alive, of being aware, of perception, was in me so keenly that it hurt. And what I was chiefly aware
of were the contradictions with which my life was hedged about. Because, although I offered no resistance to being sent to Galilee, for, to
tell the truth, I loved to go, the fact remains that this alternation, this
perpetual tearing loose of my existence each time I felt myself firmly
rooted to a known, familiar world, did me, I am sure, permanent harm.

Of course, I could have survived, even mastered the aberration of
being a man of two countries, equally a son of the stony, sunbaked
majesty of Judea, awash with hard clarity always, perpetually athirst,
so that the heat boils one's brains within one's skull—which is why my
birthplace has always been so prodigal a producer of prophets and other
madmen—and a child of lovely, lyrical Galilee, green and fragrant,
whispering with waters, flowering with lilies, whose beauty so drowns
the senses that (except, of course, for a few princely families like mine!)
in all of memory nothing has ever come from there except the *amme
ha aretz*, those ignorant of the Law, dumb fishermen and peasants,
speaking an Aramaic that is an affliction to listen to, an offense to the
ear.

But being forced to divide my life between a devout, believing
P'rushite and a worldly, doubting Zadokite was too great a burden for
my childish mind to hear. For, by tugging at me now this way, now
that, my father and my uncle split my mind, my soul, the very essence
of my being, down the middle like a gutted fish.

You see, I loved them both. And there were no two more different
men in all the world. For my father, Yehudah ben Matthya (to give
our name its Aramaic spelling), was by nature a skeptic and a doubter;

while my Uncle Hezron lived and breathed pure faith. So, in a way, they were born Sadducee and Pharisee; because, to oversimplify, the Sadducees believe in almost nought but power, while the Pharisees have so fierce a faith that they almost lose sight of life and living; "Strain at a gnat and swallow a camel," which was what Yeshu'a said of them.

With my father, I read the Greek philosophers, learned to worship reason, logic, daringly to destroy all the premises upon which religious faith can be built. In my uncle's house, I kept all the feasts with a devotion that filled my soul with peace. Of course, we kept them at home, too; but something was missing. My father, it was true, performed the holy rites with consummate grace; but there was a twinkle of private, secret amusement in his eye. His glance, meeting mine, seemed to say: "For form's sake, son! But you and I see through all this superstitious nonsense, don't we?" And my young mind leaped to agree. What were *Rosh Hashanah, Yom Kippur, Bikkurim, Sukkoth, Shemini Atzereth,*² *Hanukkah, Purim, P'sach, Lag Ba'omer, Shavuoth, Tishah B'ab,* but the remnants of the sun-blasted mindless dreams of hawk-faced desert tribesmen, retreating into these mirages of the soul because their lives were so intolerably hard? Yet, in my uncle's house, they were high, holy, splendid things! I put on the skullcap and the *tallith,* bound the *tellifin* to my head and arm, prayed with utter devotion, total faith:

"*Shema Ysroël!* Hear, O Israel! The Lord is God! The Lord is One!"

But now, the need for certitude, for peace of mind, was in me like a blade. I stood up, muttering to myself: "I'll have it out with Uncle Hezron! I'll make him tell me! I've simply got to know!"

What this muttered disjointed phrase of mine referred to, what it was I needed to know, was a strange thing indeed: How it was that alone of all the great families of Israel, mine was the only house divided against itself, the sole princely clan in which two brothers were members of our nation's most bitterly opposed sects: The Zadokim, whom you call the Sadducees, and the P'rushim, by interpretation, Pharisees.

And if it seems odd to you that I had reached and passed Bar Mitzvah age without knowing anything of my family's history, you're right. It *was* odd. All my life, such knowledge had been withheld from me. Each time I'd asked about my ancestors, about how our princely family had come into existence, how our house had split apart, I'd been put off with: "Later, when you're older, Nathan—"

Well, I was old enough now! The Bar Mitzvah ceremony, celebrated at age thirteen, admits a Jewish boy to manhood; and I was almost a year past mine. So my uncle couldn't put me off any longer. I wouldn't let him. That we were the banim Matthya, the banim Matta-

thiah, a princely house, I knew; I'd heard my uncle boast that we were
the *only* family in all Galilee that was of pure, unmixed Jewish blood.
That we were rich and respected was evident: for my father to have
been able to marry a daughter of the House of Boethus, which had
held a monopoly on the high priesthood for more than a hundred
years, was proof of that. Why, then, all the mystery? I'll have it out! I
thought again; I'll know!

So thinking, I plunged down the slope toward my uncle's house.
By the time I'd reached it, I was out of breath, so I stood there until
I'd got my second wind. Then, because the Bar Mitzvah ceremony
had taught me neither the discretion nor the sense it was supposed to,
I bawled out like a yearling calf: "Uncle! Uncle! You've got to tell me
why—"

Then old Abigail, the oldest maidservant on the place, whose in-
curable habit of scandalmongering and gossipping about other people's
affairs had so tried my uncle's patience that he had been threatening
to put her off our place for years, came out of the house and glared at
me.

"Just what are you roaring about, young master?" she snapped. "Your
uncle's gone out. Fact is, this morning before you were even up, he
went down to Kafer Nahum to attend to some business—though what
kind it was he didn't say. . . ."

I could hear the disappointment in her tone. The old witch dearly
loved poking her long nose into things that didn't concern her. I half
turned away, then I whirled back again to face her. She'd been in our
family for forty years. Surely she'd know. And if she did, it was inconceivable that she could resist telling me, especially if there was anything disreputable about my family's history, which, from the way my
uncle and my father both had evaded recounting it, I was beginning
to suspect there was.

"Abigail—" I said. "How'd my family come to live here? In Galilee,
I mean? And what *were* they, anyhow: P'rushim or Zadokim? And
why's my father one sect, and my uncle another? Tell me!"

"Why you mannish boy!" she said. "It's none of your business, and—
and anyhow, you ask Rab Hezron. It's not my place to—"

"Abigail, please!" I wheedled.

She looked craftily around her. No one was near.

"If you tell Rab Hezron that I—" she muttered.

"I won't tell him! I swear it by the Ineffable Name!"

That's the most awful oath any Jew can take. I could see it shocked
her; but it also reassured her. And, anyhow, her delight in scandalmongering was too strong.

"All right," she said. "Sit here beside me, and I'll tell you. But if your uncle finds out I did, he'll put me off the place. . . ."

"He won't find out!" I said. "You've my word on that!"

"Well—" the old crone began, "your family didn't come here. They were always here—at least the female side, anyhow. Your first ancestress was named Bernice. Bernice ha Yochanan. Her husband was the Rabbi Yochanan bar Eleazer of Kafer Tepha . . ."

"Where's that?" I said. "I thought I knew every village in Galilee, but I never heard of Tepha."

"Of course not," Abigail said. "How could you? The Goyim burned it to the ground, with the good Rab and his five brothers in it. Them and every other grown man in the *kafer*. Saved the boys and the women, though. Took 'em with them, the lecherous swine. The good-looking young women, that is. Killed the old ugly ones like me. Cut their throats. Happened about a hundred and sixty years ago, give or take a year or two in either direction—"

I stared at her.

"Abigail," I said, "why'd the Goyim run off with the young women and the boys?"

The old witch let out a cackle of evil delight.

"Look at him!" she chuckled. "The pretty innocent! Nathan bar Yehudah, you don't mean to tell me that a fine, strapping lad your age doesn't know what a woman's for?"

I grinned at her. It so happened that I did know. A maidservant in my father's house had taught me the very morning after my Bar Mitzvah, while the whole household was sleeping off the effects of the celebration. And that plump and lascivious wench had repeated the lesson to our mutual satisfaction at every possible opportunity until my mother had caught us at it. Which was why I had been sent up to Galilee so far ahead of time this year.

"But—boys?" I said.

The cackle grew even shriller.

"Them Goyim was Greeks," she said, "and Syrians who'd been taught Greek ways for over two hundred years. To them don't make no difference; a boy's as good as a girl, long as he's young'n tender—"

I thought about that.

"That's an abomination," I said.

"What the Goyim do always is," she said. "Anyhow, they took your ancestress Bernice ha Yochanan along with the rest. She was the prettiest one of all, so—"

"Abigail," I said, "why aren't we called the banim Yochanan, then?"

"Adonai and Elohim bless the boy!" she said. "A mite too smart for his own good, appears to me! Because, young Master Nathan, those pig-eaters killed the good Rab on his wedding night, before he'd properly had time to get brats on poor Bernice—"

"Then—the—the Goyim—?" I said.

"No. You don't have a drop of heathen blood in your veins, my boy. What you've got may not be exactly lawful, but by the Archangel Michael and all the Heavenly Hosts, it's the best!"

"The best? The best how?" I said.

"I'm getting to that. That Bernice was a proud one, young master. She wasn't even starting to let them as had murdered the good Rab, her husband, have their sport of her—and even less putting up with bringing forth a whelp of such jackals' breed. So when those murdering swine made camp and the one who'd won her by lot tried to make use of her, she pretended to give in long enough to get her hands on his dagger. He was too busy slobbering over her and pawing at her to notice anything until she'd pushed his own blade up to the hilt in his greasy belly. Then she broke out of his tent, and made for the hills. Nobody stopped her. They was all too busy."

"Go on," I said.

"She lived in those wild hills a whole year," Abigail said, "fed by the merciful hand of God!"

"Abi—gail—" I said.

"Well, now, I guess she did sort of help the Almighty along," the old witch conceded. "There was berries and roots and such little creatures as she could catch in the traps she learned how to make soon enough. And she wasn't above borrowing a few ears of corn or even a lamb or two in the dark o' night from the Goyim farmers in the valleys. But the Good Lord *did* put those things in her way, now, didn't he? And, anyhow—"

"She lived. And found a second husband?" I said.

"Well, now—not exactly. In those days, there weren't many Jews in Galilee, anyhow. And what with the Goyim killing our people off night and day without letup, by the end of that year, there weren't more than two, three thousand left in the whole province. But somebody got word down to Jerusalem that if help wasn't sent very soon there wasn't going to be a single Jew left alive north of Samaria. So the Government ordered Shimeon ben Mattathiah up to save our race in Galilee. You know who the Hasmonæans were, don't you?"

"No," I said.

"That's what comes of being brought up in a Zadokim house!" Abigail snorted. "You mean to tell me you never heard of the Hammers of God?"

Then it hit me. Like all Sadducean children—since the Zadokim were the worldly, international party of Judaism—my education had been more Greek than Jewish. So the minute old Abigail said "the Hammers" I knew whom she meant; *ò Makkabaioi*, the Maccabees! Yohannan, Shimeon, Yehudah, Eleazar, Yonathan, the banim Mattathiah (for the word *Maccabees*, "hammers" in Greek, is not a name, but a description, earned them by their prowess, by the crushing blows they dealt our enemies in battle) or, as they're known to history, the Hasmonæans, after their grandfather, the Rabbi Hasmoniah of Modein. Names that will roll like drums, blast like trumpets down the long history of *Eretz Ysroël!* Who remade our land. Who gave it back to us, to the *amme kaddishe elyonim*, God's chosen people!

I stared at Abigail.

"Don't tell me I'm descended from them!" I said.

"That you are, lambie!" Abigail said. "That you are for a living fact!"

"But—but—" I spluttered, "why hasn't anybody told me this before? Seems to me Father and Uncle Hezron would be proud—"

"Oh they are!" Abigail cackled. "Fit to burst when they think of it. But I guess they found explaining *how* this branch of the family got started a mite hard to put into words fit for your tender ears. . . ."

"How did it?" I said.

"Shimeon ben Mattathiah, of course. Shimeon, the Hammer. Came up here and smote the heathen hip 'n thigh. Fine-looking young fellow, Shimeon. The best-looking one of the Maccabees, I'm told. And your ancestress Bernice saw him do it. She stood there on the edge of the woods and watched him cut the Goyim to bits. And she was inspired by God, she said, to go to him."

"I grant her that," I quipped, "but which god: Eros? Aphrodite? Priapus?"

"Who're they?" Abigail said, and my Hellenistic jest fell flat, rendered harmless by her ignorance.

"No matter," I said. "Get on with it, Abigail!"

"So, being a woman, she slipped down into the valley, and borrowed herself some fine raiment from a rich Gentile farm woman's wardrobe. Then she bathed all over in a mountain stream, put 'em on, and went into his camp."

"Didn't the sentries stop her?" I said.

"No. They were all worn out after the battle, and anyhow your ancestress had learned to move like a ghost by then. Only reason she was still alive and unravished a year after her husband's death. So she got to his tent, pushed open the flap and appeared before him like a vision—"

"And?" I said.

"He just sort of sat there. Then he opens his mouth and says, kind of groaning like: 'What would you of me, my girl? Name it, and 'tis yours, though it be my life!' "

"Then?" I croaked.

"She smiled at him. You've inherited that smile, young master. That's why you can charm a bird to your hand from the thin air! Your uncle gave me orders to keep the door to your bedchamber locked every night, he's caught the younger serving maids prowling round it of nights so many times now. . . ."

I am a sound sleeper, so I hadn't known that. But the news was pleasing to me. I vowed to sleep with one eye open and the key hid beneath my pillow from now on. But I didn't tell the old witch that.

"Rubbish!" I said. "Go on with your tale, Abi!"

"Bernice sort of moved up closer to him then, reached out her sweet little hand, and twined her fingers in his curly hair—"

"Then?" I gasped.

"She answered him: 'A thing small—or great, depending upon your point of view, my lord,' she said.

" 'Which is?' the great hero asked her."

"And?" I whispered.

" 'A son of your loins, Lion of Judea!' " is what your ancestress Bernice said to him then." Abigail chuckled. "And he was happy to oblige, I can tell you that! He gave her two, twin boys, they were; but I doubt that he ever knew it—"

"Why not?" I said.

"She was proud. Prouder than Lucifer and Satan put together. When she found out he already had a dozen wives and a score of concubines in Judea, she wasn't even starting to become a member of the herd! Told him, 'If you love me, you will put them by. . . .' "

"What did he say to that?" I said.

"Says he: 'But how, O Lioness who claws my heart to shreds, can I put by the mothers of my sons? Plump and loving wenches who—'

" 'Will give you calves,' says she. 'What else can cows drop? Or sheep? What more is foaled of ewes? Or mules, for when a stallion mounts a she-ass, the colts lack all virility. While I—'

" 'While you,' says he, 'will give me such screeching, spitting, bristling, biting, clawing devil-whelps as I'll have to keep chained to a wall! Still—'

" 'Still, what?' says she.

" 'You ask too much. You demand of me a thing I cannot in honor do—' "

"And?" I breathed.

"She kind of stood there, shivering a little. And there were tears in her eyes. But she wouldn't beg. Too proud. She just put out her hand to him.

"'My Lord has spoken. So be it, then. Farewell, O Lion of Judea!' she said."

"Then—then," I gasped, "you mean we—we're bastards?"

My uncle's voice blasted the noonday air apart.

"What's going on here?" he roared.

That day, after poor old Abigail had suffered the fate my uncle had been threatening her with these several years, that is, she'd been sent back to her native *kafer*, or village, pensioned off from our service— for despite his wrath, Uncle Hezron was far too kindhearted to let her starve—for her most terrible offense, my uncle called me to his study.

"Sit down, my boy," he said sadly.

"You—you're not angry at me, Uncle?" I said.

"No," he said. "Rather, if anything, I'm angry at myself, for not giving you an account of our history, for letting you hear that silly old legend from other lips—"

"Legend, Uncle?" I said.

"Legend," Uncle Hezron said firmly.

"Then it—it isn't true? We aren't Hasmonæans, Makkabaioi?" I said, my disappointment putting a lump in my throat; for to bear that glorious blood I'd have accepted bastardy seven times over. No, seventy times seven!

"I don't know," Uncle Hezron said. "No one does. Bernice ha Yochanan *was* our first definitely known female ancestor. And her second husband *was* a banim Mattathiah—by adoption. Which is where all that salacious mischief got started—"

I waited.

"His name, actually, was Demetrios. He was a Greek-speaking Syrian. . . ."

"Then," I whispered, "we're *not* of pure Jewish blood?"

"The difference between us and the Syrians, my boy," my uncle said, "is religion and language, not race. Can you tell a member of any one of the Semitic peoples from any other until he opens his mouth?"

"That's true," I said. "Still—"

"Still, he became a Jew. A good Jew, the best—for love of Bernice. She carried him by sheer force of her indomitable will up to the Holy City, where in the month of Shivan of that same year that Yehudah Maccabaeus annihilated the Syrians under Nicanor[3] Demetrios submitted to circumcision—proof enough of his love, it seems to me,

Nathan, for you can't even imagine how hideously painful that opera-
tion is for a grown man. He took the name *Mattathiyahu,* and was, all
evidences seem to indicate, formally adopted as a son by no less than
our hero and ruler Yehudah ben Mattathiah, or as your Hellenized
Zadokim scribblers call him, Ieudas ò Makkabaios, Judas Maccabee.
And that was what caused that scandalous legend to get started. . . .'"

"How so, Uncle?" I said.

"Well—you're old enough to know the facts of life, Nathan. Let us
say that our ancestress' morals were somewhat less than perfect. By
then, she'd already borne the first males of our line, the twins Yehudah
and Shimeon, out of wedlock—to, I believe, Demetrios. But here we
have our ruler Yehudah Maccabaeus adopting as his son a man he'd
never seen before, at the behest of a woman he'd never laid eyes on
earlier, either. Why? I don't know. No one does. That page has been
torn from our history, lost."

"So?" I whispered.

"Now everyone knew Yehudah had never so much as set foot in
Galilee—so the easiest explanation, that Bernice had been his concubine
there, was out. But—his brother Shimeon? Ha! The twins, aha! What
more substantial stuff does legend need? Our King Yehudah, legend
has it, was shown the twins by Bernice, and recognized them instantly
as his nephews, saw the astounding resemblance—though two-months-
old infants don't even look human, much less resemble anybody—to his
brother, was moved to provide them with an indirect legitimacy, and a
totally legal right to bear his brother's name, to be called banim Mattathiah, at least, if not Hasmonæans—"

"But, Uncle," I protested, "it could have been that way—"

"It could have. But we don't *know* it, Nathan. We are banim Mattathiah; and men of our line have covered that name with enough
glory to make the question of whether we are Maccabees by blood or
only by adoption irrelevant. What is certain, though, nephew, is that,
even attributing our origin to Demetrios—Matthew—we boast the
purest Jewish blood in all Galilee. Of that there is no slightest doubt."

"But how could that be?" I said, showing once more that in
skepticism at least I am my father's son. "There were at least three thousand Jews here when Shimeon came north to save our people, so I don't
see what makes our blood any purer than that of their descendants."

"The fact that Shimeon Maccabaeus bore them all back to safety in
Judea with him when he went,"[4] my uncle said, "save alone Bernice,
who wouldn't go. And since she couldn't find herself a Jew to marry,
she made herself one to the terrible hurt of poor Demetrios-
Mattathiyahu's male flesh. For it is a fact of history that when fifty-six

years later Shimeon Maccabaeus' grandson Yehudah, whom your
Zadokim scribes call Aristoboulos, arrived on the scene in Galilee, and
forced every manjack of the heathens occupying this province to submit to circumcision and become good Jews, he found a flourishing
family called the banim Matthya—which is what Galilean Aramaic
had corrupted our name to by then—all the males of which had been
circumcised at birth, and whose knowledge of and devotion to the Law,
far exceeded his own.[5]

"Impressed by their bearing, their beauty, and their arrogant pride,
and even more by the fact that upon reaching manhood they invariably
went down to Judea to procure themselves Jewish wives, refusing to
soil their flesh with the ever-so-willing Goyim females, he made them
rulers in the land; and it is from those times that our family's great
wealth, power, and position in Galilee date. . . .

"But enough of this tale, for now. It grows late. Take some of the
servants, Nathan, and gather in some passersby on the highroad, or else
we'll never have a *minyan* for the evening prayers. . . ."

Let me explain that. Among us, to properly say the morning, noon,
and evening prayers, we must gather together a quorum, called the
minyan, of at least ten males of over thirteen years. And since my
Uncle Hezron had never wed, had no sons, often we were hard put to
do it.

But now, as he gave me his usual command to gather in strangers
for the prayers—who, be it said, were glad to come, since he fed them
well afterward, and crossed their palms with a shekel or two—a mocking, mischievous thought entered my head.

"If Father hadn't seen Mama first," I quipped, "you'd have a
minyan of your own by now, wouldn't you, Uncle?"

He glared at me. The corners of his mouth went white amid the
darkness of his beard. I saw, with appalled remorse, that my playful
jest had struck home.

"Uncle, I'm sorry!" I began. "I didn't mean—"

"Oh, get out of here, Nathan!" Uncle Hezron said.

Chapter II

THAT COMMAND of my uncle's to gather in a *minyan* for the prayers was, it seems to me now, another reason why I count my history as beginning on that day. For the borrowed worshiper who completed the quorum was a ragged Galilean boy called Yeshu'a ben Yosef, or, if you will, Yeshu'a ha Notzri, Yeshu'a, Miriam's son.

It wasn't strange that I had never met him before. In what land that you know does the son of a princely house consort with a carpenter's barefoot brat? But I met him then, and from that hour—though I struggled fiercely enough to free myself from him, I can tell you that! —my life was inescapably linked with his. Was, and remains. For all the years I've lived since his cruel death have been but a lingering in his shadow. . . .

He was passing through our fields with his father—that was about a year before poor Yosef died—both of them heavily burdened with ox goads, yokes, even a ploughshare or two, that they'd made in their little shop in Nazareth, and now were lugging from farm to farm to sell to the landowners like my uncle. They hadn't had much luck that day. Their faces were gray with dust, pinched with hunger. I wrinkled up my aristocratic Zadokite nose at the smell of them.

"Come," I said to them, rather arrogantly, it seems to me now. "My uncle needs you for the prayers."

"Your uncle?" Yosef the carpenter said. "And who be your uncle, young master?"

"Hezron ben Matthya," I said. "These are his fields. You're trespassing, you know."

The boy looked at me. I could see anger kindle in his eyes. Nobody had told him that he was supposed to be the "meek and gentle" Yesu then.

"These fields are—God's!" he said in his thick, countrified Galilean accent. "And we're God's creatures, so they're permitted us. Even your uncle is but a servant of *ha Shaddai*, the Almighty! And you—"

"Yisu, please!" his father said.

At the sound of the carpenter's voice, the boy's face changed. Love, tenderness, devotion, invaded it. I saw then how he worshiped his father. No wonder his teachings were afterward filled with references to a father's love. But never to a mother's. I didn't know why, then. You see, I hadn't yet met Miriam.

"I'm sorry, Father," he said, and his voice became pure music, the quality of spring, bee-drone on a lazy day, a breeze moving among the lilies. I stood there, staring at him. Was I the first to feel that quality of his, that magic that made hardheaded tax gatherers, fishermen, peasants, even a Zealot, even that tormented soul, he of Kriyoth, lose their hearts to him, count the world well surrendered for his sake?

I felt it then, so strongly that I stared at him in astonishment. There wasn't anything remarkable about him, physically. He was a skinny thirteen-year-old boy, burnt teak-color by the sun, with inky black hair, rather frizzy, almost like an Ethiopian's, a characteristic, I found out later, he'd got from his mother. But his eyes were wonderful. Don't ask me to describe them. I can't. They bored into me, flaming one instant, tender the next. Feeling that gaze, I felt strange—I wanted him to—to love me. This skinny, sunburnt beggar! This lowly carpenter's son.

I put out my hand to him.

"My name is Nathan," I said. "Nathan bar Yehudah. What's yours?"

He put down his ox goads, the yoke he bore on one shoulder, wiped his grimy, sweaty paw on his tunic, took my hand.

"Yisu," he said, and smiled. And then, truly, as I never have since— except in a different way (was it, really?) when I met Helvetia—I lost my heart.

"Yisu?" I said. "But that's not—not—"

"A name? I know it isn't. Father, what am I called in Hebrew?"

"Yeshu'a," his father said.

I put an arm about his shoulder.

"Come, Yeshu'a," I said to him. "Let's go to the prayers. Afterward, we'll break bread together. You look hungry. Are you?"

"Yes," he said simply; "but then I'm used to it. The poor often are, you know."

I turned to my uncle's servants.

"Pick up their wares," I snapped. "Carry them to the house."

The servants were outraged, but they did it. They knew better than to offend me, who was the apple of my childless uncle's eye.

When we came into the house, my uncle greeted Yosef the carpenter kindly, called him by name,[1] took his hand, gave him the kiss of peace. For, Pharisee that he was, Uncle Hezron didn't scorn the *Amme ha aretz*, the unlettered ones, when they were as godly and pious as the carpenter was. Then he turned to the boy, laid his hand upon his head, murmured over him one of the middle thirteen strophes of the *tefillah*, or, as we call it now, the *Amidah*, since we recite it standing up.

"Welcome to my house, Yeshu'a my son," he began; then he stopped. "Elohim!" he said.

I stood there, jaw-dropped. For so pious a man as Uncle Hezron to say "Elohim!" which could be interpreted as "My God!" in such a tone, was close to blasphemy. We do not mouth the Names of the Almighty lightly as the Gentiles do. But now my uncle was staring from my face to Yeshu'a's and back again.

"Heaven bless us, good Yosef!" he said. "Look at them! As the Almighty reigns, they could be twins!"

Afterward, standing with Yeshu'a by a still pool in the garden, I saw that it was so. I was not as sunburnt, I was considerably fatter; my hair was maybe a shade less kinky; but, apart from that, line for line, our features were the same.

How was I to know then that in my life, and after his was over, that whimsical sport of jesting nature was to have its sad, ironic consequence?

In fact, it had a consequence of a sort that very day, for as I walked Yeshu'a to the gate to bid him goodbye, one of Uncle Hezron's hand-maidens saw us together and laughed aloud. Turning to another, and making no effort to lower her voice, she said: "Now I know why old woodchips Yosef almost put that sly Miriam by!"

"Why?" the other *almah* asked her.

"Young Master Yehudah was a wild one in his day," the wench chuckled, "and if you want proof of it—look at the two of them there!"

I brooded over that for days before I went with it to my uncle. But the fate of Abigail had taught me a tiny bit of discretion. I didn't tell him where I'd got the idea.

"Uncle," I blurted out, "could—could Yeshu'a and I be—half brothers?"

He glared at me.

"Now where did you get *that* one from?" he said.

"I—I thought it myself. We look so much alike. And—and Father's not as pious as you are—and—people say Yosef—"

"Almost put Miriam by. He did. Saw her talking to a Roman soldier—a legionary from the Sebastian Cohort, so naturally he spoke Aramaic since that cohort is raised in Samaria. That was shortly after Miriam and Yosef had been betrothed, but before they were married. Perfectly harmless conversation, a mite flirtatious, perhaps; but that old fool of a carpenter went wild with jealousy. Yosef's not too bright, you know. . . ."

"Then—Father—" I got out.

"Look, boy, your father left here three years before you were born, and never came back. Since, from what Yosef tells me—the resemblance between you two aroused my curiosity, I'll admit—you and Yeshu'a were born the same day in Iyar[2] of the same year, you in Jerusalem, and he in Nazareth, my brother, sinful rascal though he was, didn't and couldn't have sired both of you. No; Yeshu'a is Yosef's all right. He's far better looking, but they have the same port, the same gestures, the same—"

"Uncle," I interrupted him, "why'd my father leave Galilee? Oh, I know you were the elder, so that Grandpapa Mattathiah had to leave this place to you. But it seems to me—"

"That it was big enough for us both?" Uncle Hezron said. "It was. And for the Galilean *almahim* we'd both probably have married, and the sons we'd have sired. I pointed that out to Yehudah, but—"

"Did you quarrel, then?" I said.

"No. Not really. We discussed the matter amicably enough. But your father was already a Sopher of our P'rushim sect by then, and—"

"A scribe of the Pharisees!" I exclaimed. "But I thought—"

"That he was born a Zadokite? Hardly. There aren't any Sadducees to speak of outside of Jerusalem, itself. Surely you've noticed that—"

"I have," I said; "and I've often wondered why—"

"Because the Zadokim have no other interest in life save power," my uncle said dryly, "and where else could they exercise it?"

"I don't think my father loves power," I said.

"No. But he does love wealth and ease and being numbered among the great. That's why he married Eli-Sheba in the first place. Heavens knows her looks wouldn't account for it!"

"You don't find them ill!" I shot back at him.

He stared at me. Then he sighed.

"On the contrary, Nathan," he said gently. "I do. Eli-Sheba bath Shimeon Bœthus is your mother, and my sister-in-law, which is the fault of neither of us. But Sheol and Gehenna both take me if she's not a homely little thing!"

I bowed my head a little. What could I say to the strict, if unmerciful, truth?

"On the other hand," Uncle Hezron went on quietly, and I heard again the note of tenderness that almost always stole into his voice whenever he mentioned my mother, "I have never been able to see where a woman's looks were all that important. I have never met a sweeter, nicer, kinder, more lovable woman than your mother is. The only thing I have against her personal appearance is that, knowing my brother, it makes me doubt his motives for marrying her. But that's his business, not mine—"

"You'd make it your business, and Mother, too," I thought bitterly, "if Father weren't your brother. And you might forget even that if you saw her more often, which Elohim be thanked, you don't!'

But I didn't say that. I said: "But I still don't understand why Father left here—"

"A matter of temperament, mostly. Coupled with a desire to exercise his profession—"

"And yours," I pointed out.

"And mine. Only I didn't, and don't, have to make a living by the Law—"

Wait. Let me interrupt my uncle a moment to explain something you probably don't know. Among us, the Sopherim of the P'rushim, and those of the Zadokim, for that matter, are not as your translation of it—"scribes"—would imply, writers or copyists primarily, though they can and do fill both those posts, being—as they have to be—fully masters of the difficult art of writing our twin languages, Hebrew and Aramaic. Actually they are attorneys-at-law, trained from childhood in the thorny intricacies of our sacred code. So I understood at once what my uncle meant: To a trained, professional lawyer, sleepy, provincial Galilee, lovely and fertile though it was, afforded very little scope.

"But he didn't either," I said. "You just pointed that out a minute ago—"

"Only he wanted to," Uncle Hezron said. "Farming bored him to tears. Strange. I love it."

"So do I," I said.

"You do, don't you?" my uncle said. "It's the one comforting trait you have. Anyhow, nothing could persuade Yehudah to stay here and help me farm the place. So he went up to Jerusalem and—"

"Met and married my mother," I said.

"Not so fast!" Uncle Hezron said. "That was later. Much later. First he almost starved—Jerusalem is oversupplied with Sopherim, you know, my boy. Though few or none of them could have matched his skill, or his command of languages, notably Greek. The trouble was that they had the connections and he didn't, for although our family is one of Galilee's greatest, in Jerusalem we are all but unknown—"

"We wouldn't be, if you or Father would come right out and tell people we are Maccabees!" I said.

"Which would have been tantamount to suicide as long as Herod the Great lived," Uncle Hezron said dryly, "even setting aside for argument's sake the fact that we don't know whether we are or not. You

must know that that Idumæan dog killed every member of the
Hasmonæan family he could find for fear they might rally the people
against his entirely illegal rule. Now tell me: Do you really want to
hear this, or are you going to go on interrupting me every time I open
my mouth?"

"Sorry, Uncle Hezron," I said.

"All right. Now sit still and listen. Being much too stiff-necked to
call upon me for help, your father kept soul and body together—and
just barely at that—by working as a copyist of scrolls. He was just about
to give up, and come back home, when it reached his ear that Shimeon
ben Bœthus, the merchant prince—"

"My grandfather," I said happily.

"Still to be, at the time," my uncle said. "Anyhow, Yehudah learned
that ben Bœthus, owner of Jerusalem's richest counting house, was
looking for a secretary of certain qualifications and skills, all of which
your father possessed in almost limitless abundance. So Yehudah applied at once, thus proving that he'd never been a good P'rushite at
heart, and that he'd either forgot, or had scant respect for, our family's
glorious history!"

I stared owl-eyed at Uncle Hezron.

"Why, Uncle?" I said.

"To enter that house was a sin!" Uncle Hezron thundered. "Your
mother's family are titular heads of the Zadokim sect, my boy. In fact,
so great was their power even then, that to consolidate his position,
that Idumæan dog Herod felt it imperative to take a daughter of that
house to wife, marrying your maternal Grandaunt Mariamne—the second of his wives who bore that same given name—bath Bœthus, and
by her producing your weak and ineffectual kinsman Herod[3] who—"

"But I *know* all that, Uncle! What I don't understand is why you're
so hard on father, and on the Zadokim in general—"

"Because, Nathan," Uncle Hezron said, "the Zadokim were—and
would still be, if we'd let them get away with it!—the party of
Hellenization. They'd reduce us to imitation Greeks, make polytheists
of us—destroy our Holy Covenant with God! In fact, they'd have done
so by now, if your hypothetical ancestors, the Maccabees, hadn't prevented it, and if your actual ancestors hadn't died almost to the man to
keep us Jews!"

"I didn't know that," I whispered.

"I know you didn't. But it's high time you did, which is why I'm
telling you now. That Idumæan fox Herod—"

"That's another thing I've never understood," I said. "Everyone says
he was an Idumæan. Then how'd he ever get to be King of the Jews?"

"Because Shimeon Maccabaeus' great grandson Yonathan, whom your Zadokim scribes who've forgot Hebrew and have to write in Greek call Alexander Jannæus, made the mistake that doomed our nation: that is, he did in the south what his father Yehudah, whom you, little Zadokite, probably know as Aristoboulos, had done in the north, by which I mean he forcibly converted Idumæans to our faith. Now the Syrians and Greeks of Galilee, for all their faults, had a certain nobility about them; were, I might add, sufficiently civilized to make good Jews once a generation had passed, while the Idumæans were, and remain, barbaric swine. Anyhow, by this mistaken application of his father's policy in a land where that policy couldn't and didn't fit, Yonathan bar Yehudah made it possible for Antipater, and his sons Phaesal and—worst of all—Herod the Great, to appear upon our national scene as Jews. . . ."

"So that was it!" I said. "Uncle Hezron, tell me another thing: Why does Father hate even the name of Herod so? I understand why you would, because you're of the P'rushim. But father's a Zadokite, and King Herod favored the Zadokim, even took their daughters as wives, like my Grandaunt Mariamne. But every time anybody even mentions Herod's name, for all that he's dead now and his sons have no real power, Father calls down Heaven's curses upon it!"

Uncle Hezron smiled.

"Does he, now?" he said. "I'm glad of that, Nathan. Shows your father's heart is still in the right place! We—including you, nephew!—have cause enough to curse the name of that false Jew Herod. For, as soon as he had become Governor of Galilee under the Ethnarch, Yohannan Hyrcanus the Second, his first act was to capture the Zealot patriot Hezekiah and all his band, among whose chiefs were numbered three of your granduncles, and execute them out of hand. I don't have to tell you how outrageously unlawful that was! As a Sopher's son, you must know that only the Sanhedrin has the right to hand down the death sentence. Therefore that august body summoned Herod before them; but, instead of coming in mourning garb as the Law requires the accused to do, he appeared in the Chamber of Hewn Stone, where trials are held, clad in purple like a king, and surrounded by his soldiers, so overawing the Sanhedrin that they would have acquitted him at once had not the true and noble Pharisee Shemayah called them to account. They were, men say, preparing to convict him, when the then Governor of Syria, Sextus Cæsar, uncle of the great Caius Iulius, flatly ordered the weak and muddled Ethnarch, Yohannan Hyrcanus, to liberate him, and the murderer of your granduncles went free to drown all Israel in a sea of blood.[4]

"In fact the only reason *you're* sitting here before me now to plague me with questions is because your Grandfather Mattathiah, then twenty-six years old and the youngest of the family, was out scouting when Hezekiah and his band fell into Herod's trap. Through the agency of their heartbroken wives, whom Herod allowed to visit the condemned men in their cells, your granduncles, before they died, secretly got a verbal message out to him, a stern command that he, young Mattathiah, should keep to this farm, marry, get sons, and go forth to war no more lest the banim Matthya perish from the earth. But it was not until eight years later, when Herod, Idumæan jackal, fox, dog, swine, had already become Herod the Great, King of the Jews, that your grandsire, seeing how utterly hopeless further resistance had become, settled down here, married Sarah bath Pi'abi and produced first me and then your father.

"That's why I say that to enter Shimeon ben Bœthus' house as a secretary, as your father did—easily defeating the numerous candidates for that post by his perfect knowledge of the Law, his beautiful penmanship in Hebrew and Aramaic, and, most of all, by his flawless Greek—was to betray the very principles for which his fathers shed their blood; for, whether we are truly Maccabees or not, the fact remains that your granduncles died fighting Herod and the Hellenism he stood for, and your grandfather Mattathiah escaped sharing their fate by but the thickness of a single hair. . . ."

"I see—" I said sadly.

"Don't trouble your head about that aspect of the matter, boy," Uncle Hezron said. "Truth to tell, I don't think my brother even thought about all those ramifications: all he was concerned with was keeping his belly filled, and afterwards going up in life. And that poor, sweet, delicate monkey-faced child who became your mother was no obstacle to that program, you may be certain, nephew! My brother's a handsome devil, as you know, imposing as Satanas, himself—"

"And so are you, Uncle," I said.

"I'm big enough," Uncle Hezron said, "but that's as far as it goes. Your father's too fair-favored for his own good—and so are you, or you will be if you ever attain his stature—"

"I doubt I ever will," I said morosely.

"So do I. Your dwarfishness is your mother's fault and a tribute to your Bœthusian blood. A pity you didn't inherit her sweetness of temper instead! Anyhow, poor Eli told me her heart stopped still the first instant she saw my rascal of a brother; for half a year, she suffered the classic symptoms of all-devouring love: inexplicable tears, sleeplessness, loss of appetite. None of which moved that miserable old pirate of a grandfather of yours one jot—"

"Grandfather Bœthus was opposed?" I said. "Strange! He surely dotes on Father now!"

"He should," Uncle Hezron said. "Your father saved his life. I sometimes think that the only good thing Herod the Great ever did was making it possible for your father and mother to wed. And even that he did by accident—"

"Herod the Great made it possible—"

"For you to come into this world legally and legitimately at least, for I wouldn't put it past Yehudah to have waived the rules to further his ambitions. Only he didn't have to. Herod gave your father his chance by putting your grandfather's life in jeopardy, and thus affording my brother—who had the makings of an excellent brigand anyhow before he turned scribe—the opportunity to endear himself to Shimeon ben Bœthus by saving his life—"

"When did all this happen, Uncle?" I said.

"Two years before you were born. By that time, that loathsome monster Herod was more than seventy years of age, and rotting into death while yet he lived. He had murdered our supposed kinsman Aristoboulos the Third, the high priest, for no other reason than the Maccabean blood in his veins, executed Yoseph, his brother-in-law, husband of his own sister Shelomith—or should I Hellenize that into 'Salome' the way your Zadokim scribblers do?—had the aged Hyrcanus Second, another Hasmonæan and hence one of our hypothetical cousins, whom his own father Antipater had always liked and supported, slain; murdered, in a jealous rage, his first wife Mariamne, or rather the first of his two wives to bear that name, the one who was *not* your grandaunt, but who was of the Hasmonæan-Maccabean line; killed her mother, Shelom-Zion, whom the would-be Greeks call Alexandra, for plotting against him; had Costobar, his sister Shelomith's second husband, put to death for hiding and protecting the sons of Balas, who were reputed to have Maccabean blood, thereafter putting them to the sword as well; had his own sons by Mariamne the First, Alexander and Aristoboulos, strangled at Sebaste; and beheaded his dearly beloved son Antipater, his eldest, born of his very first wife, Doris —though he never counted her as such, having put her by—for plotting against him.

"This, Nathan, only within his own household! And you wonder that we didn't boast of our alleged Hasmonæan-Maccabean blood! Outside it, he executed the ten P'rushim who had plotted a revolt against him; slaughtered the old soldier Teron and three hundred of his fol-

lowers for daring to verbally defend the obvious innocence of
Alexander and Aristoboulos, his, Herod's, sons by Mariamne the First;
he had the two rabbin, Yehudah ben Sephoriah and Mattathiah ben
Margaloth, burned alive with numerous followers of theirs for daring
to tear down the golden eagle he'd fixed above the Temple gate in
defiance of all our laws; and, last of all, feeling his own death upon
him, he had members of every prominent family in Judea confined in
the arena at Jericho, there to be put to the sword the moment his death
should be announced, thus making sure that all Jewry should weep his
passing!

"Among the prisoners so confined was, of course, your maternal
grandfather, Shimeon ben Bœthus. At that news, your father immediately did what he could to procure his prospective father-in-law's release. He was busily engaged in counting up the not inconsiderable
amount of money he had gained by then by putting out the surplus
from his salary to usury, having learned that form of genteel highway
robbery from your old bandit of a grandfather, when your mother
still-to-be, driven by desperation into an unaccustomed boldness, came
to Yehudah's room to beg him to try to save her father's life.

"When she saw what he was doing, she said: 'You mean to bribe
the guards, Yehudah?'

" 'Yes, Eli,' your father told her.

"So she asked him how much he had and he told her that, too. Then
she said: 'That's not enough, Yehudah, dearest. Wait a minute, will
you?' and skipped from the room. When she came back she had all her
jewels with her. The moneys they produced, once sold, were enough
to bribe Herod's entire army, except that your father was not so great
a fool as to attempt that or even to offer the one sentry he approached
too much. For, as he knew well, had he made the bribe higher than a
reasonable sum, the man's suspicions and his greed would both have
been aroused, with perhaps fatal results. . . .

"No, my brother's bone-deep cynicism counseled him well that time.
He offered the armored swine far too little, and allowed the man to
raise the amount by haggling to a sum actually quite modest, considering the prisoner's enormous wealth, but, naturally, at the same time,
beyond any Idumæan desert hawk's wildest dreams of avarice. The
money paid—one half down, the other to be delivered upon your grandfather's reaching safety—your father, hiding beneath his cloak a long
rope knotted at halfrod intervals to provide your grandsire a better grip,
was secretly admitted into the arena by the guard.

"But, in the end, Yehudah was forced to display our alleged Maccabean blood; for by accident—or more likely by design, almost surely

sent by the greedy Idumæan dog of a sentry to raise the price of delivery—another sentry came upon them just as Yehudah was preparing to lower your mother's father to the ground. The second sentry's mistake was major, and the last he ever made. Your father killed him with a poniard thrust to the base of the throat, the hard-driven blade itself shutting off the escape of breath that would have made audible his stuck pig's dying screech. Then, very calmly, my scribe-turned-brigand of a brother tied the rope around Shimeon ben Bœthus' waist —and lowered him who was to become your maternal grandfather to the ground."

"How'd he get down himself?" I demanded. "Did he jump?"

"No. He'd have broken his neck if he'd tried that. He merely tied the rope to one of the ornamental pillars of the arena's upper tiers, and came down it himself, hand over hand. Then he helped your grandfather up on one of the two horses he'd brought and bore him away to Jerusalem—"

Uncle Hezron stopped and let out a throaty chuckle.

"The ironic part about it," he said, "was that your father risked his life needlessly!"

"Needlessly!" I gasped. "But you said—"

"That he saved your grandfather. He did. The irony lies, Nathan, my son, in the fact that he didn't need to. For, a few days later, when Herod died, his sister Shelomith and her third husband Alexas mercifully disobeyed the orders Herod had given them before his death and freed all the prisoners without executing anyone at all.[5] So all your father would have had to do was to wait, and he'd have saved himself much danger and trouble, and his betrothed her jewels. Only he didn't know that—"

"And Grandfather?" I said.

"Realized that the bravery of the deed, and the risks involved remained undiminished by the unexpected end to the affair that Shelom and her husband provided. So he gave Eli-Sheba in marriage to your father, thus raising my rascal of a brother to the pinnacle of wealth, power, and fame in Jerusalem, and assuring him in the continuance of all these privileges by making him his heir."

My uncle stopped again, and grinned at me, mockingly.

"The end result of all these great and terrible events was, of course, you. Which is to say the mountain labored to bring forth—a mouse!"

"Oh, Uncle Hezron! What a mean thing to say!" I cried. Then, finally, it occurred to me that I hadn't asked him the principal thing I wanted to know, which was why my family's history, which now, in retrospect, seemed to me not only honorable but even glorious, had been so carefully concealed from me. So I asked him that.

"Because, until you were eight years old," Uncle Hezron said, "Archelaus, by long odds the worst of Herod's sons, was Tetrarch of Judea. He'd have been only too happy to have your father crucified or worse, in order to confiscate the Bœthus' fortune. And by killing that sentry, Yehudah had given him excuse enough. Only, in the confusion after Herod's death, your grandfather's escape and the death of the sentry went all but unnoticed. Still, you can understand why your father couldn't afford the risk of having it brought to the attention of Archelaus' spies by one of your little friends repeating your childish prattle before the wrong ears—"

"I couldn't talk about what I didn't know; I see that," I said. "But after I was eight years old?"

"Archelaus was called to Rome by Augustus and exiled to Gaul on the basis of complaints made by Jews and Samaritans both. Then Judea was made a part of the Roman province of Syria and placed under the procurators.[6] But no sooner had that particular danger vanished than the Governor of Syria Quirinius started in to take a census of the nation for the purpose of taxation. So Yehudah of Gamela and Saddock the Pharisee led a revolt against the Romans. Your father sent you up here to me to keep you safe. You were just eight years old at the time. Funny thing, Yosef the carpenter was talking about that revolt the other day while you were out playing with his son Yeshu'a. Seems he took Yeshu'a, who was also eight years old at the time, and the other children and hid in a cave in the hills above Nazareth to avoid being registered. . . . Anyhow, with the country in perpetual uproar and the procurators becoming more arrogant every year—Quirinius deposed your granduncle Joazer ben Bœthus from the high priesthood that very year, you know—I suppose keeping their mouths shut had got to be a habit with your parents. . . ."[7]

"But—but the rest of it!" I protested. "My granduncles, our descent from the Maccabees—why wasn't I told all that?"

My uncle smiled at me a little wearily.

"Because Yehudah hadn't—and so far as I know, hasn't even yet—told Eli-Sheba that decidedly murky history, Nathan. Don't blame him. A man who tells his wife that three of his uncles were decapitated as brigands, and that his family probably got started by a remote ancestress crawling into another woman's husband's bed is a fool. And whatever else he may be, your father is not a fool. Speaking of which, I'd strongly suggest—"

"What, Uncle?" I said.

"That you don't be one either. What your mother doesn't know won't hurt her," my Uncle Hezron said.

Chapter III

I SELDOM saw Yeshu'a after that day. He preferred to be alone. He had dreams to dream, plans to make; he had to prepare himself to move and shake the world. Once I found him atop a high hill, staring sightlessly in the direction of Mount Tabor.

"Yisu—" I said to him; for I, too, had learned to call him what the Galileans did, their corruption of the Aramaic short form *Yesu*, for Yeshu'a. But he didn't answer me. I called him two or three more times. He sat there, dreaming. I could see his lips move.

"*Abba*—" he whispered. "Father—"

I was frightened then. For all my skepticism, I let the thought that a demon had entered him cross my mind. I shook him, hard.

"Yisu!" I said.

His eyes cleared. He stared at me with sorrowful anger.

"Leave me alone, Nathan," he said. "I'm talking to my Father—"

"But—but, Yeshu'a! Your father isn't here! We're alone! We—"

He looked at me, and the sorrow at my incomprehension that showed in his eyes deepened, became actual pain.

"We're never alone, Nathan," he said gravely. "My Father is always here. Always. Wherever his children are. Wait for me down below. What he has to tell me is not for other ears—"

I turned then and went down the slope. It was practically impossible to disobey him, even then. As I loped downward, I met the woman coming up it. She was as broad as the earth, as dark, as fecund. She toiled upward past me, her lined, heavy face twisted with worry, sorrow. With something close to anguish, even. Then she saw him.

"Yisu!" she cried out, and her voice was a temple gong, bronze-toned, almost golden. "Oh Yisu, my son, my son!"

He didn't answer her. He went on with his dialogue with nothing.

"Yisu!" she wept. "Oh, Heavenly Father, you who look upon so small a thing as *tzaar baale hayyim,* the distress of animals, what have I done that you take away my firstborn's wits?"

He turned his eyes upon her. They were cold with contempt. That was one of the many ironies of his life. He and Miriam never got along. Never. And now they confuse her with Isis, make her—but, no; I go too fast.

"Leave me, Mother," he said quietly. "I am talking to my Father. . . ."

She hung there, her big body rigid with shock.

"Your father!" she said. "Your father is at home, worn-out and sick, working to support us, including you, you idler! Yaakob does all he can to help him, but he hasn't your skill; Yose, Shimeon, and Yehudah are too little yet; the girls of no use, a burden; and you—"

"And I—am here. Talking with my Father. My real Father who has other concerns beside ox goads and ploughshares. Leave me, Mother. I must be about my Father's business. Don't ask me what it is. You wouldn't understand. It—it isn't of this world. . . ."

She started to scream at him, then, to berate him; but he had closed his ears to her, as he had long since closed his mind, his heart. I didn't want to hear it, so I went on down the hill. But I've often wondered if Yeshu'a's unbending harshness toward the sins of the flesh was not born of the wall of mutual incomprehension between him and his mother. I loved mine past all bearing as a child; so, when I was of age, that love extended itself easily and passionately to other members of her sex. Yeshu'a was kind to women—but only because he hadn't it in him to be unkind to any living creature for very long—and they adored him, especially the mind-sick ones like Miriam of Migdal-Nunaya, that howling madwoman from the lovely lakeshore town which the Romans, with their constitutional incapacity for getting our names right, call Magdala; but he never loved a woman; never. I'd swear he went innocent of female flesh, down to his very grave.

No love is innocent. There does not exist a relation between man and woman that does not have its deep hidden, graying ember of carnality, stubbornly aglow. Not even my love for my mother. There is no friendship between man and man that does not have its twisted skein of unknowing, unacknowledged, perverted love. Not even my love/hate for Yeshu'a.

I write both these things with no intent to shock. I am trying to set down truth. And that is very hard.

For on the day I sailed away to Athens to begin my studies there, my Uncle Hezron came down to the port of Joppa to see me off. Naturally, my mother and my father both were there. My father was full of fun, making his sly little jokes, begging my uncle to say a special long-faced P'rushim prayer that I should not fall prey to Aphrodite.

My uncle muttered something into his bushy beard. Then he saw how my mother was weeping.

"Don't cry, Eli-Sheba," he murmured; and, reaching out, took her hand.

A look flashed between them. That was all.

But if at that moment I had had a blade, I would have plunged it through my uncle's heart.

The result of my youthful jealousy was disastrous: it tipped the scales in favor of my father's influence over me. I cursed my Uncle Hezron in my heart, called him pious hypocrite, would-be betrayer of his brother. Would-be. Because even then I was not fool enough to believe he'd tried to seduce my mother; or that he ever would.

"Of course," I told myself, "she'd send him packing if—"

But then I remembered her answering look, and my insides came apart. Fool! What I've arrived at since only lends splendor to them both. What other man and woman have I ever known who could or would have done what my mother and my uncle did, which was to suffer lifelong a great and terrible love, and honor God and themselves by quietly keeping to their separate ways?

In Athens I ran wild.

I came back a polished, perfect Hellenized Jew, which is the type form, description, and epitome of bastardy. Has not Saul/Paul of Tarsus proved that, fully? Did I learn anything of importance there? Little. From the hetairai, to be bold with women. To chatter away in easy, fluent Greek. From my Roman classmates, a reasonable command over Latin. Strange—it was the Latin that served me best of all.

And, upon my return, instead of passing the summer as usual at my uncle's house, I took up my abode at Tiberias, the capital that Herod Antipas had built near the warm springs of Emmaus on the western bank of Lake Gennesareth, surely the loveliest spot in all Galilee.

I chose that city out of pure, gleeful malice, knowing it was the one place on earth where my pious, God-fearing Uncle Hezron could never visit me. For, while the excavations were being made to lay the foundations of the beautiful Grecian temples and official buildings that Antipas caused to be erected there, the spades of the slaves turned up so many human bones that it immediately became apparent the spot was the site of an ancient necropolis, or cemetery.

Which meant that no pious Jew could live there, or even enter the city.[1] For merely by setting foot upon such ground, he became ritually unclean.

Antipas, therefore, had been forced to gather in a rabble of foreigners, and such Jews as could be induced, or forced, to take residence in his capital. Naturally, under such circumstances, the Jews of Tiberias were the dregs and scum of our race; in fact, they were even worse than the foreigners; and that, in Tiberias, required some small effort, shall we say?

But, as for me, as for the lecherous, drunken little imitation Hellene I'd become by then, Tiberias suited me perfectly. In a way, it prepared me for Rome, since several Roman ladies, wives of the Procurator's officers, bored with Cæsarea, or rather, tired of the reasonable degree of circumspection they had to maintain there, flocked to Tiberias that spring, on the pretext of taking the curative waters at nearby Emmaus.

Before then, I'd believed that women submitted their bodies to their husbands and their lovers, out of love, a desire to have children, duty, a simple, goodhearted willingness to please their men. I had never before, not even in Athens, where even the hetairai make a great show of modesty, met women who were rutting bitches in eternal heat, which was what those patrician matrons were.

I've often wondered why. It is not a normal thing. Now and again, among us, as among all races, you find a woman who is a prey to the demon, or the sickness of lust. But it *is* a sickness. And very rare. I think nature protects women from perpetual pregnancy by making them slow to passion, requiring more patience and more art to kindle than the average man can summon up. But, among the Roman dames, that sickness was epidemic. I think now that it was but a symptom of the wrath soon to fall upon that impious race. Whom the gods would destroy, they first make mad. . . .

I was not uncomely. In Tiberias, I had a different adulterous bedfellow almost every night. Which, as I said before, prepared me for Rome.

What it didn't prepare me for was—

Helvetia.

I have told you that no pious Jew could enter Tiberias because Antipas had defied one of our sternest laws by building it above a necropolis, a city of the dead. But there was one who could, because his piety was not of the Law, because it stood above and beyond any law, and hence nothing could profane it. I mean, of course, my brother, my friend, my dearest love, my cruelest foe, Yeshu'a ben Yosef, called ha Notzri.

He came into my lodgings at the worst of all possible moments, for
that night I was entertaining a group of my swinish friends in Roman
fashion, which is to say, most swinishly.

Yeshu'a stood there in the doorway and his nostrils twitched with
pure disgust. His gaze swept over the entwined naked forms close-
coupled—in many cases without due regard for natural gender—on the
benches, on the floor, across the banquet table itself, and returned to
my face. I wasn't, at the moment, participating in the general rut. Instead, with vine leaves in my hair, I was plucking insanely at my lyre
and chanting a *skolia,* a drinking song of my own composition, whose
lightest, least offensive word would have caused my Uncle Hezron to
wash my mouth out with wood ashes and slaked lime.

"Nathan," he said, and my soul shriveled up within me. I followed
him out into the night. We walked together along the lakeshore, northward in the direction of Migdal-Nunaya.

He didn't say anything to me, not anything at all. He didn't have to.
It wasn't even necessary. Just his being there was enough. To my
reeling, drunken mind, all the stars of heaven gathered above his head
and shed a soft radiance over him. It seemed to me his face—so like,
and so different from my own—glowed in the darkness. And the sadness in it was a reproach past all bearing, making words useless, a
reduction of meaning, a hurtful cacophony that nonetheless I had to
resort to in order to break through the crushing weight, the intensely
painful flagellation of his silence.

"Yeshu'a!" I babbled. "I—" Then the brine and bile in my throat, a
whole Dead Sea of stinging salt behind my eyes, both choked and
blinded me.

Yeshu'a turned to me then, put out his strong, sun-browned, work-
hardened hand, let it rest upon my shoulder.

"Go and sin no more, Nathan," he said.

That was all. Then he was gone. I don't know when, or even how,
he left me. It seemed to my drink-dulled senses that the stars went out,
winked out one by one in awful silence, and that the night opened up
and swallowed him. I remember that I was crying: "O Yeshu'a, Yesu,
Yisu!"

Then nothing. Nothing at all. Neither time nor place nor even tears.

An instant later, I was lying on the beach, lapped by soft and
fragrant waters and the sun was in my eyes like a host of red-hot
spears.

I got up from there and staggered home. My guests were all fast
asleep, still limb-entwined. The whole place smelled like a *lupanar,* a

brothel. It stunk of carnality, of rut, with certain coprolatic variations
produced by the activities of the sodomites. I went back into the streets,
the nausea, the disgust in me bottomless. I wandered about Tiberias
all day. When I came home at dusk, they'd gone.

How long did my mood of repentance last? Four days, I'd say. Perhaps a week. No more. Because, you see, he hadn't begun his mission
then, and to elevate me out of swinehood into virtue, he would have
had to command me to leave all else and follow him. I should have
done it, of course. Without question and at once, as all those to whom
he afterward gave that order did.

But I do think that I never really recovered my taste for, and delight
in, debauchery after that. My sins took on the curious perversity of
being in themselves a kind of punishment, since now I had almost to
force myself into them in my wild, blind, stupid efforts to do what I,
who have now lived close to ninety years, know beyond all questioning
is impossible: to escape him. To flee Yeshu'a, the Nazarene. To do that,
I shall have to die. And even then, I wonder. . . .

And I believe it was precisely my fear of him—no, not of *him*,
exactly, but rather of that high and terrible road along which, I dimly
perceived, he was already beckoning to me to follow him; that stony
path which wound dizzily up among the lofty peaks of purity, of virtue,
to plunge at the last into the dark valley of self-sacrifice—that made the
very thought of having to leave Tiberias send a shudder of terror
through me.

Because I was soon going to have to depart that capital of perfumed
vice, the hometown of every variety of perversion that diseased imagination can invent, for the simplest of all possible reasons: My father, at
the urging of Uncle Hezron, had cut off my allowance in order to
force me to return to either one of my two homes. Which meant I'd
have to settle down as a gentleman farmer upon my uncle's place, or
go to work in my grandfather's countinghouse in Jerusalem. Neither
prospect pleased me, not so much because of the work involved—I have
never really been lazy—but because of the stern supervision of my
personal life I'd be obliged to submit to.

I was almost down to my last denarius when a means of escape was
offered me. The Tetrarch, Herod Antipas, announced a series of games
in honor of both his Imperial Patron, Tiberius Cæsar, and the goddess
Flora Primavera, she who rules the spring, to be held in the local
stadium.

Now I have always been fleet of foot, largely because my small
stature made running away the only course open to me, since all the
boys of my age were far bigger and stronger than I was, thus affording

me much practice and a convincing motive for excelling at footracing. So I entered my name as a competitor in the long race, and desperately started in to train away the torpor and the fat my slothful, lecherous existence had inflicted upon me. It wasn't the prize that interested me, really; for it was far too small to solve my economic problems, but rather the tremendous amount of money I could win through bets judiciously placed, through agents, of course, and secretly, upon the outcome of that race. The only trouble was that I could never hope to cover them if I lost, and therefore risked being sold into slavery if my father or my uncle failed to come to my rescue in such unhappy case. . . .

Wait, let me put this in its proper perspective. The long race wasn't the main event. The chariot races, scheduled for the next day, were. But that unsavory collection of degenerates and swine who were Tiberias' citizens would bet on which leg a dog would hoist to wet a tree, so the importance of the event didn't matter. By the evening before the start of the games, there was almost as much money riding on my close-cropped pate as there was upon Markos, the leading charioteer for the Greens.

And I—I played it cunningly; I let myself be seen in my usual haunts, swilling wine, gay, laughing, pinching every patrician female rump I passed. But that wine had been on my secret orders watered until the color was almost gone; I slept long hours during the day, added a stade to the distance I ran each dawn, lived, while seeming not to, the life of an Essene monk.

My competitors were utterly deceived. They didn't train at all.

When I turned into the last lap, I wasn't even breathing hard. Looking back over my shoulder, I saw Yohannan bar Talmay, a few paces behind me. He was covered with sweat, and his face was distorted with pain. I looked down and saw why: the fool, who always called himself Iohannus Bartolomaeus, had had himself operated upon to restore some semblance of a foreskin, so that the spectators would not ask him why he, who swore by the whole Pantheon of pagan gods he was no Jew, had, in fact, been circumcised. He'd remembered too late that we ran stark naked; the half-healed surgery had burst, a stream of blood covered his muscular thighs.

The laughter that tore me caused me to miss my stride. Despite his pain he overtook me, came abreast. I paced myself, let him draw ahead. Then, twenty paces or less from the goal, I started to run as though this were the one-stade race, instead of the twenty-four stades we had already covered. My sight blurred, the stands, the great red velvet draperies before the judges' box, the whole circus itself, swam into un-

reality with my speed. The spectators came to their feet, racking sound
out of existence with their roars. When I crossed the finish line, I was
utterly alone.

Bending there, fighting for breath, trying to draw air into my
tortured lungs, I saw why. Fifteen paces back, poor Yohannan lay on
the track, writhing in awful agony. I whirled, ran back to him, picked
him up, leaped aside with him, just as the close-packed runners whom
he and I had left nearly two whole stades behind came thundering
around the bend. I probably saved his life, for surely they would have
trampled him.

I bore him in my arms up to the stands. Laid him down, raised my
hands toward Antipas. Toward the burly centurion at his side.
Helvetia's father. I didn't know that, then.

"*Ave*, Tetrarch! *Ave*, O Representative of Glorious Cæsar!" I panted,
in what was, for Galilee, very nearly flawless Latin. "I beg of you to
divide the prize between him who, had he not fallen, might have won,
and me!"

Why? I have an antic humor; and our rulers like such gestures. The
prize was small, a thousand sesterces; I'd gained forty times that much
in wagers won. And my empty, half-mocking gesture served me better
than I knew, for it convinced my Helvetia, whom up until that moment
I had not even seen, that I was the best, the noblest of men.

Antipas smilingly motioned me to mount the winner's dais; half
fainting, poor Yohannan stood beside me. I kept a hard grip on his
arm to keep him from falling. He looked up at me with the dumb,
grateful eyes of a wounded dog.

Then the heavens opened, and *she* came down.

Wait. What does a man see when he looks for the first time on the
woman whom afterward he comes to love? Not the reality, surely; not
the woman who is there; but a distortion, a heightening, an image to
some degree false, created by the shock of recognition at perceiving his
desire, his need, fleshed out into a form, a face, he has known always
in his heart of hearts without knowing how or why or even that he
knew. Therefore, description is useless. My Roman mistress Lydia
swore that Helvetia resembled nothing so much as a small white mouse.
Even discounting female malice, she wasn't entirely wrong. But *I* saw
a mist of sunlight on spring snow, a mouth the palest pink of roses, eyes
the color of a Tishri[2] sky. You see? A man describing the woman he
loves makes bad poetry, falsifies always, is ridiculous. Say Helvetia was
a tiny pale blond girl who was moderately pretty. Will you accept
that? It's a lie! She was the most beautiful thing who ever drew the
breath of mortal life! Don't expect truth of me. I give you Pilate's

question. To me truth is that she was Aphrodite new-risen from the foam, the quality of tenderness, all the loveliness there ever was. To Lydia, she was an albino mouse. Which is also truth, I suppose.

As she came toward me, I could see a deep violet vein beating in the base of her alabaster throat. Her skin was that fine, that transparent. I stared at her so hard, so rudely, that a tide of color rose in her face.

"Your—your name, victor?" she faltered.

"Nathan bar Yehudah!" I said loudly; then, more quietly, "And from this hour forth, your slave!"

She put the laurel wreath upon my head. Turned, and kissed my sweaty cheek, so lightly that almost her lips seemed not to touch. I have lived three score years since that day; I've been beaten, tortured, taken wounds, been baked by desert winds, seared by brazen suns; but I'll carry the feel of that kiss with me down to my grave.

She crowned poor Yohannan, too; but she didn't kiss him. As she turned to go, I gasped at her out of the depths of my anguish.

"Tonight. In the gardens of the palace. Even if it costs me my life!"

She looked at me over her shoulder. Her face was Aurora's. Her Tishri eyes opened very wide.

"You mustn't!" she whispered. "The soldiers; my father's men; they'll—"

"I'll be there!" I said.

I was. I climbed the garden wall, swung down into the fragrant dark. The garden was filled with olive trees. I could hear the Roman soldiers clanking about their rounds. Each time they came near me, I froze into tree shadow, vanished into night.

Then a door opened, and she came. The moon was high. I could see her clearly.

I stood there, unbreathing; the sight of so much loveliness was a kind of death. She peered this way and that, her face taut with anxiety in the moonlight. Though I knew it not, I had already won. But my experience with the hetairai of Athens, the patrician dames from her own country, had taught me to be bold. When she was close enough, I reached out and dragged her into my arms.

"Nathan!" she hissed. "You must go! You must! The sol—"

By then I had found her mouth.

She tore free at last. I could see the tears on her face. But she didn't reproach me.

"They'll—they'll kill you!" she breathed. "My father will order you crucified!"

"Will you come and watch me die, Helvetia?" I said; for already I had found out her name. Helvetia, daughter of the centurion Helvetius. Helvetia, Gallic rose, angel of my delight!

"Ohhhhhh!" she wailed.

"For you, I'll do it well," I said; "I'll make you proud of me. And when you're very old, you can tell your grandchildren: 'A man died for me, once. Nathan bar Yehudah. A Jew. He died very well. At the last moment, he looked into my eyes—and smiled!' "

"Oh, but you're mad!" she said. "Go, Nathan! Go now, while the soldiers are still on the other side and you—"

I shook my head.

"Don't you want me to die?" I said.

"No!" she gasped. "Oh, immortal gods! I—"

"Why not?" I said.

"Oh, I don't know! Nathan, please!"

"Kiss me," I said.

"Don't be a fool! The soldiers! I—"

"Kiss me."

She stood there. Her face was very white. Her mouth trembled. Its quiver was the most enchanting sight I'd ever seen.

"If—if—I do, will you go?" she said.

"Yes. No. Will you promise me another thing?"

We heard then, loud in the night, the clank of the soldiers' armor.

"Yes! Yes! Anything! Only go!" she moaned.

"You will walk by the lakeshore tomorrow. Very early. Northward in the direction of Migdal-Nunaya. Alone. Will you do that?"

"Nathan, I can't! You know I can't! My father—"

I smiled at her sadly. Leaned languidly back against the tree.

"Then on your head be my death," I said.

"Go!" She was really crying now. "I'll come! I'll—only, go!"

I grinned at her, perfectly at ease.

"You still haven't kissed me," I said.

Her lips were ice cold, trembling, salt at first; but I warmed them; I kissed her with a wicked accumulation of skill. I was still molding, cherishing her mouth, when the soldiers came.

I saw them just in time; dragged her into the olive shadow.

The clanking stopped.

"I could have sworn I saw—" one of them growled.

"Some wench letting a slave scullion pry her knees apart? So did I, Vulcanus! Eros and Aphrodite aid 'em, say I. Grant him a stout weapon, and her a tight sheath. We're supposed to protect his Jewish Nibs and our Captain, aren't we? And a couple o' busy belly bumpers ain't got harming nobody in their little lusty heads, so come on!"

But there was another danger. I could hear Vulcanus' breath rasp.

"Kind of like to see it," he muttered. "Never have, Lucius. Seen another couple, I mean. . . ."

"Take you down to Cyrus' Lupanar tomorrow, and have him stage a circus for you. Men, women, dogs, goats, and jackasses. But, right now, I don't aim to have to pull you off some Jew bitch who's screaming her head off. The old man's strict that way. We make our rounds, Vulcanus! Tomorrow's our night off. Wait till then."

I heard them clanking off and measured out my breath upon the dead-stopped air. Then I looked down. The tree in which we'd hid was very old, and had put up many shoots, each one of them grown thicker than a man's body over the centuries, so that one olive had become a miniature forest in itself. It was too dark for me to see her. But I could feel the long slow tremble, the desperate, hopeless way she cried.

"Helvetia!" I said. "What—"

"They—they've spoiled it!" she sobbed. "I—I was—so happy, Nathan! Then they opened their dirty mouths and spewed their filth all over—"

I stared toward that lovely face I couldn't see. I had a problem on my hands, I realized.

"All over what?" I said.

"This—" she made a poem of motion with her white hand, encompassing the garden, the moonlight, the magic of that moment, gone. "All this—loveliness. Over—us—"

You know what's the most beautiful word on earth?

Us.

Oh, God! I—

That next morning, even though I arrived by boat at the very crack of dawn, she was already there before me, waiting very quietly on the golden beach, beside the wine-dark sea. . . .

Chapter IV

I DUG the oars into blue water, drove the boat toward her so hard that its prow bit sand. I jumped out, my arms outstretched.

But she backed away, fear in her eyes. It was very clear that if I'd taken another step, she would have turned and fled.

"Helvetia—" I said reproachfully. "Why are you acting like this? After all, you did come to meet me, and—"

"Only because I gave you my word," she said. "I am a Roman, remember. We keep our word, once we give it, no matter what it costs."

Her voice hadn't the faintest trace of warmth in it. I could feel myself getting angry. In my youth, I was anything but a patient soul.

"Fat lot this is going to cost you," I said.

The heavy freight of sarcasm with which my tone was laden got over to her. She bent her bright head. Looked up again.

"My father will probably beat me to death," she said.

I said: "No!" drawing the word out, giving it the shape of astonishment.

"My sister Tercia went to the games once without his permission," Helvetia said in her grave, sweet voice. "There was a young patrician she was in love with. He was a good-for-nothing who'd run through his father's money so he'd had to hire himself out as a gladiator. When my father found it out, he hung Tercia by her wrists from the transom of the woman's quarters. By the time he'd done with her, not an *uncia*, an inch, of her back remained that wasn't in ribbons, Nathan. I went to bed, and put the pillow over my head so I wouldn't hear her screaming. It did no good. I could still hear her. She was abed—lying on her stomach, of course—three months. And she is much bigger and stronger than I am. All my sisters are."

She wasn't lying. I could tell that. I felt sick. This wasn't going the way I'd planned it, at all. I didn't say anything. To what this lovely child had just told me, what was there, really, to be said?

She looked down at the sands. Faced me again; whispered: "My skin is very delicate, very thin. I only hope my father can contain his wrath. It will grieve him terribly if he kills me. He—loves me very much, Nathan."

I stood there. Speech wouldn't come. I must have looked like a beached fish opening its mouth and gulping air.

"And yet, knowing *that*, you came!" I said.

"Yes, Nathan."

"But why, Helvetia? In God's Name, why?"

She turned away from me so that I saw her face in profile for the first time. A cameo cut by the hand of a god.

"Don't ask me that," she said.

I stared at her.

"All right," I said. "I'll ask you something else: How will your father know? I'll bring you home long before he comes off duty and—"

She looked at me.

"Because *I'll* tell him," she said quietly. "Everything, except your name. Except who you are. When he asks me that, I'll simply refuse to say anything. And that will get him so wild that he probably *will* kill me. You see, I've never lied to him, Nathan. I don't even know how to lie. And I don't want to learn—"

"Don't be a fool, Helvetia!" I said. "It's simpler to twist the truth a little than to—"

She shook her head. Smiled a wan little smile.

"It isn't simpler, Nathan. You have to prop a lie up with another lie and that one with still another until nothing remains simple or clear. Until life is all lies. . . ." She looked at me with those Tishri eyes of hers. "You think I'm a fool, don't you?" she said. "You're probably right. If I weren't a fool, I shouldn't be—here. . . ."

I have never been slow of wit. My Uncle Hezron often said I was too clever for my own good. "Borders on cunning, Nathan; which is an unclean thing . . ." he told me once. As usual, he was right.

"Am *I* among the people you can't lie to?" I asked her.

"I can't lie to anybody," Helvetia said softly.

"Then I want to know: Will you tell your father *why* you came to meet me?"

Her blue eyes caught the light in a startled leap. Then she bowed her head again.

"Yes," she said, so low I felt, rather than heard, that sound.

"And that *why* is?" I said.

"Because I gave you my word."

"All right. That, and no other reason?"

She turned away. The sun was up now, outlining her profile in a wash of light. She was silent. Intensely silent.

"No other reason, Helvetia?" I said.

"Nathan—would you strip me naked in a public place?"

I thought: With great pleasure! I said: "I don't understand you, Helvetia!"

"That's—what you're doing, now. A—certain reticence—a little modesty—are like clothing, Nathan. And you—you'd take them away from me. You—you're very hard. You really don't have much—mercy in you, do you?"

"About this, not an iota or a jot. I don't play children's games. Tell me, Helvetia, why did you come?"

Her head came up. She faced me squarely. I saw the white rush wall
her eyes out, the falling flash hang vibrant upon the defenseless quiver
of her mouth.

"Because—because I love you, Nathan," she said.

She lay in my arms in that little grove just north of Migdal-Nunaya.
I had been kissing her for the better part of an hour, so it shouldn't
be difficult to imagine the state I was in by then. But she—she remained
just as cool, just as serene.

"Helvetia—" I said.

"Yes, Nathan?"

"Not like that. Don't—clamp your teeth together. Open your mouth
a little. . . ."

I heard the ragged beat get into her breathing then. Now! I exulted.
Now! I put my hand upon her secret body, beneath her stola. Her
eyes opened, flared. She caught my wrist, hard.

"Helvetia—" I groaned.

"No," she whispered; then: "Please don't, Nathan."

"You don't love me!" I snarled.

She stared at me.

"I do love you," she said. "So much. So very much!"

"Prove it," I said.

"By—by letting you—do *that?*" she said.

"Yes."

She went on looking at me. Her eyes misted over.

"All right," she said.

But the way she said it was wrong. All wrong.

"You mean it?" I said.

"I always mean what I say, Nathan—only—"

"Only what?"

"When I go home tonight, I shall open my veins."

She had a flat, almost expressionless way of saying the things she
really meant. I didn't doubt her. I couldn't. It took me at least three
tries to get that "Why, Helvetia?" out.

"I swore before Isis that I'd come virgin to my nuptial bed. I promised her that if I broke that vow, I'd take my life. For you, I'll break
my vow. But I'll also pay the forfeit."

"Helvetia, you're mad!"

She put up her fingers and traced the outline of my mouth with their
tips.

"I suppose I am," she said.

There's a devil in me. There is! There is! I rolled away from her,

stood up. Took my dagger from its sheath. She came to her knees,
watching me.

I put the point to the great vein in the crook of my arm. Pushed it in.
The blood spurted. I stood there watching it flooding out of me with a
curious kind of detachment.

She stretched out her own milk-white arm.

"Now—me, Nathan," she said.

"No!" I howled.

"You'd leave me?" she said. "Give me the dagger, Nathan. I—I know
how. My father showed me. We've been stationed in many bad places
where there was danger of—of ravishment. So give it to me. This way,
nobody can separate us. Not even—my father. This way, we'll be together, always."

I hung there, staring at her.

"I—I don't want you dead, Helvetia," I whispered.

"Nor I, you. Give me your arm, Nathan."

I averted my coward's eye, put my bloody arm out to her. She tore off
a strip of her stola and bound it up. Then we were kneeling there
facing each other and crying. Both of us. Two children pressing hot-
wetsalttrembling mouth to mouth, bewildered by their blood.

It was then that the madwoman, Miriam of Migdal, Miriam of
Magdala, started in to howl.

I can't describe that sound. It was absolutely fiendish. It rose in
ululant pulsations that were beastlike, demented, wild.

Helvetia clung to me, trembling all over. And I knew then I could
never leave her. That she had to be mine, forever.

"What—on earth—is that?" she said.

"Miriam. Miriam of Migdal-Nunaya. The Galileans say she's possessed of seven devils. Look! Here she comes now—"

Miriam came out from among the trees. She was dressed in rags,
pieces of tent cloth, sacking, a flurry of ribbons she'd stolen God knows
where. I could see the straw and twigs tangled in her black hair. The
dirt on her face, the lines of it ground into her neck. Even so, she
was not uncomely. But even from where she passed five rods away, we
could smell her. She stank most fearsomely. She probably hadn't had a
bath since she lost her wits five years before. She disappeared again
into another clump of trees. She was still howling.

"Poor thing," Helvetia whispered; "poor lost, mad thing!"

Miriam's retreating howls beat against my eardrums. "Not only you,
Migdalene; but I, and all the world!" I thought. Then I remembered.
I had money! I'd won forty thousand sesterces in wagers on the long

race! A fortune! With that I could take Helvetia, fly to the ends of the earth, live—

"Will you—marry me, Helvetia?" I said.

The madwoman went on howling.

"What—what did you say?" Helvetia said.

"I said, 'Will you marry me?' " I shouted.

She stared at me. Miriam's voice sank into a low, tortured moaning.

"But, Nathan—we—we can't—my—my father—"

"Will never find us, where I'll take you! You'll keep your vow to Isis. I—I won't touch you till we're wed. By whatever rites you want. Before Isis. Before Ba'al. Before—"

Miriam's voice rose up, slivering the sky.

"Will you?" I bellowed, louder than Miriam could. And madder, surely.

Helvetia stared at me a long, slow, breath-halted time. I didn't even hear the madwoman's screams. The intensity of Helvi's silence drowned them.

Then, mutely, my darling nodded.

"Oh, bless you, Helvetia!" I said.

I spent the whole day collecting my bets. I didn't take Helvi with me, of course. I left her at my lodgings until that necessary task was done. By that time it was so late that night caught us before we'd got any farther than Kafer Nahum.[1] So we stayed at the inn there. I told the innkeeper we were man and wife. He winked his eye and charged me double the usual price. I lay on the floor beside the bed nightlong and listened to Helvetia crying. It was almost dawn before she slept.

In the morning, I hired horses, and rode away from there with my prize. Helvetia's eyes were swollen shut from weeping. I was getting a little sick of it by then. Normally, I should have ridden straight across Galilee, and entered Phœnicia somewhere between Sepphoris and Jotapata; but I didn't dare. Both those cities were too close to Cæsarea, where the Romans had their seat. And, surely by now the centurion Helvetius was out, fully armed, with two *decuriae* at the very least, if not a whole century at his back, searching for his daughter! So I struck due north from Kafer Nahum to Gischala, crossed into Phœnicia some ten *milia* northwest of there, kept on going until we got to Tyre.

Evil has its uses. In Tyre, wickedest city under heaven since Sodom and Gomorrah were destroyed, all things could be bought, even a no-questions-asked passage for two obvious runaways lacking even baggage on a swift coastal vessel bound for Alexandria. We put in at Ptolemais, at Dora; a thousand sesterces convinced our captain that Cæsarea, where a hundred dockside idlers would have recognized Helvetia at once, was no worthy port of call. We bypassed it, and were free.

Some days of sea and sun put the roses back into Helvetia's cheeks. She became playful, gay. Climbed into my arms, kissed me endlessly, until I snarled at her: "You want to force me to ravish you, Helvetia? Or go mad? Which?"

She stared at me then, and the first startled recognition of what love was, that "male and female created He them," came into her eyes.

"Later, Nathan—" Her voice made flute music, with cymbals underneath, velvety and warm. "After the rites I—I promise—"

"What?" I groaned.

"That I—won't fight too hard!" my Helvetia said.

There are many Jews in Alexandria. When I explained my need to the Grand Rabbi, he graciously offered me his own house for the ceremony. Moreover, he repeated each part of it over again in Greek for Helvetia's benefit. I need not mention that, traveling as she did with her father from one end of the empire to the other, she'd been forced to learn the universal language, for once you were east of Italia itself, Latin served for nothing. I had never heard the *Kiddushin*, the sanctifications, said in Greek, before. They were solemn and impressive in that language, too.

I stood under the *chuppah*, the canopy, waiting. I had my head covered, as the Law requires. A Jewish couple of the highest Sadducean rank, acting *in loco parentis* for my Helvetia, brought her to me under the *chuppah*. And so moved was that dear, sweet matron who acted as my darling's mother for an hour, that she cried, bless her!

I took the ring from the velvet cushion the Rabbi's youngest son held up. I slipped it on the forefinger of Helvetia's right hand. I said the *Kiddush*, the vow:

"Behold, thou art sanctified unto me by this ring according to the Law of Moses and Israel!"

Helvetia's mouth made a pale pink blur, so wildly did it quiver. She was sobbing aloud, as though her poor little heart were truly broken.

"Helvetia!" I said.

"Ohhhh Nathan!" she wailed. "It is *so* beautiful!"

I read the *Kethubah*, the marriage settlement:

"Upon thee, all my worldly goods I do bestow. I will work for thee, I will honor thee, I will support and maintain thee as it beseemeth a Jewish husband to do—"

Helvetia bowed her head. Her shoulders shook. The good couple stared at her in astonishment. So did I. I had never seen a Roman wedding, so I couldn't understand why our Jewish ceremony moved her so. Years later, in Rome, I did see a pair of patricians—friends of a young Roman matron with whom I was having an adulterous love affair, as usual—wed, and understood my Helvi's emotion, finally. Like everything Roman, their rites emphasized the physical over the spiritual, and were, to put it mildly, utterly obscene.

We recited the Seven Benedictions of the Newly Wed, together. Or we tried to. Helvetia was crying too hard to do more than make an incomprehensible babble of the words the Rabbi said in Greek. We drank the ceremonial wine; I smashed the glass. My voice rang out, vibrant, soaring:

"If I forget thee, O Jerusalem, let my right hand forget her cunning! If I do not remember thee, let my tongue cleave to the roof of my mouth if I prefer not Jerusalem above my chief joy!"[2]

Then I bent and kissed my bride.

"Nathan!" she whispered. "You were right! Your ways are better than ours! I—I feel so—good! The way I—belong to you is—holy. So—pure. Now I'm yours, truly!"

"And for always," I said.

In Alexandria, we were happy. It was as though we alone of all humankind had discovered, or even invented, love. The only dispute—for you couldn't call so slight a thing a quarrel—we had in all that time was religious: Helvetia wanted to make a little shrine to Isis, the Mater Dolorosa, in our home. And when I explained to her why this could not be, quoted to her the Holy Scriptures: "Thou shalt have no other gods before me. Thou shalt not make unto thee any graven image, nor any likeness of anything that is in the heaven above, or that is in the earth beneath, or that is in the waters under the earth—" and went on with the rest of it, compelled by its sonority, its majesty, saying that part about God's jealousy, his laying the fathers' sins even to their great-great-grandchildren's charge,[3] Helvetia said a thing that shocked me, but which, it has seemed to me ever since, is true:

"I don't think I like your god very much, Nathan. He's cruel. Even a man who punishes a child for what his father has done would be a monster, I think. And you say grandchildren and great-grandchildren?"

So I quoted her the next verse, the sixth: "And shewing mercy unto thousands of them who love me and keep my commandments. . . ."

She opened her eyes very wide at that and stared at me.

"So he loves those who love him? Himmmpf! Hardly generous of him, is it?"

"Helvetia!" I said.

" 'I the Lord thy God am a jealous god, visiting—' " she whispered. "I understand that. I know what jealousy is like. The other day when you admired that Egyptian girl so fervently, I wanted to die. But I loved you *before* you loved me—at the exact instant I saw you standing there like one of the earth gods, before the beginning of that race. And I'll go on loving you long after you've ceased to—remember my name. But I can't think of anything you could do that would make me want to punish you. People—and gods—who want to punish, who even think of anything but to love, to forgive—are cruel. Like my father."

I grinned at her, bent and kissed her cheek.

"Sleep well, Helvetia," I mocked. "I'll see you tomorrow. No, the day after—"

"Nathan!" she wailed. "Where *are* you going?"

"To visit the Egyptian, of course. Didn't you say that you couldn't think of anything I could do that you couldn't forgive me for?"

She stood there looking at me, and her little heart-shaped face was a picture of utter woe. Like many good and gentle people, she was sadly wanting in a sense of humor.

She bent her pale, bright head. Looked up again. The tears upon her face were a rush, a flood.

"Enjoy yourself, Nathan," she said.

That was all. But I clawed her into my arms, shaken with pure terror at the way her voice sounded saying that. She clung to me, trembling all over.

"Helvi, angel," I groaned, "if you ever see me come into this house with one hand gone and the blood spurting from the mangled stump, you'll know I've touched another woman! Because, before Adonai-Elohim and all the Seraphim, I swear I'd cut it off! I'd—"

Then she proved that she did have a sense of humor after all. A very Roman sense of humor. She gave me a squeeze, giggled girlishly, said: "Then I hope you never go further than—than touching, Nathan! I do so want—a child, you know. . . ."

It took some moments for her meaning to penetrate my mind. Then I threw back my head and roared.

I found employment in the Chief Rabbi's house as a copyist of scrolls, at which art—false modesty be damned!—I was very good indeed. Because even then I realized that, husband it as we would, our money wasn't going to last forever. And always, during those summer months, while the sun still stood high in the heavens long after my tasks were done, I'd find Helvetia waiting for me just outside that great man's door.

We wandered hand in hand like children through the lovely city. In the parks, Helvetia fed the tame gazelles, the apes, the peacocks. She loved animals, too. She loved all living things. She was feeding a gazelle out of her own slim white hand on that all but fatal evening, when I heard the clank of Roman armor. I went to the edge of the road, under the palm trees, to watch the cohorts pass by. I hadn't then learned to hate everything Roman.

Helvetia ran to me at once, took my arm.

"Don't stand there where they can see you, Nathan!" she said. She was the child of a legionary; she understood what I did not: that among the Roman officers, transferred with great frequency from one far-distant outpost to another, the chances were exceedingly good that the commander of this cohort could well be an old comrade-in-arms of her father's. More, she guessed another thing, correctly, it turned out: that the centurion Helvetius, sacrificing his pride to his rage, his grief, had had her description, and mine, sent by coasting galleys to every Roman garrison within a thousand *milia passuum* of Jerusalem.

She was too late. The stern-faced old *dux*, general, who from horseback led the armored footsoldiers, pulled up his nag so hard, that had that heat-dulled rack of bones had the strength, it would have reared.

"Seize them!" he roared. "That towhead wench! That blackskinned little bastard there!"

That's all he had time for, because I'd grabbed Helvetia by the arm; and we were off, running through the park as though Satan himself were at our heels. As, be it said, Satan was. But this time, at least, he was overmatched. The legionaries were mostly Germans, newly transferred from that miserably cold and wet clime; they were burdened with armor; they didn't know the city. Before we were out of the park we'd already lost them; a long series of zigzags through crooked streets made our escape, for the moment, an established fact. But afterward? It was that, I knew, I had to consider now.

Helvetia leaned against a wall, panting, tears of pure terror glittering in her eyes.

"Ohhhh Nathan!" she cried.

"Don't worry about it," I said. "I'll take you to the Rabbi's house and then—"

"You'll stay with me!" she moaned. "Don't leave me, Nathan! Don't leave me, please!"

"Only long enough to get the money from our place, love," I said; "though on second thought, we'd better go there now—before they've had time to find out where we live. Then, tonight, we'll take ship to—to Athens, say—"

Helvetia shook her head.

"Not Athens, Nathan," she said. "Rome."

"Rome!" I said.

"Yes. Listen to me, dearest. I—I've lived all over. As a centurion's daughter, I've had to. There isn't a city in the Empire that strangers can come to without their presence being noted within the first week— at the very best, within the first two weeks, say—except Rome, herself. The capital swallows a thousand newcomers a day. Besides, nobody'd dream we'd dare go there since all the world knows the Imperator expelled your people from Rome some time ago. . . ."

"And the first time the guards at the very quay catch sight of this beak of mine," I began, "they'll—"

"Many races have hooked noses," Helvetia said sweetly. "And since you're clean-shaven they'll think you're a Syrian or an Arab. For that matter, my pale hair is as much trouble as your nose! Where else except in Gaul or Britain or Germany, all too far away, and all miserably cold and savage country, wouldn't my blond hair be noticed? Rome is full of northern barbarians! We could lose ourselves there as we could no place else on earth! Besides, it's the last city on earth my father would even dream that we—"

I grinned at her then. "Done!" I said. "Rome it is!"

How was I to know that in the stew of iniquity there were dangers compared with which the centurion Helvetius' wrath was as nothing?

Four months from that day, we anchored offshore before Ostia, one of the three ports that served Imperial Rome.[4] I stood there with my arm about Helvetia, watching the *urinatores,* divers, plunging for coins the passengers threw them. I tossed a few, myself, until my angel stopped me.

"Don't be wasteful, dearest," she whispered; "life is very dear in Rome."

It was. Within a month, I was already alarmed at the way our little pile of coins was diminishing. So I went out and looked for work. . . .

That night—the next—six hundred nights all told—I came home and faced her.

"Any—luck, my dearest?" Helvetia said.

"No," I said angrily, wearily, despairingly. "Look, Helvetia, I have no skills beyond those of a secretary-copyist. And here people don't—"

"Hire scribes. They buy them. I know, darling," Helvetia said.

"And cheaply," I roared. "A good teamster costs more! Rome is swarming with clever Greeks, slaves one and all, most of whom have forgot more than I ever knew! Oh, Helvi—I—"

She came to me and kissed me.

"Don't worry about it, darling," she said cheerfully; "it will turn out all right. . . ."

It didn't, but she was brave to the point of gallantry. Only one thing could and did make her weep: the fact that month after month, with cruel regularity, nature brought down upon her the irrefutable evidences that she was not with child.

Still, we had each other, so we were happy. And Rome is not the worst place on earth to be poor. The games were free; and under Tiberius Cæsar, not too offensive. The Imperator was too stingy to stage elaborate ones. I loved the chariot races; at times Helvetia would even allow me to bet a sesterce on my favorites, "The Greens." Fortunately for us, I always lost. I say fortunately, because had I won, the gambling fever would have seized me, surely, and one run of bad luck would have finished our little hoard.

One morning, quite by accident, we stumbled upon a gladiatorial contest; for, God witness it, we'd have never gone had we known what was being staged that day. At first, I was fascinated by the skill the fighters displayed. I noted most of all the grace and beauty of the retiarii, the net and trident men. I found myself consciously favoring them, those slight, beautiful naked youths whose speed alone stood between them and death.

Then a gladiator's backhand stroke laid open a retiarius' thigh to the bone. I saw the flesh gape like a crimson mouth, the yellowish femur showing through before the blood flooded out, and the poor, dying bastard screamed.

The tears stung my eyes, blinded me. I bent my head and wept. At once the women nearest us began to hoot with savage joy.

"Look at him!" they cackled. "The pretty little effeminate! Crying! What's the matter, baby boy? Can't stand a little blood?"

I stood up.

"Come, Helvi," I said; "let's get out of here!"

She took my arm, her face scarlet, and we left the stands, followed by the hooted taunts of the women, more impressed by the sight of a man who wept at the spectacle of this obscene, bestial cruelty than they were by the skill and valor those poor devils displayed in dying.

"For their amusement!" I roared, after we'd got home, of course; "if they so love gore, let them cut their own throats, the rabid bitch vixens! Those were men, Helvi! God's creatures! They have souls and—"

"Yes, dearest," my Helvetia said and kissed me. "Lie back down, now. Here, take this draught. It will cool your fever and—"

I said a very obscene Latin word.

"Hades and Pluto take it. Helvi!" I cried. "I've *got* a mother! What I took you for was—a wife!"

She knelt beside my bed and held my hand.

"I—I'm not making fun of you, Nathan," she whispered. "I—I hate these things, too. I hate our cruelty. I think it will one day destroy us. And I thank both Isis and your Jewish God that you're so fine, so highstrung, so tender. I couldn't love you if you weren't. . . ."

But I'm sure she was a little ashamed of me just the same. She was, after all, a Roman.

Who was it that destroyed us finally? A neighbor, surely. Watching us going out whenever we could to the *ludi scenici*[5]—for both of us were enthralled by the pantomimes—he, greedy swine, came to the conclusion that we had something put by.

When we returned from the theatre one night, we hadn't anymore. A window had been forced, a locked cupboard pried open, our little store was gone.

I held Helvetia in my arms and listened to her cry. I didn't comfort her. I couldn't. Had I tried, my own tears would have choked my voice.

Faster now! Flip over the parchment of our days together! Look upon my Helvi. See how she's changed. No longer a radiant creature of springsnow dawnsunlight blueheavenlyeyes, is she? White, pale, drawn; her bones almost punching through her skin. That ugly, rattling sound? A cough, of course.

Starvation is an ugly way to die.

She was hidden behind the curtains when I came. I could see them shake with the silent desolate fury of her weeping. I put my hand through the opening, dragged her forth, stood there, looking at her.

She looked back. Her mouth came open. Her lips made a whitish blur.

"It—it'll grow back, Nathan! In no time at all, it'll—"

But my knees were gone from under me. I pressed my forehead to the floor.

"No man!" I howled. "No man at all! Ball-less wonder! To let you do this! To force you to sell—Oh, Helvi! Helvi! Of all of you I loved most—"

"My hair," she whispered. "It's all right, Nathan. It'll grow back. And—and—the wigmakers gave me quite a lot! You see—I've bought meat! Sit down, my dearest and—"

But I couldn't eat. Every time I looked at that close-cropped little pinkish globe that was her head—delicate and fair like all of her—the bile and blood and grief rose in my throat and choked me.

I found work. Brought home four denarii before they saw me trying to lift with two hands a beam the other *fabri lignarii*, builders, hurled upward to a companion with a flip of their wrists. I was out again. How many times? I don't remember.

I couldn't join the *collegia*, those fraternal organizations of the workers which softened the worse abuses, because I didn't stay on any job long enough to make friends with those influential *proles* who might have presented me for membership. We dared not call upon Helvetia's strapping blond sisters for help, though three of them lived in Rome with their husbands, because they'd be sure to tell her father. And marriage to a Jew was no longer taken as a matter of course. The Imperator hated our Holy Race. Just five years before, he had conscripted four thousand Roman Jewish youths, and sent them out to sure death in Sardinia, expelling, at the same time, the rest of my people from Rome;[6] therefore, I could find no aid from that quarter either. Most of the Jews left in Rome were in hiding, and were themselves starving.

Helvetia took to her bed, too weak to move. I think that in my heart of hearts, even then I knew why.

She had almost ceased to eat at all, that I might have her share.

I went mad. I prayed before every shrine, in every temple, to every god in Rome. To Isis, because my Helvetia had a special devotion toward her, I returned again and again. And one morning, it seemed to my feverish starving gaze that her dead stone eyes lifted from the face of her dead stone child, and smiled at me.

Filled with mad hope, I did the only thing left for the hopeless: I went to the gladiatorial school, and tried to sell my poor carcass to get the food and medicines to save my angel.

The lanista, for so the trainers of gladiators were called in Rome, a Gaul with a hideously scarred and brutal face, walked around me as though I were an animal. Turned to his second.

"Ho, Brutus," he said; "he might make a retiarius, don't you think? These skinny little starvelings are often quick enough to—"

I stood there sweating, hope in me like a fever. The retiarii fought stark naked, armed only with a weighted net, a trident, and a dagger. Yet, as often as not, the net men won out against the gladiators, the swordsmen. Under the crushing weight of their armor, the gladiators were slow, while the whirling, dancing, stinging insects that the retiarii were, spinning their nets like gossamer wings above their agile heads, had the advantage of lightness, grace, speed. Of course, much of the time a skilled gladiator simply disemboweled them with a single stroke; but once the net was cast, the gladiator tangled like an armored lizard in its folds. The retiarius had him helpless and could slay or spare him, as the public willed it.

Brutus looked at me. Grunted.

"I'll give him a try, Paulus; have the blunted weapons brought," he said.

Ugly as he was, I could have kissed him.

Desperation lent me the strength I no longer had; grace and speed I was born with. Three times I caught the lanista, Brutus, in my net in that first trial. The brute stood back, untangled himself, said to the chief lanista, the ugly Gaul, Paulus:

"By the tits of the she-wolf! This skinny little bastard will do!"

I took the gladiator's oath that I would suffer myself "to be whipped with rods, burned with fire, killed with steel." But there was one thing I hadn't reckoned upon: novice gladiators had to live at the school. And without me, Helvetia would surely die.

I fell on my knees before Paulus, told him of my plight, begged him to let me at least spend my nights at home. He refused, profanely.

"Hades, Nathanaeus," he rumbled; "how long d'you think you'll last if you enter the arena with your legs leaden from bumping bellies with your woman all night? A retiarius has to be fast. Speed's all he's got. And you, my boy, please me. Don't know when I've seen a beggar swift as you. . . ."

"But she's sick, Paulus!" I all but wept. "She's very sick! She hasn't eaten in God knows when! And—and—" Suddenly inspiration struck me like a light. "She's one of your own people! She's a Gaul, like you! Look here!"

I took the lock of pale sunlight hair I carried always in one of the *tellifin* along with a verse from the Song of Songs. A blasphemy? Perhaps. But does not one reverence God by worshiping the loveliest creature he ever made?

Paulus stared at that fair lock. A long time. A long, long time. Then he sighed.

"Tell you what, kid. I'll send my old woman over to attend to her. Ursilla's good at nursing. And she loves taking care o' youngsters anyhow—likely because we never had any. Tell me, where d'you live?"

He was as good as his word. And Ursilla was a saint. A real one. Or did you think saints *had* to be Nazarenes?

She lied to Helvetia out of her great kindness. Fed her, bathed her, arranged her still-short hair. Saved her life, telling her I was working as a secretary to a rich man, who had taken so great a fancy to me that he had carried me aboard his private galley within the hour that we met, and borne me away to Sicilia with him; showed her the lying missive I'd penned to confirm a tale so outrageously false that only a soul as simple, a heart as innocent as my Helvetia's would have ever believed it.

During the next six months, I lived at the school, trained endlessly, engaging in ferocious mock combats against the others, usually, when I could manage it, for safety's sake, against my new friend Andrai; ate well, slept without dreams. And, at last, Paulus having deemed me ready, I was sent into the arena, where I killed men I didn't hate, some of them my own fellows, for the benefit of that obscenely howling mob, the Romans.

I was afraid, of course. But I learned to live with that, too; to rise up in the morning, go to bed at night, live, breathe, have my being with crippling, murderous fear. . . .

Long before that full year I served as a retiarius was out, I had gained a following. All the world knew by now that no swordsman had ever succeeded in so much as breaking my skin, drawing one drop of blood from my naked hide. Women sent me love letters, tried to slip into my quarters in order to bed with me; I posed for sculptors, my beautifully muscled body oiled. . . .

I've spoken of Andrai. Like me, he was a Jew, the only other member of our race in the school; but, beyond the accident of birth, we differed in everything. He was huge, fair as a Goth, wonderously beautiful. His name, actually, was Netzer, which is the word you Greeks translate as Andrai. Netzer ben Hoseah, Andrew, son of Hoseah, you might say. I loved him. There is no other word. I hasten, lest you, being Greek, smile knowingly, to add that there was no conscious carnality in that love. He returned it with simple trust. We were brothers.

Do I have to say it? Can't you guess? He was tall and brawny, great-thewed, so they made of him a gladiator. And one day, before Great Cæsar himself, we were forced to fight each other—to the death.

I won, as usual. I knelt before his struggling, net-entangled carcass, the dagger in my hand. Raised streaming eyes to Cæsar.

"Kill him!" the mob roared.

And Cæsar turned his thumb down.

I looked down at Andrai. He smiled at me.

"You have my pardon, Nathan. Now strike quickly. And hard!" he said.

I killed him. Stood up. Hurled that bloody blade away from me. Bent and vomited upon the sand.

The spectators were astonished. They began to hoot at me.

Tiberius, Cæsar Imperator, stood up.

"What is the meaning of this, Retiarius?" he said.

"He was my friend, Cæsar; I loved him," I said.

Great Cæsar stood there, frowning. Then he said it.

"Free this man. Release him from his vows."

And all that mob of murderous sychophants, who, moments before, had been howling for my blood, split deaf heaven with their approving roars.

But now my fate had come full round again; the problem as before: how to keep my Helvetia alive. She still wasn't strong. If I couldn't procure food for her, she'd sink back again, grow paler, thinner than she was, die—

No! By Isis, no! I'd do murder first! Become a thief—

A thief? Why not? I was slim and strong, my body superbly muscled, trained to perfection. I could, I was sure, climb the highest wall, break open the strongest treasure chest, fight my way out of—

Do you know whose was the first patrician villa I broke into? Did you think I'd won free of that curious irony ruled and shaped my life as it did that of him who though not my brother was my twin, Yeshu'a ha Notzri?

Why, Lydia's, of course.

She was, as usual, waiting for a lover. And also, as usual, she was wide awake. At her first little scream, I put my dagger against her throat. She lay there with the point pressing into her flesh, and smiled at me.

"Take that thing away, beautiful boy," she cooed. "*That* isn't the blade I'd have you stab me with. . . ."

I took the dagger away.

"Money?" I growled. "Jewels?"

She laughed throatily.

"You're a beginner, aren't you, darling?" she said. "Don't worry; I won't call my slaves. But you must be nice to me. . . ."

"Nice to you, how?" I got out.

"Well, you might start by kissing me," Lydia said.

I didn't bed with her that night. I didn't. To my tattered store of honor be that one last ragged scrap laid. I was tempted to. God, how I was tempted to! Out of consideration for my poor angel's lingering weakness, I hadn't touched Helvetia since Cæsar had unexpectedly freed me from gladiatorial slavery. I was young, fully recovered, strong; my blood howled and leaped through anguished veins.

And Lydia—soaked in that perfume of hers that was almost pure musk, a gut-tangling animal scent, overlaid with a heady odor of spice, not flowers, with that languid, dark ivory body of hers clean-shaven, breasts gilded, gold dust in her black hair, her fingers straying over my lean, hard-muscled body—was enough to set a Prophet wild.

Instead, at her bidding, I told her my story. She had the grace, the generosity, or the art—or more likely still, all three—to weep.

I departed her house at dawn—after her Numidians had thrown her outraged would-be lover out when, belated and drunken, he finally did appear. And in my belt there was slung a purse. A very heavy purse. It had ten thousand sesterces in it, which Lydia had given me of her own free will.

And she, of me, had only this: My promise to return on the morrow that she might study how to aid me, how to help me escape from want, from hunger, now, henceforth, and forever more.

And I, fool that I was, kept that promise, went!

Book II

In which I lose forever my beloved, return to Judea, take refuge among the Essenes, meet Yeshu'a again, and have my second encounter with Lucius Pontius Pilatus, Procurator of Judea.

Chapter V

I GOT UP. The woman I'd shared the couch with stretched out her arms to me. I didn't look at her. The smoke from the sandalwood smoldering in the braziers was a sickness in my lungs suddenly, and the world went abruptly liquid, glittering and unclear. Then I did look at her. She was stark naked and her breasts had been gilded with gold leaf. She had golddust in her hair. Some generous soul—our gracious host, probably—had stuck an emerald as big as a wren's egg into her navel. In the flickering lamplight, it winked up at me like some misplaced Cyclopean eye.

But I couldn't call to mind who she was. At the moment, oddly enough, that troubled me. I don't know why. Her identity was a matter of supreme, almost sublime, irrelevance; she was either Delia or Fannia or Urbilia or Vivia Sabina or any of the half a hundred rather select *prostibiles* who graced our revels, all of them the best, the most expensive articles, *delicatae* and *famosae,* whose fees put them beyond the reach of any man having an income less than eight or ten million sesterces annually. A distinction of sorts, I suppose.

I stood there trying to remember what she called herself, which was the wine working in me; because it wasn't worth the effort, and, anyhow, at Avidius Publius' house, it wasn't even customary to keep the same partner all night.

"Nathanaeus," she crooned. "Caius Nathanaeus, darling—"

"No," I said, the world sliding out from under me in a belly-churning swoop, "not Caius Nathanaeus, you perfumed bitch. Nathan bar Yehudah. A Jew. Do you know who or what a Jew is? No? Ha! I don't either. One of God's chosen people, my Uncle Hezron says. Chosen for what? Death, likely. Destruction. Chaos—and—"

Then memory exploded in my entrails and I screamed.

I don't think they even heard it. They were too busy. I could see from the glazed expression in Virginus Rufus' eyes that one of Publius' little *fellatores* was at him under the table. Sextus Oppius, whose crowning vice was gluttony, was tickling the back of his throat with a peacock feather, while a naked little slave—a catamite or a prepubescent girl, I couldn't really tell which for only the backsides were visible from where I stood and those slim buttocks were no indication of the gender, if any, to which the creature belonged—stood ready with the silver basin. All the rest were shrieking with laughter, weeping drunkenly, swilling wine, cramming food down their gullets with both hands, or making love. A euphemism, that last, of course.

Flavius Dolabella had Arria Pieta stretched out on the table before him in a litter of overturned dishes, her lovely body smeared all over with greasy mess of food. He was pouring wine over her belly, loudly proclaiming that she was *secunda mensa,* dessert, and that he was going to devour her. Then he proceeded to, almost literally.

I reeled away from there, toward the *peristylium,* the roofless inner court, where at least I could breathe, cool my feverish forehead in the fountain, think—

No! God, no! Not that! I must never think again. Never allow my head to become unsodden enough to realize, remember—

I didn't see the busy couple on the floor, so I fell over them, crashed full length to the marble pavement of the *triclinium,* the dining room. I got to my hands and knees and stared at them in astonishment. They were making love by the quaint, primitive, old-fashioned provincial method, which, before I left my native Judea, I'd thought was the only way you could go about it. I started to laugh. The utter idiots! Didn't they know that such unstudied carnality often resulted in children? And nobody in his right mind wanted children anymore. Not in the Rome of Tiberius Cæsar. I was still laughing when I got to my feet.

I don't know yet at what point my laughter drowned in the rising, bitter sea-surge of my tears.

I stood there leaning against a pillar. I could hear my own voice—or its echo, for the sound of it came from nether Tartarus, beyond the Styx, across black Lethean waters, below the well-source of grief, of weeping: "God, God, God, God!"

Then I felt a hard hand come down on my shoulder. I turned and looked into that swarthy face. At first I couldn't place the man. Then it came to me. He was a newcomer, a Spaniard from Sevilla, a town far down the shores of the Iberian Peninsula, whose citizens, for some long-forgot reason, enjoy Roman citizenship. His father, Marcus Pontius, had distinguished himself under Agrippa against the Cantabrians, and had won the high honor of being given the *pilum,* the javelin, on the field. Which was why this lean and sardonic lecher had adopted the name of Pilatus, Lucius Pontius Pilatus, he called

himself now. And he aimed high. He was courting no less than Claudia, granddaughter of Augustus himself.

"God?" he said, in that sibilant jesting voice of his which made
impious mockery of every word he uttered. "And what, my dear Caius
Nathanaeus, precisely is this quality, this attribute, or—if you insist—
this being, that you call—God?"

I stood there, staring at him. From the very first instant I met him,
I instinctively loathed Pontius Pilate. Yet, strangely, he had always
shown great interest in, and even a marked fondness for, me.

Then it came to me how to answer him. I unhooked the jeweled
pin, the *fibula*, from the shoulder of my toga, loosed the silken cord
from my waist. Then, oblivious to the pain, I took a still smoldering
coal of sandalwood from the nearest brazier. With these three elements,
I fashioned a compass, and scribed a perfect circle upon the floor.

Pontius Pilatus looked down at it. His heavy brows lifted; the curl
of his lip became more sardonic still.

"And this, my dear Nathanaeus, is—your God?" he said, the lazy
Iberian accent slurring his Latin.

I nodded wordlessly.

He threw back his head and laughed. At the sound of it, the warmth
went out of the air.

"But this—" he said "—this is—nothing!"

"Exactly," I said.

He stared at me, almost serious, the smile dimming on his dark face,
his lips half hiding the flash, the glitter of wolfish teeth.

"You'd imply, then, Nathanaeus, that God is—nothing?"

I gripped his arm and pointed toward where Oppius was vomiting
up a mess of nightingales' tongues, not because he was sick, but simply
to make room for more. The cost of that one dish, some sixty thousand
sesterces, would have fed thirty plebeian families for a span of years.

"Perhaps," I said. "Perhaps that is God, Pilatus—"

He looked in the direction my finger indicated, and the corners of
his mouth tightened in disgust.

"*That?*" he said.

"Yes," I said. "Birdsong reduced to dog vomit. A form of truth, what,
Lucius Pontius?"

He looked at me, smiling with his mouth only, not his eyes, and
asked that question—for the first time. I didn't know then that I'd be
present when he asked it again.

"What is—truth, Caius Nathanaeus?" he said.

But I, at least, answered him.

"That even dogs can heave, Spearbearer! And birds—die. Their song becomes—silence. So dense you can feel it. Your ears hurt—straining for an echo of it. For the lilt and twitter of the voice—you've murdered. That."

He leaned forward, peering at me. When he spoke, his voice had something in it as close to compassion as he was ever capable of.

"Why do you weep, Nathanaeus?" he said.

I turned on my heel and left him there.

I went to Lydia's house, out on the Appian Way. So crazed was I by then that I marched straight toward it through the principal streets instead of going by a roundabout route as I usually did as a precaution against my Uncle Hezron's finding me. You see, I already knew he was in Rome, searching for me, sent (not that he needed to be, not that he wouldn't have come on this difficult errand out of the love he himself bore me) by my father to bring me home again. How my father had found out where I was, I didn't then know. It wasn't until after I was home again that he told me.

But not even my Uncle's presence in the Capital of the World crossed my mind on that day. I was going, without knowing why, nor even having the slightest desire to—to see Lydia. My mistress for the past two years. Young—for a woman of three and thirty years is not yet old —wife of Quintus Valerius Caius, senator, patrician knight, seventy-four years old, multiple—at least until my event upon the scene—cuckold, uxorious and important, besotted old fool—I am unkind. The poor old ass loved me. I have seen the will he made, leaving me his fortune, after Lydia had persuaded him to adopt me for her own purposes, the chief of those purposes being—

Ha! A linguistic, legalistic, sociological problem. If a married woman beds with her adopted son, what precisely is the nature of the crime? Adultery, I grant you! But not incest, except technically, though it delighted Lydia's evil soul to call it that. She was always saying: "Son, come to bed with Mama. Let's—"

Strange. We Jews are puritans by nature. I cannot write those words.

I went to Lydia's house. How could I? How—in the Name of Just, Jealous, Vengeful God!

When I came into the house, she was already waiting for me in the atrium. She jumped up at once and ran to me. Going up on tiptoe, she began to kiss me, those hot, wet, open-mouthed kisses that had never before failed to awake a riot, a rage, a fury of lust in my blood. But today they had the opposite effect: my heart congealed as though it had been packed in snow. More, if she had kept it up one instant longer, they'd have produced the same result as Sextus Oppius' peacock feather. I think she sensed that. Lydia was endlessly subtle. She pushed me abruptly away, laughed, and wrinkled her adorably patrician little nose.

"You stink, Nathanaeus!" she said. "Ugh! I shall have to call in the perfumers to clear away the stench of used whore you've trailed into my foyer. You've been a bad boy, now, haven't you? Come on, tell Mama what you've done!"

I shrugged, said nothing. Lydia turned to one of the slave girls.

"Caenis," she said, "go prepare the bath for my naughty son. To wash away the olfactory evidences of his naughtiness. For, oh, but he *is* a bad boy!"

Caenis grinned. She had better reasons than Lydia knew to accept her mistress' statement. So had all the other younger wenches. I don't know why. They didn't appeal to me, really. Vengeance, I suppose; cheap and shoddy revenge for the shameful bondage in which Lydia kept me.

"Come sit beside me, you mannish boy," Lydia said, "and give me one good reason why I shouldn't have my Numidians in to whip you! That's it. Now tell Mama what you've done. . . ."

My head ached dully. I shrugged again.

"You've said it. Made use of another whore. So?"

"Oh!" she whispered. I saw she'd caught the emphasis I'd put on the word "another," slight as that emphasis was. The implication didn't escape her. It was, let me say at once, totally unjust. Lydia had never sold her remarkably expert body. She had merely—in that city noted for female depravity—been more generous than most. Which was something of a feat. It had taken me months to get used to the fact that it was an utter impossibility to enter the Senate, the Thermae, any principal street, and the houses of any of my friends without meeting a minimum of two, or a maximum of five, slyly grinning acquaintances who had shared my Lydia's bed.

"Would you like some wine? Very cool wine—packed in snow. I had runners bring the snow down from the mountains at quite ruinous expense. It will refresh you, Nathan. It—"

"No," I said.

"Some fruit, then? Apples? Grapes? Pears? Quinces?"

"Nothing," I said.

She was determined not to quarrel with me. I think she knew her beauty was beginning to fade. And, anyhow, I'd spoiled things for her. Before, any man could please her if he was powerful enough. She'd brought in gladiators, boxers, wrestlers, chariot racers, all the great muscled, brutal scum that caught her vicious eye. She'd totally demoralized the Numidian archers of the Imperator's Guard, because she had had of the divine Julia herself the confident assurance that no other men equaled blacks abed. My Helvetia had so enwrapped, immersed me in tenderness, that to Lydia, whose sexual proclivities were those of a lioness, I was a relevation. I *know* she was absolutely faithful to me, a statement which, if made in public, would have caused half of Rome to collapse in helpless laughter. Yet, strangely enough, it was true. Lydia loved me. She was one of the four women in all my life who truly did.

I lay there in the bathing pool. I could feel the hot perfumed water soaking the tiredness out of my body, the long, slow ache. But where I really hurt, it couldn't reach. I kept my mind locked against that—horror. Totally. I realize now that to be able to do that—to keep my hands from raising themselves to my face and clawing my eyes bloodily from their sockets so that they who'd already seen the unspeakable, the unbearable, would see no more—to keep the brine and bile from rising from bowels quite literally torn by horror, grief, and spewing forth upon the riptide of my anguish, I had to be mad.

Lying in that marble pool, watching Lydia strip off her stola in order to join me, letting my eyes play with the ghost, the remembrance of pleasure over her rarely perfect body, I was coldly, completely, unmistakably—mad.

She plunged into the water with me, and began at once to kiss and play with me, worshiping Priapus with her hot and busy hands. I shoved her away from me.

"Nathan!" she whispered. "What's wrong?"

"Nothing," I said.

"There is!" she said. "You—you've done something! Something terrible! Your eyes—"

I stood up, stepped from the bath. At once the slave girls began to towel the water from my body. Others, the *vestiplicae*, dropped a clean short tunic and then a fresh toga over my head, began to arrange its folds. I sat down on a teak and ivory stool while Eunice, the prettiest of them all, knelt and placed my sandals on my feet, lacing them skillfully about my ankles. Then I got up again. I even think I was smiling.

"Where are you going?" Lydia said. I could hear her voice growing shrill. I raised my hand in a gladiator's salute.

"*Salve*, Lydia," I said, and my voice was gentle. "*Salve, divina imperatora mea! Morituri te salutamus!*"

Then I turned and walked out of the bathing room, through the atrium, into the street.

The shock that my words produced in her held her long enough for me to do that. Then feeling surged back in her, I think, with the recognition that I meant them. She didn't even wait to let her attendants dry or dress her. Naked as Venus, she burst out into the Appian Way in the full light of morning, the droplets glistening on her body.

By then, I was locked in my uncle's arms.

Hezron ben Matthya raised his bushy brows and glared at her. I could see his great beak quiver with disgust. And Lydia quailed before that look, before the iron sternness of the Hebrew Prophet my uncle must have seemed to her, contorted her arms and legs to cover her nakedness, opened her mouth to let a wail of terror out, only to have it drowned in my uncle's thunderous roar.

"Jezebel!"

And hearing that awful name, not even knowing the meaning of it, Lydia became a flash of snow and midnight, blurring perception as she fled.

"So!" Uncle Hezron roared at me. "It's true! You've become a fancier of strumpets, a seeker after strange women! Even a practicer of—"

"Abominations? Yes. Turn me loose, Uncle Hezron," I said.

"Turn you loose? I've come to take you home, Nathan! Away from this stew of filth! I—"

I shoved against him rudely, trying to break his iron grip.

"Turn me loose!" I yelled. "I can't stand the smell of Jew!"

He looked at me then, gravely, sadly. He didn't even take offense. All he said, and that, quietly, was: "'Tis a smell you'll never rid yourself of, my boy."

But now another antic notion possessed me. I put out my hand, began to fumble in his pelages, the sacred curls, his beard. He struck my hand away angrily.

"Just what do you think you're doing, Nathan?" he said.

I eyed him solemnly.

"Looking for a louse in the beard of God," I whispered; and before he could recover from the shock of what must have been to him *Chillul Hashem,* a blasphemy against both Holy Israel and her God, I had torn free of him, and was pounding off, up the flagtsoned Way.

I started home then. By home, of course, I don't mean the house I'd just left, Quintus Valerius Caius' imposing palace on the Appian Way, but rather the modest little dwelling near the Forum Iulium, surrounded by the towering six- and seven-story-high *insulae,* tenements of the workers, where for as many as three nights a week when I could manage to escape Lydia for so long, but always for at least one, I shared the chaste and simple bed of my Helvetia.

But I couldn't go there, yet. I simply couldn't. So, with the elaborate logic with which pure madness disguises itself, I went instead to the Temple of Isis. The temple of the tender goddess, whom all Rome called the Mater Dolorosa; who is always represented as suckling the divine, reborn, resurrected child-god Horus. My Helvetia had a special devotion toward Isis. How many times had she prayed before this lovely image of divine maternity that we be granted a child?

And now I knelt before the Holy Mother and prayed, my words a thick, hot jumble in my mouth. I started out in Hebrew. But the only prayers I know in that austere priestly language are addressed to YHWH, the invisible, the unutterable, the one; and it occurred to me at once that he who said: "Thou shalt have no other gods before me!" would hardly approve of my praying to Isis, so I switched over to Aramaic, the language we speak now. But Aramaic is the child of Hebrew, and lends itself no more to praying to a strange goddess than Hebrew does. So I compromised and spoke to her in Greek, on the mad-logical theory that the Ptolomies had ruled Egypt long enough for her to have learned it.

"Mother of God," I said to her, "you who fanned breath back into the nostrils of Osiris with your divine wings; who with your prayers caused the sailors of the boat of Ra to cease rowing so that the Disk drifted, slowed, stopped in the sea of Heaven; and Thoth himself descended from the Boat of the Millions of Years to earth, to draw out Set's poison from the veins of your dead child with spells and magic and the great word of life and the fluid of life itself which he had of Ra, thus resurrecting the divine child; you who twice have performed the miracle of restoring departed life, who saved both your husband and your son after Anubis had borne them down to Amenti, the halls of death, give me back my Helvetia! Give her back! I beg you!

"She was good! I swear it! No Vestal was more pure! Do you not revere chastity? Don't you venerate tenderness? Then why, O Mother of God, did you—"

My words drowned in the gale storm of my weeping. The goddess sat there smiling and suckling the divine resurrected child. I saw she wasn't going to answer me. Her tender eyes turned cruel. Every fiber that bound me to reason broke. I could hear them twanging like the lute strings of the demon inside my head. I got up from there, rushed out into the street, filled both my hands with asses'* droppings, a commodity of which there was never any lack in the streets of Rome, came back, and hurled the fresh, hot, stinking dung into the faces of Isis and the child.

I don't know how I escaped alive. I think her priestesses were too stunned to lay hands on me. By the time they'd recovered and rent deaf heaven with their shrieks of horror, I had mingled with the crowd, was gone.

And now, once again, I started home. On the way, I passed soldiers lashing slaves into greater speed, needfully, for once. The slaves were digging into the rubble of a seven-story *insula* that had collapsed—a thing that happened every day in Rome—burying hundreds of plebeians in the ruins. I stood there watching them dragging the grotesquely twisted bodies out. I remember that I was laughing.

"Die!" I mocked those poor, bloody, dust-covered broken carcasses. "Let everybody die! Why should you stinking scum live when my Helvetia's dead?"

That was the first time I'd said it, admitted it to myself, and it sobered me. I turned my face in the direction of my house. I could go there now. Now, I could.

Nothing had changed. The house was still buzzing with flies. She —it—that thing—still lay in the tub, where she'd been ever since I went south to Baiae with Lydia three weeks ago. The water had evaporated. The blood from the great veins she'd opened—she was a Roman, she knew how to do it well—where her arms bent, had clotted into ropes, dried, turned black.

The water had been perfumed. That smell, too, mingled with the rest. With all the other smells.

The fat, white, blind, loathsome crawling things explored— No. That's rhetoric: a despicable form of literary cowardice. The worms, the maggots—

I can't. Even yet, I can't.

All the places where my fingers, my lips—

Forgive me. But there really aren't any words, are there? Not for this. For this!

She—it—that thing—(who'd been spun sunlight, spring air whispering, a warm breeze drifting over—I mustn't make bad poetry of it, must I?) had swollen so I had to pull and pull and pull to get her out of the tub. Parts of her—parts of her—

Iesus Nazarathaeus Rex Iudaeorum! Save—Ha! Who couldn't even save yourself from jesting Pilate or your teachings from that liar and madman, Paul!

Came off in my hands.

I vomited until there was nothing left in me to heave. Until my guts tore and the shreds of them tangled in my throat and choked me. By the time I got her out into the garden what was coming up was blood.

I buried her there. With my own hands I buried her.

Prayed over her. In Greek/Latin/Hebrew/Aramaic/Coptic/Syrian. Like the uselessly erudite ass I am. Prayed to all the gods. Cursed them all. Even YHWH.

Then I tottered, staggered, fell, crawled on my belly like a snake into the house, got my sword. Crept, inched, crawled, dragged myself with the great blaze of the setting sun and my own sweat in my eyes, blood and vomit in my throat, death itself in my mind, my heart, back to her grave. Clawed myself upright by pure will, put the sword point against my throat.

It was my slave Nicodemus who tore it from my hands.

Chapter VI

I'D BOUGHT Nicodemus with money I'd got from Lydia. At the moment, seeing him standing there holding my sword and glaring at me, I was disposed to curse her for that particular generosity.

"Later!" he said. "Tomorrow. Cut your throat tomorrow, master. Tomorrow I won't stop you. But today you have better use for your blade. Like sticking pigs with it, for instance. Starting with your good friend Avidius Publius. He organized the whole thing. Led it. He was the first to—to avail himself of—"

Does it seem strange to you that one of the feelings I had then was—relief? Helvetia hadn't killed herself because I—weak and spineless sot, witless slave to my dangling gut—had gone down to Baiae with Lydia. She'd opened her veins because—

My friends: Avidius Publius, Virginus Rufus, Sextus Oppius, Flavius Dolabella, Gabinius Sergius, Calvus Crispinnia—a dozen more. Taking turns at her. Lining up—as though she were a *scorta erratica,* an *ambulatrice notiluca.* A cheap street-strolling whore.

Helvetia.

Fun. Great sport. Better than the games. "Look you, friends and lovers—our little Caius Nathanaeus, our pretty little Jew masquerading as a Roman—has gone down to Napolis. To Baiae. With Lydia, of course. Seems she can't sleep unless he's there to do what that ancient great-grandfather of all cuckolds, Valerius Caius, no longer can. If the old fool ever could, which I doubt. But do you know what our Nathanaeus has left behind? I followed him last night, so I know. A treasure. Hair like a sunset. Not bleached. Born that way. Her own. Eyes like the sea off Sicilia. Breasts—Gentlemen, I ask you: What are we waiting for?"

The rage that rose in me was, strangely, a healing thing. Because it was outwardly directed. Freed me of my self-loathing, even could be assuaged by the simple act of killing the swine who'd done this thing. Which was precisely what I meant to do.

But Nicodemus wouldn't leave me even that consolation, not even so much as that relative degree of freedom from guilt.

"—like a tigress," he was saying. "She bloodied them all with her teeth, her nails. Kept screaming: 'No! I'm Nathan's! Can't you understand that, you goats and monkeys? *I* don't count. But when you touch, profane, what's his—what's sacred to his worship, befoul my body before his *lares,* his *penates,* you—"

"God!" I said.

"She trusted you," Nicodemus said grimly. "Poor child. Poor tender, simple child. That's why I won't stop you tomorrow, Caius Nathanaeus, my master! Tomorrow I'll hold the sword for you to run against—"

Then I saw that he was crying.

"Go on," I said.

"Publius—dog and son of a dog, ditch-delivered by a drab, who conceived him by—"

"Tell me!" I said.

"Told her, then. Said: 'Why do you fight, Gallic Rose? Because of Nathanaeus? Ha! That lewd little Jew has been betraying you this half year and more with Lydia. Where do you think he is now? Where else but in Baiae, making the beast with two backs with that ancient whore who can't even get a quarter of an as for her worn-out favors anymore, and hence has been reduced to bestowing them upon your Nathanaeus?' . . ."

I hung there. What was in me had neither voice nor name. "She stopped fighting, then. No, not then. Not at that exact instant; but a little later. After a kind of—of afterthought hit her. After she'd searched her mind, put together all the bits and pieces: your frequent absences, the whoremusk of Lydia's perfume that's soaked into your very pores by now. *Moechus! Scortator!* Lecher! Whoremaster! Aye, you can have me whipped; but I call you both! Unfaithful swine!"

"Go on," I whispered.

"And it came to her that Publius hadn't lied. No! Don't look at me like that! She—didn't surrender to them, take that dirty sort of vengeance upon you for what she knew you were guilty of. She just gave up. Went limp, inert—a slaughtered lamb—a poor little creature already killed. And I—"

"And you," I said.

"I am a coward, master. You know that. But I went into your house, fought them all. Jupiter and Mars witness it! Here! Look upon me! See my scars!"

"All right," I said.

"I am an old man, master. Sixty winters have snowed my hair, my beard. They beat me into insensibility. Oppius was for cutting my throat. But Publius wouldn't let him. 'No,' he said; 'I *want* Lydia's little Jew lapdog to know—'"

I didn't say anything. I couldn't.

"They bound me to a pillar, and went about their sport. Ha! They aren't even men! I'm sixty years old, but at that game I'd have out lasted them all put together. Oppius couldn't. Too fat, I guess. His puny little—"

"Stop it!" I screamed.

"When they'd gone—she—she cut me loose. You found her—buried her. You had to touch, lift her bloated, putrid—"

"Nico, no!"

"Little corpse. But I—had to look into her eyes. That was worse, master. Far worse. She sent me to find her women. Naturally, all your brave and loyal *familia* had fled at the first howl of those wolves. I couldn't find them. I haven't found them yet. I came back and she was already in tub—already—gone. I—"

"You?" I whispered.

"I lost my senses again, seeing that. Fell to the floor. The water—was red. The bathing room smelled like a butcher shop. A butcher shop that had been sprayed with her lovely, chaste perfume. Blood and scent, together. Her eyes were wide open, staring. Upon—"

"What?" I said.

"I don't know. Desolation, I suppose. A ruined landscape in which all the trees are bare and no bird ever sang. Upon the loss of hope. Upon death—become a mercy! I was afraid. So I ran away. I didn't dare come back to the house until you'd returned, master! I'm a slave

and the soldiers would have accused me of—of complicity in it. I
couldn't bear torture. Not anymore. So now—"

"Get me out some clean clothes," I said. "Bring them with you. Accompany me to the Thermae. Agrippa's. Get going, Nico!"

He stared at me; his dark eyes filled with contempt.

"The baths," he said. "To wash, perfume, anoint himself. To make
himself beautiful for that ancient—*bustuaria!*"

I stood there, held by the matchless aptness of his term. Because, of
the twelve separate kinds of prostitutes in Rome, each class having its
distinctive name, the *bustuariae* were the worst. They—hence their
name—plied their trade exclusively in graveyards, befouling with their
nameless perversions, their utter vileness, the very tombs of the pious
dead. They profaned life and death both, it seemed to me. Which, in a
way, surely without realizing it herself, was what my Lydia did.

Then I said quietly: "No, Nicodemus. Only to spare you from having
to wash my body afterward. The reason that your great Sokrates went
to the baths in the prison. So that I may die with my flesh, at least,
clean. You don't imagine that I can do what I have to—and live, do
you?"

He went on looking at me.

"No, young master; I don't suppose you can," he said.

When I came out of the baths, clean everywhere except where it
counts, the old slave looked at me a little sadly.

"What now, my master?" he said.

It came to me then that I was honor-bound to do something for him,
who'd be left homeless and without means of subsistence by my death.
So, with him trailing behind me like an ancient, mournful hound, I
went from one of the *exedrae*, sitting rooms, of the Thermae to another,
until I found a public scribe. He made ready his instruments, and I
dictated the following note:

"To the Divine Lydia, wife of Quintus Valerius Caius, from her
devoted son, Caius Nathanaeus, greetings! The bearer of this is my
slave, Nicodemus, who, while yet I lived, rendered me signal services—"

I stopped then, looked at Nicodemus.

"Or would you rather be freed?" I said.

"To starve?" Nicodemus said.

I went back to my chore. The scribe's stylus fairly flew as he cut
the letters into the wax smeared on his tablet.

"For which, by the love you bore me, my mother, I beg you to take
him into your *familia*, your household slaves, and set him about light

and pleasant tasks. Heed this request of one who will never ask you aught else in this world, and who bids you . . . farewell, Nathan."

"Nathan?" the scribe said.

"Caius Nathanaeus. It's a form of my name. How soon can you copy it out?"

"On papyrus or parchment?" the scribe said.

"Papyrus. It's of little importance."

"Now. At once," the scribe said.

"Go to it, then," I told him.

I've told you I'd been trained as a retiarius. Yet now, that fact was of no help at all. Of course I was months out of training; soft living had diminished my speed, my skill. But that, actually, was less important than the fact that a retiarius' training is, if anything, too specialized: he must win, if at all, by lightning-fast feints and dashes; let him just once fall into the error of closing with a great-thewed gladiator, and he'll surely be disemboweled. And now, unfortunately for me, the very circumstances wouldn't permit me to use the weapons with which my skill was unmatched, for a retiarius' trident and net couldn't be employed in a confined space; in a rich man's atrium, crowded with furniture, they'd be an actual hindrance.

Therefore I chose the one weapon that requires only an arm's length for its employ, and that can easily be concealed, the *sica* or dagger, which I realized even then was a poor choice against men who had served one and all with Cæsar's legions, and the smallest of whom outweighed me by twenty pounds. The result was ordained before I had begun: My failure was both pitiful and complete.

When I came up to Avidius Publius' house, his *nomenclator* sang out my name.

Avidius got up from his couch, where his *epilatores* were removing the hair from his body—he was a shaggy beast, almost like a bear—and put out his hand to me. Then he saw my eyes.

"Your Gallic slave girl, eh?" he said calmly. "Sorry about that, Nathanaeus. I'll send you another. No, I'll send you three. You'll have to wait, though. Flaxen-haired beauties like that one are plagued hard to come by in Rome. . . ."

"You swine!" I got out and lunged at him, raising my glittering *sica* high. That was my mistake. I should have held it low, as every expert knife fighter knows, close to my thigh, and killed him with an underhanded, upward thrust which would have greatly lessened his chances of seizing my wrist.

Which was exactly what he did, easily and at once. He'd been a

centurion in the legions; his training in hand-to-hand fighting made his
countermoves instinctive. His big hands closed on mine, twisting. I
managed to bring the point of the *sica* down and rake his forearm
before I had to let go of my weapon. The cut was very slight. It didn't
even bleed much.

He heard the dagger clatter to the floor; and hurled me away from
him with tremendous force. I stood there glaring, not even aware that
those perfumed effeminates, the *epilatores*, had fled. Avidius stepped
back a pace. Clapped his hands. Six gigantic, inky black Numidians
came into the atrium. It was as if he'd summoned them up from the
bowels of the Underworld by spells and magic.

I whirled like a trapped wolf—wolf? Sheol and Gehenna, both!—
like a cornered lady's lapdog, showing its tiny fangs and snarling.

The biggest of the Africans grinned. His teeth were snowy, like
pearls encrusted in midnight. I remember that detail. Then he
brought his staff down in a smart crack that broke my right arm,
straight across and cleanly. It sounded like a dried twig snapping.

I stood there holding my arm and howling like a child.

The Numidian saw the trickle of blood running down Publius' wrist.
"Shall we kill him, master?" he said. He might as well have been
asking the time of day.

Avidius Publius smiled.

"No. Just give him a good beating and throw him out, Juba," he
drawled. Then he sat back down, surrendering his burly body to the
epilatores, who had come whining and creeping back by then. The
scratch on his arm had already ceased to bleed.

The Numidians were experts. I demeaned myself. Begged mercy.
Implored them to let me go. But they kept right on beating me. Each
time I fainted, those inky sons of sin and Satan awakened me by taking
turns at urinating into my face.

When even that device failed them, they lifted me like a slaughtered
goat, with my tunic in ribbons, sticking to my shredded back, blood
coming out of my ears, nostrils, mouth, even the corners of my eyes,
walked with me as though I were weightless, and slung my broken carcass into the street.

I wasn't entirely out. I could hear the dark-toned drumbeat of their
laughter.

Some aeons later, I felt myself being lifted again. All the places I
was broken on the inside pulled apart. My guts felt as though I'd
dined on broken glass, washed down by vinegar, brine, and gall. I
turned my head and spewed up great clots of blood.

Then I felt something warm and wet splatter against my face. For an immeasurably brief fracturing of the stuff of time, my eyes cleared. I looked up.

"Don't cry, Uncle Hezron," I muttered.

Then night itself fell out of heaven, and hit me on the head.

Chapter VII

I OPENED my eyes. The sun was in them. Its glare was a quiver full of arrows plunged into my pupils. So I turned my head sidewise. The whole horizon rose, slanting skyward with ponderous, sickening slowness. Then, just as slowly it dipped, as though something or somebody wanted to throw me off the edge of the world. I heard the creaking groan of timbers. I knew then that I was on a ship. There was no mistaking that sound. I had heard it too many times before: When I'd been sent to Athens as a youth to further my Greek studies; cruising among the islands in summer with my Attic friends; on the long voyage to Rome when I'd eloped with Helvetia—

The sound of her name, inside my mind, was the tinkling of tiny silver bells, plunged into the wind, and drowned. Then memory shaped itself into a blade and pierced my heart. I arched my head back, back, dragged a long rasp of salt-tanged sea air into my lungs; but I never got that wail of pure desolation, utter anguish out, for a hard, dry, bony hand, having the feel of parchment and a lingering smell of incense about it, clamped down over my mouth.

"Hush, now, Nathan," my Uncle Hezron said.

My eyes must have cleared then; something of the ferocious, mindless grief must have left them, for, after a long moment, he took his hand away.

I didn't say anything. I lay there, looking at him. He had on his *tzitzith*, the fringed garment that our sacred Law requires us to wear. The *tefillin*—the phylacteries, those little leather boxes with scriptural texts in them—were bound to his temples and his left arm, near his heart. He'd even attached the *mezuzah*, the sacred sign, to the gunwale of the bireme we were on, having no doorpost to nail it to as the law required. Which meant he'd been praying for me. And, at the recognition of this further evidence of the great love my uncle bore me, my heart brimmed over and blind-scalded my eyes.

"Don't weep, my boy," my Uncle Hezron said. "You've wept enough now to last you a lifetime. Console yourself. We must seek healing for your heart, and peace."

I didn't answer him. Neither was possible. I knew that. This wound would bleed forever. I turned my head toward the other side of the ship. We were clawing away from a lee shore—a long, gray-white and yellowish spine of barren rock, half sunk in wine-dark seas.

"What land is that, Uncle?" I whispered.

"The Island of Crete," he said. "We'll be home before too long. . . ."

Home, I thought; but the word awoke no image inside my mind. Home was where Helvi was, and she—

I lay there listening to the creak and groan of the ship's timbers, watching the gulls scribing white arcs against the blue of heaven, and trying not to think. My right arm ached. Looking down, I saw it was bound to a plank. Which meant it was broken. Then I remembered that it was, and why. The great tears stole down from under my eyelids.

"Nathan, please!" my uncle said.

My whole body was swathed in bandages. I had four fractured ribs, though I didn't know that then. But it was not of my physical injuries that I was dying; it hadn't been the Numidians' merciless beating which had reduced me to a rack of quite visible bones straining to burst through the yellowish gray parchment of skin that was all that covered them. No, it was something else, something that has no name. Call it total horror, insupportable grief, and you have but profaned it by setting labels thereto. Say that all of me, down to my wasted, semi-carrion flesh, had no use at all for a world that had no Helvi in it; say that mind, heart, blood, breath, spirit, had taken counsel among themselves, and unanimously resolved to die.

Which was proved one hour later, when my uncle tried to feed me. He'd prepared the lightest, most delicate of foods. But they all came up at once, as soon as he'd got them down my throat by clamping his fingers into my jaws and forcing my mouth open. As I spewed them forth, I saw they were terribly mixed with blood.

Uncle Hezron bent his head and wept. I put out a trembling hand to him.

"Don't cry, Uncle Hezron," I said.

He turned his dark, fierce-tender eyes upon me.

"You've no right, Nathan!" he said. "Suicide is forbidden us by

Sacred Law! You'd do this to your mother? Leave her with such a
memory? 'My son, Nathan, starved himself to death over a foreign
strump—'"

"Uncle Hezron!" I said.

"All right. I'm sorry. I take that back. From what I gather from your
ravings, she was good. And you married her in Alexandria according
to our rites. Would God you could have stayed there! There are enough
people of our race, our faith in that city, so that—"

"In Rome, there were even more once," I said. "When have our numbers provided us with any protection, Uncle?"

"Never. I know. But what I don't understand is you. This poor child
—by heaven, Nathan, all our patriarchs and kings took foreign wives;
but they brought them under the canopy of the Law! And this poor
child, daughter of a Roman dog though she was, had demonstrated
that she loved you enough to accept our way! Rather, it was you who—"

"Uncle," I whispered, "let's not talk about it. Let's not mouth it over.
Not now. Not yet. Please!"

He sat there, staring at me. Above our heads, the sea gulls mewed.

"All right," he said; "but, for your mother's sake, promise me you'll
try to eat at least. Promise me, Nathan!"

I lay there, thinking about that. I could feel, deep inside me, the
stirring of something mindless, ancient, ancestrally deep. I didn't know
what it was, then. I don't even yet. But it must have been that stubborn instinct which through all vicissitudes has preserved the race:
the witless, blind, unyielding will to live. In spite of all that had happened to me, in some hidden corner of my being, I had it still.

"I promise, Uncle Hezron," I said.

I tried to eat. I tried. It did almost no good at all. Every morsel that
went down my throat, came up again, mixed with blood. Or almost
every morsel. Something must have stayed down, because, as our
bireme crawled toward Cyprus, I somehow stayed alive. And conscious.
Which was the worst of all. Because, try as I would, I could not help
remembering.

"Yes," my uncle said; "it was Shimeon ben Melchi who brought
your father the news you were in Rome; and, what was worse, your
doings there, the kind of life you led. You remember Shimeon, don't
you?"

I nodded. One of my father's friends. A member, like my father, of
the Sanhedrin. Titular head of a great mercantile family, whose business called him often to Rome. For though Tiberius had expelled my
people from that city, he saw no incongruity in continuing to trade with
us, as a nation. It wasn't hard to guess what had happened: Shimeon

had seen me by chance as I wandered about the streets of Rome in company of that swinish crew I called my friends. Or perhaps not even that. Perhaps I'd been alone. To a devout Jew, my close-cropped hair, my clean-shaven face, would have been enough. We are forbidden, you know, "to put iron to hair or beard." My bare legs under my short tunic. My look of imitation Roman.

"But you—?" I said.

"Your father sent for me," my uncle said. "The degree of unrest in Jerusalem these days made it impossible for him to leave his post. The High Priest depends upon him, you know. . . ."

"And you dropped everything, came—"

"Does not a shepherd seek the lost of his flock?" my Uncle Hezron said.

As the bireme crawled homeward, leaving Cyprus behind it, and I grew daily a little stronger, I deliberately dug into my memories with conscious cruelty. You see, by then, I knew I was going to have to go on living, so I exercised endlessly with crippling pain in order to train myself to bear it. It was something to do; it filled the dull, meaningless, slow-aching hiatus of my existence; it served, much of the time, at least, to keep the sweaty, itchy torture of my broken body's healing from clawing through to the surface of my mind. But, even so, the voyage itself was over before my convalescence was half begun.

On a day of blinding sun, under a sky like hot melted pearl, my Uncle Hezron carried my broken carcass ashore at Joppa. I, Nathan bar Yehudah, was home again. Or was I? Would I ever be? If a man's home is where his treasure lies, the answer to that was simple:

No. Never.

From where I lay, I could hear my father's voice. It was curiously harsh; the grate and scrape of his irritation sounded through it.

"He just lies there, Yosef," he was saying, "and stares at the ceiling. He eats—the bare minimum it takes to keep him alive. And much of the time it comes back up again. When it does, the vomit is bloody—as though his entrails were torn. . . ."

There was a silence. In the interval, I could hear my mother crying. She had done little else since my Uncle Hezron had brought me home.

"I see," my father's visitor said quietly. I recognized his voice. Yosef ha Arimathæa, a member of the Sanhedrin; one of my father's closest friends. "What do the physicians say?"

"That he is willing himself to die!" my mother sobbed. "And, oh, good friend Yosef, it's true! What magic did that foreign harlot have that he—"

"Precisely that you wrong her," Yosef ha Arimathæa said. "I've spent much time in Cæsarea, Eli-Sheba. I've had to—this business of trying to get our Roman friends—"

"The filthy swine!" my father said. It was the first time in all my life I'd known his urbanity to desert him.

"Ah, but one doesn't say it, Yehudah!" Yosef said. "Let's say I went there to get our Roman friends—our so very kind and good Roman friends—to return the High Priest's robe.[1] And though they keep it in the Fortress of Antonia, here, one must travel up to Cæsarea to dicker with them. So I often saw that pretty child. She was daughter of the centurion Helvetius, and he is head of the Procurator's personal guard, you know. Therefore my dealings with him were direct, and frequent. A good sort, the centurion. A believer in the old virtues: *Pietas, Gravitas, Simplicitas*. We became quite friendly. I've had many a cup with that old lion. Gratus trusts him. So, whenever our good Procurator has to treat with Antipas, whom he can't stand, he delegates the chore to Helvetius. Which is *why* your Nathan happened to meet the centurion's daughter."

"Tell us about her," my father said.

"Hmmmpf!" my mother sniffed. "What is there to tell, Yehudah? We all know what Roman women are! Strumpets one and all!"

"The point is, gentle Eli-Sheba," Yosef said, with patient irony, or ironic patience—it was hard to tell which, "that we don't know what Roman women are. I'd guess that the vast majority of them are good, faithful, and pious, for the very simple reason that without those fem· inine virtues, organized society simply isn't possible. I also grant you that since great power corrupts, Roman society *is* degenerating. But not to the extent you think. Helvetius invited me to his home. I met his wife: a blond giantess bigger than he is. But a simple, pious, good woman. I know of no woman of our race who is any more decent, morally, than she is—even giving those terms the accepted Jewish sense. And I was astonished when I met the daughter. Tiny, delicate, dainty—so much so that it was strange that those two great northern barbarians—"

"Perhaps," my mother said, *"he* isn't—"

"Don't say it, Eli!" my father snapped. "Don't let your worry and anxiety over Nathan distort your judgment. Or, still less, your charity. Let us grant that Nathan's wife—"

"Wife!" my mother said.

"Wife. Married in the Grand Rabbi's home in Alexandria, before the Rabbi himself, according to the Law. By heaven, Yosef, being mother of an only son disturbs a woman's reason, doesn't it?"

"Only, or many!" Yosef laughed. "About children, women are all mother hens! In simple justice, the child was Helvetius', Eli. Looked like him, as blond, as fair. But I gather that you don't *want* to know anything about her, do you?"

"No, I don't!" my mother said. "Look at my son now! And it's all her fault! If she—"

"Did she send Nathan to Tiberias, Eli?" my father said sadly. "Will you grant at least that their meeting was an accident?"

"Yes. But you'll have to admit she ran off with him the next day after they met, a thing that no *decent* girl—"

"Eli, Eli!" Yosef said. "She's dead. She died—horribly. In defense of the virtue that you deny her—and only you, because even the filthiest tongues of Cæsarea called her nothing worse than 'snowmaiden,' attributing to coldness what your Nathan proved was honor. I think you ought to listen. Give Nathan credit for good sense. He was quite a gay lad with the women before he met her so—"

"You mean he was a lecher and a drunkard," my father said sadly. "My fault, Yosef. I undermined belief in him. And without belief, virtue perishes. Being myself a doubter, I couldn't stand— No matter. Tell us about her. . . ."

When Yosef had done with the tale—part of which he'd got from Helvetia's father and the rest from my uncle, who knew it all from my ravings during the homeward voyage—my mother was crying harder than ever. She was especially moved by the incident of Helvi's sacrificing her hair to buy me food.

"All right, all right!" she wept. "I forgive her, the poor little thing! But Nathan is dying, and we still don't know what to do!"

Yosef ha Arimathæa hesitated. I could feel that hesitation.

"There are—some people I know," he began, "who live on the western shores of the Dead Sea—at Khirbet Qumrân—"

"You mean the Essenes, don't you?" my father said. "Ha! No wonder you hesitate! I've heard it said that you, my friend, are secretly of that mad persuasion—"[2]

"I respect them," Yosef said slowly. "It seems to me that the purity of their lives merits any man's respect. But I am not of their sect. I believe a man must live in this world, and work out his own salvation in the midst of its temptations. The Sons of Zadok, as they call themselves—"

"But *we* are the sons of Zadok!" my father said.

"Yes. But, according to the Essenes, we Zadokim have departed from the true way; and they, and only they, are the spiritual heirs of Zadok.[3] Be that as it may, they believe that a man can save himself only by living apart from this world's rottenness, by ritual washings, and by stern exercise of piety. Which isn't what concerns us here. I can vouch for the fact that they've worked many wonderful cures in just such cases as this, especially among the soulsick as our Nathan is. Because many come to them to be eased, to be cured[4] and almost always they send the sufferer away from them delivered of his demons. . . ."

"Then call them!" my mother cried. "Bring them here!"

"They won't come," Yosef said. "To avail yourselves of their services, you must carry the boy to them. It's not far off—a little below Jericho, near the town of Engadi—"

"No!" my mother shrilled. "He can't be moved! He must stay here! He must—"

"So that you can flutter, and fuss, and weep over him?" my father said. "How much good has that done so far, my poor Eli-Sheba?"

"Oh, Yehudah!" my mother moaned. "He's too weak! He couldn't stand—"

Yosef cleared his voice.

"There's another consideration," he said slowly, "that neither of you are taking into account, my friends. So far, I'm sure that Helvetius doesn't know the boy is back. But how long, in this spy-infested stink of corruption that our land's become, do you think it will take him to find out? And, when he does—He's a good enough sort, of course; but he's still—a Roman—"

Even from where I lay I could hear the breath strangling in my mother's throat.

"I've been told," Yosef went on, "that Gratus is going to be, or already has been, recalled. I don't know who his successor is. Doesn't matter. In any event, Helvetius, as his chief personal officer, is sure to go back to Rome with him. So it's not all that bad, Eli-Sheba. Some months—a year at most—and you can have your darling back again, safe and sound."

"Will he—will he be—?" my father got out.

"Safe there? Perfectly. The Romans leave the Essenes strictly alone. They hold they've nothing to fear from a group of fanatics who spend all their time bathing, and afterward don't even oil their skins. I think they're wrong. I think the Essenes, or their descendants, the spiritual force they represent, will one day overturn the world. Well, my lady Eli-Sheba bath Bœthus ha Yehudah! What say you?"

"Oh, Yosef!" my mother sobbed. "I'm so afraid! I—"

"Don't be, my love," my father said. "Well, Yosef, could you—"

"Arrange it?" Yosef ha Arimathæa said. "Yes. Yes, surely. Give me until day after tomorrow, and I'll let you know. But, meantime—keep watch!"

I heard his footsteps going away. After that, there was no other sound but my mother's crying.

Chapter VIII

ONE YEAR from that day, I was sitting on a rock outside the monastery at Qumrân, looking down at the blinding silver blue of Lake Asphaltides, as the Romans, who always put fact before poetry, called the Dead Sea. I was dressed in the white robes of an Essene novice; I carried the little hoe of personal hygiene at my belt[1] but I would never become an Essene. I knew that now.

For some weeks after my father and Yosef ha Arimathæa had brought me to Khirbet Qumrân, I lay silent and remote on my bed of pain. But summer being upon the land, the Essenes bore my litter outside, and left me under the vast canopy of the night sky. Lying there night after night—some of them moon-silvered and ghostly, so that the lake was a misting, a loveliness; the others blacker than the pit, blazing with stars—I could feel the whole ponderous slow turning of the universe above me so that my heart cried out with the Psalmist:

"When I consider the heavens, the work of thy fingers, the moon and the stars which thou hast ordained: What is man, that thou art mindful of him? and the son of man, that thou visitest him?"[2]

Then I whispered to myself: "That is, if you ever do . . ." And bent my head and wept.

But that very next morning I was stronger, and felt something like hunger stirring in me. Thereafter, very slowly, I began to heal. I must admit that my progress was not steady. I fell back often enough into grief, into near madness, into ravings; and again my bowels were torn. I composed for myself, from the words of the Psalmist, a whole new litany of pain, by taking the verses out of context, and combining them to suit myself:

"My soul is also sore vexed:
but thou, O Lord, how long?
I am weary with my groaning;
all the night I make my bed to swim
I water my couch with my tears.
Why standest thou afar off, O Lord? Why
hidest thou thyself, in times of trouble?
How long wilt thou forget me, O Lord? forever?
How long wilt thou hide thy face from me?
How long shall I take counsel in my soul, having
sorrow in my heart daily? How long
shall mine enemy be exalted over me?
The fool hath said in his heart,
There is no God!
My God, my God why hast thou
forsaken me? Why art thou so far
from helping me, from the words
of my roaring?
O my God, I cry in the daytime
but thou hearest not
and the night season
and thou art silent. . . ."[3]

But life was in me, stubborn and deep; the sun came up for me ceaselessly in the morning over the bleak mountains, sank down at night beyond the bitter lake. My bones knitted themselves together; the sparse and simple foods the Essenes gave me stayed down. I rose up from bed at last, and walked.

Even after I was strong enough to have gone home, I elected to stay. At first, I worked as a domestic servant, for among the Essenes the humblest tasks are accorded honor. I cleaned the communal rooms and kitchens, swept the plaster floors, raked those of hard-beaten earth. Later, I worked in the pottery, turning the vases they used to store the sacred scriptures in; but the heat of the kilns sickened me; for the same reason, I was spared taking turns as a kitchen scullion. But outdoors, I made myself useful, and, by so doing, acquired a certain skill that subsequently was to affect my life in no small measure.

At that time, the members of the Qumrân community were building a new aqueduct, as well as repairing the old one, for nothing was more important to the Bathers at Dawn than water. Yet surely they could not have chosen a worse place for their refuge in that particular regard, for the closest available supply of abundant water was the Dead Sea, which, as all the world knows, is so salt that not even fish can live in it, and so dense that nothing, not even a man bound hand

and foot, will sink when therein thrown. Therefore, they had to bring a steady supply of the fluid without which we cannot live, from sources high in the rugged hills behind the monastery. For, by then, their numbers had grown too great to make total dependence upon the great cisterns they built to catch the winter rains possible any longer.

Now, ever since my days in Rome, aqueducts had fascinated me. How many hours had I walked beside the Marcian and the Appian arches, with Helvetia, studying their graceful sweep and soar! You'd have to be a Judean, a dweller in that parched land, baked from childhood by its pitiless sun, to understand how deep that fascination was. Even in well-watered Galilee, upon more than one occasion, I had seen my Uncle Hezron lose his entire harvest because the rains didn't come or delayed too long. So I asked to be assigned to working on the new aqueduct, which was, of course, much harder work than repairing the old, because I knew I'd learn far more about the art of building them that way. I made a fearful nuisance of myself with my questions: What stones were best to build the arches with? Wouldn't bricks do, if stones weren't available? What materials were best for lining the miniature covered canal that carried the water atop the arches? How did one maintain enough pitch over so many stadia to keep the water flowing?

It was that last question that was all important, for it is upon it that the functioning of an aqueduct depends. The correct answer, the *Paqid* in charge told me, was six *unciae*—an *uncia* being about the length of the second joint of your little finger in case you don't know— of fall in every hundred feet of length.

But there were other problems, chief among them being a source of enough fresh water in the first place. For the Essenes, with all their ritual bathing and ceremonial uses of the precious liquid, needed— and I'm being conservative in my estimate—at least ten times as much water per man as did the citizens of Jerusalem, say. They'd solved that problem handily enough, by finding a natural basin high in the hills, and damming up the lower end of it so that the water pouring into it from the winter rains couldn't run off. Thus they had made a quite respectable artificial lake, whose waters, brought down to Khirbet Qumrân by the old aqueduct, filled the local cisterns sufficiently to serve their needs all year round.

But by the time I was brought to them, not even that supply sufficed, and they'd been forced to build another artificial lake. This second lake was considerably higher, and some distance away from the old one, so that the new aqueduct had to come down to the monastery by a long, curving, roundabout sweep.

Which was why I got a chance to work on it despite the fact that they had started it more than two years before my arrival at Qumrân. You see, they'd run into problems so grave that I was up and about again by the time the new structure was three-quarters done. First of all, they had had to cut a tunnel through solid rock with hammers and chisels to draw the water off from their new lake once the rains had formed it; and now they were hopelessly halted on the edge of a gorge whose further side—that is, the side nearer to the monastery—was *higher* than the one they had reached with the aqueduct on its descent from their man-made lake. Not much higher—say a rod. But that rod represented catastrophe, because it meant not only that they couldn't maintain the needed drop of six inches every hundred feet, but that they had to, for a distance of some five or six rods, slant the bed of the little watercourse atop their arches up at an angle so steep that it was inconceivable that the water would continue to flow. They organized three nights of fasting and prayer, asking God to inspire someone with the solution to that quite insoluble problem.

Do you know whom God chose to illuminate?

Me.

Don't smile. I'd learned a great deal about hydraulic engineering by then. The Paqid in charge of the works was indulgent. And that he was almost surely more than a little flattered by my interest wasn't strange when you consider the fact that all the rest worked in stony silence, or to the accompaniment of groans designed to demonstrate how great their sufferings were! In any event, he taught me all he knew of the art, which was considerable. But, actually, I was the only one at Qumrân who could have solved the problem, because I was the sole man there who had been to Rome. To tell the unflattering truth, and to place my glorious accomplishment on its proper level in the scale of things, all I had to do was to use my memory, recall how the Romans—the finest practical engineers the world has ever seen—solved the same problem when they met it along the routes of the colossal spans they built to bring water from sources thirty *milia* and more away to Rome. Because you see they had met this selfsame problem, that of forcing water to run uphill against the whole awful down-pull of the world, and solved it!

God's illumination was far from brilliant; or perhaps, more justly, I should admit the material he had to work upon, the sodden lump inside my skull, was exceptionally poor. Be that as it may, it still took me three whole nights of cudgeling my so-called brains before I finally remembered how the first inverted siphon—the device the Romans had invented to make water run uphill—I'd ever seen looked, not to men-

tion the detailed explanation I'd had of its workings from a Roman engineer who was a friend of my adoptive father, Quintus Valerius
Caius, and, like all poor Caius' friends, one of Lydia's former lovers,
surely.

I went to the Paqid and drew the device on the ground for him with
a pointed stick. Draw it for yourself, or else you'll have no clear idea
how it works. First scribe a horizontal line, perfectly straight and level.
Now leave a gap. Then draw another horizontal line beyond the gap,
a little higher than the other. Connect the two lines with a capital letter
U, so that the end of one line and the beginning of the other touch
the tops of the U. Naturally, you'll have to make one side of the U a
little higher than the other to meet the elevation of the second line.

The Paqid stared at my drawing, shook his head. " 'Tis against all the
laws of nature!" said he. But I wouldn't give up. I built him a model of
bricks, making the channel atop my miniature aqueduct of clay. I du-
plicated the terrain to scale, gorge and all. The arches that spanned my
little gorge, instead of maintaining as near a level as possible, I made
considerably lower than those on either side, thus forming the capital
U you've drawn, so that the water coming from above roared down
into this deep-slanted, low-slung half loop with such force that it pushed
itself uphill on the other side.

He watched me pour water into the lower side of the device, saw that
water race down the U-shaped reversed arch I had made, and up the
other, higher side a hundred times before he'd believe it. Then, very
simply, he said: "So be it, my son. God has illuminated your heart."

The inverted siphon was built under my personal supervision. The
Paqid stood aside, told even members of the Elect to obey my orders.
The lesson in humility he gave me by the quiet serenity with which he,
immensely my superior in every way that counted, took orders from me,
a lowly novice, served me well. When my task was done, and the inverted siphon worked perfectly upon being tested, I quietly took my
place in the ranks without a single boast.

Thereafter, the Paqid made me his chief assistant. The last three
stadia of the aqueduct were built as much under my direction as under
his. I worked harder than any man there, studying the smallest details of the building process. You see, my interest was far from idle: I
meant to free my Uncle Hezron's farm, surely to be mine one day,
from its agonizing dependence upon the seasonal rains.

The aqueduct done, my day of glory ended, I turned without complaint to far lesser tasks. I plugged cracks in the cisterns with clay,
cleaned them when empty, used them with the other novices, apart,
of course, from the *Esath ha Yahad*, the Elect, for my daily ritual wash-

ings. I repaired roofs, I served as goatherd and shepherd; I worked as
a common farm laborer in the green fields at Ain Feshkha; my skin
burned black, my muscles corded into sinewy power; I did without protest, with peace, with joy, things that no high-born Sadducee would
have dreamed of demeaning himself to do—and was by doing them,
in a strange way, healed.

But one day, hearing that one of the *maskil*, the teaching masters[4]
was going up to Jerusalem, I went into the scriptorium and begged a
scrap of parchment, a quill, and some ink, in order to write my mother
a letter, and my position among the novices changed vastly for the
better. The Paqid in charge of the scriptorium was surprised only at
my boldness; writing is no rare accomplishment among my people; even
such sons of humble folk as Yeshu'a managed, not infrequently, to
learn to scribble a word or two. On that occasion, however, a thought
struck the Paqid. He pointed to a bench before the stone writing tables,
said to me: "Sit down, son Nathan, and show me a sample of your penmanship. We always have need here of a clear hand. . . ."

I did as I was told. Despite a lingering stiffness from the but recently
knit bones of the arm the Numidian had broken, my hand had lost
little of its cunning, its skill. The Paqid examined the biblical verse
I'd copied out. Then he said:

"You write well, Nathan. Go ahead with your missive to your
mother. Meantime, I'll ask the *Mebaqqer*[5] to assign you to me perma-
nently. . . ."

As a novice, of course, I wasn't allowed to copy any of the more
secret scrolls. For the most part, I copied the Sacred Scriptures, common
to all Jews. But some of the cryptic writing also passed through my
hands, because the Paqid saw that I could copy it accurately, though I
didn't understand it at all. Had he dreamed I would come to decipher
it, he would never have let me so much as glance at it. But there in the
scriptorium, among the soft whispering of the goosequills, I found an
interest that put back some savor in my existence: to puzzle my head
daylong, nightlong, over the meaning of the secret books. I soon saw
that they had some connection with predicting the future, an art for
which throughout Israel the *Berith Hadashahim,* the New Covenanters,
as the Essenes called themselves, were famed.

At last I connected these writings with the Essenes' practice of placing certain Elders upon the watchtowers, where they studied the movements of the heavenly bodies and recorded them on charts, using the
signs of the Zodiac.[6] As soon as I came to understand this essential
aspect of the question, it was child's play for me to break the code.

As soon as I was sure I had the method right, I tried casting a horoscope for myself. It said I would love a dark woman hopelessly through many moons, that nothing would ever come of this love, that thereafter I would marry another and by her have sons. Moreover, I would become involved in great and murky events, become a member of a new body of emergent Saints—

At which point I threw the bloody nonsense into the fire.

But my peaceful life with the Essenes soon came quite unexpectedly to an end. I remember it was a winter day, and blisteringly hot, for in that lowest spot on earth[7] the seasons were indistinguishable from one another; quite often at Qumrân the months of Shebat and Adar are *hotter* than Ab or Elul.[8] Moreover, it was shortly before, or shortly after, the anniversary of the day my broken carcass had been brought on a litter to the monastery. I sat there on a rock before the door of the novices' eating hall, and stared downward toward the harsh, metallic glare of the Dead Sea. And I'm sure it was not more briny nor more bitter than was my heart.

You see, I hadn't found there what I'd hoped to, which was the serene and lofty peace of mind that the Essenes possessed; after one full year among them, all I had was an unsatisfied hunger after that peace of theirs, that tranquility. I'd struggled, mortified my flesh, submitted zealously to discipline in an effort to find again my childhood faith in a just and beneficent God. But neither my personal history, nor that of my people, would allow me that comfort. All that had happened to my race inclined me to think that if they were God's Chosen People, it was far better to be forgot by him. And if what he had let happen to me was in punishment for my sins, he couldn't be called merciful. And if he'd used my poor sinless chaste pure good kind tender loving Helvi as the instrument of my chastisement, the mildest term I could apply to him was Monster. Therefore I was forced to the conclusion that it was less repugnant morally not to believe in God at all than it was to worship an absentee landlord of a deity on the one hand (and that, granting him the benefit of every conceivable doubt!) or Satan's own fiendish twin on the other.

Naturally I wasn't fool enough to inflict these bitter and rebellious opinions of mine upon the Essenes. But, seeing that I made no progress at all toward their peculiar and evident sanctity, they preached at and questioned me endlessly until they proved me into an exposition of my thought, to wit:

That, logically speaking, if my father knows on the first day of the week that on the third I am going to bed with a tavern slut, get her with unlawful child, kill a man in a drunken quarrel over her unwashed favors, be strangled in due course by the authorities for my crime, if, I repeat, my father knows all this beforehand and does not chain me to my bed on the morning of the third, he is guilty of unspeakable cruelty—which, I pointed out to them, is exactly the behavior of which they piously accuse their God.

That, logically speaking, if you grant man freedom of will, in order to load him like a poor braying ass with the responsibility for his sins, you hurl God down from heaven, because man can only be free to act against the will of God if God has neither knowledge nor power. For a God without omniscience and omnipotence may be whatever else you will, but certainly not a God!

That, logically speaking, God can never absolve Himself totally of complicity in mankind's evildoing, for does not the created partake inevitably of the nature of the Creator? Is not Cause—even First Cause, God—eternally, if invisibly present in Result—even final result, man? Or to put it in more mundane fashion: Would I have been a doubter had I been Uncle Hezron's son? Can my father with a clear conscience punish me for sins which are but reflections of the tendencies I got from *him*? Whoremonger, brawler, drunkard, skeptic that I am, *who* made me thus? And if you answer Satanas, I reply: Why not, then, worship him, since he so endlessly and effortlessly demonstrates that his power is greater than your God's?

That, logically speaking, that is precisely what your belief leads you to, for, if you insist upon retaining all three concepts: man's freedom and God's total knowledge, and limitless power, then you *must* dethrone YHWH and put black Samaël-Satanas in his place, for a deity that can act and won't, that knows beforehand and neither warns nor stays, and then metes out a punishment so awful that no sin any man could do is commensurate with it—for what iniquity can equal Sheol's endless night, Gehenna's eternal fire?—is Evil's pristine self!

Thereupon they dolefully shook their heads at me, and came back with the religious man's stock irrelevancy: that the ways of God are too lofty, too mysterious for our puny human intellects, that we must worship and adore Him without questioning, humbly bend our necks to his rod, kiss the awful hand that sends the pain which teaches us wisdom, that—

And all the time I was seeing that thing that had been my Helvi in that tub, until I couldn't even bear the sound of their voices anymore, and walked off and left them there.

So now I knew I could never be one of them, because I lacked the beautiful simplicity of their minds. They believed all things already explained; I knew in my bitter bones that nothing was. All I was hoping

now was that they'd give up and leave me in peace; but I knew they
wouldn't do that, either. They had set their hearts upon bringing me
into the fold. I wrote a beautiful hand; I was the son of a Sadducee
priest, and, though they denounced pride, it lingered in them still. To
gain such a one as I, would have gladdened them.

I was thinking all that when I heard footsteps, and turning, saw a
great number of them coming toward me. At their head strode no less
than the Mebaqqer, himself, accompanied by the sternfaced Paqid,
followed by the Melis, the Doresh ha Torah, and my personal Maskîl,[9]
by whom I mean the teaching master who had been assigned to me.

They came up to me, and stood there staring at me in solemn anger.

"Son Nathan," the Mebaqqer said, "what is this I hear of you?"

I prostrated myself before him with no feeling of resentment. In fact,
I felt the utmost reverence for so holy a man.

"Get up," the Mebaqqer said. "Now speak out. Is it true that you're
guilty of blasphemy?"

"I, Father?" I said, astonished.

"You. Did you not say to your maskîl that the Hymns were nonsense?"

I stared at my master. This was difficult. I had made no such sweeping statement. What I had said was—what I decided to repeat to the
Mebaqqer now.

"Yes, Father. And, no. Some are, and some aren't."

The whole *yahad* gasped. But the Mebaqqer went on looking at me
with total serenity.

"Go on," he said.

"Some are true," I said slowly. "Take, for instance:

> 'I was as one forsaken in the desert
> without refuge. And all that I'd planted
> turned into wormwood.
> My pain was terrible, there was no stopping it;
> My soul was overwhelmed,
> gone down to Sheol,
> and my spirit descended among the dead.
> My life had reached the deepest pit,
> without rest by day, by night,
> my soul grew faint—
> My bones blazed with hidden fire,
> and the flames of it devoured me
> exhausting my strength, consuming my flesh. . . .
> My arm was broken at the shoulder,
> I could not move my hand.
> My knees were dissolved in water;
> I could take no further step—'[10]

"That's true, Father. So was *I* when I came here. . . ."

"And what is *not* true, son Nathan?" he said.

> "'You will give the children of your truth
> unending joy and everlasting gladness,
> And, according to the measure of their knowledge
> so shall they be honored one more than another.'"[11]

The Mebaqqer stared at me.

"And that is *not* true, son Nathan?" he said.

"No, Father. Not now. Not while foreign barbarians hold the High Priest's robe. Not while we have to risk our lives to keep them from defiling the Temple, from setting up their *Gillulîm*, their filth, their idols, in the very Holy of Holies. Not while there is neither joy nor gladness in the land of Israel, not while we groan under the yoke of the *Kittim*, the Romans! Not—"

The Mebaqqer lifted his hand.

"It will come," he said. "They will be overthrown. The Mashiah will overthrow them, when he comes."

I stood up then, snarled at him:

"Much good that will do you or me, or any man here! For before your hypothetical Mashiah comes, our great-grandchildren will be dead!"

He shook his head.

"That depends upon you, son Nathan," he said quietly, "and upon me, and upon every man born of Abraham. For the day we achieve piety, truth, purity, that day will the Mashiah come!"

"Then, Father," I said bitterly, "he will *never* come."

The people made an outcry against me then; but their leader, the Mebaqqer, silenced them.

"Go you, my son," he said quietly. "Walk by the lakeside. Pray. Ask that a sign be given you. Then come to me, and I will interpret God's will for you. It may be that He means for you to return to the world. Perhaps your work lies there. I'd hoped, because your knowledge is great and your mind keen, that you might be granted wisdom, become one of us. But God's will, not ours, be done. Go you now. Meditate. Pray. Then come to me with your decision. May it also be—God's—"

I bowed to him again, whispered: "I thank you, my Father—" and turning, started down to the shore.

I saw the boatmen with their boats drawn up along the shore. I started to turn away from them, because all you could fish in the Dead Sea were the black masses of bitumen that came floating to the surface, and were so sticky that the boatmen cleaned their boats of the clinging tarry mess with jars of the menstrual blood of their wives and daughters, which they saved for this purpose, claiming that nothing else would dissolve it.[12] And, although I've never been especially squeamish about the body's natural functions, the process wasn't a thing any man would relish watching. But today I saw that the tar gatherers were standing together in a group, talking to one another with some excitement, while the black lumps of bitumen melted unnoticed in their craft under the blazing sun, despite the fact that it was winter now, for the Dead Sea knows no seasons.

I went towards them, a curious, anticipatory emotion prickling along my spine. But they noticed my robe's cut and whiteness and fell silent. They had a vast respect for the Essenes. From the way they looked at me, you'd have thought that I was the *Morêh Zedog*, the legendary "Teacher of Righteousness," himself.

"What's happened?" I said to them. "In God's name, good boatmen, what—"

They bowed to me first. Looked at one another.

"It's like this, Reverend Father—" one of them began.

"Speak, man!" I said to him.

"It's the new Procurator. He got here, yesterday—I mean he came down to Jerusalem from Cæsarea to put the troops up in the Holy City for the winter—"

"So?" I said. There was nothing new about that. The Roman troops always wintered in Jerusalem.

"He brought the bust of the Roman Emperor with him!" the boatman said, his voice becoming hoarse with horror; "and all the *signa* of the Legions! Slipped them into the city by night. When the people woke up this morning, they were there!"[13]

I hung there. What blazed through my veins was a great and terrible joy. I had to go home now. I had to! For surely all Jerusalem was flaming with rebellion. Then I hesitated. What the tar fisherman had told me made no sense. The Procurators knew our stern prohibition against the display of graven images in the Holy City; and always, up until now, they had respected it. What manner of man was this new Procurator? A madman, surely! What did he hope to gain by forcing the whole nation to revolt?

"Surely you're mistaken, boatman," I said. "The Procurators are charged by the Imperator himself to respect our customs—"

"Only this one's different, Reverend Father," the boatman said; "kind of cocksure. Seems he's married to Cæsar's own daughter and—"

"But that's impossible!" I began: "Cæsar has no—" Then I stopped. I had been about to say that Tiberius had no daughters, which was true. But he did have two stepdaughters, both presented to him without carnal labor on his part by the divine Julia, daughter of Augustus: Agrippina, whom Julia had had by her first husband, Agrippa—and Claudia, by God knows whom. The little Claudia who, even before I'd left Rome, the gossips were saying was going to marry—

"His name, boatman?" I said: "The new Procurator—what's he called?"

The spokesman turned to another tar-fisher, surely he who had brought the news.

"What's his name, Yonas? What's the new Roman *Epitropos*[14] called?"

The man thought.

"Pilatus. Lucius Pontius Pilatus," he said.

Half an hour later, it was all done: I had taken leave of the New Covenanters, as respectfully as the circumstances, and the furious excitement leaping and blazing in me, would allow; I procured a fast horse, paying for the beast the double of its usual hire; and now, dressed in my own rich dark clothes for the first time in more than a year, I pounded toward Jerusalem.

As I rode toward the Holy City, words sang and leaped through my head:

> "I will render vengeance to mine adversaries,
> and will recompense them that hate me.
> I will make mine arrows drunk with blood
> and my sword shall devour flesh;
> with the blood of the slain and the captives
> from the head of the leaders of the enemy!"[15]

Pilatus! Of course he had taken no part in the outrage against Helvetia; but he was of that dissolute band. And, in any event, he was a Roman! Silently I blessed him for his thick-skinned arrogance. He had given me something to live for at last.

Vengeance.

Which was, it seemed to me then, an honorable motive for continuing an existence that lacked all else.

I came up to Jerusalem by the Jericho Road, entered the Holy City by Herod's Gate. An elementary degree of prudence would have caused me to turn southward once reaching the Mount of Olives, swing half-

way around the city, and come into it by the Dung Gate, thus avoiding all danger of running into the Romans. But I remembered Yosef
ha Arimathæa had said that Helvetia's father would probably go back
to Rome with the retiring Procurator Valerius Gratus, which meant
that he was surely halfway to Rome by now; and since no other Roman
had any personal reason—not that they needed reasons, not that they
wouldn't murder a Jew for the mere sport of it!—to kill me, that danger
was greatly lessened. Besides, there was a hard recklessness in me that
panted after danger, that sought it.

I reached my father's house, plunged into it, taking all the stairs two
at a time, entered my bedroom, tore my sword down from the wall,
turned—

My father was standing there, smiling at me with quiet mockery.

"Put that thing down, Nathan," he said.

"But, Father!" I roared at him. "We can't let—"

"The Romans get away with this obscene blasphemy?" my father
said. "Of course not, Nathan. But neither can we afford the folly
of fighting them with their own weapons. We must use methods that
have some chance of defeating them, tactics which, being the barbarians and savages that they are, they don't even understand—"

"Nor do I, Father!" I said.

"Because you, too, are at least a barbarian, if not a savage, Nathan,"
my father said, only half in jest, it seemed to me. "Now put up that
barbaric instrument of utter barbarians and come greet your mother.
She'll be delighted to see you. Incidentally, so am I. I must say you're
looking well—"

I remembered my manners then, went to him, got to my knees,
took his hand, kissed it. He raised me up, and kissed both my cheeks,
warmly, murmured a prayer. I took his arm, and we went in together
to the women's quarters.

My mother's cries of pure delight could be heard at least in Athens,
if not in Rome.

When I had disentangled myself at last from her embraces, my
father drew me away with the pretext of taking me to the Temple to
receive the High Priest's blessing. I knew he was lying; he couldn't
have cared less about the High Priest, or whether I was blessed or not.
One of the advantages of being a Sadducee is that we don't believe in
the immortality of the soul or a life after death; therefore we wear the
yoke of religion lightly.

He took me into his scriptorium, sat me down, called for the servants
to bring us fruit, wheaten cakes, wine.

"I must say you at least *look* like a Jew at last," he said smilingly.
I did. In Khirbet Qumrân, I'd let both my hair and beard grow
long.

"But, Father!" I said angrily. "What are we going to do—?"

"About the Romans?" he mocked me. "What do you propose, Nathan?
That we marry—or at least ravish—all their daughters?"

He had a typical Sadducee's humor: unfeeling, harsh, and, if I may
say so, crude.

"Hardly!" I snapped. "They haven't enough of their women here to
go around; and, besides, the boot's on the other leg in that gentle sport,
Father. Wherever they're quartered, they don't leave a virgin over
twelve years old, unless she be fleeter than a gazelle. But enough of this
banter, my venerable and respected Sire! I'd still like to know what's
to be done!"

"All right," he said, and his wonderfully handsome face—would
God I'd inherited his looks!—became serious. "Word has gone out to
all the Nation. All Judea, Transjordania, Peraea, Idumæa, the Decapolis, Gaulanitis, Ituræa, Batanæa, Galilee—that every able-bodied man,
priests and laymen alike, of whatever persuasion, Essene, Pharisee,
us—"

"Go on!" I said.

"Shall march at dawn tomorrow upon Cæsarea—"

"Good!" I said.

"Unarmed," my father said.

"By Gehenna!" I bellowed. "By Sheol! That's folly, Father! The
Romans—"

"Would sweep a poorly armed, untrained Jewish rabble into the
sea, dye it red with our blood," my father said. "But a crowd of men
without even staffs, they'll dare not touch. Remember the Procurator
has to justify himself to Cæsar, and, more immediately, to the Governor
of Syria, who, I've been told, is a most temperate man—"

"Vitellius?" I said. "He is. But Pilatus isn't. Unfortunately. I happen
to know him well. In Rome, he considered himself a friend of mine."

"What's he like?" my father said.

"An unmitigated swine. An utter scoundrel. A mocker. Hard,
reckless, without scruples.[16] You know how he came to power? by
marrying the divine daughter of the divine Julia!"

My father shook his head.

"You'll have to clarify, son," he said. "I know nothing of Roman
lineage—divine or not!"

"All right. Julia is the daughter of Cæsar Augustus. She was married

twice before Augustus pushed her off upon the present occupant of the
throne, Tiberius. But, long before our great Cæsar reached the rulership of the world, Julia had adorned his forehead with the assistance
of every slave scum in Rome. 'Tis said she used even the blacks of his
Numidian guard. He bore it with resignation, not daring to offend
his august father-in-law. But someone brought the matter to Augustus'
attention. And whatever may be said of Augustus, no man can label
him unjust. He exiled his own daughter because her flagrant immorality offended him. And, while in exile, Julia bore a bastard daughter, Claudia, to a Roman knight. The child was brought back to Rome,
and made a part of Tiberius' household, when, at fifty-five years of
age, our present Imperator reached at last the pinnacle of his ambitions. Claudia was sixteen when Pilatus saw her—and by then her
virginity was not even a memory to her—"

"You've a cruel tongue," my father sighed.

"But a truthful one! Anyhow, this swart, lean and hungry Iberian,
Lucius Pontius Pilatus, saw the divine Claudia. And what cared he if
she made the beast with even the stone statues in the imperial gardens?
She was the road to greatness. He asked her hand, and Tiberius,
only too glad to be rid of this wild duplicate of Julia, gave his consent.
So, overnight, a penniless, unknown Spaniard becomes Procurator of
Judea.[17] And what's worse, one who feels himself supported by his
connection to the Imperial family, however indirect that connection is.
Father, we've got to—"

"Rid ourselves of him? Of course. But, by subtle methods, my son.
Well, will you march with us tomorrow—unarmed?"

I thought about that. But I had seen the Legions at their exercises,
and in the games. I knew what a cohort—no, even a century—could
do against an untrained mob. The Roman Legions were the closest
thing to an invincible force the world had ever seen. My father was
right: To try to fight them was suicidal folly.

"Yes, Father, I'll march," I said.

The next morning, when we set out, afoot, for Cæsarea, all the
roads were choked with men. And not only the roads, but the fields
beside them, the crests of the hills. It was like some great swarming of
insects, crawling under the brazen sun, beneath the high clear sky.

We didn't talk. We simply walked, our feet measuring off the stadia
between Jerusalem and Cæsarea. Now and again we stopped to rest,
to eat; but other groups passed by us as we squatted on our haunches
by the road, so that there was not one moment that that moving stream
of humanity was still.

And so we came to Cæsarea, dust-covered, sweaty, mingling with other groups that had converged upon the provincial capital from every point of the compass. We stood before the Procurator's palace, shouting:

"Hear us, Epitropos! Listen to us, O Representative of Mighty Cæsar! Remove the *signa* from Jerusalem! Take away the bust of your Imperator from the Holy City!"

Over and over again, never ceasing, from morning until night. All night long from sunset until dawn, taking turns so that our voices would not tire at the same time, nor fail, nor cease.

Let me say it: There was something admirable about Pilatus. And that something was his domination of his nerves. He let us stand there before his palace in a close-packed group, howling without letup, and did not appear at all.

So now, seeing what they were up against, the chief men among us organized the matter better. They counted us off into centuries, put three centuries at a time before the palace, relieved this three hundred men by a like number every hour, thus making sure we could keep up a deafening din.

Thus it was that there were long periods during those six days when we made the very heavens echo with our pleas, our cries, that I was free to wander about Cæsarea as I willed. Naturally, my first act was to seek out the Galilean delegation to see if my Uncle Hezron was among them.

He was. He embraced me, and seeing me clad in my Jewish *tzitzith*, the fringed garment, seeing my hair and beard grown long, he murmured some verses of the *tefillah* over my head, and shed tears of joy. To him I was the prodigal returned, the lost sheep of Israel brought back into the fold.

"You're entirely well, Nathan?" he said. "Yes, yes, I can see you are. I don't hold with the Essenes' doctrines, but I have to admit—"

"That they've done wonders for him," said that soft, deep voice at his side. "How are you, Nathan?"

My heart stopped still. My breath. I was blinded with joy. The day blazed with radiance. Could he do miracles? One, surely. That he made you love him beyond all else in life.

I dragged him into my arms, kissed his bearded face.

"Yeshu'a!" I babbled. "Oh, Yeshu'a!"

"Nathan," he said quietly, and smiled at me.

The lingering ache in my middle went away, disappeared as though it had never been. My blood slowed, made a kind of quiet murmuring inside my veins, like bee-drone on a lazy day. I could hear birds singing in the palace gardens through all the noise of shouting; a breeze tossed the lilies, laughing, laughing. That was what Yeshu'a ha Notzri did. That.

"My brother Yaakob is of that persuasion," he said with a little amused chuckle; "though not of the monastic Essenes. He goes to the meetings of the town ones. He wears only linen clothes, never wool; and you ought to see his knees! They're like leather, from so much kneeling, so much prayer."[18]

"You're pious enough, Yeshu'a," my Uncle Hezron said.

Yeshu'a smiled.

"But it doesn't cost me anything, sir," he said. "To me, to love man is to love God, and both are a happiness. Poor Yaakob is always weeping and wailing and scourging himself—for his sins. Strange. If you love people, you *can't* sin. You simply can't—"

I'd recovered a little from the joy of seeing him by then. And there is nothing so irritating to one who possesses neither as simplicity, as purity.

"Suppose one of those people is—a woman, Yeshu'a?" I said.

He went on smiling; answered me easily, and at once: "If you love her, her name becomes—Helvetia, Nathan. And you can't sin against her. You can't."

I bowed my head. The crystal slivers of my tears pierced my eyes.

He put his hand on my shoulder.

"Don't weep, Nathan," he said; "for whatever crimes you accuse yourself of, they are already forgiven you, my friend. Your tears have made a balm, and your sorrow has healed you. . . ."

I looked at him in astonishment. He still spoke Aramaic, but his speech was beautiful now. Only a trace of the countrified Galilean accent lingered in it. He spoke like a rab, a teacher, a sage.

He must have guessed my thought.

"I've studied with your uncle, here," he said. "For years now. Ever since my father died. And also with some of Yaakob's Essene rabbin. They're wrong. They insult life, by trying to run away from it. And thereby they insult God, who made life, although they don't mean to. But some of their ideas, I like. Their method of counting the months, the years, for instance. That makes sense, and I've adopted it."[19]

"Have you also adopted their method of foretelling the future, Yeshu'a?" I said.

He looked at me with puzzled eyes.

"I've never even heard of it," he said; "Yaakob has never mentioned—"

My Uncle Hezron glared at me.

"It's unkind to make fun of the humble, Nathan!" he said sternly. "Besides, if you were as smart as you think you are, you'd realize that Yeshu'a is no longer of the *Amme ha aretz!* I'd match his knowledge of the Torah against yours any day!"

"I wouldn't," I said ruefully, "because mine is plagued small, Uncle Hezron. I'm sure he'd leave me far behind in any discussion of the Law. And I wasn't mocking him. I don't know about the town Essenes,[20] but the Qumrân group does have a method of reading the future.[21] I don't know whether it works or not, because none of the things it predicted for me have come true so far; but I do know how to do it—"

"This is a blasphemy!" my uncle said.

"No," Yeshu'a said; "No, Rabbi[22] Hezron, no sincere search for knowledge is offensive to God. And the Essenes are sincere. You've known some of them, so you must know that—"

"Yes," my uncle said grudgingly; "I'll grant you that. They're good people. But their excessive concern with celibacy would destroy the race—"

"Ho!" I hooted. "Look who's talking! Rab Hezron ben Matthya, I salute you in the name of your many sons!"

The pain got into my uncle's eyes then.

"I could not wed," he said quietly; "the only woman for me—belongs to another. It's as simple as that. It was never a concern for any personal salvation at the expense of Israel, Nathan. Which reminds me! Now that you're recovered, we'd better look around for—"

My anguish made a ball of fire and seared my throat.

"No!" I said. "By the Unutterable Name, Uncle Hezron—no!"

"You've a duty to—" my uncle began sternly; but Yeshu'a laid a hand upon his arm. That hand was hard, work-browned, muscular. It radiated power. A power greater than its possessor knew.

"Later, Rabbi," he said; "when time has healed his heart." Then he smiled at me. "What says your prophecy as to that aspect of life, Nathan?"

"That I'll wed, and have many sons. But only after I've wasted years mooning after a woman who won't have me!"

"Because she doesn't love you?" my uncle said.

"No," Yeshu'a said suddenly, "I think it will be because she does."

"That's a very reasonable reason!" I said.

"Have you ever known a reasonable woman?" he said.

"No." I laughed.

He took my arm, said lightly, pleasantly—yet, somehow, I knew that he wasn't jesting; that the matter concerned him, that he was worried, even anxious to know: "Demonstrate your powers, Nathan; read my future for me, will you, please?"

"No," I said; "not now. You'll have to wait until tonight, after the stars are out. I need to plot their movements. . . ."

"All right. But don't forget, Nathan," Yeshu'a ha Notzri said.

But I did forget. Until midnight, it was my century's turn to scream at Pilatus. As fruitlessly as ever. When it was over, I retired to my father's tent to sleep. But, as I approached it, I saw Yeshu'a standing there. Two of his younger brothers, Yehudah and Shimeon,[23] were with him.

"We've come, O Magi," he said solemnly, but there was a twinkle in his eye, "that you tear away the veil that hides the future, and tell us what fate will befall us!"

A flicker of anger rose in me. I was dog-tired, and I didn't believe in that Essenic nonsense anyhow. But Yeshu'a smiled at me, and my anger vanished. Those other two great Galilean oafs were staring at me with their oxlike eyes. They had their father written all over them. Everything Yeshu'a had, he got from Miriam—all his intelligence, his verve, his fire.

"All right," I sighed. "Who wants to be first? I predict that you'll all be whipped, burned, crucified. . . ."

"Me!" Shimeon said. "Tell me, Rabbi, what—"

"I'm not a rab," I said, "I simply know some Cabbalistic tricks taught me by the Essenes—No, not even that. I learned from them without their realizing it, since such knowledge is forbidden. . . ."

"No knowledge is forbidden," Yeshu'a said slowly. "Tell my brother Shimeon his future, Nathan. . . ."

I had of Shimeon his birth place and date, from Yeshu'a, the hour of it. Then I plotted the signs. They fell out regularly, and in commonplace fashion. He would have sons, live many years, die in peace, full of honors. Only one thing was strange: Persistently there appeared the sign that the Essenes defined as "The Sons of the House of Peleg." And, more often than not, it was accompanied by the darker sign which meant the "dissemblers," the "furtive ones." Now that last form was perfectly clear: The symbols formed the word na'alamin, "dissemblers," time and time again. I couldn't imagine how anyone could find that characteristic in this Galilean yokel with straw still in his hair. But

"The Sons of the House of Peleg"? How did I know it meant Peleg?
All my Essenic system of plotting the signs could do was to spell
out letters. Now in Hebrew and Aramaic both, all the letters are
consonants. To write the vowels, we have to "point" them with tiny
symbols, usually dots, straight lines, or crosses, placed above, or below,
or sometimes even inside the loops of the consonants, to indicate what
particular vowel is to follow the consonant so vowel-pointed. Now
the trouble with this plotting of the signs was that there was no way
of indicating what the vowel points were. Actually the sign the Essenes
called "The Sons of the House of Peleg" was composed only of the
three letters פלג, or reading from right to left, as you must in Hebrew,
Pe Lamedh Gimel. I sat there staring at those letters, trying to imagine
what other vowel points to mark them with to give them a different
sound than "Peleg." But I couldn't think of any. I wrote that word
over and over again, until finally it came to me that if you took away
the symbol for *banim,* the sons of, which it didn't have anyhow,
which the Essenes had arbitrarily assigned to it, *peleg* didn't have to
be a noun, it could also be the infinitive of the verb "to divide"!

Taken that way, it reenforced the dark *na'alamin* symbol. The signs
were obviously trying to tell me, to warn me, that this big dumb ox
was designed to be a deceiver, and one who would divide Israel!

"Told you it was nonsense!" I said.

Yeshu'a shook his head.

"It's strange," he said; "but I believe in your powers, Nathan. Tell
us about Yehudah now—"

Yehudah's chart was much the same. But in addition to the signs
for *na'alamin* and *P'L'G,* there were more: curious, confused signs,
extending beyond his life, being torn, scattered by—by a prince of the
Kittim![24] Now I believe that by the Kittim, the Essenes mean the
Romans. But how could I be sure? I told him that. He shrugged.

"It be all tricks and fakery, Yisu!" said he.

"All right," I said to Yeshu'a; "it's your turn now. You were also born
in Nazareth, weren't you?"

"Yes," he said.[25]

He told me the season, and the hour—having had them of Miriam,
who, as mothers will with their firstborn, had fixed those quite un-
important details in his mind.

I cast the lots, drew up the signs. I did it over again three times, five.
They varied not at all. They said that he would be hanged like a
felon, like a thief, among a group of thieves.

I told him that. He bowed his head, his lips moved in prayer.

"Yes," he whispered, his dark eyes somber, big with pain. "Yes, perhaps it will be so. If it can't be helped. All right. But afterward, Nathan?"

"Afterward?" I said.

"After I am dead. After I have gone to my Father. What happens then?"

I looked at the signs. They were terribly confused. So I cast them again. And now they became clear.

And made a horror.

I looked at them. At Yeshu'a. Said: "No."

"Tell me!" he said.

"No," I answered, "it's no good. You'll do what you have to do."

He stared at me, demanded again, that authority of his that was like stone, like steel, ringing through his voice: "Tell me, Nathan!"

No wonder that even knowing it was not so, men could believe him of David's line. He could be truly kingly when he wanted to be.

"All right," I said; "but first *you* tell me something, Yeshu'a. Are you about to begin something? To embark upon some—some mission, say?"

He said: "Yes." Like that. Very quietly.

I said: "Don't."

And he: "Why not?"

"You insist upon my telling you. All right. These signs, your stars, say that if you do this thing, unknowing, it is bad enough; but if you go into it knowing, you become the greatest criminal in the long tides of human history, Yesu. Still want me to tell you?"

He said, "Yes." Just as quietly, as simply as before. With no hesitation at all.

"All right. You will drown your people, Israel, in blood. Or your teachings will. Year in, year out, they will be beaten, broken, slaughtered by the Kittim because of you—" I could hear my voice deepening, darkening, growing brazen with thunder, hear the note of prophecy getting into it. How do I know these things? I thought. But I knew them! Oh, I knew!

"Go on," he said.

I looked down at his feet. As usual they were bare. He wore but a simple, seamless robe. Wild laughter tore me. It made a taste of blood, of brine in my throat.

"Why do you laugh?" he said.

"Look at you!" I cried. "Barefoot and poor! A carpenter's son. Do you know I see temples erected in your name whose towers pierce the sky? A whole priesthood clad in silks and gold, blazing with jewels, bowing before graven images made in your likeness—though they've given you silken hair and a Kittim's, a Gentile's face! They won't even leave you your Jewishness, Yesu! They'll make of you a pagan god. A god of the gentes. And they, your priests, your Kittim, Gentile priests, clad in tall crowns and brilliant in silks, will sit in judgment over your people, Israel. And over all the earth, your people, my people, will twist in the fire, scream from the wrack, die in the chambers of the choking smoke—"

"Stop it!" he said.

—"welter in the trenches as the Kittim point the speaking spears, the flaming arrows that talk with the voices of thunder, that spit lightnings at them—"

"Stop it, Nathan!" he said.

"You will give Israel into the hands of the uncircumcised. The dead at your charge, for your iniquity, will be as the sands of the sea—"

The strength went out of me suddenly. The towering flame sank down.

"If—if you persist," I whispered, "in this—in this—"

His eyes kindled. Meeting mine, they shriveled my very soul. His anger was terrible. All the more so, because it had so much sorrow in it.

"Get thee behind me, Satan!" he said.

Then, turning, he left me there, going so quietly I heard no sound at all.

I avoided him after that. Five days later, at long, long last, Lucius Pontius Pilatus appeared at the high window, above the hoarse-voiced howling mob. He hadn't changed since I'd seen him last in Rome. His lean dark face was as mocking, as sardonic.

He raised his arms above the sun-bright glitter of his breastplate.

"My friends!" he said. "My gentle Jewish friends! I beg of you to cease your howling, and retire to the stadium. There, at the tenth hour, tomorrow, I will come and address you from the rostrum. Surely, as civilized men, we should be able to settle our differences amicably! *Salve*, O men of Judea! In the Divine Name of the Imperator, I salute you!"

Then he was gone, leaving that last deadly insult to a people to whom only God was divine, and His Name so holy as to be unutterable, lingering on the evening air.

In the stadium that next morning, I stood between my father and my uncle, waiting. Then I saw Yeshu'a standing a little way off with his brothers. They were all there: Yehudah, Shimeon, Yose, and even the wild one, the Ebionite, Essene one, Yaakob. I tried to turn my eyes away from Yeshu'a; but I couldn't. So I attempted to take refuge in anger. But I couldn't do that either.

His eyes were on me, soft, compelling. I did what he bade me without opening his mouth. I left my father and my uncle and went to him.

He smiled at me. Kissed my cheek. Said: "Forgive me my anger, Nathan."

"And you the—the things I said," I whispered.

He shook his head, a little sadly.

"There's nothing to forgive. You spoke truth—as you saw it," he said; "and I—"

But a roar broke from the crowd. Pilatus was mounting the rostrum.

He stood there, looking down at all of us, his eyes cold with contempt, his mouth curled in a smile as cruel as death.

"Disperse!" he cried. "Go back to your homes!"

"No!" someone roared. "Not until you take the Signa of the Legions and the Icon of the Imperator out of Jerusalem!"

Then we were all shouting it, cracking heaven itself with the thunder of our voices.

Pilatus raised his hand. From every side the trumpets sounded. Our voices died. There was no sound now but the clanking of the cohorts coming on. They swarmed over the stands, their armor sun-bright, terrible; they came through the gates beneath the rostra, from where the athletes and the beasts usually came. In less time than it takes to write this, they had us all surrounded.

Another signal from Pilatus, and they drew their swords. The *gladii* made a hard glitter, throwing the light into our faces.

"All right!" Pilatus mocked us, "Will you disperse, you Jewish dogs, or do you prefer to die?"

I was looking at Yeshu'a, so I'd swear he did it first. Afterward, my uncle and my father told me the movement was spontaneous and simultaneous on the parts of hundreds of men. But I saw him move forward quietly and serenely until he was inches from a legionary's blade. Then, without a word, he knelt and bared his breast. His brothers knelt beside him, did the same. I rushed to join them. Then my father, my uncle, every man there, knelt, with bared breast, with neck inclined for the cohorts' strokes.

Pilate stood there, strangling upon his rage, until his face purpled, turned black. He was gazing upon things he could never understand. The meaning of faith. The significance of honor.

Then he bowed his head, acknowledged his defeat.

"Sheathe swords," he croaked. "Leave them!"

The next day, by his orders, the Signa and the Imperator's Icon were removed from Jerusalem. We had won.

At least the first battle.[26]

Book III

In which I become entangled with the harlot Shelomith, and what was even less pardonable, Claudia Procula, the Procurator's wife, build another aqueduct, run afoul of the Zealots, and witness a baptism.

Chapter IX

"YOUR MOTHER will be heartbroken," my father said.

"Tell her it's for my health's sake," I said, "which is only half a lie, Father. Maybe not even half. Being cooped up in your scriptorium, or the High Priest's, or in Grandfather Bœthus' countinghouse, wouldn't be good for me. I'd have too much time for brooding. What I need is sunlight on my skin, air—enough hard work to make me sleep like a dead man at night. Besides, I'd even be useful. The Essenes taught me some tricks about farming that worked amazingly well in that brazen furnace where they live, so I ought to be able to at least double our harvests in a place as fertile as Galilee is. And what have I ever done in the city except to go straight to Sheol and perdition? Tell me: What, Father?"

"There you have a point!" my father said ruefully. "Well, Hezron— what do you say?"

"That I'll keep him out of Tiberias and Cæsarea, even if I have to break both his legs to do it!" my Uncle Hezron said.

"All right," my father said. "You have my permission to go up to Nazareth with your uncle. Now, tell me: How long do you plan to stay?"

"Until I'm thirty," I said.

"What!" my father cried. In that thirteenth year of the reign of Tiberius Cæsar, I was just past my twenty-eighth birthday.

"Two years—more or less," my uncle said. "It's not a bad idea, Yehudah. Or, until he's wed, whichever comes first. I'll look for a bride for him among the first families of Galilee, and you—"

"Among the ruling houses of Jerusalem. It won't be easy, Hezron. His fame has spread abroad; and, as you can imagine, it's far from savory! The priestly families won't be overly anxious to give a daughter to a semi-pagan, a blasphemer, a lecher, a wine-bibber, and a mad-man—"

"Father!" I said.

"I only repeat the comments that have reached my ears, Nathan," my father said. "They do you too much credit. You're merely a fool, which is far less interesting. . . ."

"The boy's not all that bad," my uncle said; "and here of late—"

"He's shown evidences of mending his ways. The Essenes' influence upon him. How long will it last, I wonder?"

"Well, at any rate, at my place he'll be thrown into frequent contact with young Yeshu'a," Uncle Hezron said; "and that, surely—"

"Yeshu'a?" my father said. "A dreadfully plebian name! Tell me: Who is he, brother?"

"A plebian, just as you said. Though I don't like the word. It's Roman and pagan. He comes from an *am ha aretz* family who've lived in Nazareth for as far back as the oldest citizens can remember. Father was a carpenter. Name of Yosef. He's dead now. But the mother—a most unusual woman, Miriam—"

"Ha!" my father said. "The comely widow, eh, brother?"

"Elevate your thoughts a trifle, Yehudah," Uncle Hezron said. "You've never met Miriam. She's not attractive, in that sense. At least not to me. She's one of those broad-hipped peasant women—the brood-mare type, if you get what I mean. But she's kept that family together, ruled them with an iron hand. The girls have spotless reputations. The elder, Susannah, is to be wed, soon. The younger, Yohannah, is a chit still. The boys are good, stolid, dull, hard-working peasant lads—except two. Except Yaakob—and Yeshu'a—"

"And they?" my father murmured politely. I could see he wasn't interested. He was merely indulging his somewhat garrulous elder brother.

"Yaakob's an Essene holy man. A little mad, I'd say. Like all the Essenes. No—a trifle madder than even they. He carries his religion to excess. . . ."

"Coming from you," my father laughed, "that means he's fit to be chained, cast into a pit, and left to howl!"

"Very nearly," my uncle sighed. "But Yeshu'a—is different. He—he's the most unusual lad I've ever known. There's a certain—"

"Magic?" I suggested.

"Aye! Exactly. There's a certain magic about him. He controls people effortlessly. Don't ask me how. I don't know. For heaven's sake, Yehudah! He's the young Galilean Nathan has spent so much time with here—the one who was among the first—"

"To bare his breast to the Legions' swords. Yes, I remember him. A singularly attractive face. Very like Nathan's, but—different, somehow. Strange . . . I liked him. You think that he—"

"Will have a good influence on Nathan? Yes. His purity is awesome. He never frequents women—"

"Nor boys?" my father mocked.

"Oh, for Adonai's sake, Yehudah!" my uncle said; "we don't practice those pagan abominations in Galilee! What I was going to say, what's strangest of all, is that Yeshu'a leads a life of absolute chastity, and nobody laughs at him for it! Now, do you see?"

"I think so, yes. Feminine purity is admirable; male virginity, a joke. It's always been thus, since the world began. And yet—"

"Nobody laughs at Yeshu'a, or chides him. For one thing, he's— entirely male. Women—adore him. That howling madwoman, Miriam of Migdal-Nunaya, grows quiet, pensive, almost sane whenever she sees him. And Shelomith—"

"Who's Shelomith?" I said.

"A woman—no, a girl, because she can't be more than nineteen yet —whom *you* don't need to know," my uncle said.

"Thanks, Uncle!" I crowed. "The minute I get up there, I'll go from door to door calling, 'Shelomith! Ohhh, Shelomeeth!'"

"Shut up, you fool!" my uncle said. "Shelomith, for your information, is a harlot. The worst harlot in all Galilee. Not that she's Galilean. She's from Beth Anya, Yehudah. She came to Galilee, running away from her husband. A decent man her father had wed her to."

"Accompanied by a lover, doubtless?" my father said.

"Exactly. A poor devil from Kriyoth. Ha! He has the same name as yours, brother! Yehudah—"

"Ben who?" my father said.

"Ben nobody, probably. We call him ish Kriyoth. He of Kerioth. Hair and beard as red as a fox's. Little blue eyes. Not a bad sort, or he wasn't, till she deserted him—"

"Quite a girl, this Shelomith!" I said.

"Shut up!" my uncle said. "He's become a drunkard. A witless sot. Always putting himself in that strumpet's way, begging her to come back to him. And she—"

"And she?" I prompted.

"Does the same—for Yeshu'a," my uncle said, a little angrily. "It's the most amazing thing! She—she's utterly beautiful. She's caused even men of great piety, even rabbin, to fall from grace. One of the minor priests at Kafer Nahum was ejected from his synagogue because of her. And yet—"

"And yet?" my father said.

"Whenever she can, she follows Yeshu'a about like a dog. No, like a she-wolf! I've seen her prostrate herself before him, tears in her eyes, throw her arms about his ankles, kiss his dusty feet—"

"Whereupon," my father mocked, "he spurns her?"

"No. He says to her with great tenderness, real pity: 'Poor Shelomith! Go, child, and sin no more. Return to your husband's house—ask his pardon. He'll forgive you. I promise you he will.'"

"What does she say to that?"

"About her husband, a stream of curses that blue-smoke the air. To Yeshu'a, vows of undying love. She begs him before all the world to kiss her, take her in his arms—"

"And he *doesn't?*" my father said.

"No. Once he did. He kissed her forehead very gently, as a father would. Turned her loose. She clasped her middle as though he'd stabbed her, reeled away from him, sat down on a public bench. She was there for hours, crying. But nobody dared go near her."

"Well, I can see that your Yeshu'a could be a good influence," my father said, "as long as you also guarantee me to keep this young he-goat of mine away from your Shelomith—"

"Father," I said, a little angrily, "tell me one thing—"

"What thing, my son?" my father said.

"Have you *ever* known me to frequent whores?"

"No," my father said, "though I fear me you've done worse. . . ."

"There's nothing worse!" I said. "To seduce a woman, to get her to bed with you, you have at least to be a man, Father. But to buy a piece of raddled public meat—what *do* you have to be, I wonder!"

"Don't worry about that, Yehudah," my uncle said. "When he's wed, when I've found him a bride—"

"A matter about which you'll make no haste, Hezron! You're almost as daft over the boy as Eli is!"

"True," my uncle said. "I love Nathan like a son. The son I never had. Which is *why* I'm going to make haste to see him wed—"

"I don't follow you, brother," my father said.

"I'm getting old. Once he's married, he'll have sons, of course. The firstborn we'll dedicate to the priesthood, to be reared in your house, to continue your line. But the second son is *mine*. By right of legal adoption, to continue the family, here in Galilee. And I claim that privilege now. Agreed, brother?"

My father stared into his eyes. What remained unspoken, what they didn't say, was as close to an acknowledgment of what must never be put into words between them as was humanly possible. I could almost hear my uncle say: "You've kept from me the only woman I could have loved, though you yourself, scarcely prize her highly! Therefore, you owe me this! This replacement for the son whom through your fault I never sired!"

And my father, bending his head, nodded, whispered: "Very well, Hezron. Agreed."

I started to protest, to say: "Don't you two old gaffers think I ought to be consulted about this weighty matter? After all the boy will be mine and—"

But he wouldn't be. No son that came not from Helvetia's womb would or could ever be mine, truly. What mattered it if my seed—torn from my loins by the mere heat and friction of clinging female interior flesh, wild with the race's mindless will to survive, ferociously engorging my dutifully laboring maleness—would engender this tiny, never-to-be-loved stranger, this little alien got lovelessly in the dark? It changed nothing. Let my father and my uncle divide my progeny between them, sell the surplus into slavery! It made no difference. I simply didn't care.

That summer, I worked wonders. There was, in the back lands of my uncle's estate, in the hilly part fit only for grazing sheep, a little lake. It lay very high in a basin gouged out of the very peaks of the hills themselves by the terrible earthquake that had happened some thirty years before I was born.[1] Before then, there had been nothing but a tiny trickle of a stream, flowing down by a series of laughing little cascades into my uncle's fields, making them green and fertile beyond all other lands thereabout. But the earthquake had dammed it up, and thus formed the lake which widened and deepened every year with the spring and fall rains, and the hidden sources beneath it, until it had grown to respectable proportions even then. Not knowing what else to do with it, my uncle stocked it with fish brought alive from Lake Gennesareth, so that our table never lacked speckled trout and small-mouthed bass, as well as a very oily kind of pike that I remember I couldn't abide the taste of.

But when summer lay upon the land, my uncle sorely missed the little stream that formerly had kept his fields as green as Nisan[2] even in Tammuz and Ab.[3] Without saying anything to him, I proposed to restore his stream to him.

What I meant to do was to build an aqueduct, after the Roman pattern. The materials—stones, straw and clay to make bricks with—lay to hand. I lacked only workers, and the proper tools. So I begged a whole talent[4] from my uncle, refusing flatly to tell him what it was for, beyond the fact that the use I'd put it to would repay him fourfold within two years. After I'd said it was to be employed on the estate itself, and nowhere else, he agreed.

Thereupon, I went out and looked for workers. I enlisted Yeshu'a's brothers, though, much to my sorrow, he himself, as head of the family, could not come as he had to attend to the carpenter shop. Since Nazareth had grown considerably in recent years, he had work enough and to spare to keep himself and Yaakob busy from morn till night. But Yehudah, Yose, and Shimeon came, and made splendid masons once I'd taught them what to do. I also enlisted four good friends of Yeshu'a's, men who afterward became his disciples, for part-time work, when they were not about their principal occupation, which was fishing on Lake Gennesareth. These were Shimeon Kepha[5]—that last was not his name, but a nickname meaning the "Rock" because of his immense size and strength—and his brother Netzer,[6] as well as those bull-tongued, bellowing sons of Zebediah, Yaakob and Yohannan, whom everybody called the *Boane Ragsha*, "Sons of Fury,"[7] because of all the noise they made. Actually, they were the best-hearted big, stupid Galileans imaginable, with no fury in them at all.

One other man made up the list: Yehudah ish Kriyoth.[8] I found him lying dead drunk in a gutter outside a tavern in Kafer Nahum. He was wallowing in the mud and offal, with the tears running down into his fiery red beard, and whispering: "Shelomith! Oh, Shelom, my love, my own!"

I picked him up, tossed him into my uncle's oxcart, and brought him home. Why? Because my heart went out to him who—even as I!—had loved and lost. A man who can love so terribly has to be good, I thought.

Nothing that has happened since has changed my opinion of him.

The first days, he wasn't of much use. Living upon wine and tears is scarcely calculated to maintain a man's strength. But, gradually, good plain food, hard work, and watered wine restored him. By the second week, he was taking no wine at all, but drinking only goat's milk and water. His little blue eyes followed me constantly, in wonder and in awe.

One day at the noon meal, I flopped down beside him, broke my loaf in half, and handed one half to him. At once his eyes were flooded.

"Why are you so good to me, master?" he said.

I grinned at him, answered: "Don't know, Yehudah! Perhaps because you have my father's name. I'm a bar Yehudah, you know. Or, perhaps because I, too, know what it is to suffer. . . ."

"Do you, master?" he said. His voice was soft and cultivated. His

Aramaic was so cultured that it was almost Hebrew. His accent was Judean, and it showed he'd come from high circles indeed.

To encourage him, I began to talk about myself. Alone of them all, he hadn't heard my terrible story. Not that I told him. I still couldn't talk about it directly. But I gave him, without meaning to, so many tantalizing fragments of my sorrows, that that night he demanded it all of Yose, Yeshu'a's brother.

The next morning, when we began work, he came to me and knelt and kissed my hands, called me brokenly his "brother in sorrow"—

"But mine is far worse, master," he said, "for my Shelomith lives. Your—your lady—died with honor. My heart—my soul—wallows in shame. It's a kind of disease! It is! It is! Or else—"

"Else what, Yehudah?" I said.

"She could have any man! The richest merchants of Galilee, fabulously wealthy Greeks and Syrians—we Jews haven't their head for business, you know—would keep her like a queen. But she prefers—to bide in Nikos' Lupanar! To be a common harlot—to bed with any dog —who has the price—"

"Forget her, Yehudah," I said.

"A sesterce or two. Or a denarius. Or an as. Or nothing, if the bastard pleases her! Oh God, master, I—"

"Don't weep, Yehudah," I said.

"Do you know what I was, master? The head of ben Bœzer's countinghouse! A man respected of all, for my honesty, my skill with numbers. Elias ben Bœzer looked with favor on me, would have wed me to his daughter. I should have been today as wealthy as your grandfather, master! The head of a countinghouse as great. Were it not—"

"For her," I said.

"Yes. I—I stole! I embezzled money. I thought she was greedy, because she was always asking for more, because there was never enough. But she wasn't. She didn't even keep it for herself. She—do you know what she did with it, master? Do you?"

"No," I said.

"Gave it to a dog of a Roman! She got me to run away with her. And I—I was wild with joy. I gave up Martha bath Bœzer, who was both rich and fair, gave up my future, everything, for Shelomith's sake. When we got to Cæsarea, she told me flatly, coldly, she'd come there because of him! Because of this Antonius! This Roman dog!"

"And he?" I said.

"Enjoyed both her body and my stolen gold. When Gratus, the last Procurator, was recalled, Antonius went back to Rome with him. Shelomith was sure that her lordly patrician lover was going to take her along. She prepared for the voyage, bought trinkets, clothes; talked endlessly about how she'd live on the Capitoline Hill—she said all that to me, master! To me!—until his letter came. Do you know—can you imagine—what it said, master?"

"No," I said.

He quoted it then, slowly, but without a pause, from memory. One could see it was graven on his heart:

"Farewell, Little She-Dog! The canines of your race are not allowed in Imperial Rome. I'll miss you, miss your hot bitch smell, your whimpering whines in the throes of love—at least until I find another. Which won't take me long. I advise you to forget,

One who never loved you,
ANTONIUS."

I didn't say anything. What could be said to that?

"That was when—and why—she became a whore, master. To—to punish herself—I think. To degrade herself so terribly that—"

"Perhaps," I said, not believing it for a minute, "you can still save her, perhaps—"

He shook his head.

"Only one man could save her now," he whispered, "and he won't. . . ."

"And he is?" I said.

"Yeshu'a. Yeshu'a the Nazarene," Yehudah ish Kriyoth said.

Then we had it all done. I hadn't been able to keep the secret from my uncle very long. An aqueduct isn't something one can hide. Toward the end of summer, when his fields, like those of all Galilee, were parched by the worst drought we'd had in years, he came daily to watch us work. If we didn't get the water to the fields plagued soon, there'd be no harvest for us at all. We stopped neither day nor night now; when darkness fell, we went on working by the light of torches.

Fortune favored us. And God, if He exists, must have smiled. Standing there, watching the silver water pouring through the sluice gates at the end of our soar of arches, spreading out in feathery white fingers over the parched earth, my uncle kissed me, and wept like a child.

But my feat of engineering had a result I hadn't anticipated. For, like the greathearted gentleman he was, Uncle Hezron shared his bounty with all his neighbors. Those bordering his farm were allowed to join their irrigation ditches to his own; those farther away came with oxcarts to bear the precious water to their lands in barrels. There was, of course, enough and to spare for all; our lake, fed by hidden springs the earthquake had opened was inexhaustible; but, all the same, another man wouldn't have done it. And when I realized what his generosity had brought down upon my defenseless head, I was sorry that he had!

For overnight, I had become famous in the land: "the sage who struck water from the rock!" A sort of lesser Moses, you understand. And fathers who'd called me blasphemer and whoremaster, now drove up on a Shabbat after Temple, to show my wondrous aqueduct to their daughters!

I could feel the noose closing around my neck, and panic seized me. I sat stiff and dumb at suppers I was invited to in Nazareth, in Kafer Nahum, on the nearby farms, and turned my eyes from the blushing Galilean maidens.

I told my uncle I had no desire to wed until I was thirty, if then. I hoped that by another year at least, I wouldn't see Helvetia's pure, pale cameo of a face, etched across the back of my pupils by the acid of my tears, each time I closed my eyes.

That was one thing. The other was even subtler. And the name of it was fear.

You see, I have always been a sensual beast by nature. My nurse caught me busy at Onan's sin when I was but seven years of age. At thirteen, after my mother's maidservant cured me of the solitary vice by providing me with the best of all possible substitutes for it, I made for myself the discovery that finding partners for that delicate sport wasn't too difficult if you put your mind to it. The sun swings low over Judea, and heats the blood like wine even in female veins. The women of my country, Elohim be praised!, are seldom, if ever, cold.

But now, nearly two years after my Helvetia's death, I felt not the slightest twinge of carnal desire. And I was neither sentimentalist enough, nor sufficiently a fool not to realize that that was strange. That I should never love again, so long as memory had its seat in me, I knew. That I should draw my final breath in pain, lie blinded to any other face by those Tishri eyes upon my deathbed itself, I was sure beyond all question, hope, or doubt. But being man, being male, I'd taken it as a matter of course that, having resigned myself to life, I'd occasionally feel a baser hunger for some mindless bitchthing, provocatively flaunting her anatomy before me, wiggling her buttocks just beyond my cupped hands' grasp, jiggling her breasts as close to my vulpine lips as she dared, causing my nostrils to flare as she perfumed the night, making it redolent with her high-spiced female musk.

Only I didn't. Not at all.

That worried me. Let me tell the truth: those Galilean maidens were anything but repulsive. Some of them were very fair. The fairest of them all, whom I am sure I could have learned to love, Susannah bath Yosef, Yeshu'a's sister, was already lost to me. She'd married Asa ben Micah at the beginning of Sivan.[9] His other sister, Yohannah,[10] was but a child, all eyes and legs and arms, so I didn't consider her at all then. But I probably would have given in to my uncle's anything but subtle pressures, but for one secret, galling, terrible fear:

Was I—whose male flesh had never once in almost two years risen to confound me—capable any longer of husbanding a wife?

That worried me. You cannot imagine how terribly it worried me. The essence of a man is his pride; and, among the things this feather-less biped God has made to profane his earth can and does take pride in is his randy he-goat's capacity to mount every female who carelessly leaves her thighs agape. That peerless, matchless, incomparable ability gone, he feels a sense of loss.

A great, appalling, desolate sense of loss.

I was going out of my mind. I had to put the matter to the test. So one night, after the harvesting—poor and scant that year, for my miracle had been accomplished almost too late—was done, I stole down to Kafer Nahum, and entered Nikos' Lupanar.

I assure you, upon my honor, that no thought of Shelomith had entered my head. I had never seen her, and that she was an inmate of this particular brothel—although poor Yehudah ish Kriyoth had told me that—I had quite forgot, if, indeed, the information had ever even registered in my mind.

Nikos, the *lupanarus,* the brothel-keeper, issued me into a sitting room, telling me to wait a few moments until he could parade his wares before me. There were only two other prospective clients in the waiting room: a burly bearded Jew, with eyes as hot and black as coals, and a Roman soldier so drunk he kept falling off his couch.

The third time he fell, I saw he wasn't going to be able to get to his feet again, so I picked him up, and sat him with considerable force so far back on the couch that he couldn't fall off anymore. Whereupon he thanked me in Latin so pure that I realized he was native Roman and not one of the conquered barbarians who were filling up the ranks of the Legions now.

I told him in that tongue the equivalent of "Don't mention it!" and he, as the wine-besotted will, proceeded to ask me from what part of Italia I came. Mind you, I was fully bearded and wore the fringed robe; but my Latin, aided by his wine, caused him to disregard the evidences of his eyes.

"Can't you guess?" I said to him.

He peered at me owlishly.

"Th'—south," he said. "You've got a southern accent. Sicilia, right?"

"Right," I said. I would have said "Right!" if he had said Cisalpine Gaul, or Britain, or Alexandria.

The burly bearded Jew was staring at me as though his hot little eyes would pop from his head. I smiled at him reassuringly. But, before either of us could say anything, the *lupanarus* came in, leading a parade of stark-naked harlots.

You will find this hard to believe, but I had never been in a brothel before. That I'd never had to fall back upon that pitiful recourse of the demimale unable to supply what a true woman needs, and reduced to bought acquiescence from a creature powerless to complain of his incapacity, or, at best, his mediocrity, was a part of my he-goat's pride. But now, it seemed simpler to test the degree of damage that my body, or my soul, had sustained—for which of the two bore my hidden, secret, crippling wound, if it were not both, I didn't know—in this final refuge of the absolutely unlovable. I wasn't ready for a true personal relationship yet. Better a brief squirm on well-worn sheets, paid for and forgot, thought I.

I should have known better. I should have realized that a certain degree of squeamishness—or of civilization, to accept my father's happier term for it—was a part of me. Perhaps even the essential part.

Wait. Don't anticipate me. Those girls weren't the kind of jaded hags you'd find in a Roman *lupanar*. The trade in Nahum Village was not that brisk. Mostly they were husky country girls, deep bosomed, broad of hip, with their complexions still unfaded. Of course, they had not the Roman addiction to the bath, and the smell of them, striking through the cheap perfumes they wore, was enough to bring a rush of nausea to my throat. But I should have mastered that, I think, chosen one of them at random, gone upstairs with her, except that at the last I made the mistake of looking into their eyes.

That did it. The sick self-loathing I saw there turned my blood to ice. The stunned, stolid look of creatures so beaten that they have become indifferent even to pain. The rotting carcass of a hate, now dead, for man and all his works turned inward upon themselves. The ultimate question: If *this* can happen to me, don't I somehow deserve it? Do what you like, use whatever orifice of my poor carcass that you will as a receptacle for your filth. What difference does it make?

And suddenly on the Roman soldier's body, I saw Avidius Publius' face. Gabinius Sergius' on mine; Flavius Dolabella's on the burly Jew's. Lining up to—

I whirled, already running. Then *she* came through that door.

Wait. I've said once before, in connection with my angel, that the description a man gives of the woman whom he loves is false. Allow me to say it once again, in connection with—my devil.

She came through that door, wrapped in the night cloud of her hair. I've never before, nor since, known a woman with a mane that equaled hers. When she loosed it, she could stand upon it. Naked, she could wrap herself in it, and not one *uncia* of her flesh would show. Which is not a description of her. How can I make you see her? You Greeks have no idea what a woman's like—as your female statues abundantly prove. All your goddesses are lovely, and serene—and cold. Even Aphrodite. Perhaps that's why you go aswooning after boys!

Shelomith was not Aphrodite. She was Astarte. Only we Semitic races understand desire. Which is description enough. You want more? I could almost span her waist with my two hands. Her hips were wide and undulant. When she walked by, every man within twenty rods went mad. Her breasts were two sentries armed with spears, standing at attention above the Temple gate.

Her mouth? A wound—sometimes. A great, soft fleshed puckering wound that screamed inside your mind. And sometimes the cup from which you took delirium, drew delight. Sometimes, the twin portals leading down to death. Images not as contradictory as they sound; at least not in my Shelom.

Her eyes? Doe-slanted midnight, into which all the stars there ever were have plunged and drowned. Slow-slumbrous as the Nile. Alive with all the fires of Gehenna, cradling all there ever is of Sheol.

I haven't made you see her? By Lord Satan, ruler over men's hearts! What more do you want? Details? Skin like burnt bronze with Ba'al's furnaces glowing underneath. The longest, most exquisitely formed legs in all the world. Three wild spiraling thick black tangles at her armpits and on her belly's low, because, unlike your occidental women, she never committed the obscenity of shaving. Nipples like bloody spearpoints—You fool! All descriptions are false, even this one. Maybe especially this one. I wouldn't know.

She was Shelomith. And there was no one else like her. Nowhere in the world.

She came into that room, and stood there, looking at us. At the drunken Roman. At the burly Jew. At me. Last of all, at me.

Her gaze rested longest on my face. It softened, warmed, became more slumberous. Then it changed. Something like horror invaded it.

"This one!" I said. "I'll take—"

But her voice made a dissonance, like a whipcrack cutting through the echoes of a temple gong.

"No!" she said. "The—the legionary spoke first!"

She took the drunken Roman's arm, pulled him to his feet. He swayed there, grinning foolishly. Up until that moment I would have staked my life upon it!, not a word had passed his stupid lips.

You know what I did then? I waited, refusing all the rest, for the privilege of mounting a woman rank with another man's sweat, swimming with his seed. I waited.

For that. And Satan take my pride!

When I heard the Roman stumbling down the stairs at last, muttering Latin obscenities against all the gods there ever were, I got up, pushed by him, flew up those stairs.

She lay there on the bed. The fool had been too drunk. The evidences of his haste, his failure, glistened on the burnt bronze of her thighs. The room was stifling, thick with sweat stink, made more nauseating by being mingled with perfume.

She looked at me and the tender horror got back into her eyes.

"No," she said. "You, no. Never you. Anybody else but you. It's a privilege, friend! You can boast about it. Say, 'Look upon me! The one man in all Galilee who's never bedded with Shelomith!"

I hung there, trembling.

"I don't want that privilege," I got out; "besides, you're wrong. I'm not the only one—"

"Who else?" she taunted. Then, I think, I must have smiled.

"Aren't you forgetting—Yeshu'a?" I said.

She came up off that bed before I saw her muscles tense, her fingers curved into talons, raking for my eyes. She was soaking wet, and glistening. I needed all my strength, my skill to throw her, hold her down.

I clasped both her wrists in a grip like iron, pressing her body against the bed with the weight of my own. Her eyes were the eyes of a lioness, flaming through all the jungles of the night.

Then they changed. The fire in them went smoky, dimmed. She smiled at me. Have you ever taken the butt end of a lance shaft full in your big gut? That was what that warm red lip curl, slow quivering, did to me then.

"Turn me loose," she said. "You've won. I won't fight anymore. What have I got to fight for anyhow? Huh, Nathan?"

I stared at her, said, "You know my name! How—?"

"My secret," she said. "Turn me loose—will you, huh? Please?"

I turned her loose. Her hand blurred sight as it plunged beneath the pillow to come out with a knife. She put the point against my throat with one smooth practiced motion. Held it there.

I leaned upon it, hard.

She drew it back at once, said: "Yes. You would, wouldn't you? But there's one thing you won't do, couldn't stand . . ."

She reversed the blade with matchless speed and skill. Put the point against the lovely darkness of her left breast, pushed in so deep that I thought it was never going to stop and terror hit me in the gut like an armored fist.

"Shelomith!" I screamed.

Then she did stop, and lay there looking at me and smiling a little with that knife in her so deep that to get it away from her I would have had to ruin her, leave that sweet flesh butchered torn. More than it already was, I mean. Because the blood was flooding up about that blade already, making thick black-scarlet rivulets all over that—that glory.

"Two of us," she said. "You want that, Nathan? Your—divine Helvetia—and a whore! They'll make ballads about you in Tiberias tomorrow. In Cæsarea, the day after; next week in Jerusalem! You'll be famous! Nathan bar Yehudah, for love of whom a patrician Roman—and a dirty Jew bitch—died. Both—the same way. You want that? You want *her* name forever linked with a harlot's in men's minds?"

I got up from there. Stood bent over, abject and trembling with defeat, looking at her. Passed a tongue tip over bone-dry lips. Said: "Why?"

She kept her fist curled around the hilt of the knife as she spoke. It must have hurt dreadfully because it was in her deep; but she gave no sign of that; no slightest grimace betrayed the pain she surely felt.

"Because—you look like him. Just like. So much that I—I couldn't stay apart. So much that it would become a—a betrayal. And I've never betrayed him! You understand that? Letting a hairy, stinking lout make use of this wornout carcass doesn't count. As long as *I* stay out of it, Nathan! As long as the—the real me, who sometimes lives inside this putrid corpse—Oh, always, when he's near!—is absent, so that there's nobody home when all the—the filth goes on. What's done to meat, to a sack of guts and blood and dung, is beside the point and puts no horns on his sweet head. You understand that, don't you?"

"Yes," I said. In a way, I did. And respected it. Whatever desperate last ditch is held against all odds in defense of honor, however you define honor, no matter how meaningless, tattered, long lost, gone—is worthy of respect. I knew that, even then.

I turned to go. My gait was shambling, tired, old.

"Nathan!" she called out to me.

I turned. Saw that she was crying.

"You—you aren't *good*, are you?" she whispered. "I mean, like him? You wear his face. His eyes—his mouth. You even have his voice. But you aren't good, are you? Because if you are, it would be too much! I'd have to—"

I saw her hand tighten on the knife handle, and screamed: "Shelomith!" High, and thin and wailing. Like my despair. My grief.

"—push this blade on in. Make the sky come tumbling down. The night. I couldn't stand it if you were good! *One* of him is killing me by inches now, but *two*—"

I smiled then. My mouth hurt. My throat was full of bile, but I managed.

"No, Shelomith; I am not good," I said.

Chapter X

THAT NEXT DAY, to employ one of my father's favorite phrases, I was fit only to be bound hand and foot, thrown into a pit, and left to howl. I wandered all over my uncle's place without aim or direction. Inside my ravished carcass, my head and my heart waged bitter fratricidal war.

You, who've read all our modern lovesick Latin poets, can give me by rote, I'm sure, their finest lyrical cries of pain over love unrequited, denied, outraged, betrayed. But tell me, friend, is there among their splendid verses one line dedicated to the lover who is *not* deceived, who sees clearly the body of the death which inflicts him, the loathsomeness of the disease, recognizes the biting bitterness of the poison; and yet, eyes wide open, brain reproachful and clear, knowing full well what he is doing, goes step by hopeless step to his own ruin?

Yes. There *is* one. I recall it now. From the pen of Ovidus Naso: *Video meliora proboque; deteriora sequor!*[1]

For I couldn't get Shelomith out of either my mind or my heart. I told myself I'd carry her away by force, elevate her from that life, convert her by tenderness into the wife of my bosom who—

Who already had a husband, a good, sober citizen of Beth Anya. Who'd run away from him, tricking poor blind ass ish Kriyoth into turning thief in order to obtain the funds to sinew her flight; who'd tossed Yehudah Blind Ass ish Kriyoth into the gutter in his turn, once she'd reached her goal, the seamy, adulterous bed of a dog of a Roman. Who, deserted by said imperial son of a canine, turned to her natural bent, the profession to which, perforce, she had been born: that of harlotry. And I, who knew from my Roman days how chillingly remote are the possibilities of reforming any human heart, was fully prepared to outdo Yehudah of Kerioth in asininity by braying lustily down the road to my own doom without even the saving grace of being blind.

It's the only cure, I told myself. Have her! Bed with her! Sicken yourself into satiation upon her used whore's flesh! And thereafter—

I closed my eyes. And saw Helvetia standing there with her head bent, that day in Alexandria I'd jestingly sworn I was going to visit that Egyptian wench. The pain that bit into my middle was so great then that I had to clamp my teeth together, or else I would have cried aloud.

"No," I whispered. "No—not ever. No other woman. I'll go back to the Essenes. Become a monk. Die with the taste and feel of your mouth —only *your* mouth on mine, Helvi, I swear—"

But there is something in me basically irreverent, unsentimental, brutal, true.

"And Lydia's?" it jeered. "And Cænis'? And Eunice's, and all the other slave wenches in Caius' house, whose names you can't so much as call to mind, whose faces are a composite blur in the stagnant pool of memory? You weren't even faithful to poor Helvi while she lived, so what in the names of Satan, Sheol, and Gehenna are you piling Hedron on Carmel for, at this late and festive date? To bury the gnat-sized cadaver of your scruples? Ha!"

I opened my eyes, and saw Yehudah ish Kriyoth standing there. The last man on earth I wanted to see, now. My "brother in sorrow," he'd called himself. But, from what he'd said, she had at least let him—

I whirled away from his murmured "Master—" to see the *vexillum*, the banner, of a Roman cohort coming up the hill.

But it wasn't a cohort. It wasn't even a century. It was approximately two decuriae, twenty men, led by a lowly decurion, a commander over ten. From the *vexillum* itself, I could see that they were from the *Cohors Sebastenorum*, so I leaned back against a fence post and waited for the trouble I knew was coming.

Wait. Let me explain. By that time, Rome had conquered all the world, but she simply hadn't men enough to hold it. So she hit upon a very nearly infallible device: Divide and Rule. There was, in that thirteenth year of the reign of Tiberius, one *Cohors Italica* in all the province of Syria; just one. All the rest of the cohorts were drafted from the local populace, with the sole exception of the members of my race, who, because of our religious scruples—we would not worship the Imperator's bust, or bow to the graven Eagles of the Legions—were allowed to escape conscription by means of paying a tax.

Which meant that the Roman garrisons in the land of Judea were made up of Greeks from the Decapolis, Syrians from the desert country, Idumæans from the south, and, worst of all, Samaritans from Samaria, all of these races our hereditary enemies, men who'd have been pleased to eat a Jew for breakfast every morning. Especially my uninvited guests on this particular occasion, legionaries of the Sebastian Cohorts, who were actually Samaritans—for when Herod the Great razed the ancient city of Samaria to the ground, and built Sebaste on its ruins, he installed the old population in the new city, which did nothing to change their swinish natures.

As they came toward us, clanking up the hill in their armor, I glanced at Yehudah. His whole face had changed. It had turned a reddish purple. His nostrils flared. A little knot of muscle appeared above his temples and jerked. The whites of his eyes disappeared, dyed scarlet by the rush of blood behind them.

"Romans!" he said. He made of that one word, soft spoken, almost quiet, the filthiest obscenity in all the world.

"They're not," I began; "they're only—"

"Samaritans. I know. But they wear the Legions' armor. Bear their standards. So that makes them—Romans. Romans and Samaritans! Can you think of a bloodier abortion, master?"

"No," I said.

He closed his eyes, whispered: "O God, when the Mashiah comes, may it be in my lifetime! May I be there beside him to strike like thunder, make my sword eat flesh, my arrows drink blood! May—"

"Shut up, Yehudah!" I said. For by then the troops were upon us.

The decurion was a Philadelphian and a Greek. By which I mean he came from the city of Philadelphia in the southerner corner of the Decapolis, not far from the borders of Peræa, that is, close to the lower part of Antipas' tetrarchy. I was glad of that. The Philadelphians were usually reasonable men.

He saluted me smartly with his sword, sheathed it again, said:

"You are ben Mattithias' nephew, aren't you?" He gave my uncle's name the Greek form, although he spoke in Aramaic.

"Yes," I said in Greek. "I have that honor."

"And honor it is," he said pleasantly, switching with evident relief into his native tongue. "There is no finer gentleman in Galilee than Hezron son of Mattithias. No one disputes that. But it is with *you* that I have business, Nathanaios, son of Ieudas, not your uncle. . . ."

"And that business is?" I said.

He pointed with his hand toward my aqueduct; said: "That."

"It's entirely within the borders of our lands," I said quietly. "Even its source is, so it seems to me that your jurisdiction—"

"No, no!" he said quickly. "Don't mistake me, Nathanaios! You were entirely within your rights to build it, and it is in no way subject to tax. Rather I was sent here to ask a favor of you: that you call upon the Epitropos at Cæsarea, as soon as you conveniently can. . . ."

I was astonished; but he had been uniformly courteous, so I thought it better to match his tone.

"May I ask why, good Decurion?" I said.

"A piece of bad luck, uios Ieudas! The chief engineer of the *Cohors Italica* has fallen desperately ill. In fact his life is despaired of—"

"A great pity, Decurion," I said.

"It is," he agreed, "the more so because the Epitropos was planning to build a new aqueduct to bring down to Jerusalem the additional water that the continual growth of the capital's populace causes her to need—"

Now I was more astonished than ever. Had Pilatus been so impressed by his defeat at Cæsarea that he'd decided to court our favor? I glanced at ish Kriyoth. The red-bearded one shook his head warningly. It came to me then that he understood Greek. Which, when I came to think of the walk of life from which he originally had descended, was hardly strange.

"That's why great Pilatus would like to talk with you, Nathanaios. The fame of your feat of arch building here has spread throughout Galilee, and has reached his ears. May I examine your aqueduct? I'm requested to bring back a report upon it. . . ."

He put everything, politely, as a request; just as though it were within my power to refuse!

"Of course," I said.

"But first, when may I tell the Epitropos you will call?"

I thought quickly.

"Day after tomorrow," I said. "But please warn him that my skill hardly extends to such mighty works as—"

"The principle is exactly the same," the decurion said. "And yours has been supplying water to all the farms hereabouts for more than a month now. With unlimited funds, uncounted workers, it is easily possible that you might construct a deathless monument to your own fame—"

"Or Pilatus'?" I asked dryly.

"Oh, he's willing enough to share!" The decurion laughed. "He told me to tell you that a bronze plate bearing your name as builder would be affixed to the work in a prominent place. Now I'll go look at this one, if you don't mind—"

"My house is yours," I murmured politely, and bowed to him.

After he had inspected my aqueduct with what seemed to me a most professional eye, the decurion took his leave, trailing his grim Samaritan wardogs silently behind him. As soon as they were out of sight, I turned to Yehudah.

"Well, Yehudah," I said, "what do you think?"

But before he could answer me, we had another demonstration of the fact that the wonders of that day of wonders were not yet over:

Before our startled eyes, a clump of wild grass rose up from the ground. By the time it reached the level of our knees, we could see it had a man's head under it; and that the man in question was standing in one of the pits out of which we had dug clay to make bricks for our aqueduct. Which was why we hadn't seen him. It didn't occur to me until long afterward how professional his mastery of the military art of concealment had been.

"*Shalom Alechem!*" the man said. "Peace unto you!" And scrambled up out of the pit.

"And unto you, brother!" Yehudah said in an astonished tone. "Tell me, how's the climate down there in Sheol?"

I felt a twinge of envy at not having thought of that one myself; but the black-bearded visitor from the nether world answered imperturbably: "Hot! And Satan's stoking up Gehenna for the Romans! A word with you, young master?"

Then I saw who he was and a trembling got into my knees. For our troglodyte was none other than the burly blackbeard who'd shared Nikos' sitting room with me and the wine-sodden Roman as we waited for the *leno'* to herd his she-goats in.

"Of course," I said.

"All right," he growled. "But first a straight answer to a straight question: be you in their pay, or d'you otherwise favor them?"

"Neither," I said.

"You speak the truth?" Blackbeard said.

"Don't be stupid, man!" Yehudah said. "If you're from hereabouts, you should know that until they changed Procurators, there was a price of twenty thousand sesterces on his head!"

Which was a detail I hadn't even known before, but it turned out to be true. Helvetius' fellow officers got together and put that much up to insure the return of my angel to her father's house. Yehudah ish Kriyoth may have been a fool about women, but—I take that back! As far as Shelomith was concerned, from what man who ever saw her didn't rationality depart?

One. Yeshu'a ha Notzri.

"Why?" Blackbeard said.

Yehudah looked at him, then at me.

"Tell him," I said.

"He ran off with the daughter of the centurion of Gratus' Prætorian Guards," ish Kriyoth said.

Blackbeard threw back his head and roared.

"Ho!" he guffawed. "That I like! Paid 'em back in style, eh? The horny bastards! Where they're quartered, you have to keep your old grayhaired granny hid, or else they'd plug even her! So you knocked off one of their women, eh? Great, sez I; and here's my hand on it!"

I looked at him coldly.

"You're speaking of—my wife, friend," I said, "my dead wife—"

"Who was ravished and murdered by the Romans!" Yehudah said.

Blackbeard bowed his head. Looked up at me from under the thicket of his brows.

"I'm sorry, young master," he said, almost gently. "I didn't know."

"It's all right," I said.

He turned upon Yehudah.

"But if she was Roman herself, I don't see—"

"It was in Rome," Yehudah said, "after Tiberius expelled our people. The Romans didn't like the idea of her being married to one of us, and by *our* rites at that. It made her fair game—"

Why is it that the truth, oversimplified, becomes far worse than any lie? Not one word that Yehudah ish Kriyoth had said was less than perfect truth; and yet—

A look of craft got into Blackbeard's eyes.

"What would you do to even the score with them as killed your lady, master?" he said.

"Nobody killed her," I said evenly. "She killed herself."

"Because of what they'd done to her!" Yehudah said.

"Then it's the same, ain't it?" Blackbeard growled. "Kind of looks to me like you ought to be pining for vengeance, master."

"I am," I said.

"All right. You're a cool one. But that's all to the good, appears to me. You was palavering with the decurion in Greek, just now, wasn't you? Nearly everybody knows some Greek. But the other day at—" he saw Yehudah's eager little blue eyes, and halted—"at that place, you was jabbering away with a member of the *Cohors Italica* in his own tongue! Now, wasn't you?"

"I speak Latin, yes. I lived some years at Rome."

"Then, young master, how'd it strike you if you was to find yourself with a villa in Cæsarea? A little house in Tiberias, too? All your expenses paid, including the price of an occasional hot 'n willing piece o' tail?"

"In exchange for what?" I said.

"Keeping your ear to the ground. Making the right friends. If you was to shave off your beard, clip your hair close—"

I smiled.

"I wore it that way for years," I said. "My hair, I mean. And I was clean-shaven, too. But the Torah says—"

"That any sacrifice made for the Lord God of Israel," Blackbeard said fervently, "is justifiable in His sight!"

"Then—my villa, my shorn locks and beard, the befoulment of my body with harlots are all—justifiable sacrifices before the Lord?" I said.

"Yes!" Blackbeard said. "Look, master, you ever hear of—the Zealots?"

I stared at him.

"Then you—?" I said.

"I am called Shimeon Zealotes.³ Which is enough. I have no other name. You know us. You know what we do—"

"Yes," I said. I did know. Alone of all Israel the Zealots continued to fight and die for what they believed. Men called them brigands, *sicarii*.⁴ But it was the Romans, and those who supported them, whom they robbed and killed. I could feel the excitement moving in me. And the doubt. The fear.

"How much better could we do it," Shimeon Zealotes said, "if we knew when a cohort was being sent out, or an ala of cavalry, or when a century, or merely a decuria—"

"Or when the Roman paymaster sets out about his rounds?" I said dryly.

"Yes! Yes!" Shimeon the Zealot said. "Even that! Don't they wring that gold out of the sweat of our foreheads, master? Could it not be used to provide food for the widows and the orphans they have made? Weapons for us? Is it robbery to take back our own?"

"Do it, master!" Yehudah of Kerioth said. "You've the perfect opportunity! This aqueduct Pilatus wants you to build will give you excuse enough to pry into—"

"I—I'll have to think about it," I said slowly. "If my uncle sees me returning to that way of life, it may kill him, Yehudah. Surely it will break his heart. That's one thing. Another, O Shimeon, is this: Will your people trust me when they know my lineage? My mother is a bath Bœthus, Zealotes! Her first cousin is Yosef ben Kaiapha, the High Priest, son-in-law of the hateful Annas ben Seth. Half my blood is Bœthusian, friend. The blood of those of whom you sing:

> 'Woe is me for the House of Bœthus; woe is me
> for their clubs!
> Woe is me for the House of Annas; woe is me
> for their whisperings . . .' "[5]

Shimeon smiled.

"A man is of his father's house, master. Which makes you of the banim Matthya, a good Galilean. A son of the land which has never produced a traitor yet!"

"Pray God that I be not the first one!" I said.

"Do it, master! Join them!" Yehudah ish Kriyoth said.

But I stood there. Deep inside my mind, I could feel a subtle inquietude. It was if I felt, not heard, the echoes of the alarm bell, clamoring across the desert air from the furtherest outpost, long before the enemy has reached the gate.

"Tomorrow," I said slowly. "Come to me at sunset tomorrow. I will give you my answer, then. . . ."

Shimeon studied me. His hot black eyes clouded over with doubt.

"So be it, master! Until tomorrow," he said.

I had no one to turn to; no one at all. And the burden of my now tripled perplexities was terrible. For the first one, whether or not I should enter into some sort of so far undefined relationship with Shelomith, I had not the remotest possibility of obtaining useful advice from anyone; and, anyhow since I knew myself only too well, the possibility of my acting upon that advice once obtained—especially if it made sense—was remoter still. In fact, it was nonexistent.

But, when I had had time to examine my two new problems— whether I should help Pilatus build his aqueduct, and whether I should or shouldn't become a paid informer, or to put it crudely, a spy, for the

Zealots—I found to my great surprise that they both fell into the same category as the question of Shelomith, at least in one regard:

By their very nature, they were the sorts of things about which advice, even from the wisest of sources, was likely to be prejudiced, misinformed, or wildly, dangerously wrong.

Because to judge them fairly demanded an experience and a temperament that almost no one in Israel had. The question of the aqueduct required a cosmopolitan, worldly, almost pagan point of view. Had Pilatus known us, or even been seriously concerned about gaining our favor, he would have built a new imposing synagogue, totally free of graven images, and offered it to the Nation. Or less than that! Had he appeared daily in the Temple, offering sacrifices to Invisible, Unutterable, Unknowable God, all Israel would have sung his praises.

But offer us cool, clean water to drink and to wash our sweaty hides in, the means toward an almost acceptable degree of personal cleanliness, the way to stave off an epidemic or two, and what will my goddrunken, otherworldly people say?

"*Water*? For what? To drink? Hath a pest destroyed the vineyards? To wash? But we *do* wash! We lave our hands before each meal, just as the Law—Our *bodies*? Well—once a fortnight say, if the weather's fine. And for that it seemeth me we have water and to spare—"

My uncle, asked, would snort: "Neither their gall nor their honey!" My father would spin the matter out into a gossamer web of philosophical speculations having neither beginning nor end, nor head, nor tail. And Yeshu'a—who knew what Yeshu'a would think or say? What value had the thoughts of a carpenter's son who in all his life had never strayed ten leagues away from the sleepy Nazareth of his birth?

There, at least, I think now, I was wrong. I should have asked him. But I didn't.

I had to decide that question for myself. And I, who was half a pagan, remembered Rome, where one spent half one's life in the baths, where even the plebes rarely offended one's nostrils, where it was possible to kiss one's beloved all over from the soles of her dainty feet to the top of her delicate head, as I'd often kissed my Helvetia, and risk neither asphyxiation nor nausea! Besides, Jerusalem, high, parched, dry Jerusalem, needed water. Needed it desperately. And if even such a swine as Pontius Pilatus was prepared to supply that need, it seemed to me criminal folly not to ally myself with him in that one regard.

That decision made, I felt better. But the question of becoming a Zealot spy was a much more thorny, hurtful thing. Like every son of Abraham, I was prepared to give my life to free my land from Rome. But I was approaching the age when one begins to painfully accommodate one's self to bitter fact. And the bitterest fact I had to swallow was this:

Under the then present circumstances, Israel stood in far greater danger from those who loved her most than she did from her cooler, more indifferent sons, or even from her foes. For only such as the Zealots, inflamed with the rage of a man forced to watch helplessly the brutal ravishment of a beloved bride, were likely to provoke or force the Romans into destroying the Land, the Nation of Judea.

Among my contemporaries I was almost unique; alone among all my friends and acquaintances had I traveled widely enough to know the overwhelming nature of Roman power. A man has the right, perhaps—though our Law forbids it—to take his own life. But when he sets in motion a chain of events that will doom inevitably a whole people to death and slavery, he becomes a murderer and worse. And that, through their isolation-born provincial ignorance, was precisely what the Zealots would surely do.

It would have been so easy to join them, become their spy, help them to fall upon Roman patrols, rob the paymasters, poniard traitors! The blood leaped and sang in my veins at the prospect. Perhaps one day, along a lonely road, I'd even meet Avidius Publius sent out to Judea—

To feed my idiotic fantasies, my sick, impotent lust for vengeance. Nothing more. Because, unlike Shimeon Zealotes and his friends, I hadn't the excuse of their honest belief that tiny, naked, unarmed Judea could vanquish mighty Rome. Nor did I have the Essenes' faith that the Lord God of Hosts would come down and scatter the Kittim like dead leaves before his trumpets' blast.

No.

I'd called on him too many times in my awful, bitter need. I knew in my bleak and barren heart, his silence. I knew from experience he was capable of letting innocence die—horribly, as my Helvetia died. And that to ask me to even believe in, not to mention to venerate, to worship, a God who could and did allow me to live on as I lived now, with the petal-soft tenderness of a kiss branded forever on my mouth, obscenely mingled and combined with the smell of putrefaction, the feel of rotting flesh pulling ropily, sicksweetly away from slender, achingly beloved bones as it came off in my hands, was asking too much.

Like any rational man, I prefer atheism to demonolatry.

Nor did I believe the Mashiah would ever come to deliver my people, Israel. More, I hoped for his own sake that, if come he must, he would choose another epoch, era, age. Because I knew what would happen if Israel's Savior came to free us now and here:

The Romans would take him like a thief, and hang him from a tree.

So it was that in the red glow of that next setting sun, I faced Shimeon Zealotes, and said very quietly:

"No."

And he: "Why not, young master?"

"It wouldn't work. And, anyhow, spying is beneath me. I find the very idea demeaning."

He stood there and the sunset got into his hot black eyes, turning them blood red. But he didn't say his thought. He said only: "So be it, master!" And turned, and left me there.

And I, fool that I was, did not recall until far too late, that to a Zealot, he who is not a friend is, inevitably, a foe. And that to their foes, the Zealots have but one answer.

Death.

I went up to Kafer Nahum. I could not stay away. But once there, neither could I bring myself to direct my footsteps towards Nikos' ill-famed house. I wandered about, hoping to encounter Shelomith by chance. My uncle had said she often left the *lupanar,* usually to throw herself in Yeshu'a's way when he came up to Kafer Nahum to visit Shimeon Kepha, Netzer, and the sons of Zebediah. And I did encounter her. But not at all by chance.

I was sitting on the prow of a beached boat, watching Shimeon Kepha and his brother Netzer mending nets. A little way off, Yuani—for such was the affectionate diminutive that the Galileans made of the Hebrew name Yohannan, Yuhanni in Aramaic[6]—bar Zebediah, was amusing himself by trying to spear fish in the shoal waters with a trident. He was having no luck at all, but the combination of net and trident woke memory in me.

I saw quite suddenly the other Netzer, the other Andrai I had loved, halfheartedly fending off my trident and my net before the fiendish, roaring mob at Rome. Andrai whom I'd loved—and murdered. To save less my own life than Helvi's. And remembering that, I bent my head, there by the shore, and wept.

"What ails you, Nathan?" Shimeon Kepha bar Yonah said.

"Nothing," I muttered: "I—"

But that was as far as I got, for I saw Yose, Yeshu'a's youngest brother, running toward us on the sands.

I leaped from the boat. He threw himself on his belly before me, began to pound the sandy beach with his two hands.

"The strumpet!" he howled: "The harlot! The whore! Oh, Nathan, I—"

I raised him up; said: "Where is she?"

There was no need to say the name.

"Back there. In the main square. With a crowd of gladiators, charioteers, and some soldiers from the Sebastian Cohort. She—she's drunk. They're tossing her in their cloaks. When she goes up you can see—can see—"

"What?" Yohannan bar Zebediah said.

"Everything!" Yose wailed.

It came to me then that he loved her, too.

"This I got to see!" Yuani laughed.

I raised my hand.

"No," I said. "You stay here, Yohannan; there's likely to be trouble. Now give me that trident."

"Whaaat?" Yuani said.

"You heard me. Your trident, Yuani! And you, Shimeon, a piece of net. There—that smaller one will do—"

"But what are you going to do, Nathan?" Netzer, or Andrai, if you prefer, Shimeon's younger brother, began.

"I propose to teach those swine a lesson," I said. "And a trident and a net, plus this dagger I already have, are enough and to spare to do it with. Thank you. Now all of you stay here. One man alone can do this, but five would provoke a slaughter. I command you, by the Ineffable Name, to stay out of this!"

"But what the devil d'you mean to do, exactly, Nathan?" Shimeon Kepha said. "What can a man do with a net and a trident except—"

"Fish!" I said: "But this time—men!"

When I came into the square they were still at it. And my Shelomith, be it said, was enjoying the sport as hugely as they. Each time she soared aloft, displaying her lissome thighs, her lovely hips—even, upon occasion, the night plume of her sex—to the public view, she loosed the silvery flute notes of her laughter.

The rage that tore me left me almost blind. That nakedness was mine! A wife's nakedness was her husband's! And I—

Was a poor fool standing there watching a runaway adulteress, a public whore, disport herself with exactly the kind of panimperial brutal oafs she was divinely suited for!

Or was she? Was the woman who had been prepared to die rather than profane one last curiously chaste and simple love really suited to consort with the offal and the scum of earth, the scourings of the whole Roman world? Wasn't she at heart a poor romantic fool deliberately destroying herself in this nauseous way in order to punish herself for bitterly regretted sins?

That was Yehudah ish Kriyoth's theory; but he, as his subsequent actions proved, was a true romantic. The truth was somewhat less accommodating. I'd say that Shelomith was equipped from birth to become a saint or a whore, like every woman born. Just as every man is born both high priest and thief; both pious rab and murderer. The Essenes would have blamed it on her stars, you Greeks, on the Fates; I, on nothing more than the fact that man is essentially lost and mad, eternally tormented by Nature's cruelest jest: to have been granted simultaneously both knowledge and impotency.

And—desire.

The crowd was of divided mind. Some were enjoying the spectacle, others shook pious heads at its wantonness. Being Galilean Jews, the pious were the majority. That decided me. I'd take the chance. All through their history the Galileans have died for liberty. And this profanation, this insult to their piety, their peace, was excuse enough for them to aid me. But then I stopped dead, for that ice-cold something at the center of my being, had asked the right question:

What right did I have to involve these poor unarmed innocents in what was sure to be a slaughter?

While I was debating that one with myself, an old man, white-bearded as a Prophet, ended the matter for me. He lifted his staff.

"Thieves and harlots!" he quavered, his voice breathless and sobbing, feeble with age, torn by grief. "Practicers of abominations! Brigands! Despoilers of—of Babylon's daughters!"

"Just how many of her does he see?" I thought; but I had no time for more, because one of those Samaritan bastards of the Sebastian Cohort whirled upon the poor quivering ancient and slapped him to the ground.

The crowd roared at that. Whereupon the legionaries drew their swords and charged. The Galileans broke, scattered, trampling each other in their wild flight. I managed to draw the old man aside in time.

"Go home, my father," I said to him. "God in his own good time will punish, will avenge—"

"No, no!" he wept. "I've waited too long now! I'll die without ever having seen—"

I propped him up against a tree.

"Just keep your eyes open then, father!" I said.

The Sebastians were coming back, now. I saw with some relief there was no blood on their blades. They were laughing.

Then I stepped out into the square and met them. They stopped cold. The sight must have been a rare one: A small and slender bearded Jew, clad in his holy fringed garment, but carrying a trident and a fishnet in his hands.

"Are you," I said harshly, "men of honor, or the dogs you seem? If dogs, I bid you put your tails betwixt your cowardly legs and scurry off to your kennels!"

I could feel Shelomith's great eyes on my face, pouring sunlight against my cheek. They made a burning.

"If men, I challenge you! Choose among you your mightiest champion. Let him come armed as he will to meet me in a contest to the death. I ask only that should I lose, you do not profane my body—"

"And should you win?" a gigantic, brutal Goth said mockingly. "What, then, Maccabaeus?"

"That you all will abide by the fortunes of war," I said, "and let me depart in peace, taking with me—this woman!"

"Why, I like that!" Shelomith said. "Why you bandy-legged little he-goat of a Jew, I'll—"

"The gods help him if he wins and tries to spend a whole night with little Shelom!" a Sebastian laughed. "She won't leave a rag of flesh on his puny bones. What say you, boys, shall we let Thor eat him alive?"

"Agreed!" they roared. "Let Thor, the gladiator, butcher him!"

I stepped back. Stripped off my long fringed robe. Stood before them entirely naked. I could feel Shelomith's gaze crawling over my body, feel the warmth get into it, kindle, take fire. It was a curiously shocking thing. If you know anything about women, you know they *never* look at you. Not the way a man looks at a woman with longing and with lust. Women are tactile beasts; their desire lies just beneath their soft skins. You have to stroke it, pet it into life. It never leaps full armed into being at a glance, a glimpse of an inch of forbidden, secret flesh, the way male lust does. But Shelomith stood there staring at me, and the nipples of her breasts rose up like tiny twin *phalli*, pressing visibly against the thin stuff of her harlot's robe.

I didn't know then that she was putting *his* head on my shoulders. It wasn't until later that I found that out.

I stooped, picked up my dagger, sheath and all, and buckled it about my waist. It wasn't until I bent the second time, and came up with my trident and my net, that it came to them that they'd miscalculated, that this game wasn't going to be the child's play that they'd thought.

"A retiarius!" Thor bellowed. "A Jew retiarius! By Vulcan, who ever heard—"

"Well, you have now," I said, and put that trident almost into his little blue eyes.

He leaped back a rod, came roaring in. I played him as the bull dancers do the bulls in the arenas of Crete. I moved in and out of the flashing circle of his blade, until Shelomith stuffed all five fingers of one hand into her mouth. Else she would have cried out from horror and from fear. She had no idea how hopelessly unequal that contest was. I could have killed Thor within the first five minutes had I wanted to; but the vein of cruelty in me stood up and beat with my ardent blood. I ripped his face open to the bone. Gashed his sword arm, perforated one massive thigh. All with lighting-fast jabs of that wicked three-headed spear.

Then I stood back and looked at him as the bull slayers gaze upon the tormented, crippled bull whose death is but a single stroke away.

"Acknowledge yourself defeated," I said, "and I'll spare your life."

"No!" he bellowed, and came limping in. I lifted the net, set it aspin. It billowed up and out, gossamer and iridescent in the sun. I gave my wrist a flick, opened my fingers, let the net soar. It lifted high, came down over Thor's great bloody head, settled down over his huge body. He hung there for a breath-gone moment, then he began to tear at it. While he was so occupied, I put the shaft of the trident between his massive legs, and spilled him to the ground. He shook the earth with his impact, lay there, motionless, stunned.

At once I was upon him, dagger raised and glittering; but at the last moment, I stayed my hand. Down to my bones' marrow, I hated killing —even such a beast as this.

"Well, Shelomith," I called out. "Shall I spare this swine?"

She didn't answer me. And I didn't see her. I turned my head. Then I did see her, too late. Her—and the huge stone she held high in both her hands, the exact moment before she brought it crashing down upon my defenseless skull.

My head ached damnably, which proved at least I wasn't dead. I put up my fingers and felt it. They came away covered with blood, but the bone wasn't broken, which, considering the size and weight of that stone and the force with which my beloved Shelomith had thrown it, was something of a miracle.

"Ha!" one of them sang out. "The beggar revives! Now what shall we do with him?"

"Push fishhooks through his balls and hang him by them to a tree!" Thor, the gladiator amicably suggested.

"Tie him to a green log, over a slow fire," another said.

"Cut him all over, smear him with honey, and stake him above an ant heap," still another said.

"No," my darling's voice came over to me, throaty with laughter, slumberous and deep. "I was the victor in that fray, so he's mine. I'll propose the penalty. What say you, boys?"

"Agreed! Agreed!" They laughed. "Let little Shelom decide!"

"That is," a Sebastian drawled, "if she doesn't decide to fornicate him to death . . ."

"That way she can kill me!" another legionary roared.

"And me! And me! And me!" the rest of them bellowed.

I opened my eyes. Grinned at her.

"Go to it, Shelomith!" I said. "Proceed to execute the Legions!"

She smiled back at me. I have never seen anything as cruel as that smile.

"Boys," she said, "he's a Jew. And our Law says: 'Accursed of God is he who's hanged.' Therefore I propose that you—crucify him."

"By Tartarus, Shelom," Thor said, "that'll take too long! He's a wiry bastard. He's good for three, four days. And we have to get back to barracks tonight. Leave's over, as you know damned well. . . ."

"I'll keep watch," she whispered. "You send the boys who come off duty tomorrow—to take turns at him. And they, those of the day after, and they—"

"Hades!" One of the Sebastians laughed. "It ain't a half bad idea. Drag him up to that grove by Migdal-Nunaya. Make a cross and—"

"Done!" the others said; "Here, Phillip, you tie his hands!"

Since the sect of the Nazarenes, or, as you call them, the Christianoi, have extended throughout the world, including your native land, you've probably acquired an image of that fiendishly cruel death that is somewhat, though not entirely, false. Having wisely decided to convert their original shame at the knowledge that he who founded their sect was hanged like a felon into a point of honor, they've spread their little T-shaped crosses through all the world, with the image of poor, pitiful Yeshu'a upon them nailed. In this they are correct, for so did my loved and hated friend/brother/foe actually die.

But that wasn't the usual form of crucifixion. Among other things, the upright is almost never extended above the crossbar as it was in Yeshu'a's case so that Pilatus could affix his blasphemous mockery above his victim's head. And the Romans, those past masters in the art of

prolonging pain beyond all endurance, seldom nailed their victims to
the tree, since experience had taught them that that way they always
died too fast. No, they usually bound them to the cross with ropes, and
left them to dangle there until—sometimes up to a whole week later—
they died.

But there is nothing worse. Not even burning at the stake. At the
very worst, with green wood, a slow fire, before an hour's up, your
burnt victim's awful agony is over. Less than that, if he has the wit to
breathe in the flames. All other tortures, designed to reduce the victim
to a cringing wreck over weeks until he confesses or reveals what his
tormentors want him to, have their intervals of relief, of surcease.
Crucifixion has none.

I know, because I was crucified.

They kicked my poor trussed-up carcass through the town, and out
upon the northbound road. Naturally, my progress toward the other
world did not go unobserved. Among the people who saw me pass were
Shimeon and Netzer bar Yonah, Yaakob and Yohannah bar Zebediah,
Yose, the brother of Yeshu'a, and a dozen more who knew me.

But nobody lifted a hand. I think the Sons of Fury, the *Boane
Ragsha*, Yaakob and Yohanna, were going to, because their faces
turned black with rage. I warned them off, shouting:

"Go to my uncle! Tell him—"

Then one of my captors slammed me in the mouth with his fist.

My friends did as I bade them, and raced down to Nazareth to tell
my uncle. Then everything went wrong at once. My uncle with all that
crowd, including Yeshu'a himself, running at his mount's heels, took
horse for Cæsarea!

Which was logical enough. The Procurator Pontius Pilatus had his
seat there; and they'd told Uncle Hezron I'd been arrested by the
Romans for coming to the defense of Shelomith. And he didn't think
to ask which way my captors had taken me, nor did those thick-skulled
Galilean bumpkins remember to say that when they'd seen the so-
called arrest, the Sebastians were clouting and kicking me *northward*
toward Migdal-Nunaya, directly opposite the direction they'd have had
to go to take me to Cæsarea.

The result of all this confusion was simple: It gave dainty Shelomith and her gentle friends time and to spare to murder me.

Along that road, I kept glancing at her, to see if I could surprise pity
in her eyes. There was none. Instead she sang snatches of love songs,
gathered an armful of the wild roses that grew along that way. And it

came to me then that this lovely, savage creature was more than a little
—mad.

They made an x-shaped cross—the best and most stable form, since
it has both bars embedded in the ground instead of only one, which
proved they were experts—and bound me to that, spraddle-legged.
Thor pulled off his swordbelt, brass-studded, the buckle end out, and
handed it to one of the Sebastians. He couldn't use it himself, because
I'd crippled his arm for him.

"Here," he said. "Use this on the bastard. Every third stroke betwixt
his legs. Cure him of his ambitions toward our little Shelom—"

But Shelomith got up then, faced them.

"No," she said calmly, "he's mine. I claim the right to torture him!"

"How?" Thor rumbled. "With those?"

He pointed to the spray of Sharon roses she had picked along the
way as her louts had kicked and dragged me toward Migdal.

"Why not?" she said. Then lightly, playfully, she began to strike me
across the face with them, until the petals showered down, rained about
my feet.

"Hades!" Thor rumbled; but then he saw how I was bleeding.

They watched it, fascinated: her hands striking lightly, playfully,
as a kitten strikes a captured mouse. And each time those thorny stems
tore my face, brought blood.

"You—won't—" she chanted, in rhythm with her blows, "look—like
him—any—more. . . . You won't—look—like—Yesu—any—more. . . .
You will not look—like him—I love—never like him—I love—Never
never never—like beautiful beautiful Yesu I love! Never like—"

"Oh, for Jupiter's sake, Shelom!" one of the Sebastians said. "It's
getting late and we'll have to go before you even get a yelp out of him!
Let me—"

"No!" she said. Then: "You want to see him go out of his mind?"

"Yes!" they chorused. "That's just what—"

She moved back, a dancing step. Unhooked the great bronze clasp
that held her broad-belted girdle around her slender waist. Let it drop.
Pushed her silken dress down off her shoulders. Stood there before me
as naked as the day she was born. I saw the ridged crusting of dried
blood on her left breast where she'd stabbed herself to escape me three
days (years? centuries? ages? aeons?) ago. It was healing well and
cleanly.

"By Pluto!" one of the Sebastians said. "Didn't I tell you? She's
gonna ravish th' bastard to death!"

She came up to me, step by step by step. Stood inches away from me.

So close that I could smell her. I knew then that she was right. That very shortly, I was going out of my mind.

She went up on tiptoe, and found my mouth. An X-shaped cross is plenty low enough for that. I was no love sick half-virgin boy; I'd been kissed by experts; I had been, among other things, you may recall, Lydia's lover. But never until that hour had I known what it was to have my being, my identity, my pride of self, my will, drawn out of me through every pore of the underflesh of my sweetlyhotlywetlysavagely-tenderly assaulted mouth. Her tonguetip was the Serpent in the Garden, and Gan Eden was suddenly commingled with dark Sheol; her lips bloomed on mine like great hot fungus flowers, blood-gorged, absorbent, and what they drew from me was but my soul.

She moved in then, working her body into mine until the contact between flesh and flesh was very nearly total. She writhed against me until every nerve I had was screaming, until in one second more I'd have disgraced myself, showered and drenched her, belly and thigh, externally with my seed.

But I was saved from that minor disaster, for suddenly I felt the splash and scald against my face, on her wide lips tasted the sting, the salt. Her mouth hard-pressed against mine still, she moaned: "Oh, Yesu! Yesu! My love, my life!"

I tore my mouth free of hers, said: "If you use my body as a substitute for his, I'll kill you, Shelomith. Though I have to come back from Sheol itself to do it!"

She stared at me. Her eyes flamed. Her black-maned head was like night itself, crashing down from heaven. Her mouth smashed into mine like the blow of a fist. I opened my mouth to speak, to say—what I'll never know, because she caught my underlip between her perfect, savage teeth. At the same time her hands clawed down, down to where a man is most potent and most weak, most naked, and most vulnerable.

I felt her teeth and her nails at the same time and screamed.

"Pretend to faint!" she hissed at me.

She'd given me too much credit. It wasn't pretense at all.

When I came to myself, I was alone. I could hear the bass rumble of their voices dying out of time and mind, and through it the silvery lilt and soar of her laughter. Night was slanting along the land; the shadows grew and grew and all the trees were ghostly.

And then again as on that long lost golden morning when I lay with my Helvetia in this selfsame grove, I heard Miriam, the madwoman of Migdal-Nunaya, howl.

Hope rose in me. Miriam was mad; but she was endlessly kind. She brought home crippled animals, fledglings fallen from their nests, all small lost, forlorn things, nursed them in her clumsy way, mourned them when they died, as they usually did. If I could attract her attention! If I only could!

"Miriam!" I cried.

She came toward me very slowly. Her eyes were enormous in her ravaged, filthy face.

"Miriam!" I moaned. "Get a knife! Cut me loose! Do you hear me! Get—"

But she had sunk to her knees before me, her hands folded in the attitude of prayer.

"Bless me, my lord Yeshu'a," she said.

I tried to talk some sense into her. I tried. But I am not Yeshu'a. I am me. Her attention soon wandered. She got up and left me there, still dangling in awful agony from my cross, still bound. The ropes bit into my arms and legs. I knew without being able to see them that my hands and feet were turning blue. That was one of the effects of crucifixion. Often they started in to rot, long before the victim died.

I hung there all night long, tightening my belly muscles so that my guts would not sag down. When they did, that was the beginning of the end. You lost control then, defecated upon yourself, which brought the flies. Some people think it is the flies that kill you finally. Certainly they are what drive you mad. They crawl into your eyes, your nostrils, your mouth. They explore your ears, your navel, your rectum. And you can't drive them away. You hang there with your flesh puffing, turning black around those ropes, spurting dribbles of bloody urine down between your feet, and pray for the death that will not come.

I must have fainted again, or even slept. But I woke with the sun in my eyes. Twisted, strained my arms, my legs, turned my head—

And Shelomith was there.

She looked like the great-grandmother of all the whores on earth. Her dress was in ribbons, in tatters. Her eyes were blue-ringed, sunk back into her head. Her mouth was one great bruise. There were teeth marks on her throat, nail furrows in her shoulders. Death and bitter Sheol in her tortured gaze.

The self-inflicted wound in her left breast had reopened. It was bleeding sullenly.

When she came close to me I took the stench of twenty intermingled male carnal sweats full in my nostrils. I bent my head and vomited upon the ground.

Then she cut me loose. I slumped to the earth and lay there while she massaged my legs, my arms. The blood forcing its way back into my all but collapsed veins was an agony almost impossible to bear. But I bore it staring at her all the time she worked at me.

"I couldn't come before," she said; "I couldn't, Nathan! They wouldn't let me leave the barracks. . . . They thought I'd turn you loose. They thought that there—that there was—something—between us—"

"Isn't there?" I said.

"Oh, God!" She wept. "You know as well as I that—"

"That what?" I said.

"That—nothing—" she moaned. "I'm—a filthy harlot—I am not fit to —to—I—I had to lie with all of them, Nathan. Some of them two and three times—until I'd worn them out. They kept giving me wine, but I spat it out. And when they were all snoring their swinish heads off, I got out of there—and—"

"And now?" I said, death in me up to the iron hilt.

"Can you walk?" she said. "Here, let me help you up. That's it. That's it! Another step—Good! Oh, Nathan, Nathan, I—"

"Thank you," I said.

"For what, Nathan? After all, I—"

"For getting my name right. At last. For not calling me—Yeshu'a."

"Ohhhh!" she moaned. "Don't make it worse! I'm being pulled apart in two directions now and—"

She looped my arm over her shoulder, and started off, half dragging me. We must have been a sight, Shelomith in rags, and me stark-naked. But neither of us thought about that then—or ever.

Because half a stade beyond the woods, we met Shimeon Zealotes. He had been searching for me, nightlong. When he saw who I was, he drew his knife.

He got that blade three quarters of the way to my poor defenseless hide before Shelomith fully realized his intentions. Even so, she managed to knock his arm aside. But not far enough. That razor-sharp blade slid along my rib and made a gash fully twenty *unciae* long, from which a river, a flood, a sea of blood ran down.

What saved me was that Shelomith started in to scream. And that Shimeon had no stomach for butchering a woman. Besides, from all the blood that soaked my naked hide, he must have believed me finished, done. Anyhow, he turned and loped off, like a clumsy wolf.

And Shelomith screamed and screamed and screamed, tearing the sky apart, slivering the day, until the people in nearby Migdal-Nunaya heard her and came.

By that time, I was out again. But not too far out not to hear her pray:

"Oh God, if you save him, spare his life, I'll be good! I'll leave this life! I'll worship and cherish him—all my days . . ."

Or was it "cherish you" she said? I was too far gone to be sure, lying there in a muddy pool of my own blood. In that particular phrase, as you can readily see, the difference between "you" and "him" is enormous.

Great enough, in fact, to wreck my life.

Chapter XI

THE FIRST THING I saw when I opened my eyes again was that I was in my own bedroom in my uncle's house. The second was that Shelomith was sitting in a chair beside my bed looking at me.

And something in the way she looked then, at that moment, stopped my heart. I had never seen anything like her in all my life, except—

No. That's not right, either. I'd started to say "except Helvi." No. That's one of those statements that seem to make sense, but don't, really. Because, you see, they were both perfect. In different ways. And comparisons, contrasts, between perfections of distinct orders are meaningless. Helvi was—Helvi. And Shelomith was Shelomith. Total opposites. In everything. Except that they both managed to break my heart.

I saw another thing, too: We'd been there for some time. Shelomith had on a rough woolen robe surely borrowed from one of my uncle's maidservants. She had had time to bathe, even to scrub herself, for her skin was literally glowing. There wasn't a trace of a harlot's paints, powders, rouges left on it. She'd piled that demonic witch's mane of hers high in a soft mound atop her tiny, arrogantly queenly head. She wasn't Astarte anymore. She was Esther. Ruth. Seeing her like that, seeing the nineteen-year-old girl miraculously reborn out of the jaded whore, I wanted to cry.

Wanted to! Sheol and Gehenna both, I did!

Instantly she was on her knees beside my bed. Her hands came out, cupped my fevered face between them, holding me like that while she stared into my eyes.

"Nathan!" she said, her voice a little strident, hoarse. "What's wrong? Do you hurt? Is there anything I can—?"

Wordlessly I shook my head. As much as I could shake it with my bearded face imprisoned between her strong and tender hands. She tightened her clasp, held me like that, so that I could not escape her eyes.

"Tell me!" she said.

"I—" I got out; "I—"

"Yes, Nathan?"

"Oh, God, Shelom; I love you so!"

Her hands came away from the sides of my face, made a silken rustling through my beard, were gone. She knelt there facing me, and her eyes melted. There is no other way to describe it. They melted and poured down her cheeks.

In all my life, neither before nor since, have I seen or heard a woman cry like that. I never want to again.

Her lips were heavy-fleshed, wide. Her tears caught on the corners of them, danced on that wild, hopeless quiver as though an invisible idiot were juggling jewels. Then they flashed white fire and slanted downward, penciling light across her chin. The sobs came up out of her throat and made a tearing.

"Shelom—" I groaned: "Oh my love, my own—"

She shook her head. "No!" she sobbed. "I am not fit! You shouldn't —you mustn't—say—"

"What?" I whispered.

"That—you—that you love me. You mustn't, Nathan!"

"Why not?" I said.

"It's—too—cruel! You—shouldn't cast what's—holy—before a she-dog!"

"You're not!" I got out. "You never had a chance! From now on, I'll—"

"Don't be a fool, Nathan!" she said harshly, angrily. "I had every chance! I come from a good family in Beth Anya. My—husband was —the kindest, the best of men. Only, he bored me. Oh God, how he bored me! I needed Antonius. I *needed* that kind of putrid filth, don't you understand? Oh, Nathan, Nathan, you sweet damn fool, I was born a whore!"

"Nobody is," I said tiredly: "Shelom, what I offer you—"

"Is water in a cracked cup—to a woman dying of thirst. It runs out and the earth drinks it, makes mud of it, before she can get it to her mouth. Food two rods from a famished she-beast, howling in her cage, unable to poke her muzzle or her paw far enough out to reach it!"

"You mean you don't love me," I said bitterly.

She shook her head.

"No, Nathan," she said quietly. "I mean I do."

I stared at her.

"If I didn't, I should grab you, you fool! Fly to the ends of the earth with you! Devour you with kisses, use that slim, strong, beautiful man's body of yours that just to look at makes my middle melt and run down my thighs. Only, I do love you, so I can't. You see, I love you, Nathan bar Yehudah Yeshu'a ha Notzri—"

"What!" I said.

"Who are the same man divided in two to make a mirror image. You're the him who is gay and worldly and manbeautiful and who starts a fire in my belly and makes my breasts hurt. And he's the you who is gentle and godlike and angelbeautiful so that I want to kneel down and kiss his feet. I did once. Kiss his feet, I mean. Only—"

"Only?" I whispered.

"You won't stay apart!" she wailed. "Sometimes he's manbeautiful, too; and I want him the bad way, just like I want you all the time. I've wanted you like that from the first moment I saw you in the street and realized that you weren't, couldn't be, him and followed you. When you turned around, I ran and hid. That was when you first came here, you know. . . ."

"Go on," I said weakly. This was too much. I could feel the strength slipping away from me now.

"And sometimes you are angelbeautiful, like when they hung you on that cross, and—Do you know *why* I did that, Nathan?"

"Why you did what?" I whispered.

"Hit you in the head with that rock. I had to, love! If you'd killed Thor they'd have butchered you like a sacrificial lamb no matter what they'd promised. So I let you have it. And, Oh Lord, I was so afraid I'd killed you! And afterward I got them to crucify you because I figured that since they were sure to do something awful to you anyhow that was the only thing I could think of that would give me time enough to come back and save you. Never figured on that black-bearded bastard Shimeon! Anyhow, what I started to say was that when they hung you on that cross, and that light came out of heaven and hovered about your head, you looked just like an angel the way Yeshu'a always does, and I—"

"Shelom, you're mad, you know," I croaked.

"I am. Howling mad. For you, like a chained-up bitch in season. For him—"

"Shelom, don't!"

"Like a worshiper before the Holy of Holies, kneeling. All he has to do is smile and the morning and the evening stars sing together, and all the Cherubim and Seraphim come down! While you—"

"While I?"

"You're good too. Brave and gallant and gay. The sort of man I should have married instead of that pious old fart! I—I'd have been faithful to *you*, Nathan! Oh, I would! I would! I would!"

"Shelom, don't!" I groaned. "Please don't cry! Not any more! Please!"

"Only, what have I to offer you? Used, dirty, diseased—no. I was. But he cured that."

"He—Yeshu'a cured you—of—"

"An issue. A running issue. Ugh! What a beastly thing! I don't suppose he even knows he did. I met him in the street and made a fool of myself over him, as usual. Crawling on my belly, embracing his ankles, kissing his feet. He—he raised me up—and kissed my forehead. And it went away. Like that. Two days later, it was gone—"

"Shelom, I don't believe—"

"It's true, I tell you! Nathan—"

"Yes, Shelomith?"

"I want to kiss you. Right now, I mean. Oh, Nathan, I want to kiss you so damn' bad!"

"Me—or him?" I said bitterly.

"Both. But right now, you. Kiss you as though I were a—good girl. A—a virgin. And you were my betrothed. Nobody—*ever* kisses me like that! All sweet and gentle and trembly—and—and—"

"Tenderly," I said. "Come here, then."

I kissed her like that. For me, then, at that moment, she was my bride-to-be. My virginal, spotless bride.

It broke her heart. She clung to me and sobbed and sobbed until my uncle came through the door with his riding whip in his hands.

He caught her by the hair and jerked her from my bed. His first blow caught her across the face, and her flesh broke open like a ripe plum. She carried the scar of that down to her grave.

Then he was beating her beating her beating her and she simply covered her face with her two hands, but made no further effort to stop him. I saw his whip cut through the wool of her robe like a knife, and under it her flesh open up like two long bluish white lips and turn scarlet in the middle and drip red, and he crossing that with another and that with still another until I was out of the bed and between them and the whip was whining and singing and whistling and biting into me too and I, going down into red fire into Sheol's blackest pit into utter night, screamed at him: "You fool! She saved my life!"

Then his eyes cleared. He saw me lying on the floor. And that knife wound had come open. I was bleeding like a bull calf bleeds in the Forum Boarium when they cut his throat all the way across, slowly.

Shelomith knelt beside me. She had both hands stuffed into her mouth. Then she took one of them out. The right one. It snaked for my uncle's belt, closed around his dagger. He reeled back from her, sure that she meant to kill him. He was wrong. It was not him she meant to kill.

He saw her raise that blade high above her left breast, hold it there pointing at her heart a long moment while her lips moved, murmuring a prayer. He saw her teeth clench in mad determination and he hurled himself upon her just as she started blueglittering death whistling downward to end her, and my, world. He was in time. My uncle is a big man and a fighter. But it took all his strength to get that dagger away from her. He threw it out of the window just to make sure.

Then she was standing there facing him and crying in that awful insupportable way I'd already found out she could cry, and saying, not loudly, not screaming, but flatly, calmly, softly: "He's dying. When I had him saved. So now I've got to die, too. And I will. Tonight. Tomorrow. The next day. You can't watch me all the time. I can't live without him. I don't even want to."

My uncle looked at her then, at me. Groaned: "Daughter, I—Oh God—I—"

And it was then that Yeshu'a walked through that door. He'd seen my uncle passing through the village on his horse. So he'd left his little shop and walked all the way out to our place to see if there was news of me. I loved him beyond all reason; but he loved me, too! If I have no other cause for pride, I have that.

He asked no explanations. He simply bent and picked me up. Laid me on the bed. Ripped open my robe with his strong and tender hands. Turned to Shelomith, said: "Water. Cloths. Quickly now, Shelom!"

So you might list me among the first of his miracles. Oh, he did all of the conventional things! He packed that wound, bound me up. But it was his fingertips that did it. The endless compassion there.

In any event, I was still alive, though weaker than a maiden's love-sick sigh that next morning when the Roman century came.

A whole century. One hundred men, under the command of a stern-faced centurion. They'd come to arrest me—for not keeping my promise to appear before Pilatus.

You see, my uncle had never got to see the Epitropos, the Procurator.

Pilatus was not one to trouble his head over the problems or complaints of one lone Jew. The best my uncle had been able to do was to talk with the decurion Telemarchos who had visited our place to inspect my aqueduct. The decurion had investigated, and told my uncle that no order had then been issued for my arrest, advised him to ride home again, go to Kafer Nahum, begin his inquiry there.

And even now, by immensely good, or enormously bad, fortune, Telemarchos' decuria was one of the ten squads of ten men each that made up this particular century. Or maybe it wasn't even accidental, because the centurion turned in his direction and ripped out: "Decurion Telemarchos!"

Telemarchos came forward on the double, saluted his commander.

"You know Ieudas Nathanaeus by sight, don't you?" the centurion said.

"Yes, my captain!" Telemarchos said.

"Then come with me. The old man swears his nephew's desperately wounded. Some sort of criminal attack. But you know what slippery beggars these Jews are. I just want to make sure that there *is* a wounded man in this house, and if there is, that he's actually Nathanaeus, so come on!"

"At your orders, my centurion," Telemarchos said.

They stood beside my bed, looking at me.

"Yes, it's him, all right," the decurion said.

The centurion turned to Shelomith who was crouching on the other side of the bed, her eyes big with terror.

"Lift his robe up, wench," he said. "I want to see this wound!"

Shelomith did as she was told. My side was still bleeding sullenly. The bandage showed a great splotch of red.

"Hmmmmnnn," the centurion said. "Whoever did this wasn't playing games, was he, Telemarchos? I wonder why in Black Hades' name he, or they—"

"Couldn't it have something to do with the—aqueduct, my centurion?" Telemarchos said.

"*What* aqueduct?" the centurion said.

"The one our Epitropos wanted him to build. He's an expert engineer, you know. If the Zealots ever got wind of his doing a job for us, or even agreeing to, they'd—"

"Ohhhhhhhh!" Shelomith wailed.

The centurion glared at her.

"What ails you, wench?" he said.

"The Zealots!" she wept. "Oh, my lords, take him away! Hide him! For they—"

"What in the name of Pluto and Persephone both are you talking about, girl?" the centurion said.

"The Zealots! They—they never give up, O noble lords! They'll finish him off the next time, sure! And it *was* them! It was! It was Shimeon Zealotes who struck him down! I was with him! I saw—"

The centurion stood there. His heavy face went heavier still.

"Call for litter bearers, Telemarchos," he said tiredly. "The wench is right. They never give up. Best we keep the young man in the Prætorium under guard, or he won't stay alive long enough to slap mortar to a stone. Hades take me, but their spy system's getting better all the time! This poor bastard didn't even get to appear before Pilatus; they got him *first!* And Telemarchos—"

"Yes, my captain?"

"Bring the wench along. She *saw* it. So put her under protective arrest, too. Damn' pretty hunk of hot 'n juicy Jew meat. Shame to let 'em disembowel her. *That's* what they do to their women who favor us, you know—"

Telemarchos looked at her then. For the first time.

You say there's justice in heaven? Ha! Then explain to me why it didn't strike that smooth-tongued Greek bastard dead!

That's unfair. He was a good man. A good, kindly, civilized man who had a wife and five children in Philadelphia. Which didn't change the fact that what any man was, or had, became curiously beside the point the moment he looked upon my Shelomith.

And to tell the truth, to give Telemarchos his due, it wasn't entirely his fault, anyhow. He was greatly aided by fate's pure malice. And by—
Claudia.

I don't believe in miracles. I know, or at least my Greek-trained reason does, that nature's ways are invariable, or that God—if you need that hypothesis—does not violate the laws that He himself made. But if there ever was a miracle, an event that defies explanation by natural causes, it was that I endured being litter-borne all the way from Nazareth down to Cæsarea under a blazing sun and got there alive. Just barely, but alive.

They didn't take Shelomith and lock her in one of the dungeons under the Prætorium, which was what they'd have normally done with her. You see, the centurion, with a certain logic based on the fact that the decurion Telemarchos actually did know more about the ramifications of this case than anybody else, left the whole thing in his hands. And, after watching what Shelomith's hips did, walking all the way from Nazareth to Cæsarea, by then Telemarchos would have given her his head with the blood pouring from his severed neck, if she'd asked for it. But she didn't ask for the decurion's head, more's the pity! She merely knelt before him with tear-scalded eyes, her hands folded in the attitude of prayer, and begged to be allowed to stay with me.

He granted her that. I suppose he was sure that the guards placed outside the door of my bedroom provided sufficient security for us both against the Zealots' *sicarii* murderers. And, as he told me afterward with a mocking laugh: "I knew I didn't have to worry about your tugging those glorious thighs apart, not considering the state you were in, then, Nathanaios!"

Pilatus looked in upon me that same night. Of course I was unconscious and did not know that then. But Shelomith told me that he stared at me a long, long time, bent close enough almost to kiss my cheek, muttered an oath in Latin, then said in Greek: "I'd swear I've seen this face before!"

Two days later, I was lying there fully conscious and in considerable pain, when a stranger entered my room.

"What in black Satan's name d'you want?" I croaked in Aramaic; but the blank expression on his face told me he hadn't understood a word I'd said. I studied him more closely, then. And something about him—not his dress, of course, for in my times Roman and Grecian dress were exactly the same—told me he was Greek. And by the fairness of his skin, I judged him to be European Greek, from Hellas, itself, not from one of the colonies. So I said the same thing over again in that tongue, substituting "Hades" for Satan, since he wouldn't have known who Satan was.

He gave a little dancing step of delight at hearing his native tongue spoken with such flawless accent, and bowed with a mincing grace that caused me to see another thing, too: he was of that most peculiar persuasion in sexual matters so prevalent among your people.

"I am His Excellency the Epitropos' personal barber, my lord," he lisped. "My master has ordered me to shave you, and cut your hair . . ."

"Shave me! Cut my hair!" I roared. Or rather I meant it to be a roar. What it was, actually, was a dry rasp, barely audible.

"Yes, my lord," he cooed. "You see, my master is convinced he's seen your face before—but your beard keeps him from being sure. Please allow me to shave you, my lord, or my master will be wroth with me. I—I fear his wrath! 'Tis most terrible—"

I remembered then that in Rome, Pilatus had shown a marked fondness for me. Surely no harm could come of his learning my identity; and, besides, I was in neither the position nor the condition to resist.

"All right," I whispered. "Get to work, Shear-locks!"

"Oh, that's a good one!" the barber tittered. "I must remember that! Shear-locks, Barber to Most Noble Lords! Oh, good! Quite! My master commands me to advise him the minute you're shaven and shorn. He has a great curiosity about you. My lady, too. In fact, I'd think that the divine Claudia Procula has even more desire to find out who you are than my master, the Epitropos. The decurion Telemarchos, y'know, is a part of my master's personal guard—and he's told her the wildest tales! How the Zealots tried to kill you because you're the only man in Galilee who knows how to build aqueducts—"

"It was less than that," I croaked, in order to plague him. "Shelom, here was involved—"

He looked at her where she sat in a big chair by the window. I saw his nostrils quiver in pure disdain.

"Oh, really?" He pouted. "Well, there's no accounting for tastes, is there? Will you turn your face a little more to this side, m'lord?"

He was very skillful. In a few moments—or maybe it was longer, because I confess I dozed while he was about his labors—he had shaven me and cut my hair. What brought me to awareness again was the warmth of his gaze.

"Well," I got out, "what are you going to tell His Excellency Lucius Pontius Pilatus, Procurator of Judea, and his lady, the semidivine Claudia Procula?"

"That you—are the most beautiful man I've ever seen!" the barber breathed.

At which Shelom loosed a belly-deep hoot of laughter.

"Oh, get out of here, Shear-locks!" I said.

Lucius Pontius Pilatus, in his overwhelming arrogance, made at least four disastrous mistakes in his life. The first was bringing the Eagles of the Legions and the Imperator's Icon into Jerusalem. The second was seizing the sacred Temple treasure to build his damned aqueduct with, then murdering the people who protested. The third was condemning the Nazarene to the cross. The fourth and last was massacring the followers of the Samaritan Prophet, for which crime, at last, the Governor of Syria, Vitellius, removed him from the Procuratorship, and sent him under arrest to Rome.[1]

But, in addition to these major public mistakes, he made at least two private ones which were hardly less serious. Of these, the first was marrying Julia's daughter in the first place, knowing full well that Claudia must inevitably inherit her mother's ungovernable blood.

The second was ever letting Claudia lay eyes on me.

When she and Pilatus came into my bedroom, I was awake once more, and had been for more than an hour. Shelomith was feeding me fine wheaten cakes, soaking them in wine. She was also singing to me, teasing me, saying things like: "Oh, Nathan! You are so *pretty!* Without your beard, I mean. Sure you aren't a girl?"

"Just you crawl under the coverlet with me—" I was saying in the cadaverous croaking whisper that was all I could manage, when I heard Pilatus' dry, amused, sibilant voice ring out:

"It is! By Jupiter Thorens! Caius Nathanaeus in the flesh!"

I looked at him and smiled. At least I made a fearsome grimace that was supposed to be a smile, and croaked: "I give you greetings, Lucius Pontius!"

It was then that Claudia spoke, and that I saw her for the first time.

"Don't try to talk!" she said sharply. "Oh you poor, poor boy!"

She came forward then, and sat down on the edge of my bed.

"Here," she said to Shelomith, "give me that. I'll feed him. You may go away. I'll call you when I need you."

Pontius Pilatus chuckled at that, drew up a chair, sat down, said: "She's *not* a slave girl, dear."

"Then what is she?" Claudia said.

I let my breath out slowly, slowly. Because by then I was almost sure that Claudia was going to escape alive. The black, sulphuric rage that had flamed in my darling's eyes was dimming, dying down.

"Our Nathanaeus' mistress, I rather think," Pilatus said.

"Then you think wrong," I croaked.

"Oh, come now, Nathanaeus; you're among friends!" Pilatus said.

"Ask—her—" I got out.

Claudia smiled. She had the smile of an angel. Pure, sweet innocence. When you got to know her, it was the most shocking thing about her.

"I'll ask her," she said. "I'm interested; truly I am. What *are* you, girl?"

Shelomith looked at her. I expected Claudia's milkwhite skin to crisp, crumple up, turn brown. I was truly surprised when it didn't.

"A harlot," Shelomith said, her voice flat, harsh, dangerously calm. "A common harlot. The worst harlot in all Galilee. Or the best. Depends on your point of view."

I was surprised at the fluency and purity of her Greek. I shouldn't have been. Nearly all the legionaries of the Decapolis Cohort were Greeks. In a country like mine, the crossroads of all the world, who has better opportunity, or greater need, to become polyglot than a whore?

"I'd say the best," Pontius Pilatus said. But Claudia was gazing at Shelomith with an expression that I shouldn't have been surprised at either. But I was. It seemed to me a combination of admiration and awe.

"Pontius!" she said gleefully. "You must give her rooms in our apartments! You must!"

Pilatus lifted a quizzical eyebrow. It was plain that the little Claudia amused him greatly.

"And why must I do that, dear?" he said.

"So she can teach me things!" Claudia squealed. "Oh, Pontius, darling, don't you see the opportunity's priceless?"

And now the rage was gone from Shelomith's eyes. Entirely gone. What had taken its place was laughter. The wickedest laughter in all the world.

"I must say you're a game girl, aren't you, my lady?" she said. "What is it you want me to teach you?"

"Everything!" Claudia exulted. "How to drive a man wild, crazy, insane, howling mad, out of his stupid mind!"

Shelom looked at me; winked one great, gorgeous, night-black eye.

"I'll do my best, my lady," she said.

After that, they were the best of friends, and inseparable. And if my Shelomith was truly teaching Claudia the art of driving a man right out of his feeble mind, which I doubted, because again that is one of those things that certain women are born knowing, and the rest never acquire, it was also evident that she was learning a great deal from the Procurator's girl-wife.

For one thing, Shelom no longer looked like a whore. She gave up the use of cosmetics, which she didn't really need, almost entirely. And the little she retained, she learned to apply with great subtlety, marked restraint. You needed to look close to see that they were there. Her dress became quiet, tasteful, refined. And though Claudia lavished gifts upon her, she learned to wear just the right amount of jewelry. And instead of those cheap whore's scents she formerly used, which hit you in the nostrils when she passed by two stadia away, her perfumes became delicate and fine.

Even her behavior changed. She was by nature affectionate; but her affections were apt to be expressed in a vocabulary that would have made a worker on the docks of Joppa cringe. Now, her speech itself changed. She imitated Claudia's beautiful, almost classically pure Greek. And, strangely enough, that discipline carried over into her Aramaic, which remained delightfully racy; but crudities like using the bodily functions as expletives, and references to male and female genitalia, disappeared from it. In short, in all ways now, her presence became an unfailing joy.

She was, I afterward found out, beginning to dream, to hope. Her husband was much older than she—perhaps he'd die. Or maybe he'd be kind enough, understanding enough, to give her a divorce. And since there was no deception involved, since I knew her former life, it wasn't beyond possibility that the love I gave her daily proofs of could be sanctified before God, and its fruits to His service.

She was right. I'd have wed her without a second thought. But there was Telemarchos.

And Claudia.

I was six weeks abed. During that time, the decurion Telemarchos, aided and abetted by that little witch, who had him assigned to her personal guard and then gave him all the time he needed away from his duties so that he could further her own plans by removing the chief obstacle to them, never lost an opportunity to press his suit. And, thanks to Claudia, opportunities he had in Satan's own plenty! Besides, he was a tall, striking, handsome man, clever, gay, witty, and fluent. How clever he was, you may judge for yourself, from the account I attach here although I did not know it then, for it was months later when I learned it from Shelom's own lips under such terrible circumstances that—but let me reserve those circumstances until I come to them, for fear of destroying your interest in my tale.

Telemarchos had the supreme intelligence not to lie. For lying, like every human act, is neutral; it is the circumstances surrounding it that give it its moral coloring. Only one thing about lying is certain: whether a lie is a kindly act designed to save or salve wounded feelings, or a cruel one, deliberately designed to hurt, it is always, without notable exception, stupid. So the decurion came right out and admitted to Shelom he could never marry her because he had a wife and sons already.

"But," said he, "how much better off will you be in a little house covered with rambling roses, a servant to attend you, good food, good wine, clothes and gifts within the limits of my possibilities than in Nikos' Lupanar? I'll admit those possibilities aren't great, but—"

Shelomith was only human. She was, she admitted to me frankly when she told me this bitter tale long after, tempted. It was a good life in comparison to the one she'd had; and it was close at hand, while her chances of marrying me—a detail I foolishly insisted upon—were still icily remote.

"And—Nathan?" she faltered.

And here, it seems to me, it was that Telemarchos played his master-stroke. A stroke of almost infinite cunning and subtlety. Far from damning me, he praised me to the stars. Lying there in Shelom's arms beneath the black canopy of the Zealot brigand's tent in the Judean desert, listening to her tell it, I found that my rage, my jealousy were vanquished by my admiration for the absolute brilliance of his tactics.

"Nathan is a great man, Shelom," he said solemnly. "Surely he is a genius. Fame awaits him. In fact, it's already beckoning. Do you know his history? He is, on his mother's side at least, of Judea's highest lineage. Of the House of Bœthus—of the family of the High Priests, my poor dear. On his father's, he is of Galilee's noblest line as well, a descendant of the patriot and soldier Mattithias; from the time of the Maccabees on down, that family has been famous—"

"So?" Shelomith whispered.

"Do you, my poor forlorn lovesick girl," Telemarchos said, "believe you have the right to—destroy his chances?"

"Destroy them?" Shelomith said. "But how could I—"

"How couldn't you, poor child?" the decurion said. "Let's consider the fact that, being already wed, you can't marry him, can never be more to him than a concubine. He *has* to marry. He is the last of his line and owes that duty to his father. What will you do on the day he brings home a bride? Could you bear knowing that the sons you've given him are outcast bastards and can never inherit? What will you do when he stands smiling at her under your Jewish canopy and slips the ring—"

"Cut my throat," Shelomith said. "From ear to ear."

"Don't be a fool, Shelom! Listen to me. Suppose that, miraculously, your dreams come true: that your husband falls down the front stairs and breaks his neck; or that he wearies of waiting and puts you by with a bill of divorcement. Don't you know, little fool, that all the doors—like this aqueduct of Pilatus'—now opening before Nathan, will slam in his face once he's saddled with a wife whose ill fame extends from Beth Anya in Judea, through Cæsarea on the coast, to Kafer Nahum in Galilee? *The* most widely known whore in all the Jewish Nation? Don't you know his uncle will cut him off without a Temple shekel? Don't you realize that his father, who is the *ab beth din,* the vice president of the Lower Sanhedrin, will be forced to disown him? How many commissions will come his way when people point at him and whisper: 'His wife is Shelom! Shelom the Harlot'? How many, I ask you?"

"Ohh, Telemarchos!" Shelomith wailed.

He took her in his arms, kissed her right tenderly, whispered: "Come with me now, little Shelom! Let us be off to—"

But she tore free of him.

"No!" she sobbed. "I'll go to Nathan; tell him—"

"What, child?" Telemarchos said.

"Oh, I don't know!" Shelomith cried, and fled.

My luck was at its miserable worst that night. Because when she got to the Prætorium, she was so troubled that she went first to see Claudia Procula. She confided in her, asked her advice. Need I tell you what counsel dear Claudia gave her?

Two days before the charming interview I've just described to you had even taken place, they captured Shimeon Zealotes.

They brought him before Pilatus. And the Procurator, having that very morning seen the sketches I'd made for the proposed aqueduct, decided to offer me the sweet savor of vengeance.

By then, I could walk about a bit; but the Epitropos' physician considered it unwise for me to overdo it. So they brought me down to the judgment hall on a litter.

Shimeon the Zealot stood before the Procurator's chair. He was in chains, his hair, his beard were matted, his skin was broken in a dozen places by their blows; he was utterly filthy; his stench filled up the hall. He stood there like a boar at bay and glared at me with his hot black eyes. I could see his nostrils quiver.

"Well, Caius Nathanaeus, my friend," Pontius Pilatus said. "What shall we do with this ugly beast? Shall I crucify him outside your bedroom window so that you may enjoy his groans the while?"

"And my curses, traitor!" Shimeon spat.

Fortunately for him he spoke in Aramaic, of which Pilatus understood, at that time, not one word.

I looked at Shimeon, and pity entered me like a blade. Pity, and something more. Admiration, perhaps, for his courage, his dignity. Wholehearted sympathy for what he and his were trying to do, however dangerously, suicidally wrong, mistaken their methods were.

He had tried to kill me, but I felt no hate for Shimeon Zealotes. He was a patriot, a man. By his lights, he'd done his simple duty when he'd stabbed me. Then, suddenly, it came to me how he might be saved; how, in fact, I might save him. The Romans have absolutely no interest in Jewish crime, as long as that crime is internecine, fratricidal, and has no political connotations whatsoever. For Shimeon

Zealotes to stab me to prevent my building Pilatus' aqueduct was a direct attack on Cæsar's power, and called for the death sentence; but for him to stab me because—

"I'd suggest you—release him, great Epitropos," I said slowly in Greek, knowing that Zealotes had some small knowledge of that language.

"What!" Pilatus said. "You mean—"

"That he is not guilty of any crime of such a nature that warrants your august attention, Representative of Cæsar. He stabbed me, true; but, so far, it has occurred to nobody to ask why—"

"Then I ask it," Pilatus said. "Why did he stab you, Nathanaeus?"

I smiled.

"Three nights before—we, he and I," I said mockingly, "met by chance—in the hall of Nikos' Lupanar. You've seen Shelom, so you won't doubt me when I tell you he was inflamed with desire for her—"

"And?" Pilatus said.

"There's no accounting for tastes, noble Procurator! She—she chose to go upstairs—with me."

Pilatus threw back his head and roared.

"And for *that* he butchered you like a calf?" he said.

"A most excellent reason, don't you think, Epitropos? Especially since on the occasion of the plain and fancy carving of my poor hide, he met Shelom and me coming out of the woods under such—well—circumstances as would suggest—at least to a man of his fiery temperament—that we—"

"Had just repeated the offense!" Pilatus fairly rocked with laughter. "By Vulcan, this is rich!" He turned to Zealotes. "I say, you bloody beggar, if I turn you loose, as Nathanaeus, here, suggests, do you promise to leave his skin unperforated in the future?"

Shimeon turned his hot little eyes on me.

"Nathan," he said, "do I understand aright? Is he going to—to free me?"

"Yes, Shimeon, my friend," I said.

"You call me friend!"

"Let's not talk about it now, Shimeon. Do you promise not to try to kill me anymore?"

"To kill you? By Sheol, boy, from now on, I'm your slave!"

I turned back to Pilatus.

"He faithfully promises to leave my hide intact," I said solemnly. "Well, O Representative of Cæsar?"

"Release him!" Pontius Pilatus said.

That next day, the Procurator, alone and unattended, visited me in my rooms.

"I'd like to ask a favor of you," he said without preliminaries. "Put it this way: D'you think you need those two stout fellows before your door any longer? You said the quarrel between you and that black-bearded scoundrel was personal. Over Shelomith. I can well see why. She's enough to start another Trojan War. So, if the Zealots really aren't involved, d'you think—"

"No, I don't need them," I said. I thought: How the devil do I know? Shimeon is but one Zealot, and there are hundreds of them. Maybe thousands. But perhaps he'll tell them I saved him. Perhaps—

I took what comfort I could from that thought.

"You see, I have to go down to Jerusalem today—and Claudia's worried. One of those famous dreams of hers! She insists that I take her personal guardsmen, too. Swears that if anyone tries to enter her rooms, she'll set Shelom on them! Tell me, Caius Nathanaeus, is that wild creature as fierce as she looks?"

"Fiercer," I said.

"You've survived—" He laughed, then turned serious again. "I'm not a believer in dreams, but Claudia's has the point that it coincides with what my spies tell me. There's marked unrest in Jerusalem. And I have to stay there a whole week. I could, of course, call on other units; but—frankly I don't trust them. Local beggars, so, who knows? That's why I'm taking the *Cohors Italica,* full strength. Of course, if you feel insecure, I'll send you a couple of the Sebastians—"

"Pontius," I said then, dryly, "I'm a Jew. Your Sebastians are Samaritans. Send me Zealots instead. I'd feel safer!"

"Oh, your petty little internecine wars! How they bore me! But you've a point about the Sebastians. Slippery beggars, aren't they? Then I leave you unguarded? Don't like the idea, really. Where'll I find me another engineer if they cut your throat?"

"They won't. Don't worry about it. Tell me, why do you go to Jerusalem, Lucius Pontius?" I said.

"To procure funds for our aqueduct, Nathanaeus. You don't imagine that miserly old skinflint in Rome would advance me moneys to so favor Jerusalem, do you? And, by Pluto, your priestly rulers equal him! You'd never think—"

"That they'd be reluctant to finance an aqueduct? Why not, Pilatus? They see no special virtue in water, being neither Romans nor Essenes. Tell them you're going to build a temple to the One True God, entirely free of icons and images, and see how fast they'll cover you with gold!"

"The One True God must have sealed nostrils and an iron stomach," Pilatus sighed, "if he can stand his people's stench. But, by High Olympus, I mean to clean the beggars up—to civilize them, if such is possible!"

"How, Lucius Pontius?" I asked him quietly. "Would you teach them to throw naked, weaponless men to famished lions? To make whole armies of captives butcher each other for no other reason than to amuse the plebes? To have thousands watch breathlessly as the public executioner violates a fifteen-year-old virgin before her father's eyes, in the arena itself, and then strangles her for the high crime of being the daughter of the man who at the same time is being hideously tortured to death for the higher crime of having by some idle, careless remark offended Cæsar! Your delicacy, your civilization, extends to this, that you can't execute a virgin, under the law. Oh no, you have to rape her first. In public. Is it by such marks, tokens, signs, that one is supposed to recognize the superior civilization of the Romans?"

Pilatus stared at me. Then he nodded his head. He was a curiously honest man.

"Y'know, come to think of it, you're right, my dear Caius Nathanaeus," he said solemnly. "We're barbarians, too. Only I like our barbarity better. It's more amusing! *Salve*, Nathanaeus!"

"*Vale*, Procurator," I said morosely. "Go with God!"

That next night, I lay fretfully abed, wondering why Shelomith hadn't come to kiss me good night as she always did. The reason she hadn't was that Telemarchos had upset her so with his absolutely truthful, mercilessly accurate analysis of the situation in which we found ourselves that she wandered about for hours trying to think— a labor for which she was singularly ill-fitted. She was made to be, to feel, which was enough and a glory. And, after that, she consulted Claudia Procula—that treacherous little bitch!

I remember there was no moon. The night was thick, hot, oppressive, blacker than the pit. The oil in my lamp burned out, leaving an acrid stink lingering on the air. I hadn't any more oil. "I'll ask Shelom to bring me some," I thought uneasily, "when she comes—"

Because she had never failed to visit me before. Never. The hours dragged on. I could hear the frogs in Pilatus' pool, croaking. They sounded like damned souls in Sheol. I held my hand up before my face, moving it toward my nose in an attempt to see if there were any visibility, but it smacked against my nose and I couldn't see my fingers.

Then the hinges of my door creaked. I heard it groan open. I saw —no, not saw, perceived, realized, because without light sight is impossible—that the lamp in the hall had gone out, too. It hadn't, really, being much bigger than my own, and holding oil enough to last all night. It had been capped, extinguished. But I didn't know that then.

I felt, sensed, a figure glide, drift into my room, black upon blackness, a shadow moving. The hinges creaked again, I heard the sodden little thud as she closed my door.

She.

Because my wondrous great Jewish beak had come into the play. I smelt perfume. And woman's flesh. Perfectly clean, recently bathed woman's flesh. So recently that the smell of olive oil soap was even stronger than her perfume. And when a woman came directly from her bath to a man's room, that meant—

I concentrated upon that perfume. Recognized it! It was the kind that Shelom always wore now. A quiet, delicate scent. She came closer, and my blood rose up in my veins and beat and beat. Because she was making the night go thick with her own wild female musk, striking effortlessly through all that cleanness, soap scent, perfume. . . .

"Shelom!" I got out; but she only hissed: "Shhhhhhh!" And slid into my arms. She was stark-naked and totally ready. And I hadn't had a woman in more than two years. What saved me from the lovesick boy's failure of immediate explosion was my body's terrible weakness. I was slow to respond. So slow that impatience got the better of her. She ground her mouth into mine, writhed against me, moaning.

And every possible conceivable thing went wrong.

You see, by then I knew Shelom's mouth, her body, better than I knew my own. There had been no carnal love between us—no. That's not true. Not entirely. God, but this is hard to explain! These things should not be written about at all. Sheol! I don't mean in deference to the Nazarene, Christianoi concept of sexual morality, but because words falsify them, give them the aspect of the *porna-griffe*, whore-scratchings above a brothel door, when between two who love they are close to sacred, more than half divine!

There is no division between body and soul. It is they who artificially make that separation who have filthy minds. Say then that the carnospiritual love between my Shelomith and me had not reached consummation. When I was still too weak to move, blue with chills, my teeth chattering, she had lain stark-naked in my arms, held me to her, warmed me. Made of her body one long bifurcated kiss, drawing the freezing cold that is one of the alternations of wound fever out of me. When I was burning up, she sponged me with cool water, kissed my fetid, fevered mouth to stop my ravings.

But, when I grew stronger, and she noted my male flesh's response to her caresses, her tenderness, she reduced both, placed me on a starvation diet of affection for fear that we might slow or even reverse my convalescence by surrendering to our mutual pure and lovely desire before my poor, half-slaughtered carcass was ready for it. To distract me, she asked me to teach her to read and write. I tried, but beyond getting her to the point that she could scrawl her name, I failed. Her wisdom was of the earth, not of the intellect. It was seated in her generous, tender loins, not in her head.

All right? You're convinced now that I could know tactilely Shelom's body without actual sin—especially in my sense of the word, by which I mean I had never violated, humiliated, shamed the *person* that she was? If you aren't, it matters not. It is enough to say that in half a heartbeat, I knew the woman in my arms was not Shelomith.

How? For one thing, her lips were thin. Cruel thin like all the white-skinned races. Her skin had that faintly soured milky smell that I'd been able to endure even in Helvetia only because I loved her. She didn't have Shelom's Æthiopic steamfurnace meltingtender great-lipped mouth, nor her hot rich burnt bronze odor, nor those wide-spaced softcushioned firepoints stabbing me into delirium, nor—

Oh God, here we go again! Let me not offend your delicate sensibilities if you have any such; and, if you don't, I refuse to accommodate your prurience.

Say merely that the woman in my arms was clean-shaven, a Hellenic/Roman practice which my Shelom rejected as a final offense against the irreducible minimum of modesty. "If God had meant for us to be naked as babies, He would let us stay that way, Nathan," she said. "But He doesn't. Not after we're twelve years old. So—"

So I held clasped to me—an intruder. A woman who had no idea what I was like. Who thought I could be—used.

There is no more deadly insult. I shoved her away from me, hard. Got up from there, groped on my table for my flint, my steel, my lamp. Struck down a shower of sparks upon the wick. It smoldered red, went out. Then I remembered that all the oil was gone.

"The one in the hall has oil," that soft, sweet girl's voice said. "I put it out. Wait, I'll get it for you. Give me your fire-making things, won't you, Nathanaeus, darling—"

I stood there, frozen. Because my life was over. Entirely over. Within a week, or perhaps a little more, I knew, I'd be groaning on another cross, with no possibility of being taken down while yet I lived.

"Claudia!" I said.   She came to me then. Straight to me. Perhaps, being the witch she was, she could see in the dark. Went up on tiptoe, kissed my mouth.

"Who else?" she said. "Were you so great a fool as not to know—"

"What?" I groaned.

"That I love you. That the first time I saw you I—no matter! Give me your fire things, Nathan."

I gave them to her. Hear her girlish skip and scamper as she went. Heard the door hinges groan, and after that the sharp little splat and splatter of flint striking steel.

She came through the door with the lighted lantern in her hand. Her hair was loose. It hung down about her shoulders. The lantern poured warm yellow light upward into her face. She was a Claudian —and her father surely must have been a handsome man, because, for all her promiscuity, Julia's taste was good—which meant that she was lovely. She was very small and slender with firm little breasts not much bigger than apples. She was Augustus' granddaughter, and through her, this sardonic Iberian scoundrel she had married might one day reach the Imperator's throne, become Master of the World. And yet for a whim, born of boredom, surely, she was prepared to risk—

Nothing! Lucius Pontius Pilatus would close his eyes to her adulteries, as Tiberius had closed his to Julia's! He hadn't married her for love, but to further his ambitions. And for those ambitions, he'd suffer—

No. Nor that. He didn't have to suffer anything. He wouldn't have to arm a scandal by a public execution. He'd merely call in a hired assassin, have me knifed to death, and blame the whole thing on the Zealots. *After* I'd built him his aqueduct. Until then he'd not even show his displeasure. He'd simply keep her away from me—quietly.

She put the lantern down on the night table and turned to me. I must admit she was a *very* fetching sight. Ninety-eight women out of every hundred look far better with their clothes on. The female figure, because of buttock waggle, belly bulge, breast sag and dangle, or their opposites, want of flesh, pipestem arms and legs, thighs you could drive an oxcart through, no breasts at all, usually needs the help, the concealment, the disguise of clothing.

In that regard, I'm a thoroughgoing pagan. No woman ever interested me for five minutes flat who couldn't have gone proudly, arrogantly naked under a noonday sun.

Helvetia. Shelomith. And now, Claudia.

"Nathan," she breathed, "kiss me?"

"No!" I growled.

"Why not?"

"My lady Claudia," I began.

She stamped her foot.

"Don't call me 'my lady'!" she said.

"Then what shall I call you?" I said.

"Anything you like—except that. Call me something sweet. No! Call me something exciting!"

"Such as?"

"Concubine. Slut. Bitch. Strumpet. Harlot. Whore."

She said those words with a sweet and childish patrician lisp that made them doubly awful.

I glared at her.

"*Meretrice, Prostibula, Lupa, Doris, Bustuaria, Scorta Erratica, Ambulatrice Notiluca, Gallina, Foraria, Blitida, Diobolaia, Quadrantaria,*" she chanted in her soft, delicate, little girl's soprano.

You know what those words mean? No? Well you won't from me, beyond the generality that they were the names of the different classifications of the whores of Rome, in descending order both according to the filthiness of the perversions they were willing to practice and their price.

This child, this sweet child of imperial line, with the blood of divine Augustus coursing through her veins, should never have even heard of those utter obscenities, much less have known what they meant. But she did. And also how to go about the nauseous acts involved, with sickening expertness.

Oh, yes; I found that out. But not that night. I've never denied being the sensual swine I am; but there are limits even to swinishness.

She locked her slim arms about my neck, glued her sweet child's mouth—wide open, of course, with her hot little tongue busily athrusting—into mine. I tore away, glanced at the door.

She loosed a peal of pure delighted laughter.

"Don't worry about *her*, darling," she giggled. "She won't come. Not tonight. Not ever, for that matter—"

I dug my fingers into the soft milky whiteness of her shoulders, thrust her an arm's length away from me, held her there.

"What in black Hades' Name do you mean, Claudia?" I said.

She sighed.

"Now I'll have to prove it to you. And I didn't want to. It would have been ever so much nicer if you'd loved me for myself. All right. Turn me loose, Nathan."

I turned her loose. She went to the door, stopped at the table beside it. The table that held that Roman copy of the Aphrodite by your greatest sculptor. You know it, the one that's distorted into the ugliest, most indecent posture possible because she's shown trying to cover all her strategic areas with her arms and hands. You fools! Don't you know that everything a beautiful woman has is beautiful?

Claudia put out her hand and picked up a little scroll. Evidently she had laid it there between Aphrodite's feet when she'd come into my bedroom in the dark. She came back slowly, quietly, imitating, I was sure, Shelomith's divinely provocative way of walking. She did it well. It was at least amusing.

She extended the scroll to me. I took it from her hand, unrolled it. The hand was strange. A slave scribe's, of course. I've told you, I think, of my failure to teach Shelomith to do more than scrawl her name. I glanced at the bottom of the scroll. That was hers, all right. The signature, I mean. It was her back-slanted, uneven, sprawling scribble, the letters of different sizes, ill-formed and childish. I read:

My Own,
I am going away. With a man. I don't love him. I love you. But I cannot ruin your life. That's all I would do if I stayed. So forgive and forget her who will stop loving you the day they put the silver shekels on her eyes to hold them shut. Maybe not even then if the P'rushim have it right.[2]

Forever,
Your,
SHELOM.

She'd looked at it, tried to read it before she'd sent it off to me, because it was blotched and splotted with her tears.

I sat down then. I had to. I couldn't stand up. I bent my head and cried noisily, terribly, like a wounded ass braying out my grief, my sorrow against the night.

Claudia sat down beside me, put one arm around my neck, rested her delicate little head against my shoulder.

"Poor Nathan. Poor, poor Nathan!" she said, and wept, too, moved by my naked hurt.

I swear to you that nothing at all happened that night. Nor the next, nor the next. It wasn't until the night before Pilatus' return that I allowed myself to be elevated to the imposing position of his wife's official lover.

I was not made of iron. The hurt, the grief, the rage in me, needed some surcease, some relief, if nothing more original than thrusting mindlessly into Claudia's scalding, undulant, wildly twisting loins, closing my ears against her algolagnic screams, arming my tortured nerves, my lacerated flesh against the red murder in her teeth and nails.

For that, this granddaughter of Emperors served. As well as any other harlot would have, I suppose.

Perhaps better. For harlots sometimes complicate matters by having hearts.

Chapter XII

I STOOD there beside the windlass, watching four of my strongest workmen, two to each side, wrestling with the huge crossbars that turned the winch, slowly coiling the rope as thick as a man's arm about it. They were a sight to see: Their great blackbronze biceps knotting like gigantic pythons, the sweat on their bodies glistening, as they bent that rope around and around the bole of the windlass, so that the immense, rough-hewn block of stone lifted, lifted, borne aloft on ropecreak, timbergroan, until it was high enough for the stonemasons atop the rapidly growing arches of my—and Pilatus'—aqueduct to catch it with their grappling hooks, swing it in toward the top of the arch itself, then signal the winch men to slacken off on the windlass far below, and allow the stone to thud into place.

It was going well. I was pleased with it. To be the engineer in charge of the greatest work ever seen in Judea—for my aqueduct would be all of four hundred stadia long by the time we'd finished it—was no little thing. And not the least of my satisfactions lay in the circumstance that since we were bringing the water down to Jerusalem from the Pool of Solomon,[1] which lay very near the village of Bethlehem, the City of David, from whence the Prophecy said the Mashiah was to come,[2] I was, and would be, for some considerable time out of the reach of Claudia's hot little hands; and, by that very token, safe from the risk that her utter recklessness would force Pilatus to loose a hired assassin upon me.

I use the word "force" deliberately. I honestly don't believe that Pilatus would have cared if Claudia had worked her way horizontally through every cohort of the Legions, so long as her activities did not interfere with his progress towards the Imperator's throne. But he would be forced to have me—whom he was genuinely fond of—killed, because, should it be noised abroad that his wife, the at least semi-divine Claudia, was cuckolding him with a Provincial, and what was even worse, a Jew, the gale of laughter sweeping from one end of the Empire to the other would scatter his ambitions before it like so much chaff.

Only by my death could he then regain his dignity, command the respect of men, resume his march toward the rulership of the world. This ironical set of circumstances seemed to me an insanely ignoble reason to die. To be cut down over a chit of a girl who represented, from my weary point of view, only the nightly use of a commodity I could have procured with much less bother (though that I could have found dear Claudia's peer in enthusiasm, expertness, and single-minded devotion to sheer carnality, I pay her the sincere and respectful compliment of doubting!) in any of the better *lupanares* of Tiberias or Cæsarea, and at the orders of a man who'd stifle a yawn with the back of his hand as he gave them, made the whole thing singularly unap-pealing. If die I must—and for no such noble cause as my people's free-dom—let it at the very least be for love!

I was thinking about all this when I saw the horseman coming to-ward me. Of course my Decapolian guards stopped him long before he got even within bowshot of my precious hide. They had their orders from Pilatus. For, once again, it was clear that the Epitropos had his reasons for believing my life in danger: his first act upon his return to Cæsarea from Jerusalem had been to inform me flatly that under no circumstance whatsoever, not even to visit my parents, was I to enter the Holy City, although we should begin work upon the aqueduct near Bethlehem of Judea, only a few *milia* away; and his sec-ond, to place the two burly Italians once again before my bedroom door where they stayed until I had—again at the Procurator's orders—left Cæsarea under heavy guard to begin work in Judea.

Those two brawny members of the *Cohors Italica* whom Pilatus had provided for my protection during my last days in Cæsarea re-mained a nagging, aching source of worry to me. For, unless they were stone blind, between three and four o'clock of every morning that I was obliged to linger at Cæsarea, they had seen Claudia, wrapped in a silken robe made of cobwebs and moonmist for all the concealment it provided her lovely body, parading, not furtively, but proudly, like the queen she was in some ways, into my chamber, after having waited that long to make sure the brew of poppy seeds with which she had dosed Pilatus' wine had had the desired effect; and, unless they were hopelessly deaf, they had heard—what they had heard. I hoped with all my heart that they were tongueless mutes, or had the wit to pretend to be; which last, be it said, wasn't at all unlikely. Romans born, they'd long since learned how dangerous it was to their own continued existence to let their tongues wag about the amatory escapades of the great.

But now, one of the Decapolians who had detained the horseman came up to me and saluted smartly.

"It's a man of some rank, sir," he said, "to judge by his dress. By race, of your people—though he speaks Greek better than I do. Says he's a friend of your father's and that you would recognize him. Shall we permit him to pass?"

"Yes, Decurion," I said slowly, "but under guard until I've seen whether or not he's telling the truth. This work's not popular, you know."

"Don't I, though!" The decurion laughed. "But I wouldn't worry about that if I were you, sir. We took very good care of those beggars in Jerusalem!"

I wondered what the devil he meant by that, but I didn't ask him. It was absolutely necessary to impose some respect for my position if not for my person upon those Jew-hating Greeks of the Decapolis Cohort. And one of the basic rules for maintaining discipline among men more or less under your command is not to talk to them beyond the giving of direct orders, to enwrap yourself in lofty dignity, to keep apart.

A few minutes later, the decurion came back again, leading the visitor's horse. The man, in his vigorous middle years, rode surrounded by a glittering forest of spears. My Decapolians were being zealous, to say the least.

But then I saw who he was and leaped down from my high perch beside the windlass, ran to his horse, took his hand, and kissed it with real respect. At the sight of that, the legionaries fell back.

"Leave us!" I said.

Yosef ha Arimathæa climbed down from his beautiful Arabian and took me in his arms.

"God make the Light of His Countenance to shine upon you, Nathan," he said, "and grant you peace!"

"Amen," I said. "And upon you, likewise, respected friend of my father!"

He glanced at my clean-shaven face disapprovingly.

I raised a hand to the indecent nakedness of my cheeks and chin.

"It is necessary for the moment, my master," I said. "As soon as this work is done, I'll be able to return to the dress and the customs of my people—I hope, forever."

"Good!" he said. "Nathan, I've come at your father's request, and also of my own free will, to warn you. This work is highly unpopular in Jerusalem—even among us—even among your own—"

That surprised me. I'd taken it as a matter of course that the P'rushim with their maddening concern with every vowel point of the Law would oppose it; and that the extremists among them, the Zealots —for the Zealots were not, as some have written, a separate party from the Pharisees, but were themselves Pharisees, differing only from their fellows in their advocation and use of violence—would carry that opposition to the point of drawing steel. But that my father's party, the Zadokim, the Sadducees, being the pragmatists that they were, would raise their voices against so obviously necessary a thing as supplementing Jerusalem's pitifully scanty water supply, astonished me. I said as much to Yosef ha Arimathæa.

"You're right, as far as you go, Nathan," he said. "The aqueduct *is* necessary, and from that standpoint will be a blessing to the city. But when in our history has the necessary taken precedence over the Holy?"

"I don't understand you, sir," I said.

"Don't you know how and where Pilatus got the money to finance this work, my boy?" Yosef said.

"No," I said.

"He seized the Qorban," Yosef ha Arimathæa said quietly.

I stood there speechless. The Qorban was not the ordinary Temple treasure, but a special fund for purposes so sacred that only the High Priest and his council in the Sanhedrin knew what they were. The word itself means *secret,* or *tabu.*

"But why?" I said. "He could have used the ordinary Temple funds. There's a Mishna which states that they may be used for public works, specifically including aqueducts, if I remember right."[3]

"I know. But apparently your friend Pilatus considered the ordinary fund insufficient."

"There wasn't any trouble?"

"There was, Nathan." I could hear Yosef's voice thickening with pure rage. "I'm happy to learn you began this work without knowing that. By the way, I should like you to take your sacred oath before me now to that effect."

"By the Ineffable Name, I swear it!" I said at once. That is the most awful oath any Jew can take. "But why did you require of me my oath, sir?"

"Because," Yosef said sternly, "people were killed, Nathan. A good many people. He—your very good friend, the Procurator—was so very well prepared that there's a rank odor of treachery about the whole affair. He had enough soldiers dressed in civilian garb and hiding clubs beneath their robes among the mob to turn the mutiny into a near massacre within minutes. They clubbed the people down, splattered their blood and brains upon the walls of the Antonia, on the cobblestones of the streets. Dozens more were trampled to death by their fellows in the wild rush to escape Pilatus' murderers. In my life I don't recall having seen a more horrible sight!"[4]

"Master," I said quietly, "is it being said that I—"

"Informed him of the proposed mutiny? Yes. Why, yes, of course. Or it was. Your father and I silenced that rumor by submitting to the Sanhedrin, when that august body was on the point of ordering your arrest, a letter from your uncle proving that for weeks before the event you lay at death's door in the Prætorium at Cæsarea, a prisoner of the Romans, and hence couldn't posssibly have even known what was going on in Jerusalem. Unfortunately the effect of the letter was somewhat lessened by your uncle's overscrupulous inclusion of the fact that it was Shimeon Zealotes who stabbed you—"

"Over a private matter!" I said.

"Your mutual rivalry for the favors of the harlot, Shelomith," Yosef ha Arimathæa said dryly. "You wouldn't have wanted us to introduce *that* in evidence, would you, Nathan?"

"Yes!" I said. "I loved Shelomith! I was prepared to marry her; I—"

"There is," Yosef said, "to quote your father, no worse fate than that of having been born a fool!"

I bent my head. Looked up again.

"One," I said quietly; "that of being, or even seeming—a traitor."

"I agree," Yosef said; "but no one accuses you of that anymore. Now they say the reason the Epitropos wears the adornments you've placed upon his forehead with such easy grace is he finds the information which the Lady Claudia obtains from you while sharing your pillow so valuable that—"

"Ha!" I said. "They flatter me! What secrets of state am I supposed to have possession of? And if they knew anything about Claudia, they'd know—"

"What, Nathan?" he said quietly. Too quietly, which should have warned me. But my father was right: there's nothing worse than being a fool.

"That she never wastes time in talk. Or leaves me breath enough to—"

Then I saw his eyes.

"So," he whispered; "it's true!"

I bent my head; said: "Oh, Sheol!"

"Nathan," he said then, "I bear a command from your father. A formal command that you yourself have just made unconditional. You're to wed. As soon as this work is done—I don't suppose you could leave it, could you?"

"Yes," I said. "At the expense of being hung from, or maybe even nailed to, a cross."

"I thought as much. All right. But as soon as you've finished this, you're to return to Galilee. Your father doesn't want you in Jerusalem until the anger touching your involvement with the procurator, and the scandal over your relations with his wife, have died down. During that time he, or your uncle, will have found you a bride, if either can encounter a family who can support your reputation sufficiently to give you their daughter! Which is why you are also free to find a wife for yourself, providing her Jewishness and her morals are above all question. But within a year, you must be betrothed, if not wed. Since, as your father says, your hot blood leads you forever into folly, why not cool it honorably and to some purpose? You've something to say to that, my boy?"

I bent my head, stared at the ground. I knew where Shelomith was by then. In that little house covered with climbing roses, just outside of Cæsarea, where nightly the decurion Telemarchos—

I looked at Yosef ha Arimathæa then.

"Tell him I hear—and obey," I said.

Thereafter, a madness fell upon me. I drove my men without mercy, to the degree they probably would have mutinied but for one thing: I worked with them, with my own hands, outdid them all at the murderous tasks of chipping away at the stones with hammer and chisel, especially those which had to be carefully shaped to fit into the arches, their long, sloping sides keying into one another to hold the entire U-shaped bridging up; lifting the finished stones into the oxcarts by main force; winching them upward, swinging them into their final resting places; carrying sand and mortar on my back, all of which I did like the commonest laborer to their unmitigated astonishment and delight, what this strenuous work did to my but barely postconvalescent body was nothing short of astonishing. I had always been slim and strong, but now I became a miniature Hercules. I grew no taller, because I was past the age for natural growth; but I broadened until I took on the look of one of the professional wrestlers of the games. And, because I greatly feared that the great thews with which I had roped and burdened my body would greatly diminish my speed and skill at the one warlike exercise I knew, that of retiarius, I commanded certain of my guards to meet me in practice with imitation weapons.

To my delight, my speed had lessened but little, while my strength, my endurance, had at least tripled. The Decapolians, who had thought me mad to work like a Canaanite slave among the laborers and who had all but openly laughed at me for it, now saw the result, and ceased to smile. I beat them all, even their best swordsmen, with mocking ease. Whereupon, one of the youngest and slimmest of their officers, the decurion Aristides, offered to teach me the art of sword and shield play, lanista style, if, in return, I'd teach him the retiarius' art.

I leaped at the chance, and thereby acquired the one thing needful to make me a leader of the people when the Zealots in their mad folly forced the Romans into war—that is, a full and rounded command of the use of arms. For, beyond swordplay, I could and did train myself secretly and apart with the light-armed trooper's weapons: the javelin, the bow, and the sling.

The work went on until toward the end of the fourteenth year of the reign of Tiberius, we'd brought our arches to within sight of Jerusalem. I never ventured there, thus obeying the Procurator's orders, and my father's, which had the accidental effect of reinforcing one another. Although I could look down, longingly, upon the twinkling oil lamps of the city, I slept in a tent under the stars.

One night Aristides, who had become my trusted companion and my friend, came to me.

"My lord," he said, keeping his voice low, but not so low I couldn't hear the note of astonished delight in it, "there's a woman outside the camp—asking for you. By Aphrodite, what a creature! Hair so long she has to loop it over one arm to keep it from sweeping up the sand. A pair of tits bursting out of her tunic, hips—"

"I know," I said, forcing the words out through the strangling in my throat, the constriction in my lungs, the pain in me like a death-stab to my gut. "Go tell her that by Sheol and Gehenna both, I mean by black Hades and Tartarus, I—"

"She said I was to give you this," Aristides said.

I took the little scroll. Carried it over to my lamp. She had written it, herself. The formation of the letters was atrocious. She'd also left out the vowel points, so that some of the words could have meant any of three or four different things. I've often thought of inventing extra letters for the vowel sounds, as in Greek, so that Aramaic and Hebrew would cease to be the at times maddening code ciphers that they are. But how could I get my ultraconservative people, and especially our scribes, who have a vested interest in our languages' difficulties, to adopt them?

Only one thing about her letter was clear: that she had been crying when she wrote it. It was plentifully blotched and splattered with what could only have been her tears.

I puzzled my head over it. Finally I got it to make some sense by quite arbitrarily reading into some of Shelomith's incomprehensible hen scratchings meanings that accorded with the parts I actually could decipher. I read:

"My Own. If you don't come to me, I shall die. And maybe if you do, you will kill me. Better that way. By your sweet hand I—" here a long phrase impossible to decipher—"gladly." I read it as "From your sweet hands I would accept death gladly" or "would consider death a gift" or "a boon" or some other such rubbish. The rest of it was the word "please" repeated ten times, followed by a phrase that surely meant "come to me" and that by a line written with the greatest care, startlingly different from the rest, though I could see it was still her hand—"I love you, Nathan. Your, Shelom."

There were no explanations in it. No word as to how, or why, or even if, she had left the decurion Telemarchos. No hint of how in Satan's Name she'd come to Judea. Nothing.

I sat there a long time, staring at that letter. A long time. A very long time. I said—aloud, because afterward Aristides told me he heard me—"Fool! Fool! Fool! Idiot! Ass! Braying ass who—"

Then I put on my cloak and went. Aristides went with me. Which made no difference. I don't think she even saw him, was so much as aware of his existence, much less his presence. I stood there with my arms held rigidly down at my sides and stared at her by the light of the torch that Aristides held. There was no moon at all. Nor any stars. The night was overcast. But for the decurion's torch, I could not have seen her.

I stood there and inside my veins my blood was screaming. The way a prisoner screams when the torturers are at him. My skin burned alive from the tactile memories crawling all over it, from blind, mindless, will-less recall of how every inch of her felt. My mouth hurt, tormented past all bearing by both memory and desire, savoring the taste of her, that wild, sweet venom whose absence was draining me of manhood, of life. My head went dizzy from her perfume, from her own absolutely maddening, tart, hot, feral, female smell. My father had it right: I was, I am, a fool.

I put out my arms to her.

I heard the sob tear her throat as though it were clawing her entrails upward through her mouth. Then she was in my arms, and climbing all over me, kissing me everyplace she could reach, grinding the barrier of our clothing into her own flesh and into mine so that afterward I found actual lacerations on my hide from the terrible, agonizing, and real—I swear it!—hunger of her embrace. And all the time she was crying. Her mouth tasted like the waters of Lake Asphaltides do in Ab: hot and briny, a little sulphuric—the mouth of a damned creature escaped for one brief moment from the pit.

I was aware then that darkness had fallen between us. Jerking my head, I saw Aristides' torch bobbing away toward the camp. He had left us alone. The fool. The dear, kind, romantic fool.

Shelomith's voice was a sea surf in my ears; a rush of foaming, briny waters.

"Come," she was saying. "Come with me—over there—those trees—it's darker—come—"

I took her by the arm. Walked over the warm sand, the scale rock, toward the trees. A tiny animal, a lizard surely, made a skittering. There was no other sound except the rasp of our breathing, the rustle of our clothing.

We reached the trees. I turned to her, said: "Shelom—"

And hands caught my wrists, jerking my arms almost from their sockets, twisted them behind me. I exerted all my newly acquired strength, tore free of my assailant, slammed my fist down to my belt, closed it around the hilt of my *sica*, held it there; for a broad-bladed *gladius*, a sword, was already pressing into my throat; a half dozen spearpoints bit my flesh simultaneously—not fatally, or even deeply, but enough to bring blood, to convince me that to try to fight was folly. Suicidal folly.

"Tie the Roman-loving little bastard up," a great voice said.

We rode down a rocky, dried-up stream bed and then southward toward the Dead Sea. The cords binding my arms bit into my flesh. But they'd assumed I could ride because they hadn't tied me in the high-pommeled desert rover's saddle. Ahead of me a burly brigand pounded southward at a gallop, tugging at the bridle of my mount, who followed him as the wind follows a driven cloud.

We were in desert country now, because the hoofbeats became noiseless, muffled by the drifting sands. I made it a point of honor to hold myself erect, ride like a prince instead of a bound captive. I wondered how, in what manner, they would kill me. I hoped that I'd die well, without crying out. But I doubted it. From their Roman masters, such brigands as these had learned too well the art of inflicting pain. More likely they'd have me screaming like a woman in childbirth before half an hour was up.

Then, toward the east, the night broke loose from the edge of the world, and a pale, pearl gray band stole up from the Great Sea, yellowed, grew bright. Now I could distinguish Shelomith among this pack of desert wolves. She rode a snow-white mare. Her hands weren't bound. She had her head up as though to sniff the air. She rode proudly, like a queen.

I was still watching her when the long, low sprawling black humps of the tents came in sight. We pounded up to them on those tireless desert horses. A great shrill and gabble of women and piping of children boiled out to meet us. The warriors pulled up their steeds, leaped down.

I was surrounded. The women peered at me timidly. Some of them were comely. All of them had their faces unveiled. Then I saw why. They were Jewish, not Bedouin. Some of them, I saw from their features' fineness, had been gently born, city bred. The children stared at me with the eyes of owls. Their soft little mouths made great O's in their burnt-black desert faces. They were beautiful children: well fed, sturdy, strong; a race to make the Romans tremble when they came of age.

Then the leader came toward me. He was short, only a little taller than I am, but at least twice as broad. He had a thick, squared-off night-black beard. His great bole of a chest, bared to the morning sun, was covered with hair like a beast's. His muscles made the ones I was so proud of appear the products of starvation, of some wasting disease, by comparison. His hair was short and curly. He wore a single heavy golden earring in the lobe of his left ear, but none in his right. I wonder what, if anything, that meant. His weapons were Roman, stolen or wrested from some legionary. Wrested, surely. For no man could stand up to this earth-broad Kolossos, this Herakles, and live.

"Nathan bar Yehudah!" he boomed in a voice that was great as the rest of him. "I give you greetings, and pray that you accept our hospitality!"

"For how long?" I said bitterly. "Until you can erect a cross, or build a fire?"

He looked at me, and loosed the dark thunder of his laughter.

"Neither, by Sheol!" he said. "You'll find that we'll treat you right tenderly. For one thing, we had of Shimeon how you spared his life when you had it in your power to revenge yourself on him for that scratch he gave you; for another, dead, you're but another lump of flyblown stinking carrion, vulture food; alive you're worth your weight in gold!"

"You mean—ransom?" I said. "My father's far from rich, and my uncle—"

"Don't be a fool, bar Yehudah!" he said. "We're Zealots. We don't prey on our own. But will not the Epitropos pay us well to return him the one man in all Judea who can complete his watercourse? Or, better still—" he looked around until he found Shelomith, and grinned at her with jobial malice, "will not the Lady Claudia urge him to pile up the talents so that her lover can return to her bed?"

I saw Shelom's lips go white. If I had desire or need of vengeance for her treachery, I had it then!

"So you'll write the Epitropos a letter, bar Yehudah! Another to the little Claudia—now there's a bit of dainty tail I'd have you share with me! *That* one will be a cunning missive, penned in goat's blood, enclosing the finger of another captive, with that ring you're wearing on it! But you we will not harm. You're our guest. Our honored guest. In fact, you can have Shelom for your bedmate. I'll send her to you come dark, bearing with her a whip for you to beat her with. Treacherous little bitch, isn't she? But don't beat her too hard or you'll make her useless. Do those cords hurt? I'll cut them loose if you'll swear by the Name not to try to escape. . . ."

"I swear it by the Name," I said.

He came and cut me loose. Helped me down from my mount. I stood there, rubbing my half-paralyzed arms.

"Might I know your name, good Captain?" I said.

"Of course. It's Yeshu'a," he said.

Now the name Yeshu'a, "He Who Saves," or, as some interpret it, "The Help of YHWH," is a common one among us. It is but a variant of the Hebrew name Yehoshu'a, which in your tongue would be Joshua.[5] But somehow I couldn't help resenting this great thewed animal's having the same name as him I loved.

"Yeshu'a what?" I said.

"God knows!" he laughed. "Most people call me 'Son of the Father.' Probably because I never had one. Or, if I did, his name was legion. Are you hungry, bar Yehudah?"

"Very, bar Abbas!"[6] I said; "in fact, I'm starving."

The midmorning meal consisted of huge slabs of roasted sheep, served desert style, and washed down with endless flagons of wine. While I ate, Shelomith sat apart, staring at me. She picked at her food listlessly; I saw no single morsel of it reach her mouth. Her face was utterly wretched. She seemed to be fighting back her tears.

For dessert, we had clean locusts[7] broiled in wild honey. They were delicious, though I had to close my eyes to get the first one down.

After that, they took me to a great tent. In it was a table with writing materials already on it. I offered no resistance, but wrote as they told me to. What cared I if Pilatus had to loosen his purse strings in order to buy my freedom? And, as for the letter to Claudia—written in my purest Greek, employing the blood of a freshly slaughtered goat as ink —my resentment over the casual way she'd used my body as an instrument for achieving pleasure caused me to make a little masterpiece of it. The blood I was writing this with, I told her, was drawn from my opened veins. I was being submitted to the most fiendish of tortures; I hoped she would not despise me when she saw how hideously I'd be scarred.

There was among them, of course, one who knew enough Greek to vouch for the fact that I'd made no trickery of either missive. Then Yeshu'a bar Abbas demanded of me my ring.

"Look, good Chieftain," I said, "you really aren't going to cut off a man's finger in order to—"

"Yes," he said cheerfully, "but don't you worry about it, bar Yehudah. He won't feel a thing. Bastard up and died on me this morning, before we could get out of him where he had his silver hid. . . ."

That night, as bar Abbas had promised me, Shelomith came to my tent. Also, as promised, she had a great whip in her hands.

Tremblingly, she held it out to me. I shook my head, said: "No."

And she: "Please, Nathan."

"You *want* me to beat you?" I said.

"Yes. Oh, yes! I'd feel—less—less filthy, then! Nathan, I—"

"Sorry," I said; "I won't oblige you. And you may go back to wherever you came from. I don't soil my flesh with—other men's leavings. Offal. Treacherous offal, at that."

She stood there and took that, and she didn't cry. Instead she whispered: "Nathan—"

And I, wearily: "Yes, Shelomith?"

But she didn't answer me. She couldn't. The tears burst, exploded from her eyes. In the lamplight, they looked like yellow diamonds, like a spray of stars. A low, keening ululation came from her throat.

"Oh, for God's sake!" I said.

"Nathan," she said, shredding my name upon the pulsations, the

torn thrustings of her breath, "you—and—and—Claudia! Tell me it—
it's not so! Tell me that, even if you lie!"

I looked at her. Remembered that little house with the roses climbing
all over it. The house near Cæsarea. The house where she and
Telemarchos—

The rage that tore me was all the more hurtful for being cold.

"Yes, of course it's true," I said. "Why not?"

Her hands went beneath her cloak, came out with that knife. Then
she was kneeling before me with it lying across the palms of her hands
like a votive offering.

"Take it," she said harshly, "and kill me, Nathan. Finish killing me,
I mean. Because you already have. Do for me what you'd do for any
coursing hound bitch of yours who came home dragging her guts on
the ground out of her belly where a boar had ripped her open. That's
what it feels like. And I can't do it myself now. I haven't the right to,
anymore. If I could, I would; but I can't."

I stared at her.

"You want to die," I said, "because I lay with Claudia? With one
girl-child, while you—"

"It's not the same!" she stormed. "It isn't, Nathan! I—I'm dirt! What
I do with this ruined, rotten carcass doesn't count—as long as I'm not
in it, then! I told you that once! And I *never* am, except with you!
Never, Nathan! What I had with you was—was holy—and now you—
now you—"

"Oh, Elohim and Adonai both!" I said.

"You've dirtied it! With her! So kill me! Don't leave me hurting like
this! Don't leave me to go through life dragging my guts on the ground,
with my insides screaming 'cause I hurt so! I hurt, I tell you! I hurt!
I hurt!"

"Shelom, for the love of God!" I said.

"No. For the love of you. Who were getting to be more *him* every
day. So that the light was always there on your forehead and you were
more shining bright angelbeautiful like he is every minute and I
didn't even need to tell you apart anymore! You had no right to dirty
that, Nathan! To smear the spit of her filthy kisses all over your
Yeshu'a-face, her rutting bitch stink over your angelflesh! You who
were the Yeshu'a I could have, who could belong to me, had no
right—"

I hit her then, as hard as I could. Open-palmed across her mouth.
Her head jerked sidewise. A thread of scarlet from where her great
warm wonderful lips broke against her teeth, stole diagonally down
across her chin's tremble.

She bent her head and cried, hoarsely, terribly. Looked up at me and said: "Kill me. It's easy, Nathan. Like a she-goat. You put the blade here and—"

I, who was already killed. She couldn't understand that, comprehend the death in me, the utter weariness. I couldn't explain to her in a way she could grasp that the only thing worse than rejection is—substitution.

Far, far worse. This poor dumb little bitch couldn't see, perceive, my horror at the very idea of being used as an icon, an image of flesh, to be inhabited—through her longing, her imagination, her need—by another soul. Unlike her, I couldn't escape my body. For good or ill, I was always its indwelling gnostic host, though not entirely its master, even when it was engaging with Claudia in acts that have no name, and are utterly vile. So I couldn't make room in it for her lovelust-longing sculptured idol of Yeshu'a ha Notzri. My body was not meant, or even fit, to be a shrine.

"No," I said, the weariness, the death in me, drowning, stifling, sinking into primordial soundlessness my voice; "if you want to die, you'll have to do it yourself. I won't stop you. I don't think anybody ought to be stopped considering what life's like, what it is. But you can't ask me to become a murderer in order to arrange the mess you've made of your life. . . ."

"It wouldn't be murder. To kill a bad-hurt she-dog is—a kindness, Nathan. A mercy. I'll write that down! I'll tell them why!"

"No," I said.

Her eyes turned inward, then, as she considered the matter.

"I can't kill him," she said, talking to herself, not to me; "I can't kill my little Yeshu'a. Because I'm going to name him that no matter what Telemarchos says—"

I sat down. I had to. I couldn't stand up anymore.

"You mean that you—that you're—"

"With child? Yes. I wanted him to be—yours, Nathan. Only they—Telemarchos and your Claudia, the filthy little bitch!—told me what would happen to you if I stayed with you. How your family would disown you. How nobody'd give you work. How you'd starve. All because of me. And they were right. That's what makes it so awful—"

I didn't say anything. What can you say to the truth? To that kind of curdog bellygrovelling truth? Except that it represents—surrender. Of yourself. Of what you are. Of everything in you that makes you a man. And castration, my friend, however it's done, is—vile.

"So I went away with Telemarchos. He's a good man, Nathan. He's kind to me. I could be happy—if it weren't for you—"

"You mean if it weren't for Yeshu'a," I said.

"No, you. Because you're human, sort of. You *could* be mine—if people would leave us alone! But Yeshu'a I couldn't ever have because he's—"

"What?" I said.

"An Angel. A real one, I mean. I don't think that carpenter was his father! I think that an Angel, or God himself, came down and—"

I couldn't let that blasphemous nonsense pass, that Hellenistic reduction of Almighty God into a rutting swine like your Zeus, Roman Jupiter. As low as man. Having attributes no more divine than animal lust. I said, using the literal, filthy, gutter words, the utterly obscene equivalent of: "And had sexual intercourse with Miriam?"

But she wasn't shocked. She said: "No. Just touched her with His hand. Just sort of—hovered over her in a cloud of—of light. And then he—Yesu—was there in her womb without all the sweat and stink and panting and—and ugliness. Tiny and pure and angelbeautiful with all the sin left out. Mine, too, sort of—"

"Shelom!" I said.

"'Cause when Telemarchos and I were—were doing that—I knew we were making him. I knew it, Nathan! So I prayed to God to make him look like you—and *be* like Yeshu'a . . ."

She was mad, of course. But madness is sometimes beautiful. I wonder if sanity *ever* is?

"Then," I said, "if you were so content with your Greek paramour, why did you—"

"Leave him? I didn't, Nathan. That big wild boar bar Abbas dragged me off. Had it all planned, like that kind know how to do only too well! Waited until Telemarchos had left the house to stand guard before the Procurator's palace, then came bursting in. Shimeon Zealotes had told the big bastard you were crazy over me. So he threatened to kill me if I—I didn't betray you into his hands this way. I told him to go ahead. That I'd die first. So he put his knife against my belly, swore he'd disembowel me. They do that, you know. The Zealots, I mean. Open women up from crotch to navel, let everything spill out. Mostly women who've lain with Roman soldiers. Women like me. But I was already two weeks overdue for the second month in a row. I remembered that. Remembered my little Yeshu'a—"

I put my arms around her then.

"Poor Shelom," I said; "poor little Shelomith—"

She stayed there with me until it was dawn, until the sun came up like a shofar blast over that bitter lake, that lifeless sea. I didn't touch her in that way. I had not the slightest desire to. That was over now. Forever over between the two of us.

Somehow, on that dreadful night, we'd killed it.

Chapter XIII

WHEN I came out of my tent the next morning, I went in search of bar Abbas. I found him readily enough, for I was guided to the place he was by the clash of arms, and his own bull-roaring.

He was training the boys. He'd assembled all those sturdy little beggars between Bar Mitzvah age and—seventeen, I guessed, and was making them fight each other in companies. They were armed with wooden swords and leather shields. I stood there watching, and shook my head. The way he was training them, we would never beat the Romans.

He saw me and came up to me with a white-toothed grin, flashing pearls amid the sooty midnight of his beard.

"Well, bar Yehudah!" he roared—he always roared; I don't think he even knew how to talk quietly—"what d'you think of my Jewish Liberation Army?"

I looked him straight in the eye and told him the strict and bitter truth.

"They're hopeless. A Roman decuria could sweep a cohort[1] of men trained like this off the face of the earth."

His brows crashed together over his broad, blunt nose. I half expected to hear a thunderclap.

"You're saying," he bellowed, "that *my* training—"

"Is poor. Worse than that, it's dangerous. They'd fight better without it."

He glared at me.

"*You* could do better, I suppose?" he said.

"Yes," I said.

He grinned at me then, a savage grin, filled with unholy glee.

"Prove it!" he said.

"Prove it how?" I said.

"Meet me in single combat! Sword and shield. Spears, daggers—anything. What say you, bar Yehudah?"

"Done!" I said at once, and grinned back at him.

That disconcerted him. He had expected—fear.

He half turned.

"Wait!" I said.

He looked at me out from under his shaggy brows. I could see why Shelomith called him a wild boar.

"I'd advise you not to assemble the people," I said quietly. "And to send these boys away."

He glared at me and his nostrils twitched. I'd already learned they did that when he doubted your word, suspected treachery.

"Why?" he said.

"Because I have no desire to become the leader of this band of brigands," I said evenly. "And when your people see how badly I'm going to beat you, they may insist upon that. Your authority rests upon your reputation as a fighter, bar Abbas. I'd not rob you of it."

"By Sheol!" he bellowed. "I've met some nervy little bastards in my time, but you—"

I grinned at him.

"You haven't asked me what weapons I want," I said.

"All right. What weapons do you?"

"A fishnet, a dagger, and a trident."

He shook his head.

"Impossible. We're not fisherfolk. What use would we have for—"

"Then a spear, four square rods of tentcloth, and a dagger," I said.

He studied me.

"You'd hold *me* to fighting with this mountebank's combination of yours?" he said.

"No," I told him. "I'd prefer that you came to meet me fully armed: breastplate, buckler, shield, sword. Spear, too, if you like."

"A spear, no," he growled. "Beyond throwing it or holding it out to break a charge, a spear's no good. Now come with me."

"Where?" I said.

"To the center of the camp—where everybody can see me eat you alive, bar Yehudah!"

"That's not wise, Chief," I told him. "When the people see—"

"Oh, fæces!" he said. "Come on!"

When I went into my tent, Shelomith was asleep. But as I stripped off my clothing, and prepared a loincloth—after all, there would be Jewish women watching this contest, not Roman matrons nor Greek hetairai—she woke up and stared at me.

"Nathan—" she whispered. Then her face turned green. She leaped up, staggered through the opening, and started to vomit. I came to her at once, took her arm.

She looked up at me with tears in her eyes, but her smile was a glory.

"There!" she said triumphantly. "That proves it! I am!"

I managed a sickly grin. You see, I'd thought she was concerned about me.

Then she saw how I was dressed, or rather how I wasn't dressed.

"Nathan—" she breathed. "You—you're going to—to fight somebody!"

"Yes," I said peacefully; "bar Abbas—"

"Oh, Nathan, no!" she wailed. "He's made out of iron! He'll—"

"Get the worst beating he ever took in his life. Remember what I did to Thor?"

"I do, and what they did to *you* afterward!"

"At *your* suggestion, Shelom, darling," I said.

"I know. But these wild beasts—Oh, Elohim! Here they come! Nathan, don't! I—I'll die! I'll lose my baby!"

"Go inside then," I said; "don't watch."

"And when they bring you in there all bloody and broken and—and dead?" she whispered.

"I thank you for your confidence in me, Shelomith," I said. Then I whirled her around, and smacked her bottom smartly with the palm of my hand, propelling her through the tent flap.

Yeshu'a bar Abbas saw that and roared with laughter.

"At least you know how to handle women, don't you, boy?" he said.

"And weapons," I said. "Look, good Captain—let's place some conditions on the outcome of this contest—"

He stared at me. His nostrils twitched.

"Such as?" he said.

"If I win, I want three things: Your promise to send Shelomith back home to Cæsarea. She's gravid, and hence of no use to me. It is our custom to abstain from women in that state—"

"Done," he said. He knew nothing of Zadokim customs, so he was willing to take my word for it. In truth, we do have such a custom; but it is far from always held to. "And your second condition is?"

"That *I* be allowed to train the boys."

"Agreed," he said. "By Sheol, you can do that even if you don't win, if your showing's good enough. It's a chore I don't have time enough for, really—"

I saw then, with some relief, that he meant neither to kill nor maim me.

"And the third?" he growled.

"That I be allowed to ride at your side when you go forth to war," I said.

He shook his big, bushy black head.

"No," he said; "that, no. You're too valuable to us all in one piece. Sheol, bar Yehudah! What do *I* gain by whacking you about the way I'm going to?"

I grinned at him.

"Send Claudia another finger. Ask for twice as much," I said.

The outcome was a foregone conclusion. I'd been trained by experts; he, not at all. It was like the bull slayer's art: the beast's enormously greater strength counts for naught against the speed, the skill, the intelligence of the man. I won't bore you with the details of it. It's enough to say that I bloodied him all over with dozens of spearpoint pricks, netted him with the tentcloth, tripped him with the spear shaft, hurling him to earth while he was trying to fight free of it, put the spearpoint against his throat, held him there.

" 'S not fair!" he roared. " 'Tis magician's trickery! Why—"

I took the spear away.

"Get up," I said. Then I turned to one of his—decurions, I suppose I'll have to call them, though how many they commanded, I truly do not know. "Give me a sword and a shield," I said.

"Armor?" the man asked.

"No. Just the *gladius* and your shield. I don't need more," I said.

I didn't know that Shelomith had come back out of the tent. And it would have made no difference if I had known. I gave them a dazzling exhibition of lanista-trained swordsmanship. I touched him at will, while he, great-thewed, sweating, panting, winded, slow, could not lay a blade on my naked hide.

He stepped back. Threw down his shield, his sword.

"You win, bar Yehudah!" he panted. "By Sheol, I've never seen the like!"

Then he stepped up to me and almost crushed me in his great embrace.

When he released me, I turned and saw Shelom lying on the ground. She had seen the last of his desperate thrusts from such an angle as to make it seem to her he had me, and had fainted dead away. I'd never known her to show a jot of weakness before. Tears, fury, passion, yes; but weakness, no. Her condition was responsible for it now, I supposed.

She kissed me goodbye with a soft, sweet tenderness that sent pain screaming through my veins. I helped her up on the white mare, watched her ride away. "I'll never see her again," I thought.

I was wrong. It was not to end like that. Neither so cleanly nor so well. God, or fate, whichever you believe in, or the malicious, mindless, perverse blind accidentality that I'd swear rules life is—as all of human history demonstrates—simply not that kind.

I was, I am, as my father always said, a fool. But I have two qualities which have always served me almost as well as intelligence: a retentive memory, and a great curiosity about the why and how of things. And now, as I set about training the Zealot boys, they served me well.

By the very nature of things, the Zealot brigands had to be poorly armed, their only weapons being those they could make themselves, or steal. Now the Romans, as you Greek did before them, rather despise light-armed missile troops. I don't mean they despise the use of missiles. Far from it! Their employment of the various forms of *katapeltes*, of huge stone and fire-dart throwing artillery, has never been equaled by any other nation. But slingers and archers they give no importance to, largely, it seemed to me, because among them, both were so ludicrously, pitifully inadequate. No, less than inadequate: bad.

There were two exceptions to this rule: Whenever they could, they enlisted Numidian and Scythian archers into the ranks of the legions. In the hands of the great blacks, and in those of the slant-eyed Asiatic barbarians, the bow was a terrible weapon. I've seen, at the games, a Numidian slay a lion with but a single arrow; and the Scythians could drive their iron-pointed *attrakoi* through a bronze breastplate with ease.

But Roman and Greek archers are so bad that any good javelin thrower among them can achieve greater range with his light spear than the bowmen do with their arrows.[2] Which was why it seemed to me that a first-class troop of *Kataphracts* was precisely what we needed to beat the Romans. To try to fight men equipped with the world's best weapons, trained all their lives in hand-to-hand combat, was folly. No, our only chance against them was to slaughter them from afar, rain arrows down upon them from a distance so great that their formations would be broken up before they ever reached us. Therefore I set myself the task of producing a good copy of the long Numidian bow, or the short, double curving, terribly powerful Scythian one, which only the strongest men can pull. Do you know what happened?

I failed. Completely. The materials for the manufacture of such splendid weapons just were not available in my country. Judea is sand

and rock, with almost no trees. The ones that do grow there produce a rigid, sunbaked wood that is brittle, has no elasticity. Oh, it's good enough for javelin shafts, for spears; but for making bows it's useless. In Galilee, well-watered Galilee, I might have done it. But I wasn't in Galilee; I was in Judea.

Sorrowfully, I put that idea by. My boys were good slingers. They often killed desert hares with their stones. I improved the sling, made the thongs longer, taught them to select carefully the roundest, smoothest stones. But to hit hard enough to kill a man, you need something far heavier than a stone in your sling. I knew, of course, that hundreds of years ago, your Greek slingers used molded leaden bullets in their slings. And when one of those murderously heavy leaden balls struck a man on the forehead, he died. Any other place they hit him, they left him crippled. But I hadn't any lead either. So the slings remained an annoyance, a toy.

I was in despair. To train these splendid, beautiful youths as lanista swordsmen was to condemn them to death. There was no way at all to provide the logistics which supports a Roman legion. Say I could get them to equal a legionary's skill with javelin, heavy spear, *gladius*, shield. It would make no difference. Unless I could supply them with the weapons in quantity and quality to equal the legions', and procure enough of perfectly trained, perfectly armed young fighters to outflank at least a cohort, it was assassination to send them into battle. And I had neither the weapons nor the numbers of men.

I was thinking about that, when I chanced upon a crooked piece of root lying on the ground. Something in its shape intrigued me. It looked like a reclining capital letter L. I picked it up, a dim memory prickling me. But it was all of two days later before it came to me: One of my foster father's friends, famed as a traveler, had described in Caius' house in Rome, how a tribe of smallish African blacks, not quite dwarfs, but almost, hunted gazelles, brought them down on the run with the combination of—a throwing stick—and a spear.

A throwing stick. This! My letter L! I could see in my mind's eye the drawing he had made of that curious weapon. You pass a loop of leather thong through a hole bored in the longer end, wrap the thong about your wrist. You rest the butt end of the javelin against the upright, short bar of the L. You hold the throwing stick tightly with all the fingers of your right hand, except the thumb and forefinger which alone lightly clasp the javelin's shaft. Then you throw, releasing the javelin only, not your L-shaped throwing stick. The vertical bar of the L catches the butt of the shaft, whips against it with a force at least triple of what you could manage to put behind your cast without it,

sends the slender shaft whistling through the air to achieve a range
rivaling that of the arrows of a Scythian bowman.

I tried it. It worked. It worked beautifully. I could double my best
range by using the throwing stick. I set my boys to manufacturing
throwing sticks, and a lighter, longer javelin. I made them practice
with this new combination weapon from morning until night. Betimes
I taught them swordplay, which they loved, holding javelin throwing
rather cowardly. But I insisted upon javelin practice with those
L-shaped sticks.

Yeshu'a bar Abbas watched it, grunted: "Not bad!" and rode off to
raid a Roman supply train.

No sooner had his troop disappeared behind the hills, than a century
from the Sebastian cavalry wing rode into sight, raising a cloud of dust
visible to us from some twenty stadia away. It was hopeless. There was
no doubt that those horsemen from the *Ala Sebastenorum* had seen us.
Against the golden sands, our black tents were visible from even that
far away.

They had, I discovered later, been sent out to search for me by
Claudia's express command. She missed me. Wanted me back. Was
sure she could keep me as her tamed beast, useful bedfellow, amusing
lover-pet, as long as she wanted to now. And as openly. Because she
had found a way of tying Pilatus' hands, of making him absolutely
powerless to gainsay her.

I assembled my boys. Commanded the women—including the charming little bedmate bar Abbas had cheerfully assigned me (Why describe her? She didn't matter. She was complaisant, dutiful, good in
bed. That's all. And, besides, I cannot call anything else about her to
mind)—to take themselves and the children to the rocky hills behind
the camp. I sent ten boys to bear the water and the food, and to serve
as guards. The weakest, least reliable boys. The rest I kept.

Then we retreated to some rocky outcroppings to the left of the
camp and waited for the Roman cavalry to come close enough. In that
natural fortress, I could stand off an army. From the highest rock of all,
I killed the centurion leading the Sebastians with a single javelin
hurled over a distance so great that I myself could scarcely believe
my luck when I saw him reel from the saddle with that shaft protruding from his throat.

At once the Sebastians were thrown into confusion. Watching them,
I thanked my stars it was they, provincial conscripts, we were confronting, and not members of the *Cohors Italica*. They hadn't even
seen where that spear had come from. They milled about, tugging at
the bridles. The horses neighed shrilly. And that gave me an idea.

"Aim for their mounts!" I commanded. A horse is a much bigger and easier target to hit than a man. Besides, in the Roman cavalry the mounts bore no armor.

My youths fitted the javelins into the notched hooks of the throwing sticks. Bent their glorious sunblackened bodies far back. Hurled the slender shafts upward, retaining their grips on those wickedly simple javelin launchers, so that the throwing sticks whipped around one hundred eighty degrees of arc still glued to the butts of the javelins, adding all that tremendous propulsive force to them before the singing spears left them, flew free.

Below us, the carnage was terrible. The horses screamed like women, threw their riders, bolted. Within minutes, it had turned into a stampede. When bar Abbas—after whom I'd sent one of the younger women, wild as she-hawks themselves, riding one of the half-tamed mares of our herd—got back, all he could do was half crush my ribs with his bear hug, and to set his brigands to poniarding the wounded Romans. Because we wouldn't have time to take prisoners. They would slow us too much. And now we had to get out of that particular stretch of desert, fast.

Two weeks after that, bar Abbas' scouts found the bag of gold he'd demanded as my ransom in a certain hole in the rocks not far from the Essenes' monastery at Khirbet Qumrân, where they'd instructed the Epitropos' emissaries to leave it. In parting, bar Abbas shed tears before them all, kissed me, called me brother.

Then they broke camp again, put the reins of a magnificent mare in my hands—for, like the Bedouin, the Zealot brigands favored mares as mounts over both geldings and stallions—and rode away, leaving me alone there in the desert. I watched that brave and gallant crew of brigands, ruffians, *sicarii*, murderers, who were Israel's only hope, who were to be the cause of her despair, until they were out of sight. Then I mounted and rode down to Qumrân, to the monastery of the Essenes, where my escort of Decapolians awaited me. A whole century, armed to the teeth. My captivity was over. Or was it?

Had it not, truly, just begun?

For, that night, after I'd given commands to my work crew to demolish the half stade of aqueduct they had built during my absence, getting the pitch hopelessly wrong so that the water would have ceased to flow, I was sitting in my tent with my friend Aristides, telling him neither the truth nor the romance he wanted to hear, but rather a judicious mixture of both, with enough pure unadulterated lies added to cement the whole fanciful structure together, when a strange legionary was escorted to my tent by the sentries. Strange to the Decapolians, that is. I knew him at once: The centurion Costobar, commander of that century from the *Cohors Sebastenorum* that had been assigned to Claudia as her special guards.

He saluted me, and handed me the scroll. As I opened it, a cloud of perfume rose about my head, that scent become doubly maddening, because, besides being Claudia's own, it was the kind she'd taught Shelomith to use. In many a romance you will find a lyrical passage in which a whiff of scent reminds a lover of his dearly beloved; but even in this, reality crossed and cursed me; the perfume that will haunt my nostrils till I die awakes in my memory the image of not one woman but two. And worse, when I tried to counteract its insidious effect by calling Helvetia's favorite scent to mind, I found to my abysmal shame and disgust that I could no longer remember it. The reason, of course, for that sad state of affairs was simple: neither as her father's daughter nor as my wife, had poor little Helvi had the money to buy a scent that any slave girl couldn't have worn. She bought what was cheapest: during our last days together, an attar of roses. But its odor was not distinctive. I do not remember it.

Now, as I looked up, I met Aristides' delighted, half-mocking grin. He was not envious. Vicariously, I think, he enjoyed my affairs more than he did his own rather base and boring conquests, which consisted of slave girls, whores, an adulterous wife of a merchant traveler, female riffraff of that sort. He had seen Shelomith, seen how she'd half devoured me when we met, which was enough to cause him, as far as women were concerned, to freely award me the victor's palm. And now this missive, brought by a full centurion, penned in a hand that half a glance showed him was the daintiest of feminine scripts—and in Greek, at that! He leaned over my shoulder, shamelessly.

"Aristides!" I said.

He drew away from me with an injured look. But then that dull ass of a centurion spoiled all my precautions.

"The Lady Claudia said I was to bring an answer, my lord," he said.

I glanced at Aristides. He was hugging himself with pure, if unholy, glee.

I sighed, long and deeply.

"Tell her—I hear and obey," I said.

That night, out of sheer necessity, disobeying my father and Pilatus both, I rode up to Jerusalem, entering it not by the Damascus, nor Solomon's, nor any of the principal other gates, but by the Dung

Gate, through which, after midnight, the carts carried away mountains of human offal to be buried or burned. I chose that entrance because it was by it that I ran the smallest risk of accidentally encountering anyone I knew. But also because it seemed to me a singularly appropriate entrance.

That was what I felt like. Dung.

A slave girl opened the door of the house to which Claudia's letter had directed me. I followed her through ghostly, silent passages to her mistress' bedchamber. She opened the door. I entered.

And stood there just inside it, unbreathing, shocked beyond the use of speech.

The girl who came toward me was almost unrecognizable as the Claudia I had known. She was no longer slender, she was skeletal. Her eyes peered out of their sockets as from a death's-head, a skull. Her cheeks were inhollowed, her lips bluish. In her bare arms, her shoulders, I could count every bone she had. I had the feeling I could encircle her throat with the thumb and forefinger of one hand. An exaggeration, of course, but not as great a one as you might think.

I hung there, staring at her.

"Nathan!" she breathed. "Oh, Nathan!"

Then, in one wild rush, she was in my arms.

I held the long slow quiver of her to me, feeling down to my bones' bitter marrow the way she cried. I had been the cause of too much female sorrow already in my life; I had believed Claudia beyond the reach of any emotion more profound than lust; but now I saw that I'd been wrong. I was not Yeshu'a ha Notzri's twin for nothing; I shared—in lesser measure, of course—his awful, terrifying power to inspire—love.

"Don't," I whispered. "Don't, Claudia! I am not worth—"

She pushed away from me a little, stood there looking up at me, peering at me, really, trying to discern my face through the wild white curtain of tears that surely walled it out.

"Not worth crying over, you mean?" she said quietly, almost calmly. "To me—you're worth everything. Even the life you almost cost me—"

I stood there looking at her, and a quivering stole along my limbs. I was held in the grip of winter frost, iron chill.

"Don't get me wrong; I didn't do this—on purpose, Nathan," she said then, quickly. "I am not the heroine your Helvetia was. I'm a selfish, spoiled little bitch to whom nothing and nobody matters. I wouldn't prick my little finger for any man alive. Not even you. Or so I thought. Only my—my body knew better. It knew that it hurt all over inside and out from wanting you. So it—it refused food. Not I,

Nathan—it! My dumb beast body, starving for your caresses, ravenous to—to engorge—to be impaled upon—your hard male flesh. So it decided to starve itself in all ways, to end a suffering it couldn't bear. *It*, not me! I tried to eat, Nathan! I tried! I simply couldn't get food down. It wouldn't pass that knot of—of pure damned screaming agony in my throat. And what little I did force down; hhhhupppp, right back up again! Pontius' physician says I'm in a decline. That I'm going to die. I've lost half a talent[3] by weight, already. I, who never in my life could afford to lose an ounce. Only now—"

The shaking in my limbs was noticeable now, even to her. I was remembering Helvi. Remembering the awful rents she'd made in her whitesweettender flesh, because of me. And a grief, both new and old, sprung from triple sources—my Helvi metamorphosed into a bloated, unrecognizable mass of putrefaction; my Shelomith gravid with another man's child; my Claudia—yes, yes, *my* Claudia!—reduced to this—rose up and blindscalded my eyes.

I felt her mouth against my cheek. It went away. Then it pressed, opened and quivering, against the other.

"*This*—was the medicine I needed," she said.

We talked all night long. Or rather Claudia talked, and I listened.

"Oh, I planned it so well, darling! Would you believe that hungry Iberian boar I married is capable of love? Well he is, just as though he were actually human—"

"Isn't he?" I said.

"Human? No, of course not? From his brains, I'd say his mother was a sly and cunning vixen; but his father surely was some species of swine. Oh, he's clever enough; but the only real emotion he feels is— ambition. He isn't even jealous of me. I could make the beast with two backs with half the Roman Empire and he wouldn't care—as long as I was discrete enough not to wreck his chances. He's jealous of *you*, though, darling. You may be sure of that!"

"Why?" I said.

"Because—because he knows I love you. As distinct from—from doing—this—"

"Stop it!" I said. "You're not strong enough, Claudia . . ."

"Aren't I? Just you wait, my lover! I'll give you such a demonstration that you'll beg for mercy! Later. Now I want to talk . . ."

"Thank God," I said.

"Anyhow, I found out about his Myrtilene. A Greek. A former hetaira, married to one of our duces—our generals. A slave—at my orders, of course—stole a first draft of one of his letters to her. Actually schoolboyish! The syrupy endearments in it would have turned your stomach—"

"I'm listening," I said.

"So I had my loved and respected foster father, the more-than-divine Tiberius—he'll do *anything* to keep me quiet, you know, darling— send her out *here* with her fat fool of a husband. You should have seen my Pontius, hopping from foot to foot like a schoolboy who wants to go to the latrine and dares not ask. He couldn't wait to send that fat fool Malvidius on extended tour of Idumæa, Peræa, lower Judea—all the awful desert countries where he couldn't possibly take his wife along. Then I did my bit for the cause: I offered her a house I own in Jerusalem, telling Pontius at the same time that she got on my nerves, and I wanted her as far away from Cæsarea, and me, as possible. A detail he was entirely prepared to believe and which delighted him. I waited until I was sure. Until my spies had brought me proof he was bedding with her. Then I invited Vitellius—"

"The Governor of Syria?" I said.

"Yes. You know how upright *he* is! I asked him to come to see me on an urgent matter. I am nobody, really; but I'm still the granddaugh- ter of Cæsar Augustus, so he came. I took him, with his guards—to *her* house. The house I'd had assigned to her. Even the slaves in it were my own. It wasn't a matter of breaking in; I had a duplicate key to every door, every closet. We stood in the doorway and watched them bucking and gasping and pounding away—Zeus, what an ugly sight!"

"It's not made for watching," I said.

"No—for doing, for participation," she said, and kissed me. "We watched them for at least five minutes—no, ten. With *her*, he was good. She screamed the roof down. Like I do with you, darling—"

"Claudia, please!" I said.

"Then I put on the required performance. I swooned into the august Governor's arms. There was a great deal of shouting. Vitellius was for placing Pontius under arrest, and shipping him back to Rome; but I asked time to think it over, time to talk to my erring spouse—"

"And you said to him?"

"'Have fun, you lecherous swine! Only I'm free, too; understand? We're friends, you and I, Lucius Pontius. I'll help you get to the throne. Sit there beside you smiling—your loving, dutiful wife, your divine Empress. Everywhere, except in bed. Which shouldn't trouble you. You have this greasy Greek slut, don't you? And I—' He cut me off. You know what he said?"

"No," I said.

"'And you, my dearest, your cut-tipped little Jew. My engineer—

whose skill extends beyond building watercourses. It would seem he also plugs them, doesn't he?'"

"Claudia, in God's Name!" I said.

"I know. He's vile. So am I, I fear. Only you—are sweet, Nathan. And then—"

She bent her head, quite suddenly, and cried.

"Claudia!" I said.

"That same night, they brought the news. That the Zealots had seized you, carried you off. Pontius was sure they'd kill you. He'd had the brains beaten out of hundreds of people in Jerusalem over that accursed aqueduct, you know. He was terribly upset. It was awfully unflattering but instead of being happy to see the man who'd cuckolded him killed, he put three whole cohorts out to search for you!"

"And?" I said.

"Two days later—they brought me your letter. I didn't read it, Nathan. Because, when I opened the scroll, that awful, bloody—"

I lifted up my hand with my ten fingers spread wide.

"Ugh! What a filthy trick!" she said. "I—I threw up. Then I started screaming and rolling on the floor and tearing my hair out by the roots. Because that finger with your ring on it, to me meant that you were—dead. It never occurred to me to read the letter, or even that there *was* a letter. Pontius had his physician give me a sleeping potion. It didn't work. I lay there crying all night long. In the morning, a servant brought me my breakfast. But, by then, my body, my poor, dumb-beast body that needs you more than it needs food or clothing or baths or ointments or perfumes, had already decided what to do, quite independently of me, entirely apart from my mind, or will. I tried to get my breakfast down. It was like trying to eat a nest of serpents, trying to swallow offal. All my meals after that were the same—"

"Claudia," I said reproachfully, "you shouldn't have ever—"

She smiled at me then.

"I didn't want to live without you, Nathan. No more than your Helvetia did. Oh yes, I know about her. Poor little fool! What a thing to die over! The one part of us that *can't* be damaged, really. Did she think you'd leave her when you found out? Why? It wasn't her fault. I don't see—"

"No," I said. "She had a conception of herself that was very high, Claudia. Almost as high as the one I had of her. She knew that purity is not just a word. That our bodies—hers and mine—were temples, sacred to each other's worship—and hence not to be profaned. Which is why—"

She lay there, looking at me; and now her eyes eclipsed her tiny, emaciated face.

"—you have never loved anyone else," she whispered; "why you—you can't—That's it, isn't it, Nathan?"

"That's it," I said.

She went on looking at me. Then she raised up and found my mouth. For the first time since I'd known her, she didn't kiss me like a hungry she-beast, ferociously grinding mouth on mouth. Instead she clung her lips to mine as lightly as a breath, slow moving, salt with tears, while her fingers moved with awful, lacerating tenderness amid my close-cropped dark, wiry hair.

She drew back at last, and let the endless white star-tracks pencil her face.

"They had to—to force-feed me like a German goose, finally—to save me, Nathan," she whispered; "and now—and now I wonder why—what for?"

"Oh, Claudia!" I groaned.

She smiled at me then, through her tears.

"Except maybe to prove that I—have love enough in me for us both," she said slowly. "And that this—temple—ruined, ravaged, violated, profaned—before it knew the—the unknown god it was dedicated to—is sacred to your worship still. That it will always be. As long as there's life and breath and blood—and hunger—in me. Oh, Nathan, I—"

I took her in my arms then. And we made love. Very gently, and with great tenderness.

In some ways, that was the greatest sin of all.

Chapter XIV

THINK ABOUT IT. There are layers, depths, to any relationship between two human beings. And nothing in life stands still. For, when stillness, quietude, finally comes to us, we have a word for it. We call it by the name that fits it: Death.

Granted that there was no going forward with what existed between Claudia and me, it would have been far better to have floated, while yet we could, mouth locked to mouth and limbs entwined, upon the foaming surface of sweet simple lust, giving and taking our fill of mindless carnal joy. Add, if you will, even the valid excuse that it was circumstances beyond either her control or mine, life's own malicious mockery, call it, which plunged us down to depths of feeling, where the *what* we were, man and woman, male and female, two bodies duly equipped with complementary genitalia, with, moreover, the instinctual needs, the acquired skills, the somewhat perverse imaginations required to make rarely excellent use thereof, became irrelevant before the *who* we also were, before two beings of something more than flesh, having hopes, dreams, feelings seated elsewhere than in our loins, possessing minds (of dubious value) powers (limited) of thought, I, Nathan, and she, Claudia, highly complicated, intricate, pitiful, farcical, doomed, damned, laughable, at best (lend us a little dignity, will you!) tragicomic compendiums of two distinct racial memories, tortured into abrasive individuality by all that had ever happened to us, both together and apart; yet, even conceding us that mitigating palliative of blind accidentality, I repeat: the fact remains that we should have thrashed upward at once toward where sunlight and air could have bathed our twisting naked bodies, where pain itself existed only on the level of a playful bite, or a passion-convulsed indriving of nails. For, to linger at this unsought-for depth, where the sudden, almost stupefying recognition *that* she was Claudia, and I, Nathan, began appallingly to matter, where other faces, breasts, vulvae, phalli, gonads simply wouldn't do, where the flesh became not the instrument of pleasure but of fusion, of making us twain one soul, was (since that depth demands continuity, a future of sorts, an end to proceed toward, or to) profoundly, even terribly—a sin.

Shall we have a go at defining that elusive word?

You'd probably say, good Nazarene, Christianos, that I have imagined you to be, that sin is what is offensive to God. But there you lose me. And not, as in your pious wrath or wrathful piety you would surely accuse me, because I am incapable of grasping so vast a concept. God's vastness does not elude me; what escapes me is His morality. I'd say, to judge by what He permits to happen daily in His world, that absolutely nothing whatsoever offends Him, no matter how fiendishly cruel or nauseously vile. I *saw* how He allowed my Helvi's goodness, chastity, fidelity, piety, purity to be rewarded; I *felt* the glutinous, obscenely stinking mess that once had been her sweet flesh, pull free in my hands. I *witnessed* your Lord's death in awful agony upon a felon's cross. With that horror I could fill pages, and granting the logorrhea from which I suffer, I probably will. I lived through the pogroms committed against my (and supposedly His!) defenseless people in Cæsarea and Alexandria, I saw babies' heads smashed against walls, maidens stripped naked and forced to eat swine's flesh in the theatres before being violated to the vast edification of the roaring mobs. Permit me, then, to pay your God the respect of disbelief for, by the plain evidences of history, in the moral sense he is, at best, irrelevant; and, at worst, a monster. And, even by my definition of it, demon worship is a sin.

I pray you accept that definition. We can argue later. When I have done with this. When all the evidence is in. It is very simple: To me, any relationship, any act, which involves the humiliation, the wounding of a human soul—another's or my own—is sin.

Which is why my love affair with Claudia became so. Yes, *became.* It hadn't been before. Before it had hurt nobody: not Pilatus, busy about his ambitions, his own swinish loves, a permissive cuckold, not even deceived; not Claudia who'd used my body as an apparatus of pleasure, a sort of fleshly puppet dancing to the strings of passion; not me, because I simply hadn't cared. Not even poor Shelomith, really, although she thought it did; for, examined truly, the wound of which she was dying had another source.

For now I was going to have to hurt Claudia, hurt her terribly. Or destroy myself. For life at a standstill is a kind of, and soon becomes an actual, death. And that's all my life with Claudia was, or could be: dead stopped, arrested now. With no future to it. None.

She knew that when the aqueduct was done I was going to leave her. That I had to. I had explored every possible blind alley, dead-end street, of existence already; now I had to find, or make, my road. I owed my family sons, myself continuance. I could no longer proceed by blind accidentality; if life has no meaning (and I, having passed far beyond mankind's allotted span, have found no trace of any rationally acceptable significance in it) we have to erect what useful counterfeit of that quality to support our days we can.

"When you go," Claudia told me, "I'll open my veins, just as your Helvetia did!"

But I knew she wouldn't. She was not the kind of antique Roman that my Helvi was. She'd go on living, after a fashion. Slip from one facile love to another, as a well-worn coin slips from hand to hand. Until even the image, the numerals upon it are eroded away by too many too easy contacts that haven't even the virtue of hurting a little, that blur in the mind, that wear down smoothly into nothingness.

At least I had given her a memory. Sharp-edged. Hurtful. Rimmed about with pain. As she had, me. We'd recall each other's faces until

we died. Remember a glance, swift seeking, a mute imploring look
that conveyed more meaning than all the ink-profaned scrolls of this
world, a silent gesture that sang or screamed; a timbre of voice that
deepened or belied the sense of what words we were at any given moment saying; the tortured unto death grimaces of love; the long sweet
clinging lassitude of accomplished desire, when other voices, faces,
limbs, circumstances, loves, have faded forever out of time and mind.

And that, at the very least, is not to be sneered at, my friend!

I was sitting beside her at the games that Lucius Pontius Pilatus
was giving to celebrate the completion of his aqueduct. On the other
side of her, a burly bodyguard sat, a naked sword across his knees,
pledged to give his life for hers. Then Myrtilene. Beyond her, her
husband, the General Malvidius. Another guard; then Pilatus. Behind
us, all the seats were filled with guards in civil dress. To our right and
left, the same. It made general conversation difficult; but it allowed
Claudia the opportunity to both do and say to me things she shouldn't;
that were useless now, lacerating, a gratuitous addition to already
more than sufficient pain. But no Zealot daggerman was going to
get close enough to any of us to use his blade. Of that, the Procurator
had made sure.

"And this Iohannus Baptistes, Pontius," the Dux said in his heavy,
dull voice; "what of him?"

He said it like that, combining the Latin form of the name Yohannan with the Greek word Baptistes. He had to. There was, at that
time, no word for *Baptist* in Latin; it was Yohannan himself who
forced the Romans to invent that barbaric transliteration from the
Greek, *Baptisterius*.

"Refer the question to our Nathanaeus here," Pilatus said carelessly.
"He's my expert on Jewish affairs."

Claudia jerked my hand downward, violently. She had had it halfway to her mouth—again.

"Well, Nathanaeus?" Malvidius said.

"That's difficult to answer, my General," I said, raising my voice
so that it would carry. "Yohannan bar Zachariah, in himself, is nothing. A typical Essene holy man. A harmless sort of lunatic. But his
effect upon the people—I'm not so sure I like it, sir—"

Claudia had my hand in her lap. She'd covered both it and her own
with her shawl. She was fondling it, tracing upon my palm with her
fingertip our private code symbol for the phrase "Let's make love." She
was a little crazed by the imminence of our parting. It was making her
reckless.

So was I. But it was making me morose. Sad.

"Why?" Malvidius said. "I've been told he's merely a religious fanatic. Wants everybody to share, down to their shirts and their bread. Even dips tax collectors in that muddy creek of yours,[1] warns 'em not to be greedy. Baptized a few legionaries, told 'em to stop extorting and bullying;[2] damned if I see the harm in that. The man's not one of these political rabble-rousers who—"

Pilatus threw back his head and laughed aloud.

"My dear Malvidius!" he said. "One can see you haven't been in Judea very long. It's impossible to separate religion and politics, here. To a Jew, his state is a theocracy; his only ruler, God. That awful, invisible, untouchable, tasteless, odorless God. Only Jew who doesn't stink—their God. Saving Nathanaeus, here; and he's more than half a Roman—"

"Oh, but you're wrong, Epitropos!" Myrtilene said. "He *does* have an odor. He smells of perfume. Claudia's. Does he steal it, or do you give it to him, dear?"

"I apply it to him, personally," Claudia said. "All over."

"Good!" Pilatus said with perfect equanimity. "I hereby commission you Head Perfumer of the Realm, my dear. You may proceed to scent them all!"

"The harm, my General," I said quickly, trying to head off a screeching cat fight, "lies not in the Baptist's teachings, but in his prophecies. It seems he predicts the immediate coming of the Mashiah—"

I didn't say *Mashiah*. I said the Greek word *Christos*. They both mean "The Anointed of God." But whether Greek-speaking people understand by Christos what we do by Mashiah, I do not know. Considering what the Christianoi Ekklesia teach now, I doubt it.

"That's another thing I don't understand, Nathanaeus," Malvidius said fretfully. "This *Christos* of yours. One is forever hearing of him. Who is he? What's he supposed to do?"

"Cut our throats—" Pilatus yawned "—push our Legions into the sea. Occupy Rome. Make slaves of us—"

I laughed at that. But my laughter was bitter. 'If only that were possible!' I thought.

"Why do you laugh, Caius Nathanaeus?" Pilatus said with mock solemnity. "Do not your Holy Writings say:

> 'On him was conferred sovereignty,
> glory and kingship
> and men of all peoples, nations, and languages
> became his servants.' . . . ?"

He quoted that in Greek, of course. From the Septuagint. Because, even as far back as the time when Ptolemy Philadelphus reigned in Egypt, there were enough of our people who'd already lived in that country, mostly at Alexandria, so long that they'd forgot Hebrew, making it necessary to translate the Holy Scriptures into Greek for them. That happened about two hundred fifty years ago.[4] It's a good text. I like it.

But I was a little astonished to find out that Pontius Pilatus had gone to the trouble to read the Septuagint. Was he seriously trying to understand us better? If so, knowing him as I did, it was very likely for the purpose of discovering a subtler, more effective means to provoke us into the revolt that would give him excuse to slaughter us to a man. Starting with me, of course.

But two can play at that game of quoting Scriptures—at which, I'm told, even the Devil is adept.

"Or, if you will, great Epitropos," I said evenly, "our Scriptures also say this:

> 'Who could believe what we have heard,
> and to whom has the power of YHWH been revealed?
> Like a sapling he grew up in front of us
> like a root in arid ground.
> Without beauty, without majesty
> no looks to attract our eyes
> a thing despised and rejected by men
> a man of sorrows and familiar with suffering
> a man to make people screen their faces;
> he was despised and we took no account of him.
> And yet ours were the sufferings he bore.
> Ours the sorrows he carried.
> But we, we thought of him as someone punished,
> struck by God, and brought low.
> Yet he was pierced through for our faults
> crushed for our sins.
> On him lies a punishment that brings us peace,
> and through his wounds we are healed . . .'[5]

"That, also, is our Mashiah, Pilatus! The suffering, sacrificial lamb, taking upon himself the sins of the people, being slain, for:

> 'By force and law he was taken.
> Would anyone plead his cause?
> Yes, he was torn away from the land of the living;
> for our faults struck down in death . . .'[6]

"Doesn't seem to me you Romans have much to fear from such a Mashiah, does it? On the contrary, I'd think—"

I got no further, for my words were drowned out in the roar of the mob. The games had begun.

At that same precise instant, I saw Shelomith. She'd come late, with Telemarchos. He was helping her to a seat in one of the higher tiers. He had to help her, because by then she was very great with child. I looked at her, and—

How can I describe it? How can I tell you how I felt? Or what? For the sexual relationship has occupied the quills of men ever since humankind learned to draw, much less write. Perhaps because it is the greatest, the most terrible of hungers; but more, I think, because it is so many-sided, touches every other conceivable aspect of life. And, because of that, all the words have been written, said, the coinage of language debased by overuse, making it, for instance, difficult, to say "I love you" to a woman whom you *do* love, because you have systemically reduced the content of precious metal in those particular coins, robbed that phrase of meaning, by saying it to so many wenches you merely lusted after, so many facile little bitches who amused you.

So now, I hadn't any words left to say that Shelomith was—lovely. Soft, rounded, the image and type-form of sweet maternity. No phrase, clever or dull, to tell you that my bowels yearned for that unborn child, who should have been mine; that the knowledge that he wasn't, that I'd never hold him in my arms, say to him, "My son! My son!" was a sickness in me, a pain to stop my breath.

I stared at her, and—forgive me the the well-worn phrase! But must I invent a new one, when the old, ground thin and slick by overuse, was in that awful moment true?—my heart was in my eyes. So much so that Claudia saw it, and dug her feline claws into the palm of my hand. It made no difference; I went on staring just the same. But now another thought struck my semidivine Imperial mistress. She leaned suddenly close to my ear.

"Yours?" she hissed.

I shook my head. "Do you think I'd be here, with you, if it were?" I said.

"That's insulting, Nathan!" she began.

And I: "Or that I'd leave *you*, if you were going to bear my son?"

Claudia's eyes opened very wide. Her hand closed around mine, hard.

"Nathan—" she whispered.

And I: "Yes, Claudia?"

"I—I took precautions! But now—"

"But now?"

"I—I won't anymore! God, no! What could be more—glorious? Yours —a little you—to hold—to keep. . . . To melt my breasts down his tiny throat. . . . To watch him grow more like you, every day. . . . Nathan, come to me, tonight. Come and help me make—a god! Because he will be! Beautiful like you! Fierce like you, tender—"

I shook my head. "No," I said.

And she: "Why not?"

"I'll not give Pilatus the son he cannot sire himself," I said flatly, "nor risk that a manchild of my loins might sit one day upon the throne of that monstrous perversion of power into crime that Rome is. My son, if I ever sire a son, will be a priest of the Most High God. The God I don't believe in. Perhaps that will be some recompense, some atonement for my unbelief. What think you, my dove?"

"I'll leave him!" Claudia wept. "I'll come to you! Live with you openly; be your wife! I'll—"

"Do you know how long the life we'd have together would last?" I said.

"Yes," she said, bitterly: "Five minutes. Or less. Yours, at least. He'd have to kill you then. He couldn't face a public scandal. But he wouldn't dare kill me. I'd have to do it myself. And I would. I may even do it now—tonight, when you go. . . ."

"Children!" Myrtilene said mockingly. "Don't quarrel! This is no day for a lovers' fight. . . ."

"We weren't fighting, Myrtilene," Claudia said. "I was merely envying that woman over there."

"That pregnant sow?" Myrtilene said.

"That pregnant sow. Especially and precisely that. That she can be. That she has the right to give the man she loves—a son. Can you think of anything more—beautiful?"

I shook my head, said: "You're wrong, Claudia. She hasn't that right. She's breaking her heart this minute because that child weighting her down isn't—"

"Yours!" Claudia spat.

"No. Because it isn't Yeshu'a ha Notzri's."

"Who's he?" Myrtilene began; but the beast-bellow of the mob cut her off.

Looking down, I saw why. The new gladiator, one Longinus, whom Pilatus had brought out from Rome at ruinous expense, had won again. With one back-handed stroke, he'd disemboweled the retiarius opposing him. That poor devil knelt there on the bloody sands, busily engaged in trying to stuff his guts back into that gaping slit in his belly with his two hands. He couldn't do it. They were too blood-slimed, slippery. They looked like thick pink sausages slipping through his fingers. The crowd watched him and roared with laughter.

With a mocking grin, Longinus came up to our box, saluted Pilatus. He was as hairy as a bear. He reminded me in that regard of Avidius Publius. In itself, that was enough to make me hate him. But the arrogance of his stance didn't help my temper either. Then Claudia tugged at my arm.

"Nathan," she whispered. "Why is she looking at you like that?"

I raised my eyes toward where Shelom sat in one of the upper tiers. She had a seat at the end of the row, next to the stairway, so I could see her well. Her face was absolutely gray. Even from that distance, I could see her lips tremble.

I knew why at once. I had been a retiarius. She'd even seen me fight as one. She was putting me, in her imagination, in that poor dying devil's place.

Then Pilatus gave the expected signal. The only one he could give now; that was a mercy: *Pollice verso*; thumbs down.

Leisurely that hairy bastard sauntered over to where the pain-crazed dying retiarius knelt, clutching at his blood-slimed guts and screaming. And, instead of drawing his *sica* and plunging it into the retiarius' throat, providing him thus a quick and merciful death, he gave him another end, just as quick, and perhaps even more merciful; but, to look upon, a horror. That is, he swung his *gladius* with sickening force, and cut off the kneeling man's head. It rolled, mouth open in a silent scream that, lacking lungs, no longer had air to give it sound; eyes glaring in ferocious anger upon death, blood pouring from the severed neck.

I turned, looked up at Shelomith. She had hid her face, was leaning up against Telemarchos, shuddering.

And quite suddenly everything got to be too much: Myrtilene's mockery, the crowd's bull-bellows, Claudia's perfume in my nostrils, Shelom shuddering in Telemarchos' arms, Melvidius' laughter, the infinitely subtle malice and mockery of Pilatus' smile.

I stood up. Ripped my tunic over my head. Then, stark-naked, I leaped down into the arena.

Longinus stared at me. I hadn't so much as a *sica* in my hands. But I didn't run. I walked step by step by step through total silence—for no man or woman in the stands was breathing now, I'd swear—to where the fallen retiarius' weapons were, and picked them up. Then I turned.

"Well, Longinus," I said, "shall we begin the dance?"

He hung there, still frozen, until I put the trident into his face and deliberately opened his right cheek to the bone. Then he came roaring in.

In seconds, I saw my life was probably over. Never in my professional career had I met a swordsman of anything like his skill. Nor, to give my Lord Satan his due, had he met a retiarius of mine. We were matched to a hair. Time and time again I felt the wind his blade made on my naked hide as I leaped aside. Fifty times or more I lifted my net to cast, only to find him gone from there. Not for a moment did the crowd stop screaming. I could hear Claudia's voice fluting above the din: "Oh, Nathan! Nathan! Oh, Great Zeus, I'll die!"

But I didn't hear Shelomith's. Nor did I have time to seek out her face. To me the crowd was but a blur, a voice; one total unceasing obscene bestial bellow.

Then it happened. By accident or design, Longinus had worked me into that part of the arena where my predecessor had been butchered. And nobody had had time to cover his thick-pooled blood with sand, as was always done between the bouts. I stepped into the ropy, thickening mess, my foot slipped, I went down. At once Longinus was upon me, his *gladius* shortened for the fatal stab.

I heard, in that immeasurably brief fracturing of the stuff of time, Claudia's scream tear the day apart. It saved my life. For the quality of it, its unbelievable anguish, horror, grief, so shrill you felt it like slivers of glass slammed into your ears, a real and unbearably physical pain, paralyzed every man and woman there. Including Longinus. Briefly, of course. For the barest subdivision of a second. But long enough for me to ram a kick up between his thighs that almost emasculated him, and to roll free, just as his blade bit earth at the exact spot my throat had been before. He staggered away, his face white with the agonizing pain he must have felt; and I set my net awhirl, released it, let it soar.

And murdered him. Quite coldly. He was out on his feet. I pushed all three tines of the trident through his neck, sent him over backward, pinned him to the earth. Then I looked up. I couldn't see Claudia. The reason I couldn't was that she was bent far over with her head down between her knees to keep herself from fainting. I raised my eyes upward toward where Shelomith should have been. She wasn't there either. And Telemarchos was running like a madman down the tiers, hammering people out of his way with both his fists, and screaming:

"Shelom! Shelom! Oh, dear God!"

The crowd was on its feet roaring, applauding me. But where Telemarchos plunged downward a little knot of people were bending over something in the lower stands.

Over Shelomith.

When she'd seen what had seemed to her—as it had to all the spectators except those directly in front of the place where I had fallen—Longinus' murderous thrust strike home, she hadn't screamed. She had merely stood up, hung there with her face graying out of life, swayed, tottered, put out her two hands blindly as if to seek support, bent forward, leaned, loosened all over, gave, and pitched headlong down the stairway between the seats, for fully twenty tiers.

I saw them pick her up. From the way her left arm dangled, I knew it was broken. All the lower part of her skirt was soaked with blood. I stood there watching them bearing her away but I couldn't move. I wanted to; but I couldn't. Then my knees turned to water. All the bones in my legs melted. And I was lying on the ground, pounding the blood-soaked earth with both my fists and screaming the way the other retiarius had when Longinus had spilled his guts for him. No, worse. Louder, shriller, more terrible.

They bore her away while I was screaming. And, one hour later, she lost her child.

"Oh Absalom, Absalom! My son, my son! Would God I had died for thee!"[7]

That next morning, I went to see her; but Telemarchos stopped me at the door. Not in anger, but in grief.

"It's better that you go, Nathan," he said quietly.

"Why?" I said, "I haven't come—"

"To take her away from me? I know that. You can't. You're too late. God, your jealous, vengeful Jewish God—"

I hung there. My lips shaped the words "No Oh no Oh no Oh No—No!" And though they had all the throat-tearing stridency, the briny, bloody anguish of a scream, no sound accompanied them, no sound at all.

But Telemarchos shook his head.

"She's not dead, Nathan," he said, his voice the scrape of sand over brass. "He wasn't even that kind. She's—"

"What?" I fought the word out, clawed it bloodily out from where it was tangled in my lungs, my guts.

"Mad," Telemarchos whispered. Then he closed the door in my face. Quietly.

But that's the way the world always ends, doesn't it? With an all but noiseless thud. An almost soundless whimper. Then—

Silence.

Chapter XV

IT WASN'T until the next morning that an idea penetrated my thick cranium, which, if I had had any brains at all, would have occurred to me in the first place: If, as all the people who'd been close to her swore she had, Shelomith had fainted and fallen down those stone stairs between the rows in the stadium at Cæsarea because she'd thought me slain, might not I, by presenting her with the irrefutable proof her eyes had deceived her, restore her to her senses?

I leaped from my bed, threw a short tunic over my body, rushed out into the street, and—stopped dead.

At this hour, Telemarchos would be on duty before the Prætorium. Shelom would be alone, except for her maid. And, oddly, instead of seeming to me a divinely glorious opportunity, the whole thing seemed rather, in some vague way, wrong. Now I'll admit the ethics of the whole matter were damnably obscure. Shelomith was Telemarchos' kept mistress, not his wife. Moreover, he'd robbed me of her, by telling her—the strict and literal truth. For me to have married Shelom would have doomed us to exile. Because we couldn't have lived in the Land of Israel; with all that was against us, we would have starved.

Besides, I'd cost him—a child. A son. That he had five others by his wife made no difference. Any man would have put a bastard got upon Shelom before a prince born of a queen. Any man at all. And Telemarchos loved her. As much as I did, maybe. For him, for any man of woman born, to love her more wasn't possible. More; it wasn't even conceivable.

He'd robbed me of her. But I had returned the compliment a thousandfold. I'd robbed him of their child, him of her, the world of her, her of herself! I wouldn't try to take her away from him, now. The only thing I wanted to do was to see her, try to restore her, nothing more. So I couldn't go sneaking into his house like a thief. I'd go to him, get his permission first, tell him why. . . .

He came out of the guardroom at once, walked with me down the palm-shaded street. Heard me out.

Then he said: "You're wrong, Nathan. By your awful God, if I thought it would do any good, I'd send her to you. I'd give her up completely. If saving her required my life, I'd open my veins here, now, on this street. You've known her. You know that any man who has been blessed with Shelom's company—her company, damn it! Not the other —although she has no equal in *that* either, as you know—"

I shook my head.

"I don't, Telemarchos," I said.

"Ha! Late for gallantry now, Nathanaios!" he grated: "Why lie to me? You and she—"

"Never. By the honor of my mother. By the Ineffable Name of God, I swear it."

He stared at me. A long time. A very long time. Said with commiseration, compassion, even pity: "You poor bastard. You poor, poor bastard." Then: "She said the same thing; but I didn't believe her."

"You should have," I said.

"No matter! Shelom is—an angel. A trifle soiled—fallen, if you will, but—an angel. I'd do anything for her. Anything, Nathan! And that anything includes giving her to you, if I thought it would help. But it wouldn't. In fact, it would make her worse. Which is why I tell you now, that if you go near her, I'll kill you. Not out of jealousy. But because the sight of you would take away the last hope I have of saving her—"

I looked at him; said: "Why would it, Telemarchos?"

"You're a man, Nathan. A brave man, as you demonstrated by killing Pilatus' imported butcher before his eyes. So you can stand the truth. She didn't love you. She doesn't love me either, but she was fond of me. She was *not* fond of you. How could she be? She didn't even know you. Your identity was never—clear to her. She—"

"Confused me with Yeshu'a ben Yosef. Yeshu'a ha Notzri. I know that, Telemarchos."

"You know it. But have you grasped all the implications of it? When she went down that stairway—and I wouldn't swear she didn't throw herself down it deliberately—she screamed not your name, but *his*. She didn't go mad yesterday, Nathan. She has been sliding out of reality, out of this world, a long time. She is—delicate, dainty, fine. Don't look at me like that! That business of whoring—was self-punishment. For the sins her youth, hot blood, and inexperience pushed her into. The inexperience that kept her from being able to distinguish between men—and swine. Like that Antonius. That prevented her from realizing that human beings—even such miserable examples of so-called humanity as ish Kriyoth—are not to be used. So she learned what shame was. And, being by nature immoderate in all things, she converted shame, which is permissible, even necessary, into self-loathing, which is neither—"

"So," I said, "to punish herself, she turned to whoring?"

"Exactly. And it nauseated her. So once driven by despair, by self-hatred into that life—from which there is no escape, you know, Nathanaios—she evaded it by—"

"Training her mind to leave her body. To abandon it. 'So that there's nobody home when all the filth goes on.' She told me that once. Only—"

"She trained it too well. And now it has abandoned her for good. Months ago, I found out that she'd come to believe that our baby was—miraculously conceived. That I'd had nothing to do with it. That a cloud of light came down from heaven, and—"

"Hovered above her. And he was in her womb, tiny and pure and immaculate, with all the sweat, the panting and the stink left out. Her little Yesu—"

"My God!" Telemarchos said. "She told you that, too?"

"No. She said that of the original Yeshu'a. The man she's in love with. That's her theory of how he came into the world. Do you know him, Telemarchos?"

"Know him—no. I've seen him, yes. And I've a much simpler theory of his origin."

"Which is?"

"Your father was a Galilean. And lived near Nazareth."

I shook my head. "Yeshu'a and I were born the same year. I, in Jerusalem, he, in Nazareth. My father had left Galilee long before. And, until this business of our demonstration before the Epitropos here, I know for a certainty he's never been back."

"Then—your uncle. For, Zeus Thunderer take it, if you and he aren't twins!"

"Nor that. My uncle's an upright man, Telemarchos."

"All right," he said grudgingly; "but there *was* something. Some sort of scandal. Nobody knows anymore what it was. I've heard that Yosef, the carpenter, was on the point of putting her by. Something about a Roman soldier—"

"Called Pantera. A lie. A calumny. You don't know Miriam. I do."[1]

"All right. But I was *born* here, Nathanaios, though I'm a Greek. I know your customs as well as I do our own. Why was it, then, that Yaakob, the second son, was dedicated to the priesthood from his birth, and not Yeshu'a? You Jews always dedicate the firstborn male of your house to God!"

I stood there, staring at him, appalled. He'd hit home now. I'd never thought of that. And why, by everything unlovely, was Yeshu'a so different from his brothers?

I smiled a little sadly, said: "Let's say Shelom's right. Let's call him the child of the Holy Spirit . . ."

"Making him a holy bastard instead of an unholy one, and your God a fornicator like our Zeus? All right. I won't argue the point. The only interest I have in Yeshu'a ha Notzri is the absolute necessity of putting my hands on him today. At once. Now."

"So that you can kill him, because Shelom loves him? Tell me, Telemarchos, what good would that do?"

"None at all," Telemarchos said quietly; "and you mistake me, Nathan. I'd like to find Yeshu'a because I think that if any man alive can bring her out of this—horror, it is he—"

I stood there, looking at the decurion.

"How?" I said. "How could he?"

"Hades in Tartarus, I don't know! All I know is that she's obsessed with him. I think that if he were to show her a little kindness instead of consistently rejecting her, as he seems to have done—"

"Not 'Seems,' has. Does this 'little kindness' of yours include lying with her, Telemarchos?"

He stared at me. Twin knots of flesh stood out above his jawbone, twitched. But, when he spoke, his voice was calm.

"Yes," he said, "even that. Understand me, Nathanaios! It is *Shelom* I'm trying to save, not my mistress. Giving her up would be a little like dying. No, more than a little. But, you see, I love her. And love has nothing to do—with possession. If I have to go through life seeing her married to you, or to him, if it takes that to make her happy—"

"Neither is possible. And I don't think happiness exists in the sense you romantics believe it does. Contentment, yes. A sort of not-too-abrasive resignation. But happiness, no. And we reach a man's estate the day we accept the fact that we've got to live without it. That it isn't even necessary—"

"Spare me your sermons, Priest!" he said. "You said that it wasn't possible for either you or him to—"

"Marry her. No, Telemarchos, my friend, it isn't. I can't, because she doesn't even love me; and making use of me as a fleshly icon in substitution for the worship of her—god—wouldn't help her madness. You pointed that out yourself, a little while ago—"

"True. And he?"

"Has surely taken a vow of perpetual chastity. He has never been known to frequent women. Never."

"Ha!" Telemarchos said. "That merely means he frequents boys! It's one or the other. A man has to have some outlet. Normal or perverted, he has to!"

"And sometimes both." I smiled. "But Yeshu'a, no. Neither one. I'd stake my life on that. Perhaps Shelom's right. Perhaps he wasn't the result of ordinary human copulation. Perhaps that cloud of light did come down and—"

"Dung!" Telemarchos said. "Asses' dung at that! So you think that he wouldn't help her?"

"If it comes to making the beast with two backs with her, no. Apart from that, yes; surely. He's the kindest human being I've ever known. And the strangest. If you're willing to take the risk that this absolutely mad passion Shelom feels for him won't get worse, and drive her even further out of her wits than she already is, I'll find him for you. I'll ride up to Nazareth today and—"

But Telemarchos shook his head.

"It's not that easy, Nathanaios," he said. "Do you think I haven't sent for him already?"

"You mean he—he *refuses* to come?"

"Refuses? No. Of course not. I mean he isn't in Nazareth. He isn't even in Galilee anymore. He left here the day before those accursed games to go down to Judea to be baptized by the new wild man of yours."

"Then," I said, "it's merely a matter of waiting until he comes back and—"

He glared at me like a wild man himself.

"Waiting!" he said. "She—she sits up in bed with a bundle of rags in her right arm. The one that's not broken, not in splints. She—sings to it, Nathanaios. Croons lullabies. Calls it her little Yesu. Puts it to her breast, frets because it doesn't suckle enough. Yahweh, Elohim and Adonai! And whatever else you call this invisible faceless eyeless blind monster of a God of yours! You think I can stand that? I'll go mad, too. I will, Nathan. It's killing me! It—"

And there in a public street, dressed in full legionary's armor though he was, the decurion Telemarchos bent his head and cried.

I put my arm about his shoulders.

"Don't weep, Telemarchos," I said. "I'll find him. I'll bring him to you."

He looked up at me, his strong face streaked and wet.

"When?" he said.

"As soon as I find him. I'll leave within the hour. And it shouldn't be difficult. The mobs that follow bar Zachariah are so great that finding the Holy Man will be easy, surely—"

"But Yeshu'a—" the decurion said; "he's been gone three days—"

"Walking. I'll be riding Bedu."

"Bedu?" he said.

"My Arabian mare, given to me by the brigand bar Abbas. Swiftest creature you ever saw. I'll probably get there before he does—"

He looked at me then, and asked me one more question, the bitterest of them all: "Will—the Lady Claudia Procula—even let you go?"

"She hasn't any choice in the matter," I said, and put out my hand to him. "Until we meet again, Telemarchos!"

"Until we meet, Nathanaios," he whispered; then: "Go with God!"

From Cæsarea there is a well-built Roman road slanting southeastward to Samaria (rebuilt and renamed Sebaste by Herod the Great) and from thence to Sychem. About three Roman *milia* further on, at the spot traditionally held to be the well of Yaakob, son of Abraham, he who wrestled all night with the Angel, the road turns due south and runs almost directly down to Jerusalem.

But I didn't want to go to Jerusalem. I could have, of course, if I had wanted to, at the small cost of defying my father. For Pilatus' prohibition against my entering the capital had been lifted by then, for the very simple reason that, his aqueduct finished and my relations with his wife being what they notoriously were, to have the Zealots knife me in some crowded street would save him both the trouble and the expense of having to hire someone to do it himself.

But it wasn't either my father or the Zealots—bar Abbas had convinced me that I had nothing to fear from them—which kept me out of Jerusalem. Rather, it was my pride. You see, I was only too well aware that in my birthplace I was an object of contempt, of scorn. To meet Claudia there, as I had upon my return from captivity at the hands of Yeshu'a bar Abbas, had been a monumental piece of folly. I knew from my father's furious letters that our night of love had been known throughout the city before it was even over with; that—here I quote my father—"had you raised your lecherous head from your scarlet woman's pillow long enough to look out the window, you'd have seen a mob of curious people peering at that house 'ere dawn!"

How? The servants, of course, were Jewish. And I am of the Houses of Mattathiah and Bœthus both. Nothing I did, in those days, could escape notice. What that particular piece of folly had accomplished was to block completely my father's negotiations with a priestly family for a younger, singularly ill-favored daughter with but scant dowry to become my wife. He hadn't any choice, really. It was Susannah bath

Zakkai, or nobody. And after Claudia's own servants spread that business of her and me abroad in Jerusalem, it was nobody. Even a greedy
old thief like Zakkai ben Yishmaël couldn't stomach the idea of giving
his daughter to one of such tainted fame.

As dearly as I longed to see my mother, I decided to bypass Jerusalem
completely. I knew where Yohannan bar Zachariah, called Baptistes,
was, more or less. He was in southern Peræa, the lower end of Herod
Antipas' Tetrarchy, on the far side of the Jordan. More specifically,
those of whom I had inquired told me he kept close to the place called
Beth Anya, which was not the Beth Anya, or Bethany, from which
Shelom came,[2] but only crossing place in the river itself, and not a
village at all. For, had it been a village, that wild man, Yohannan
Baptistes, would have had nothing to do with it.

So when I got to Beth El, I deliberately cut cross-country until I
came to Jericho. There I watered my mare Bedu, the sweetest, most
docile creature I've ever known, the *only* female I have ever met who
didn't give me trouble; and ate a frugal meal of wine, bread, cheese, and
dates. I was tempted to linger, for Jericho is a garden spot, presenting
one of the loveliest vistas known to man, and I was very tired. But
Telemarchos' description of Shelomith, cuddling a bundle of rags,
crooning lullabies to that pitiful substitute for the child I'd cost her,
rose up and tiptoed through my mind with icy feet, setting me ashiver.
I mounted once more, took the Gilgal Road, and crossed the river by
the Beth Anya ford itself.

As I had anticipated, finding Yohannan the Baptizer was no problem at all. But what I'd known from the first *was* going to be a problem, that is, finding Yeshu'a among all the other idiots surrounding
that raving lunatic,[3] was an impossibility.

I couldn't get anywhere near Yohannan, not that I wanted to, for
I'm sure, had that been possible, his smell would have distressed my
nostrils as much as his aspect did my eyes. He was truly a madman, a
savage creature: great matted black beard, a lion's mane of hair, dressed
in absolutely filthy camel's wool, with a broad leathern belt about his
waist, bony arms and legs as hairy as a monkey's—altogether a most
unappealing sight. But, having nothing to stuff into my ears, and not
being—at that moment at least, unfortunately—deaf, I couldn't help
hearing him.

"Snake's brood!" he was roaring. "So you've come to me, eh? Trying
to get out of what you've got coming to you? If you've repented, prove
it! By the fruit it bears, shall your contriteness be known! And don't
give me that business that you're Abraham's children, and that that's

enough to insure your being blessed! I tell you that from these stones, the Almighty can raise up children unto Abraham!"

That last phrase was beautifully turned. You can't do it so well in Greek. In your language stones are *petroi,* and children *paidía* or *uioi,* so it doesn't work out. But in Aramaic, stones are *abanim* and children, *banim,* making a wordplay that came over with terrific force. The people roared at it.

Yohannan went on preaching what he'd always preached. He'd repeated it so often by then that it must have been graven on his tongue: The barren tree—that is, he who produced no good works—was going to be cut down and thrown into the fire; the necessity of sharing our worldly goods, the wickedness of certain abuses, such as overtaxing, extortion, et cetera, et cetera, et cetera.[4] And repentance. I smiled bitterly at that one. From what I'd seen of the rewards of virtue, it seemed to me more logical to thoroughly enjoy one's sins. But, now, he was boring me. By the fruits of Tantalus, how he was boring me! I sat there on Bedu, gazing over the heads of that mob of bumpkins and morons, and my eyes closed. I was dead tired. I slumped there, half asleep in the saddle.

Then a Galilean—who else but a Galilean!—asked that question, committing mayhem and murder upon the helpless body of Aramaic as Galileans always do; and it woke me up.

"Rabbi!" the oaf cried out. "Be you the Mashiah?"

The silence at that was so thick I could feel it. It crawled like ants over the surface of my skin. I thought: "You ass, don't you know you're asking him to condemn himself to the cross?"

Because he was, you know. To the Romans, the word *Mashiah* meant a warrior king. And the only king they intended to have anywhere they went was Cæsar. The bad part about it was that it meant the same thing to the majority of us, as well. Yeshu'a was the only man I've ever known who took seriously that passage in Isaiah I'd quoted to Pilatus at the games. Which was the error he was to die of, finally.

Then Yohannan spoke:

"I baptize you with water; but he who will come after me is greater than I am. I'm not big enough to run behind him, carrying his shoes.[5] He'll baptize you with fire. His fork's at hand, to winnow out the chaff from the good wheat. He'll put the wheat in his barns; but the chaff will be burnt in everlasting fire!"[6]

Then, at that precise moment, to my surprise—for I'd been sure it was going to take me far longer to find him—I saw Yeshu'a. He was standing a little way behind the Baptist. And that last phrase of bar

Zachariah's had had a strange effect on him. His face had gone white. He had his eyes closed. He seemed to be praying.

"Come!" Yohannan bellowed. "Let us go down to the river. All you who have truly repented, and want to be baptized, follow me!"

I rode along behind them choking on both the dust they raised and their collective stench. I don't think you have any region in Grecia as dry as Peræa is. It's all rock, and low clumps of brush, and blinding sun. A country for demons—and for wild men, like this one.

I couldn't get anywhere near the baptismal place. Down near the river, of course, there were shade trees, and green grass; but I tugged Bedu's head about and rode back to higher ground, so that I could see it. The repentant sinners formed a line. They came to the wild man who was standing up to his breast in the muddy water of the Jordan. He'd say a word to each one as they reached him—"D'you repent?"— I'd guess, and Splaaaasssh! down they'd go, to come up choking and spluttering, with their sins, presumably, washed away.

Some of the younger women were a sight to see, when they came up out of the water with their wet robes clinging to every inch of them. I was beginning to enjoy this baptizing business!

But also, I was getting plagued hungry. Then, suddenly, I realized the implications of my own instinctive reactions, and sat there upon Bedu, appalled. I had come down to Judea on a terrible errand: to find Yeshu'a so that he might, if he could, if he were able to, do something about Shelomith's blasted mind. I myself had been the cause of that madness. I had cost the life of an innocent, unborn child. I had left behind me still another woman—Claudia—weeping bitter tears. I had made my mother so sick from worry that she had taken to her bed; I'd aged my Uncle Hezron by at least ten years, taken all the savor out of my father's existence. Yet, here I was, casting an expert and appreciative eye over the way wet woolens clung to breast, buttock, and belly of these hysterical country wenches, and concerned mainly about the rumbling in my swinish gut!

I threw back my head and loosed a peal of wry and bitter laughter. So be it! I was myself, and had to live with my lack of sainthood, of piety. Besides, if I fainted from hunger, as I was very likely to, in this waste of sand and rock, I shouldn't be able to accomplish my errand of mercy either. The problem was serious. Almost surely it meant that I was going to have to cross back into Judea, and ride all the way back to Jericho again before I could sup.

"Oh, well," I thought, "I can hold out until I've laid hands on Yeshu'a. Take him back with me. Bedu can carry the two of us that far—"

Then I saw the boy. He was standing a little way off with another group of spectators. From his gestures, he was obviously trying to sell them whatever it was he had in the basket under his arm. But he wasn't having any luck. The Pharisees and the Sadducees both were too engrossed in the spectacle, clearly finding the watery circus as amusing, as ridiculous, as I did.

I called the boy over. As I did so, I noticed that Yeshu'a was only two or three penitents away from Yohannan. So I roared at the little bumpkin: "What have you got in that basket?"

"Pigeons. No, sir—one pigeon. Sold the rest, already—"

"For the sacrifices?" I said.

"No, sir. To eat. My pa sends me out with 'em to sell to the pilgrims who come to the Prophet—"

"*What* Prophet?" I said.

"Him," the boy said, and pointed. "Pa says he's Elijah, the Forerunner of the Mashiah. According to Pa, Elijah never died, y' know—"

"True," I said solemnly; "he went up to heaven in a chariot of fire. So the bird's eatable, eh? Come on, let me see it."

The boy opened the basket, took the pigeon out. It was a lovely plump creature, white-plumed and glowing.

"How much?" I said.

"A shekel," the boy said.

That was outrageous, but I wasn't disposed to argue. I groped in my hand-embroidered purse—Claudia had made for me with her own semi-Imperial, demidivine hands, and, to tell the truth, I rather treasured it for that reason—for the coin. But, at that moment, one of the Zadokim let loose a bull-bellow of laughter. I looked past him toward the river and saw what he was laughing at: as the plump wench just ahead of Yeshu'a in the line had come up out of the Jordan, she had slipped and fallen back in again. Now she was thrashing about in a wild panic. Yohannan reached down and yanked her out of the muddy water by the hair. It *was* funny. And pitiful. And ridiculous. And sad. All at the same time, as most things human are.

At that, the Sadducee roared louder than ever. His guffaws startled Bedu. She danced nervously, and her flank banged into the boy. To keep himself from falling, he turned the pigeon loose. The bird leaped upward in a clacking clatter of wingbeat, soared skyward, arrowy and swift.

"Oh, Sheol!" the boy said. "Pa'll have my hide!"

"No," I said; "here's your shekel. It was my fault. I should have reined in my mare. . . ."

"Oh, thank you, master!" the boy said.

I turned away from him. Yohannan had his hands on Yeshu'a's shoulders. He didn't say anything to the Nazarene, nothing at all. I think he was in a foul humor because of that fat clumsy wench who'd spoiled the dignity—if any—of the proceedings. He didn't look at Yeshu'a ha Notzri,[7] or ask him any questions at all. He simply slammed poor Yeshu'a down into the slow-moving half-stagnant waters, and brought him up again. Which was why, I think, Yohannan had to send his messengers to Yeshu'a to ask him, "Are you the one to come, or are we to expect some other?"[8] Certainly nothing about Yeshu'a struck or impressed the Baptist at the time.

But then I heard an outcry from the people. A sudden shaft of sunlight had burst through the heavy dust-haze of evening. And, confused by it, my escaped supper fluttered downward so low that he almost touched Yeshu'a's dripping head.

"Sheol!" I thought. "If Yeshu'a would just raise his hands a little, neither of us would have to go hungry tonight, because I'd share with him—"

Then the pigeon recovered its equilibrium, beat downward sharply with its wings, raced skyward, and was gone. Yeshu'a stood there in the Jordan staring upward. From the expression on his face, I'd have sworn that the bird—or something—had spoken to him.

But he came out of the river on the Judean side, the opposite bank from where I was. And again I lost him in the crowds. You cannot possibly imagine how many thousands were there. Their numbers were symptomatic of something: of my people's weariness, born of centuries of oppression, of their soul-sickness; of their need for surcease, for relief. In that fifteenth year of the reign of Tiberius, I shouldn't have liked for anyone to have compelled me to find him a Jew of Judea, or a Galilean of Galilee, whom any discerning physician would have certified as entirely sane.

Certainly not one Nathan bar Yehudah!

I forded the river again, went in search of Yeshu'a. But, in those latitudes, night falls out of heaven like a stone. I was in despair, worried about Shelom, my legs caked with that peculiarly foul-smelling Jordan River mud, my belly gnawing me from nerves and hunger both, blundering about on a worn-out, skittish mare, trying to keep her from crushing some pilgrim new-washed of his sins under her hooves and thus sending him straight to Gan Eden, when I saw a man sitting by a campfire. He was bent forward. From the way his shoulders shook, I could tell that he was weeping.

I started to go on by him, when suddenly, unaccountably, everything about him was familiar to me. I danced Bedu in close. Then I sat there looking at him, so long and hard that my gaze, boring into him, performed its curious alchemy inside my mind, and caused him to look up. His little blue eyes locked with mine, and something very close to madness flamed in them. His hand flashed downward toward the hilt of his dagger. But my voice itself, the weary calm in it, stopped him.

"I shouldn't do that, if I were you, Yehudah," I said.

Yehudah ish Kriyoth took his hand away from his *sica*; sighed; said: "You're right, master. *You* did nothing. You merely butchered a Roman swine who'd killed too many of our people already. You didn't make her throw herself down that stair. And from what Olympia says—"

"Olympia?" I said.

"Her slave girl. A mixed Greek-Syrian bitch that I make use of, and obtain information from, once I've worn her out. Bought for Shelom by this uncircumcised dog, Telemarchos—"

"The uncircumcised, I'll grant you. The dog, no."

"He stole her from *you!* And yet—"

"How could he steal from me what was never mine? There is but one man in all of earth she loves, Yehudah. Even when she *thought* she was fond of me, it was because—"

"You look alike. I know. That's why I came down here. To find him, to bring him back, to force him to—"

"But you lost him in this stinking herd of superstitious cattle. I know, Yehudah. So did I—"

"But I didn't," ish Kriyoth raged. "I found him, master! Only he—he—"

"What, Yehudah?" I whispered.

"Refuses to come! Says Shelom can wait! That he must be about his father's business. And that that business requires him to go and fast and pray in the wilderness of Judea—you know that wild country near Lake Asphaltides, don't you?"

"Aye," I said. "Farewell, Yehudah!"

"Nathan!" he cried. "My master! Where are you going?"

"After him, of course. No man could live one hour in that country under a noonday sun. Unless he finds a cave for shelter, he'll—and even so, there's no water. None at all. You go back to Nazareth, Yehudah. Tell my Uncle Hezron I'll return as soon as I can—"

I spent the remainder of that night at the Essenes' monastery at Khirbet Qumrân. My ex-companions welcomed me back with simple goodwill. And, at the first hint of dawn, I began my search for Yeshu'a ha Notzri.

I didn't find him that day, nor the next, nor the next. But on the fourth day, the kites and vultures were circling above him, and that led me to him.

You have no idea what that country is like. There is nothing worse, not even your Tartarus. Our Sheol, our Gehenna combined, couldn't begin to match it. The wind blows off the Dead Sea, laden with salt crystals, and half blinds your eyes within minutes. The sun is a naked, blazing ferocity. The rocks are all jagged, sawtoothed, destroying the stoutest sandals before an hour is out, bringing blood from a man's feet two minutes after the protection of leather is gone. And, as I'd told ish Kriyoth, once the rainy season is over, there is not one drop of drinkable water to be found, not anywhere from one end of that murderous waste to the other.

So, when I found Yeshu'a, he was a pitiful sight. He'd torn off strips from his robe and bound them around his lacerated feet. He wasn't even trying to walk anymore. He was sitting there under that blazing sun, talking to himself, or to something his heat-stricken mind told him was there.

"No!" he was saying fiercely. "Get you gone, Satan! You shall not tempt the Lord, your God!"

I went up to him and dismounted. I took him by the hand. He flashed me a smile of dazzling sweetness, and said quietly: "I knew you would come, Suriel. . . ."

I was so startled I almost dropped his hand. For Suriel is the Angel of the Presence.

"Suriel?" I said.

"And that's great Metatron with you, isn't it? I give you greetings, Angels of my Father. Greetings to you, Michael, Gabriel, Rafael, Uriel, and Sandalfon. You came in time. Samaël[9] had me much troubled. He came with his hosts. Ashmodai and Lilith, the night-lying demon, were leading them. But I bested them. I bested them all!"

As I raised him up, my eyes were blind-scalded, both because I loved him and from the bitterness of my despair. How could a madman drive out a woman's madness? In the name of everything unholy, how?

I got him up on Bedu somehow, and mounted behind him, holding him up with my two arms about his waist. All the way back to the monastery, he babbled in his delirium as the sunstricken will: how Samaël/Satan had tempted him to turn stones into bread in order to still the pangs of his hunger; how he'd been borne aloft on Samaël's black wings and shown all the kingdoms of this world; how Satan had promised him dominion over them all, if he'd stoop that once to demonolatry; how the Lord of Evil had then set him upon the parapet of

the Temple in Jerusalem, saying: "If you are the Son of God, throw
yourself down; for Scripture says: 'He will give his angels orders to take
care of you;' and, again: 'They will support you in their arms for fear
you should strike your foot against a stone—' "

"Then I said to him," Yeshu'a's voice soared up, rich and strong,
" 'You are not to test the Lord your God!' "[10]

"I know," I whispered; "I heard you, Yesu—"

By the time I got him to the monastery, he wasn't raving anymore.
He was unconscious, slumped over against my arms so that I had all
I could do to hold him in the saddle. At my outcry, a crowd of novices
came and lifted him down. They bore him to one of the cells, and
went to get the Medical Paqid.

That wise man looked at Yeshu'a and shook his head.

"Four days in the wilderness?" he said. "Then he'll die. I've never
known any man to survive more than two. Even so, most of them don't
recover their wits. That sun broils a man's brains inside his skull,
leaving him—mad."

"But you must save him, Holy Paqid!" I wept. "You must! Too many
things depend upon this life! A woman's wits and—"

"Perhaps even yours, son Nathan?" the Paqid said dryly. "To say I
must save him is to ask too much of me, and perhaps even of God.
What I must do, nonetheless, is to try—"

Thereupon, he got to work. He bathed Yeshu'a, oiled his body to
ease the terrible blisters the sun had raised on it, despite the fact that
to oil the skin is against their teachings.[11] Then he forced a few drops
of water down the unconscious Nazarene's throat. He turned to me.

"I charge you, son Nathan," he said, "to give him six drops of water
every two hours. Nothing more. If you give him more at any one time,
he will go into convulsions, and die. If you fall asleep, and omit the
water, he may die of dehydration. Can I trust you, my son?"

"For him?" I said. The way I said it, made of my question an answer.

"Very well," the Paqid said. "If he regains consciousness, you can
give him a spoonful. If he stays conscious, increase the amount by
another spoonful every hour. Then in the morning, give him a cup of
water. By noon of the first day that he has stayed awake for at least
six hours, let him drink all he wants. After that, you may feed
him. . . ."

"I thank you, Holy Paqid," I said.

But it wasn't even that simple. Instead it was a torture of waiting, a
perfect horror of almost maddening alternations of hope and despair.
Yeshu'a was unconscious two whole days and nights. Except to an-

swer the most pressing needs of nature, I never left his side during all that time. Even when I did, I had a novice to stay with him.

He didn't toss about or rave. He just lay there. And, just as quietly, on the morning of the fourth day, he began to recover. But his recovery was very slow. It took a full thirty-six days, counting from the morning I brought him into the monastery at Khirbet Qumrân, before he was well enough for us to start home again.

Strange. Thirty-six days in the monastery, plus the four he spent in the desert, suffering heat, hunger, thirst, sunstroke, delirium, madness, make a total of forty days in the wilderness, just as your Scripture says.[12]

I bought a scrawny mule for him to ride on. He wouldn't let me buy a horse. He accepted the mule only on the condition that once we'd got back to Galilee, I should put that ugly beast out to pasturage long enough to cover its bones, then work it, on my Uncle Hezron's place. That is, he'd take it as a loan, not a gift.

"You're too proud, Yeshu'a!" I said to him.

He shook his head, smiled at me.

"No, Nathan; it isn't pride," he said softly. "You know me better than that. Perhaps I've been exposed to Yaakob's Essene friends too much; but it seems to me they're right about the possession of worldly goods. I don't need a mule. I don't need anything but time—enough time to—"

"What?" I said.

But his smile had darkened.

"You'll see," he said.

On the way up to Galilee, we didn't talk much. I asked him about his family. What I wanted to ask him, I didn't dare: the truth about the mystery—or scandal—surrounding his birth. So I put the question to him in another way, phrasing it so that if he answered it, he'd be forced, all unwittingly, to tell me what I wanted to know.

"Yeshu'a," I said, "why weren't *you* dedicated to the priesthood instead of Yaakob? You're the eldest and—"

He frowned.

"I don't really know, Nathan," he said. "I've guessed that there was some—trouble, between my mother and my father, over me. And my father wouldn't. Later, when I was about six years old, he changed his mind. I remember that I did something, said something—I don't know, or remember what it was—and he stood there staring at me like a madman. Then he took me in his arms and kissed me a hundred times, I'd swear, and wept. He kept saying, 'Yesu! Yesu! My son! My son! Mine!'

Then he got up from there and went to look for my mother. I followed him. When I came in the house, he was kneeling before my mother like a slave, kissing her hands and crying. I heard him say, 'Forgive me, Miriam! I've been a fool—' and then my mother raised him up and kissed him. She was crying, too. But you know *her*, Nathan! All she said was: 'Hummph! What *man* isn't, Yosef? Go call the children. It's time for the noonday prayers.' And, after that, as far as my father was concerned, nothing was too good for me. . . ."

"You loved him very much, didn't you?" I said.

He bowed his head, looked up again. Even then, even after so many years, his eyes were wet.

"With all my heart," he said. "In my father, I was blessed, Nathan."

"But not in your mother?" I said.

He thought about that.

"Yes," he said; "yes. In Mother, too. She's a good woman, Nathan. Of course she irritates me. As I do her. It's mutual. Let her lose a penny, and she'll turn the whole house upside down to find it, in spite of the fact that among all our earnings, she's managed to save up quite a little hoard.[18] To me, she's too occupied with this world; to her, I'm too little. One of the reasons I came away was to avoid quarreling with her anymore over Yohannah—"

"Your little sister?" I said. "But why should you quarrel over that sweet child, Yeshu'a?"

He smiled.

"You haven't seen her in a long time. She isn't a child anymore. She's seventeen, now, Nathan. Quite pretty. And, at the moment, as girls of that age will, every two weeks she's in love with a different boy. Or she would be, if Mother would let her alone! The trouble is that Yohannah's latest light of love is a totally illiterate farm laborer who hasn't a denarius. I don't approve of him, either; largely because I'm sure he's going to be a swinish lout all the rest of his days. But if Mother would shut up for an instant, Yohannah would forget him, as she has all the others. Only, my mother's not very smart, Nathan. She screams the house down, demands that I—"

He stopped short, in some confusion, stared at me. A tide of color rose in his face.

"That you?" I prompted.

"That I—bring *you* over to dine, Nathan. You who are handsome, cultured, and *rich*."

I looked at him, grinned.

"I accept the invitation with pleasure, Yesu! Especially since you say that little Yohannah's got to be—"

"Pretty? She has. Only, Nathan, my friend, you can't accept my invitation, because—I haven't offered it."

I stared at him, and hot anger rose and beat inside my skull.

"You mean you think I'm not good enough for your sister, Yeshu'a?" I said.

"I don't think it," he said quietly, "I know it. And not because she's my sister. You're not good enough for any decent girl, Nathan. What you did with Shelomith—was bad enough. But your adultery with the wife of the Epitropos was even worse. For one thing, it was cowardly. You knew the people wouldn't stone you for it as they would have if she'd been Jewish. You are—my brother, and I love you. But your sins cause me great sorrow. Have you no care for your soul? Don't you think it's about time you mended your ways, began to live a clean life?"

I was furious. I opened my mouth to say: "I saved your life, and now you reproach me! Sheol take you, Yeshu'a, I—"

But I couldn't. I simply couldn't. The anger drained out of me. Under his gaze, with those great eyes of his boring into me, searching my soul, stripping it naked, all I felt was—shame. Deep, abysmal, abiding shame. In a way, I had caused Helvi's death. I had killed, to my certain knowledge, at least three men—no, more, if I counted, as I had to now, those I'd cut down in the games at Rome. I had cost Shelom her child. I had left Claudia weeping her poor, sinful little heart out, totally disconsolate.

In spite of myself, my eyes hazed over, salt-stung, half blind. I bent my head. Then I felt his arm about my shoulder.

"Don't weep, Nathan," he said; "I didn't mean to hurt you—"

"You didn't," I said. "Or at least you couldn't, if what you said weren't true. Swine have no mirrors, so they don't suffer from what they are, since they can't see themselves. But you turn your eyes on me, and they become mirrors, Yesu! I see my soul reflected in them. And the sight's not pretty. In God's name, brother! What—"

"Don't blaspheme, Nathan," he said. "Why don't you go up into the hills behind your uncle's place, and pray? That helps, you know. God will give you the strength to lead a better life. You have goodness in you, that I know—"

"Yeshu'a—" I said to him then.

"Yes, Nathan?"

"If I—I demonstrate to your satisfaction I've reformed, would you withdraw your objection to my marrying Yohannah?"

He smiled at me.

"How do you know you'd even want to?" he said. "You haven't seen her in years."

"Don't need to see her. That she's *your* sister is enough. I'll love and cherish and honor her all my days."

He put out his sun-blackened hand and let it rest on my arm.

"Yes, Nathan," he said; "though chiefly to give you some reason to try to lead a cleaner, better life. Beyond that, I can guarantee nothing. You'll also have to win her love. I warn you that will be difficult. She —as who hasn't, hereabouts!—has heard in great detail the story of your sins—"

"Including those I didn't even commit. I'm supposed to have fathered upon Shelom the child my folly caused her to lose, am I not?"

"Yes," he said.

"I am—guilty of Claudia, Yeshu'a. I'm ashamed of that; but I am. Of Shelomith, I am innocent. I swear that by the Name!"

"Don't swear, Nathan. It's an ugliness. And, between us, unnecessary. I accept your word. Poor Shelom! I only hope I can help her—"

"You can!" I said at once. "You have—strange powers, Yeshu'a. You're the only person who can quiet Miriam, the Migdalene. When those Sebastian swine had bound me to the cross, she happened by, and knelt and worshiped me in your name as though I were a god! She thought I was you. We do look alike, you know. . . ."

"Yes," he said; "and when you've let your hair and beard grow as the Law requires, we'll be even more twinned. As for Shelom, I'll try. But I haven't any strange powers, Nathan. Truly I haven't—"

"Oh yes, you have!" I said.

We came up to Cæsarea together. When we got to Telemarchos' house I could see Yeshu'a's eyes were sick with trouble, filled with self-doubt. Some time during his slow convalescence from heat stroke, dehydration, and starvation, a goodly part of that perfect surety of self, that calm, confident belief in his mission, in his powers, had gone from him.

It was my good fortune, or my unpardonable crime—for who can say with certainty which it was? And evil Pilatus posed the greatest question ever asked!—to restore it.

I put my hand on his shoulder, gripped it, looked him in the eyes, said: "Go on, Yesu! You can do it. Only you of all men under heaven can."

He smiled at me, but that smile was doubtful and shy.

"I hope so," he whispered, and went into the house.

Half an hour later (half an eternity had gone screaming along my nerves) Yeshu'a ha Notzri came out again, leading my Shelomith by the hand. One look at her, and pity tore me with iron claws. My heart, my bowels bled. She was a walking skeleton, thinner than Claudia had been when bar Abbas finally released me. She was palsied all over; her midnight hair was streaked with white. But her face was still beautiful; not even the scar my uncle's whip had left across it could mar that. Only now it had the beauty of a saint's, enduring martyrdom by starvation. But her eyes—her eyes!—Blessed be Yesu the Nazarene through all eternity!—were cool and sane.

Yeshu'a smiled at her.

"Who is this, Shelom?" he said.

"Nathan," she whispered.

I didn't say anything. I couldn't. How can a man talk when he's stopped breathing?

"And I?" he said.

"Yisu," she said, and her voice made the air, the house behind her, the solid earth, melt and flow away. It was tenderness; the thing, itself. The quality of unutterable longing.

I died. Sheol take you! You think a man dies but once? I died that day I found Helvi in that tub. I died this golden morning, hearing Shelom make all the echoes, nuances above and below the range the human voice is capable of go vibrant with a desire—a love—so anguished, so agonizing that the "No!" that never reached my tongue, my lips, was, even though suppressed, nonetheless a cry of desolation and of pain. And, though I didn't know it then, I was to die again.

"And this?" Yeshu'a held it out to her.

"A bundle of—of rags," she got out.

"And your baby?"

"Dead. I lost it when I fell down the stairs the day I thought—"

"What?" his voice was harsh now, stern.

"That—Nathan—had been—killed."

"You haven't got us—confused with one another anymore?" I said.

"No, Nathan," she whispered.

"What are you going to do now?" Yeshu'a asked her.

"Go back to—to Beth Anya. To—my husband. Beg his—forgiveness. Be—a good—and faithful wife to him—all the rest of my days—"

And it was then, at that precise instant, that I began to hate Yeshu'a ha Notzri a little. I didn't stop loving him. I simply hated him on top of that. Or beneath it. I wouldn't know.

For one of the things that Shelomith and I had talked about, during the time I lay all but helpless in the Prætorium, was her husband. What he was like. The kind of man he was. Good? Of course he was good! But have you lived your thirty-nine years without learning how often men can be good and still, at the same time, insufferable? If the two qualities aren't always combined. Which was what I was thinking as I looked at Yeshu'a now.

"Yesu—" I said; and he, patiently: "Yes, Nathan?"

"You can't do this. You can't!"

His face darkened. Some of that explosive, terrible wrath of his that your pious scribes so conveniently forget when they write about him now, got into it.

"Why not, Nathan?" His voice was quiet, but lightning crackled in it.

"Because she'll be back in the streets—or in a whorehouse in half a year. Less. Don't you know *anything* about people, Yeshu'a?"

He stared at me, whispered: "You're saying that—men and women —have no powers of will—no control over—"

"Themselves? Almost precisely that, my brother! As far as the flesh is concerned, at least, so little that they don't count, you monster of piety. Which is why the institution of marriage is necessary. Not just for children. But to cool the heat, the ardor of the blood before it makes us run wild! Have you *never* felt desire?"

He bowed his head, looked up at me again.

"Yes," he said, "terribly."

"And?" I grated.

"I mastered it," he said. Like that. As though he were saying: "I drank a cup of water." Or "I washed my hands."

"You—you aren't human!" I howled at him.

Then I heard Shelom's voice: "No, Nathan. He's—an angel. Half, anyhow. I told you that."

"He's a monster!" I said. "He'd send you back to an old fool, forty years older than you are, all but impotent, a bore, and what's worse, a talkative bore, who—"

"Nathan," Yeshu'a said.

"Yes, Yeshu'a!"

"Don't judge others, unless you want to be judged yourself."[14]

I glared at him.

"I can stand judgment, Yesu! I'm a sinner, all right. A lecher, a drunkard, a murderer, if you will and—an adulterer. But, thereby— human. Thereby knowing, instructed by my own, that the flesh is weak and must be helped to virtue, not *ordered* to it! You—you demand perfection of people! I tell you, my brother, nothing's more cruel than that. You'd have me—have Shelom—lead blameless lives? All right, I'll tell you how, and only how that can be done!"

"All right," he said evenly. "Tell me, Nathan."

"Find me, help me find a wife I'll love so much that I can see no other face. Don't expect a starving man not to steal! Obtain a divorce

for Shelom from that ancient, creaking fool her father sold her to because he was in debt, and the prospective bridegroom promised to pay
his debts in exchange for his daughter. Then find her a young husband,
handsome and gay, who'll tease her, pet her, sing love songs to her—
wear out a mattress with her every night, so that the blood will flow
sweet and quiet through her veins and she'll stop dying by inches of
love for *you*, my friend! I tell you—"

He looked at me, and his face was as stern as YHWH's must have
been on the mountaintop, as He gave unto Moses the Tablets of the
Law.

"Marriage is sacred, Nathan," he said. "Whom God has joined together, man must not separate."[15]

I should have given up then, but I tried once more.

"Shelom," I said. "You can't! You *know* you can't!"

She looked at him then, and her eyes were a glory.

"Yes, I can, Nathan," she said. "For him—I can do anything!" Then,
very quietly, she turned and went back into the house.

"Yeshu'a!" I said to him then, tears in my throat, almost imploring.
"You can't do this! You can't condemn her to spend the rest of her life
with that pious old fool!"

He looked at me.

"Enough, Nathan!" he said, and that terrible authority that he had
in reserve always, spoke to me out of his eyes like lightning, made
brazen thunder of his voice. "You cannot make of Shelom an adulteress
again. I won't allow it. For truly, I say to you: A man who divorces his
wife and marries another commits adultery; and anyone who marries
a woman divorced from her husband commits adultery in his turn!"[16]

I gave up then. I, like all men born of women, was powerless against
him when he stood tall in that power of his, that awful simplicity that
cut through to the bitter bone of things, and counted not what hurt it
did to tender flesh.

"All right, Yeshu'a," I said tiredly; "have it your own way." Then:
"You aren't angry at me, are you?"

"No," he whispered.

I shot a glance at him and saw that he wasn't. That he'd had one
of his dazzlingly swift changes of mood that made him so difficult to
understand. He was looking at me now with a questioning, speculative
gaze; and I should have sworn some of that doubt of self I'd thought
I'd ridden him of, lingered still in his eyes.

"Nathan," he said; "may I keep the mule until tomorrow?"

"You may keep that ugly beast forever, as far as I'm concerned," I said. I was staring at the door through which Shelom had gone. I pitied her with all my heart.

"No, just until tomorrow," Yeshu'a said.

"All right," I said tiredly. "Let's go, Yesu. It's far to Nazareth, still. . . ."

You know what he did? That same night, instead of going home, he rode over to Migdal-Nunaya, and cast all seven devils out of that howling mad woman, Miriam.[17]

But the legion of fiends that shrieked inside my heart, he couldn't reach. Perhaps because they were truly part of me. A man is less simple than he thought. We need our devils, too.

Cast them out, and you maim us.

Book IV

In which I become more deeply involved in the affairs of Yeshu'a the Nazarene, witness some miracles, work two myself; and, at the cost of considerable hurt to my poor flesh, acquire myself a bride.

Chapter XVI

THE WINTER that encompassed—by your Roman calendar, of course—the end of the fourteenth and the beginning of the fifteenth years of Tiberius Cæsar's reign, had been an exceptionally rainy one; so much so that it seemed that nature, out of some inner sense of balance, wanted to make up for the drought of the previous summer. In Judea, at least as far as I was concerned, the almost continual downpour had had no more serious effect than to slow the work upon Pilatus' aqueduct to the extent that I hadn't been able to complete it until spring; but, to the north, in Galilee, and especially on my Uncle Hezron's estate, it proved a near disaster.

All my uncle's terraces had been damaged by the great sheets of water pouring down from the hills on and behind his domain. Even our lake had overflowed at one time, with the result that much valuable topsoil had been washed and scoured away from our best vineyards and from our orchards of fruit trees, both of which stood on terraces cut into the slopes of the hills, since, naturally enough, we reserved the richer lowlands for the more important grain crops and vegetables as the custom was in Galilee.

So it was hardly to be wondered at that, on my return from my errand of mercy, I found my Uncle Hezron—by nature inclined to a melancholy that neither the loneliness of his life nor the behavior of his lone, dearly beloved nephew were calculated to ameliorate—in a state bordering upon despair.

Therefore, I decided to do something about the condition of the estate. In sober fact, I had to. For, to follow my father's example and to enter into the priesthood as cynically as he had, or more so, because he, at least, retained some faint vestiges of belief, while I had none, seemed to me an outrage against my personal integrity, my dignity as a man. And the only other two professions I had any command of, those of a professional scribe and a builder of aqueducts, were certain to keep my belly constantly groaning from hunger. A scribe simply wasn't paid enough to live in the rather luxurious manner to which I had become accustomed; and, since Cæsar had sent out another engineer to the *Cohors Italica* to replace the one whose death had given me the opportunity of building Pilatus' aqueduct, I wasn't likely to get a chance to construct another watercourse as long as I lived. Now the choice between almost any kind of work and starvation is easy enough; but in my case, it was made easier still by the fact that I actually liked farming, and preferred country life to being cooped up in the city. In any event, to end my days submerged in the miserable boredom of my Grandfather Bœthus' countinghouse, the sole other chance I had, was the one thing I wasn't going to do. I honestly believe I would have starved first, so much did I hate the very idea.

My Uncle Hezron's estate would afford me opportunity enough, for it was one of the biggest in Galilee. Managed right, it would provide us with real wealth. But it wasn't being managed right. My uncle's methods were too conservative to permit us to get the profits, the yields from the really rich and fertile land he owned, that we should have. I knew, from my year with the Essenes, what scientific farming could do, even on lands as miserable as theirs were. The same excellent methods applied to my uncle's wonderful stretch of fields would perform miracles. I knew the methods. I'd learned them firsthand working on the community farm at Ain Feshkha under the direction of the Agricultural Paqid of the Qumrân sect. All I needed to apply them were men and money. Or rather money and men, in that order. For once I'd pried the money out of Uncle Hezron, I could easily hire the men. But when I opened the subject for discussion, they must have heard him yelling as far south as Idumæa.

"Money! For what? To procure yourself another harlot? Or a whole brothel full of strumpets? To spend your nights in drunkenness and wallowing with the Procurator's wife in Cæsarea?"

I have an antic sense of humor. I couldn't resist saying: "That didn't cost me anything, Uncle. Not even a quadrans or an as. Quite the contrary. And you've given me an idea! If you don't advance me the miserable three or four minae I need, I'll go to dear Claudia. She'll be most happy to let me have—"

My uncle actually tore his *simlah* robe, so greatly was he outraged.

"A he-whore!" he roared. "A male harlot! Don't tell me that vile Roman strumpet actually paid you to—to—"

"To do what, Uncle?" I said, my voice all sweet boyish innocence.

"Elohïm and Adonai!" my Uncle Hezron screamed.

"Neither one," I said solemnly; "Eros and Aphrodite, maybe. A little Astarte. Just a touch of Ba'al—"

Uncle Hezron lifted his staff, brought it crashing down. Only my training as a retiarius saved me from a broken head. I danced away from his blows until he was so out of breath that he could no longer strike or speak. Then I stood there grinning at him a long moment before I said: "My revered and respected Uncle Hezron, I plan to marry soon—"

He brought one great brush of an eyebrow down over one baleful eye and glared at me out of the other. "Who?" he croaked.

"Yohannah bath Yosef," I said recklessly. "Yeshu'a's little sister. That is, if she'll have me—"

"Hummmphf!" my uncle snorted. "Don't see why not! Yeshu'a is a good lad; but the rest of 'em are *amme ha aretz* and dirt-poor to boot—"

"Aha!" I said. "Now you've conceded me my point! Since the dear child cannot bring me other dowry than her sweet person, it behooves me to have a thought about my future, don't you think? Starting with this latifundium which you, Rab Hezron, respected Uncle, have let go to wrack and ruin—"

He stared at me in outraged astonishment.

"I'm not responsible for acts of God, Nathan!" he said. "And that's what those rain storms were!"

"True," I said. "Man cannot control the weather. But if, in times of drought, he can bring water from three stades away, in wet spring weather like this, he can—"

"What?" my uncle growled.

"Do a number of things, all of which require workmen, Uncle. Who, in their turn, require wages. Of course we can piddle and fiddle away at it for half a lifetime with the hands we have. Or you can let me have four minae, exactly one hundred shekels,[1] with which to hire one hundred *l'qutoth*[2] for as long as I need them. Day laborers, Uncle. A few women to cook and wash for them, not for—" I started to say something absolutely outrageous, but I changed my mind—"not for lascivious purposes . . ." I finished lamely.

I could see from the expression on Uncle Hezron's face that I was convincing him now. Since I'd built him the aqueduct, he was beginning to concede that I wasn't altogether worthless.

"Sit down, Nathan," he said quietly; "tell me what you propose to do—"

By the time I'd finished, he was almost smiling. I was going to re-terrace all the slopes with retaining walls of stone. At intervals of every dozen feet, I was going to leave a drainage opening, so that the press of water behind them in the rainy seasons wouldn't tumble them down, as it had the old ones. That done, I proposed a major earth-moving project: my *l'qutoth*, armed with shovels, would spade the accumulated mud washed down from the hills onto our flatlands up into carts, and carry it back where it came from in the first place. There, well mixed with a compost of manure and rotted leaves, it would make the finest orchards and vineyards in all Galilee.

Uncle Hezron was tightfisted and a conservative; but he knew sense when he heard it. And, being a practical dirt farmer, he put his finger on the one weakness of my scheme at once.

"Carts," he said. "We'll need dozens of them—four and five times more than we've got. And only temporarily, nephew. So it'll make no sense to buy them—"

"I know," I said; "I've thought of that. But did you ever see a farm that didn't have one or two laid up for repairs? I'll get Yeshu'a or Yaakob—or, if they can't leave the shop, as most likely they can't, Shimeon, Yose, and Yehudah to repair them, at *our* cost, Uncle, on the condition that their owners lend them to us for the duration of the work—"

"Fair enough," Uncle Hezron said. "Draft animals?"

"We'll have to hire them," I admitted.

My uncle figured rapidly inside his head.

"Four minae won't be enough," he said; "I'll give you five. But one thing, Nathan!"

"Yes, Uncle?" I said.

"*You* supervise the work. Which means you stay out of Cæsarea, and also away from little Yohannah. She's a sweet child. Virtuous. Decent. Since you plan to marry her—and I reluctantly approve, though her family are humble folk, in view of the fact that your outrageous behavior has cost you any chance of marrying among our own class —leave her that way!"

"Uncle Hezron," I said quietly, "I'm going to tell you something strange: I haven't seen Yohannah since she was thirteen or fourteen years old."

"What!" my uncle said. "You mean that you—"

"Plan to marry a girl whom I know nothing about, except that she's the sister of the man I love like a brother. I believe her to be good, dutiful, pure, and not uncomely. But, from what I've seen of love, it seems to me the worst possible reason for getting married. Besides, my love has unfailingly brought disaster to every woman upon whom I've bestowed it. Helvi. Shelom. Claudia—"

The glare was back in Uncle Hezron's eyes. His right brow crashed down like a thundercloud.

"You said the bastard Shelom lost at the games—" he began grimly.

"Wasn't mine. I repeat it. If you want me to, I'll swear by the Name. But only because she left me, so that the burden of her reputation wouldn't ruin my life. Out of a certain generosity, Uncle. She loved me. She proved that, at the games."

"Hummmphf!" Uncle Hezron said; but his tone wasn't entirely scornful. "And this—imperial adulteress of yours?"

"Lies ill abed now, because I left her. Not because I didn't love her, Uncle. I did. With me, she was at least becoming something very fine. But there was no future in that. And I'm—tired—of the life I've led. I'd like to see a good woman, my wife, sitting by that fire now, carding and spinning, with my sons playing about her skirts. I'm sick to death of—of disorder, impermanency, lack of peace. Since, with the women I love, I never find those things, I'm prepared to sacrifice love, Uncle Hezron. But I must marry. Can't let the banim Matthya die out, you know. Ours is a great strain—poets, prophets, warriors—"

"You're warlike enough," Uncle Hezron said. "Did yourself a lot of good hereabouts with the younger men by killing Pilatus' butcher. All the poor devils sent against him were Jewish prisoners, as you know. And Shelom's fainting and falling down those stairs has helped you more than it's hurt with the women. I've heard things that—"

"What things, Uncle?" I said.

"Things you won't hear from me! You're arrogant enough a gamecock now! But, Nathan—"

"Yes, Uncle Hezron?"

"I told you to stay away from that child. I take that back. You'd better call. Have you spoken to Yeshu'a?"

"Yes, Uncle. He approves—with reservations. He wants to see some evidence that I've retired from the competition to gain the prize as Champion Whoremonger of Galilee—"

"What competition? You've won the prize already," Uncle Hezron snorted. "And that of Judea as well! Hundreds of people standing in the street staring at her bedroom window while you—"

"Performed in my own inimitable style," I quipped; then, soberly: "There'll be no more of that, Uncle. I promise you."

He stared at me; saw I meant it.

"Good!" he said. "Now you get over there. This business of the carts will provide you with excuse enough. Put on your best robes, a bit of jewelry. Ride Bedu. Fortunately—or unfortunately—you're much too

handsome for your own good. A brave show never hurts with an
almah. . . ."[3]

"I hear and obey, Uncle!" I said.

But I was strangely reluctant to go. From what I remembered of
Yohannah, a sapling thin slip of a girl, all arms and legs and eyes topped
by a great mane of black hair almost like Shelomith's, I was afraid that
growing fond of her might prove too easy. And I didn't want to love
her. A curse lay upon the women that I loved. Had I not already had
proof enough of that?

Yet, in the end, I prepared to go. I bathed and perfumed myself
first, put on my best robes. Stuck a jeweled *sica* in my belt, hung a
heavy golden chain about my neck. I must have made a splendidly
barbaric sight, for as I rode away on Bedu, all the younger serving
wenches in my uncle's house came out and squealed at me.

I worried my addled head all the way to Nazareth over what excuse
I could give Yeshu'a that would cause him to invite me into the house,
which was behind the shop itself. "With my luck," I groaned inside my
heart, "sure as Samaël rules men's hearts, she's gone berry picking or
out walking with her latest light o' love or—"

I was wrong. My luck was magnificent. The first person I saw when
I turned into that street was Yohannah herself. She was leaning up
against the doorpost and crying her eyes out.

The clatter of Bedu's hooves on the cobblestones startled her. She
whirled, and, for a moment, I thought she was going to run. But then
she saw that I was neither a Roman cavalryman, nor even one of
Antipas' cutthroat swine.

She hung there, eyes and mouth both opened wide. My heart sank
to the soles of my Roman *caligulae*, the short, smart riding boots I
wore. She looked like what she was: a small-town Galilean wench.
Worse still, at that moment, her astonishment caused her to look like
what she wasn't—as I was very soon to learn—a stupid one at that.

"I give you greetings, Yu-Ann," I said, giving her name the Galilean
form, but not quite. You see, I cut the final *ah*[4] off it, which made it
sound languidly elegant, a trifle Hellenistic.

Her mouth closed, but her tear-brightened eyes got even bigger. Like
that, I could see what Yeshu'a meant. She *was* pretty; decidedly so.
Strange, but you can nearly always trust a brother's description of his
sister. The other way around, no. Most girls are blinded by their fondness for their brothers; but take away the possibility of desire—we're
not Egyptians, nor Ptolemies,[5] you know!—and a man sees a woman
clear.

Yohannah was pretty, and something more: she was also—interesting.

I suppose that at this point, some comparisons are in order. Physically, of the four women in my life (for Lydia never counted!) she was the least attractive. About Helvi, it is utterly impossible for me to be objective: she was my first real love, and all my memories of her are distorted by that fact. I know well she wasn't as beautiful as I thought her; most people who knew her called her "a pretty girl," though some were kind enough to add the qualifying adjective "very." But to me, she was, and remains, the most beautiful thing who ever drew the breath of mortal life. Shelom, now, was barbarous, splendid, exotic, gorgeous; her beauty was the sort that drives men mad; and no one who ever saw her—including Uncle Hezron—ever called her anything less than beautiful. For, oh, she was! She was!

Claudia—a pure and classic loveliness on your Grecian mold. She might have posed for a statue of Aphrodite except that she was rather too slim for your tastes, to judge from your sculpture. Strange: she was so perfect, so harmonious of line, so cleanly carved of feature that she looked—cold. The last thing on earth she was, really.

But as this child, this pretty Galilean child, stared up at me, I saw—intelligence, speaking with the voices of angels out of her great dark eyes. I saw—perceived, rather—that here was a person, with the force to match her mother's, and the mind to soar above all her brothers', save alone Yeshu'a's, effortlessly. Besides that, the way she looked—and she was comely enough, mind you; few Galilean *almahim* could have matched her in physical beauty—didn't matter. With a woman such as this, life would be pure paradise, or Sheol piled atop Gehenna, with the damned souls screaming round my bed. One or the other, with nothing in between. Which made the whole thing vastly interesting.

"I said, I give you greetings, Yu-Ann," I repeated a trifle sharply, the battle between us already joined, the tension already crackling like hidden lightning upon the dead still air.

"I return them, Nathan bar Yehudah," she said quietly. "And say, farewell."

"Farewell?" I said. "Are you going somewhere?"

"No," Yohannah said. "*You* are."

"I?" I said. "Where?"

"That's up to you, friend of my brother. Anywhere at all, as long as it's away from *here*."

I smiled at her, then. I had a good smile in those days. Many was the maid and matron who had told me so.

But she didn't waver. She said: "Be so kind as to leave me, Nathan; now."

I swung down from Bedu, came toward her. A lesser one would

have shrilled and scampered away by then. But Yohannah didn't move. She stood there looking at me with her eyes getting bigger and bigger until they almost eclipsed her tiny, heart-shaped face. But, when I was close enough, I could see the anger in them. It was cold and still —like—like frozen flame.

"Why do you want me to go away, Yu-Ann?" I said.

"Because I'm alone in the house. Mama and my brothers have gone after Yesu. To bring him back. They think he's gone mad."[6]

"Why do they think that, little Yu-Ann?" I said.

"Because he's left the shop. Now he's going around preaching—as though he were a rab. When he found out that Herod Antipas had put Yohannan Baptistes in prison, he—"

"Yohannan in prison!" I said. "I didn't know that!"

"There're a great many thing you don't know, my lord bar Yehudah! But now's not the time to talk about them. We've troubles enough in this family without your adding to them. Just when we were beginning to lift our heads a little, Yesu has to turn Galilean itinerant![7] Oh, the disgrace of it! So now, goodbye!"

"Now, Yu-Ann," I said gently; "that's no way to treat an old friend. . . ."

The icy wrath in her eyes took fire, flamed, crackled, stood tall.

"You're no friend of mine, Nathan bar Yehudah!" she said. "And you're becoming less one, every second that you stand there!"

"Why?" I said.

"Because you're—you. You've been here five minutes, at least. Long enough to cause talk. If you stay here another five, I'll be in serious trouble. Half an hour, I'd might as well go down to Kafer Nahum, and take *your* Shelomith's place in Nikos' Lupanar for all the reputation I'll have left. So will you do me the great favor of getting back upon that horse and riding away from here?"

I liked the way she said "*your* Shelomith." It had a trifle too much edge to it—a fine excess of bitterness. I knew then I had some hope.

I didn't say anything. The time for talk was past. What was needed now was action. I stepped in close to her, caught her face between the iron fingers of my left hand, bent and kissed her mouth. A good long time, before she tore it away from mine with a strangled sob.

I was poised to catch her hand as she swung it to slap my face. But she didn't even attempt to. Instead, she said in a tone of voice that was like broken glass grating over rock: "Don't go. Wait here a moment."

Then she whirled, and went back into the shop. Three minutes later, no more, she came back again. She had a basin in her hand, a clean white cloth, a jar of soft, homemade wood ash and olive oil soap. She put the basin down upon the doorstep. Then, with her great eyes locked upon my face, holding me like that as effortlessly as Yeshu'a himself could, she proceeded with slow ceremony, with appalling dignity, with ritual care, to scrub her mouth.

The insult was absolutely deadly. The rage that hit me was like a poniard hard-driven and quivering in my gut. But it was coupled with sickness. Because she had beaten me. This slip of a girl, armed and girt about with that monumental dignity of hers, had beaten me. By maintaining a self-control I'd never seen before in a woman. By showing me not anger, but contempt. And that knife wasn't in my big gut anymore. It was further down. Such things as this emasculate a man.

I turned away from her, marched back to Bedu, swung myself into the saddle with less than my usual grace. Sat there looking at her, until I saw that cold, still anger in her dark eyes thaw. But not into rage this time. Into—confusion? Pity? Remorse? I didn't know.

And I didn't need to. Something in me instructed me—Uncle Hezron would have called it my unclean cunning; I, by bonedeep knowledge of the ways of women; but it was something else, something deeper, even more worthy than either—what to say. So I said it, slowly, clearly, and with great calm:

"Farewell, Yohannah! Scrub away. Use a stronger soap. Put hot irons to your lips. But you'll carry the feel and taste of my kiss down to your grave—for all the good that it will do you now!"

Then I yanked Bedu's head about, and rode away. As I reached the corner, I looked back. Even from there, I could see the great tear streaks penciling her face. But I rode on without stopping. To have returned then, would have spoiled things, softened the impact of the blow I'd clearly dealt her. And I didn't want to soften it. I wanted her to reflect upon it, feel it like a bruise deep in her heart, her mind.

I rode away from Nazareth up the Roman road that runs through the village of Cana to Migdal-Nunaya, and from thence to Kafer Nahum. I went that way, because simple logic demanded that Yeshu'a should begin his preaching somewhere along that road, since it ran through the most thickly populated part of Galilee. I was terribly worried about him. The fool! Hadn't the news of Yohannan Baptistes being thrown into Herod's dungeon shown him what happened to anyone who attracted too much attention, now?

I was right. Before I got to the great town—almost a city, for even then, the word *kafer*, "village," no longer described it—of Nahum, I saw the crowds. They were immense; as great, or greater than those who'd followed Yohannan.

From my high vantage point on horseback, I could both see and hear Yeshu'a. He was preaching to the people in parables. I listened long enough to hear that he told them exceedingly well; but, though I have a collection of his words written by Matthya, the publican, I cannot remember which of the many parables therein contained he spoke on that particular day.[8] Besides, once I saw that there were neither soldiers nor any known spies about, I realized that the danger of his being arrested on that particular day was slight, and that his technique of speaking in parables was a wise one, so that even if he were hailed before Antipas, nothing rebellious could be proved against him. Therefore I had time. I began to look about for his mother and his brothers, so that I might talk to them about the necessary work of saving my uncle's farm. Despite Yohannah's icy and insulting rebuff of me, I was far from despairing, or losing all hope of winning her love. But, even if I should fail to win her, the work must go on. I had to wed, preserve my father's line. That was my sacred duty. I wasn't in love with little Yu-Ann yet; though, knowing myself, I sadly feared I could get to be; and in the worst of cases, should she reject me, I could easily find another winsome Galilean lass with less scruples as far as wedding a man of my fearsome ill fame was concerned, especially when my actual rank and reputed wealth were taken into consideration.

But I didn't find Yeshu'a's family at that moment. I might not ever have found them if a little group of women standing nearby had not let out an astonished gasp at the sight of me. I didn't know any of them, but the face of one, a really lovely woman about thirty or thirty-five years of age, was strangely familiar. "I've seen that one before somewhere," I thought, "but where? In the names of Ba'al and Beelzebub, both, where?"

And then, as though beckoned by my eyes, that woman separated herself from her companions and came up to Bedu's flank.

"Sir—" she said in a soft, dark-toned, honey-dulcet voice. "Who are you—that you look so very like our Lord?"

"Nathan bar Yehudah," I said shortly.

"Oh!" she gasped. "He—of whom they say—that—Shelom the harlot tried to kill herself over! And that the Epitropos' wife and—"

"Half a hundred more," I said wearily; "take care I don't add you to my list, O dark sister of my heart! Now tell me, who are those women?"

"That one's Yohannah, the wife of Chuza, Antipas' steward. That's Susannah, and that's Miriam, mother of Yaakob, that's Shelomith, and that's—"

"Enough!" I laughed. I need not mention, of course, that the Shelomith she indicated was not *my* Shelomith, any more than the Yohannah,

Chuza's wife, was *my* Yohannah. We have a strange paucity of women's names, which makes for great confusion. And the commonest name of all among us is Miriam. I've known at least twenty Miriams in my lifetime.

"Now tell me, lovely creature," I said, "to whom presently I shall offer my vagrant heart, just who are you?"

"Miriam," she said simply.

"Miriam what?" I said.

"Miriam of Migdal-Nunaya,"[9] she said.

I came very close to falling from the saddle. Of course I'd known that face! But this was the first time I could remember seeing it clean. She was well dressed, too, in simple robes that were nonetheless of rich stuffs. I knew she owned a latifundium, not much smaller than my uncle's, inherited from her father on his death; and it was a tribute to the superstitious awe in which mad people are held in Galilee that not a *zereth* nor a *tofah*[10] had been stolen from her boundaries. But she couldn't have put it back into cultivation yet. Since I'd brought Yeshu'a back from Judea, there simply hadn't been time.

"That's a very pretty dress, Miriam," I said.

"It was—my mother's," she said. "I found it in the great chest in my house. Oh, I might as well tell you, since you probably know all about me. I had to search for clothes when I went back home—after he, my sweet Lord, cast seven devils out of me. Before that I was mad. That's why I went around in rags and was so—so filthy. Ugh! So don't offer me your heart. I belong to him, and only him. Besides, I don't want your heart. It's a very wicked one, from all I've been told—"

"Oh, Sheol!" I said. "Tell me, Miriam Migdalene—do you know where I can find his mother and his brothers?"

"Yes," she said. "Get down from your horse, and I'll take you to them."

As I walked along beside the Migdalene, I couldn't help but stare at her. Clean, neatly dressed, her hair combed and perfumed, she was a woman of extraordinary beauty. But she wasn't—entirely present, not completely there—if you understand my meaning. Yeshu'a had calmed her, made her almost sane. I say *almost*, because there were signs that madness lingered in her still. Even her simplicity, her serenity —were odd; her total obliviousness to the grins and meaningful looks that were cast at her as she walked by my side. For Yohannah had been right: For a woman to be seen with me was to risk her reputation —so great and so widespread was my evil fame.

When we came up to the place where Yeshu'a's mother and brothers were standing, on the edges of the crowd, I could see the despair in their faces. Yaakob, of course, wasn't with them; to him, I realized,

Yeshu'a's behavior couldn't have been a cause for grief, because it differed but little from his own, except I'm sure he would never have thought of preaching. But, to the other members of the banim Yosef family, it was a disaster. You see, they were beginning to go up in life: the shop was prospering; Susannah, the elder daughter, had married very well indeed. People were beginning to consider them a cut above the *amme ha aretz*, the poor unlettered peasant stock from which they sprang; Miriam's ambitions for her sons were towering; and now here was Yeshu'a disgracing them all, descending to the level of the wild itinerant preachers whom the idle city mobs and ignorant country yokels delighted in. We produced a flock of these half-mad fanatics every year, spitting on people to cure them of their sicknesses, and performing all kinds of trickery, which the simple-minded Galileans saw as miracles. Of course it is written in the Talmud and Midrash that such learned doctors as Rabban Yochanan ben Zakkai and Eliezer ben Hyrcanus, his disciple, performed true miracles;[11] but though ben Hyrcanus was of my—and Yeshu'a's—generation, I never had the chance to see him. And, as for the wonders that Yeshu'a himself worked—and he *did* work wonders—I shall write of them at another time.

But now, seeing the tears misting his mother's eyes, I pitied her with all my heart. Yet I was a little angry with her, too. She was concerned with pride of place, with familial shame; while I was concerned with— saving his life. For what he was doing now, however innocently, was sure to get him hanged. Yohannan Baptistes, who had done no more than this, who had preached no more revolutionary doctrine than repentance of sin, was already chained in a dungeon in Herod Antipas' fortress at Machaerus; and anybody who knew how Antipas' mind worked wouldn't have given a fig for the Baptist's chances.

"Well, there they are," Miriam the Migdalene said; and turning, left me there. I was glad she was gone. Trying to talk to two Miriams at once would have been too great a strain.

I came up to where Yeshu'a's family stood, and bowed.

"My lady Miriam, the banim Yosef," I said, "I give you greetings, mother and brothers of our newest prophet!"

Instantly they whirled upon me, their faces black with anger. Then Miriam saw who I was, and her face softened.

"Don't make mock of us, Nathan, in the hour of our trouble," she said.

"I'm not," I said. "I honestly believe Yeshu'a is a Prophet, not merely a holy man like Yaakob. But, just as honestly, I think that these are no times for prophecy—that all exercising such powers as Yeshu'a possesses will get a man nowadays is the opportunity to decorate a cross with his poor carcass. That's why I came—"

Her broad, lined dark face paled a little.

"You think that—that the Romans—" she began.

"Or Antipas," I said dryly. "Yohannan Baptistes did no more, and look where he is now, my lady Miriam. All Israel is dry tinder waiting for a spark. And, all unwittingly, men like Yohannan and your Yeshu'a could provide it. The meek. The terrible meek, whose innocence is—deadly . . ."

"Now look, Nathan!" Shimeon began.

"I am looking, Shimeon!" I said. "And what's more, I have eyes with which to see. And what I see is that Israel should lie quiet, like a field left fallow, until the Romans destroy themselves, as they will, as the power-drunken always do. But I've traveled, lived abroad: in Athens, in Alexandria, in Rome—"

"Which is why men call you traitor, Nathan!" Yehudah ben Yosef said.

I shrugged.

"Words. If you send a coursing hound out to attack a lion, what happens to that hound, however brave? You were not yet born when the last revolt occurred, Yehudah, the one in which Archelaus, Herod's son, mingled the blood of three thousand Galileans with that of the sacrifices within the Temple itself. But ask any man of more than forty years of age how it was to see the roofs of the Temple buildings burning, and the Roman Dux Sabinus marching away with the Temple treasury, more than four hundred talents, in his hands. You're proud of Yehudah bar Hezekiah here in Galilee, but what was the result of his bravery? Sepphoris, his city, reduced to ashes, every inhabitant, man, woman, or child, sold as slaves. At that same time, two years before Yeshu'a and I were born, there was the slave Shimeon of Peræa, the shepherd Athronges in Judea, making themselves masters of the country until Varus came from Antioch in Syria with his legions. Ask my father what it's like to see two thousand men being crucified at the same time.[12] So many that no matter which way you looked from Jerusalem, the horizon was black with crosses, and the air itself darkened with the carrion birds come to beak their eyes, their poor blackened, swollen tongues, while yet they lived! I tell you, friends, that bravery without means is criminal folly. Call me traitor, coward, what you will; but I'll oppose any revolt against the Romans now. Not because I love those filthy swine—"

"Their women don't displease you," Yehudah sneered. "That you've proven, Nathan. Twice!"

"Stop it, Yehudah!" Miriam said. "Listen to Nathan! He speaks truth!"

"Their women don't displease me," I said quietly. "True. One I loved more than life, married her in the synagogue at Alexandria, by our law. The other—also I loved. Enough to sin—before Israel, and our God. Of which I have much shame; but that is neither here nor there, now. What is at hand is the fact that to arm a revolt now would be to condemn all Israel to death and slavery, which is why I, or you, or all of us have to stop Yeshu'a, persuade him from this folly—"

"My brother doesn't preach revolt, Nathan," Yose, the youngest, said.

"He doesn't have to. Let him mouth one unguarded word, and it'll start of itself. You know how these people are, Yose! But that's not the point. Listen to me, in God's Name! I love Yeshu'a. I want to see him live out his years. Don't you see, you fools, that he doesn't have to do anything more than he's doing now—attract attention, draw crowds like these—for Antipas to do with him what he's already done with Yohannan Baptistes? Who in the name of Heaven ever told you that a man had to be *guilty* of rebellion in Galilee to be hanged for it?"

They stared at me, appalled. All they'd thought of was their prickly pride, the shame of being laughed at as the family of a madman. Not this. Not this true and terrible danger.

"Nathan!" Miriam said. "Go to him! Tell him that—that we're here. Ask him to come to us!"

I held her with my eyes.

"Will he?" I said.

"I—I don't know!" she moaned. "He—he's so strange, Nathan! We've never been close. All his life I—I've quarreled with him. I wanted him to wed, to get grandsons for me, and he wouldn't. I wanted him to live —at least a little like other men. He's neglected the shop for years. He doesn't care whether we have anything to eat or not, he—"

"I know, Miriam," I said pityingly. "I'll go call him, now. Yose, hold my mare for me. . . ."

But I couldn't get anywhere near him, for the crowds. So I did the the next best thing: I asked the people to pass the word from one to another that his mother and his brothers were without the crowd, waiting for him. The people did so right gladly, happy to have a chance to do some small service for the new Prophet. By the time the message reached him, the distance was too great for me to hear it said to him. But I heard him, all right. He stood up, and his eyes flashed a wrath that made the man who'd brought my message tremble.

"Who is my mother?" he thundered. "Who are my brothers?" Then slowly, impressively, he waved a hand over the heads of the crowd. His voice deepened, darkened, as he said: "Here are my mother, and my brothers. Whoever does the will of God is my brother, my sister, my mother!"[18]

I came away from Kafer Nahum with them. I pointed out to them, truthfully, that the danger of Yeshu'a's being arrested by either the Romans or Herod Antipas was not immediate; I promised them that I would use whatever influence I had with Yeshu'a to get him to desist from this folly. But my words helped little. They were all downcast, angry, and terribly ashamed. I was simply angry. Yeshu'a's public rebuke to his family seemed to me both outrageous and uncalled for. To get their minds off it, I started telling them of my plans for Uncle Hezron's place, asked their help. They agreed readily enough. For one thing, I was willing to pay them well, and they needed the money. For another, even Yehudah and Shimeon, neither of whom particularly liked me, were a little chastened by Yeshu'a's action. Besides, the whole family knew I'd saved his life in the desert of Judea, because he'd told them that.

The business of the carts settled, there remained one great problem: that of Yohannah. I had sense enough to realize, for once, that cunning, deviousness, would get me nowhere. With these lowly uncomplicated people, honesty was not only the best, but the only feasible policy. But I hadn't counted upon two factors that, knowing men, I should have: plain rut-dog male jealousy, and the unexpected depth of Shimeon's and Yehudah's dislike for me.

That jealousy, that dislike, had a most understandable basis: Everything I was—rich, well born, even handsome—they would have liked to be; everything I'd done—traveled, drunk deep of life, fought and killed the bravest foemen, lain with the most excitingly forbidden of foreign women—titillated their dull imaginations, and awoke in them that most miserable of all emotions—envy. But I was too intent upon my course to realize that, then.

"My lady Miriam," I said, "would you oppose my paying court to—Yohannah? With the intention of marrying her, I mean?"

"What!" Yehuda and Shimeon bellowed in one voice. Yose said nothing. Yose had always liked me, been my friend, almost as much as Yeshu'a himself.

Miriam's great dark eyes—Yeshu'a's and Yu-Ann's were the same, and got from her—softened. Miriam, too, was fond of me. I was—within certain limits, of course—precisely the kind of man she had wanted Yeshua' to be. Besides, to the mother of a marriageable daughter, I had a great deal to recommend me: I was, on both sides, from almost princely family; and I was—or would be surely when I inherited from

my mother and my uncle, both—rich. In fact, though I knew from
Yeshu'a that Miriam had dreamed aloud of just this possibility, I don't
think she'd dared consider it seriously. The banim Yosef were *amme ha
aretz*, the outcast of Israel, those ignorant of Torah. Of them all, only
Yaakob and Yeshu'a could read or write their names, I was sure. That
Yohannah could, too; that Yeshu'a had taught her, never occurred to me.
Even among us, even among the highest families, few women could
read or write.

But my lifelong devotion to Yeshu'a must have given Miriam some
hope, my hurrying down to Judea to search for him had surely added
to it; and, as for my sins—no real woman is every truly or deeply offended by male sinfulness, with the sole exception of infidelity to her
fair self, which, without knowing it consciously was how Yohannah
looked upon my behavior, hence her fury. Women, my friend, are
merciless toward the frailties of their own sex, while on ours they cast
a most indulgent eye—one of the wise provisions of benevolent nature,
I believe.

"Nathan," Miriam said now, slowly, "are you—serious?"

"Absolutely," I said.

She went on looking at me; then she said: "You are a banim Matthya.
Of the House of Mattathiah, Nathan. The greatest in all Galilee."

"Hardly the greatest," I said.

"Yes. The greatest. And your mother is a bath Bœthus. The highest
priestly family."

"So?" I said.

"You're—very rich. We're poor. Ignorant—"

"Mother, stop it!" Shimeon said. "Haven't we been shamed enough
today? I tell you, Nathan, clearly, I'm opposed! You frequent the Roman Epitropos. You're his wife's lover! You made a scandal with the
harlot Shelom that—"

I looked him straight in the eye. Here, I had him. Him and Yehudah,
both. Not Yose. Yose was too young, too timid, too shy to—

"All right, Shimeon, you're opposed. And you, Yehudah?"

"Opposed!" Yehudah said.

"And you, Yose?"

"I—I don't know, Nathan," Yose faltered. "People say—"

"Too damned much!" I said. "So now, let's have this out. Yeshu'a,
the head of your family, since I must remind you, is not opposed to my
marrying Yohannah. I know that because I asked him first. He merely
asks that I try from now on to lead a clean life, which I mean to do—"

"Ha!" Shimeon said.

"All right, Shimeon!" I said. "You begin to tire me, you know! Let's

examine my sins: I eloped with the girl I loved, whose chastity was
beyond question, and married her, under our law. It's none of your
filthy-minded business, but Helvi came virgin to my marriage bed. My
sins with Shelom are totally nonexistent, whether you believe me or
not. I did not father the child she lost at the games. I have never had
carnal knowledge of her, nor of *any* harlot. Can you, either of you, say
the same? All right, you don't believe me. Let us put the matter, then,
upon another level. Shelomith left Nikos' Lupanar and followed me
throughout the land. Is it my sins that offend you, or your envy of
them? You, who waste half your wages and more at Nikos' place?
Would you find me nearer to your approval if I had had to seek Shelom
there, and pay her for her favors, as you do your strumpets? And, as
for the one sin I do confess to, that of Claudia, what boots it really, to
either of you? A woman loved me—enough to risk her high position and
her life. And which, my dear Shimeon, calls for more gallantry, manhood, nerve?—my dalliance with the Epitropos' wife, guarded by a full
Roman Legion, or yours with Akiba, the fishmonger's, guarded by nobody once her ancient, half-blind husband is out of sight? Where's the
keener sport, the greater danger, the possibility of truer delight? And
you, Yehudah—"

Yehudah raised his hand.

"I withdraw my opposition," he said. "Don't shame me before my
mother, Nathan!"

Miriam was glaring at them both.

"Fine thing! Fine thing!" she began. "A pair of—of lechers! My sons,
the whoremongers! I like this! I like it fine! Spending the money we
need on harlots! Why—"

"Miriam, my lady," I said, "leave them be. They're young, unmarried
—and men. Don't expect sainthood of them."

She turned upon me then, her eyes afire. You see, to her, I had already joined her family; I was her son-in-law, and she wasn't going to
let me off any easier than the others.

"And well does it seem, Nathan bar Yehudah," she said, "that you're
much too proud of your sins! I'll have to think well about this business
of my Yohannah's marrying you! Why—"

That was a little too much, and I lost my head. I'd had a bellyful
of these prickly peasant yokels by then.

"And I also, Miriam ha Yosef!" I said. "Or is it Miriam ha Pantera?
Oh yes, thinking's called for! Yu-Ann is, after all, *your* daughter; and,
like all men, wifely fidelity is a virtue that I prize!"

Her lips went absolutely white. She bowed her head. Those three big oafs stood there like the great stunned oxen that they were. Then Shimeon recovered. I saw his hand snake for his knife.

"Put that thing up, Shimeon," I said wearily. "Beyond the fact that you wouldn't have a chance against me, I set another, more important now: I won't fight you. If you can stomach killing a man who refuses to draw steel, go ahead. But I won't fight you. I can't."

"Put it up, Shimeon," Miriam said. Her voice was toneless, dead.

I did what I had to, then. I, of princely, priestly rank, knelt in the dust before her, took her hand.

"I have done many evil things in my life, my lady," I said, "but none more evil than this—none of which I am more ashamed!"

She stretched out her other hand, and let it rest on my head.

"Get up, Nathan," she said. "My son, Nathan. Who is impetuous, hot as fire, rash, and a fool. But not wicked. The wicked never humble themselves—and you're willing to. Now, tell me something: You say you're innocent of Shelom the harlot. Can you *prove* it?"

"No," I said, "I can't. But I swear it, by my mother's honor; by the Ineffable Name of God!"

"Don't swear," she said, and now I saw again where Yohannah got her dignity from. "Swearing is a wickedness. I believe you. Now hear this, Nathan, for the first time, and the last, from me, in all your life, for this shall never be mentioned between us again: Neither could I prove my innocence of that which I was accused of—And it almost—wrecked my life. Yet, I was innocent. And, being a woman, I suffered more. I'm suffering still. For that—shadow—almost cost me my husband's love, and *has* cost me my eldest son's. Because of it, Yeshu'a grew up—strange . . ."

"Mother!" Yose wept. "You don't mean—"

She smiled at him tenderly, through the great rush and glitter and scald of her tears.

"Yes, Yose; sweet Yose, my son, my son—who bears the name your father wouldn't give our firstborn because of this: Your mother was once young and giddy and a fool. But nothing more—nothing worse. I ask you to believe that, without proof, simply because you love me. Do you?"

"Yes, Mother!" Yose said at once.

She turned to the others.

"And you, my sons?"

They hesitated, just a shade too long, before they muttered: "Yes, Mother. . . ."

'You poor devils,' I thought, 'this is going to haunt you both, life-long—'

I went up to them.

"Let there be peace among us, my brothers," I said. "When I am angry, my tongue flies much too free. I beg your pardon, both of you, right humbly. And I ask you to consider this, as men who've worked long hours at backbreaking tasks, and still, despite your labors, have suffered privation, want, and the scorn of those who hold you their inferiors: What real harm can come to the House of the banim Yosef by linking itself through marriage to the House of the banim Mattathiah?"

Even stupid as they were, that got to them. They wanted to go up: here was the ladder! Who in Galilee would dare scorn a family any longer whose daughter had married into the House of Matthya? What doors would remain closed to them now? What opportunities couldn't this arrogant little gamecock of a brother-in-law—like him or not—provide them with the wealth at his command?

Sheepishly, they grinned at me.

"You're right, Nathan," Shimeon said. "All of us were a mite too hot with our talk. I welcome you into our family. . . ."

"And I," Yehudah said. "Sheol and Gehenna! A man's a man. As you said, our own robes are far from clean. Agreed. And here's my hand on it, brother!"

I took their hands. I even went further. I kissed them both, which startled them. They hadn't expected that from one so far above them.

But the problem, itself, remained. After all, it wasn't Yohannah's *family*, I wanted to marry, but her wild sweet self.

I took Miriam's arm.

"Please," I said; "walk apart with me a little, my lady—Mother! I must tell you, I must say—"

"All right," she said, "but you don't have to apologize more, Nathan. Let us forget all the hard words that have passed between us. I—like you. I think you'll make my daughter happy. And I shall be proud to have you for my son. But, tell me this: What does your *uncle* say? Have you—have you—"

"Asked him? Of course! He approves. You know how fond he is of Yeshu'a. He's all for it. Says Yu-Ann will cure me of my wildness. And that's just the rub!"

"What's the rub?" Miriam said.

"Yu-Ann. She—she despises me. I have a confession to make: I went to your place this morning. Of course I wanted to see her, but I didn't expect to find her alone. Or else I shouldn't have gone, I swear it! Actually, along with seeing her, I wanted to talk to Yeshu'a and the others about this business of repairing the carts. And, I hope you'll forgive me, but she was so pretty and sweet, that I—I kissed her—"

"And she slapped you blind!" Miriam said with a low, throaty chuckle.

"Would God she had," I groaned. "Worse than that: she went, got water, and washed her lips!"

"I see," Miriam said. "That's grave, isn't it?" She stood there, thinking. "Nathan—day after tomorrow, my cousin Tabitha's son is marrying Rebekkah bath Yehoiakim at Cana. You come. I extend the invitation now, in their names. Yohannah's one of the bridesmaids. Then, we'll see. . . . Of course, the wedding feast won't be much, because they're poor as we are, but—"

"I won't be interested in food," I said. "Yu-Ann's got me so terrified that—"

"Good!" Miriam laughed. "That's the way it should be! Lord, but I'm tired!"

I turned at once.

"Yose!" I called. "Bring Bedu here! That's it. Now help your mother up on her. . . ."

We came into Nazareth like that, with me walking, leading Bedu, and Miriam sitting sidesaddle, proudly, like a queen. One of the dearest of a woman's pleasures is the opportunity to kill her neighbors with pure envy; and it was that opportunity I provided Miriam ha Yosef then. But, as we turned into their street, Yohannah came out of the house and stood there, looking at us. That is, she looked at the others. At me, she glared.

"So," she whispered. "You've won Mother over! Well, it won't do you any good, I can tell you that!"

"Won't it, my lady wife-to-be?" I said; then I kissed her again, there before them all.

This time she did slap me, hard. I don't know which hurt my ears worse: her hot little hand, or her brothers' roars of laughter. But even that was progress of a sort, after all. At the wedding at Cana, I would make more.

Chapter XVII

THE HOUSE of the banim Lameth was a little white house set down in a grove of cypresses and poplars just outside of Kafer Cana, the village of Cana. It was a very poor house of very poor people, but now with the afternoon sun on it slanting through the trees it was beautiful. I sat there in the yard next to Yeshu'a ben Yosef, and I was happy. I hadn't been happy in a long time, so the feeling frightened me. It was a good feeling, soft and warm and true, and I was afraid of it.

"Yisu—" I said, calling him by that Galilean dialectical corruption of his name that neither of us had used since we were children.

He put his right hand on my shoulder, smiled at me, and said: "No, Nathan. Let's not talk about it anymore. You said once that I would do what I had to. Don't you remember that?"

"Yes," I said; and the happiness went away. "But they'll kill you, Yeshu'a! They'll put you in prison just like Yohannah—"

"They haven't killed him, at least," Yeshu'a said.

"But they will," I said morosely; "they will!"

Then I saw Miriam. She was sitting with her cousin Tabitha, the mother of the groom. They were talking about me. I could see Miriam looking at me, and her face was filled with pride. She was giving me too much credit. The idea of sending over two wagonloads of ducks, geese, pigeons, chickens, fine wheaten bread and cakes, all sorts of vegetables and fruit, had been my uncle's, not mine. The other wagon he'd also sent was late. It was the one with the tall wine jars in it. Therefore, it had had to go slowly, so that the jars wouldn't bang against one another and break. The only idea I had had, besides that of making a present of two hundred shekels to the bride and groom, I still had in my purse. It was a string of pearls—a very lovely string of pearls—that I meant to give to Yohannah.

But I hadn't been able to get anywhere near her. Every time I'd started in her direction, she had turned away with an angry toss of her head. Yeshu'a saw me looking at her now, and smiled.

"Let her alone awhile, Nathan," he said. "I know my little sister. It's going to be all right."

"But—she hates me!" I said.

He laughed then.

"And you're supposed to know so much about women!" he said.

I looked at Yohannah. She had very long legs, and was as slim and as graceful as a gazelle. Her hair was just like Shelomith's. The wind was in it now, blowing it about her small, heart-shaped face that wasn't pretty but was something else, something better than pretty, something very fine and true. I loved her very much, mainly because she'd rebuffed me; and I was afraid of that feeling, too.

Then Miriam got up from beside her cousin Tabitha, the mother of the bridegroom, and came over to us. I could see the expression of worry on her face before she got to us.

"Yesu," she said at once, "there's no more wine!"

I wasn't surprised. Tabitha was a widow; and Boaz ben Lameth, Tabitha's son, a small holder. They were barely able to make ends meet with land they owned. In spite of which Boaz, driven by the hungers of the flesh, had had to get himself married, and soon there'd be a dozen mouths to feed on a farm that now couldn't decently support two.

Yeshu'a looked at his mother, and his gaze darkened. His dislike of Miriam had deepened, I saw that very clearly.

"Woman," he said evenly, "why turn to me? My time hasn't come yet."[1]

I stared at him. To address his mother as "Woman" was plain, down-right rude.[2] But I kept my mouth shut. Today, I couldn't afford to quarrel with either of them.

Miriam's face tightened. But, when she spoke, her voice was as even as his had been, as controlled.

"Something must be done," she said. "Thanks to Nathan, there's more to eat than even this mob will be able to pack away in a week. Naturally, Boaz and Cousin Tabitha didn't figure on so many coming. And they wouldn't have either, if it weren't—" She looked at me, and stopped. She didn't dare say her thought. The bulk of the country-side had come out of curiosity to see either Yeshu'a—or me.

They'd come to see Yeshu'a, because on yesterday, he'd healed a boy of epileptic fits. Oh, yes; he could do that. He could do a great many things that are difficult to explain. If you insist upon calling miraculous any phenomena we don't know the explanation for, I'll grant you that, by that definition, he could work miracles. But don't try to tell me there were no explanations. He himself always denied that. He said that when he cured a sick man, it was because that man had faith. He was right. That was the root of all his powers. Later on, when the occasion arises, I'll give you my theory of how his powers worked. And also, since you say that you respect the truth, that to you it is the highest good, of how a number of wonders he didn't do at all came to be attributed to him.

But they'd also come to see me for reasons on the opposite end of the scale of human values. Miriam, poor dear, hadn't been able to resist bragging that I was going to marry Yohannah, which, considering the class distinctions between us, was a greater wonder than any of Yeshu'a's in the minds of the Galilean country people. Besides, my absolutely horrendous reputation as *moechus* and *scortator*—adulterer and whorehopper—had the women, at least, fairly panting to eye me, and had caused not a few quarrels, one or two of which had already extended to the administration of a husbandly beating.

Be that as it may, the result of my presence, and Yeshu'a's, was that Boaz had been overwhelmed with uninvited guests, whom, our traditions of hospitality and his own prickly Galilean pride being what they were, he couldn't turn away. My uncle's generosity with provisions for the banquet had solved half the problem for him; but the slowness of the wine cart—which he didn't even know was coming—had aggravated the other half.

Yeshu'a went on looking at his mother. He didn't even stand up as he should have, and I had already, done.

"All right," he said shortly, "I'll do what I can."

Miriam turned to the servants.

"Do whatever he tells you," she said. Then she went away and left us there. As soon as she had gone, Boaz, the bridegroom, came over to us. I think he meant to appeal to me for help. But Yeshu'a didn't even give him time to open his mouth.

"I know," he said, his voice harsh, metallic; "there's no more wine. Tell your people to fill the wine jars with water, Boaz—"

Boaz stared at him. He'd heard the story of the miracle, too; but this command of Yeshu'a's puzzled him. It shouldn't have. Yeshu'a was in bad humor so all he meant was that lacking wine, the guests could damned well drink water as far as he was concerned. But then, at that very moment, I saw my uncle's cart with the full wine jars coming up the road. An unholy glee possessed me. I've always been like that. Nothing gives me greater joy than making sport of fools.

"Fill 'em up, Boaz!" I said. "Water never hurt anybody!"

He turned away, gave the orders to his hired hands. I saw them lugging the wine jars off around the side of the house. After a while they came back, empty-handed, and started toward their master. Boaz waved them away angrily. But, by then, my uncle's cart was almost there. The well itself was behind the house so that you couldn't see it from where Boaz and Rebekkah bath Yehoiakim, his new bride, sat with their guests; and I, aided by all the wine I'd drunk, had already seen the possibilities in that.

I got up, went through the gate, and down the road to meet my uncle's cart. I stopped it before it got to the gate where it could have been seen by Boaz or some of the guests, and spoke to my uncle's people. I didn't explain anything to them. I simply told them to drive the wagon on down the road until they were past the house, and to bring the wine jars in through the rear gate. It seemed reasonable enough to them; and, even if it hadn't, given the fact that a favorite saying among the people on Uncle Hezron's place was, "The young Master is as crazy as a body can get and still escape being chained up!" they would have done it without question, anyhow. They took the wine jars down one by one and carried them to the well. And, as I'd told them to, every time they put a wine jar down, they picked up one of Boaz's jars that was filled with water and carried it back out to the wagon. They kept that up until all the jars had been exchanged and even after that they went on bringing jars. Only now they weren't taking any away because there had been more jars on the cart than Boaz had had in the first place. When they had finished, I gave them each a drachma and sent them on their way.

Then I went back outside and stood in the road at a place far enough away from the house that I could see both the banquet tables and the well at the same time by merely turning my head a little, which wasn't possible inside the garden. Poor Boaz was at the table, nursing along the wine that was left in the pitchers. But it gave out, in spite of all his efforts. His face was pitiful. You have no idea what a proud people even the poorest of Galileans are. That pride—and I've already given you an example of it in the way Yohannah's brothers had opposed at first the very idea of my becoming betrothed to her—was tormenting poor Boaz now. He picked up a pair of pitchers and turned away from the table where his fair Rebekkah sat prettily blushing among their guests. And, as he started down the path toward the well, his gait was shambling. I think the reason he didn't send one of the help, as he ordinarily would have, to fill those pitchers was because he was still desperately trying to think of something: some ruse, some trick, to stave off disaster.

I watched him until he reached the wine jars. There he hesitated. I suppose he was hoping against hope that the residue clinging to the inside walls of the jars would color the water enough so that the guests wouldn't notice the difference. But, realizing there was no help for it, he tilted the jar and poured. When he saw the color of the liquid spurting from the mouth of the jar, he almost dropped the pitcher. The wine Uncle Hezron had sent was of the very best vintage, so much darker and richer than the pale, vinegary, and probably watered brew that Boaz had been inflicting upon us before, that our host could see at a glance how different it was. Nevertheless, being a peasant, with all a peasant's innate suspiciousness of mind, he tasted it.

Then he turned and stared at Yeshu'a. When I saw what was in his face then, the awe, the wonder, the worship, I was a little ashamed of the trick I'd played. So I stepped up to the fence quickly, and said: "Don't tell anyone, Boaz! He wouldn't like it!"

Boaz turned to me, his young, dull, oxlike Galilean face actually working from emotion.

"But how?" he got out: "In heaven's name, young master—how?"

I looked him straight in the eye with long-faced gravity, and said: "He has great—powers. Now go serve your guests. They're parched!"

He lifted up his head and called to the servants: "Bring pitchers!"

The hired hands came with the pitchers. One of them actually dropped and broke his when he saw what was coming out of the jars that he himself had poured water into. Boaz swore at them fiercely, swore he'd have their hides off them in strips if they opened their mouths about what had happened; but, as they turned away to carry the brimming pitchers back to the tables, I could hear certain words afloat on the current of their murmurings: "Sign—wonder—miracle!"

The very first pitcher, naturally, they put down before Nathanael bar Talmay,[3] Boaz's best friend and the younger brother of that worthless swine, Yohannan bar Talmay, whom I had beaten in the long race at Tiberias on the occasion that I first met my Helvetia. I say naturally, because young bar Talmay, a good sort, vastly different from his brother, had been chosen *Symposiarch*, or Master of the Revels.[4] One of your customs we'd adopted, of course.

With a grin, Nathanael bar Talmay lifted it to his lips, drank deep. Then he roared out: "Boaz, you trickster; blessed if I can understand you! Everyone serves the best brew first, and waits till the crowd's too drunk to tell a hoe from a handcart before bringing on the cheap stuff! But Gehenna shrivel my thirsty soul if you haven't saved the good wine for the last!"[5]

I saw Yeshu'a tasting the contents of his cup. He raised his eyes and stared at me. I grinned at him and went on about my way. I knew that if I went anywhere near him, he'd have the truth out of me in less than a minute. I never could lie to him; and I never met anyone else who could, either. But my diabolical sense of humor, aided and abetted by all the wine I'd already put away, unmixed with enough solid food to absorb its effects, just wouldn't let me spoil that really first-class Galilean-style miracle so soon!

Within a quarter of an hour or less, my Uncle Hezron's excellent brew was beginning to have its effect upon the gathering. That wedding feast was becoming decidedly gay. As for me, I was feeling very little pain, myself. The good ruby-colored wine pooling warm and soft inside my belly was making me amorous—never, I confess, a difficult feat in those days! So I went in search of Yohannah. I found her easily enough; but, unfortunately for my by then distinctly censurable intentions, but surely fortunately for my future, I found her surrounded by a group of girls.

From the sullen expression on her face, I could tell that those Galilean *almahim* were plaguing her. At once it came to me it would be very useful to overhear what was being said. Both from her friends' remarks and from her responses to them, I was fairly sure of being able to get some idea of where I stood with my darling. So I moved noiselessly around the grape arbor until I was just back of them.

"Well," one of them laughed, "if you don't want him, Yunna, darling, you can give him to me! Is he ever the handsomest thing!"

"All right," Yohannah said, "take him!"

"Why, Yunna!" they chorused. "You don't mean that, and you know it!"

"Of course I mean it!" she said furiously. "He—he's awful! I wouldn't marry him if he were—"

"The—last—man—on—earth!" they chanted; and dissolved into great gales of silvery feminine laughter.

"Well, I wouldn't," Yohannah said.

The one who had spoke first, a bold and buxom country wench whom on any other occasion except this one I should already have sneaked away to the nearest strawheap, put her arm about Yohannah's neck.

"Now, Yunna, honey," she said, grinning, "I wouldn't go around tempting Providence like that! Not to mention this pack of panting females you call your girlfriends—which includes me. If he was mine, I wouldn't leave him alone with any woman here for five minutes flat. Including the Rabbi's wife. And if I had to, I'd make sure she still had her *ketoneth*[6] on when I got back!"

Yohannah stared at her.

"You know, Rhoda," she said, "I think you have a perfectly filthy mind!"

"Don't I though!" Rhoda laughed. "That's why nine times out of ten what I think is so. Now, c'mon, Yunna; tell us all about him! Bet when he kisses you, your toes curl up!"

"They do *not!*" Yohannah said.

This time the shrieks of girlish laughter split the sky.

Tears of pure exasperation stood in Yohannah's eyes. She had a great deal of Yeshu'a's absolute simplicity. She was no match for Rhoda in this kind of a contest. Perhaps she wasn't a match for any of them, on that level. But, in another way, she was. On her own high plateau of simplicity, purity, she was a match for anybody. As she proceeded to prove.

She said very, very quietly: "I have never even kissed a boy. Or let a boy kiss me. Except—him. Except Nathan. And he did it by force. And afterward I went and got water and washed my mouth in front of him."

"Lord, Yunna," one of the others said, "if he ever kissed me, I'd *never* wash. At least not till he did it again. I'd go 'round with my hand over my mouth, just trying to keep it there!"

I saw Yohannah's great dark eyes soften then, turn inward. My blood went singing along my veins with joy. But she didn't say her thought.

"Well, I did wash, Dorcas," she said. "And I won't marry him, ever! Because—"

"Because of his women?" Rhoda said. "Lord, Yunna, are you ever a fool!"

"You shut up, Rhoda!" Yohannah flared. "You're a bad, wicked girl yourself, and I—"

"No, I'm not, honey," Rhoda said calmly, "more's the pity! Sometimes I wish I were, but I'm not. I've just got a tongue that's loose on both ends and hinged in the middle, that's all. But, if I lived somewhere else—up at Jerusalem, say—I wouldn't bet a Temple shekel on my virtue. Here, I'm a good girl for the same reason every one of us is —except maybe you—and that's because I've got sense enough not to want to end up in a *lupanar*. You tell me, Yunna, who could get away with being bad in a Galilean *kafer?* Wasn't for that, I'd take your Nathan by the ears or the beard and lead him off into the woods as soon as it gets dark!"

"I—I think you're horrid!" Yohannah said.

"And I—think she's—truthful," the one called Dorcas said soberly.

"And I," another girl said. "Sometimes—it's awful—waiting, isn't it?"

That was the first time in my life I'd heard girls talk when they didn't know there was a man around. It was proving instructive.

Yohannah's eyes darted from one face to another. I could see she was shocked. But from the reflective expression on her face, I could see that a goodly part of that shock was that of—recognition. She had been tormenting herself, as the innocent always do, accusing her warm and lyrical blood of depravity because of its response to me.

"It is, Bernice, it is!" Rhoda said. "But what else can we do? Being a woman's plain rotten. See a boy who sets you wild, and you can't walk up to him and say: 'Look, Nathan, darling, how's about you and me coming to an understanding?' "

"Stop saying 'Nathan'!" Bernice said. "After all he *is* Yunna's, and—"

"No, he's not!" Yohannah said. "He's a bad, wicked man and—"

Rhoda threw back her head and laughed aloud.

"And what more could you want, Yunna?" she chuckled. "Listen to your wild, wicked, little old friend, Rhoda. You know what's the one thing worse than a *bad* man?"

"No," Yohannah said.

"A *good* man," Rhoda said.

"I—I don't understand you," Yohannah said.

"Know you don't, lambie. Let's see if I can explain it to you—in a way that won't shock you too much . . . Oh, Sheol! Take Boaz, for instance. He's a good boy. Never had the time, nor the money, nor the nerve to be anything else. Tied to his mother's apron strings, up until now. Good. No question about it. But I," and she shuddered visibly, "would sure hate to be in 'Bekka's place tonight! An oaf. A clumsy oaf, scared spitless. A Galilean yokel. Ugh!"

They were all staring at her, their mouths making delicious little O's of horrified fascination.

"Now take your—Nathan. Oh, Sheol and Gehenna both, Yunna; but if you really don't want him, give him to me! I'd never run away from a man who can look out of the corner of one eye and have the grand-daughter of the Roman Emperor following him around like a pet lap dog!"

"She's a bad woman, too!" Yohannah said; "And besides—"

"There's Shelom, the harlot. That's what you were going to say, wasn't it? So, all right. You know my oldest brother, Toma, don't you? Well, he was plenty wild until he got married and settled down. He used to—to frequent girls—like Shelom. And you know what he said?"

"Noooh!" all the others breathed.

"That they *hate* men. That they've seen so much, been so tormented and abused by men that they can't stand 'em. And here you have Shelom, the harlot. So what happens, Yunna? Shelom's awfully pretty. Sheol! She's beautiful! Let's be fair. She knows *all* about men, honey-lamb. She's not just guessing, the way I am, plague take it! She's had her fill of the creatures. And what happens?"

"What?" the girl called Dorcas said.

"She leaves the *lupanar* and follows him up to Cæsarea when the Romans arrested him. After that, she's right behind him every living place he goes. And, even after he took up with the Epitropos' wife, she couldn't forget him. I'd say that when a girl like Shelom, who knows more about men than any of us will ever learn—throws herself headfirst down a flight of twenty stairs because she thinks he's been killed, that man's got something little Rhoda is perfectly willing to partake of. And if that's what you call bad, Yunna, honey, you're looking at the original Scarlet Woman straight out of the Holy Scriptures!"

"Well," the girl called Bernice said, in a subtly insinuating tone of voice that combined sober reflection with the barest hint of mockery, of doubt, "Couldn't it have been, Rhoda, dear, that she just didn't want to see the—father—of the child she was carrying—killed?"

I wasn't prepared for what happened next. Nor were any of them. Yohannah's eyes took fire. I didn't even see her hand move. But she slapped Bernice so hard that if Rhoda and Dorcas between them hadn't caught her, dear Bernice of the poisonous tongue would have surely measured her length upon the ground.

Then Yohannah whirled and ran away from there as though pursued by all the fiends from Sheol. The girls stood staring at her, appalled. But I didn't. I pushed my way through the vines and started after her. When they saw me, they let out a flute run of squeals.

"Your pardons, fair Virgins of Galilee!" I mocked, and ran down the path that Yohannah had taken. Then I saw her. She was bending over the fence by the road, and crying in a way I'd seen only one other woman cry: Shelom. The way I'd sworn I never wanted to see anyone cry again.

I started toward her, slowly. Before I got to where she was, I saw another thing: one of the Gentile farmers—Galilee was full of foreigners, you know, so much so that at times we Jews were actually outnumbered there—had sent his swineherd up that road to drive home his pigs. I wondered bitterly if the bastard had had to come that way, or whether, having heard of the wedding, he'd offered us this deliberate insult to our customs and our laws—but then I pushed the matter from my mind, and went up to where Yohannah bent over the gate fighting back what were, I saw now, spasms of actual nausea.

"Yu-Ann—" I whispered.

She straightened up. And what was in her eyes now was horror. Combined with—loathing.

"Don't touch me," she said. "Please don't touch me, Nathan."

"Yu-Ann!" I groaned.

"If you do—I—I'll kill myself. Because I'd never be clean again. I—I didn't know about—the child. That it was—*yours,* I mean. And I—I was beginning to—to let myself like you—a little. You—you monster! You —despoiler of women. Killer—of babies. Leave me, Nathan. Go away. I beg you. Please."

I took the case with the necklace out of the purse that swung from my belt. I laid it very carefully on the top rail of the fence—within her reach.

"A gift in parting, then, Yohannah," I said. "Something to remember me by."

Then I turned away. As I did so, I saw Yeshu'a coming toward us. He looked angry. His face was set and stern. I suppose he thought I'd been up to my usual kind of mischief. He had none of the clairvoyance your scribes attribute to him now. In fact he could be exasperatingly dense at times. But then he looked past me and I saw his expression change. He was staring at his sister. I half turned. Yohannah had opened the case. She had that string of pearls in her hands. She was fondling them tenderly, her eyes veiled by her long lashes, her mouth aquiver. They lay between her fingers like moonmist, milky bluewhite and shimmering.

She stood there like that, holding them with love and longing, cupped between her hands in that dead-stopped hiatus, that absolute suspension of time, until, finally, she raised her head and saw me staring at her. Something broke up behind her eyes, shattered into the jagged slivers of unutterable pain and grief; her mouth made a grimace that even in the unmatched purity of her face was distorted, ugly. She looked at me, then down at the string of pearls. Her arm came back, made a blur, moving. The pearls for one brief flicker of an instant made an incredibly lovely perfect oval on the hard bright evening air. Then they struck the road. The string broke. They bounced, rolled, scattered —balls of moonlight dancing—making a loveliness for another, slightly longer, instant, before they were trampled under the feet of the on-rushing swine.

Yes, that's where he got it from. The best, the most telling of his metaphors.[7] But, of course, I didn't know that then. What I felt at that moment has no words—except to say that that, too, was one of the times I died.

I walked away from there. I went very fast without looking back. It was a pity I didn't. For, if I had, I should have seen Yeshu'a holding his little sister in his arms, talking to her very gently. And what he said to her was the very best defense I could have had: He told her what Shelomith herself had confessed to him about her relations with me, adding: "She didn't lie, Yohannah. Have you ever known anyone who could lie to me when I looked them straight in the face?"

Only I did not know that then. And a fat lot of good it would have done me if I had. That was one of those days when gratuitous evil rains down from heaven, the kind on which a man is ill advised even to get out of bed. Because before I got to that part of the fence to which I'd left Bedu tied, I saw a whole century of Samaritan legionaires, from the *Cohors Sebastenorum,* of course, coming up the road. And in their midst—

That splendid traveling cart, drawn by eight snow-white mules.

I didn't even need to see that it was canopied with the finest silk, nor that the emblem on the ridgepole of that canopy was that of the Procurator. I knew with icy, dead-sick certainty that Pilatus wasn't in that cart. He never traveled in that effeminate sort of luxury. He was proud of his skill as an equestrian. He always rode a magnificent bay.

No. It was, it had to be: Claudia. And I was ruined. I'd lost Yohannah, now. Lost her forever.

The centurion leading the Sebastians stopped before the gate. He said, in the perfect Aramaic of a man native to this land: "Is Nathan bar Yehudah here?"

I came forward then. Just before I reached the cart, I looked back. Yeshu'a had come around the house with his arm about Yohannah. They both stopped dead. Then one of the Sebastians threw the canopy back, and Claudia stepped down from the cart.

She was absolutely gorgeous. She was coiffed, perfumed, painted so, that only one as close to her as I was could see Sheol and Tartarus both, screaming in her eyes.

"I—I've come to your wedding, Nathan," she said. "Aren't you going to present me to your bride?"

I smiled at her then. It cost me agony, but I managed it.

"You've been—a trifle misinformed, my lady Claudia," I said. "A wedding it is; but not mine. Come. I'll present you to both the bride —and groom."

She stared at me. I could see her mouth quiver.

"Don't—lie to me, Nathan!" she said.

I took her by the arm. Led her to the table. Nobody was breathing. Especially not my prospective mother-in-law. Miriam's broad face was turning slowly purple with the purest, most exquisite rage. But she didn't say anything. The silence was absolute. Even the wind had died.

"Boaz, my friend," I said easily—because I was beginning to enjoy myself by then; the whole thing was so criminally, idiotically ironic that it awoke the night-black devilish humor in me—"the fair Rebekkah, your wedding has been singularly honored. May I present my lady Claudia, wife of the Epitropos?"

Boaz almost bumped his head on the ground. Rebekkah got up from her place, her head as white as death. She bowed, too.

Claudia looked at them. Then she said, in the slow, halting Aramaic that I'd begun to teach her: "You—are—bride and groom? This is *your* wedding?"

"Yes, my lady," Boaz said.

There is a certain advantage to having been born to the purple. Claudia showed it now. She smiled, said, haltingly: "May—I a cup —have to—to drink your healths?"

Boaz almost knocked the table over reaching for that pitcher. He spilt wine all over everything, filling the cup.

"You—too," Claudia said, nodding toward Rebekkah. "And—your husband. And Nathan. All of us."

I lifted my cup. Then I saw Yohannah's face. It was whiter than the snows atop Mount Hebron. The tears were a flood on her cheeks. But she wasn't even aware that she was crying. She was staring at Claudia as one might stare at the ax which will end one's life, just before the executioner brings it whistling down. I tore my gaze away, looked back at Claudia. She put her cup down, took off the spray of emeralds she wore about her throat. They were worth more than my Uncle Hezron's whole estate. Then she dropped them into her cup, held it out to Rebekkah.

"Now you—you—" She halted. "Nathan," she said in her swift, idiomatic Greek, "how does one say 'change with me' in Aramaic?"

I told her.

"Now—you—change with me—my dear," she said to Rebekkah.

"It's a gift," I said to Rebekkah. "Take it. You must. You can't offend the wife of the Representative of Cæsar—"

Rebekkah drained the cup. Stood there peering into it. Claudia put out her hand, took the cup from her, fished the dripping necklace out of it, fastened it about Rebekkah's neck with her own slim, semi-divine hands.

And thus did Boaz ben Lameth and his bride become the greatest landowners in that part of Galilee. The money they sold that gaudy bauble for was enough to buy them a latifundium bigger than my uncle's. You've been plaguing me for months now for an account of Yeshu'a's miracles. Well, how do you like mine? The two I'd performed

—or caused—that day, really weren't too bad for a beginner, now were they?

"I—I thank you, great lady!" Rebekkah wept.

"It is nothing," Claudia said; then turning to me, she switched into Greek. "I'd give more than that. I'd give all the jewels in this world, for this—relief. Only—" she lifted her regal little head, and her fine nostrils flared—"it isn't going to last very long, I see. *That's* the one, isn't it? The lovely little creature who's devouring you with her eyes?"

"Yes," I said; "that's the one."

"And that beautiful, beautiful man beside her? Oh, Nathan, he looks just like you!"

"Her brother," I said.

"Call them over," Claudia said.

"No," I said. Like that. Flatly.

"Don't, then," Claudia said, and strolled gracefully to where they were.

I shall be spared Sheol when I die, for I have had it on this earth. In that long moment Claudia stood there staring into Yohannah's face, I paid fourfold for every sin I've ever done, and stored up pardons for all I'll ever do.

"You," Claudia said, "are—Nathan's—girl?"

Yohannah didn't answer her. By that time I was at Claudia's side.

"No," I said slowly in Aramaic. "She's not, Claudia. I'd hoped so. I should have given—my life, to make it so. But now—"

"I've spoiled it?" Claudia said.

"We've spoiled it," I said sadly. "You and I—and maybe even—God. Yohannah doesn't look kindly upon adulterers, my dear. Being what she is—an angel—she can't comprehend the ease with which mere mortals fall into sin—"

"I didn't understand that," Claudia said in Greek.

I said it over again, in that tongue. Yohannah was staring at me in awe.

Claudia reached out suddenly, and took her hand.

"Listen!" she said. "Don't be—a fool. One life is all. Is very short. Happiness—is—like emeralds—like pearls. Precious. He—is—a god—"

I saw Yeshu'a's eyes speak fire at that.

"Yes, yes, a god! No one else is—can be—like him. Sinner or not. Bad or not. Doesn't matter. One hour his love worth eternity without. Worth—Tartarus—no, Sheol—forever. You understand?"

Yohannah nodded dumbly. She saw how Claudia was crying now, and she was too astonished to speak.

"Make him happy, girl! Him—I cannot—have. So—tonight—I die. The cup's prepared. No more in your way. Without him life is nothing, no taste, bad—better to die—"

Then Yeshu'a's voice came over to us, measured and slow.

"No," he said. "You haven't that right. God promised happiness to no one in this world, my lady. Peace, yes. A peace beyond all understanding. But your life isn't yours to take. You can't destroy yourself, nor destroy Nathan, the way you're doing now. For you, even you, are a child of God, put into this world to do good—"

She turned to me, her eyes grown great in her face.

"Nathan!" she said. "I don't know your language. Not really. Not beyond the little you've taught me. But how is it that I—understand every word, every single word he says? Just as if he were speaking Greek?"

"I don't know," I said. "Men call him a wonder-worker—a Prophet. But I don't know. Listen to him, child."

She turned then, stretched out her lovely hands, and took Yeshu'a's arm impulsively.

"Come, master," she said in Greek, "let's go over there under the trees. Where you can sit and talk to me. Say wondrous words in your wondrous voice—that heals me—heals my heart. Come!"

Yeshu'a smiled at her. I would have sworn he understood her.

"Very well, newborn daughter of God," he said.

I was left there, staring at Yohannah.

"Yu-Ann," I whispered.

"He—my brother—says that—that the child—wasn't yours, Nathan," she said.

"It wasn't," I said.

"And that you were—never—guilty—of Shelom—"

"To that extent, no," I said.

"In that—I was unjust, then," she whispered; "I'm sorry, Nathan."

I put out my arms to her. She stiffened, backed away.

"No," she said.

"Why not?" I said.

"The man I wed—must belong to—to *me*," she said. "I won't share him with anyone. Not even—princesses—who come with troops, and banners. Besides—she—she is—*very* beautiful, Nathan. I understand now why you—you love her. I'm not. I'm homely. Besides I'm only a poor *am ha aretz* girl who can only stand here with my mouth open, gaping like a fool, while you chatter away in all the tongues spoken of man. She is very beautiful, and even if I were silly enough to—to wed you, you'd never be mine. Not really. And—"

"And what, Yu-Ann?" I said.

"I don't think I could stand that. My heart would break. I'd—I'd die."

"You wouldn't have to stand it!" I said. "There's no one but you. No one in this world. Not Shelom—not Claudia. No one. Please, Yohannah!"

She went on looking at me. Then she said:

"I don't know. I'm afraid. Nathan—would you wait—until after next Pesach? Not this Passover. The next one?"

"But, Yu-Ann, that's more than a year from now!"

"I know. And even then, I promise you nothing. And I don't ask you to promise me anything, either. If you see—another girl—you can love—you're free to—"

Her voice choked off, died.

"Am I, little Yu-Ann?" I said.

"Oh, I don't know!" she wailed. "I'm so confused! It's been an awful day! But I need time, Nathan. To—to get to know you. To stop being —afraid. If I can. . . . And you don't know me, either. Maybe, when you do, you won't—"

"Love you? Ask me to stop breathing, Yu-Ann!"

Then I put my arms around her. And suddenly, wildly, she began to cry.

"Yu-Ann!" I said.

"Oh, Nathan! Those—those pearls! They were so beautiful! And those awful old smelly pigs—trampled them! Ohhhh, Nathan!"

"I'll bring you another set as soon as I can, Yu-Ann. Next week. I have to go down to Cæsarea for them, so—"

"No!" she said fiercely. "Not Cæsarea, Nathan!"

"Why not?" I said.

"Because—because that's where *she* lives! And I hate her! I—I hate her—and that's grave, isn't it? I haven't any right to hate her. Only she's *so* beautiful and she has everything in the world and still she comes swooping down like a she-hawk on a barnyard to take—"

"What?" I said.

"You," she whispered, and hid her face against my breast.

"And you don't want her to?" I teased.

"No. I don't want her to. Nathan, don't buy me any more pearls. I don't want them. It—they wouldn't be the same. I only want those —the ones I threw away—"

"Those are ruined, I'm afraid," I said.

"Doesn't matter. I don't want any more. Now, turn me loose," my Yu-Ann said.

"Why?" I said.

"When you hold me—I feel—queer. I don't like the way I feel. So turn me loose."

"Kiss me," I said.

"No!"

"Why not, Yu-Ann?"

"Because that would make the queer feeling worse. Please, Nathan, let go of me!"

"Elohim give me patience!" I said, and opened my arms.

She stood there, looking at me, and the evening wind was in her hair, blowing it about her face. Then she turned, and ran, wildly, like a child, back to where the others were.

And one thing more: I saw Claudia only once more after that day, on a terrible errand that did not lend itself to love. She removed herself very quietly and completely from my life. Nor, to my vast astonishment, and the world's, did she take any other lovers. Her behavior became all a young Roman matron's should have been, even by the austere standards of the antique Republican days, before wealth and world dominion had corrupted that conquering people beyond repair. You've written me repeatedly for details of the signs and wonders that your Mashiah, your Christos, Yeshu'a ha Notzri, performed. I give you that one. There you have a miracle of the truest sort.

For nothing is harder to change than is the human heart.

Chapter XVIII

I SHOULD have wagered money, at any odds at all, that I wasn't going to be able to sleep that night. I had drunk too much wine at Boaz's wedding, without putting enough food atop it to hold it down; and I had the distinct impression that a flock of small, furry, batlike creatures, duly equipped with leathern wings, were fluttering about inside my middle. The sensation was hardly pleasant. And my memories of all that had happened that day helped it not at all. Yet, to my surprise, sleep I did, almost as soon as my head touched the pillow.

But not for long.

For, hard upon midnight, my door crashed inward, torn from its hinges by one mighty blow, and the flare of three great torches blinded my half-opened eyes. Then a voice I half recognized, cried out: "You see! You were wrong. I told you Nathan wouldn't! It stands to reason that a man who asked permission from the first—"

The torches lifted, and I saw their faces; Yohannah's brothers: Yaakob, the wild man, looking for all the world like a young Yohannan Baptistes, Yehudah, Shimeon—and Yose. It was he who had spoken, of course.

I sat up, covering my nakedness with the sheet, and stared from one to the other of them. They were at that moment sheathing their blades. All except Yose, that is. He had never drawn his, believing, as he did, against all available evidence, in me.

I looked from one of them to the other. Sleep had gone from me. My brain was icily awake. And I, the emotional, feeling, dreaming I, was trying to arm my thresholds against the invasion of—knowledge. But I couldn't. I'd had to face truth's ugliness so many times by then, that accepting the world as it is, and people as they are, had got to be a habit.

"Yohannah?" I said. "She's—run away. That's it; isn't it?"

They didn't answer me. Their faces went green-sick suddenly. Yaakob's and Yose's from shame, because they shared—to a lesser degree, of course—that curious purity of their elder brother's; but Shimeon's and Yehudah's from rage, from grief, at the awareness of what this was very likely going to cost them.

"The stupid little slut!" Shimeon raged. "By God, I won't leave a strip of hide on her back when I find her! I swear it!"

I swung my legs sidewise from the bed; put my feet on the floor. Tried to get up. Found, to my not very great surprise, that I couldn't. For one thing, I'd downed enough wine at the wedding to drown a medium-sized camel in; for another, the obscenely precise vision that invaded my mind—complete with sight, sounds, smells, all of which my own brilliant career of lechery afforded me—of my Yu-Ann twisting enraptured and naked in another's arms, hit me in the gut like the yoke pole of an oxcart. I bent my head and gave way to my utter nausea. Part of my sickness was, of course, the result of overindulgence. I admit that. But the rest of it was grief.

At once Yose was beside me on the bed, his arm about my shoulder. "Nathan, don't!" he said. "After all, we don't *know*—"

"What is there to know?" Shimeon snarled. "His woman, the Epitropos' wife, came after him to the very wedding. That got Yohannah wild. So she decided to get even. What else?"

What else, indeed? I thought.

"Yose," I said, "what happened? Tell me!"

"You guessed it," he said sadly. "Yohannah's left home. Sometime after we'd all gone to bed, she got up and left the house. I should have known she would! Because, when she came home from the wedding, she was terribly upset, Nathan. She didn't stop crying for a minute all evening long. Yeshu'a tried to comfort her; but even he couldn't. She kept saying, 'I threw him away—I threw him away—' Meaning, I suppose, that because she'd more or less rebuffed you, you'd turned again to—"

"Yose," I said, "tell me something: Did she say anything about pigs? About swine?"

"Yes. I didn't understand her, though. I thought she was calling *you*—"

"A pig? No. Though she had every right to—" I stopped short then, because the joy that invaded me at that moment was almost as hurtful as my grief had been. I straightened up, looked at all of them.

"Shimeon," I said, "when I find your sister, I'm going to kneel before her, kiss her feet, ask her pardon for having let you make me think evil of her even for a minute. And then, by Sheol, you're going to do the same, or I'll break your filthy neck. Now wait a minute. I'm going with you. In fact, I'm going to take you to where she is—"

"So you know!" Yehudah grated. "That means—"

"That you're a fool. You and Shimeon both," I told him. "Don't make me waste time having to half kill you. The Gentiles won't respect her if they run across her. And there're too damned many of them up there where she is. . . ."

My very assurance halted them. They waited there, while I slipped a short Roman tunic over my head, pushed my feet into my sandals, turning my eyes betimes with a shudder from the stinking pool of winy vomit on the floor, and stood up.

"Aren't going to arm yourself, brother?" Yaakob said.

"No, Yaakob. Arms aren't necessary. I suppose you walked over here, didn't you?"

"How else?" Shimeon said bitterly. "We haven't anyone to give us emeralds worth a fortune—"

I stared at him. The disease of envy is almost as ugly as leprosy, I thought.

"You know where the stables are," I said. "You and Yehudah go saddle mules for all of you. Wake the stablekeeper, and tell him to prepare Bedu and bring her here. That's all. Now hop to it!"

They glared at me a little, but they went.

"Nathan—" Yose began, "how do you know—"

"Where to find Yu-Ann? *You* told me, brother. Because she didn't say, 'I threw *him* away.' She said, 'I threw *them*.' And the pigs settled the matter."

"I—I don't understand you, Nathan," Yose said.

"Ah, but you will, brother! You will!" I said.

Yaakob, the Essene wild man, stared at me; then, very slowly, he put out his huge, hairy hand.

"Yeshu'a is right," he said simply. "You *are* good. Your sins surely don't extend to your heart. And I think now you've done with them."

I took that big paw. I felt both humbled and honored. For the banim Yosef produced *two* saints, not just one. And Yaakob the Just was very nearly as great a man as his elder brother. In some things: fidelity to the Law, respect for our traditions, the unique quality of Jewishness without which we are nothing, he was, perhaps, even greater. And he died just as cruelly for his faith. Remember that. For your whole Christianoi tradition is a subtle distortion of the way things really were. 'Tis that I would set right while entertaining you with the story of my days. . . .

They came back with the mules, and the stablekeeper brought me Bedu. Then we all mounted and cantered off.

Northwestward—toward Cana.

She was exactly where I'd known she'd be: crawling about on her hands and knees in the road outside Boaz ben Lameth's fence. She'd stuck her torch upright into the ground. But it didn't give enough light. She was scrambling about like that and crying. When she heard the hoofbeats she came to her knees, and stared toward us in real terror.

But, by then, I was down from Bedu, and beside her.

"Get up!" I said sternly, and put out my hand to her. She took it, got clumsily to her feet.

Then I knelt in my turn.

"Nathan!" she gasped. "Why—"

"I promised God and myself that when I found you, I'd do this," I said quietly; then I prostrated myself before her and kissed her feet. Both of them. They tasted of dust and sweat, and—and the way unwashed feet always do, I suppose. I'd never kissed anybody else's before —except Helvi's. And *they* smelt and tasted of attar of roses.

She stared at me, then she sort of crumpled. It was as though her bones were breaking up inside her. She came to her knees. Put her hands down and clawed her fingers into my hair, tugging at me, and sobbing.

I got to my knees, and she had her arms about me, and was saying,

"Nathan oh Nathan oh Nathan Nathan—" like that, over and over again, and was kissing my face with hot salt wet clumsy kisses that tore my heart to tiny singing bits with this absolute proof of her innocence, her purity, that she didn't even know so simple, so instinctive a thing as how to kiss, until I put my hands under her armpits and raised her to her feet.

"Now, Shimeon," I said. "You!"

"No," Shimeon growled. "I won't kiss her stinking feet. She probably hasn't washed them in a month. But I will beg her pardon. I do. Forgive me, Yunna—"

She stared at him.

"For—what, Shimeon?" she said.

"For—thinking ill of you, my sister!" he said. "We went to Nathan's house, broke in upon him with naked blades in our hands, expecting to find you in the same condition in his bed. We were wrong. I beg your pardon—I am sorry. . . ."

Her eyes opened very wide; her mouth trembled.

"Ohhhh, Shimeon! How could you?" she wailed.

"Easily enough. *He* thought worse. That's why he kissed your dirty feet, sister. He thought you'd taken vengeance on him because of the wife of—"

She whirled upon me, her eyes afire.

"Nathan!" she hissed. "Did you think *that?*"

"Yes, Yu—" I began; but that was as far as I got; for half the stars in heaven exploded inside my head. I reeled away from her, deafened, blind. Lord, what a temper she had!

When my eyes cleared, I saw that Yose had thrown himself down from his mule and had caught her by both her wrists. She was struggling with him furiously.

"Yohannah!" he said. "You savage little beast! I've a good mind to take an ox goad to you! By heaven, you've neither manners nor sense!"

"I—I'm supposed to thank him for thinking me a—a harlot?" she raged. "Am I, Yose? I'm not his Shelom, nor his Claudia, either one! That other one I didn't know, but—"

"Turn her loose, Yose," I said wearily.

"No!" he said. "Listen, Yunna! Nathan doesn't know you that well; and any man has the right to think what he pleases of an unmarried girl who runs away from home in the middle of the night! That's one thing. Another is that a man who cares enough about a girl to—to get so sick that he loses his supper when he thinks she's betrayed him; and then to kiss her feet—setting aside the fact that Shimeon's probably right when he says you haven't washed them in a month—deserves better treatment from her!"

She stopped struggling then; stared at me; whispered: "Turn me loose, Yose."

He released her.

She came up to me. Then blindly she went up on tiptoe and kissed my mouth. It was exactly like butting into a fence post in the dark. She had her teeth locked shut, her lips compressed into a thin line. It was absolutely the damnedest, poorest excuse for a kiss I've ever had. Worse than even Helvi's at first. But it stung my eyes. Broke my heart. And healed it at the same time.

I grinned at her.

"How many have you found, Yu-Ann?" I said.

"Five!" she wailed. "Oh, Nathan! D'you suppose those filthy old pigs *ate* them?"

"No. I think the swineherd came back before you did." I turned to the others. "Get down, my brothers," I said. "Light all the torches. We're going pearl fishing—on dry land!"

Between us, we found another five. Less than a fifth of the whole string.

"I'll buy you the rest, enough to make up the string," I began; but she flared up at me again:

"You will *not!* If I ever hear of you setting foot in Cæsarea for any reason whatsoever, Nathan bar Yehudah, I won't slap you; I'll take a stick to you! So there!"

"Lord!" I laughed. "Does this mean we're engaged, Yu-Ann?"

She stared at me.

"No—" she whispered.

"We're not engaged, but if I go to Cæsarea, you'll—"

"Take the hide off you in strips! Yes, Nathan. Because I sort of think that most likely we *are* going to be betrothed. After *next* Pesach, just as I said."

"Now, Yu-Ann," I groaned, "that's not—"

"Fair? I know it isn't. But it—it is practical. All my life—is a long time, Nathan. And if you can't stay away from other women until after next Pesach, what won't you do, once we're wed? I—I'm jealous by nature. I know that. I don't want to be tormented into an early grave like poor Papa was—"

"Yohannah!" Yose said. "Father had no reason at all to—"

"I know he didn't," she said quietly. "But he thought he did, and it was enough to kill him. That's why I don't want to have any doubts.

I want to *know* my man is mine and not Claudia's or Shelom's or—or— what was her name, Nathan?"

"Helvetia," I whispered. "But she—she's dead, Yu-Ann!"

"I know that, too. Which makes her the worst one of all. Makes her seem—perfect to you now. A living girl, I can manage. But having to fight against your memories of one who didn't live long enough for you to get tired of her, is too much, to my way of thinking. . . ."

I stared at her. The spine holding this slender body up wasn't of mere bone as is the case with the commonality of women. No, it was—like her mother's—of finest tempered steel.

That was all right. Sons got of her would be a pride of lions, a glory unto Israel. But life with her might well be Gehenna piled atop of Sheol unless I curbed this very quality of hers, this formidable valor of the lioness she was.

"All right," I said. "Shelom's gone. And Claudia, whether you believe it or not, is also out of my life. But what, I ask, am I supposed to do about—Helvi, Yu-Ann?"

She looked at me, and her eyes were the flaming swords the Angel put before Gan Eden's gate.

"Forget her. Forget her completely, Nathan. Don't even remember she ever lived!" she said.

I stood there looking at her. When I spoke, my voice was quiet.

"Do you know what you're asking, Yu-Ann?" I said. "Do you know what Helvi was to me?"

"Yes," she said sullenly. "They say—she was your—your wife. . . ."

"*They* don't say it. God says it. Wedded to me under the *chuppah,* by our sacred Law. But set that aside, let it go. You're asking me to forget the girl who sold the hair off her head to buy me food. Who starved herself almost to death so that I might have the crusts that would have been her share. Do you know how she died? Have they told you that in this kingdom of the ever-wagging tongues?"

"Yes," Yohannah said. "She killed herself."

"And do you know why?"

"I know why."

"And left all my days signed, sealed, and encompassed round about with her honor. All right. Since we've cleared every jot and tittle of possible misunderstanding between us away, I ask you only this: Do you put my forgetting Helvetia as a condition of my marrying you?"

She didn't even hesitate.

"Yes!" she said.

I held her with my gaze; put out my hand to her.

"Goodbye, Yohannah," I said.

I assumed, of course, that the banim Yosef would not come to work for me once I'd broken off with their sister, that their stiffnecked Galilean pride wouldn't let them. And, in the matter of repairing the carts, I needed them badly. Short of going to Kafer Nahum itself, I couldn't hope to find *po'el* of their skill. Worse, even if I should find hired artisans in the city, I had no assurance they'd be willing to come so far away as a farm beyond Nazareth to do a few days' work. I was very nearly despairing, when, two days later than the date they'd promised to, they finally came.

Yose, who loved me like a brother, explained the matter candidly, the first time that he and I found ourselves alone.

"Mama *ordered* us to," he said with a sad little laugh. "You didn't think she was going to give up the best catch she's likely to find for Yunna in all her life just because Yunna's a spoiled brat and a jealous little idiot, did you? Besides, Yunna will come around, Nathan. Have patience. You were absolutely right. Marry her on her terms, and she'll turn out to be a worse shrew than Mama was with poor Father, and that's a feat, I can tell you!"

"I see," I said.

He looked toward me a little anxiously.

"Nathan, you didn't mean—" he faltered.

"To give her up forever?" I said. "No, of course not. I merely meant for her to learn a wife's place and her duty. But, for God's sake, don't tell her *that!*"

"Don't worry, I won't," Yose said.

But, even on that basis, I found that I missed Yohannah appallingly. I didn't seek out another girl, not so much out of fear of offending Yu-Ann beyond her forgiving me when she heard of it, as from the simple fact that I had absolutely no desire for any other female face or form. On my uncle's place, I worked like a madman. Each night I went to bed, too wearied to dream. But with my hired laborers, and the borrowed carts that the banim Yosef repaired for me, I turned my uncle's farm into a little Eden. What's more, by so doing, I insured it almost totally against the accidents of nature. My aqueduct kept it fresh and green in the hottest days of summer, my thick stone walls, shoring up the terraces, protected the vineyards and orchards against the erosion of the winter rains. I had reason for pride, could have been content, were it not for the aching void in the exact center of my life.

From time to time, we had news of Yeshu'a. He was healing the sick, even, some had it, raising the dead. For the first time, I heard the word "Mashiah" mentioned in connection with his name. But most

of the people scoffed at that. "Who ever heard of the Mashiah's coming
from Galilee?" they said. "The Scriptures put it plain enough for any
fool to see. The Mashiah is to come from David's line; and from Beth
le Hem, The Bakers' Village, David's own town in Judea!"[1]

But I kept away from him, away from all his brothers, after they'd
fixed the carts for me, because of that hurtful business of Yohannah.
The only thing I may have done for Yeshu'a in the early days of his
ministry was to provide him with another Galilean-style miracle. Or
rather, my Uncle Hezron probably did, through my instigation. That
is, if either of us did. What follows is admittedly conjecture on my part.

What is certain is that on a day I called my uncle and pointed at the
crowd pouring across our place to go hear Yeshu'a preach at one of the
isolated lakeshore spots he always chose for fear of Antipas' agents.
They were wet, and muddy, and tired. Some of the women had babies
slung on their backs; but they pressed on, in pursuit of the new Prophet,
desperate for a little surcease, a ray of hope to illuminate the grim
bleakness of their lives.

"Strange," I said; "not one of them has a basket, or even a sack with
him. What in heaven's name will they eat? It will be nigh onto dark
before they get there and hear his words, too late to send into town
for food. . . ."

"He does God's work," my Uncle Hezron said. "And the Almighty
has blessed us through the things you've done here, Nathan. Order the
steward to send after them three carts of bread and the morning's
catch of fish from our lake."

I looked at him. Uncle Hezron was the most generous of men. He
was only tightfisted about spending money on himself, or letting me
have it when he thought I was going to use it to get into mischief with.
Apart from that, he was the number-one easy mark for every lying
mendicant, fake cripple, and imitation blind man in Galilee. I started
to protest, but thought the better of it. It made him feel good, and it
would fill those poor bastards' bellies for once. So I went, and gave the
orders.

That very next morning, I heard how Yeshu'a had fed five thousand
people with five loaves and two fishes on the shores of the Galilean
Sea.

It was only an hour after I'd heard that wondrous news, that
Yehudah ish Kriyoth came.

The moment I saw him coming toward me, I knew that something
was wrong. In the first place, I hadn't seen my Brother in Sorrow, as he
called himself, or my fellow cuckold, as I called him—thus mocking
both him and myself with complete impartiality—since I had witnessed

the baptism of Yeshu'a in the lower reaches of the Jordan, at the hands of that wild man, Yohannan Baptistes.

But now as ish Kriyoth loped across my uncle's lowlands in my direction like a red-bearded wolf, his little blue eyes aglitter, I groaned in my heart: "What now?"

"Master!" he cried out. "Have you seen Our Lord?"

I stared at him.

"Since I haven't the faintest idea who your Lord is—" I began.

"Yeshu'a," he panted, being much out of breath by then, "Yeshu'a ha Notzri! I tell you, my young master Nathan, that he surely is the Mashiah!"

"Now that's a pious thought!" I quipped. "But no, I haven't seen him, Yehudah. Should I have?"

"Don't make mock of me, young master," Yehudah groaned. "We, his disciples, are much worried about him. Someone brought him news that Antipas has had Yohannan Baptistes' head separated from his shoulders, and—"

"No!" I said.

"Yes," Yehudah said sadly. "Antipas had Yohannan executed. At the instigation, I've heard, of that vixen Herodias, and even, some say, of her daughter Shelomith. I don't believe that. Antipas isn't that much ruled by his women any more than his father was. Anyhow, Yohannan's dead, and buried somewhere under that grim rockpile at Machaerus. But that's not the point. The trouble is the news so upset Our Lord, that he's disappeared. Nobody's seen him since yesterday morning, when he fed the multitude—"

"With five loaves and two fishes," I said solemnly.

"And had twelve baskets of scraps left over!" Yehudah said triumphantly.

I shook my head in pure admiration. What can stand against the invincible force of human stupidity?

"Have you any idea—?" Yehudah ish Kriyoth was saying.

I thought. Then I turned to the worker who had been setting up some beehives under my direction, and said: "Get on with it. When you've done, go up to the house and tell my uncle I've been called away. An emergency, in connection with Yeshu'a ha Notzri. He is not to worry. I'll come home as soon as I can. . . ."

Yehudah looked at me. Some of the anxiety lifted from his brow.

"You're going to help us find him, master?" he said.

"Of course. Where are the others?"

"At Kafer Nahum, or thereabouts. They're thinking of putting out in a boat to search for him along the lakeshore. Only the lake is so big and they don't know where—"

"I'd say on the other side," I said. "In Gaulanitis, somewhere between Julias and Gergesa—"

Yehudah stared at me in awe.

"Men say," he whispered, "that you, too, have strange powers—that since your sojourn with the Essenes, you—"

"That, my dear Yehudah, is pure, unmitigated dung of asses," I said cheerfully. "Now come on!"

"Where?" he said.

"To the stables. I have to saddle Bedu. You can ride behind me as far as Kafer Nahum. Then you get in the boat with the others. Tell them to row straight across the lake to Gergesa. They're not to stop in either Bethsaida or Julias. You understand me, Yehudah?"

"But, master," he whispered, "you seem so *sure!*"

"I am sure," I said; "but before you make a miracle of it, I'll explain it to you. It's what's called deductive reasoning. I know Yeshu'a. I've known him most of his life. Even as a child, when something upset him, he preferred to be alone. Now, where could he go on the Galilean side of Lake Gennesareth to be by himself, Yehudah?"

Ish Kriyoth thought.

"Nowhere," he said.

"Exactly. But since, up to now, he has neither taught nor worked miracles in Philip's Tetrarchy, or in the Decapolis, his fame is so far confined to this side of the lake, right? So, needing to get away from all the people who crowd around him, not to listen to his teachings but to see him perform a wonder, including your gape-jawed dozen of assorted pious idiots, he—"

But the mockery of my tone was not lost on Yehudah ish Kriyoth.

"Master," he said, "you don't believe in his—powers, do you?"

"I don't believe in any man's powers, Yehudah," I said slowly. "I don't believe that God violates or even permits the violation of the immutable laws that He himself made. And I think that any man who attempts to set them aside is guilty of blasphemy. More, if he deceives people knowingly, he is a charlatan and a liar; if he does so unknowingly, being himself among those deceived, he is at best a fool, and at worst, a madman."

"But, master! I was there! I saw—"

"What you *wanted* to see, Yehudah. Just as you and I both saw love shining in dear Shelom's eyes. Would you swear, Brother Cuckold, My Brother in Sorrow, that when the heart's involved, the eyes always see clear?"

He stared at me, and his face became troubled. Was it then that the tiny worm of doubt began to gnaw at his ardent heart? Can I swear that it was not *I* who first put it there? Yehudah, my brother! Brother in all things: pain, sorrow, confusion, anger, sin—and doubt. Bone of my bone, blood of my blood, deceiver, betrayer, madman—

Even as I, as I!

"You—may be right, my master," he muttered.

"I *am* right, Yehudah!" I said. "Now, come on!"

By the time we got to Kafer Nahum, the weather had turned positively foul. The disciples, all twelve of them,[2] had taken shelter in Shimeon Kepha's house. The rain came down in sheets, wind-driven, and the lake was wave-torn, angry.

They weren't even talking to one another. They sat there, staring out of the window, their bearded faces bleak with worry.

"Have you no faith?" I mocked them. "Surely, with his powers—"

To my surprise—though God knows why it should have surprised me, knowing Galileans as I did—they brightened at once. Four or five of them began to tell me in loud, excited voices, interrupting each other, falling all over themselves in their eagerness, how they'd been out on the lake with Yeshu'a, and he'd gone to sleep in the boat, a storm had come up; they'd almost drowned; and he, when they'd awakened him, rebuked the wind and wave so that a dead calm fell at his spoken word.[3]

I stared at them in wonder; what was truly miraculous was their power of self-delusion. They knew Lake Gennesareth; knew that one of its commonest habits was the sort of thing they'd just described. I've seen it happen a thousand times: A wind comes up, raises a line squall, then dies. One minute, if you're in a boat, you think you're going to drown; the next, the lake is like a sheet of glass.[4] But before I had my mouth half opened to point this out to them, my small store of charity restrained me. Why take away men's illusions, when illusions are all they have?

But then, that oily scoundrel Matthya, the tax collector, was bowing before me. He had a parchment scroll in his hands.

"I crave your indulgence, my master!" he said. "But would you be so kind as to have a look at this account that I am writing of Our Lord's life? I'm told that you alone among us all knew him as a child, so—if you would be so kind?"

"I'd be glad to, friend," I said, and took it from his hands. I carried it over to the table where they had a lamp lit, because it was getting close to night by then, and the storm had drowned what little daylight there was left. Then I began to read.

Wait. I shall tell you first of all only what it did not have in it that your present *Besorah*, or *Evangelion*[5] according to Mattithias (need I tell you that Matthya the publican had little or nothing to do with this one?) has. It had none of your obscene Greek blasphemy of a fornicating Holy Ghost ("The Gospel According to Shelomith," I've always called that one!) because that doctrine of poor Miriam's conceiving while still virgin—would she ever have been surprised, if anyone had dared tell her that!—I attribute to Shaul ish Tarsus, or, as some call him now, Paulus ha Shaliach,[6] that ugly little epileptic half-blind madman, and had occurred to no one at that date. Nor did it have the mysterious three Magi following a star from the East to worship the divine child, for the very simple reason that the future Emperor Nero would not yet be born for another two or three years, so that Tiridates of Partha had not yet set out from his wild homeland accompanied by the three Magi laden with gifts for that newborn imperial monster whom they worshipped as the Lord God Mithras, to suggest that idea to your fanciful scribes.[7] But it did have the long genealogical table proving that poor, illiterate Galilean Yosef was of the royal Judean House of David,[8] which the book you sent me still has, and which was as resounding nonsense then as it is now. I ask you only to compare it with the other table by your newest Greek mythmaker[9] and see how they gainsay one another in every single detail. That they might not agree as to who poor Yosef's great-grandfather was, is understandable; but that they don't even agree upon his father and his grandfather is evidence enough of their total want of credibility, it seems to me.

Matthya's manuscript was very short. He had not, heaven be praised, got very far along with it.

I looked up, glared at him. He was no fool; he quailed before my gaze.

"Well?" he quavered.

"Burn it!" I said.

"But, master—" he began.

"That's the simplest way. Or else someone might ask you how a Galilean carpenter who couldn't read or write his name happened to be descended from Judea's royal house. Or how we Judeans, who literally worship every offspring of that line as *gaon* or prince, ever let one of them wander off to Galilee and sink so far in life. Or, once you've got a woodchips-bedizened scion of David here, sawing and hammering away to the destruction of all the laws of probability, why he had to drag his poor gravid wife all the way across Sheol and

Gehenna both down to Beth le Hem; I mean, of course, apart from the fact that the Prophecy says the Mashiah's got to be born there?"[10]

A stubborn look got into his eyes.

"The census, of course, master," he said. "Every man had to go back to his hometown to be registered, and—"

"If you'd bothered to ask Miriam, you'd have found out that Yosef's hometown was Nazareth," I said; "but, beyond that, how old is your Lord, Yeshu'a?"

"About thirty—"[11] Matthya said.

"All right. Who ordered the census? I don't mean Cæsar Augustus. I mean what officer of his?"

"Quirinius," Matthya said.

"All right. How old am I, would you say?"

"About—thirty, also, master," he said.

"Right. Well, Matthya, Robber of the Poor, when Publius Sulpicius Quirinius was appointed Governor of Syria, I and Yeshu'a both were already eight years old.[12] I *remember* the uproar the census caused."

"Well—" he began unhappily; but I cut him off.

"And here you say that Herod the Great ordered all the male children of Beth le Hem slaughtered, and that Yosef and Miriam had to run away to Egypt because of that. Aside from the facts that no one could have convinced Herod he had anything to fear from a carpenter's son, and the last time I was in Beth le Hem the streets were thronging with men my age, don't you, my poor fanciful fool, *know* what's wrong with your attempt to fulfill all the Prophecies[13] with your un-anointed Mashiah?"

"No," he said glumly; "what?"

"Herod the Great died two years before Yeshu'a and I were born.[14] So, if he ordered any babies slaughtered, he did it from beyond the grave. You know Yeshu'a's mother; why don't you ask her if she's ever been to Egypt?"

"Well," he said, and I could see that stubborn look getting into his eyes, that Galilean fanatic's easy rejection of truth when truth interfered with what he wanted to believe; "what do you suggest, master?"

"That you record his words. And the things you, yourself, see him do. Not what other people tell you. They don't exactly lie, but they do exaggerate, say. Will you do that, Matthya? That way, you'll render the world a service. Elsewise—"

I never finished my thought. For it was at that moment that Shimeon the Rock, son of Yonah, cried out that the wind had died.

Thereupon, I, upon my horse, and they, in their boat, set out in search of him.

Which is, I sadly fear what half of mankind has been doing ever since. But once they find him, and see his rude, rare contours—like some monster's from the sea—they throw him back again, putting in his place the image of a plaster doll, polychromed and bright.

For he, the man himself, was, is, and always will be, just what he predicted: the bringer of the sword instead of peace, the sunderer of families, the purveyor of that hateful, hurtful thing, the truth.

And hence too much to bear.

Chapter XIX

BUT YESHU'A wasn't where I thought he'd be, so that if Yehudah ish Kriyoth had ever bothered to remember the matter, which he didn't, my reputation as a prophet would have suffered considerably. Instead of somewhere in the area between Bethsaida-Julias and Gergesa, where, by all logic, he should have been, I finally caught up with our carpenter-turned-prophet much further south than that, beyond Hippos, to be exact, walking along the shore of the southeastern end of the Galilean Sea.

By the time I found him, my mood was almost as foul as the weather. For one thing, I was sick with worry. I'd told the disciples to row straight across the lake in the not unreasonable assumption that the storm was over and done with. I should have known better. An hour after I had set out, riding around the northern, and broader, end of Lake Gennesareth in the direction of Bethsaida, the winds came back again, worse than ever. In two seconds, I couldn't even see poor Bedu's ears, not to mention any sign of the disciples' boat. The waves became black howling mouths, white-fanged with foam.

I kept peering out across the waters in hopes of catching at least a glimpse of them. But I couldn't. They had simply disappeared amid that shrieking waste of wind and water. Now I was genuinely fond of Shimeon the Rock, his brother Netzer, and the banim Zebediah; I respected that sturdy old brigand, Shimeon Qana,[1] or Zealotes, in spite of the fact that he had tried to kill me—and I pitied ish Kriyoth. The rest of them I didn't really know except Matthya the publican; and him

I despised. But my dislike of that tax collector, that robber of the poor, didn't extend to wanting to see him drown, especially considering the fact that eleven other good, pious, stupid, lovable men would certainly drown along with him.

There was nothing I could do about it, though. I didn't even have your believer's recourse of prayer. I don't mind admitting that I prayed anyhow, in spite of that. God, if he exists, might hear an unbeliever's prayer; and, if he doesn't, I could afford the slight waste of thought and breath the gesture entailed.

So I urged Bedu on into the teeth of the storm. On the other side of the lake, the wind lessened somewhat, and the going was easier. I bypassed the towns, stopping only once on the outskirts of Bethsaida-Julias to wake up a shopkeeper sleeping just behind his stall, in order to buy a little food and drink. Then I rounded the headwaters of Lake Gennesareth/Tiberias/Sea of Galilee, and headed southward.

I didn't ask after Yeshu'a in any of the hamlets I passed through for two good and sufficient reasons: first, I was sure he'd avoid any populated place; and, second, nobody on the eastern side of the lake knew him anyhow. I reasoned he would walk along the beach, therefore I kept to it. I was practically certain he'd do that in order to catch some glimpse of the disciples' boat, knowing, as he did, that they were sure to come in search of him.

They were nearly all lakeshore dwellers; it was logical to assume they'd use a boat; and, besides, he had used it with them often enough, usually to escape the crowds who came to see his miracles, and who, to his mounting disgust and despair, failed completely to understand what he was trying to say to them.

I had passed beyond the town of Hippos and was headed southward toward Gadara when I saw him. It must have been about three o'clock in the morning, but flashes of lightning lit up that shore like day. He was standing before a deserted fisherman's hut and peering out to sea. I could tell the hut was deserted, because the door hung crazily from one hinge, and the wind was banging it about.

And it seemed to me then—why, I don't know, some trick of the lightning and black cloud billowings, the wave reach and soar and shatter before him, my own bone-deep weariness, the awe he effortlessly inspired in all those who loved him—that he towered into the lightnings, that his head overtopped the pinnacles and peaks and airy billowings of the clouds, reached into heaven, serene and bright.

My anger left me. I leaped down from Bedu, calling, "Yesu! Yesu!" like a lover.

He turned, smiled at me, said: "Nathan—"

And became my size again.

Now everyone who ever saw us together marveled at the likeness, the resemblance between Yeshu'a ben Yosef and me. Which means that he shouldn't have been beautiful, for, by black Samaël-Satan and all the fiends in Sheol, I am not. Yet he was. Line by line, feature by feature, we were nearly twins, except—

For whatever it was he had inside him: that tenderness, that compassion, that awful anger, that shattering power.

"Yeshu'a," I groaned; "the others—they set out in the boat—they—"

"They'll be all right, Nathan," he said. That was all. But I believed him at once. If you loved him, you always believed him, even when what he said made no sense at all. As now. Twelve men in a little boat on an angry sea in a storm like that one could not by any stretch of the imagination be presumed to be all right; yet, when he said that, I believed it. He had a faculty for suspending disbelief while you were with him that was nothing short of awe-inspiring.

So I took his arm, and we walked along the shore together. I could see—no, not see, perceive—nor that!—sense that he was troubled. He was often troubled. Like most men of genius, he was more than a little mad.[2] The reason his madness wasn't noticeable was that all Jews, after having endured Herod the Great's reign, that of his sons, and the abysmally cruel tyranny of the Romans, were just as mad as he was, though in a different way. A way more worldly, perhaps. God knows I was. And, in the scale of history, I prefer our commonplace Jewish madness to his extraordinary exalted insanity. Ours did less harm. Preserved the race. His all but destroyed it.

"Nathan," he said; "remember your prophecy?"

"Yes," I said. "Utter rot."

"No," Yeshu'a said. "It may turn out that way, if—"

"If what, Yeshu'a?" I said.

But he didn't answer that. Instead, he said: "Nathan, do you believe that all the prophecies in the Holy Scriptures *must* be fulfilled?"

I thought about that. Then I said: "No," raising my voice so that it could be heard above the shrieking of the wind.

"Why not?" he said, *not* raising his voice. Yet, all the same, I could hear him. His voice, too, had an effortless power in it.

"Well—" I floundered, not wanting to upset him by stating my reasons for doubting the very existence of God; "for one thing, Yesu—how d' we know they are all from God? Might not Satan—"

He nodded gravely.

"That's a good answer," he said. "For, if they all must be fulfilled, then I cannot be—"

"What?" I shouted above the wind.

"What it seems to me—I am," he said quietly. "What something within me has whispered to me I must be—since my childhood. Yet, all the prophecies say—"

"That *he* must be of David's line," I said, "and born in Judea. In Beth le Hem, the Baker's Village, even as David was. That's it, isn't it?"

"Yes," he said quietly.

"Yesu!" I said. "You mustn't! Forget this madness! Where are your armies? What do you know about weapons? About fighting?"

He stared at me.

"Weapons?" he said. "Fighting?"

"The Mashiah must overcome our enemies," I told him; "he must give us sovereignty over all nations."[3]

He held me with his gaze. I couldn't tell whether the lightning illuminated his eyes, or flashed from them.

"Could he not conquer, gain sovereignty—by love?" he said.

"Love!" I cried. "Explain that to the Romans! Explain that any supposed so-called Mashiah is *always* a poor, half-mad, deluded devil and not a King guilty of *laesa maiestas* against Imperial Cæsar! Just whisper the word *Mashiah* into the wind, and the *delatores*, the informers, will run to Pilatus so fast that—"

"No," he said; "I shall never say it. It must be revealed by God Himself, if it be true—"

Then, I thought with relief, we have nothing to worry about! But I didn't say that. In fact, I didn't say anything, for that was when we saw the boat.

That they'd managed to find us wasn't strange, once you stop to think about it. Having landed at Gergesa and discovered that we weren't there, they'd embarked again, headed southward, because, even as dull-witted as they were, they realized that Yeshu'a wouldn't go northward to Philip's capital, Julias. That would have been too dangerous. Julias, or Bethsaida, was located at the place where the Jordan enters Lake Gennesareth, and therefore is a frontier town, since the Jordan itself divides Antipas' tetrarchy from Philip's. A good many people from there had heard Yeshu'a preach, had witnessed his miracles. We all knew that Philip would throw so dangerous an exciter of crowds into a dungeon as fast as Antipas had Yohannan Baptistes, and separate his head from his shoulders faster still. For, of all Herod's sons, Philip was the most pro-Roman. He wasn't a bad sort, really; but no Jew trusted him because of that.

So, counseled by ish Kriyoth and Matthya, who were both, unlike their fellows, shrewd articles, they had headed south. And now they had found us; but it wasn't likely to do them any good. Because, by then, the winds had shifted, and were blowing them away from the shore. The waves were mountainous; and, after rowing all night, they were exhausted. They had all they could do to keep their prow into the wind. If they lost steerageway, turned broadside, those waves would swamp them. Both of us could see that.

Yeshu'a didn't even hesitate. He started running toward them, straight into that terrible sea. I knew I had to stop him, that what he proposed to do was madness. By the time he was waistdeep, I'd caught up with him, locked my fingers into his hair. You cannot imagine how strong he was. He didn't even notice that I was yanking at him. He went on dragging me behind him into the sea. I was sure we'd both be drowned, and opened my mouth to scream at him; but, at that moment, we were hit by the biggest wave in all the world.

When I came to myself, half-strangled, blind, I lay against the side of the deserted hut. I was vomiting tons of sea water. But, when I looked up, I saw Yeshu'a had recovered faster than I had, and was again headed for the sea.

"Stop!" I screamed at him. "There's a way! The door, Yesu! The door!"

He turned then, and saw me struggling to tear the door away from the one hinge it had left. He came to me at once, and, putting out his hand, wrenched it free without visible effort. Then we carried it to the edge of the sea.

I held it in the boiling surf while he mounted upon it. Then it came to me what we'd both forgot.

We had neither pole nor oar.

"Wait!" I cried. "An oar—a pole—something—"

But the surf boiled outward, and he was gone.

It was the damnedest thing you ever saw. He stood on that massive door as though he were on dry land. Occasionally he shifted his feet to keep his balance. If I hadn't known better, I should have sworn he was skipping, dancing, over the waves themselves.

The disciples saw him, and started rowing toward him. Shimeon bar Yonah cried out something, but the wind snatched his voice away so that I couldn't hear what he said. But the wind was driving Yeshu'a straight toward them; and, if their rowing advanced them not at all, it at least kept them standing still so that the wind could blow him to them.

Then, when he was very close—a rod or so only from them—that big idiot Shimeon Kepha cilmbed out of the boat and started toward

him. Naturally, the "Rock" sank like the pristine marble he had between his ears. The lightning flashed, and flashed again. There was a
confused struggle, and then I saw that a wave had thrown Shimeon
and Yeshu'a both against the boat.

I stood there, holding my breath. But the others leaned over and
clawed them up over the side. I let out my breath slowly, measured it
out into the wind shriek, flying spray. I saw the boat move out, scudding
to leeward before the gale.[4]

Utterly drained, totally spent, I stumbled back to where Bedu was.
But I didn't mount her. Instead, I tied her to a rock, and entered the
deserted hut. I don't even remember lying down. But I must have. For
at six o'clock that morning the thunderous quiet wakened me. I opened
my eyes and was half-blinded by a glorious ray of sun.

I rode homeward again. I wasn't worried about Yeshu'a and his
Twelve. I knew very surely that while he was with them, they would
find the strength to overcome any sea whatsoever. What I was thinking
about, actually, was Yohannah. My reason, and my experience with
women, both, told me it was utter folly to seek her out, after what had
happened between us; but what were reason and experience when
confronted with desire?

I could see her still, the day of the wedding at Cana, with her night-
cloud hair blowing about her face. I remembered the way she moved,
walked, ran, as graceful as a gazelle, with nothing—not so much as a
promise of it in the future—of her mother's heaviness about her. Even
the explosive flare and flash of her anger enchanted me, because, I
realize now, it was a trait she shared with Yeshu'a. Still, I feared that
anger—in both of them. Compared with their swift, towering, shattering rages, wind, lightning, thunder, storm were as nothing at all.

And I was too lonely, now. I was prepared to surrender. I knew
that if I did so, Yu-Ann would make my life a daily Sheol; but, I
groaned within my heart, could that, could anything at all, be worse
than the Gehenna her absence inflicted upon me now?

What saved me from folly was a meaningless accident that had
nothing to do with my beloved whatsoever. I came, dreaming still,
cherishing my memories of Yohannah, to the outskirts of Gergesa. And,
suddenly, without any warning at all, Bedu neighed shrilly and reared,
her forefeet pawing the sky.

Only my years of practice as a horseman saved me from being
thrown. I tightened my hands on her bridle, dug my knees into her
sides, hung on, fought her down again. Then I saw what had frightened her.

A man stood in the road, clanking the broken links of chain attached to the manacles at his wrists and ankles at her, and screaming like a beast. He was dressed in rags and tatters; his beard reached to his navel. There were twigs and straws in it, and in his shoulder-length matted hair. The stench of him was enough to make a goat heave. He stood there, screaming at me—his mouth a red, raw cavern in the darkness of his beard, his teeth yellow fangs, what there were left of them, his huge, thick tongue an utter vileness.

I hadn't even a dagger. Nor a whip, for I have never needed one with my docile Bedu. The only thing to do was to ride away from there as fast as Bedu could carry me. The man was obviously mad, and what was worse, the kind of madman who was dangerous.

Only, I hated to run. That kind of pride is stupid, I know; this poor, demented devil lacked any capacity even to accuse me of cowardice. Before I was out of sight, he would have forgot I existed. I hung there, staring at him. He came toward me, howling.

Then, just before he reached me, a crowd of men came running down the hillside, and fell upon him. For several minutes, he was more than a match for them all. But, finally, they overpowered him. When they had him bound wrist to wrist, and ankle to ankle, they fell to beating him unmercifully with staves.

"Stop it!" I said, "Can't you see he's mad?"

They stared at me. Then they bowed, touching their foreheads and their lips in the age-old gesture of respect. Because, you see, to them, a man dressed the way I was and mounted on a horse like Bedu, had to be a prince.

"Why beat him?" I said. "It won't do any good. He doesn't know what he's doing—"

"We know that, my lord," one of them said; "but his devils do. He's possessed of so many of them that he calls them Legion.[5] We're only trying to drive them out of him before they can do some more harm—"

"Harm?" I said. "What harm can this poor idiot's imaginary devils do?"

"Plenty," another of them said angrily. "Especially when they've got a crazy Galilean prophet to help 'em along!"

"A Galilean prophet?" I said.

"Yes," the man said. Then he stopped, gazed at me, jaw dropped, staring. "By Ba'al! You're—him! Or his brother!" he bellowed. "For, if I ever set eyes on two faces more alike—"

"Wait, Ephraim!" the man who had spoken first said. "He does *look* like that crazy prophet; but if you had any ear for talk, you could tell this young master isn't a Galilean at all!"

Thank you for this relief, I thought. I needed it. Their faces had become distinctly threatening.

"You're right, friend," I said. "I'm from Judea. Jerusalem, in fact. But tell me about this prophet. What did he do?"

"Came over here," the man called Ephraim said; "and this wild man jumped out at him. That's all his demons generally make old Legion do: try to scare people. But this Galilean—and by Ba'al, he could be your twin, young master, begging your pardon right humbly—started in to talk to him. And the more he talked, the wilder old Legion got. Took up a stick and started a beating our pigs. The boy we had herding 'em got scared spitless and run away. And old Legion, here, chased all the pigs right down into the lake. Drowned 'em. Cost us a pretty denarius, I can tell you!"[6]

I stared at them.

"And what did this—prophet say to that?" I said.

"Nothing," the man said disgustedly. "To a Jew like him, seeing pigs drown must have pleased him mightily! Anyhow, he went right on talking to Legion. Calmed him down. For almost two weeks, this crazy bastard was as sane as you or I. Then his devils came back, worse than ever.[7] He always swore the prophet put 'em into those pigs he drowned; but—"

"But if I were you, friend, I'd let him keep his devils," I said dryly; "for who knows what or *whom* they'll enter into next, if you beat them out of him?"

They looked at each other then in pure dismay.

"By Ba'al, he's right!" one of them said.

I bade them farewell, and rode away, sure that they would treat the madman right tenderly from that hour on.

But the thing itself made such an impression on me that though I didn't actually forget my intention of seeking Yohannah bath Yosef out, throwing myself at her feet, I put off doing so. It seemed to me that I'd better join the throngs that followed Yeshu'a about, and see for myself what he was doing. Because that was the only way to get at the truth. By then, after a hundred years of unspeakable sufferings, my tormented people had lost all contact with reality.

Yet, strangely, I didn't do that either. Fatigue held me, a certain lassitude, a failure of nerve, of will. Which was just as well.

For, on the third day after my return from Philip's Tetrarchy, a little boy brought me a note from Yohannah herself!

You cannot possibly imagine my astonishment. I knew Yeshu'a could read and write, because my Uncle Hezron had taught him. But, in

Galilee, the only other person I knew who was not of the priesthood, or of the wealthy landowning class who had mastered that accomplishment, was Matthya the tax collector, and he—at least until Yeshu'a got hold of him—used his skill to defraud the poor. For nearly all Galileans were *amme ha aretz*, those ignorant of Torah. More, the writing of Hebrew and Aramaic is extraordinarily difficult. My own mother, till the day she died, never really mastered it, beyond the simplest kind of words. But, looking at Yohannah's note, I saw that the script was dainty, feminine, the mode of expression characteristically her. I read: *Nathan: I must see you. I need your help. Yohannah.*

The spelling was perfect. The grammar, likewise. The vowel points were all exactly where they should be. The formation of the letters was beautiful. I raised the scrap of parchment to my lips.

The grimy urchin who had brought it grinned at me. Then he blurted out: "She said I was to tell you she was going to visit Rebekkah ha Boaz at Cana this afternoon, and if you wanted to come, she'd—"

I could have killed him. It was well past noon now. By the time I bathed, dressed, and rode up to Boaz ben Lameth's place, it would be—

I got a grip on my nerves. Let her wait! If I went rushing up there like a madman, I'd only throw away whatever advantage I'd gained over her by my firmness. That is, if I'd gained any. For there wasn't the slightest hint of warmth or affection in this note of hers.

So I gave the little beggar a whole shekel and sent him on his way. Thereafter, I bathed, perfumed myself, dressed, with a leisurely slowness that set every nerve I had a screaming just below my skin. On the way to Cana, I held Bedu back. For some reason—probably because my own excitement had communicated itself to her—she would have set off at a pounding gallop had I given her her head. But, as I said, I held her back, and rode up to Cana as slowly as I could.

At the sound of Bedu's hoofbeats, Yu-Ann and Boaz's wife came out of the house together. By then, Rebekkah was noticeably pregnant, and it became her. I climbed down from the saddle and greeted them both, with a studied calm that brought the taste of blood to the back of my throat, so much did my self-control cost me.

But, if my absence had had any effect on Yohannah, I couldn't see it. She was just as I remembered her: slim, graceful, lovely. A little more tense, though. I could see her hands clenching and unclenching. The great vein at the base of her throat stood up and beat with her blood.

"Bekka—" she whispered; "would you—leave us—alone? I know it's not right, but—"

"Of course, infant!" Rebekkah laughed. "I was in love once myself.

And look what it's cost me!" Then she patted her bulging belly, said mockingly: "Now you be careful, children!" and left us there.

I stood there, looking at Yu-Ann. By Lilith the Night-flying Demon, by black Samaël and all the fiends in Sheol, I'd be double damned and hurled into Gehenna's hottest pit before I'd make the first move!

"Nathan—" she got out. My name seemed to strangle her.

"Yes, Yu-Ann?" I said.

"Aren't you—aren't you going to—to kiss me?" Yohannah said.

I considered that. A long time. A very long time.

"No," I said.

She took a backward step.

"Why not?" she said.

"Why should I?" I said. "What good would it do?"

She bent her head. Said, her voice falling to the ground somewhere in the general neighborhood of my feet: "No good, I don't suppose. . . ."

"All right," I said cheerfully, "that matter settled, why did you send for me, Yu-Ann?"

She looked up at me, and now I saw the tears in her eyes.

"It's—it's Yeshu'a!" she wailed. "He's given notice that he—that he's going to preach at our synagogue this Shabbat! And they—and they—"

"They?" I prompted her.

"They're going to kill him!" she sobbed. "They're going to throw him off the cliff! I heard them say it!"

"Lord God, Yu-Ann!" I said. "Why should they do that?"

"They—they're furious at him! For being so presumptuous, I mean. They say a—a carpenter's son's got no business pretending to be a rab! They're going to ask him for—a sign! And if he can't give them one—if he doesn't work a wonder before their eyes, they—"

"I see," I said.

"Nathan, save him!" she wept, "You do—and I'll do—anything—for you! I—I'll marry you—right now! Please, Nathan!"

Then she hurled herself upon me, wrapped her arms about my neck so tight she almost strangled me.

I put up my hands and broke her grip. Pushed her away from me. Held her at arm's length. I felt sick. You see, I'd seen, heard, felt the shudder with which she had pronounced the words "marry you."

"I'll do what I can," I said quietly. "But for *him*, Yohannah. For him, I'd offer up my life. Not for you. I don't want a bought bride. Even if the coin's gratitude, it's still—payment. And I won't make my marriage a blasphemy before the Almighty, or my wedding night—a species of—whoring."

She stared at me. Her great, dark, glorious eyes—so like his—drowned all the light there was in the sky.

"Nathan—" she whispered. "You—you don't—love me—anymore, do you?"

I sighed.

"That's hard to say, Yohannah. It's—difficult to love a girl who says 'I'll marry you—' and shudders in horror at the same time. It's not even pleasant to kiss a girl who clenches her teeth and tightens her lips into an icy piece of whipcord while you're at it. Still—I'm afraid I do love you. I'm trying to cure myself of it, though. Because clearly there's no future in it, none at all—"

She went on looking at me, but now, again, her eyes filled, brimmed, spilled. She didn't try to hide it. She just stood there, looking at me, and let the great tears chase one another down her cheeks.

My heart chanted hosannas at the sight; but I didn't relent. I knew better.

"You—you *will* save him, anyhow, won't you?" she said.

"Of course. If I can. If it's possible. But you can be sure of one thing, Yohannah—"

She waited silently.

"If I fail—if I can't save his life—you won't be able to reproach me. For in such a case—"

"Yes, Nathan?" she whispered.

"You'll have to bury me—along with him," I said.

She hung there. Her hand clutched her middle as though I had hit her there with my fist. Her lips went whiter than the rest of her face.

And I—I was very wise that day. I didn't spoil it. I simply said: "Goodbye, Yohannah bath Yosef!" and mounted Bedu. As I rode away, I could see her standing there like Lot's wife, gazing back at the Cities of the Plain.

But it wasn't a pillar of salt I'd turned her into, that day. Rather, it was—a woman. Only I didn't know that, then. I had to wait until that fateful Shabbat to find it out.

There remained, of course, three days before the Shabbat. So I went in search of Yeshu'a. Knowing his stubbornness, I had little hope of persuading him not to preach at Nazareth, but I meant to try. I toyed with the idea of arranging a miracle in order to win his fellow townspeople over. That idea I discarded almost at once. Nobody who had seen Yeshu'a sawing, hammering, boring holes, hard at work in his father's carpenter shop was going to be convinced of his powers. They'd examine any sign, any wonder I staged much too closely. And the essence of any successful miracle is that it be surrounded by circumstances that don't permit men to look at it too hard.

So, once again, I went in search of Yeshu'a ha Notzri. My luck was miserable: every single time I reached a place I'd been told he'd be, he had just left. And worse, when I asked after him, I'd be delayed an hour or even more while they babbled out accounts of his miracles.

The trouble was, I couldn't conceal my skepticism, which moved them to prove their words. So, after talking to a dreary collection of deranged people convinced they'd been possessed of devils, ex-blindmen whose eyes showed no organic defects, cripples whose unwasted muscles clearly demonstrated that their disabilities had existed only in their addled heads, I'd move on, each time a little more angry and disgusted with Yeshu'a for sinking into a Galilean itinerant's cheap fakery.

But gradually an element in all the tales of "signs and wonders" came home to me: these people weren't lying. Their sincerity was so obvious as to become, by accumulation, overwhelming. What difference did it make if a man was not really crippled, blind, that all demons are figments of a disordered imagination, when you consider the bitter fact that—for reasons unknown to us, unknown even to the victim himself, some horror graven upon his tender mind in childhood, perhaps—he believed himself to be with all his soul? The answer to that was so simple as to be almost rhetorical: none.

Such a one was as lost to society as a real blind man, a real cripple, one incurably insane. And Yeshu'a's miracles, seen in that perspective, became what they were—true miracles, as they had to be, for he, the man himself, had not one jot of falsity in him.

That, I was willing to accept. That idea I could live with. So I forgave him his interference with the workings of nature, until the morning I rode into the little town of Nain and found that now, truly, he had turned my world upside down.

The whole place was in an uproar. The words, "Sign! Wonder!" rose above the excited babble of the crowd. "He is Elijah!" someone screamed out. "No," another bellowed. "He's Yohannan Baptistes come back from the grave!" And there, before my eyes, the proponents of these two eminently sensible theories came to blows.

I rode on, forcing Bedu through the sweaty, howling, stinking pack of crazy Galileans until I came to where a dense mass of them were standing before a certain house in silent awe. From within that house I could hear the sounds of hysterical weeping, mingled with laughter. But even the weeping sounded joyous, it seemed to me.

"What in Satan's name is going on here?" I demanded. That is the proper way to address Galileans, especially if you're richly dressed and mounted on a beautiful white mare. They took me for the lord-ling I wasn't, and answered me, their voices hoarse, dropping into horrified whispers.

"He—he's in there. The widow's son. He was—dead. We were carry-ing him on our shoulders to the graveyard, when the Prophet Yisu—"

I got down from Bedu, giving the reins to a beggar boy.

"Hold her for me," I said, and entered that house.

The woman—in her early forties—stopped her hysterical crying and laughing. Turned her son loose. He was a handsome lad, about twenty years old, a trifle delicate, a little too pale. I could see he had been sick a long time. But—and it was this that gave me pause—both he and his mother were clearly upper-class Galileans. Fallen on evil days, perhaps, but clearly not *amme ha aretz*. Their faces were fine cut; their eyes intelligent. They were not the kind of people to go about howling, "Wonder! Sign!"

"My—lord?" the widow whispered. Her voice was cultivated, soft-spoken, gentle.

"I give you greetings, my lady," I said politely. "I am looking for Yeshu'a ben Yosef—Yeshu'a ha Notzri. I was told that he—"

"Restored this, my son, to life. My only son," the widow murmured. "He did. In this house, my lord, his name will be blessed forever!"

"Tell me about it," I said.

Whereupon, she did. At times she was torn with tears, stricken with joyous laughter; but her account was rational, and she wasn't lying. She wasn't lying at all. I sat there listening to her, and my blood turned ice. Yeshu'a, by this impeccable eyewitness' account had brought this pale young man back from beyond the grave.[8]

But as I turned to go, a thought entered my reeling head.

"Has your son," I said to the widow, "ever fainted? Has he ever lain in a deep trance, scarcely breathing?"

"Why, yes," the good woman said; "several times. Once or twice before, I'd thought him dead. But it never lasted so long as this! He was never so pale before, so unmoving. And after he'd lain like that for hours, I called the rabbi, who certified that my son—"

I smiled at her. I knew the rabbi of the synagogue at Nain. Rab ben Zahvli, ninety years old, totally senile, almost blind.

"—was dead," she went on; "so we performed the rites. I washed him with my own hands. We put him on the bier and started to the burial place. And it was then that we—"

"Encountered the Nazarene. I know," I said; and bade her fare-well, stepping out into the good, solid streets, of a good, solid town, on this good, solid earth that was mine again, that she had given back to me.

I found him the next day, the day before the Shabbat. He was teaching by the lakeshore. I listened to him in awe, for surely no man ever spoke more beautifully. Here, I think, lies the chief value of your *Besorahim*, your Gospels; thanks to me, to my forcing Matthya the publican to set them down, they report Yeshu'a's sayings accurately enough. Which is why, also, I have not repeated them in this account, this interweaving of my life with his. It is my intent, my design, to correct error, and his words, except for shadings, nuances, a deliberate distortion or two, you have mostly right.

But when I tried to approach him to begin my pleas that he stay away from the village of his birth, I was unable to, for a man called Jairus, president of one of the synagogues at Kafer Nahum, rushed out of the crowd like a madman and threw himself at Yeshu'a's feet.

"Master!" he wept. "You must come! You must! My little daughter is dying! Oh, my child, my child!"

Yeshu'a got up at once. I followed, trying to force my way through the press of the crowd to get close to him. I couldn't. It was simply impossible. Not even when a new commotion broke out—some silly woman touched him, and afterward made a great outcry that the miraculous powers woven into his cloak, or soaked into it by his sweat, maybe, had cured her of whatever she was convinced was wrong with her[9]—was I able to get nearer than fifteen or twenty rods of him.

But I kept on trying. I'd reduced the distance between Yeshu'a and me to about ten rods, when a relative of Jairus'—a brother, I think—came toward us and said:

"The child's dead, Jairus. So you'd might as well leave the Rabbi in peace—"

Jairus stopped still. So did the whole crowd. They stood there, making a sea of opened mouths, turning the air miasmatic with their garlicky breaths.

Then Yeshu'a spoke.

"Don't be afraid, friend Jairus," he said gently. "Just have faith—"

At that, we all started out again. Before we came to the house, we could hear the hysterical shrieks of the women within. But, once we'd got there, Yeshu'a wouldn't let anybody come in except Shimeon Kepha bar Yonah and the banim Zebediah, Yaakob and Yohannan. Followed by them, he took Jairus' arm, and entered the house.

But I wasn't having any of that. If Yeshu'a was going to raise the dead child, I wanted to see it. So I hammered my way through the crowd with my fists until I was standing before the president's house. And now, again, my bearing and my dress stood me in good stead. I stepped boldly up to Jairus' door, knocked on it. The servant who opened it, gave one look at me and bowed.

I said: "The bedchamber?"

And he: "Follow me, my lord."

Yeshu'a was bending over the still form of the little girl. Behind him, the women of the household rocked back and forth and moaned. I pushed Shimeon Kepha aside and approached the bed. On a table near it were flasks of medicines, and a silver spoon, used, obviously, to give the child her draughts. I picked the spoon up. It was very bright. I put it forward just beneath the child's nostrils. At once her breath clouded it.

Yeshu'a's head jerked up. He stared at me. Then, angrily, he turned to the women.

"Stop that noise!" he said. "The child's not dead. She's just asleep."

Then he turned back to me, held me with his gaze. I think he sensed my opposition, knew how I hated charlatanry. He put out his hand, took the still, white fingers of the little girl:

"*Talitha cum*," he murmured, and his voice was a tropic tide, warm with a melting tenderness. "Get up, my child—"[10]

You know the rest. It *was* a miracle. I couldn't have done it, nor you, nor any man alive. That twelve-year-old girl was comatose, in a trance so deep that only his matchless force, his shattering tenderness could reach her. Yet she rose at the sound of the angel music in his voice, walked about, had her being.

After it was over, after he'd told them to feed her, warned them not to talk about this sign, this wonder—for by then, I think, he'd come to realize how self-defeating his miracles were—I walked arm and arm with him through the town.

"Yeshu'a," I said, "don't preach in Nazareth. Please! They'll kill you! They're angry at the very idea that you, Yosef's son—"

"I know," he said sadly; "not even my brothers believe in me. . . ."[11]

"Then stay away!" I begged him. "Your mother, Yu-Ann, both say—"

"Nonsense, as usual," he said tiredly. "I'm sorry, Nathan; but I must. Will you come to hear me?"

I stood there. Then, again, I signed away my life, for love of him. "Yes, Yeshu'a. Yes, of course," I said.

Chapter XX

I HAD bathed and perfumed myself as I always did before going to worship; but, when I got down from Bedu on that Shabbat morning in Nazareth, I could smell myself. Fear does something to a man's sweat, and I was afraid. I don't know why. I was more than a match for any of the Nazarenes in a fight; I had a better-than-even chance of standing off the lot of them if it should come to that, yet the ugly, acrid stink of fear oozed from my pores, rose up and stung my nostrils.

"Fool!" I said to myself, "a shepherd boy with a stave can take an armored warrior who's got a fluttering gut, so tighten up your anus and—"

Then I started toward the crowds who were pouring into the synagogue. But before I'd taken two steps I stopped, appalled by the loud clanking my scabbard had made as it struck against my thigh. A man wasn't supposed to go into the Temple of the Most High, armed. That was one thing. Another was that if I displayed my weapons openly, I would have thrown away the one tactical advantage I had: surprise.

Then I remembered that Yohannah had said that the hotheads among Nazareth's citizenry meant to throw Yeshu'a from the cliff. And it came to me she meant the top of the hill, because I couldn't remember any precipice hereabouts.[1] So I turned my back to the synagogue and climbed up the hill. I stopped near the top, and hid my curved Arabian sword and my dagger among the rocks where I could find them readily enough should the necessity of making use of them arise.

I had just put the last rock over the little hollow I'd scooped out to conceal them when I saw Abal, the village idiot, coming toward me. He was grimacing, jerking his head from side to side, talking to himself, and laughing. There was, of course, absolutely no way to tell from his behavior whether or not he had seen what I had done. Considering where he came from, I was practically certain that he must have, so I wasted another minute or two debating the advisability of moving the sword and dagger to another hiding place. After all, who in black Samaël's name knew what an idiot might not do if he got his crazy hands upon cold steel?

But, in the end, I didn't move them. For one thing, there was no time; for another, I doubted that Abal would remember what he'd seen me do for as long as five consecutive seconds—that is, if he had even seen it. So I went back down the hill, feeling the fear inside me deepening, darkening, becoming another thing: a kind of foreboding, a premonition.

The first person I saw when I got back down to Nazareth's ugly and shabby little synagogue was Miriam ha Yosef, bustling toward it, leading her brood, which, on that Shabbat morning, included not only all her sons—save alone Yeshu'a himself—and Yohannah, but her elder daughter, Susannah, her son-in-law Asa ben Micah, and her two grandchildren as well.

I was horrified, because, from what Yohannah had told me, I was sure there was going to be at least a riot if not a stoning. Why, in God's Unspeakable Name, hadn't Yohannah told her mother that there was likely to be trouble? Then it came to me why. She hadn't dared. As formidable as Yohannah was, she was still no match for her mother. Miriam, I could see, was dressed to kill; and from the triumphant expression on her face, all set to fill her conversations for weeks thereafter with irritating digs at her female neighbors, demonstrably mothers of lesser men.

Then I stopped looking at Miriam. After the briefest flicker of a glance over the faces of Yeshu'a's brothers, I locked my eyes upon Yohannah's graceful form. Almost instantly, as though she'd felt my gaze, Yohannah raised her eyes to mine. Our gazes held each other for one of those long, long moments during which everything stops as though Yehoshua's ghost had once more halted the sun, until her lips moved in silent supplication, imploringly; and then she bowed her head.

The fear was gone from me now, all gone. I knew with absolute certainty that this day I was going to make her mine, or die in the attempt. What I didn't know was how close I was going to come to doing both.

I kept staring after her as long as I could, because I realized I wouldn't be able to see her again until after the services, for, as custom demanded, all the women in the synagogue sat in the balcony and were hidden from the lascivious gaze of men by high latticework screens. Then I went into the Temple and sat on a bench from which I could watch the altar, the balcony, and the door, all at the same time.

Yeshu'a was already there. He was sitting on the first bench, facing the seats of the rabbi and the president of the synagogue. He was very calm. But I became aware, almost at once, of the intense hostility

toward him that showed on the faces of the would-be worshipers. I
tried to analyze its cause. Yeshu'a, so far as I knew, had done nothing
to offend his former neighbors. Up until that time, he'd preached a
doctrine of tenderness, of love. And even if, because of the miracles
attributed to him, a fool or two in the lesser villages had already
pronounced the word "Mashiah" in connection with his name, he himself had never publicly made such a claim, knowing as he did that he
was not of David's line, or house.

That claim, of course, would infuriate any pious Jew; first, because
in the son of a Galilean carpenter, it was patently absurd; and second,
because an attempt to take upon himself the prophecies, the powers
and honors due the Anointed of God would clearly be false prophecy
on the part of this *am ha aretz* carpenter, and, as such, punishable by
death.

But Yeshu'a had made no such claim, except privately and indirectly,
to me. I don't think he was at that time as sure of his divine anoint-
ment as he afterward became. So, as I turned from glittering eye to
quivering nostril to hard-clamped mouth on every side of me, I simply
couldn't fathom why they should hate him so.

Even his brothers—except Yose—shared the congregation's anger. I
could see that now. And that gave me a clue. Yeshu'a's brothers, I was
aware, accused him of bringing their family's name into disrepute,
of making a laughingstock of the banim Yosef, by becoming a crazy
Galilean itinerant, a breed of which the province had all too many
now. Could it not be, then, that all Nazareth felt much the same
way about it? Had not, perhaps, people from the other towns mocked
them about their new "Prophet" so that Yeshu'a had already become
an offense to them?

I looked up toward the balcony, wondering if Yohannah could see
me through the latticework screens which hid her from my view. The
second thing those screens were supposed to do was to insure male
piety by keeping the temptation of luscious female flesh from our eyes.
As far as I was concerned, they didn't work because they forced me
to substitute unbridled imagination for sweaty, pimply, or otherwise
blemished fact. And my imagination was already a-tiptoe, preparing
to steal away down fragrant, flowering paths away from every "Thou
Shalt Not—" in the Book of Deuteronomy, when, with an exaggerated
sweep intended to convey his mockery, the president handed Yeshu'a
the scroll.

Now, among us, any man can read from the Scriptures and
expound therefrom if he has the knowledge. Then it hit me. If he has
the knowledge! That was the point! Except for the president, the

rabbi, and Mattathiah the tax collector—and of course the other pub-
licans, for every Galilean town had a swarm of those leeches sucking
away its life's blood—no one in Nazareth could read or write his own
name. So they were convinced that Yeshu'a was faking, that he was
pretending to knowledge he didn't have; and now they were sitting
there almost holding their breaths, waiting to see him shown up as the
charlatan they were sure he was.

Yeshu'a took the scroll calmly enough. Then, upon opening it, he
saw that the president had handed it to him upside down—surely as
a trick to reveal his ignorance, his illiteracy, so just as calmly, he
reversed it, and began to read. I don't know whether he chose the Sixty-
first Chapter of Isaiah on purpose or not, but if he did, the choice was
unfortunate. For what he read was:

> "The Spirit of the Lord YHWH has been given me;
> For YHWH has anointed me.
> He has sent me to bring good news to the poor,
> To bind up hearts that are broken,
> To proclaim liberty to captives,
> Freedom to those in prison
> To proclaim from YHWH
> A favorable year . . ."[2]

As he rolled up the scroll, and gave it back to the president, I could
hear the whispers.

"How'd *he* learn to read? Where'd he get an education from? Old
Woodchips Yosef's son, ain't he? His ma's sitting right up there behind
those screens. His sisters, too. And look at his brothers over there.
Yaakob, Yose, Shimeon, Yehudah. Plain folks just like us. None of 'em
can read a line. Funny business, if you ask me!"[3]

Yeshu'a opened his mouth. His words rolled forth, majestic and
slow:

"Today—in your very hearing, this text has been fulfilled in
me. . . ."

At once the bull-bellow of the congregation drowned him out. All
the burly, bearded Galileans were on their feet as one man, shaking
their fists and shouting at him. Which didn't surprise me. For
this carpenter's son to say, or at least to imply, that a text which read:
"The Spirit of YHWH has been given me; For YHWH has anointed
me . . ." had been fulfilled in him, was indisputably a blasphemy. It
meant that he was claiming to be the Mashiah. For that was what "The
Anointed of the Lord" meant.

"Stone him!" the voices roared. "Kill the blasphemer!"

"No!" Levi ben Halphai, the brother of Yeshu'a's own disciple, Yaakob ben Halphai, mocked. "Let him give us a sign! Let him do a wonder here, like they say he's done in Kafer Nahum!"

"A sign!" another took it up. "A sign, Prophet! Give us a sign!"

One of the banim Sheatiel brothers ran out of the Temple, and came back, pushing Abal the idiot before him.

"Look, O Rabbi," he bellowed. "Here, O Great Prophet, is your chance! Drive the devils out of Abal's addled head! C'mon! Give us a sign! A sign!"

I looked up toward those maddening screens. I wondered if Yohannah were crying. I could picture her lovely face streaked with the tears of rage and shame. I was prepared to cut a throat for every tear; to wash away this insult with their loutish blood. Then I looked back at Yeshu'a. I saw the lightning of his terrible wrath flashing from his eyes.

"Physician, heal yourself!" Levi mocked. "A sign! A sign!"

"No," Yeshu'a said coldly. "You're not worth it. You've broken your covenant with God. So now he'll turn to others. Remember that there were many widows in Israel in Elijah's time; but God sent him to the Sidonese woman. And what leper was healed in Elisha's days? Naaman, the Syrian!"

"He insults us!" a woman's voice shrilled down through the screens. "He mocks Israel! He says God favors foreigners!"

"No," Yeshu'a said, his voice harsh, grating, filled with a bitterness hard to listen to; "I say that a Prophet is honored everywhere except in his hometown; except in the bosom of his own family!"

Then they were upon him, worshipers in the Temple of the Most High, transformed into a howling mob, committing sacrilege themselves in their terrible rage.

I did what I had to, what was, I knew, the wisest thing to do: I dashed through the door, out into the street, and started up the hill to get my sword and dagger. But before I had gone twenty yards, I heard someone screaming my name, and, looking back, saw Yohannah racing after me.

I stopped, and she came up to me. Her face was terrible, amid the wild tangle of her hair. Her eyes were blind-scalded, her lips foam-flecked; and there was no reason in her, none at all.

"Coward!" she hissed. "Look upon him, Almighty God! Look upon this—thing—I thought a man. That I was even going to marry. And if you're still Gideon's God, and Shaul's and David's, I ask you to strike him dead!"

Then, as hard as she could she smashed her closed fist into my face.

I reeled away from her, went on up the hill. Explanation would have taken too long, and she wouldn't have listened anyhow. Breathlessly, I bent above the place I'd left my blades, and stopped, appalled, seeing the stones scattered and my weapons gone.

"That idiot!" I swore. "That raving, blithering—"

Then, a little way off, I saw the glitter. Abal hadn't kept my weapons. As usual, his attention had wandered and he'd thrown them away from him. I ran to that spot, bent again, picked up my sword. I couldn't find the dagger, but that scarcely mattered. I turned, sword in hand, and waited for the mob.

They were pushing Yeshu'a up the hill, clearly intending to throw him from the crest of it. Yohannah and Susannah both were screaming at them, while Miriam's great voice rent the sky. But I didn't see his brother-in-law, nor his brothers. I didn't see them at all. And Yu-Ann had call *me* coward.

I waited until they were almost upon me before I spoke. I didn't shout. I only raised my voice enough to carry.

"Turn him loose," I said. "Or, by heaven, I'll disembowel the lot of you!"

They stopped there, glaring at me. But the sunlight fell on my blade and made a hard, bright blaze. They had heard about my killing Pilatus' gladiator at Cæsarea—as who hadn't? Their hands fell away from him.

But he didn't run. He stood there, looking at me. Then he said: "I thank you, my brother; though I'd not have had you use such means as these—"

At that, he turned slowly, impressively toward his tormentors, walking directly at them. They divided like the Red Sea did for our Father Moses, and he walked straight through their midst and was gone.[4] There was something mysterious about it. Something almost magical. He was at the foot of the hill before the trance that held them broke, and they began to stir.

"Don't move!" I warned them. "Samaël take your murderous souls to Sheol, don't even breathe!"

I held them like that until he was out of sight. Then, just as I was about to lower my blade, bid them disperse, I heard that senseless cackle, that high-pitched, almost feminine laughter. But, because I recognized it at once as the idiot's, I paid it no attention at all. Which was my mistake.

I heard Yohannah's scream tear the day apart, so that the sound of it and the white fire that entered me, plunging sickeningly between my ribs, became one and the same thing. I turned and saw Abal grinning at me, his right hand empty now, but covered with what could only be my blood. I looked down over my own shoulder, twisting my neck until I could see the handle of my own dagger protruding diagonally from the small of my back. The handle. Because the blade was in me to the hilt, and I had found my death.

I turned then, fixed my eyes on Yohannah's face. I didn't say anything. The pain hadn't come yet. I knew that when it did come it was going to be very bad. I don't know whether I thought about the matter consciously or not, but I suppose that something in me decided to make of my dying a proud thing, since it had to take place before her eyes. I went on looking at her until a trembling got into her. She shook all over. Her mouth came open, not entirely, but half opened and half closed so that the cry that came out of it made an awful, deadly, gurgling sound, and the ague which had possessed her unlocked her knees and she went down upon them like a worshiper at prayer. But she didn't pray. Instead her mouth cam all the way open and she screamed and screamed and screamed making a hideous noise that could only be my name. Then, seeing me stagger, totter, start to fall, she got up from there and started running toward me still screaming like that until she and the pain both crashed into me at the same time and the world slid out from under me with a sickening swoop and shudder and I was going down down down into blackest Sheol, into Gehenna, and her arms were around me and scalding droplets were falling onto my face and she was saying slowly, clearly: "I've killed him. I've killed—Nathan. Abal had nothing to do with it. It was me. I asked God—" Then, her voice thickening, the grate and scrape of horror getting into it, but sounding more distant so that I knew she'd raised her face toward heaven: "Why did you answer me? I've prayed before and never—not even once—Didn't you know I didn't mean it? Couldn't you see I loved him? Can't you understand anything about people? Or don't you care? What good are you? I ask you, what good at all?"

After that, I couldn't hear her anymore; and maybe even God didn't want to, couldn't stand what she was saying, because that was when night fell out of heaven like a stone and He, or somebody or something, took a great breath and blew out the sun.

This part I didn't witness. This part was told to me.

Yohannah looked at my Uncle Hezron. He had his prayer shawl around his shoulders and his skullcap on his head. He'd bound the little leather boxes to his arm and temple. He'd ripped his fringed robe down to his navel so that the white hair with which his big chest was thatched gleamed like a forest covered with snow against his dark skin.

He was rocking back and forth and crying aloud. The tears trickled down into his beard, and he was sobbing: "Nathan! Nathan! My son! My son!"

Yohannah wasn't crying. Her face was very still. She had on black, like a widow. She said: "He's not dead yet, is he?"

"No, not yet," my uncle said.

Yohannah said: "My brothers are building the *chuppah*. They should be here with it within the hour. . . ."

And my uncle: "The canopy?"

And she: "Yes. So I can marry him. So I can be his widow, anyhow. You don't object, do you?"

And my uncle: "He'll die childless. He has no brother to take you in his stead as the Law—"

And Yohannah: "I know that."

And my uncle, snarling: "You'll mourn a while. You who killed him. Who caused his death. Then you'll find consolation. You're young and comely and there's no reason why—"

And she, facing him, saying it, her voice very low, so that until he died he swore it was the voice of Ruth from the Holy Scriptures speaking through her mouth, even the language changing from that she ordinarily used, becoming stately, liturgical:

"I shall never take off my mourning robes while I live. I shall never raise my eyes to another face. If any man look upon my countenance and find it fair so that it awake desire in him, I shall cut my cheeks with knives, burn my lips with coals, rub salt and earth into the wounds until my beauty's gone."

"And if you should see some fine young fellow," my uncle began; "you're only human, you know—"

"And if these eyes of mine look with favor upon another face," Yohannah said in that same still, terrible voice, "I shall lay two live coals on them and not cry out no matter how great the pain is, until my sight is gone. I swear this by the *Shem ha Meyuhad*, the Ineffable Name of God."

My uncle stood there, looking at her.

"All right," he said at last; "this was his house. You shall dwell in it—as my daughter. For he was a son to me, and more."

But she knelt before him, took his big hands and kissed them; said: "As your daughter, no. I am not fit. But as your handmaiden, your servant, and your slave."

"No!" my uncle thundered. "I'll not have—"

And it was then that three of her brothers, Yaakob, Shimeon, and Yehudah, came bringing the rabbi with them.

Yose wasn't with them. The reason he wasn't was simple: He had
gone racing after Yeshu'a. To bring him back. To ask, or force, him
to work one more wonder in order to save my life. You see, Yose
loved me as much as Yeshu'a did; in some ways, more. That was why
he went flying after his brother. And it was he, of course, who, some
weeks later, told me what happened next:

Yeshu'a hadn't seen Abal stab me. And his own achingly bitter
failure at Nazareth almost broke his heart. He took his disciples and
started north toward Sidon and toward Tyre, swearing never to set
foot in the village of his birth again.

But he had scarcely reached the place where the others waited when
he heard somewhere behind him a voice desperately calling his name.
He turned and they saw his brother Yose running toward them covered
with dust all over except where it had been penciled through by the
white streaks of his tears.

"Yesu!" he cried. "You must come! You must! Nathan—"

Yeshu'a stood there. His eyes went very dark.

"They've hurt him," he said.

"No, Yesu; they've killed him!" Yose said. "Abal the idiot put a knife
through his back—just after you left. For your sake, brother. He's
dying, I tell you! You must come! You—"

But Yeshu'a shook his head.

"I have sworn before my Father that I shall never enter Nazareth
again," he said.[5]

Yose hung there, staring at his brother. When he spoke, his voice
was thick with horror.

"You—monster!" he said. "You ungrateful monster! He—he saved
your life!"

But Yeshu'a shook his head again.

"No, Yose. God saved my life. Nathan was but his instrument. As
he will save Nathan's. As he already has. Go back to Rab Hezron's
house, O you of little faith, and see what you'll see."

I don't suppose that miracle was spectacular enough for them to
remember it, put it in their Gospels. Or perhaps it was too closely
connected with his most notable failure, the one thing they were
unable to conceal, as they concealed so many others. Why think you
he hated so for the reports of his signs and wonders to be spread
abroad? I'll tell you why: He never knew when his powers were
going to work and when they weren't, for it depended more on the
sufferer's belief in him than upon himself, so he avoided wonder-
working all he could.[6]

Anyhow, when Yose got back to my uncle's house, he found his sister, now my wife—though I didn't even know she was—weeping beside my bed. I was comatose, but still alive. I stayed that way for twelve days more before I began to mend. So it wasn't spectacular enough. I didn't leap from my bed the exact moment he pronounced the words, "As God will save Nathan's. As he has . . ." I went right on teetering between this world and the next. But it *was* a miracle for all that. With a wound like that, I should have died. What kept my flesh clean? Why didn't the wound suppurate, drip stinking pus? Of course Yohannah washed it, applied herbs, changed the bandages constantly once the bleeding had stopped; of course Miriam, herself, bathed me, fed me, tended me with her strong and capable hands while I lay there unconscious; of course my Uncle Hezron spent day and night upon his knees beseeching the Almighty to spare my life. A miracle it was; but—whose?

On the thirteenth day, I opened my eyes. All I could see was a huge blurred form. So I closed them again. Some time later—minutes? hours? I'll never know—I opened them once more. Magically, miraculously, the world clicked into place, and I saw my Uncle Hezron sitting by my bed.

"Uncle Hezron," I said; or thought I did; but I was too weak to give sound to the words. He went on sitting there, while I tried desperately to talk to him, moving my lips like a mute, and he, lost in thought, in prayer, didn't notice it until the tears of pure exasperation had flooded my face, and a single ray of sun came through the window and made them blaze. Then he saw them, and tiptoed to the edge of the bed, stared into my opened eyes a minute, two, three, before his big head went back, back, and his great voice crashed against the ceiling, rising from its normal bass to break like an adolescent boy's, like a woman's, into the crystalline slivers of purest joy as he cried:

"The heavens declare the Glory of God!"

When Yohannah and Miriam came running into my bedroom they had to actually pry me out of his arms before he crushed me to death.

Miriam kissed me, and smoothed my covers, and wept and fussed over me and thanked God at least seventy thousand times, but Yohannah stood in the corner of the room and stared at me without saying anything. I could see she was crying. I wanted her to come to me, but she wouldn't. She had on black.

When I saw that, pain hit me in the gut like an iron fist.

"Yeshu'a!" I wept. "They caught him! They—"

And so great was my anguish that it lent me the strength to force my babbling into sound.

Then she was there, kneeling beside my bed.

"No, Nathan," she said. "Yeshu'a's all right."

"Don't—lie—to—me!" I got out, forcing the words out on gasping spurts of breath. "You've—got on—black—Yu-Ann!"

"That was—for you, Nathan," she whispered. "I'll go take it off now, if you'll promise me you'll live!"

I looked at her. She was still crying. But now the tears were dancing on the upturned corners of her mouth as she smiled at me. That, in itself, was enough to heal me then and there.

"I—promise, Yu-Ann," I croaked.

Miriam got up then, took my uncle's arm.

"Come, Rab Hezron, let's leave these children alone," she said.

But I still didn't know we were married. And Yohannah didn't tell me. For one thing, I had quite a serious relapse that same night, and it wasn't until four days later that I became conscious again. After that, I really began to get better.

By the middle of the next week, when it was obvious that I was going to go on profaning the world for a good long time, she marched into my bedroom and said: "Nathan, will you give me a bill of divorcement?"

I stared at her, said: "Whaaaat?"

"A bill of divorcement. Because it wasn't fair. I only did it because I thought you were going to die, and I wanted to be your widow at least, but before that you'd said that you were trying to stop loving me because I wasn't even a real woman and I didn't even know how to kiss and—"

I sat there, propped up on my pillows, with my mouth opened wide. Then I said: "Yu-Ann, will you tell me what in the name of Sheol and Gehenna both you're talking about?"

"I—I made the rabbi marry us!" she wailed. "While you were—unconscious, Nathan! I told him—you'd asked me to, and your uncle backed me up! Only Rab Hezron didn't know you'd—you'd jilted me for being so mean and bad and crazy jealous! So it wasn't fair! It wasn't, Nathan! So now—"

I kept my face serious, although all the Seraphim in Heaven were singing hosannahs in my heart.

"Do you *want* a divorce, Yohannah?" I said solemnly.

"No!" she sobbed. "I want to be your wife! For always, Nathan!

Forever and ever and ever, Amen! Ohhh, Nathan—will you keep me?
I'll be good! I'll be so good that—"

I smiled at her.

"Come here—wife," I said.

She came to me, very slowly. Knelt down beside my bed.

"Now, kiss me," I said.

It was still like butting into a fence post. I pushed her away from
me, grinned at her.

"Here commenceth the first lesson," I said.

Chapter XXI

"BLESS HIM," Yohannah said.

I was sitting in a big chair outside my uncle's house. Yohannah
sat on a cushion on the ground and rested her head on my knees.
It was early in the month of Adar[1] and all the world was beginning
to leaf, to bud, to flower, to sing. Like my heart.

"Bless whom?" I said.

"Abal," Yohannah said.

"Elohim and Adonai, Yu-Ann, why?" I said.

She turned and looked at me solemnly.

"Because Pesach isn't until next month," she said.

"So?" I said.

"The Pesach I was going to make you wait until after before I'd
agree to us even getting betrothed. That's why I say bless Abal. For
being crazy. For not even knowing what a knife was, really. Wasn't
for him, I'd have missed so much—"

I grinned at her.

"So much—what?" I said.

Her small, tender, wildwoods-thing face went scarlet.

"You know," she said.

"No, I don't," I said.

"Oh yes, you do!" she flared. "You're just trying to make me say
something immodest. You're a bad, wicked boy, Nathan, and—"

"And aren't you glad," I said.

She looked at me and loosed a soft purr of warm, deep-throated laughter.

"Yes," she said. "Yes, I am glad. Nathan, you remember that time I sort of shuddered when I said I'd marry you if you'd try to save Yesu?"

"Yes," I said. "That was before you asked God to strike me dead."

She jumped up as though I'd hit her, and clamped her hot little hand over my mouth.

"Don't say that!" she said. "Don't say that out loud! It might remind Him, and—"

I pulled her hand away from my mouth.

"I take it, then, my lady Yohannah bath Yosef ha Nathan, that you no longer want me dead?"

She put both her arms around my neck. Slim as she was, she was very strong. She almost strangled me.

I kissed her. A long time. A very long time. It was no longer like butting into a fence post in the dark. Not at all.

She pulled away from me, put her mouth to my ear, explored it briefly with her tonguetip, whispered: "No, I want you alive. Like you are now, at least. Besides, you haven't got a brother."

I considered that. Among us, when a man dies childless, his brother must lie with his widow in order to preserve his name and line.

"So," I said, "for lack of a suitable replacement, you'll resign yourself to me?"

"Yes," she said. Then she stared at me, her dark eyes very wide. They were also troubled.

"Nathan—" she breathed.

"Yes, Yunna," I said.

"Don't call me Yunna! I hate it! Everybody calls me that. Call me Yu-Ann, the name *you* gave me. D'you know, that night after the first time you said it—the day you kissed me and I washed my mouth—I whispered it to myself all night long, trying to make my voice do what yours does, saying it. Only I couldn't. So you mustn't ever call me anything but—"

"Yu-Ann. All right. Now, what were you saying?"

"Nathan, do you think I'm—wicked?"

I threw back my head and roared.

"Wicked? Compared to you, my dove, all the Seraphim in heaven are fiends. And the Cherubim. And the Angels of—"

"Nathan, don't blaspheme! But I *am* wicked. I must be. At least—depraved—"

I stared at her. She hid her little face against my chest.

"Because—because what I thought was going to be—to be horrid—

isn't. I—I like it. I like it—too much. More than you do. The only times
I get angry with you now are when I wake up in the middle of the
night and there you are sleeping like a log, and I daren't shake you or
anything—"

"Why not?" I said.

"Because you'd think—"

"I'd think 'Glory to God in the Highest who male and female made
he them to be fruitful and multiply and replenish the earth!'" I said.

She giggled then, girlishly.

"You're going to be sorry you said that!" she said. "Because now you're
never going to get any sleep." Then: "Oh, how I wish it were night,
right now!"

I bent and swept her up into my arms.

"Who ever told you it had to be night, Yu-Ann?" I said. "He said
'Be fruitful and multiply'; but he didn't say when."

"No, Nathan," she said; "please, no. And not tonight, either. You
see, I've got to ask Mama something first—"

"You have to ask that old battle-ax if I, your husband, can—"

"Make love to me? Yes. Only don't call Mama a battle-ax. She's fond
of you, Nathan. Very fond."

"I know," I groaned; "but what I don't see is why, after all these
months, you—"

"Have to ask her that? Well, let me see—Put it this way: Even if you
did have a brother now, and something—which the Almighty forbid!—
happened to you, I wouldn't need him."

I almost dropped her. I said: "Yu-Ann!"

"That is, unless it's going to be a girl. But, according to Rab Hezron,
the P'rushim hold that even a girl counts—so you be careful. I don't
want to be a widow. I want—"

"Yu-'ann," I got out. "Are you *sure?*"

"Yes. So I have to ask Mama if it does any harm to—"

"Poke the little bastard here and there and jiggle him about?" I
said.

"Oh, you're wicked!" she said. "And don't you call my son a bastard
and—and—You're right. Something like that, anyhow, only put in a
nicer way. So put me down, Nathan."

I put her down. She stood there, peering up at me with the eyes of
a tender and bemused little owl.

"Nathan—you—you aren't *sorry*, are you?" she said.

"Sorry?" I said. Then I threw myself down and turned three cart-
wheels in a row. I could still do that. But now I felt the scar tissue
in my side pull. It hurt. I paid no attention to it. When I came to my

feet again, I put my head back and yelled. It sounded like somebody blowing the shofar. It echoed from all the hills.

My Uncle Hezron came out of his study and glared at me. He had been reading the Torah, as usual.

"May I ask what all the bellowing is about?" he said.

I caught him in my arms, lifted him up, big and heavy as he was, whirled him about. Yelled again.

"Put me down, you fool!" he said. "What in the name of everything unholy has got into you?"

" 'Make a joyful noise unto the Lord, all ye Lands!' "[2] I said. "You, Rab Hezron ben Matthya, are going to become a grandfather; no— a granduncle. Or something. Anyhow—"

"Put me down, Nathan," he said.

I put him down. He kissed me on both cheeks, and wept. Yohannah stood there looking at that. I could see the tiny flare of jealous anger getting into her eyes. She adored Uncle Hezron, and now he was more or less leaving her out of his joy.

Only he wasn't. He turned to her, his big arms opened wide.

"My daughter," he said; "My dearly beloved daughter, with whom I am well pleased!"

"Oh, Rab Hezron!" Yu-Ann sobbed. Then with a wild little skip and scamper, she was in his arms.

And we were, all three of us, happy. Too happy. I should have known better.

For it was that very night that Yehudah, he of Kerioth, came.

The moment I saw ish Kriyoth, I reailzed something was wrong. For, as I knew from my many conversations with him, My Brother in Sorrow was a most intelligent man. I'd say he had more intellect than all the rest of Yeshu'a's disciples put together. True, he could be, and often was, swept along by his enthusiasms, his passions, as his mad—and lifelong—infatuation with poor Shelomith proved; but being, alone among the Disciples, a Judean, he was, unlike the Galileans, capable of long, long second thoughts. And now, as we sat alone under the arches of my aqueduct, it was apparent that he was beginning to have them.

"You were right, young master," he said harshly, "I was a fool. I saw what I wanted to see. But now—"

"Now?" I echoed.

"He is a madman! A dangerous madman. A false Mashiah who will bring disaster upon our people Israel!"

I held him with my gaze.

"Why have you turned against Yeshu'a, Yehudah?" I said.

His head came up. His eyes met mine squarely.

"Turned against him?" he whispered. "I? No, Nathan, my master—I love him, still. I love him with all my heart!"

"And yet—" I prompted him.

"I hold to what I said! Yeshu'a ben Yosef is mad! You know how I feel about the Romans, don't you, master?"

"Yes," I said; "I do."

"Well, while we were wandering around up there in the neighborhood of Cæsarea-Philippi—that is, the Tetrarch Philip's Cæsarea—not the one down on the coast—a man came to him and asked him straight out: 'Look, master, if a Roman legionary comes up to me and orders me to carry his pack for him, what should I do? According to *their* law, they can load us down like a jackass over a distance of one *mille* without having to pay us a denarius for it. And if we don't do it, they beat us. On the other hand, do it, and all our people laugh at us and call us cowards. What do you think we ought to do, Rabbi?'"

"And what did Yeshu'a say to that?" I said.

"'If any man slaps your face, hitting you on the right side, turn the left side toward him, so that he can hit you there, too,'" Yehudah quoted solemnly; "'and if he makes you carry his pack for a mile, carry it of your own free will for two; for, by such mildness, such forbearance, you'll heap coals of fire upon his head. . . .'"[3]

I looked at ish Kriyoth, but I didn't say anything. To that kind of philosophy, what was there, really, to be said?

"He's convinced the others that he's the Mashiah," Yehudah went on worriedly. "At Cæsarea-Philippi, he more or less forced Shimeon bar Yonah to say he was. And when bar Yonah—I know why they call him kepha, now, Master Nathan; they're referring to that boulder he's got atop his neck—came out with that one, he said: 'No man told you this, Shimeon Kepha; this knowledge came from God, himself. . . .'"[4]

"So?" I said. "Perhaps he *is* the Mashiah, Yehudah. We don't really understand God's ways. If it pleases him, he can change his mind, you know—just as he gave Abraham that sheep as a substitute for his son Isaac as a sacrifice. . . .[5] So maybe he'll use a barefooted Galilean, son of a carpenter, born in Nazareth, a town without a history, as his Anointed, instead of a Prince of Judea, born of The House of Bread, in David's village, and of that kingly line. . . ."

Yehudah caught the deep-hidden note of mockery in my tone at once. I saw then that the quiet, the opportunity for reflection that

months of following Yeshu'a about had afforded him, had both sharp-
ened and quickened his wits.

"You don't believe that," he said harshly. "Sometimes I don't think
you believe much of anything—"

"There, you're right," I said. "Peaceful way to live, Yehudah—"

"Ha!" he snorted. "To hold that the soul is breath, the body, carrion,
the way you Zadokim do, is to rob God of all meaning, Nathan!"

That was the first time he'd omitted that unctuously respectful
"master," and it pleased me.

"Whereupon," I said calmly, "you have absolutely no desire to kill
people over such esoteric questions as whether his name is YHWH,
Zeus, Jupiter, or even Ba'al. You can enjoy a fat slice of pork upon
occasion—and even leave your infant son's poor little pecker uncut.
Hurts like Sheol, y'know, Yehudah—"

He smiled.

"Now you're plaguing me," he said. "Your son, when he's born, will
be circumcised. I know that. And you follow the Kashruth practices to
the letter. Don't tell me it's only to please Rab Hezron! It's because
they appeal to you—to something in your nature. Now don't they,
Nath—master?"

"Let's drop that 'master' business for good," I told him. "We're
brothers, aren't we? If only in sorrow. Therefore there can be no master-
servant relation between us. You worked for me once, but that was
a long time ago—so forget it, will you?"

"All right," he said, obviously pleased. "But, Nathan, about the
dietary laws, the—"

"As far as you go, you're right, Yehudah," I said slowly. "I think
that life is meaningless, without form. And that it's up to us to give
it whatever counterfeits of significance and symmetry we can devise
in order to make it as endurable as possible. Surround it with rites
and ceremonies, invent glorious myths to lend some not altogether
laughable imitations of dignity to all our brothers in sorrow, mitigate
our condition of being pallid, ambulating carrion temporarily provided
with breath. Supply the merciful lies, up to and including the one
about a God who cares about us, which is the first and greatest of the
myths—"

"And the most necessary," Yehudah said. "Even granting you that
He could be a myth, which I don't; though I have had moments of
weakness when I've thought that, too—"

"You'll have them again," I said.

"True," he said quietly; "I'll have them again. But I hope to overcome them in the future, just as I have in the past. The loss of belief, of faith, is a painful thing, Nathan—"

"So's the loss of virginity, Yehudah," I quipped; "but once the bleeding stops, the soreness is gone—"

"Your comparison is false," he said dryly. "The loss of faith—in—a person—dearly beloved, is like a suppurating sword wound in your guts. It—rots you, living."

I looked at him.

"You're talking about Yeshu'a—or Shelomith?" I said.

"About Yeshu'a," he said. "Shelom's out of my life for good. I've forgot her."

I doubted that. I doubted it profoundly. But I didn't tell him that. I said: "Why have you lost faith in Yeshu'a?"

He thought about that. Then he gave the correct answer; the true one.

"Because I'm not a Galilean," he said. "You're a Judean, yourself, Nathan! So you know we're not easily impressed. Or, if we are, the effect wears off quickly enough. For them, he can fail fifty times; but let him succeed just once, and the fifty failures are forgot. While for me—"

"It's just the reverse, isn't it?" I said.

"Exactly. Look, Nathan, he claims—or causes those peasant yokels to claim for him—that he's the Mashiah. All right. I'll grant you that in the matter of his signs and wonders he succeeds more often than he fails. But the Mashiah would *never* fail. . . .

"Another thing that bothers me is that he doesn't know his own mind," Yehudah went on. "He's always contradicting himself. One minute he says, 'Whoever is not against us is for us . . .'; and the next, 'Everyone who is not with me is against me.'⁶ Then he says: 'I didn't come to overthrow the Law, but to fulfill it,' and: 'I tell you heaven and earth will vanish before one vowel point in the Law shall be changed . . .'"⁷

"So?" I said.

"Fine!" Yehudah said angrily; "but in the next breath he's talking about how *new* wine has to be put in *new* bottles,⁸ feasting without washing his hands, and cropping wheat for us to eat on the Shabbat.⁹ Another thing more serious to me is that he isn't—brave. I'm sick of hiding out with him, wandering about, avoiding the towns. If he *were* the Mashiah, Nathan, would he give a fig for Herod Antipas? Wouldn't he rally the people to him, and—"

I looked at ish Kriyoth in wonder.

"But, doesn't he?" I said. "When he preached in Galilee, the crowds—"

"Then, yes," Yehudah said; "now, no. I'll explain why in a minute. But my explanation is based upon a knowledge of politics that I'm not sure that you, a pampered rich man's son and a Zadokim to boot, also have. Tell me, Nathan, if you can, who—I mean what party— are the most liberal, the most advanced thinkers in Israel? What group has wholeheartedly the people's repect? Not necessarily their love, for a good many *amme ha aretz* fear and even hate them. But respect, yes. Tell me that."

"The P'rushim," I said. "The Pharisees."

"Exactly. At first the P'rushim thought he was one of them, and listened to him with respect. But they soon found out he was no Pharisee! When they saw him eating with whores and tax collectors and making light of the law—"

"The P'rushim make it too heavy," I said. "Elohim blast them! They drown you in legalisms. I know they don't mean to, but they do make ceremony seem more important than morality!"

"Still, their concern for every jot and tittle of the Law, exaggerated as it is, has one great virtue, Nathan—"

"Which is?" I said.

"It keeps us—Jews," Yehudah said.

"Ha!" I said. "You call *that* a virtue?"

"Yes," he said quietly, "the *amme kaddishe elyonim*, God's chosen people. The eternal race—who suffer and endure. Kingdoms and empires wax and wane, and sink at last into dust and rubble, but we persist, Nathan. We remain. Why? Because we're possessed of a God so high you can't even see Him, so all-powerful that attempts to reduce His likeness to stone or bronze or gold only insult Him. Whose Temple is inside our hearts, so that it can never be thrown down, nor His idols smashed, because He hasn't, and doesn't even need any—"

"And you attribute *that* to the P'rushim?" I said.

"Yes. Look at what happened to the other peoples who've dwelt in this land, my brother! The Egyptians came and they became Egyptians; the Babylonians, and they turned Babylonians; the Assyrians—"

"I follow you. And when those races perished, they, the changelings—"

"Who, instead of clinging to the Most High God, had turned to the worship of the brutal, animal gods of every passing conqueror, to burning babies in Ba'al's belly, sacrificing to Golden Calves, wallow-

ing with the Temple Whores of Astarte, bowing down to a god with
a vulture's head—"

"A hawk's," I corrected him.

"A hawk's," he said. "What difference does it make? They, the people,
with nothing peculiar about them, with no concepts of their own,
without—"

"Stubbornness—" I suggested. "Obstinacy—"

"Even that. It's a virtue in defense of our God, Nathan. The people
who didn't have it, perished. As those who still don't, will. Lacking
even the anchoring weight of a true identity, a knowledge of *who* they
were, they were so much dust to be swept along behind the chariot
wheels of every race of brawling bloodswillers who passed through on
their way to—nowhere. But God—the God who said, 'Before Abraham
was, I *am!*'—remains. And so do we. We're a peculiar people, Nathan
—and for that blessed, saving peculiarity we have the P'rushim to thank.
Which is why I say we ought to be grateful to them for their maddening
habit of splitting hairs over the slightest, least important aspect of the
Law, because it is precisely that—since it preserves our Jewishness—
which makes us go on, endure—"

"And Yeshu'a?" I said.

"Would take no account of that. He'd lessen it. With his argument
that the Shabbat's made for man, and not man for the Shabbat,[10]
he reduces the distance between us and the idolaters. I grant him he's
right in part; but—Sheol take him!—it's *safer* for humanity to believe
they were made for the Shabbat, for servitude to God, rather than
the reverse! But that's not the worst of it—"

"What is the worst of it?" I said.

"The point I was coming to: How he came to lose the people. He
attacked the P'rushim, who didn't hate him, who were ready to claim
him as one of themselves until they saw how he played fast and loose
with the Law. In fact, it was they who warned him that Antipas was
out to take him,[11] which is why we went over to the Decapolis in the
first place. But, instead of being grateful for that, what does our
Prophet-Mashiah do?"

"What does he?" I said.

"Calls them a nest of serpents, whitewashed sepulchers, swears that
every tax collecting thief and every public whore in Israel will enter
Gan Eden ahead of them!"[12]

"Injudicious," I said.

"Folly!" Yehudah said. "Madness! So now, in self-defense, the P'rushim have turned the people against him. No more crowds, Nathan,

my brother! A few stragglers, that's all. The lame, the halt, the blind, begging to be cured—"

"And lepers?" I said. "I've heard—"

"Lies. As usual. I did see one leper call out to him from a distance, and he said to the poor bastard that his sins were forgiven him, as if that would stop his carcass from rotting while he lived, his nose, ears, toes and fingers from dropping off! But you know perfectly well that lepers aren't permitted to live in towns, and on the very, very rare occasions that one of them happens accidentally to come close to healthy people, all and sundry take sticks and stones and drive him away. So, except for that one poor putrid devil, we didn't even so much as *see* a leper. How could we? We'd have had to visit the camps and caves to which they're confined by Law for that.[13] And he hasn't that much stomach, I can tell you—"

"I see," I said. "Then he's lost the people. Which means—"

"That as the Mashiah, he's already failed," Yehudah said grimly. "Without the people, where will he get his army?"

"I don't think he even wants an army," I said. "I'm afraid he and you have a vastly different concept of the Mashiahship, Yehudah."

"I know that. The Isaiah prophecy. The suffering servant. The sacrificial lamb. I don't object to that conception, brother! If Yeshu'a's committing suicide would cause God to overthrow the Romans, I'd tie the rope to the branch so that he could hang himself, damn him! Only—"

"Only?" I prompted.

"It won't," Yehudah whispered; "and I—God help me!—I love him, still . . ."

"So?" I said.

"So, for the time being, I go along with his mad belief that God will, when he, Yeshu'a, asks Him to, destroy our enemies without our having to lift our hands, but—"

"You don't believe it?"

"No. Have you ever known God to do anything for a man who did nothing to help himself or his people, Nathan?"

"I've never known God to do anything for anybody, period," I said. "Have you?"

"Well—" he hesitated.

"Did He stop you from stealing money to give to Shelom? Or her from giving it—and her nicely rounded little fundament—to Antonius? Or Antonius from leaving her? Or her from leaving me? Or—"

"God's not concerned with rutting swine, Nathan!"

"Isn't He? Then why'd He make so many of them?" I said.

"All right! All right! Let's not split theological hairs. Put it this way: I *know* Yeshu'a ben Yosef is not the Mashiah—"

"If you'd known poor old Yosef, you'd have known that from the first," I said.

"Very likely," Yehudah said. "Any man who would endure Miriam for five minutes flat couldn't have been much. But that's not what I'm referring to now. I mean Yeshu'a lacks the attributes. Among other things, he has no gift for prophecy—"

"Hasn't he?" I said.

"No. He sent us out in pairs, warning us that we'd be persecuted, that we'd likely suffer even martyrdom. And what happened? We were received everywhere with open arms. All the idiots who believe they're possessed of devils—"

"Ha!" I said.

"Yes," he said sadly, "it rubs off on me, your skepticism. It seems I must be a follower, a disciple, never a leader; but I preferred—I prefer —being *his*, to yours. Anyhow, he sent us out, warning us not to go to any Gentile town, to keep the blazes away from the Goyim—and we obeyed him. And, as I was saying, the soul-sick—or, to be conventional, the devil-possessed—came to us, and we cured them. Even I. Even I—" He paused, his voice drowning in the dark sea of his own wonder. "But when we came back to him, where do we find him? In deep conversation with a Canaanitish slut who was begging him to do something for her—"

"Ha!" I said again.

"Not *that*," Yehudah said sternly. "You know him, Nathan. He's no lecher, God knows. She wanted him to cure her son, or her daughter, or her husband, or somebody—I didn't hear that part of it. So he said to her, 'I was sent only to God's people. It's not fit for their bread to be cast before dogs!' But she saw through him at once, and answered him with that fake humility that is those swine-eaters' stock in trade: 'Even dogs are allowed to eat the scraps that fall from the children's table, aren't they, master?' "[14]

"And he?" I said.

"Blessed her, and praised her faith. So even that distinction he'd break down. We must always stay apart, my brother! We must! Or else we'll drown in a sea of alien blood, mongrelize the race, perish—"

"Through copulation," I said; "not a bad way to die, Yehudah!" But, like all fanatics, he was without a sense of humor.

"For the individual, perhaps not. For the race, it's ignominious," he said. "What we have to offer, our concepts—"

"Ethical Monotheism," I said.

"Don't put Greek sounding tags to it!" he howled. "Don't reduce *Shema Ysroël!*—'The Lord is God! The Lord is one!'—to your foreign polysyllables, Nathan!"

"All right," I said wearily; "I won't. Now, besides all this, why did you come, Yehudah? Not just to complain of Yeshu'a, surely?"

"No—" he said; "to save him, Nathan. Or to ask you to. He—he's decided to go up to Jerusalem for Pesach. To preach there. To work wonders—if he can. For, here of late, his powers seem to have deserted him. He believes that God is going to come down from heaven and establish the Eternal Kingdom at his, Yeshu'a's, demand—or command. Because he has his relative position, and God's, a trifle confused by now. And you know Pilatus. Well enough, it would seem, to tumble his wife with impunity—"

"That's not exactly the instrument I used," I said solemnly, "but let it pass! Tell me, Yehudah, my brother—what do you think will happen there?"

His voice made a whipcrack: "The same thing that you think, Nathan!"

"Which is?" I whispered.

"That the Romans haven't forgot how to make crosses, nor the use of them," Yehudah ish Kriyoth said.

Yohannah looked at me, but she didn't stop crying. She couldn't.

"Now, Yu-Ann," I groaned, "he'll be all right. I promise—"

"Hush, Nathan!" she said. "Don't promise! I love my brother. I don't want him to die. But I'd rather that he—"

"Yohannah!" my Uncle Hezron said.

"Yes, Rab Hezron," she whispered. "You're right. I shouldn't say that, should I? Yesu hasn't a wife. Nor a child. And Nathan has—both, now. I want my baby to have his father—and—and—brothers! Dozens of them! So all I'm asking is that—my husband stays home with me. That he doesn't go up to Jerusalem with my crazy wild man idiot brother and get himself killed along with him! Please, Nathan! I almost got you murdered because of Yeshu'a once already! So I ask you, I beg you to—"

"Desert him?" I said. "Let him—die?"

My Uncle Hezron looked at me.

"Can you prevent it?" he said sadly.

"I think so, yes. According to what ish Kriyoth said, they should be close to the borders of Samaria by now. On Bedu, I can overtake them easily enough. I'll talk to him, persuade him—"

Yohannah shook her head.

"You can't. You know you can't, Nathan. Have you, has anybody, *ever* been able to stop Yesu from doing something once his mind's made up?" she said.

She was right. I knew that. But there were other factors involved, now.

"All right," I said; "I grant you that, Yu-Ann. But, all the same, it would be better for me to be in Jerusalem when he gets there. It won't be a matter of my facing down a mob of Galilean yokels with my sword in hand. Rather, it would be an exercise in diplomacy—in which I, a kinsman of the High Priest, a son of a member of the Sanhedrin, would be able to bring all sorts of pressure to bear to prevent his ever being arrested—"

"That is, as far as your Bœthusian-Sadducee party is concerned; and even there, you'd have your work cut out for you," my uncle said. "They'd arrest him at the first hint of a popular outcry—in order to keep the Romans off their own precious necks. And it would never occur to any Zadokim—not even to my loved and respected turncoat of a brother—that a self-proclaimed Mashiah *could* be anything else but a radical revolutionary. They'd maintain their policy—their only policy—that it's far better for one poor deluded Galilean madman to die than to have the Romans decimate us. That policy which is cruel, unjust, and—absolutely correct!"

"I agree," I said. "Only—"

"Only you think you may be able to persuade them to overlook whatever blasphemous folly poor Yeshu'a is sure to commit in Jerusalem. All right. Say you can. I doubt it; but, for argument's sake, let's say you're successful with the priestly party. Can you also—so persuade—the Romans?"

"I'd be admitted to Pilatus," I said. "I have his ear—"

My uncle looked at me.

"Or his wife's," he said.

I saw all the color leave Yohannah's mouth, but I didn't hesitate.

"Or his wife's," I said.

Yohannah faced me then. When she spoke, her voice was quiet. I could feel the grate and scrape of anguish in it; but I couldn't hear them. Which made it worse, somehow.

"Nathan—" she said.

"Yes, Yu-Ann?" I whispered.

"Yesu—wouldn't have his life from you at such a price. You know him, my husband. You *know* he wouldn't."

I did know that. I knew it very well.

"All right. Claudia's out. I won't try to save him that way," I said.

"Promise," Yohannah said. "Swear it—by our son."

"All right," I said again; "I swear it."

"By our son!" she insisted.

"By our son. And by the love I bear his mother," I said.

She came up to me, put her arms around my neck.

"Nathan—" she said.

"Yes, Yu-Ann?"

"Don't get killed. Don't *you* get killed. Not even if—"

I put up my hands and broke her grip.

"Don't say it!" I said. "Don't put that condition on it, Yohannah!"

"Why not?" she said.

"You can't weigh my life against *his*," I said. "He's unique. Yu-Ann. There has never been anyone like him before. There never will be again. I don't count. He does."

"More than—us?" she whispered. "More than our growing old together? More than the children you'll never give me?"

"More than that. More than anything," I said.

She hung there, staring at me. Then she went up on tiptoe, and kissed my mouth.

"All right," she said. "I come third. After Yesu. After Helvetia. Doesn't matter. I haven't any pride. Can't afford it, now. Go. Save my crazy brother. Then come back to me. Because if you don't—"

"If I can't, you mean."

"Whether you don't, or can't—won't change anything. *She* left all your days—sealed with her honor. You said that. So—I'll just seal—your memory—with mine. Oh! Not what you're thinking! I only meant that you'll condemn me to a widow's weeds, forever, Nathan. And your son—to your absence. But, if Yesu means that much to you—go!"

He did. I went.

Book V

In which I follow Yeshu'a ha Notzri up to Jerusalem.

Chapter XXII

I CAUGHT up with them on the very borders of Sebaste, or Samaria; and, for several moments, it looked to me as though I were again going to have to use my sword. You see, what your *Besorahim* don't make clear is that Yeshu'a had many more people with him than just the Twelve, more, in fact, than even the seventy-two he'd sent out to preach in the villages.[1] Some of his followers had brought their wives, and there were as well even a few unmarried pious women who had contributed materially to the support of the disciples—among them, I noted at once, the lovely Miriam of Migdal-Nunaya, as calm, as absentminded as usual, but with the seven devils he was supposed to have cast out of her hovering almost visibly about her in the evening air.

But now that herd of superstitious Galileans—more than a hundred people, all told; perhaps more even than two hundred, it was hard to tell—were packed together in a dense mass, all shouting and shaking their fists and staves at the same time. As I rode forward, I heard the bull-bellows of Yohannan and Yaakob, the banim Zebediah, drowning out the rest. The *Boane Ragsha*, Sons of Fury, were being precisely that, and themselves, as usual.

"Master!" they roared. "Let us call down fire from heaven and burn the bastards up!"[2]

Then Yeshu'a spoke, and all the shouting died in that instant, all the upraised fists and staves remained in midair in a sudden arrest of motion, a kind of halting, a petrifying of fury that should have been comic, but, strangely, wasn't.

"No," he said quietly; "burning and killing is not our way. Come, let us go eastward through the Jordan Valley. We'll pass through the forest,[3] and no man will harm us."

I could see the fists and staves drifting downward—slowly and reluctantly, for Galileans are *not* a peaceful people—and I made my way toward him, wondering, as I rode, for perhaps the ten thousandth time at that power, that authority of his, which could halt a raging mob with a slow, soft-spoken word.

He saw me then, towering above the crowd—I was mounted on Bedu —and smiled at me. And, as always, the world renewed itself; the air became smoky pearl, fragrant with flowers; in the tamarisks, the nightingales sang, although it was still day.

I leaped down, clasped him in my arms.

"How is Rab Hezron?" he asked me. "And my little shrew of a sister? Tell me, does she still beat you?"

"No!" I laughed. "Yohannah's a perfect lamb. She has been ever since Abal stuck my own dagger into me—"

"For my sake," he said quietly.

"For your sake, brother," I said; "and no more—or even less—than you would have done for me. Uncle Hezron's fine. Sends you his love, and several camel loads of advice, which I'll spare you. *My* news is that you're to become an uncle, and I a father, some eight months hence. How does that strike you, Yeshu'a?"

I saw at once that it saddened him, even before he opened his mouth. For the first time I realized how much he missed, and would have loved to lead, a normal life, if his bone-deep conviction that he was the Mashiah, and had to carry out his appointed role, hadn't prevented it.

"I envy you, Nathan," he said simply. "The foxes have holes, the birds have nests, but the Son of Man has no place to lay his head. . . ."[4]

That was also the first time I'd heard him use the expression *bar enosh,* "Son of Man," with its Messianic implications, in reference to himself; but to quarrel with them would have doomed my mission to failure at the outset, so I let that go by without comment.

Instead, I asked him: "What was all the uproar about?"

"Our friends the Shomroni," Yeshu'a said, calling the Samaritans by their ancient Hebrew name, "objected to so many of us passing through their territory. One or two would be all right, but more than two hundred are two hundred times too many. Yehudah ish Kriyoth says it's because our numbers reduce their chances of robbing and murdering us. He may be right, for all I know. . . ."

"He *is* right. Slippery beggars, the Samaritans. So that was what got the banim Zebediah wild?"

"Doesn't take much," he chuckled; "I despair of ever taming them. But tell me, brother: why have *you* come? It would seem to me that with Yunna pregnant, you'd be needed at home. . . ."

"There you've hit the mark," I said slowly. "The trouble is that she, and Rab Hezron—and I—are worried sick over your going up to Jerusalem. . . ."

He looked at me then. My bones, the very marrow of them, trembled under the terrible authority of his gaze.

"So you've come to dissuade me?" he said.

I thought about that. Then, almost instinctively, I took the right tack: "No," I said. "To try to safeguard you after you get there."

That pleased him. Your *Evangelionoi* to the contrary, he had no desire to die. Life was a sweetness in his veins still, slow-running, powerful, deep. He was hoping against hope that the bitter cup could be put by.

He said: "Come, Nathan, let Shimeon Kepha lead your horse while you walk with me for a space so that we can consider the matter between us. For you're right: you can help me. It lies within your powers to—"

"How?" I asked him.

"In various ways. First, I'd ask you to ride ahead and find lodgings for me. At Beth Anya, not in Jerusalem itself."

"That's smart," I said, meaning it.

He looked at me; but he apparently didn't want to consider the implications of my remark.

"I'd suggest you try the house of Shimeon, the Essene,[5] first of all," he said. "You know him, don't you?"

"Yes," I said. I did know Shimeon. He'd come out to Qumrân for a period of meditation while I was recuperating at the monastery from my physical injuries and the soul-sickness my Helvetia's death had left in me. Many of the town Essenes did that from time to time, to purify themselves and to renew their faith. He was a good, pious, simple man. I remembered that I had liked him very much.

"And if, for some reason, Shimeon can't take you in?" I said.

"Then try the house of Miriam and Martha, who'll be glad to," Yeshu'a said. "But, since there is no man in that house, I'd prefer Shimeon's. I care not a fig for wagging tongues, ordinarily; but what I have to do in Jerusalem is too important to allow it to be distorted by scandalmongers. . . ."

He was right, of course. The risk of scandal involved in his staying alone in the house of two not uncomely women, still in their middle thirties, was great. For you see, Miriam and Martha hadn't any brother name Eleazer, or, as you call it, Lazarus, or anything else. I think your most fanciful scribe borrowed Lazarus from a parable I once heard Yeshu'a tell, in which a sinner asks Father Abraham to send the dead and blessed Eleazer/Lazarus back to life so that he could warn the sinner's equally sinful brothers of the folly of their evil ways. Not even the fact that in Yeshu'a's parable Father Abraham refused the requested resurrection stopped your mythmaker from attributing actual existence to an imaginary being, in order to credit Yeshu'a with still another miracle.[6] But, of course, all that lay far in the future still, so the only effect Yeshu'a's remark about Miriam and Martha's unguarded state of innocence had upon me was to awake my black, antic sense of humor.

"And should the good, devout sisters fail you," I said, "how about my getting you a room in the house of Shelomith and her husband? They live at Beth Anya too, you know."

He shook his head, said "No." Like that, without explanations. It was one of the things that added to his dignity, his authority: he could, and usually did, state his intentions flatly, feeling no need to support them with the whys. It is a curious fact that the proffering of your reasons unasked inevitably weakens your position, which was one of the many, many things he knew.

"All right," I said. "No Shelom. What else can I do for you there?"

"You can buy me a donkey. A young donkey. A colt. You're family now, so I'll accept that gift from you."

I stood there, staring at him. Then it hit me. I went on standing there, lost in admiration at the beautiful subtlety of it. There is, in the Book of Zechariah, a passage which reads:

> "Rejoice heart and soul, daughter of Zion!
> Shout with gladness, daughter of Jerusalem!
> See now, your King comes to you;
> he is victorious, he is triumphant,
> humble and riding on a donkey,
> on a colt, the foal of a donkey.
> He will banish chariots from Ephraim
> and horses from Jerusalem;
> the bow of war will be banished.
> He will proclaim peace for the nations.
> His empire shall stretch from sea to sea
> from the river to the ends of the earth . . ."[7]

Every Jew knew that passage. So when he came riding into Jerusalem like that on an ass's foal, they'd know that he came as the Mashiah. But the Romans wouldn't. They'd see a simple Galilean rab, mounted on a donkey. And since what they'd expect in any self-proclaimed Jewish Mashiah would be somebody like the brigand Yeshu'a bar Abbas, armed to the teeth and mounted on a splendid horse, surely they'd let my brilliantly mad brother-in-law enter the city without interference.

That way maybe he'd live a day or two longer, giving me at least

the chance to forestall the Zealots—who had always rejected that
conception of the Mashiah, logically enough considering that what
we needed to free us of the Romans was a fighting hero-king, and certainly not a suffering, sacrificial lamb—before they fell upon him in
their fury; and perhaps even the chance to talk the P'rushim, my
uncle's sect, and the Zadokim, my father's, out of stoning him to death
for the monstrous blasphemy of claiming that he, a lowly Galilean
carpenter, was, or even could be, a rod of Jesse, a branch out of David,
the expected Mashiah, a Judean, and a King.

"Consider it bought," I said; "what then?"

"You leave it in a place that I'll decide upon later, after we get
there. I'll do the rest. That's all—except one other thing: could you
—in absolute secrecy, of course—procure us for the one night of Pesach,
a house with a dining room big enough for me and my twelve to eat the
Passover in?"

"Yes," I said; "there's a house I happen to own—"

"No!" he said at once.

"Why not?" I said.

His face darkened.

"Because," he whispered, "if it goes wrong, I shouldn't want you to
suffer because of me."

"Don't worry, I won't," I said. "No one knows I own this house—"

That was true. It had been given to me by Claudia, by letter, in
memory of the nights of love we'd spent there. And that, too, I admit
now with shame, appealed to my outrageous sense of humor. Did his
powers extend to converting my private Temple to Aphrodite and
Eros into a suitable setting for our noblest rite? "I'll have to have it
aired," I thought, "lest the lingering odors of whoremusk and used
harlot profane the festivities. . . ."

"How will we find it?" he said. "Because above all things, *you*
mustn't—"

"I know," I cut him off. "For Yohannah's sake, and my son's, my
discretion is increasing by the hour. Tell you what: I'll send a servant
to the well at Beth Phage, the House of Wild Figs. When you see a
man drawing water, which is a thing that usually only women do,
follow him into the city, and he will lead you to it. I shall be waiting
for you there."

"No," he said; "if there's trouble, you—"

"There'll be no trouble," I said. "Would you deny me the joy of
eating the Paschal lamb, the bitter herbs, the unleavened bread, and
drinking the four cups with you, my brother?"

He considered that.

"All right," he said. "The risk is small, I suppose. No man can make a crime of eating the Passover. But remember we celebrate it two nights before you Judeans do, for we use the Essenes' Jubilees calendar—"[8]

"I'll remember," I said; then: "Yesu—do you think there's going to be trouble?"

"I don't know," he said honestly. "There could be. Remember your prophecy, Nathan?"

"Forget my prophecy," I said. "Rather remember what it says in the Wisdom of Solomon:

'Let us lie in wait for the virtuous man, since he annoys us
and opposes our way of life,
reproaches us for our breaches of the Law,
and accuses us of playing false to our upbringing.
He claims to have knowledge of God,
and calls himself a son of the Lord.
Before us he stands, a reproof to our way of thinking;
the very sight of him weighs our spirits down;
his way of life is not like other men's,
the paths he treads are unfamiliar.
In his opinion we are counterfeit;
he holds aloof from our doings as though from filth;
he proclaims the final end of the virtuous as happy
and boasts of having God for his father.
Let us see if what he says is true,
let us observe what kind of end he, himself, will have.
If the virtuous man is God's son, God will take his part
and rescue him from the clutches of his enemies.
Let us test him with cruelty and with torture,
and thus explore this gentleness of his,
and put his endurance to the proof.
Let us condemn him to a shameful death
since he will be looked after—we have his word for it!' "[9]

He looked at me and his black eyes burned me, living; I was cindered, consumed in their night-shade flame.

"He's right," he said; "Solomon, or whoever it was who really wrote those words. I shall be looked after. My Father will take care of me."

"Your—father?" I said. "But your father's—dead."

He shook his head, and his eyes swam the sky dizzily. Slow thunder rolled beyond the world's rim, shaped itself into words.

"Not my earthly father," he said: "My heavenly Father—God."

I hung there. What he had said was enough to earn him his death, even if spoken before the most liberal Jew on earth. It was not blasphemy, under our Law, but something worse: It was *mesith*,[10] the crime of setting up "Other Gods Before Me," and enticing the people to worship them. For his idea of being God's son in a special way destroyed the lonely uniqueness of our Deity, made of Yeshu'a himself a demigod like the host of holy bastards in your ancestors' religion, reduced our faith to the same kind of lecherous farce that your ancient myths are. But I didn't tell him that. I couldn't. And he wouldn't have understood me, anyhow.

"Do you remember the day of my baptism?" he said. "You must. You witnessed it."

"Yes," I whispered.

"God spoke to me then. He hovered above me in the form of a dove. I heard his voice. He said, 'You are my beloved son, in whom I am blessed; for this day I have begotten you.' "[11]

I still didn't say anything. What could one say to that?

"Because you see, Nathan," he went on quietly, "you have never understood what my mission was. You—and Shimeon Zealotes, and Yehudah ish Kriyoth—and perhaps even the banim Zebediah—would reduce me to an earthly king, diminish my task into something so paltry as overthrowing the Romans. They will be overthrown, of course; but none of us shall have to lift a finger to do it. No. My mission is a greater thing—"

"What is it." I said.

"To usher in the Kingdom of my Father, God. For I say to you that there are some here present who will not die before they see the Kingdom of God come in power."[12]

"Yeshu'a—" I said quietly.

"Yes, Nathan?" he said.

"I'm not interested in the Kingdom of God. I don't give two figs on a barren tree for the Kingdom of God. What I want to live to see is the Kingdom of Israel—free of the Romans."

But he didn't get angry, as I fully expected him to. He said: "That, too, will come. That is also part of it."

I thought: "The rest you can keep!" I said: "And without hands?"

"And without hands."

I couldn't help it; I burst out: "Yesu, you're mad! They'll kill you! At best they'll stone you. At worst, turn you over to the Romans and let them crucify you! For Yu-Ann's sake, for the sake of your unborn nephew, don't get yourself slaughtered for the imaginary kingdom of your mythical god!"

He stared at me; said: "Poor Nathan! It's hard to live without faith, isn't it?"

"Yes," I whispered; "but to die for a piece of monumental folly is harder. Or at least to me it seems so—"

"I shan't die," he said. "Now go. Ride on ahead and prepare the way for me. I can depend upon you still, can't I?"

"Yes. Why yes, of course," I said.

So it was, that mounted on my fleet Bedu, I got to Jerusalem long before Yeshu'a and his followers did. After my mother's outcries of joy at the sight of me had subsided, I did what I could to prevent a major celebration of the news that the banim Mattathiah would go on, would continue in time, that I was not to be the last of that august line. My father would have invited half Jerusalem—the half that counted, of course—to feast this news with him.

"No," I said; "better wait, Father—until you see whether it isn't a girl. Or a hermaphrodite. Or a monster with at least two heads . . ."

"Or an idiot," my mother sniffed, "considering from—or rather *what*, you married!"

I hadn't thought of that, though I should have. Galilee is much more democratic than Judea. Among us, it is written that a pious man may marry the daughter of one of our great men, the daughter of the president of a synagogue, the daughter of a teacher of children; but then the text adds sternly: "But let him not marry the daughters of the *amme ha aretz* for they are loathsome, and their children are abominations, and of them, the Scripture says, 'Cursed is he that lieth with any manner of beast!' "[13]

I took the letter out of the bosom of my robe. I had found it hidden in the change of clothes Yohannah had prepared for my journey. Except for being tear-spotted, it was beautifully written. For, despite the childlike simplicity of her speech, Yohannah, in large measure, shared her brother's artistry with words. I have often wondered where they got that trait. Not from Miriam, surely.

"Can you read this, Mother?" I said, and passed it over. There I had her. Like many another spoiled and pampered daughter of our upper class, my mother was intellectually lazy. She could read, of course; but just barely. But, before you scorn her for her ignorance, allow me to point out, in her defense, that the languages she had to read were not Latin and Greek, but Aramaic and Hebrew. Suppose *you* had to read a language that is all consonants, whose vowels are indicated by little marks on which the scribes themselves are not always in agreement and often leave out altogether; suppose you had to determine the tense of a verb that when written in the future tense can be converted into the past by merely marking the letter *vav* with either one of two tiny symbols, do you honestly think you could do it?

When one has been trained to it, as I've been, and have practiced it daily, as I have, reading our twin languages becomes second nature, and one does it without conscious effort, or taking thought. But it is not easy. I could see my mother moving her lips, struggling over Yohannah's somewhat archaic Galilean turns of phrase. After a moment, she gave it up, and passed it over to my father.

"Read it aloud, Father!" I said. "I want Mother to hear it."

My father read:

> " 'My heart goes with you,
> Where you go.
> And though you leave your life in me
> You take away my life.
> You deny me even the surcease
> Of dying.
> You force me to live in order to care for
> Him
> Who will torment me all my days
> By being your image, by being my memories
> Fleshed out, by being you
> Resurrected, continued, carried forth
> In time.
> So be it. If it must be so,
> I am resigned.
> You do what must be done, as always,
> And count not the cost to yourself
> Or me. But if Heaven grant that you
> Live and come back to me, my Hosannahs
> Shall strike through the floor of the sky
> And deafen God.
> Either way, so be it.
>   I love you.
>   YU-ANN.' "

"My wife wrote that, Mother," I said quietly. "And you couldn't even read it. So I ask you, Who is the *am ha aretz*? She—or you?"

My father was staring at me now, long and thoughtfully. In a way, I'd turned his world upside down, too. In theory, we admit that the *amme ha aretz*, "Those Ignorant of Torah," can become *Haberim*, "the Learned"; practically, we doubt it. But to witness the proof that it can happen gnawed away at the bulwarks of class, of pride. Only my father was a ben Matthya, a ben Mattathiah, and hence, by pure instinct, a gentleman.

"You have married very well indeed, my son," he said.

"And *she* badly," I said. "Well, Mother?"

"Forgive me, Nathan," my mother said. "That she loves you so greatly and so purely is enough for me. You must bring her here. I do have some right to both my daughter and my grandson, don't I?"

I could picture those two ferociously jealous she-lions in the same house. But I didn't say that. Instead, I said: "Father, there's a thing I'd consult with you. Let's go into your scriptorium, shall we?"

"Oh!" my mother said.

"It's politics, Mother," I said, knowing how that subject bored her.

"Then go," she said; "but come back as soon as you can. I want to hear all about Yohannah and—"

"Oh, all right, Mother!" I said.

"You mean your brother-in-law is actually going to proclaim himself the Mashiah?" my father said.

"Yes," I said.

"He's mad!" my father said.

"I know that," I said. "But that's not the point. The point is: How can I save him?"

My father considered the matter, slowly.

"If he claims to be the Mashiah aloud, now, no way," he said.

"Father, couldn't you intervene in the Sanhedrin? Tell them he's sick! Tell them he's devil-possessed! Uncle Hezron says your influence in the Lower Court is growing yearly—"

"He's right. In fact, I've been made *ab beth din*, vice president of the Lesser Sanhedrin, through the influence of your so dearly beloved cousin, Yosef ben Kaiapha, the High Priest. I'm not proud of the fact. So far, I haven't even written Hezron about it. So I could intervene in your crazy brother-in-law's behalf. But what good would it do? If he claims the Mashiahship in Jerusalem, the crowds will take it up and use him—or even force him—to lead an outbreak against the Romans. They're still burning to revenge themselves for the people Pilatus had clubbed to death when they protested against his seizure of the sacred fund to build *your* aqueduct—"

"As a result of which we have enough water for the first time in centuries," I said bitterly, "but let that go. I tell you that Yeshu'a will be neither tricked, nor forced into leading a revolt against the Romans. His idea of the Mashiah is that the Anointed of God is to lead us into

ways of purity and thus bring into being God's Kingdom of Peace and
Plenty—"

"Not only crazy, but stark, raving mad!" my father said. "You mean
he is *that* ignorant of human nature? Or does he simply disregard it?"

"Both," I said. "He believes in the infinite perfectability of man—"

"And I—and you, I suspect—in humanity's utter vileness—"

"Not vileness," I said; "stupidity. But this is getting us nowhere!
Father, couldn't the Sanhedrin simply ignore him?"

"And leave him to the Romans? Him and the city mob—who'll surely
seize upon his every word, or any other madman's, for that matter, as
an excuse to revolt—and sweep all Jeruselem down to ruin? What more
delightful present could we give to the husband of your whore?"

I let that go by. I had to. My father was a Sadducee, and the Zadokim don't mince words.

"Couldn't you just arrest him—and give him a beating, say? Throw
him and his fellows out of town? Warn them not to come back?"

"And have Pilatus shake the horns you've affixed to his forehead at us
and accuse us of treason, for not delivering a criminal guilty of *laesa
maiestas* against Cæsar up to him? The Romans oversimplify, you
know. The Mashiah, by definition, is king of the Jews. But *Cæsar* is
king of the Jews. Cæsar is king of all the world. Hence, Mashiah equals
rebellion, revolt, treason. Besides, there's another difficulty—"

"Which is?" I whispered.

"False prophecy. Unless he can *prove* he is of David's line, he's
guilty of it. Can he?"

"No," I said; "for the very simple reason that he isn't."

"Hence, to be stoned, by our Law. Only *that* won't happen—"

"Why not?" I said.

"Yosef ben Kaiapha hasn't the testicles," my father said. That was
another Sadducee trait: crudity of speech. "If your Yeshu'a proclaims
himself the Mashiah, he'll have the city mob behind him on the spur of
that same instant. The fools will never stop to consider how preposterous
those claims are. So our fine High Priest—a slippery swine if there
ever was one!—won't dare have your Galilean idiot stoned. Nor will
he dare release him. No, he'll find some way to shift the onus onto the
Romans and thus save his precious hide from our howling rabble. That's
one tactic he might use. Another would be delay. You say that your
Yeshu'a is a man of peace, that he inclines toward the sacrificial lamb
concept of the Mashiah, doesn't he?"

"He's asked me to buy him an ass's foal for him to ride into Jerusalem
on," I said.

"Ha!" my father said, recognizing the reference at once. "Do it, for heaven's sake!"

"Why?" I said.

"That way you get *our* buttocks out of the wine press! Let him come as the man of peace, and the mob themselves will kill him in their disappointed rage. Or at least the Zealots among them will. I tell you, son, there is only one way to save ben Yosef—no, two. . . ."

"Which are?" I said.

"Persuade him *not* to proclaim himself Mashiah," my father said.

I shook my head.

"Nothing or nobody could do that," I said.

"Then keep him the Sheol out of Jerusalem!" my father roared.

"Nor that," I said.

My father looked at me.

"In that case, buy a grave plot for him, Nathan," he said gently, "for he is already a dead man."

I stood up.

"Where are you going?" my father said.

"To see Yosef ha Arimathæa,"[14] I said.

Yosef of Arimathæa was much more sympathetic than my father had been. Which was why the fact that he confirmed my father's analysis in every detail left me in even greater despair.

"So you think there's no hope?" I almost wept.

He looked at me. Then he said it: "One. Is he—strong?"

"Very," I said.

Yosef hesitated.

"You were at Khirbet Qumrân," he said at last. "How much do you know of the New Covenanters' medical, even magical, lore?"

I looked at him, hope leaping and blazing in my eyes.

"A great deal," I said. "Do you think—"

"If he can endure crucifixion several hours," Yosef murmured; "if we can delay the execution so that by nightfall—when according to our laws his body must be taken down—he's still alive . . . If you can get to Qumrân and back with—what we'll need . . . If we can persuade some woman to take the risk—the woman make a soporific, you know, to help those poor devils not to suffer too much . . . It's even customary—"

His voice trailed off.

But he'd already said it all. Except the one thing I needed to know. So I said it: "Why?"

"I heard him teach once—in the Decapolis," Yosef said. "He is very close to God. Such a man should be saved."

Despite his age, and the respect I owed him as my father's friend, I clasped him to my bosom and kissed him. So great was my hope, my joy, that I wept.

Yosef ha Arimathæa pushed me away from him gently.

"Now sit down, son Nathan, and let us plan it carefully," he said.

Chapter XXIII

WHEN I came out of the house of Yosef ha Arimathæa, it was already night. I flapped along in my long Jewish robes like a bird of darkness, beaking my way through layers of stenches, for to get home, I had to cross a broad belt of taverns and brothels, all of them redolent with stinks that my nose ticked off, inventoried: vomit, offal, urine, dung, wine, sweat, carnal sin. There were sounds: a drunkard's bellow, whoreshriek, the sodden thud of blows on flesh. I moved on, hope afire in me, a drunkenness, the blood in my veins new wine, but alternating with the ice of fear.

I have to sleep, I thought; I have to. Start out tomorrow with my tail dragging, and I'll muck it. Yosef's right. It's the one way out—if all else fails, as sure as Sheol it's going to. But it has to be—perfect. Anything less—one little slip, and Yeshu'a—

A woman stepped out of the shadows and took my arm.

"What's the hurry, Prince of Judea?" she murmured. "Surely a rich young ruler like you has an hour—or even a night—to spare for the delights of love?"

"Let go of me, whore!" I hissed. Then I stopped. Not only my voice, my feet, but all of me. My breath. My heart.

"Shelom—" I said, tasting her name in my mouth like ashes, gritgray; but with live embers underneath. Coals. That burned me still. "Oh. Shelom!"

"You know me?" she said. Her voice coiled about me, serpentine, caressing, warm; but with an edge hidden in its purring felinity, a harshness, a grate. "Then you must know I'm the best—"

Across the narrow alley, a tavern door crashed open. A drunken roisterer half staggered, half fell out into the street. He reeled away from there, muttering curses, leaving the door ajar. And the warm yellow lamplight from inside the tavern washed over my bearded face.

Shelomith took a backward step. She brought her two hands up (golden lotus blossoms, Nile-borne, floating, floating!) and clapped them to both sides of her face. The lamplight from the tavern pooled in her eyes. But it wasn't warm anymore. It made wintry fire, Gehenna's flames congealed, turned ice, turned screaming, night-black Sheol.

Then the trembling got into her. It was a curious thing to watch. A tiny tremor began down low, somewhere in the neighborhood of her ankles. It climbed up her legs, her thighs, her belly, her breasts, reached her throat. There it halted, lingered, grew, became a drumbeat, rolling, rolling, silent, of course, unheard; but in that filthy alley of greasy taverns, of strolling whores, it was the after-ache of thunder, the toothed and vibrant echoes of pure, shrieking anguish within my deaf-slammed ears.

I couldn't take my eyes off that quiver in her throat. I stood there watching while it beat and beat and beat. Then it leaped the gap to her chin, her mouth. Her lips fluttered so they made a blur. Only her right cheek was still, where the scar of my uncle's whip slash had left a kind of slight paralysis, I suppose. I couldn't stand it. I tried not to look at her. But I couldn't do that either.

"Shelom—" I said again, and took a step toward her. But her knees unlocked themselves with a curiously awkward, jerky motion; the thud they made striking the cobblestones juddered through my heart. I put my hands down to her; but she wasn't within their reach anymore. Instead she lay on her belly like a wounded dog, and wrapped her two arms about my ankles.

I felt the great hot wet fungus flower of her mouth pressing against my dusty flesh. Then she turned her head sidewise, cradling it against my feet; and flooded them both with the slow brim and scald of her hurt, her shame.

It was too much. I bent, put my two hands under her armpits, feeling the perfume and sweat-matted thick she-animal growth there, and raised her up.

"Shelom—" I said, or rather groaned.

And she: "I told you I was born a whore! I told you, Nathan!"

And I: "No, Shelom—"

And she: "Why'd it have to be you? Of all the men in Jerusalem, Judea, Galilee, the world—"

"Because it had to be," I said. "Come, I'll take you home, now—"

"Home?" she said dully. "Home?"

"Beth Anya. Your husband's house—"

She said: "Ha!"

And I: "Why not? Aren't you—don't you—?"

"Live with him anymore? No. He swears that if he ever catches me with a man, he'll have me stoned as an adulteress. God knows he can; that's the Law. Go to him! Tell him I'm here! By the time you get back, I'll be stretched out across a table in that tavern with one of those drunken bastards on top of me pumping away. Give him his proof—so he can have me stoned!"

"No," I said.

"Nathan, hit me. Knock me down. Walk on me. Spit in my face."

"No," I said.

"You know what I do now? What I let them do to me?"

"No," I said; "and I don't want to."

But she told me. There wasn't any way to stop her. She said it, speaking slowly, clearly, explicitly through the lurch and shudder of my quivering gut, using words as vile as my nausea. No. Viler.

"I charge extra for that. The old ones, mostly. Who've lost their powers. Who can't get it up. Who—"

"Stop it!" I said.

"And what I do to them? The ones who're queer that way? Or maybe just lazy. I make 'em wash, first. When I'm not too drunk to remember. Even so, the smell, the taste—"

I hit her then, hard across the mouth. Her great, fleshy lips broke against her teeth. From both corners of her mouth a flood of black scarlet gushed, dyeing her quivering chin, dripping upon the paving stones, making splotches as big as denarii.

"Oh, Shelom!" I groaned; but, by then, she had my right hand, the one I'd hit her with, between both of her own, and was pressing her hot salt-wet bleeding mouth to it in an agony of tenderness, in gratitude for its having granted her this kind of pain: hard, bright, hurtful, sudden, physical, which broke through and dulled for the moment the other which was none of these, and of which she was very slowly and terribly dying.

I tore it from her grasp.

"Shelom," I said, "this has got to stop! You weren't made for this life; you—"

"Wasn't I?" she said. "Want a demonstration? Come with me to Zeno's, and I'll show you. Gratis. Free. Maybe *then* you'll despise me. After I finger you and mouth you and make you perform the Roman abomination on me and the Egyptian and the Greek—"

"No," I said slowly. "You can't, no matter what you do. How can you make me despise you, when you've never been able to make me stop—loving you, Shelom?"

She stood there, looking at me. Then she started to cry. That bad, awful, unbearable way she could. That listening to wasn't the kind of torture that killed you, but something worse: the kind that didn't, that wasn't even merciful enough to.

"Nathan," she said; "come with me. To—to—my place. You—you don't have to—do anything. Just hold me. Just sit and talk to me. I don't even want to. At least not very much. Sheol! Why lie? With *you* I always want to. But I won't. For your sake. Who knows but what I don't have something loathsome by now? Please, Nathan? Oh, love, I want— I need you so!"

Slowly I shook my head. I was tempted to go with her, though not out of lust. Rather I was driven by the most difficult of all emotions for me to resist: pity. Yet, I couldn't. Tomorrow I had to be in full control of myself. I needed a head as clear as spring water, as subtle as a serpent's, as wily as a fox's, to do what I had to do. What was sure to fail; but what had to be tried, anyhow. If I spent the night with Shelomith, even sinlessly, I should be lost.

"Shelom, I can't," I said; "tonight I—"

She stared at me. Her gaze plumed the night with black, sulphurous flame.

"Tonight you're going to—her. To Claudia Procula. To your imperial whore. Did you think I didn't know she was here?"

"No," I said tiredly. "Tonight I'm going home—to my father's house— to sleep, if that's possible."

"Don't lie to me, Nathan!"

"I never lie," I said. "You ought to know that. I don't want a woman. I don't need one—yet. You see, I left a wife in Nazareth, Shelomith. Left her gravid with my child."

It cost her a full minute to get that one word out. I could see her trying to force it into sound, through the visible strangle in her throat, the wild shudder of her chin, her mouth.

"Who?" she grated, finally.

"Yohannah bath Yosef. Yeshu'a's sister," I said.

"Oh," she said. Like that, very quietly. "Then he'll be a—a god. The child, I mean. *Your* son—and with Yeshu'a's blood in him, too, from the mother's side. What are you going to call him, Nathan?"

"Don't know. Yehudah, I suppose. My greatest ancestor was called that."

"No, don't. It's such an ugly name. Call him—Yeshu'a, won't you,

Nathan, huh? After—*him*? Oh, I know, I know! The law says you can't name a child after a living person. But there must have been at least one Yeshu'a among your forefathers, so that you—"

"There was. Yeshu'a ben P'iabi, who was kicked out of the High Priesthood by Herod, in order to put another great-granduncle of mine, Shimeon ben Bœthus, in. Seemed His Royal Wickedness wanted to marry Shimeon's daughter, my grandaunt Mariamne. But that's ancient history. Now you tell me: Why should I name my firstborn Yeshu'a?"

"So it'll be like *him*. Like my—our Yeshu'a. That way you'll make sure your son will be beautiful and good and—"

"As it made sure that bar Abbas is all those things?" I said.

"Oh!" she said. "That big hairy ape! I forgot about him! Ugh, how I hate him! When the Romans crucify him the week after Pesach, I'm going to watch. Damn him, I'll enjoy it!"

"The Romans are going to crucify Yeshu'a bar Abbas?" I said.

"Yes. He got caught robbing a storehouse.[1] Killed a guard. Even so, he was lucky. The storehouse belonged to a Jew. A Zadokite. Roman sympathizer, of course. But they can't *prove* it was political, so some people say he might get off, even yet—"

I bowed my head. I'd admired Yeshu'a bar Abbas. But I couldn't save him and my Galilean would-be-Mashiah brother-in-law at the same time. One Yeshu'a was all I could manage, not two.

"Nathan," Shelomith was saying, "Do you—love her—very much?"

"Love whom very much?" I said.

"Your wife. Yohannah."

I thought about that.

"Yes, I love her very much," I said.

"Oh," Shelom said. "Is she—like him? Like Yeshu'a, I mean?"

"Yes," I said; "very like."

"Oh," she said again. "Then it's all right. Then I understand it. Funny—I can't even hate her. Nathan—"

"Yes, Shelom?"

"What's the easiest way to die?"

"Good God!"

"Don't blaspheme. Tell me, what is? I'm not brave. Not anymore. Not like I was when I first met you. I've lost that. It's gone. Last week, I tried a knife, but it hurt so I couldn't finish the job. And hanging, if you don't tie the knot right, you strangle—slowly. . . . A Greek apothecary I know brought me some poison. All it did was to keep me vomiting every half hour for a whole week. And I can't even get into any building that's high enough to throw myself off, make sure I wouldn't only be bad hurt and crippled—"

"Shelom, child, listen to me—" I began.

"No. What have I got to live for now, Nathan? Tell me that!"

I tried to remember some of the things I'd heard Yeshu'a say—about repentance. About peace beyond all understanding. About the Kingdom of God. But I'm not good at preaching, and I don't believe those things myself, even. I believe that life's a wasteland without form or meaning, and that what happens to people is a perfect demonstration of that fact.

"Try to live, little Shelom," I finished lamely; "things will change for you. I know they will. You'll be happy and—"

She looked at me, said: "Oh, shit. Now you're being tiresome. Nathan, kiss me good night—no, goodbye—and go home."

"Which is it?" I said. "Good night, or goodbye?"

She thought about that.

"Good night," she said. "I'm not brave enough yet. Don't know whether I'll ever be. And don't worry, I don't have anything you can catch. At least not by kissing me on the mouth. So kiss me, will you, huh? Please?"

I kissed her. The tenderness of her mouth on mine was shattering. I turned her loose, stepped back. She clutched her middle as though I'd hit her in the belly with my fist, and moved off, like that, down that narrow, crooked alley. I hung there, watching her go, sick in all the bad, hurtful, gut-ripping ways a man can be, and not die of it. At least not immediately. And my alleged gift of prophecy deserted me in my hour of need. I no more thought than you or any other man under those circumstances would have, that this chance encounter with a public harlot in a noisome street could possibly affect my chances of saving Yeshu'a ha Notzri's life.

But it did. Terribly.

That very next morning, I presented myself at the Tower of Phasael in Herod's palace, where during the eight days of the *hag ha mazot*, the Feast of Unleavened Bread, the first one of which being Pesach, Passover, our greatest festival, the Romans had their Prætorium.[2] The Procurators always came up to Jerusalem for the Feasts because that was usually when all the revolts started.

But I didn't know whether Lucius Pontius Pilatus would receive me or not. His aqueduct was built now; he had no earthly use for me. I'd heard that he and Claudia were reconciled; that his Greek mistress had been sent away. There was a decided risk in my attempting to see him: his memories of me must have been bitter. I had publicly humiliated him by killing his gladiator in the games at Cæsarea; all the world whispered I was his wife's lover still. But I gambled on his curiosity, on the way his tortuously, deviously subtle mind worked. He might have me killed, but not in the palace, and not today. If he received me at all, I could count half my battle for Yeshu'a's life already won.

And receive me he did, not in his public audience hall, but in his private study, getting up as I came in, and shaking hands with me in the curious Roman fashion in which each man clasps the inside of his friend's elbow at the crook of the arm so that the whole length of the forearms are in intimate contact.

"Nathanaeus!" he said in his dry, light, sibilant voice. "Just when we thought you'd deserted us completely! Claudia's been desolate. . . ."

"And you, Lucius Pontius?" I said.

"I? Less, being male!" he laughed. "Still, I *have* missed you. There have been times when your insight into the workings of your compatriots' minds would have been priceless. Tell me, where have you been? Jupiter Thorens, but you're thin! What's happened to you? When you butchered my gladiator so tidily—that *was* unkind of you, Nathanaeus! —you were a miniature Hercules; but now—"

"Now, I'm a wreck," I said soberly; "the chief reason being—this." I lifted my robe, exposing my buttocks—among us a deadly insult, which made the subtle game I was playing all the more pleasing—in the process, and showed him the scar where the idiot Abal had used my own blade on me.

His face darkened with real anger.

"Again!" he said.

I'd known he'd think that, just as I knew that the source of his anger was not the hurt to my poor flesh, but what he took to be Zealot defiance of Roman authority.

"Yes," I sighed. "Costly business being known as a friend of Cæsar's, Pilatus!"

He peered at me mockingly.

"Are you really, Nathanaeus?" he said. "I've heard it said that you are—merely—a friend of Claudia's—"

And now the battle of minds, the duel of wits was truly joined.

"I resent that 'merely,' Lucius Pontius," I said. "I consider the small kindness that the Divine Granddaughter of the Divine Augustus has occasionally shown me great honors indeed—"

He smiled.

"And I wonder at the terms 'small' and 'occasionally,'" he said; "but let us not quibble over words. I repeat my question: Are you really a friend of Cæsar's?"

"No," I said flatly; "I hate his ugly, miserly guts. But I *am* a friend of the Jewish people, which to all intents and purposes amounts to the same thing—"

He threw back his head and laughed aloud.

"You, my dear Caius Nathanaeus, have more damned nerve than a brazened-bellied Ba'al!" he said. "But your thought is devious! How can being a friend of the Jewish people amount to the same thing as being a friend of Cæsar's? Precious few of your fellow countrymen would agree with you, as they've demonstrated most succinctly by carving you up—twice!"

"I know that," I said; "but I'm different from the rest of the Jews in one small detail which is, none the less, great: I've been to Rome."

"So?" he said.

"So I no longer labor under the delusion which makes the Zealots the most dangerous enemy my people have: That it's possible for a handful of bearded idiots clad in prayer shawls and led by their eyeless, faceless god, to overthrow the mightiest empire the world has ever seen, or every will see. I don't love Rome, Lucius Pontius. I hate the slavery you impose on us. But I am an oriental, a Semite, with an oriental's patience. I believe that if we wait, endure, you will fall of your own weight, your own vices, of the luxury that is ruining you. You're no longer the lean, hungry Italian wolf pups who conquered the world. You're fat and soft and effeminate. You love boys as much as the Greeks do. As far as women are concerned, you've forgot what your phalli and your gonads are for, so busy are you at switching ends. Which means you don't produce children to maintain your undisputed military and governing genius. Your legions are filled with towering blond beasts from your dark northern frontiers. People who have neither wine nor sun nor song in them, who have nothing in them but their abysmal cruelty, who can *never* be civilized, who can only imitate, counterfeit civilization, while remaining northern barbarians to the end of time—"

"You've a rough tongue in your head, Nathanaeus," he said; "but, I fear me, an honest one. . . ."

"You know I don't lie, Pilatus!" I told him. "I believe our only hope is to wait until you destroy yourselves. I won't see it. Nor my son. But perhaps my great-great-great-grandson will. I believe my people are unique, that their conception of God—in which I, personally, don't believe—is the noblest mankind has ever seen. And that's why I fight the Zealots; why I've twice been at the door of death from their blades.

For, if they force my people to revolt, you can and will destroy us, destroy a people superior to yourselves in everything but brute force —a crime from which I'd save you—"

He stared at me.

"Hades take you, but you're intelligent, Nathanaeus!" he sighed. "If you'd come to me protesting your great and abiding love for Cæsar, for Rome, for me, personally, I shouldn't have believed a ruddy word of it! But now you force me to—"

"Because I know that you, too, are intelligent, Lucius Pontius," I said; "which is why I didn't waste your time or mine trying to lie to you. Nor will I tell you now that I've come to save you from a grave error, one which could conceivably result in your being recalled to Rome to give account for your actions here. Of course, it might have that effect, too; but, from my point of view, that's only incidental—"

"Ha!" he snorted. "*Now* I begin to doubt you, Caius Nathanaeus!"

"Don't. Since I've seen you last, Lucius Pontius, I've got married. My wife and I await a son—"

"Congratulations!" he said. "Wait till I tell Claudia this!"

That effect was calculated, too: that he'd feel relief at my news, take it as the removal of a threat. And that he'd enjoy tormenting poor Claudia with it. "Thank you," I said. "I only told you that to get to my essential point: my brother-in-law, my wife's brother, is a little mad. Here of late, he has fallen into the delusion of believing himself the Mashiah. And he's coming up to Jerusalem with a band of disciples—"

"Ha!" Pilatus said again. "Jupiter Thunderer be praised that I already have three whole cohorts here!"

"As far as he's concerned, you don't even need one," I said. "He conceives of himself as a suffering sacrificial lamb, prepared to die to lead our people to virtue, not to war. He personally instructed his followers not to resist the *angaria,* your military requisitioning of labor and transport. He advocates meekness, submission, love. He has already got the Pharisees against him because he'd lessen their strictness in the interpretation of the Law. The Sadducees fear him because they've fallen into the same error I'm trying to save you from: they fear he will start, or even accidentally provoke, a revolt. . . ."

Pilatus smiled at me; said in that hateful, jesting voice of his: "Go on. . . ."

"Now, when my brother-in-law and his little band get here, any one of several things can happen: First, nothing, which is what I fervently hope. Second, the people, led by the Zealots, will flock to him, and proclaim him King, thus forcing you to crucify him, which you'll do only if you're an utter idiot—"

"Why so?" Pilatus said.

"Because, if you wait a week or two and let those fools find out his pacificism, his total horror of war and bloodshed, his mystical, spiritual concepts of kingship—he thinks of himself as a priestly Mashiah, a sacerdotal Christos, not a warrior king—they'll kill him for you, if I can't get him away from them first, out of their disappointment and their rage. And I don't think crucifying a man whose every teaching reinforces Cæsar's rule, as his followers can produce hundreds of witnesses to prove, will help your standing with the Imperator—"

"Interesting—if true," Pilatus said.

"Very true. I appeal to your self-interest, Lucius Pontius, not to your nonexistent charity! The people are burning for revenge because of the heads you cracked when they protested against your robbing the sacred treasury to build *our* aqueduct. That's another reason you have to believe me. I'm inevitably associated with that cruel and stupid business in the people's minds. If they succeed in getting you recalled—as they're trying to—*I* won't stay alive an hour thereafter. And I've a great deal to live for now!"

I could see I was convincing him, finally.

"So?" he said.

"So it's to the interest of the Sadducees to deliver him to you, since they fear the people's wrath. Neither they, nor the Pharisees, nor any other vested interest, want a Mashiah, a Christos appearing now to turn their cozy little world upside down. So—two birds with one stone, Pilatus! They make you crucify this harmless idiot of a brother-in-law of mine, and afterward they force Vitellius to have you recalled by proving, as they can, that Yeshu'a ha Notzri, was a friend of Cæsar's—"

"There's something wrong with this," Pilatus mused; "but I can't put my finger on it. You're a cunning devil, Nathanaeus! I have the feeling that were I to examine this matter closely, I'd find every word you've said today is—true. But what are you leaving out? Don't you realize that a man who has survived as long as I have in the world I've had to live in, knows as well as you do that while lying to an intelligent man is the act of a fool, telling him *all* the truth is the procedure of a jackass? Your community of interests with me—you'd save me from an error that might threaten my career because you don't want your wife's brother killed, because if I'm recalled, the Zealots will murder you, because your patriotism extends to treason against your people's ideals, knowing as you do that the practice of those ideals would give us the exquisite pleasure of slaughtering the most exasperating race of prickly bastards we've ever encountered anywhere to the last bearded, louse-infected man—is just too *neat*. Do you think I've lived all these years without finding out that there's always a hangnail, a burr, a jagged edge, something that doesn't fit? When you present me with such symmetry, Nathanaeus, you make me suspicious. You remind me of a counterfeiter they caught at Antioch because his tetradrachmae, his denarii were better executed than the official coinage. Therefore, don't you think that—as friends, and equals in intelligence—you'd be wiser if you told me *all* the truth?"

I gambled then. I had to.

"I have told you the truth, Lucius Pontius," I said; "whole, complete, and naked. If you don't believe me, I'm sorry. Why don't you plant one of your spies among the Galilean's followers? That would be easy. Even I wouldn't be able to pick him out until too late. That way you can surely get at the truth of my claims. . . ."

He stared at me. Then he smiled, said: "Oh, I'd never do that, Nathanaeus! That you propose it, shows how futile it would be—"

But he would. I knew that. And he knew I knew. I had won the first battle. Unfortunately, in my hopeful enthusiasm, I allowed myself to forget the oldest military axiom:

The only battle that really counts is the last.

All of the next day I spent at Khirbet Qumrân. I had to persuade the Medical Paqid that no harm would come to the New Covenanters by lending me a detail from his vast knowledge of drugs in order to balk, to frustrate the Kittim, the Romans.

I won him over at last. I rode back to Jerusalem, singing, with the herbs and powders—combined they were bitterer than gall—in my pouch. But I'd won more from the Paqid than a supply of the most powerful soporific known to man, capable of producing for some hours a state almost indistinguishable from death; I had gained his wholehearted cooperation. For, when, quite by accident, I mentioned that the rab whose life was in danger was the brother of Yaakob, called Tzaddig the Just, the Paqid's eyes flashed angry fire.

"If you can get him down from the cross with life still in him, bring him here," he said quietly. "For the brother of Yaakob ha Tzaddig, we will accept the risk and gladly. Because, as you know, Yaakob ben Yosef is of us, of the New Covenant—not only that, Nathan, my son, he is the best of all the town-dwelling Chasyaim[3] and has brought many sinners to our way. . . ."

Of course I was almost sure by then that I was going to be able to safeguard Yeshu'a against falling into the hands of the Romans at all, by convincing Pilatus that the Bœthusian-Sadducean priesthood were planning to use the Galilean as a lever to pry him, for all his Iberian cunning, out of the Procurator's chair; but I dared not leave everything depending upon so exquisitely devious a scoundrel as Lucius Pontius Pilatus. I hoped for the best, but I prepared for the worst. What I meant to do was to save Yeshu'a ha Notzri—without a scratch on his mad, deluded hide, if it could be done that way, or three-quarters dead, covered with blood, dust, dung and flies, if I had to; but, anyhow, to save him.

After I was home again, it came to me that I still hadn't done what Yeshu'a had asked me to, so I sent servants to the cattle market and had them buy a pearl-gray little jackass almost too small to carry a grown man's weight. But he'd insisted upon that detail, that the beast had to be a foal, never before mounted by anyone, so that the prophecy be fulfilled to the letter. I told them where to take the colt, and gave them the code phrase already arranged between Yeshu'a and me. If anyone tried to untie the colt, they were to say: "Why are you taking that colt?" And if the man taking the little ass answered, "My master needs him," they'd know he was from Yeshu'a, and let him lead the animal away without hindrance.[4]

I also sent handmaidens of my father's to clean and air and perfume the house tht Claudia Procula had given me. In the dining room, I had a seven-branched candlestick placed. I ordered the little table that had served Claudia and me for intimate suppers taken away, and a huge one brought. It was so big that they had to take it apart to get it into the house; but when it was set up again, I saw it would hold the place settings for at least twenty people.

Now there was nothing to do but wait, and that was the worst of all. I knew Yeshu'a was at Jericho, and that on yesterday, a blind man had greeted him as "Son of David."[5] It surprised me that, from the accounts my informers had brought me, Yeshu'a hadn't rebuked the poor devil for giving him a title he had no right to. But he hadn't. That worried me. Had he fled so far from reality that he now believed himself of David's line? He'd merely comforted the blind beggar—not cured him as your *Besorahim* say, because this man was authentically blind.

But on the morning of the ninth day before Passover, my servants came running into the house and burst into my bedroom, as I had ordered them to, without even knocking.

"Master!" they panted. "They have taken the foal!"

I leaped from my bed.

"Who?" I said. "Describe them!"

"Queer-looking fellows. A huge man," they got out; "blackbearded, with a big head. Fellow with him was smaller, but not much. They looked alike. Kinsmen, probably—"

I flung on my fringed robe as they talked; but, from their description, it was apparent I had nothing to fear. It was not a trap: the men who'd led the little donkey away were Shimeon Kepha bar Yonah, and his brother Netzer, or Andrai.

I left the house and raced toward the Valley Gate. I was in time, Yeshu'a and his followers hadn't reached it yet. But someone else had. Among the crowd of curiosity-seekers already assembled there—for the wildest kind of rumors were already flying about—my eye jarred to halt on a tight-packed group of men whose dress was—strange. They wore long cloaks, but those cloaks were not of a Jewish cut, nor were their edges fringed. These men were clean-shaven, and of short, stocky build. They could have been Hellenized Jews, because they were as dark as we generally are; but something about them, an almost indefinable difference, told me that they weren't. Then, as one of them turned to the man, clearly their leader, who stood in their midst, surrounded by all the others, I saw the sudden glint of a blade.

Romans. For no Jew would have borne a weapon during even the preliminaries to the festival. The very idea of it was contrary to every concept of our Law. Legionaries from the *Cohors Italica* surely, because there was not a Gallic or a Teutonic face among them, not one blond head or blue eye. And in disguise, wearing a bad imitation of our robes over their armor. Pilatus, then, was repeating the tactic he'd used to put down the revolt over his seizure of the Temple Fund to build the aqueduct: he had his legionaries ready to mingle with the crowds, and strike without mercy at the slightest sign of an upheaval. Repeating it and improving upon it, for the man standing in the center of the group was—he, himself.

I didn't even hesitate. I walked straight toward him. At once every hand slapped audibly upon a sword hilt, except his own.

He recognized me. A sardonic smile twisted the contours of his vulpine mouth.

"No," he said in Latin, "this one is a friend—for the moment, anyhow. . . ."

"Lucius Pontius—" I said reproachfully. "I told you—"

"That there was no danger," he said. "Of course not! But what harm is there in a little extra insurance against your compatriots' folly, my dear Caius Nathanaeus? Come, stand beside me, here. Would it be asking too much to request of you the favor of pointing out your dearly beloved brother-in-law to me?"

I looked him in the eye.

"Yes, it would be, Pilatus," I told him.

"Then don't," he said with perfect equanimity. "Just stand here where I can use you as a basis for comparison. I have already had of dear Claudia—accidentally, of course, a mere slip of the tongue, I assure you, Nathanaeus; you know how women are!—the information that you and he are identical. So much so that my informants from Galilee tell me that the rumor's current there that your father was once a *very* naughty boy—"

"That's a lie," I said.

"Is it? I'm told your Christos is vastly different from his brothers in wit, beauty, verve, intelligence, fire. And that he's estranged from them. Incidentally, I also know your second—and exceedingly honorable—scar, was got on his behalf. Dealt you by the village idiot. Have the Zealots begun enlisting idiots to their cause, my dear Nathanaeus?"

"As far as I'm concerned, they all are," I said.

My sally pleased him, as well as those of his officers who could speak Greek. They explained it to the others in Latin, and the laughter became general.

Pilatus gripped my arm momentarily, said: "We'll have to have another chat, Nathanaeus—to clear up the question of how many more lies you told me the other day. . . ."

I didn't answer that, now only because no useful answer came to me, but because it was then that Yeshu'a and his followers came in sight.

Wait. This is difficult. To your Christianoi he is—or has become—a god. And broad-hipped, shrewish, bossy, fussy Miriam a new Isis. The event I'm about to describe is what you call The Triumphal Entry into Jerusalem. I'm sorry. I didn't see that. I saw my brother-in-law jogging along on a little jackass so small that Yeshu'a had to bend his knees awkwardly to keep his feet from dragging on the ground. He was sitting on a pile of the disciples' sweaty robes instead of a saddle in imitation of Jehu[6] and all those Galilean yokels as well as a goodly proportion of our local idiots were scattering green grass and branches torn off trees before him and bellowing:

"Hosanna! Blessings on him who comes in the Name of the Lord! Blessings on the coming Kingdom of our father David! Hosanna in the heavens!"[7]

Then someone in the crowd said it.

"Hosanna to the Son of David!"[8]

And the faces of most of the people, of the overwhelming majority of the multitude who were watching this ridiculous spectacle silently, went dark with anger. A Pharisee cried out to Yeshu'a at that: "Rabbi, restrain your people! Don't permit them to bear false witness!"[9]

Yeshu'a hauled back on the bridle. The little jackass, unaccustomed to such treatment, danced. I could see that awful anger I knew so well kindle in Yeshu'a's eyes. His voice, speaking, wasn't loud; but, as always, it carried.

"I tell you," he said, "that if my disciples were to hold their tongues, the very stones would shout aloud!"[10]

"Who the devil is he?" somebody said.

"Another Galilean rab. Every time you overturn a stone, one of these wild itinerants crawls out from under it—"

"No," another said, "he's a Prophet. A real one. Name of Yeshu'a—the Nazarene. Raised a man from the dead in a place called Nain in Galilee. My brother wrote me about it—"

I turned toward Pilatus. His lips were twitching with ill-suppressed laughter.

"Is *that* your brother-in-law?" he said.

I nodded grimly.

Pontius Pilatus turned to his followers. They were all grinning at the sight of this Galilean rab riding along on a little jackass two sizes too small for him, surrounded by a raving, bellowing, sweaty, stinking crowd of madmen.

"Well, gentlemen," he said, "it appears the Empire's safe for a day or two longer, doesn't it?"

And they, all of them, threw back their heads and roared.

That night, I went in search of Yeshu'a at Beth Anya, for he didn't stay in Jerusalem very long that day, nor did he perform anything of note there.[11] But I didn't find him. The reason I didn't was very simple: I was prevented from continuing my search by Yehudah ish Kriyoth.

He, my Brother in Sorrow, lay in a gutter. He was roaring drunk, and all the urchins of Beth Anya were standing around him in a circle, laughing at him. I drove them off with a few well-directed blows of my staff. Then I bent and picked ish Kriyoth up. Drunk as he was, he recognized me at once.

"Nathan!" he wept. "My master! She—Shelom—"

"Oh Sheol!" I thought. "Just what I needed to run the cup of my joys over!"

"She refused me!" he wept. "Again! She was with a mincing little effeminate of a Greek and—"

I sighed, possessed of a great and terrible weariness.

"Come home with me now, Yehudah," I said.

I should have watched him more closely. He was far less drunk than he appeared. What he was, actually, was mad, of rage, of hurt, of grief. And I was tired, depressed by the ludicrous spectacle Yeshu'a had afforded all the world that day. Rather than face another sleepless night, I mixed myself a tiny portion of the drug I'd got from the Essene Paqid for the ultimate emergency, and took it. I'd no sooner got it down than my bed, my pillow, rose up and smote me in the face.

When I woke, sunlight was streaming in all the windows and Yehudah ish Kriyoth was gone.

"Rushed out of here like a wild man," my manservant said, "just after dawn. He was blaspheming and swearing something awful, master! Kept saying over and over again: I'll fix her! I'll fix her! She won't live another day!"

I got to my feet. The room reeled dizzily. Sheol and Gehenna both, but the draught was strong!

"Saddle Bedu," I said. Walking was out of the question now, and I knew it.

The first thing I saw, as I was passing the Temple, was that mob. They all had stones in their hands. Ish Kriyoth was leading them, of course. Beside him walked an old man, his weak white-bearded chin trembling and jerking in his rage.

"The bitch!" he quavered. "Told her I'd have her stoned! Told her if I ever caught her with—"

Then I saw Shelomith. Two of those pious ruffians were hustling her along between them. There was blood in her face from a cut above her right eye. The whiplash scar my Uncle Hezron had given her in defense of my nonexistent honor was livid against her cheek. She moved like a sleepwalker, her eyes already emptied of life. It was very clear that she was content to die.

The despair that tore me then was very nearly mortal. I hadn't even one of those little knives you use to cut writing quills with. There was no way I could save her, no way at all. And nothing, not even cruci- fixion, is uglier or harder to watch than death by stoning. Very often the eyes are knocked completely out of the victim's head. The teeth. Long before death came, I knew, this sullen, barbaric, achingly beloved, beautiful face, would be unrecognizable as anything human.

I had to stop it, but how? In God's Unspeakable Name, how?

Then Yeshu'a ha Notzri came out of the Temple. He didn't say anything; he just stood there, looking at them. His gaze moved from face to face, flickering over them like dark and silent flame.

Yehudah ish Kriyoth fell back. It seemed to me he was trying to hide himself in the crowd. But one of the two oafs who had been pushing Shelomith along, a Sadducee, surely,[12] though not of the highest class, by his dress and speech, cried out: "Master, this woman was taken in adultery. Caught in the very act. According to our Lawgiver, Moses, such creatures are to be stoned. What say you to that?"

Yeshu'a didn't say anything. He simply knelt and wrote with his finger on the ground. I couldn't see what he wrote, both because I'd got down from Bedu and because I was too busy watching Shelom's gaze caress Yeshu'a's countenance, turn itself into female fingers and rove over his bearded face.

But the Zadokite could see what that writing was. His face turned white above the great brush of his beard. He stepped back, muttering.

His companion, the one who was holding Shelomith by the other arm, shouted then: "What say you, master?"

Yeshu'a wrote another word. I saw the shaking get into the second pious ruffian's knees. His mouth came open, pouring enough wine and garlic stench out into the air to kill a passing fly.

"But how—?" he got out. "How—?"

Then Yeshu'a spoke. His voice was quiet, serene; but laden with that terrible authority of his.

"Let he among you who is without sin," he said, "throw the first stone—"

And then, as though they were not even there, he bent once more to writing on the ground.

They melted away. It was the damnedest thing to watch. As he wrote what I was sure by then was each man's most private, secret sin upon the earth, judging each of them with uncanny accuracy, I could hear a slow glissando rain of stones upon the hard-packed clay, as unnerved fingers unlocked, released, gave.

Finally, only Yehudah ish Kriyoth was standing there. And now, because the others had gone, I could see what Yeshu'a wrote. I'm sorry —if the word he'd written about him of Kerioth had been "traitor," this would be a better tale, demonstrating his omniscience. But it wasn't. It was "coward."

Which was equally true, of course. Ish Kriyoth hadn't had the balls to use a blade, take upon himself the consequences of killing Shelom, as—had he been possessed of manhood, male pride—he'd have been forced to do. Instead, he'd arranged a judicial murder, a legal assassination, dragging along her fatuous old fool of a husband and three witnesses to show them Shelom naked and asleep in the arms of a pretty Greek boy of dubious gender, to whom she had given herself without payment in search for surcease, for relief from the grief and shame she was dying of.

Yehudah didn't let the stone he was carrying drop. He threw it down, hard, between poor Shelom's bare feet. It ricocheted, made a spark. My Brother in Sorrow turned. But, just before he loped after the others, he looked at Yeshu'a.

In all my life, I have never again seen so much hatred contained and concentrated in a single gaze.

Yeshu'a looked up. Shelom stood there, clad only in her *shimlah* tunic, alone and trembling. He recognized her, of course; but he didn't call her by her name. Don't ask me why. I don't know. What man of woman born can truly say why Yeshu'a ha Notzri did the things he did?

"Woman," he said gently, "where are your accusers?"

Shelom's mouth opened a little. Quivered.

"Gone," she said.

"And none of them has condemned you?"

"No—master," she said.

"Then neither do I condemn you," Yeshu'a said. "Go and sin no more."[13]

And I knew then that Pilatus had been wrong. The Empire *was* in danger. The force in this little skinny, bearded Jew would one day shake it down. Would leave not one stone standing on a stone. Would conquer Rome.

Rome—and all the world.

Chapter XXIV

YESHU'A DIDN'T LINGER; he went back into the Temple almost at once. After he had gone, I turned to Shelomith.

"Come," I said.

But she didn't answer me. She was staring toward the Temple, and what I saw in her eyes then was a thing that doesn't go easily into words, embracing, as it did, not only the opposing extremes of lust and love, but all the shadowy territory lying between, so that it was simple and complicated and beautiful and terrible all at the same time, the way the deeper emotions of a really female woman always are. Anyhow, watching her eyes commit both abominations and tendernesses upon the very door he'd gone through was an intolerable invasion of her privacy, so I put my hands beneath her armpits and boosted her up onto Bedu. She didn't protest. She was still staring toward the Temple door. I don't think she was really aware of my existence. I mounted and we moved off, clipclopping through the streets, with Shelom leaning against me, her two arms wrapped around my waist as though I were the pillar of her salvation. Then it came to me that I didn't know where we were going, where I was supposed to take her.

"Where's your place?" I said. "Your room, I mean; not your booth in Zeno's Lupanar. . . ."

"My room," she said in a low harsh tone of voice that had ashes in it, "you mean my hole in the ground that I run to so I can hide, and—and lick my hurts like bad-off bitch-things do. It's in Beth Phage, the House of Wild Figs,[1] Nathan. But I can't go there now. Not anymore. Not even to get my things."

"Why not?" I said.

"Because I took Demos there. That poor little bastard of a Greek. He doesn't even like women, really; but he was drunk and sad and so was I. I never took anybody home—to my place, that is, Nathan—before. And, of course, that whining old lecher ish Kriyoth had to follow us. So I can't go back. The people I rented that place from didn't even know I was a harlot. I never even used paints and powders over there."

"I see," I said. "Then where shall I take you?"

She shuddered.

"Sheol," she said. "Gehenna. Maybe both."

"Oh, for heaven's sake, Shelom!" I said. "There must be somewhere—"

She shook her head. I could feel the motion.

"No, there isn't," she said; "no place in this world. Unless you want to take me to Zeno's. I'm always welcome there."

The very thought sent a green tide of nausea surging through my gut.

"You want to go back to the brothel?" I said, controlling my voice, keeping it neutral.

"You heard what *he* said, didn't you?" Shelom whispered. " 'Go and sin no more.' So I'd die first now. Cut my throat. From ear to ear."

"That's a sin, too," I said.

"Yes. But a different kind. Killing yourself to keep from whoring is almost—decent, Nathan. So now, I—"

"Shut up," I said. "Let me think."

I sat there on Bedu, feeling her two arms around my waist and the heat of her against me. Which wasn't exactly conducive to either accuracy or clarity of thought. And thinking was what I had to do now. Where could I take her? Both my father's house and the one I'd had of Claudia Procula as a gift were inconceivable; my father's, for obvious reasons; Claudia's because I'd pledged it to Yeshu'a as the place where he and his disciples could eat the Passover. Yeshu'a might have been, and probably was, a Prophet; but that didn't alter the facts that Shelomith was a whore, and he, my wife's brother.

Then it came to me. I knew a woman who rented rooms by the week or month, but only to respectable people, and only for respectable purposes. She was a widow, very old, and nearly blind. It was old Sarah's want of sight that I was gambling on now. Because Shelom, clad only in her undertunic, her face bruised and swollen, smelling of stale perfume, her own and Demos' sweat, wasn't exactly an object to inspire confidence.

I kicked Bedu into motion.

"Where're we going?" Shelom said.

"A rooming house. Decent place. You keep your mouth shut when we get there. Let *me* do the talking. And the first thing you do, once you're inside your room, is to take a bath. Really scrub. Old Sarah's nearly blind; but there's nothing wrong with her nose. Besides, she's as inquisitive as the devil. So the first time she gets to spend five minutes alone with you, I want you to neither look nor smell like a whore."

"Oh!" Shelom said; then: "All right, Nathan. But, lover—what will I wear?"

"Don't call me 'lover.' I'll bring you your things," I said.

I got Shelomith past old Sarah easily enough. I told the old witch that Shelom was a young widow come up to Jerusalem to remake her life. I said that in Shelom's presence, knowing I could count upon her natural inventiveness to sustain and even embroider the tale. And I paid Sarah one year's rent in advance, with the thought that even should the pious old busybody find out the truth, returning that much money would be more than she could bear. I had another reason for my extravagance: If Shelom really meant to abandon the practice of harlotry, not having to worry about paying her rent would help her do it. Food was a much smaller problem; and she already had enough clothes to outfit a whole *lupanar*. Unfortunately, that's what they looked like they were made for. I knew that, because I brought them over from her old place in Beth Phage along with all the bottles and flasks of female sorcery that she used to cheapen and debase her natural beauty. Not that she knew that, of course; she thought she was heightening it.

I took a hundred drachmae out of my belt purse; but at the sight of it, she flared up at me.

"Put your money up, Nathan!"

I grinned at her, said: "I'm not trying to buy a small portion of your dainty anatomy, Shelom. Consider this a gift. Or a loan, if you must. You've got to eat, you know—"

"Do I?" she said morosely. "Why, Nathan? And, as for buying me, you couldn't. And I wouldn't, free. Not even with you. 'Specially not with you, now—'cause that would be the worst sin of all. . . ."

"Why?" I said.

"I love you," Shelomith said. "And you're married. To Yeshu'a's sister, at that."

"And those are supposed to be good reasons why not?" I said.

"The best," Shelom said. "So keep your drachmae, Nathan. I don't need them. I've got enough saved to last me more than a year now that you've paid my rent. Funny what men will give to wallow with a fly-blown, putrid carcass with no one in it. Lying there making like it was alive—"

The bitterness of her tone was a hurting in me, a wound.

"No," I said; "that's not what they pay for, Shelom."

"Isn't it?" she said. "Then for what, Nathan?"

"Dreams," I said. "A counterfeit of love, an imitation of tenderness. Things we have to have. That we'd die without. What would all the poor bastards of this world do, if they couldn't have girls like you, Shelom? One day they'd find out that they're not only loveless, but unlovable. Then they'd run through the streets, howling mad. It would be a disaster. No—catastrophe."

"So?" Shelom said.

"So, Dream-vendor, Merchant of Surcease," I said solemnly, "they couldn't have paid you enough. Not you. The others, maybe. But you, no. What you had to offer—one bright memory to light up a lifetime's darkness was—priceless. You got cheated. There isn't enough money to pay for you. Nowhere in the world."

She looked at me and her eyes went brilliant with tear glitter.

"Nathan—anybody ever tell you you're a fool?" she said wearily. "A sweet, dear, kind fool—but still a fool. I got paid for lying there with some hairy stinking ape on top of me, and wiggling a little. Or for the other filthy tricks I told you about. Nothing more. Oh, I know what you're doing: you're trying to make me quit hating myself. Only that's not the way to do it."

"Then what is?" I said.

"Come back in a year from now, and eat the Passover with me," Shelom said. "See what I'll be like by then. My talk, my clothes, everything. How easy it'll be to treat me like a lady. 'Cause I'll be one, Nathan! I will! All I need is a quiet time. To pray. To ask God's forgiveness. To earn it—by being good. Really good, in every way."

"You're good now," I said.

"No," she said. "Because my breasts still hurt when I look at you. My insides melt. I've got to get over that. Not over loving you, 'cause I can't and don't even want to, and, anyhow, loving, by itself, isn't really a sin. But wanting you the way I do—"

"—and the way I want you—" I said truthfully.

"—is. So, Nathan bar Yehudah, love of my life, will you go through that door and not come back for at least a year? Will you, huh? Please?"

"All right," I said, meaning it, for both her sake and mine, because though it was going to be bad not seeing her, it couldn't be as bad—as ugly, cruel, gut-crippling bad—as seeing her daily and not being able to do anything about it would have been, for nothing this side of Sheol could have matched that. "All right, Shelom—"

But I did go back. The very next day. And thereby ended all her dreams, her hope. But it wasn't my fault. It was Yeshu'a ha Notzri's. Or Yehudah ish Kriyoth's.

Or, maybe, even God's.

Because, you see, when I came out of old Sarah's place, I found my Brother in Sorrow waiting for me, just outside the door. I looked at him from head to foot, and back again, slowly.

"You swine," I said. "You utter, filthy swine."

"I know," he said; "I was. I am. I thought I was over her, but I'm not. And I guess I'll never be. But what I did yesterday was evil. Cowardly—just as he wrote on the ground. That's why I've come: To try to make up for it, Nathan."

"And not to slip a blade into me for having spent the last few hours with her?" I said.

"No," Yehudah said. "She wouldn't, with you. She told me that. Because you look too much like him. She's afraid of that. Of the confusion, I mean. Of what it might do to her mind—"

"All right," I said. "What do you want from me, Yehudah?"

"That you come with me. To—to save him, Nathan! He's going to get himself stoned, as sure as Gehenna's afire!"

"How?" I said. "What's he planning to do?"

"Cleanse the Temple!" Yehudah groaned. "That's what *he* calls it, anyhow!"

"Calls what?" I said.

"Driving the dove sellers and the money changers out of the outer courts. Of course the bird offerings, the *kinim,* are pure robbery, and those money changers would cheat their own mothers; but their sins are on their own heads, and their booths are not located inside the sacred courts, and what they have to do is absolutely necessary as anybody but a Galilean yokel like your brother-in-law would have known!"

He was absolutely right; but I wasn't going to give him the satisfaction of agreeing with him. So I said: "He *told* you he was going to do that?"

"Me, no. He doesn't seem to trust me anymore. He told Old Marble Head, Shimeon bar Yonah. And Shimeon told me. Fairly bursting with admiration over the scheme, the big idiot! Never occurred to him, or to any of them, that forcing the High Priest's hand like that is sure to get Yeshu'a stoned—"

"We can't stone anybody anymore. The right of capital punishment has been taken out of our hands, Yehudah.[2] Or at least restricted greatly. Seems we have to consult with our Lords and Masters before battering out anyone's brains or thrusting a burning wick down his throat or gently strangling him. That's another thing you should have thought of yesterday. If you'd got poor Shelom battered to death, some of her clients among the Roman legionaries would have seen to it that you'd be crucified for murder."

"And I should have deserved it," Yehudah said morosely. "But that's neither here nor there, now. In Elohim's Name, Nathan! We'd better get started if we ever hope to get there in time—"

"All right," I said. "Come on."

As we started toward the Temple at a fast trot, I looked at Yehudah out of the corner of my eye.

"Yesterday, it seemed to me you'd have been glad to see him arrested, Yehudah," I said.

Ish Kriyoth sighed.

"Yesterday, I should have," he said. "Today, no. He was right, yesterday. What I did was cowardly, wrong. But today, he isn't. So today, I pity him. A man shouldn't die because of his ignorance, Nathan. When I die, God grant it be for sin, not folly!"

"Amen!" I said. But I doubt that he heard me; for, by then we were close enough to the Temple for the uproar in the outer courts to drown out even thought.

Before I even got through the gates, I could hear the crash of falling bird cages, the clatter of the overturned tables, the clinking of silver on the pavement, the bestial bull-bellow of the mob. I ran through the gates and stopped. I couldn't breathe. I was sure that my heartbeat had halted, too.

Yeshu'a was there—at the epicenter of all the confusion. His face flushed with his terrible anger, he was laying about him lustily with a whip of cords. And he had the mob with him. For, to be quite fair about it, the abuses of the money changers and those who sold the pigeons for the *kinim* sacrifices were flagrant. They robbed the people blind. So now, for the first time since he had come up to Jerusalem, Yeshu'a had the common people, nearly all of them, on his side. Especially the street idlers, and the grimy little urchins who specialized in begging from the pilgrims come up to the Holy City for Pesach, picking their pockets, and guiding them—once the festival was over—to the various houses of ill fame.

Those were the ones who were taking the lead in smashing the bird cages, wringing the necks of the pigeons, and stuffing the still bleeding carcasses under their tunics to serve as their suppers that night. It was they—especially the urchins—who were scrambling like wild beasts on the pavement, for the coins that rolled in every direction from the money changers' tables that Yeshu'a and his followers overturned. It was they who were engaging in fist fights over the spoils.

And, in the center of it, sublimely oblivious to the disgraceful, sacrilegious riot he was causing, Yeshu'a ha Notzri, my brother-in-law. I felt sick. The shame was in me like a fist to my gut, until it was replaced by fear.

Because, for the first time, I saw the Levite porters—as the Temple attendants were called, though in truth their duties included that of acting as police should the occasion or the necessity for such action arise—standing on the edges of the courts with their staves in their hands. Then I saw that they were arresting nobody, and not even cracking a few heads with their clubs as, under the present, sickeningly shameful circumstances, they should have, as I would have had I been in their place, as *you* would today if a Jew were to invade one of your *ekklesia*, and start throwing down your collection plates, and beating your ushers.

Moreover, I realized with a giddy surge of relief that left me breathless that they weren't going to; that their very *segens*, their officers, were restraining them, surely on the direct order of the Head Segen, the commander of the Temple police, who was, I saw now, also present. I turned to ish Kriyoth.

"They aren't—" I began.

"Doing anything," Yehudah said. "Of course not. You're of Zadokim parentage, Nathan. You ought to have known what the policy of the Sadducean priestly party would be in a case like this—"

"To tell the truth, I don't, though," I said. "Of course, I've been away from Jerusalem a goodly part of my life now; and it never occurred to me to ask my father about such a thing, for the simple reason I never dreamed it could arise. Why haven't they arrested him, charged the mob, cracked a few heads, stopped this madness?"

"Out of patience," Yehudah said. "Out of wisdom, and even out of piety. Whether your father ever told you so or not, it's been the fixed policy of the Zadokim for years *not* to confront the city mob whenever they can avoid it. Send the Levite porters in and the riot that would start would bring the *Cohors Italica* down from the Baris of Antonia, from the Tower of Phasael, on the double to make all the gutters run red with Jewish blood. So they won't arrest him—*now*. They won't build this up into a full-dress revolt—"

"But if a legionary or one of their officers were to happen by—" I began.

"He'd consider this a minor squabble over religious questions peculiar to that peculiar people, the Jews," Yehudah said bitterly. "He'd stand there and split his sides laughing at this farce—this obscene farce staged by a Galilean yokel who has already committed suicide—"

"Yehudah!" I said.

"Because Yeshu'a doesn't even know that the dove sellers and the money changers are necessary, and that their setting up their booths here in the outer courts, which aren't a sacred site, is by no stretch of the imagination a profanation of the Temple. You ought to tell him that, Nathan. You ought to ask him if he thinks that worshipers, however pious, are going to buy their birds in the common market, lug them all the way up here, across the whole city in cages, and then run the risk of having them rejected for some imperfection by the priests. And you might also ask him—if they don't take him tonight, if he hasn't been delivered to Pilatus for this outrage before morning—where pilgrims coming from all over Israel, from the Decapolis, even from abroad, are going to get coins that don't have Cæsar's image on them to buy the seals for the Temple offerings. Or would he prefer that we commit the blasphemy of offering God coins with graven images on them—'Thou shalt not make unto thee any graven image, or any likeness of anything that is in the heavens above, or on the earth beneath, or in the waters under the earth!"[3]—after he's chased the money changers out?"

I looked toward Yeshu'a. He'd finished it now. He'd just given the last red-faced, furious money changer a smart swipe across his fat ass as the burly thief ran through the gates. He was standing there with an expression of triumph on his face. I felt sicker than ever.

"They're thieves, Yehudah," I said; "they rob the people, they—"

"I know," Yehudah said. "But is *this* the way to correct the abuses, Nathan? Couldn't he have gone—or better still sent *you*, who are kinsman to all the powers that be in Jerusalem—to the High Priest, and suggested that a special *segen* be put over these courts to watch those thieving scoundrels, to receive and act upon complaints from the people? Wouldn't that have been the logical, the civilized way to do it? Did he have to commit a major outrage to cure a minor one?"

He had me there, as, with his ice-cold intelligence, he nearly always did. So I left him, went up to Yeshu'a, took his arm, said: "Come, Yeshu'a, before they seize you. You've been a fool, a Galilean wild man; but there's no helping that now. The money changers are necessary because of the images on the coins, and—"

"Then let them set up their tables elsewhere, Nathan!" he said flatly, "Not in the House of the Almighty! For is it not written, 'My house shall be called the house of prayer for all people . . .'? But they've made it a den of robbers!"[4]

I saw that there was no reasoning with him so I didn't even try. I refrained from reminding him that he who claimed that the use of force was always wrong, advocated turning the other cheek, was making a remarkably ludicrous spectacle of himself with his whip of cords, standing there amid the smashed bird cages, his clothes splattered with pigeon dung, while snot-nosed urchins scrambled for coins spilled from the tables of men engaged in—sharp practices aside!—a legitimate, even necessary business (Have you learned to support your *ekklesia,* your churches, without funds? If so, I pray you tell me how!) on the paving stones. All I did was to take his arm, and lead him away from there. As we moved off, the people formed a double row on both sides of us, so that the *segens* couldn't get anywhere near us—not that they even tried to—and cheered him as he passed.

"Hosannah in the Highest!" they roared. "Blessings upon you, Son of David!"

Yeshu'a was a dead man then, at that moment. They'd condemned him the instant they said that. For they were calling him the Mashiah. Which was the one thing that neither the priesthood nor the Romans could permit. The High Priest couldn't, for unless my wild man brother-in-law really were the Mashiah, or could prove at least that he was of David's line, the claim itself was, by a technicality too difficult to explain here and now, false prophecy, and punishable by death. And the Romans couldn't, for to them the word *Christos, Mashiah,* meant "king," and hence the man bearing that title was guilty of treason against the Imperator, rebellion against his authority.

So, Yeshu'a ben Yosef, called ha Notzri, stood condemned, unless I could save him. He had made his position in Jerusalem impossible by offending the very highest powers in what was after all a theocratic state. All that was keeping him alive now was the fact that the Bœthusian-Sadducean priestly party feared the people. As long as Yeshu'a could keep the people's favor, the danger while great, was not immediate. How was I to know that he was going to lose even that, and infuriate the Pharisees of Jerusalem—the one group who might have defended him, since his teachings only differed from theirs in emphasis, in detail—as well?

As I led him away from that debacle, it seemed to me that nothing or nobody could make his position worse.

But he, himself, could. And did.

Chapter XXV

WE GOT out of Jerusalem without any trouble at all, crossing the Kedron ravine, and climbing up the slopes into Beth Anya. But, by the time we got to the house of Shimeon the Essene, the exaltation that had possessed them all during what had seemed to them Yeshu'a's singularly heroic feat, had drained out of them. I could see my ancient enemy, Shimeon Zealotes, frowning like a thundercloud, largely, I guessed, because he couldn't determine the logical next step from that messy little scandal-provoking affair in the outer courts, to the full-dress, grand-scale, first-class revolt against the Romans he was still hoping for. Shimeon Kepha and Andrai, his brother, were looking throughtful and grave. It interested me most to watch the speculative cast that stole over the face of Matthya, the former tax collector. Already, I was sure, his head was busy with his literary labors, seeking somehow to transform that disgusting and ridiculous spectacle into the triumph your *Besorahim* make of it now.

When we entered the house, apart from greeting our host, nobody talked. Yeshu'a, himself, was utterly calm. I could see the others staring at him. Nathanael bar Talmay, and Philip, who was half Greek, had their heads together, and were whispering in that language, probably to keep the rest from understanding them.

"Do you think they'll come after him tonight?" I heard one of them say.

Then the two sisters, Miriam and Martha, came and began to prepare the evening meal.

We ate it in silence. None of us ate very much. Yeshu'a ate nothing at all. He sat there, rapt, lost in contemplation of—I guessed—what your *Besorahim* now call "the pangs of the Mashiah," of "the abomination of desolation," or maybe even of himself, the *bar enosh*, the Son of Man, coming in the clouds with great power and glory to gather up his chosen from the four winds, from the farthest bounds of earth to the fartherest bounds of heaven.[1] He was, I knew, convinced that all this was going to happen now. Within days, perhaps even within hours, not in some far off, remote future. Which was another thing I had to save him from: the danger that when he found out his deepest concepts were irrelevant to the world that exists, to life as it is, the shock might upset his already delicate equilibrium altogether and drive him, truly, mad. . . .

That was the state we were in when Shelomith came through the doorway.

Every man in that room stopped breathing, except, of course, Yeshu'a, himself. Women—even glorious creatures like Shelom—simply had no visible effect upon him. But that night, had he not been so lost in his apocalyptic visions, had he even bothered to look at her, I am sure he, too, would have been moved.

I heard Miriam and Martha gasp, paralyzed in the very act of serving me more soup; I felt against my eardrums the short, explosive expulsion of their horror, shock, outrage. And though they didn't say it, I could feel their minds shaping the words: "Strumpet. Slut. Harlot. Whore."

Some of the men shared their disgust, especially our host, Shimeon, the Essene. Others, the Boane Ragsha, for example, Zealotes, bar Talmay, Yehudah ben Yaakob, Philip, fell—through sheer habit, I'm sure—into the slack-lipped, salivating gross expressions of easy lust.

But two of us, Yehudah ish Kriyoth—my Brother!—and I, suffered the crippling, murderous anguish of those who truly—love.

There is, my dear Theophilos, as you who write, who are a most worthy scribe, must know, a law of diminishing returns in the use of words. There are no words for absolutes. Words are, by their very nature, approximations. And approximations will not do. Not for this, for this!

So I ask you to aid me. Lend your warm heart, your generous imagination to my task. Don't ask me to do the impossible. Help me. Enter into that little house in Beth Anya on a night fled into the dark abyss of time more than fifty years ago, with me, now. . . .

Listen. Hear how her bare feet whisper across the tiles. Strain your ears—catch that sound. There is none other like it. Slowly. Slowly. There! And the rustle of her robes. See them. Close your eyes and see them in your inner, spiritual eye. They are ragged. You can distinguish the torn places where she ripped away the broideries, the filigrees, the ornaments of whoredom. They look odd. They have been altered, patched, added to in all the places where before they flaunted flesh to catch the eyes of the goats and monkeys of this world. Their awkward, anguished gropings toward modesty, toward chastity, break your heart. Or at least they broke mine. And Yehudah's. There are tears in his little blue eyes, now. And in my black ones. My tears blind me. They scald my throat.

She is clean. Her dark skin shines. Her cheeks are reddened, roughened, she has scrubbed them so. There is no paint on her face, her mouth. She smells only of soap. A strong, acid soap; the kind women use to wash clothes with.

Her hair is loose. I fight the similes (night descending from heaven without a star, the darkness of the deep before light was, the blackness of deepest Sheol) and write: It is very long, and very black, and thick, and wild, and beautiful. Words! I wanted to claw my fingers into it, ram it against my mouth, make a noose of it and die sweet-strangled! Words. Her hair. Shelom's hair.

Her mouth. Shelom's mouth.

Trembling now. A little opened. A smoky flash of pearl between. My own mouth hurts. From memory. From hunger. I can taste her three rods away. From across the room.

Her eyes. Shelom's eyes.

Distilling diamonds—no! That's false. Spilling tears. Ordinary human tears. But hers. Hers! Running molten through my heart. Which is not false. That's what it felt like then.

She has a little flask in her hands. As she comes toward him, toward this man capable only of a kind of love she cannot understand, her hands tear at the stopper, making convulsive motions, those same convulsive motions that the hands of a criminal who has been tortured too long make just before he dies.

She has the cap—the stopper, the cork—how do I know which it was? —off now. She is very close to him. She puts out her hand—see it shake (a lone leaf on a slender limb, winddriven) and pours the contents of her flask over Yeshu'a's head. Now she kneels and pours what is left over his feet. The room fills up with the smell of purest nard.

Her tears fall on his feet now (as once they fell on mine, on mine!) and she is kissing them (as she once kissed mine) blessing them with her tears, and drying them with (black glory, silken tenderness) her hair.

Martha said: "Adonai!" at that, which broke the spell. They all found voice.

Shimeon the Essene grumbled: "Can't he see what kind of a woman this is? A sinner and—"[2]

And, at my side, my brother Yehudah began, speaking out of his hurt, his jealousy, his grief: "What a waste! That spikenard's worth three hundred denarii! It could have been sold to feed the poor instead of—"

But Yeshu'a had put down his hand, let it rest on Shelom's head. Then he looked at ish Kriyoth, at the others who had taken up the complaint: "A waste. A criminal waste. Expensive stuff like that. Three hundred denarii—spilt—"

"Wait," he said quietly, "don't reproach her. The poor you have with you always. But I am going away from you soon, now. . . ."

He looked down at Shelomith, stroked her head. She gave an ecstatic shudder, as a dog does when caressed.

"You're preparing me for burial, aren't you, child?" he said. "You think—or know—I'm going to die. That's it, isn't it, Shelom?"

She nodded dumbly. Her bent form sculptured anguish out of the naked, scent-drenched air.

Yeshu'a looked up. Said softly, slowly: "I tell you this: Shelomith will never be forgot. Wherever in the world my word is taught, men will remember her because she honored me—"[3]

Then he sought and found my eyes.

"Take her home, Nathan," he said.

So I took her home. On the way we talked, using the broken phrases, the disjointed words, sentences that make the very air vibrate with tension, that shoot it through with the unseen lightning of what they don't say, leave out.

"Shelom—"

"He's going to die. They're going to kill him."

"Who?"

"Don't know. The Zadokim. The High Priest. Pilatus. The Romans. After what he did this morning, they've got to. Only—"

"Only what, Shelom?"

"They'll have to turn the people against him first. Won't be hard. The fickle bastards. They'll figure out a way to make it look like—"

I said beneath my breath: "Shelom. My love. My own."

She didn't hear me. She went on: "—he favors the Romans. Any filthy trick will do. He's not smart. He's too sweet to be. Too filled with love—"

"And I—and I—and I—" I thought or maybe even said.

"Nathan, what are we going to do? To save him, I mean. To get him out of their clutches. To—"

Then I told her. When I'd done with it, she kissed me. On the mouth. I'll carry that one down to my grave, too. Like the first one Helvi gave me.

"Bring me the stuff," she said. "Now. Tonight. Show me how to mix it. I'll bring it there. The soldiers will let me. They all know me. They ought to. The dirty pigs."

"All right," I said.

"Soon as he passes out, appears like he's dead, you go to Pilatus—"

"No. Pilatus wouldn't trust me—" I said.

"Ha! He shouldn't!" Shelom mocked. "Considering what a pair you hung on his forehead, he—"

"That's not why. Anyhow, Yosef ha Arimathæa will do that. He looks wise and trustworthy and—"

"And you look—wicked and sensual and beautiful and—so now you turn yourself around and march yourself home and get that stuff. You can come in then—long enough to explain it to me. Then you get out. Before I spoil everything, I mean."

"Spoil it how?" I said.

"Claw you bloody. Bite your lip through. Put my thighs around your hips and break your backbone. Drain everything out of you so you won't be any good to any woman anymore. Not even—your—your wife —God, how it kills me to say that word!"

I grinned at her, said: "What a way to die!"

But she said: "No, Nathan. I won't. It's all—talk, now. It's got to be. *He's* forgiven me. Blessed me. I feel—clean. I want to stay that way. You—damn you!—bring out the rutting bitch in me. So go. And when

you come back it's—that stuff for him. How to mix it, I mean. Nothing
else. You understand that, don't you?"

I did. And it was.

All that night, I shared my bed with fear. It came flapping through
my window on leather wings, heavily, slowly. It stank. Of carrion. Of
death. It hadn't any form, but it had weight. It perched on the window-
sill and looked at me out of the eyes it didn't have, either. There were
only two holes in its head, but I could feel its gaze. Then it belched
putrefaction, until the air went thick, and flapped over and sat on my
chest. It was heavy. It weighed ten tons of utter vileness sitting there
on me, clucking kitetalk, crowtalk, vulturetalk, dropping offal on my
belly, half-masticated carrion meat stinking, stinking into my face. And
it wouldn't let me breathe or move or even come awake.

I lay there with it sitting on me clucking away until day began to
carve gray form out of blackness, unfurl blue-smoked pearl across the
bottom of the sky. Then I heaved up, and threw it off me. It rolled
itself into a noisome ball of midnight, flapped through the window, and
was gone.

I got up from there, attended to the unlovelier functions of the
human body, washed, cleaned my teeth, dressed, went down into the
street without having eaten anything, strode through the thinning
dawn mist out of the city, crossed the ravine, climbed up to Beth
Anya.

I found Yeshu'a where I'd known he would be, standing on the
higher slope beyond the town and gazing across the ravine at Jerusalem. He was murmuring something. I caught the words: "Oh Jerusalem, Jerusalem, city that murders prophets and stones the messengers
sent you—" and I knew that he, too, felt what I felt, that, like me, he
was troubled and afraid.

"Yeshu'a," I said to him, "don't go into the city. Not today. Let them
cool off. Forget. You mustn't enter Jerusalem. They'll take you. Stone
you. Crucify—"

He looked at me; said: "Are you prophesying again, Nathan?"

"No," I said. But all the same I saw a cross black against an angry
sky, saw—"No!" I said again, louder.

He smiled.

"It isn't written that it will happen thus, Nathan," he said. "Today
I'll be safe. Today's the Shabbat, remember—so they won't touch me.
Will you come with me, my brother?"

"Of course," I said. But that evil bird was back again, clawing at my
gut. "Of course I will, Yeshu'a," I said.

I went with them. I put a dagger beneath my robe and went. I didn't know what in the name of Satan, Samaël, and Beelzebub a single blade would serve for; but, all the same, it was a comfort to have it there.

The crowds met us at the gates and escorted us into the Holy City, crying "Hosanna to the Son of David!" and stretching out their hands to touch him as he went by. But, as soon as we entered the outer courts, I saw a group of the highest priesthood waiting for us, surrounded by their *segens,* clubs in hand. They were Zadokim one and all, many of them cousins of mine on my mother's side, Bœthusians, kindred of the High Priest, Yosef ben Kaiapha. So I edged in closer to Yeshu'a. He smiled at me.

"Don't worry about me, Nathan," he said.

They came up to him and addressed him sternly:

"Rabbi, by whose authority did you act yesterday?"

He looked them up and down from head to toe, slowly. I didn't do that. I peered into their faces, trying to read them, make out what they were thinking, know—It was very hard. Their eyes were troubled. They were, after all, men, despite their priesthood. Neither especially good nor especially bad; but burdened by their tenuous and uncertain authority as the leaders of a state occupied by a foreign power. And, to make bad matters worse, leaders of a theocratic state, groaning under the heel of an all but godless power.

Fear clawed my gut again, blew its putrid breath into my face. They, these imposing, godly men, were prepared to kill him. They didn't want to—as they had proved yesterday, and as their eyes showed now—but they were prepared to; and for the best of all possible reasons: To save their people, Israel.

Your *Besorahim,* your Gospels, have made criminal monsters of them; but they weren't. They were just men, troubled men, the oldest of whom had seen the sky black with Roman crosses on which the sons of Israel moaned; the youngest, witnessed (through my fault, through my fault, through my most grievous fault!) Jewish brains splattered against the walls of the Antonia, Jewish blood running like water through the gutters of Jerusalem.

Men. Standing there confronting another wild man. Another crazy prophet come down from Galilee to stir the people up, to set them mad, to send them howling to the attack once more, once more to die like slaughtered animals under the swords of the best, the most efficient butchers in all the world.

So now they asked it again: "By what authority did you—"

And I knew. Quite suddenly and appallingly, I knew. They were trying to make him hang himself in a noose of his own words, commit in their presence and before witnesses the terrible crime of *mesith*.[4] In their eyes, he was guilty of it already, this crime of enticing the people to idolatry. For *mesith* included setting oneself up as a god, and allowing people to worship one as such. I was getting sicker by the second. How many times had I heard Yeshu'a call God "my Father"? And not in the acceptable sense of God's being the collective father of all men, but *his* father, who had begot him as a new soul when he arose from the waters of the Jordan after his baptism by Yohannan.

They had him now. All he had to do was to answer—as he was sure to—"I acted upon the authority of my Father, God—" and he was a dead man. I hung there, waiting for him to speak.

He smiled at them, said: "You'd have something for nothing? I'll strike a bargain with you: You answer me my question, and in fair exchange, I'll answer yours. Mine is: Did Yohannan, called Baptistes, baptize from God's power, or merely from the authority of men?"

I stood there, looking at him. What a Pharisee he was when he wanted to be! Yesterday, I had almost agreed with ish Kriyoth in calling him a yokel. And now, very simply, he'd asked the subtlest brains in Israel a question so subtle that either way they answered it, they were lost.

I could see the mob crowding in close now, mouths agape, making the air in the outer courts miasmatic with their garlicky breaths, as they waited for the priests to answer. For they, the people, had adored Yohannan the Wild Man. Many of them believed that he had been Elijah returned. All of them held that he was a Prophet. So now, if the priests answered that Yohannan had had his powers of God, Yeshu'a would ask them, "Why then didn't you believe in him?" and the crowds would rock with delighted laughter. On the other hand, should my lordly kinsmen and venerable priestly fathers reply, "From men," the mob would set up such a howl of rage as to cause the very walls to shake; for that answer was tantamount to declaring their beloved and martyred Yohannan hadn't been a Prophet.

I could see their confusion. I watched them whispering among themselves. Then they decided upon a prudent answer:

"Master, we don't know."

Yeshu'a smiled.

"Then neither will I tell you by what authority I act," he said serenely.

I let my breath out slowly, into the rising ripple of the people's laughter. Yeshu'a had answered not only like a Pharisee, but like a lawyer of the Pharisees, like a P'rushim scribe.

But the Zadokim weren't disposed to give up at that. While the priests and *segens* consulted among themselves, talking in hoarse-voiced mutters as the Sadducees will, some of their laymen pushed forward, determination on their faces.

I knew them all. Two or three of them were former friends of mine. For now that I had openly associated myself with the Nazarene, I could have no friends among the Sadducees. But, knowing them as I did, I feared them less than I did the priests. The lay Zadokim are a hearty, beefy lot, full-fleshed and unsubtle. I knew Yeshu'a was more than a match for their dull wits. The people I truly feared were the P'rushim, the Pharisees.

But seeing me now, recognizing me, some of those Zadokim louts in whose company I'd gamed and wenched many the night away, came forward, seeking to strike at him through me. They ringed me round about, grinned at me mockingly, said:

"Nathan bar Yehudah, whoremonger turned saint, ask your master about the seven brothers with but one wife among the lot of them!"

That was the hoariest of Zadokim chestnuts. They were always using it to mock the P'rushim. Briefly, it goes like this:

Among us, a brother must marry the widow of his brother who has died childless, in order to preserve his name and line. So the Zadokim propose a ridiculous tale of a woman who successively survived seven brothers in turn, all without fruit from their labors upon her, in order to ask: "At the resurrection of the dead, whose wife shall she be?"

Thus cast they mockery upon the central P'rushim doctrine: The resurrection of the dead; the immortality of the soul.

I looked them in the eye, grinned back at them, said: "Don't need to. *I* know the answer."

"Which is?" they demanded of me.

"None of theirs. A bitch with a poisonous tail like that would never get into Gan Eden."

They set up such a roar of laughter, that Yeshu'a heard them, turned, came back to me, said: "What is it, Nathan?"

"Rabbi," I said solemnly, "these friends of my youth would pose you a riddle."

He looked at them calmly.

"Propose it, then," he said.

They did. And his answer was another marvel:

"You're wrong. I don't believe you know either the Scriptures or God's power. In heaven there's neither marrying nor giving in marriage, for men and women don't carry their lustful bodies there, but only their pure souls. . . ."

He went on teaching them, expounding to them as though they were children, until a Pharisee who stood nearby was moved to ask him: "Master, what is the first and best of the Commandments?"

Yeshu'a lifted up his head and made the Temple courts ring with that greatest, that noblest of all cries:

"*Sh'ma Ysroël!* The Lord is God! The Lord is One!" Then, more quietly: "And you, my son, must love him with all your heart, your soul, your mind, your strength. That is the first and greatest of the commandments. But the second is important, too: You must love your neighbor as yourself."

The Pharisee bent his head, looked up again. And once more I saw Yeshu'a's truest miracle, the one he effortlessly and endlessly performed: The P'rushite turned wax, melted under the matchless tenderness, the shattering authority of his gaze.

"You're right, master," he said. "To obey those commandments is enough. More than enough. It is far better than burnt offerings or sacrifices."

Yeshu'a put out his hand and let it rest on the P'rushite's shoulder.

"My son, you're not far from the Kingdom of God," he said.

I was beginning to relax now. To feel good. The danger was passing. Then I looked into the faces of the assembled P'rushim, who had so far held themselves aloof from their enemies the Zadokim, saying nothing, taking no part in the debate, and my fear came back with a sickening rush. Because their eyes were glittering in their faces like those of so many wolves. And it was precisely this surrender to the power in him, the magic, the authority, the love, by one of their own that had got them wild.

Heaven witness he had *earned* their enmity! When he had first started to teach, the P'rushim had welcomed him as one of them, warned him against his foes,[5] invited him to their houses.[6] But when they'd ventured to rebuke him, mildly enough, God knows, for making light of, and even setting aside, the Law, things for which they could have stoned him to death in the purest, most indisputable legality had they wanted to, he, instead of accepting a reprimand very largely just, had turned upon them in one of his towering rages and called them things *I'd* have killed him for, or at least been tempted to, if he'd said them to me.

So now I loosed my dagger in its sheath. But a moment later, I took my hands off it altogether. For, watching them narrowly, I saw from their looks, their gestures, that they weren't going to use force against him; they were going to continue the Zadokim's tactic of making him hang himself in a noose of his own words. But now the danger was real, and terrible: the Zadokim were bluff, hardy, crude; but the P'rushim were the most subtle dialecticians in all the world.

They hit him at once with the obvious. He hadn't rebuked the grow-ing number of people who were calling him the Mashiah. More, he'd declared in public that if they kept silent, the very stones would speak. He had proclaimed himself the cornerstone of the whole vast edifice of our Faith. He, this carpenter's son, this wild Galilean rab! It was enough to madden saints, which the Pharisees, for all their self-righteousness, had never claimed to be. But, being P'rushim, they didn't ask him straight out: "Are you the Mashiah?" Instead, they put it to him quietly:

"Rabbi, must the Mashiah be David's son?"

It was, I saw, a question both edged and barbed. Any way he an-swered it, he'd be wrong. For if he said, "Yes," they'd follow with: "And are *you* of that princely descent?" If, on the other hand, he said, "No," they'd demand of him: "Show us one line in the Holy Scriptures that justifies your contention! Our fathers have taught us that God's Anointed must be David's son."

But I, as well as the P'rushim, had underestimated him. He was not to be trapped into denying his role, nor into the lie of claiming descent from David.

He said to them evenly: "How can your sages say the Mashiah is David's son? For David himself says in the Book of Psalms: 'The Lord said to my Lord, "Sit at my right hand until I make your enemies your footstool."' Thus David calls him 'Lord'; how then can he be David's son?"[7]

I could see them considering that, and nodding gravely among themselves. Being Pharisees, they could even appreciate it, take a som-ber pride in his skill. For, to them, he was one of themselves, an erring brother who had strayed from the path.

The people, too, nodded just as gravely, as if they'd understood him, which, of course, they hadn't, and crowded in closer to hear more. I could see the Pharisees staring speculatively at the mob, *amme ha aretz* in their vast majority, with a sprinkling of Zealot firebrands among them. I think that was what gave the P'rushim their matchless idea, the exquisitely subtle tactic by which they destroyed him. They must have recognized the Zealots in that crowd; they had—which I didn't—ways of knowing them. So they dealt him their masterstroke, and left him defenseless and without hope.

"Master," their spokesman said, "we know that what you speak and teach is sound; you bow your head to no man living, but teach honestly

God's way. So tell us: Are we or are we not permitted by our Sacred Law to pay taxes to the Roman Emperor?"

For the twentieth time that day, I ceased to breathe. They had him. They had him inescapably, with no way out. For if he said: "We are not allowed by Law to pay taxes to anyone but God!"—which was the truth—he'd be guilty of public treason to Cæsar, and his poor carcass would decorate a cross before morning. And if he said, "We are so permitted—" the Zealots in that crowd would cut his throat like a Paschal lamb as soon as the sun set, that is if the mob itself didn't forget that it was Shabbat and they were in the Temple courts, and rend him limb from limb the moment the words were out.

For nothing was so oppressive or so hated as those taxes, which was why the nation had risen in revolt against Publius Sulpicius Quirinius, the Governor of Syria, when he'd called a census to count us for the tax in the year when Yeshu'a and I were eight years old.[8] They violated our belief that we owed allegiance only to God; and made, from the economic standpoint, the lives of the people all but unbearable.

Yeshu'a stood there, looking at the P'rushim; and his dark eyes went sick with rage and grief. But he controlled himself nobly, said:

"Show me a silver denarius."

The P'rushim instantly produced two dozen. Yeshu'a took one of them, stared at it. Then he said, very quietly: "Whose head is this on it? Whose inscription?"

"Cæsar's," the P'rushim said.

"Then pay Cæsar what is due to Cæsar, and God what is due to God."[9]

It was a wondrously skillful answer. Because to buy the Temple script offering with coins bearing *iconoi*, graven images of living men, upon them was a violation of the Ten Commandments, and tantamount to idolatry. Which was why the money changers he had driven out of the outer courts were absolutely necessary: they exchanged the image-bearing coins the people brought them for Temple shekels free of the idolatrous icons. But the effect of Yeshu'a's clever answer was only to blunt the crowd's anger enough to allow him to escape alive. Your Gospels make of it a triumph. It was, unfortunately, the exact opposite, his single greatest failure. Because at one stroke it lost him the people's love, which was the only protection he had against his enemies.

I could see the faces of the crowd. They were disgruntled at the least. Some—the Zealots, I guessed—were black with anger. Even his disciples looked at him with troubled eyes. I could hear the grumbles:

"The Mashiah? Ha! The Mashiah would lead us against the Romans, push 'em into the sea! And this Galilean itinerant—"

"Would pay 'em, the bloodsuckers! He's—"

"No Mashiah. You heard him! He just admitted he wasn't of David's line. So now he has to prove it. Look at him. Scared shitless. Give to Cæsar—Ha! What *isn't* Cæsar's due, according to them? Your house, your land, your money, your labor, your wife's sweet wiggling tail, and your daughter's, too! I tell you—"

I moved in close to him, my hand on my dagger. Then he made another mistake: he lost his temper, and began to berate the P'rushim.[10] The people listened to his tirade a while, but now they saw it for what it was, the anger and chagrin of a defeated man; so it bored them. They began to drift away. By the time he got to the end of it, repeating the same words he'd said that morning—

"O Jerusalem, Jerusalem, city that kills the prophets and stones the messengers sent her! How often have I longed to gather your children, as a hen gathers her brood under her wings, but you wouldn't let me. Look, look! Here is your temple, forsaken of God. And I tell you, you'll see me no more until the time comes when you say: 'Blessings on him who comes in the name of the Lord!' "—they were all gone, and only the P'rushim stood there listening to his words, hearing his fury-shaken voice with complacency, with contempt. . . .

I took him by the arm, gently but firmly.

"Come, Yeshu'a. Come with me now," I said.

He allowed me to lead him away. His eyes were dark with anguish. His death was already upon him, and he knew it.

As we went out the gate, Shimeon Kepha looked back at the Temple and murmured, wonderingly: "What fine buildings, what mighty stones. . . ."

Whereupon Yeshu'a turned upon him, raging: "I tell you, Kepha; and all the rest of you: Not one stone will be left upon another! All will be thrown down! All!"[11]

I tugged at his arm. I could feel him trembling. So I said to him with infinite patience, total weariness:

"Come, Yeshu'a, my brother. Don't talk anymore, I beg you! Forget Jerusalem who isn't worthy of you. Or you of her. Or something. Anyhow, come."

Chapter XXVI

AND NOW, finally, all things ran downhill like a millstream to their end. We had one day of quiet after Yeshu'a's disastrous debate with the Pharisees, the day you call Sun Day, and use for your Shabbat, having borrowed it from the Mithraists, to whose religion your faith has far more resemblance than to anything that Yeshu'a ever taught. I don't know why we had that day of grace; probably because the Sadducees had decided to move with prudence and caution, to make haste slowly, as it were . . .

I don't even remember what, if anything, happened on that Sun Day. But on the second day of that week whose sixth day marked the beginning of the *hag ha mazot*, the Feast of Unleavened Bread, those seven days from the fifteenth to the twenty-first of the month of Nisan, during which we are forbidden to even keep leaven in the house for fear we might violate the Sacred Law by accident, Hagar, my mother's maidservant, brought my breakfast in to me.

I took one look at it, and a scalding tide of nausea exploded up from my belly, filling all my throat. I choked it back down again, said: "Leave it there on the table, Hagar, and get out of here!"

"Your Lady Mother says—" Hagar began.

"Sheol and Gehenna!" I howled. "Leave me in peace! You and Mother both!"

Hagar backed out of the door. I lay there eyeing my breakfast. There was nothing wrong with it. It was a perfectly good breakfast: fruit and wheaten cakes and cheese and a little watered wine. Yet to me, it might as well have been a nest of coiling vipers, a mess of loathsome, crawling things. And the reason for that sad state of affairs lay not in my breakfast, which had been prepared by my mother's own loving hands, but in me.

Fear strangles a man's gut. Terror, anticipated anguish, lived with too long, tears them, rips them apart. Before, upon my return from Rome, I had almost died, not of my physical injuries—which were grave enough, God knows—but of what intolerable horror, unspeakable grief, the loss of hope, had done to my insides, which was to claw them

into bloody shreds. History was repeating itself: the same thing was
happening to me all over again, now.

What will I tell Yohannah? I thought. How will I face her, say:
They hung him on a cross. It didn't take too long. He died—very well.
Very bravely. He—

But would he? Could he? Could any man of woman born bear the
obscene horror of being crucified? I had to save him. Get him out of
Jerusalem. Now. Before Passover. Before—

I'll knock him on the head! I raged inside my mind, tie him up,
bear him away as the violent bear away God's Kingdom and—

Then, suddenly, I *saw* him hanging there. With the flies at him.
With his swollen tongue protruding from his mouth. Dripping greenish urine down his own sweat-glistened thighs, a flux of liquid fæces
befouling the backs of them. And the vile green tide came up my throat
in a foaming rush. I opened my mouth and spewed it forth. It was at
least three-quarters blood.

I got out of bed, clawed myself erect by pure will, hung there,
swaying like a reed in a winter wind. Fool! I cursed myself, give in now,
surrender to your cowardice, become a ball-less wonder and—

The weakness ebbed. I washed my mouth out, cleaned up the bloody
vomit from the floor so that Hagar wouldn't see it and tell Mother,
bathed, perfumed myself. Which did no good at all: I stank like a
rutting billy goat from the ice cold sweat of fear.

I combed out my hair, my beard. I'd just finished dressing myself
when Hagar came back again. She stared at my untouched breakfast,
but she didn't say anything about that. She knew I was perfectly
capable of telling her to shove it up one of the more intimate apertures
of her anatomy, so she said: "Young master, there's a man outside,
asking for you . . ."

"What sort of man?" I said.

"A queer-looking man. Talks almost like a rab, but different, somehow. Little fellow, sort of bent—"

Shimeon the Essene, I guessed at once. Come to remind me of my
promise to provide a place for the Seder. They're all as nervous as I am.
Or worse. Because why else would he come today? Pesach isn't until
the end of the week. Shabbat eve, in fact, and—

"Tell him I'll be down directly," I said.

Pesach, Passover, is always celebrated the fifteenth of Nisan, the
first day of the Feast of Unleavened Bread. Which means, since our
day ends at sunset, we sit down to it shortly before sunset of the day
before. It is a very solemn occasion: We eat the Pesach, the sacrificial
lamb, drink the four cups of consecrated wine, and accompany the

meat course both with the matzah, unleavened bread, and the bitter herbs, in memory of our people's sorrows.

Now the eve of Passover is called Preparation Day. On it, the priests kill the paschal lamb for us according to the Holy Ritual, and that, surely, was what Shimeon had come to remind me of; but what I couldn't figure out was why, in the name of everything unholy, he had come to me so far ahead of time. For Pesach that year fell on the eve of the Shabbat, and this was only the second day of the week, the day that you pagans—I beg your pardon!—you Christianoi call Moon Day. So, when I got downstairs I asked Shimeon that.

He smiled at me and said: "But I haven't come too soon, son Nathan. You see, *tomorrow* is Preparation Day."

I looked at him as though he were mad. I've already told you that Pesach fell on the sixth day of the week that year. This was indisputable because our astronomers had already calculated that the first full moon after the vernal equinox would appear on the fifth day of the week, the fourteenth of the month of that thirty-second year of my—and Yeshu'a's—singularly unquiet existences. So Pesach *had* to be celebrated on the sixth day, the eve of the Shabbat, because, by our rather complicated lunar calendar, any time the full moon didn't appear on the equinox itself, we had to celebrate Pesach the night after it did appear.

Bear with me. This is important. It is because they knew nothing of Jewish Law and customs that your scribes got the events of what you call Holy Week all wrong.

But here was this sober, pious member of the New Covenant of Saints, informing me that the third day of the week, the twelfth day of Nisan, was Preparation Day, and that the fourth of the week, the thirteenth of Nisan, was Pesach.

"But Shimeon!" I told him. "Aren't you a little mixed up? Preparation Day isn't until—"

He stopped me with a majestically lifted hand.

"No, son Nathan," he said; "it is you people of Jerusalem who are confused, not us. Why do you think that Israel suffers? Not only have your false priesthood profaned the Temple with their unlawful practices, but how can you expect the Lord to bless festivals celebrated according to the calendar of those worshipers of *Gillulim*, of idols, the Greeks. It is *we* who preserve the ways of the Patriarchs, the Fathers! Our system of counting time was used by Ezekiel, by Moses; by Ezra and Nehemiah. If you calculate the days, weeks, months as the Goyim do, how can you truly worship God?"[1]

There he had me, and I wasn't disposed to argue the matter anyhow. From what I'd seen of God's loving kindness and tender mercy, the question of which days one celebrated the festivals, or even if one celebrated them at all, was, to me, a problem whose interest was something less than burning, a cloud-cuckoo-land debate for yawning over, if that.

"For," Shimeon went on sternly, "Pesach must be celebrated on the first day of the week and—"

I couldn't let him get away with that. Not that I cared, really, but now he was contradicting even himself, because he'd just reminded me that according to the Essenes' Jubilees calendar, Pesach was day after tomorrow; and if the day after tomorrow wasn't the fourth day of the week, what in the name of all the Angels of the Presence was it?

I asked him that.

"The first day of the week," he said solemnly. "On what day did God create the heavenly luminaries, Nathan, my son?"

I searched my memory until the answer came.

"The fourth," I said.[2]

"Hence, for mankind, the fourth day became the first day, because how could there be—to human perceptions, I mean—day and night before the sun and moon existed so that we could tell light from darkness?"[3]

I should have known better than to argue with an Essene. Actually, what I was thinking about was why the meaning of the difference between their calendar and ours hadn't ever really struck me before, since I had spent more than a year among them. But now that I'd come to think of it, the reason was really very simple: I had been carried to Qumrân in a semiconscious state; and when I returned to consciousness, I'd been for a long time, half mad of grief and pain. So, when I came to myself, and they'd told me a certain day was Shabbat, it never even occurred to me to question their word. Nor had I any contact with the outside world to show me that our days and theirs were different ones. Even when I came back into the world, the circumstances—Pilatus' violation of our prohibition against idolatry —had been so dramatic that I hadn't had time to think about what day it was. The first occasion on which I'd become aware that there *was* a difference between their reckoning of time and ours was when Yeshu'a himself had told me he'd adopted from his brother Yaakob, called Tzaddig, the Just, a fervent member of the Nazareth community of the town-dwelling Essenes, the use of the New Covenanters' calendar.

But now, at long last, a sudden, wild stab of joy penetrated me. Whatever action the High Priests and their *segens* planned to take against Yeshu'a for his outrageous behavior in the Temple courts, for his megalomaniacal claims of Mashiahship, for his close to *mesith* assertion that he was *the* son of God, for representing a danger to the peace and order of the Holy City, they weren't likely to take it until the *hag ha mazot* was over,[4] and the pilgrims, especially his own crowd of Galileans, were on their way home. That moment, one minute after sunset, when our day officially ends, when Pesach and the seven days remaining of the Feast of Unleavened Bread that followed it were barely over, would be the best conceivable moment to seize him, since very likely he could be arrested then without danger of crowds being present. But now, according to what Shimeon the Essene was telling me, I could have my wild, crazy, mad, but still achingly beloved brother-in-law safely out of town before my cousin Yosef ben Kaiapha and his band of pious frauds were ready to strike, because the Essene Passover preceded the official one by nearly three days.

I could have kissed the pious old fool; but I didn't, for surely such a familiarity would have shocked him. Instead, I said: "Tell your master I hear and obey. Don't forget to look out for the water carrier, about the fourth or fifth hour tomorrow—"

"Very well. My blessings upon you, son Nathan," Shimeon said; and took his leave.

But on that tomorrow, the twelfth day of Nisan by official reckoning after I had the matzah, the unleavened bread, the bitter herbs, and the wine prepared, I ran head on into a difficulty that, had my own piety been a trifle more exemplary than it was, I surely should have foreseen: the priests flatly refused to sacrifice my paschal lamb on a day that to them wasn't Preparation Day at all.[5]

I started to argue with them, but I closed my idiotic mouth just in time. Because, to convince them, I'd have to explain to the group of men whom Yeshu'a's very existence most outraged, that he and his band were going to celebrate Passover two days ahead of time.[6] And, even had I held back both names and details, I should have wakened their suspicions or their curiosity enough for them to have me followed in order to see who it was that planned to violate Sacred Law in this mad fashion.

In fact, from the way they were staring at me now, I saw I had better offer them some reason for requesting that they sacrifice my lamb for me on the wrong day that would quell their curiosity, their suspicion and their ire.

"Forget it, good Rabbin," I said carelessly; "it's not important, really. I'll bring the lamb back day after tomorrow, then. It's just that we have a venerable guest at home who happens to be an Essene. He insists that today is Preparation Day, and that our calendar is mistaken. Out of hospitality it didn't seem to me wrong to humor him in this; but, since you say it is, I bow to your great wisdom—"

To my surprise, my remarks caused a verbal civil war among them. I found out then that a good many of the P'rushim among the priests held that the Essenes were right in this matter of the calendar.[7] These fell to battling with their colleagues, both the Zadokim and some priests of their own party—for, within certain limits, the P'rushim embraced many different degrees or shades of opinion—brandishing quotations from this or that sage as though they were so many swords.

I got out of there, leaving them at it; but I had scarcely gone beyond the outer courts before one of the P'rushim rabbin came flying after me, his *tzitzith* shaking in his rage.

"Wait!" he cried. "I'll sacrifice your Passover for you, young man! Here and now! Oh, the idiots! The fools! The—"

Whereupon, he did.[8] Now we were not at the altar of the sacrifices, and he was too angry to get the ritual right; but he was, after all, a priest. With that, I was well content, though I had no intention of telling Yeshu'a more about the matter than he needed to know. Of that, you can be sure!

It wasn't long after I'd accomplished the major feat of getting a Jewish priest to kill the Passover lamb on the wrong day that I ran into my Brother in Sorrow, Yehudah ish Kriyoth.

He was weaving and bobbing along with a dazed expression on his face so that, at first, I thought he was drunk. But he wasn't. Coming closer I saw the bloody furrows somebody had clawed into his forehead, cheeks, throat, upper chest. Somebody? Ha! His *tzitzith*, his fringed robe, was ripped almost to his navel.

I looked at him, said: "You swine. You filthy, lecherous swine."

He cocked one glassy, glittering, bright blue eye at me and said: "I didn't. I couldn't. She is a lioness. You know that."

And I: "Good!"

And he: "There's a devil in me. Or a host of them. But it's not lust. Not really. No other woman affects me like that—"

"Then what is it?" I said.

He looked off, down the street, in the direction of the Temple. Then he said: "Despair."

"Despair?" I echoed.

"Yes. Of all the pleasures we're promised in life, what other isn't disappointing? What other is not only as good as anticipated, but—"

"Better," I supplied him, "unimaginably better. None. Except, maybe, sitting on *his* right hand amid the clouds when he ushers in his kingdom—"

Yehudah said "Ha!" at that, and spat into the street.

"Don't you believe him?" I said.

He looked at me, and his face was terrible, suddenly.

"No," he said.

"Why not?" I said.

Then he said it, his voice very, very quiet. As death is quiet. And as final. It made my torn gut ache. If I had had one ounce of intuition in me, I should have drawn my dagger and killed him then.

"I'd hoped for so much," he almost whispered. "At first—no, not at first. In those days, he seemed to me but another rab. Then he grew in my sight. This man, I said to myself, is a Prophet—"

"So?" I said.

"So, all right. A Prophet. But at Cæsarea-Philippi, he—almost convinced me. That he was the—Mashiah, I mean."

"That wasn't the impression you gave me," I said.

"I know. When I talked to you, I was fighting against that feeling. But it had hope in it, Nathan! The one thing no man can live without. I've clung to that hope until now. Because he *could* be of David's line. All you've got to do is to look at him to see that Miriam—"

"No!" I said. "I won't permit you that, Yehudah!"

"Permit it or not, it's true. And if not of Davidian descent, at least of the banim Matthya, and your half brother. Good stock, Nathan!"

"Nor that," I said. I thought then, suddenly, how glad I was that I *knew* when my father left Galilee, so that now I didn't have to worry that the marriage between Yohannah and me could be an abomination, capable of producing monsters, and incest before the Law.

"Sheol!" Yehudah howled. "How do *you* explain him, then?"

"I don't," I said. "To me he's unique, and beyond explanation."

"Beyond comprehension, you mean," Yehudah said. "So—despair. Look at my life, Nathan! A failure. A total failure. I didn't marry Martha bath Bœzer. I didn't become rich. I became a thief. A drunkard—whining after the—the skirts of a whore. Tell me something: you still say you've *never* lain with Shelom?"

"I never have," I said.

"Do you swear it?" he said.

"By the Name," I said.

He looked at me.

"You were—fortunate," he said.

"Fortunate?"

"Yes! Yes! So now you're not dying by inches the way I am! And don't tell me you can imagine what it's like. You can't. I've had other women, too. Comparison isn't even possible. I'll go on wanting her until I die. I'll scream her name throughout all eternity in Sheol. And Yeshu'a—"

"Yeshu'a?" I said.

"Would deny me that. He demands impossibilities of men, not being one himself, being less—"

"Or more," I said.

"Or more. That's one of the reasons I hate his unnatural guts—"

"Yehudah—" I said.

He went on as though he hadn't heard me.

"I'd thought I could exorcise—Antonius, through him. Not revenge myself upon the Roman swine who took the gold I'd stolen, took her, used her narrow little—"

"Yehudah!" I said again, outraged now, truly outraged.

He grinned at me like a red-bearded wolf.

"Passage into Gan Eden, into Paradise," he said. "Better, Nathan? You want euphemisms? All right. I—and Shimeon Zealotes, and the Boane Ragsha at least, had dreamed of that. Of his leading us on that glorious day when we'd gut the Legions like so many fish, throw their stinking tripes to the kites, the vultures. They—gave up that dream. He talked his soft, womanish dung of asses—no, not of asses, for asses have balls!—mule dung, excreta of born castrates, to them, and grudgingly they accepted that idea of the scapegoat Mashiah—"

"The scapegoat isn't killed," I pointed out.[9]

"I know it isn't," he said; "I've witnessed the Day of Atonement, Nathan!"

Then suddenly hope leaped in me, flamed, stood tall. For on our Day of Atonement, the goat marked for Azazel, the ancient desert demon, has all our sins placed on his head, and then is led forth into the wilderness and set free, bearing our lust, greed, blood guilt, iniquity away with him.[10] If Yeshu'a were God's scapegoat, might he not be merely exiled instead of—

But Yehudah read my thought and grinned at me mockingly.

"No," he said; "the other one. The one without sin who's sacrificed to YHWH. For what sin can be laid on *his* head?"

I'd forgot that. There are *two* goats employed in the rites of our Day of Atonement. And the first one, the white, spotless innocent one, is killed before the altar of the Most High God, while the other one, the mottled, ugly one, goes free. . . .

"Yet," I said, "you hate him."

"Yes," he whispered; "for lifting my hopes so high, then hurling them down. I couldn't accept that castrate's philosophy, Nathan! I still had —Antonius before my eyes. The violater of my—love. The ravisher of —Israel. I had to be free of him. Of all the Kittim, the Romans! I thought that here in the Holy City, this center of our faith, our race, Yeshu'a would do mighty works, confound the Zadokim and the P'rushim both, crush the Romans like cockroaches beneath his feet, make even doubters, skeptics like you, bow before his majesty. I wanted a king, Nathan! Not a bleating, sacrificial goat! Instead—"

"Instead?" I whispered.

"What do I see?" Yehudah said, his voice a groin-deep groan of naked sorrow.

"What?" I got out. There were fishhooks in my gut now, brambles, thorns, broken crockery, knives.

"No signs. No wonders. No mighty deeds. An obscene, sacrilegious farce in the outer courts, that's all. No one conquered. No enemy subdued. He tells us to bow our necks. To—Antonius! To the violater! To the ravisher of—of Shelom! Of all our women . . . To pay them Cæsar's coin, turn our cheeks to their blows, bear their stinking packs another *mille!* He curses the P'rushim, the best and noblest of our people, swears the Temple will be torn down, rants and raves about Israel's sins. Dung, Nathan! Mule dung! What plan has he for Israel's redemption? How will we be freed of the violator, the ravisher? By paying taxes? By turning our slavish eunuchs' cheeks? By bending beneath the yoke? And this man, who I thought—"

I could taste the blood in my throat now, the green vileness.

"—was the mashiah, this beguiler, this deceiver—"

"—who leads astray," I finished for him, "the Law commands to be killed without pity or compassion or forgiveness. Do you plan to lead another stoning party, Yehudah?"

He looked at me, his rage-filled, more-than-half-mad eyes unblinking.

"I?" he said. "No—that is, I hadn't thought it through so far. Only —the sin. Not its consequences . . ."

"Think about your own, Yehudah!" I told him.

"Mine—are normal. Loving, lusting after a woman who despises me. Desiring a used, filthy—"

I hit him then, hard across the mouth.

He bowed his head. Slowly he turned the other side of his face toward me.

"The other cheek, Nathan," he said with icy mockery. "Go on! What

are you waiting for? See what a good disciple of his I am? Strike me.
Slap—"

I turned away from him. One second more, and I should have
killed him.

Oh, God, how I wish I had!

That night, they came filing into my lust-profaned love nest which
was to serve them as a Holy Site. Yeshu'a and his Twelve. Shimeon
bar Yonah, called Kepha, the Rock. Netzer, his brother, whom you
called Andrai. Matthya, the tax collector, who set down the words of
his Lord. Yohannan and Yaakob, the banim Zebediah, called the Boane
Ragsha. Nathanael bar Talmay, from whose elder brother I won a
footrace, and thereby my Helvetia. Philip, half Greek, half Jew. Toma,
called Didymus, the Twin, wearing as always, his skeptic's wry, mocking smile. Shimeon Zealotes, my ancient enemy who'd carved his me-
morial into my hide. Yehudah ben Yaakob, called ben Taddai, Son
of the Beast, for his shaggy roughness, or sometimes ben Lebbai,
Son of the Heart, for his impulsive good nature. Yaakob ben Halphai,
from another family of tax collectors, his brother Levi having been for
a time a disciple. And—my Brother in Sorrow, Yehudah bar Shimeon,[11]
called ish Kriyoth, after the little town in Judea he came from. There
were, of course, two other persons present: Shimeon the Essene,
and myself.

I sat there, looking at Yeshu'a and wondering if he would perform
the rites, or ignore them, as he often had, to the fury and the despair
of the P'rushim. But, on that final night of fellowship, there were no
P'rushim present, and he could afford to follow the dictates of his
conscience and his heart.

So, he performed them all. He had water brought, and pronounced
the benediction prescribed for the washing of the hands. After we had
washed, he said the first *Kiddush*, the Inauguration of the Festival,
then, taking up the bread, he said, his voice warm, vibrant, filled
with his own peculiar magic: "Praised be You, O Lord, our God, King
of the Universe, who brings forth bread from the earth! Blessed are
You, O Lord our God, King of the Universe, who has sanctified us
with your commandments and ordered us to eat unleavened bread . . ."

Then he broke the bread and gave it to us; poured out for us the
cups of wine.

We, each of us, drank the four cups that every adult male Jew
must drink on the Eve of Passover, and pronounced the appropriate
benediction over each. Then we ate the paschal lamb, the bitter herbs,

the unleavened bread in memory of our people's sorrows. And, as always, we said the Grace after Meals, and sang the Hallel.

I found the whole thing intensely moving. Such rituals are—beautiful. They lend dignity to life. They distinguish us from beasts. What further meaning do they need?

I still remember the sadness in Yeshu'a's voice when, after drinking his fourth cup, he said: "From now on, I tell you, I shall not drink wine until the day I drink the new wine with you in the Kingdom of my Father—"

But that was all he said about the wine; and about the bread, beyond the two benedictions always said over it, he said nothing at all. He didn't say of the bread, "this is my body." Nor of the wine, "This is my blood, the blood of the New Covenant, shed for many for the forgiveness of sins."[12] He didn't command us to eat his flesh, drink his blood. He was a Jew, not a cannibal. He had no wish to disgust us, leave us all outraged.[13]

No. That Pesach was like all others I have eaten except that it was more impressive, more solemn. I found that I had tears in my eyes. So did all the others—except ish Kriyoth. His glittered—it seems to me now in retrospect, though almost surely I didn't notice it then— with madness and with hate. Before the end of the Seder, he whispered something to Yeshu'a, got up and left the room. I thought at the time it was strange that he didn't come back again.

But Yeshu'a did *not* predict his betrayal, or point the traitor out by a sop of bread, or any other means. He didn't know Yehudah was going to betray him. Nor did any of us, not even I—at least not that night. Good God! What kind of eunuchoid, effeminate gutless wonders do you think we were? You mean you actually believed that the Sons of Fury, or Zealotes, or Yehudah ben Yaakob, the Shaggy Beast, or *I* would have let ish Kriyoth get out of that house alive if we had?[14]

After Passover—at least that Essenic anticipation of it—was over and done with, I went home and tried to sleep. But I couldn't. Not even the fact that Yeshu'a and his disciples, through ignorance or out of fear, had violated one of the sternest commandments, that no man should leave the City during the night on which the paschal lamb was eaten—for in the Book of Deuteronomy it is written, "You must cook it and eat it in the place that YHWH your God chooses, and in the morning you are to return and go to your tents . . ."[15]—and had gone back across the Kedron ravine and up into the Mount of Olives, was sufficient to still my unrest. I lay there with the sickness mounting in me, with iron claws ripping at my gut.

"Why?" I asked myself. "He's safe for now. The Zadokim won't make a move until Pesach, the real Pesach, not this Essenic anticipation of it, is over. They fear the people too much. They think there'll be riots. Only there won't be. The P'rushim have seen to that with that business of the taxes. There's not an *am ha aretz* born who'll lift a finger in defense of a man who advises him to pay his hard-earned coin to Cæsar. And, as for the Zealots—"

I sat up in bed, the pain in me so deep I almost cried aloud. Would the Zealots wait? Had they ever waited? Hadn't they repeatedly violated even the Shabbat to strike a hated traitor down? And that was what Yeshu'a was to them, surely, now. He, who had had the crowds at his beck and call, had preached submission to the Romans. Yeshu'a bar Abbas would cut his throat like a goat's for far less than that!

But then I remembered that bar Abbas was in jail, doomed, Shelom had told me, to be crucified. Only Pilatus' clemency could save him; Pilatus who had never given evidence that he even knew the word. Fat chance my onetime abductor had!

Still there were other Zealots. Thousands of them—"Adonai," I prayed; "Elohim. Save him. He is a little mad, but he is innocent. His teachings are beautiful. Impractical, but beautiful. And he loves you, God, with all his oversimple heart—"

It was then that I heard—or thought I did—the noise of shouting, and the sound of marching feet. Those sounds stabbed into my bleeding gut. I leaped from my bed, wound a simple linen wrapper around my naked body, and ran from the house.

The street was silent. Too silent. I wondered if I'd dreamed those sounds I'd heard. But I couldn't afford to chance it. I started off, at a hard run, straight toward the city gates.

I crossed the ravine, climbed up the Hill of Olives. I searched for them there. Your Gospels say they were in a garden called Gethsemane.[16] Sorry. I've never heard of it. I don't believe there ever was any such place. The word is wrong, written by a foreigner, surely, for he has combined *gath*, a wine press, with *shemen*, olives. That isn't Hebrew. Nor is it Aramaic. In fact, it isn't any language I ever heard of. If he meant to write the Garden of the Olive Press, why didn't he say so? We have a perfectly good word for olive press; it is *beth habad*. But Gath-Shemene! Good Lord! Besides there were many olive presses on the hill, so even so, his designation is meaningless. Did he mean to write *Beth-Shemanaya*, the House of Wine and Oil? But *that* was a hall in the Temple itself where the offerings in kind were stored. Forget it. It's not important, now. What matters one more error in Sacred Books whose every other word is wrong?

In any event, I found the disciples on the crest of the hill itself, among the olive trees.

They were all fast asleep. Shimeon the Rock and his brother Netzer had swords in their hands. None of the rest of them were armed.[17] Not even the Boane Ragsha. I suppose Yeshu'a didn't trust their fiery natures. He was right, though, as a matter of fact, he was in far greater danger from all his disciples' full bellies and sleepy heads.

Yeshu'a wasn't with them. He was a little higher up, alone. He knelt on the rocky ground, beneath an olive tree, and prayed. I stood in a wash of moonlight, but under the tree, where he knelt, it was very dark. It was—a peculiar kind of darkness. There was no light at all, but I could see into it. I could see him very clearly. The reason I could was because that darkness wasn't just tree shadow on a moon-lit night. It was a quality. It was nadir. Death's epicenter. It emanated from the horror in him, from his utter, final loss of hope.

I stood there looking at him, and what I felt has no name. There are no words small, short, simple, chaste, pure enough to tell you what it was like. Put it this way: No shriek defines horror the way a whisper does. A whimper is more expressive of hope gone than a cry. And what I had come to now, looking upon him I love more than life, was— silence. The silence beneath sound. The mirror image, the reverse of all the screams that ever tore a human throat; the vibrations, echoes —above, below the range our ears can catch—of every bloody, gut-ripping sob that every poor bastard come to his personal limits, gone beyond them all for nothing, ever uttered in this bleak, miserable, stinking world.

I could see him. He was trembling all over. He sweated like an overdriven horse. The drops on his forehead, his throat, his arms were huge. In the shadow where he knelt, they looked like clots of blood.[18]

His voice was—anguish. No—agony. The thing itself. It clawed my gut. It pierced me like a host of swords. I wanted to go away, but my feet wouldn't move. I didn't want to listen to him, but his voice was in my ears like the ugly scrape of glass on stone. I didn't want him to demean himself like that. I wanted him to preserve my illusion— the only one I had left to my name—that *he* was somehow not of common clay; that he was braver, finer, nobler—that, in some inde-finable way, he *was* the only begotten son of the god I'd long since banished from my personal cosmos anyhow; that I, who believed in nothing, not even the simpler *lares* and *penates* men live by—my father's honor, my mother's virtue, the fidelity of my pregnant bride— could somehow believe in him.

And now he was robbing me of even that. He was crying, begging his Father, God, to take away the bitter cup. He sounded the way a child does when he's about to be whipped for some prank or fault. He said it over and over again:

"Father, take away this cup, this cup—"

The sickness rose in me, made a knot of vileness at the root of my tongue. I thrust two fingers down my throat, and brought it up. It was pure, unmixed blood this time. It wasn't even streaked with bile. So, instead of the relief I sought, weakness invaded me. I reeled away from there, caught a gnarled olive branch, clung to it. If I hadn't, I should have fallen to the ground.

And it was then that Yehudah ish Kriyoth and the *segens* of the priest, leading the Levite porters, the temple police, came.

The rage that tore me left me all but blind.

I knew him! I howled inside my heart; I knew this cowardly Judean dog! He who brought a mob to stone Shelom, not having testicles enough to do his own killing! Who now—

Had given the High Priest the one thing that he needed: time. Time to arrest Yesu, try him, condemn him, before the Laws with which Pesach and the Feast of Unleavened Bread were hedged about, made trial, arrest, condemnation, execution impossible, since no such ugly, mundane things are permitted on our high and holy days. For Yehudah's betrayal consisted in this only: that he'd warned the priests that Yeshu'a had already eaten the Passover, according to the ancient Jubilees calendar, and would surely depart from Jerusalem on the morrow, before they could lay hands on him.

I could see Yeshu'a standing there looking at the *segens* and the Temple police—for, of course, your Gospels' contention that the high priests and the dignitaries of the Great Sanhedrin accompanied them to make the arrest is utter nonsense; Jewish high priests don't engage in manhunts any more than your Christianoi bishops do—and though his face was white, he had somehow—clawing loin-deep, groin-deep, or maybe below even that, inside himself to the roots of his own manhood, the seats of atavistic male valor—recovered his control, his self-mastery. His voice rang out then, slow, deep, majestic.

"I was with you in the Temple day after day, and you didn't lay hands on me. But now you come with clubs and swords to take me like a thief in the night. Now—in the dark, in this hour of cowards."[19]

I looked around for Yehudah. I had no weapon, but I meant to strangle him with my bare hands. But he was already gone, slipping away into the night that was his mother and his father both.

He'd done all he had to do. For your Gospel writers were lunatics, surely, men who couldn't even manage to tell convincing lies, because their addled pates held no seat of memory. Answer me this, Devout God Lover: Why should ish Kriyoth have kissed Yeshu'a ha Notzri to identify him to the same Temple police who had seen and heard him preach in the outer courts every single day for more than a week? Do you believe that they—the same Levite porters who stood helplessly by, clubs in hand, chewing upon their rage while Yeshu'a upset the money changers' tables, smashed the cages of the dove sellers—had *forgot* how he looked? Don't you realize that when everyone down to the serving wenches at the High Priest's house could identify not only Yeshu'a, himself, but your Kepha/Petros as a follower of his, all Jerusalem could have drawn his face from memory by then?

I didn't hear any more, because the Temple police laid hands on him, then fanned out to arrest us all. Somebody—I think it was Shimeon Kepha—lashed out with his sword, and cut off a dark-skinned porter's ear. Then all was confusion. The disciples broke loose and went galloping off in every direction like a herd of stampeding goats. The *segens* let them go. I don't think they were seriously interested in arresting anyone else but Yeshu'a. I felt someone grab at my linen wrapper. I tore free of him, and ran off, as naked as the day my mother bore me.[20]

I managed to get into my father's house without waking anyone. I dressed quickly, took a dagger, and hid it in my robes. A sword wouldn't do. The *segens* wouldn't let a man bearing a sword get anywhere near the *lishkat ha gazit*, the Chamber of Hewn Stone, in which all trials were held. But if I went there apparently unarmed, they might let me approach it. That depended upon whether they'd forgot my horrendous reputation in Jerusalem, or whether they'd think of me as the son of the man who had recently been appointed the *ab beth din*, the vice president of the Lesser Sanhedrin (the Greater Sanhedrin *never* tried capital cases) and who might have got to be *Nasi*, president of it, if my behavior hadn't made them look upon him with doubt, as being, perhaps—since he hailed originally from Galilee —the source of my wild and rebellious blood.

But they didn't have Yeshu'a imprisoned in the dungeon beneath the Chamber of Hewn Stone. The Sanhedrins no longer met there, as I should have known if I hadn't been out of Jerusalem so much in those last few years.[21]

Where they had taken him, I finally found out, was to the Booths of the House of Annas, a temporary prison near the great house in the upper city where the Doyen of the high priests, Annas ben Seth, and his son-in-law, Yosef ben Kaiapha, the actual High Priest, lived.

So I went there. The *segen* on the door—a surly, suspicious brute if there were ever one!—wasn't inclined to let me into the courtyard; but the serving wench he was talking to[22] recognized me at once.

"Let him in, Yonas," she said. "He's the son of the *ab beth din*, the Rab ben Mattathiah. . . ."

At that, the holy brigand stood aside. I entered that courtyard where they had Yeshu'a bound, awaiting the rising of the sun, when his trial could begin. I know that two of your *Besorahim*, your Gospels, say that he was tried that same night, but that only proves your scribes' total ignorance of Jewish Law. Neither the Lesser Sanhedrin of twenty-three members, nor the Greater Sanhedrin of seventy-one, *ever* met at night. The Lesser Sanhedrin met from the close of the morning prayers until noon;[23] and the Greater Sanhedrin met from the hour of the morning sacrifice when the whole east was alight with dawn, until the hour of the evening sacrifice at half past the third hour of the afternoon.[24] Only your third Gospel has it right: They tried him at the break of day.[25]

I waited there in the courtyard. After a while, I saw Shimeon bar Yonah, called Kepha, the Rock, come stealing up to the gate. He stood a little way off from it, and the shame and grief in his face, blazed white against the darkness by the guard's flaring torch, were a kind of nakedness. I went out to him, took him by the arm, and led him through the gate. The surly guard made no objections. By then, two or three others had confirmed my identity, my high lineage, my august connections.[26] As we passed his booth, the bastard even bowed to me.

Poor Kepha, or, as you call him, Petros, which means the same thing, was trembling all over. He was afraid, but he had come back. He was the best and noblest of them all. They'd all played the coward, but only he had found the valor and the love to risk his life to return to his Master and his Lord.

During the remainder of that long night, we sat huddled around the fire, and watched the Temple police as they mocked and abused poor Yeshu'a. They didn't really torture him; but they were rough enough, God knows. They blindfolded him, spat on him, knocked him about, saying: "Now, Prophet, who hit you? Tell us that! Prophesy who's going to hit you next!"[27]

But there was nothing we could do to help him. My head ached with contradictory plans. If they condemned him to be stoned, I meant to rescue him from the stoning party by force. But if they turned him over to the Romans, as I was almost sure they would, on a trumped-up charge of treason, I'd have to try to carry out that plan that Yosef ha Arimathæa and I had conceived—that wild scheme of drugging him into the appearance of death, and getting him down from the cross alive.

And there was one more immediate problem: nobody in Jerusalem could positively identify me as one of Yeshu'a's followers, though now and again I'd been seen with them, because, just as often I'd been seen with Pilatus, or with my father, the vice president of the Sanhedrin. But Shimeon Kepha risked his life by coming there, as was immediately proved. For a pert and perky serving wench came up to us and stared at him. It was a measure of my misery that I scarcely even noticed what a splendid little mare she was for nightlong riding, nor did I speculate upon her walk, trot, canter, gallop, or any other change of gait.

She opened her eyes very wide and said to bar Yonah:

"You're one of them! You were there too with Yeshu'a of Galilee! I saw you!"

Shimeon's face went gray. He shook his head.

"No," he muttered; "no. I don't even know the man."

But the saucy little minx turned to the others, and shrilled: "This fellow was with Yeshu'a ha Notzri!"

Shimeon's face went grayer still.

"I swear by the *Shaddai*, the Almighty, that I don't know him!" he said.

But one of the men looked at him, hard.

"You're one of them," he growled. "That thick Galilean accent gives you away!"

"I'm a Galilean all right," Kepha almost wept; "but I swear that I know nothing of—"

Then he stopped, looked at me. His face was pitiful.

"Nathan," he whispered, "what hour is it?"

"Hard upon cockcrow," I said.

For even in this, your scribes reveal their appalling ignorance. All of them say that poor Petros *heard* a cock crow. If so, his ears were capable of greater wonders than any Yeshu'a ever performed. There weren't any fowls in the Holy City. There haven't been for centuries. The Talmud puts it clearly, "They may not rear fowls in Jerusalem because of the hallowed things."[28] Fowls dig in the earth, track dead things into the house. The Sages held that they'd have kept our homes in a perpetual state of ritual uncleanliness. Hence, no cocks. Not ever. We use the ancient expression "cockcrow" to denote the hour before the dawn.[29]

But, hearing my words, poor Shimeon Kepha bent his head and

wept. Afterward, he told me how Yeshu'a had predicted he'd deny him thrice before the rising of the sun. And it was his tears that saved him, for they moved the wench to pity. Besides, Shimeon bar Yonah was a big, strikingly handsome man.

"Oh, leave him be," that toothsome bundle of high-spiced and savory she-meat said. And, probably because they all entertained hope, or cherished memories of the sweet nightlong use of that talisman she wore between her thighs, they let poor Kepha/Petros be.

And now, seeing that he was for the moment safe, he began to question me.

"Why now, Nathan?" he groaned. "Why didn't they wait? I was so sure—"

"That he'd be safely on his way to Nazareth before they made their move?" I said. "So was I, Shimeon. Only Yehudah—"

"That filthy swine!" Shimeon Kepha said.

"Amen. That poor sick wounded filthy swine. Like you. Like me. Our brother, Shimeon. Sharer of our cowardice, weakness, envy, pain—"

"All right!" he said angrily. "That's how they knew he'd already eaten Passover. Because of ish Kriyoth. But why'd they have to arrest him that same night? It seems to me they had time—"

"No," I said. "They didn't. Day after tomorrow's Pesach, Shimeon. Theirs, anyhow. The Passover of all Jewry, not merely the one you half-Essenes celebrated ahead of time. . . ."

"So?" Shimeon bar Yonah said.

"So, they have only today to try him. Today, Shimeon! The thirteenth of Nisan. To try him, and find him guilty, as they will. Even so, they can't pass sentence on him until tomorrow—"

I stopped then. My breath stopped. My heart. Because it had hit me, then. They had to hand Yeshu'a over to the Romans. They had to!

"I don't understand—" Shimeon Kepha began.

"I know you don't!" I said. "Look, Shimeon. Forget this Essene nonsense! *Tomorrow* is the Eve of Passover. The Sanhedrin is forbidden to meet on a Shabbat, or even on the eve of a Shabbat, lest the case have to be postponed until the following week, if they don't come to an agreement. Because if they don't hand down on Shabbat Eve, they *can't* on Shabbat, because even condemning a man to death constitutes work. Since writing is explicitly forbidden on the Holy Days, even the court clerks could keep no records, which in itself would invalidate a trial. The same principles apply to Festivals,[30] according to my father. And he's the vice president of the Court. So they've got to try him today. But that's not the worst of it . . ."

"What is the worst of it?" Shimeon said.

"They can acquit him today; but if they condemn him, they can't pass sentence until tomorrow. The fourteenth of Nisan, the Eve of Passover. For it is written: 'If they find him innocent, they acquit him at once; otherwise his sentence is left over until the morrow. In the meantime they should go together in pairs, eat little, drink no wine, discuss the matter carefully all night, and come to court early on the morrow with their final decision.' "[31]

"And?" Shimeon bar Yonah, called Kepha, said.

"That means they have to turn him over to the Romans. Have you ever heard of anybody's being stoned on Preparation Day, Kepha? It's impossible. The streets are empty. Everybody's at home preparing the matzot, the herbs, the wine. Where'd they get a stoning party from? How would they, the priests, even find time to gather enough people together to kill a man by throwing rocks at him? Remember what they have to do on Pesach Eve, Shimeon! They have to kill hundreds, even thousands of paschal lambs for the Passovers of not only the citizens of Jerusalem, but all the pilgrims, too. So they couldn't execute sentence on that day. And if they don't—"

"If they don't?" Shimeon said.

"They'd have to bind him over until the Festival is finished. Until twenty-second Nisan. Eight days, Shimeon. Time and enough for his Galileans to raise a riot, to attack the prison, free him. Over two hundred people came with him here, you know. You think that ben Kaiapha and the Zadokim would take that risk?"

Shimeon Kepha looked at me. Slowly he shook his massive head.

"Small risk, Nathan, if the rest of the Galileans are as arrant a pack of cowards as we were," he said. "But you're right. The High Priest and his Council won't. So—"

"The Romans. Who are pagans. To whom our Feasts mean nothing, or less. Who'll gladly oblige by crucifying—"

"The *bar enosh*. The Son of Man. God's Anointed—the Mashiah," Shimeon said.

And it was then that I heard their footsteps coming on. I looked up, and saw them: The Nasi, Yosef ben Kaiapha, High Priest and president of the Lesser Sanhedrin of Twenty-Three, which always tried cases involving the death sentence. The *ab beth din*, my father, Yehudah ben Mattathiah, Father of the House of Judgment, or vice president if you will, of the Court. The twenty-three judges, including one called Yosef ha Arimathæa. The one man I could count on. Because my father and the Nasi would only be called on to vote if there wasn't a clear majority for one verdict or the other. Then came the two clerks, one of whom stood on the right, and the other on the left of the semicircular seats, in order to record the votes for acquittal and condemnation respectively. The two messengers who would bear the message of the verdict to those in charge of executions. They all came on slowly, impressively.

And the dawn broke above the roofs of the Holy City, hard and bright and sudden like a shofar blast.

Or a cry.

Book VI

In which I witness two trials, a crucifixion, and a resurrection.

Chapter XXVII

FROM WHERE I sat, high in the little balcony that was reserved for the very few spectators that the Lesser Sanhedrin occasionally admitted to capital trials, I could see them all. I swept my gaze around the semi-circular arc of daises upon which the judges sat, moving my eyes from face to face of the Zadokim majority, since the few P'rushim didn't count, searching, not for a vestige of mercy—I knew better than to expect that from a Sadducean court—but for a flicker of indecision, a hint of honest doubt. Being, as they indisputably were, men of the highest probity and honor, that little would have been enough to save him. But, except upon the deeply troubled countenance of Yosef ha Arimathæa, I didn't find it. I didn't find it at all.

Not even upon the face of my father.

The *ab beth din*, I thought. The vice president of the Court, by virtue of your marriage to a daughter of the House of Bœthus. A member of this time-serving, slavish Sanhedrin that's but an instrument of Roman power, because ambition in you outweighed principle, so that you left the Pharisees, who, for all their faults, are still men of mercy—as they've proved by hedging the Law about with so many precautions against the too hasty shedding of possibly innocent blood, that were this a P'rushim court, condemning this poor, mad dreamer of dreams would be practically impossible—to join the Zadokim, to whom mercy is but a word. Was it worth it, Father? Do the privileges you enjoy, wealth, honors, position, compensate for the shame that must come in the night to claw your gut?

He felt my eyes become augers, boring holes in his skull just above his forehead. He looked up at me, and frowned.

If it does . . . if it does . . . I thought. How much shame have I ever felt, who am your son, and far worse than you ever had the imagination to be? You went from P'rushite to Zadokite, Father; but I, from Jew to Pagan, and from pagan to—nothing. Which is a longer, darker road. All downhill, with a grade too steep for climbing back.

Destination—Sheol. So forgive me, Yehudah ben Mattathiah, my father! For, as he you're going to help murder put it, these hands have forfeited the elementary right of throwing stones. . . .

Beside me, I could feel Shimeon Kepha bar Yonah tremble. And turning, I could see his eyes aflame with hope.

Poor devil! I thought. Poor *am ha aretz* fisherman devil. Who left your simple catch for far more dangerous prey: men. Unfinned, lacking scales, but filled with a black, sick evil that forever stifles the hypothetical souls he taught you that they have. Who're capable of swallowing you whole and never vomiting you up, poor fisherman! Don't hope, Kepha, Petros, trembling rock of uncertain faith, who ran away, who denied your Lord. Hope's a bauble for fools and children. The outcome's not even in doubt. Don't quiver in suspense. Sit still, as a rock ought to. Freeze your heart, let it go to powder under the weight of this crushing, ice-cold inevitability. You don't know the Law—blessed be your ignorance!—but I do. I have lived, breathed, had my being, forever surrounded by its thorny technicalities. Petros, Kepha, Rock of Faith, I tell you this: They could stone him twenty times over in strict conformity with the Torah for the things I, myself, have heard him say, seen him do. I beg you, Shimeon bar Yonah, noblest, best of men, for all the base, crumbling shale rock of which you're made, don't hope, don't hope!

The Nasi, the president of the Court, Yosef ben Kaiapha, High Priest and—damn him!—my cousin by virtue of the fact that his mother and mine are half sisters, my maternal grandfather having married twice and had nothing but daughters by both his wives—stood up.

"Let the witnesses be brought," he said.

The messengers opened the doors, and herded in at least twenty men.[1] Recognizing several of the Galilean P'rushim, who, as usual, had come up to Jerusalem for Passover, among them, I bowed my head. Because what little hope I'd struggled to maintain was gone now. You see, in Jerusalem, Yeshu'a had neither done nor said anything for which he could be put to death; even his childish and stupid action of driving the dove sellers and the money changers from the outer courts was only a misdemeanor, punishable by—at worst—a whipping, at best, by a few days' imprisonment and a fine. But in Galilee, he'd done and said things for which they could have hung his broken, stone-battered carcass up as a deterrent to sinners two dozen times. So once they'd produced witnesses to his outrages against Torah in Antipas' Tetrarchy, he was, to put it simply, doomed.

Ceremoniously, my father got to his feet. As *ab beth din*—literally "Father of the Court," which, with a view to making it comprehensible to Greek-speaking people like you, dear Theophilos, I translate "vice president," interpreting it according to what the man holding the office does, rather than according to what the words themselves mean, just as I've called Nasi—actually "The Prince"—"president of the Court," because that's what the Nasi now is, no matter what our quaint and archaic expressions say—it was his solemn duty to instruct the witnesses. And I must say he did it well.

"Perhaps," my father began quietly—he had a beautiful speaking voice; and how he loved the sound of it!—"your testimony will be based upon mere supposition, by which I mean circumstantial evidence, or on hearsay, or on the statement made by another witness, or you may say to yourselves, 'We heard it from a man who is trustworthy.' I tell you that none of these is acceptable, but only that which you saw or heard yourselves. . . ."

"Perhaps, too, you are not aware that before this trial is over, we will investigate your testimony, by examination and cross-examination. I tell you, therefore, to be very careful of what you say. And be advised, finally, that there is no similarity between civil and capital cases: in civil cases, one may pay money and so make atonement; but in capital cases, the witness is answerable for the blood of the person he caused to be wrongfully executed, and for the blood of the children who would have been born to him, had he been allowed to live, down to the end of time."[2]

My father then straightened himself up to his full and impresive height—my short stature is a testimony to my Bœthus blood—and glared at them.

"Have you well and fully understood what I said to you?" he thundered.

The prospective witnesses nodded dumbly. I could see that he had frightened most of them out of their wits, which was precisely what he intended to do. Now he turned to the two messengers.

"Take them out again," he said.

After the witnesses had been herded from the court, once again Yosef ben Kaiapha, the Nasi, stood up.

"Bring the first pair of witnesses before me," he said.

I have wondered about those first two witnesses ever since. Did my august cousin, the High Priest, allow them to remain among the others to demonstrate the fairness of his justice? Or did he feel that the solemnity of the occasion needed a little comic relief? Or did he depend upon their testimony—totally unactionable though it was—to prejudice the P'rushim members of the Court against Yeshu'a, and thus achieve his goal of an unanimous verdict?

I don't know. I shall never know. What is certain is that the writers of your Gospels have used the testimony of those two clowns, and ignored, suppressed, that of the eighteen other witnesses who followed them.

They were street beggars of the lowest sort. One day they might be cripples, the next, blind men. Their art extended even to the imitation of raw running sores. But today, before the Sanhedrin, they were their natural selves—ugly enough, God knows—and, even, surely for the first time in all their filthy lives, reasonably clean.

The Nasi addressed them.

"With what do you charge the prisoner?" he said.

They looked toward where Yeshu'a stood between the two *segens* charged with guarding him. Not even his hands were bound. Their eyes went red.

"With blasphemy!" they said.

At once my father left his dais and bowed to the president.

"My lord Nasi," he said gravely, "before these witnesses proceed with their testimony, it seems to me, considering the social stratum from which they come, that they should be warned, and instructed in the proper manner of testifying to this particular offense, lest they, themselves, fall accidentally into the very crime of which they accuse the prisoner. Do you agree, my lord?"

"Agreed," ben Kaiapha said. "Please do so instruct and warn them, honorable Father of the Court."

My father turned to those two new-washed but still grimy swine.

"When charging a man with blasphemy," he began, "you may not repeat his exact words, for if he *has* blasphemed, you would repeat the offense, and become guilty of it yourselves, by saying what he said. Therefore, in every instance where he pronounced the Divine Name, you must substitute for it the common name Yose, which has the same number of letters, but which is totally inoffensive. Is this clear?"[3]

The two beggars looked at each other.

"But he didn't say the Divine Name," one of them muttered; "he said—"

Yosef ben Kaiapha got up again, waving my father to his seat.

"What, precisely, is the nature of the blasphemy that you charge the prisoner, Yeshu'a ben Yosef, called ha Notzri, with?" he demanded.

"He said," one of the beggars declared, " 'I will throw down this Temple, made with human hands, and in three days, I will build another, not made with hands.' "[4]

At that, Yosef ha Arimathæa got up, bowed to the president of the Court, and to my father.

"My lords," he said suavely; "is this a court, or a lunacy commission?"

As solemn as the occasion was, three quarters of the judges rocked with laughter at his words.

"There is much reason in the member from Arimathæa's question," the High Priest said. "My lord *Ab Beth Din,* will you instruct the witnesses as to *what* constitutes blasphemy under the Law?"

My father got to his feet.

"Know you, witnesses," he said sternly, "that *megadeph,* blasphemy, consists solely of cursing one Name of the Almighty with another, which is why we substitute the formula 'May Yose curse Yose' for it, lest we unwittingly become guilty of it in court ourselves by repeating the offender's words—"

Thereupon, he explained it fully. But to follow the circumlocutions he employed to avoid the crime of *megadeph* himself would cost me twenty pages. And, since to you the offense is all but meaningless, and I don't believe that God—if he exists—is so small of spirit as to even take notice of such petty human nonsense, allow me to indulge in a little quiet blasphemy in order to explain it to you.

If we use one divine attribute to curse another divine attribute, we blaspheme. As for instance: "May the *Shaddai* (the Almighty) smite the *Zebaot* (The Lord of Hosts)!" Or, "May the *Hannun* (the Gracious) curse the *Erech Appayim* (the Long Suffering)!" I once made the mistake of trying to demonstrate to my Uncle Hezron how ridiculous the whole idea is. He broke his staff across my back, and chased me from the house.

On a more serious level, some sages insist the blasphemer must pronounce the *Shem ha Meyuhad,* the Real Name of God, that Yod, He, Vav, He, that we don't know how to pronounce anyhow, as a part of his curse. That is, to blaspheme, Yeshu'a would have had to say: "I curse Aleph, Daleth, Nun, Yod—" employing those four letters we substitute for the Unutterable Name, and which we call *Adonai,* although we're not sure of that pronunciation either.[5]

So it was no wonder that my father concluded his long address with:

"Therefore this charge you make against him is nonsense. The Sanhedrin is not concerned with the vain boasting of a fool. The day you find him, or his like, busy at the Temple's walls with ram, pick, and iron bar, then return to us. Or is it your intent to prove him mad? If so, the Court will gladly entertain testimony to that effect. But know you, since madness negates responsibility, he must then be freed."

"No," the beggars muttered, "he's not crazy. Sounded like a blasphemer to us, talking about the Holy Temple that way, but his head's screwed down on his shoulders tight enough. . . ."

My father turned to the Nasi.

"These witnesses have proved nothing illegal against the prisoner, my lord," he said.

"Dismiss them!" the High Priest said.

Shimeon Kepha's grin had split his black-bearded face in half. He was sure that Yeshu'a would be freed now. Even I was beginning to hope.

That new-fledged hope lasted exactly three minutes. Directly below me, one of the twenty-three judges leaned forward and whispered something to his neighbor. Now they were too far away from me for what they were saying to reach my ears clearly; but one word did, because, I think, they raised their voices each time they pronounced it. And the word they were uttering with the accents of horror, shock, and rage was *mesith*.

Pain made a fist, and slammed itself into my bleeding gut. How many times had I heard Yeshu'a speak of god as *his* father, in a peculiar way? When had I ever heard him say "our Father God," which was acceptable, instead of "my Father," which wasn't, which constituted the crime of *mesith*, that of enticing people to idolatry, and was punishable by death?

For, among us, if a man sets himself up as a god, and induces, or even allows, people to worship him, he is guilty of the crime of enticing people to turn from our high, incorporeal, spiritual God to the worship of an idol; the idol being, in this case, himself. You, who've read your *Evangelionoi*, your Gospels, until you have them by rote, don't need me to point out to you the thirty-odd occasions in which Yeshu'a either permitted people to kneel to him to beg for some favor, or to otherwise worship him, or failed to rebuke him when they called him "Son of God."[6]

I looked at him where he stood between his guards. His face was serene to the point of vacancy. He had retreated beyond the reach of judges, courts, or even executioners. He—the essential he—simply wasn't there.

But one of the two whispering judges got up from his seat, and approached the dais on which my father sat. And again, instead of speaking out what he had in his head, he whispered it into my father's ear.

My father frowned, made a gesture of disdain; then turned to the High Priest, and spoke to him in a low voice. But so sure of himself was Yosef ben Kaiapha that he answered my obviously troubled sire aloud.

"Could the charge of *mesith* be proved against the prisoner?" he said.

"Yes, my lord," my father said, with an unaccustomed hint of hesitation in his voice. "Indisputably; but—"

"But what?" the Nasi snapped.

"It would take too long. Tomorrow is the Eve of Passover, my lord."

He didn't need to finish his thought. On a Shabbat, the eve of the Shabbat, on a Festival such as Pesach, and on the eve of a Festival, as I'd already pointed out to Shimeon Kepha, the court was forbidden by Law to meet.[7] So what my father—like all converts, more Sadducee than the born Sadducees—was reminding the High Priest and president of the Lesser Sanhedrin, Yosef ben Kaiapha, was that bringing up the intricate and technical charge of *mesith* against Yeshu'a at this juncture involved the risk of drawing the trial out so long that they couldn't get finished that same day, the thirteenth of Nisan, which meant, that since the fourteenth was Passover Eve, and the fifteenth not only Passover, but the beginning of the *hag ha mazot*, the Feast of Unleavened Bread, the prisoner would have to be bound over for a total of eight full days, far too long both as far as the Law was concerned, and when the notorious temper of Galileans, which all his followers were, was taken into consideration. No; to get this filthy but necessary job done before the evening sacrifice, the charge had to be simpler, more easily proven.

To find that charge cost them no difficulty at all. For the next two witnesses were both Galileans, and not only Pharisees, but Sopherim. Which means they were highly educated men, for among us, the duties of a Sopher, or scribe, range from the copying of manuscripts to the teaching of children, from the drawing up of texts, to expert analysis of the Law. In fact, a scribe was more a lawyer than anything else, as these two proved by the manner in which they responded to the question put them by the Nasi.

They said, speaking not in the more usual bad Galilean Aramaic but in courtly Hebrew: "We charge the prisoner, Yeshu'a ben Yosef, called ha Notzri, the Nazarene, with false prophecy on the score of publicly abrogating Mosaic Law!"

The trial was over then, at that moment. The rest of it was pure routine. Witness after witness got up to say:

"We saw him and his disciples gather corn on the Shabbat which is clearly work. When rebuked by our leader he said, that he, calling himself the *ben adam*, or rather, since he speaks only Aramaic, the *bar enosh*, the Son of Man, was ruler over the Shabbat."[8]

Other witnesses declared:

"He healed a man of a withered arm on the Shabbat. When rebuked, he declared in mockery or in ignorance: 'Is it permitted to do good or to do evil on the Shabbat; to save life or to kill?' "[9]

At this, once again good Yosef of Arimathæa got up and made one more attempt to save him.

"But, my lord Nasi, honorable *Ab Beth Din,* and respected fellow Judges," he began; "what is this but the *Pikuah nefesh doheh shabbat?* All the sages agree that the Shabbat not only can be but *must* be broken in order to save the life of a man who is in possible danger of losing it!"

At that the Rabbi Gamaliel, surely the most distinguished member of the Court,[10] rose very quietly and said:

"It is true, good Judge from Arimathæa, that the *Pikuah nefesh doheh shabbat* commands us to profane the Shabbat to save a man in danger of death even when that danger is somewhat remote. But in this case, the danger was nonexistent. The cripple had lived many years before that day with his withered arm. The cure—if there was such a cure, which with all due respects to the witness, I doubt profoundly —could easily have waited until the next day. It seems to me the charge stands: ben Yosef, called ha Notzri, both profaned the Shabbat and abrogated the Law. And either of those two crimes is punishable by death."

I looked at Yeshu'a then. He seemed not to have heard a word of the debate. His lips moved. I could see that he was praying.

Other witnesses easily and quickly proved that he'd advocated the abolition of our Kashruth laws, saying aloud to all the people: "Listen to me, and understand this: a man is not defiled by what goes into his mouth, but by what comes out of it!"[11] Still others, that he'd openly abrogated the Law of Divorce.[12] And finally, the last two witnesses reminded the Court that he had profaned the Shabbat not only by gathering corn on the Holy Day,[13] but also by kneading, since he'd spat on the ground, mixed earth with spittle, and anointed a blind man's eyes,[14] both of which acts being listed among the thirty-nine classes of work forbidden us on the Shabbat.

And as if that were not enough, the Galilean Pharisee scribe on the witness stand added solemnly: "It surprises me most of all, my lords, that no Judean witness had come forward to charge him with an act of openly and flagrantly defying and abrogating Mosaic Law that I, myself, saw and heard him do, *here* in the Holy City—"

I caught my breath. I'd assumed that no witness was going to mention that unsavory business of Yeshu'a's "cleansing the Temple" as he, himself called it, because there my wild-man brother-in-law had the weight of public opinion on his side. But if the witness did bring it up, it certainly wouldn't help Yeshu'a's cause with such stern advocates of law and order as the members of the lesser Sanhedrin.

But the witness was speaking again, and hearing his words, understanding them, my heart turned to stone and the last faint flutter of hope died within me.

"They had," the Sopher said suavely, "taken a *sotah,* an adulteress. This woman, my lord Nasi, honorable *Ab Beth Din,* venerable Judges, had been found naked and abed with a foreigner, a Greek. She, herself, admitted her guilt, confessed that she had left the house of her husband, a respected citizen of Beth Anya, to indulge in lewdness and the practice of harlotry. But, as they were about to stone her— and this my lords, I *saw*—the Accused intervened. How I do not precisely know, except that it seemed to me a sort of sorcery, a practicing of the black arts, Yeshu'a, son of the carpenter Yosef, and of the woman Miriam, herself of somewhat uncertain fame among us—"

My father was on his feet. His anger was both sincere and terrible.

"Clerks!" he thundered. "Strike that last remark from the record! The mother of the Accused is not on trial here, but rather Yeshu'a ben Yosef himself. Witness, I warn you, if you do not confine your remarks to the case at hand, your testimony will be disallowed, and you, yourself, fined!"

Smoothly that Galilean swine bowed his head.

"I crave the Court's pardon," he said. "I went too far. My lord *Ab Beth Din's* rebuke is just . . ."

"Proceed," my father told him.

"Yeshu'a ben Yosef intervened. By some mysterious means, which seems to me even yet to have been sorcery, the Accused forced the stoning party to release her. Then a fine young gentleman—"

He raised his eyes and let his gaze flicker with deliberate insolence over my face—

"—bore her away on his white Arabian mare . . ."

My father's eyes were coals of fire in his head. They seared my face. Of course that P'rushite bastard had recognized me; but, being as subtle as a serpent, he hadn't accused me. Instead, by that excess of detail: "white Arabian mare" when "on his horse" would have been enough and to spare!—he was revenging himself with exquisite P'rushim subtlety upon my father for his public rebuke, by letting him know that his son was both a whoremonger and an adulterer. It was beautifully done. Not three people in that court knew I owned a white Arabian mare. But my father did, and now even his possible aid was lost me.

When that last, sublimely malicious witness had done with pulverizing Yeshu'a's last hope, the High Priest and president of the Court,

Yosef ben Kaiapha, rose and asked: "Has the prisoner or his friends provided any witnesses to gainsay these charges?"

Surely it is here, or at least so it seems to me, that your writers have most deeply misunderstood Jewish jurisprudence. A prisoner is *never* called upon in our courts to either defend or condemn himself. If a witness charges him with murder in Jerusalem on a Shabbat, say, he must produce another witness who will swear he saw the alleged assassin praying in the synagogue at Kafer Nahum on that same Shabbat, whereupon one witness is considered to have cancelled the other, and the charge remains unproved.

I know how your Athenian trials work, for I have seen them. Your speechwriters provide eloquent discourses for the accused to make in his own defense. It is very exciting and moving; beside it, our Jewish method seems dull and tame. Nor will I argue which system arrives more closely at true justice; both are good and well suited to the temperaments of the people in question, for Greeks are not Jews, nor vice versa. I point this out to you only to indicate how impossibly wrong your *Besorahim/Evangelionoi*/Gospel accounts of Yeshu'a's trial are.

My father, a little sadly, it seemed to me, answered the Nasi.

"No, my lord, no witness has come forward in his defense," he said.

"Then, honorable *Ab Beth Din*," the High Priest said, "I bid you charge the judges."

My father's charge to the twenty-three judges was a little masterpiece. The fact that he gave it reluctantly, that he liked Yeshu'a, that he was troubled by the fact that the accused was "family" through my marriage to Yohannah, made it all the more moving. I heard it through the contrapuntal rasping of Shimeon Kepha's breath.

"My lords," my father began, "it is written in the Book of Deuteronomy: 'But the prophet who shall speak a word presumptuously in My name, which I have not commanded him to speak, or that shall speak in the name of other gods, that same prophet shall die. And if you say to yourselves, "How shall we know the word which the Lord has not spoken?" When a prophet speaks in the name of the Lord, and the thing which he has promised does not happen or come to pass, that is the thing which the Lord has not spoken; the prophet has spoken it presumptuously, and you shall have no fear of him.' "[15]

My father paused and raised his eyes toward my face. It seemed to me that a pleading note crept into his voice. My father loved me, desired my love, and he feared now that he was going to earn my hate.

"This Court," he said quietly, "does not claim that Yeshu'a ben Yosef, called ha Notzri, spoke in the name of other gods, except in so far as he commanded or permitted other men to worship him, boasting of some special relationship with the Almighty. But that constitutes the crime of *mesith*, enticing to idolatry, with which we have *not* charged him, being, as it always is, too difficult of proof. . . ."

My father paused, swept his gaze over the judges, began again.

"It is very clear that the accused has spoken many a word in the Name of the Lord which the Lord has not commanded him to speak. But since the proof of that charge is the fulfillment of prophecies which not even our great-great-grandchildren will live to see fulfilled—"

An appreciative titter rose from the judges at this irony. Sternly my father raised his hand.

"But, in the interest of justice, the Court will not press this charge, for should one prophecy of the prisoner be fulfilled before the world comes to its end, we shall have condemned him unfairly. . . ."

Again my father paused, looked up at me.

"This charge, however," he said solemnly, "we do press against the accused: that he, Yeshu'a ben Yosef, publicly did prophesy to uproot not only Torah but *halakah l'moshe misinai*, the Laws that have come down from Moses on Mount Sinai. For, without exception, our greatest sages have declared that any attempt to overthrow Sacred Law also constitutes false prophecy and is punishable by death through strangulation.[16] For it is written in Deuteronomy: 'All I command, you must keep and observe, adding nothing to it, taking nothing away.'[17] You have heard sober and truthful witnesses testify that the prisoner repeatedly has advocated the abolition of Shabbat observance, of Kashruth, and of the *halakah l'moshe* concerning divorce. . . ."

My father halted then, raised his eyes to mine; but now I saw both anger and authority in them. The anger, his next words proved, was largely directed at me.

"You have heard the last witness," he said, "set forth how, even here in Jerusalem, the Accused openly defended a *sotah*, a suspected adulteress, though 'suspected' is hardly the word for a woman taken in the very act! Thus again did ben Yosef set aside one of the sternest of our laws. Further, we do charge him with personally having profaned the Shabbat by curing people of illnesses which in no way threatened their lives, and also by performing two of the thirty-nine forbidden classes of labor upon the Holy Day, in defiance to the Fourth of the Ten Commandments. . . .

"For in the Book of Exodus it is written: 'Six days shall you labor and do all your work, but the seventh is the Shabbat of the Lord your God. On it, you shall not do any work, neither you, nor your son, nor your daughter, nor your male or female servants, nor your draft ani-

mals, nor even a chance visitor staying with you. . . .'[18] This, too, is
a capital offense, punishable by stoning. . . ."

My father stopped, looked around the court for a long, long time.
Then, lowering his voice still further, but calling upon its full musical-
ity, its depth, its remarkably rich timbre, he said:

"It will be argued—in fact it has been argued, notably by my own
son here present among the spectators—that Yeshu'a ben Yosef, called
the Nazarene, is only a mild sort of lunatic, and therefore should not
be held responsible for his crimes. As much as it pains me to disagree
with this view, and more especially with a dearly beloved son" (Was
this irony, or truth? Or for my benefit, or was it aimed at that sly,
malicious P'rushite Sopher?) "who has gladdened my heart by returning to sober, clean, and industrious ways of life, I hold that Yeshu'a
ha Notzri is a danger to Israel, and hence must be sacrificed. Even
were he innocent, he would be so great a trouble among us that we
should be forced to exile him at the least. But he is *not* innocent! And
the danger he represents is terrible. Since his arrival in Jerusalem, he
has done nothing but stir the people up! First he staged a 'Triumphal
Entry' into our Holy City, mounted on an ass' colt, which, had not
the Romans laughed themselves sick over the comical farce it was,
might have caused them to arrest him and insured the outbreak of
terrible riots. Secondly, he preached daily in the Temple, attacking
both us of the Zadokite party, and our respected colleagues, the
P'rushim, with bitter and mocking words. Third, he himself physically
assaulted worthy and honest merchants and traders in sacred things in
the very outer courts of the Temple! We refrained from arresting him
then, lest the noisy and tumultuous rabble who follow him provoke
such a riot that the Legions would have been forced to intervene and
once again make all the gutters of Jerusalem run red with Jewish blood.
And fourth, he set himself up as a judge in the case of the harlot
Shelomith, causing that woman of notoriously ill fame to be freed from
stoning for an adultery of which she was proven guilty. . . .

"This man, I contend, if acquitted and allowed to follow his mad
course, which includes, I'm told, the megalomaniacal pretension of
being our nation's Mashiah, a charge we have not brought against
him as being too ridiculous to warrant the august attention of this
Court, will soon have our cities and our countryside flaming with
revolt—a revolt that all of recent history demonstrates we cannot win.

"Therefore, if I may quote the words of our honorable Nasi and
High Priest, I, too, feel that it is better that one man should die than
that the whole people should suffer.[19] My lord Nasi, venerable Judges,
I have spoken. . . ."

My father sat down then; but there was no triumph in his face. He had done what he had to do; but he didn't like it. Nor did I, but I couldn't blame him for it. I was trying to save Yeshu'a; he, Israel. And all that has happened since that day convinces me that he, not I, was right.

The President rose.

"Honorable Judges," he said, "you have heard the *Ab Beth Din's* charge to you. What is your verdict?"

One by one they rose and gave it: "Guilty!" It was unanimous. Even Yosef ha Arimathæa voted against him.

I stared at my father's friend and mine in astonishment. He caught my look and made a quick, short, tossing gesture of his left hand. I understood at once that his vote was strategy; but, beyond that, I couldn't imagine what he proposed to do. But he showed me that very next moment, in a masterly demonstration of his intelligence and his command of legal technicalities. He rose to his feet, saluted the High Priest, my father, and the court.

Then he said: "My lord Nasi, honorable fellow Judges, the prisoner stands condemned—and by my vote as well as yours. But, as you all know, sentence cannot be passed upon Yeshu'a ben Yosef until to-morrow, since the Law provides that a night of reflection must intervene before a death sentence can be confirmed. I should like to remind this court that tomorrow is the Eve of Pesach, and therefore all delay must be avoided. For that reason, I beg of you, that in your sober reflection you consider this: You have condemned the prisoner, Yeshu'a ha Notzri, Yeshu'a ben Yosef, on two different charges, carrying two different forms of execution: if he is a false prophet, he must be strangled; if a profaner of the Shabbat, stoned. Therefore, since one method of putting him to death negates or violates the other, it seems to me they cancel one another, and the prisoner must be freed."

Then, having so quietly tossed that legal thunderbolt into the court, Yosef ha Arimathæa sat down.

Shimeon Kepha threw his huge arm about my shoulder and crushed me against his chest.

"A Daniel!" he exulted. "A true Daniel! Oh, what a wise and mighty judge!"

But the Rab Gamaliel, that subtlest of all Pharisees, was already rising to his feet. Now Gamaliel was a most humane man. But, I think, he disliked Yosef ha Arimathæa, and was offended by my old friend's ability to very nearly rival his own intellectual powers. And these things—accompanied in great measure by all the P'rushim's anger at Yeshu'a's largely unwarranted attacks on them—made him forget his habitual compassion, drowned it in his zeal to score a point in learning over Yosef. It is, of course, a shame that a man's very life can depend upon such intangibles as these; but it can. And—in every court of law conducted not by angels but by men—it does.

"My lord Nasi," he began, "honorable *Ab Beth Din*, respected fellow judges, and especially my most brilliant colleague from Arimathæa, whom I congratulate on his knowledge and his zealous efforts to safeguard us against error. Permit me to point out that this conflict is more apparent than real, for if my brilliant colleague cares to renew his indisputably profound acquaintance with the Holy Writ, he will discover that the Book of Deuteronomy provides no specific manner of carrying out the execution of a false prophet at all.[20] It merely says in one instance, 'he shall be put to death;' and in the second, 'that prophet shall die . . .'

"Now our Sages, ever merciful men, have provided that whenever the method of exeuction is not stated in the Law, the culprit is to be strangled, because it is the least cruel manner of putting a man to death.[21] Therefore, here, we have no conflict. We have merely an unspecified death sentence, and a specified one. Whichever of the two we choose, either the recommendation—never a law, my good colleague from Arimathæa!—of the Sages, on the one hand, or the method of stoning, on the other, we are legally justified. . . .

"In which regard, My Presiding Lords, and the Court permitting, I'd suggest we follow the Sages. On the Eve of Pesach, it will be impossible to assemble a stoning party, while the public executioners, our own servants, can easily—"

My father raised a warning hand, stood up.

"No," he said, seeing Gamaliel about to take his seat, "remain standing, wise Rab Gamaliel, for this is not a point of law. It is rather a matter of caution, of elementary prudence. We dare not execute this man in secret, for when it is noised abroad, as inevitably it must be, the wild rumors will make rioting among the tumultuous certain. On the other hand, if we stage a public execution, carried out by our own executioners on Pesach Eve, we court disfavor from people in all walks of life. I confess I see no way out of this practical difficulty—"

Hearing his troubled words, the Nasi Yosef ben Kaiapha stood up. He was smiling.

"Honorable Judges," he said, "calm yourselves. Since you are all agreed that the prisoner is, indeed, guilty, allow me to handle the matter. . . ."

With what was surely a double sigh of relief, my father and the Rab Gamaliel sat down.

And it was then and only then that the High Priest and president of the Court finally did do what your Gospels said he did in the first place. That is, he spoke directly to Yeshu'a ha Notzri.

"Tell me," he said, in an ordinary, conversational tone of voice. "Are you, Rab Yeshu'a ben Yosef, the Mashiah, the Son of David?"

The whole court sat gape-jawed with pure astonishment.

Even Kepha/Petros turned to me with questioning in his eyes. But I had no time to explain to him that what Yosef ben Kaiapha had just done was actually inexplicable, for surely the president of the Court knew that the *first* rule of Jewish jurisprudence was: *Ain adam mesim atzmo rasha;* no man can incriminate himself.[22] So strict are we about this point, that among us it is impossible to convict a man of a crime to which there are no witnesses; let him confess it from the rooftops, he will still go free, because all confession serves for in Jewish Law is to ensure the sinner's right to *helek l'olam habo,* a share in the world to come.

I leaned over the balcony, staring at Yeshu'a. "Blaspheme!" I begged him silently. "Please, Yeshu'a, blaspheme! Curse them by all the terrible Names of God! Befoul each separate Name by another! For your sake, for Yu-Ann's, for mine, blaspheme!"

From the way Shimeon Bar Yonah was staring at me, I could see I'd whispered those words at least loud enough for him to hear them.

"Why, Nathan?" he got out. "Why should he—?"

"Because it takes precedence over the crimes he's charged with!" I whispered. "And since they haven't passed sentence, they have to try him for it, too! Because to do that, being themselves witnesses to it, they'd have to disqualify themselves, call another court with different judges, appear before the new court not as judges themselves, but as witnesses,[23] because tomorrow's Pesach Eve and they can't! Because if they lock him up for eight days, I'll free him from prison, bear him away by force even if it costs me eternal exile to do it! Because—"

But Yeshu'a's voice rang out, awful in its majesty:

"I am he. And you will see the Son of Man seated on the right hand of Power, and coming on the clouds of heaven."[24]

I sank back. He was lost now, totally lost. For he hadn't blasphemed, which alone might have delayed matters long enough for me to save him. He hadn't once used the word *God,* or even *Elohim,* or *Adonai.* He'd said *Geburah,* Power, a very ordinary and acceptable synonym for the Almighty.

But I still couldn't see what my miserable scoundrel of a cousin was getting at. He, himself, soon enlightened me.

"Honorable Judges," he said gently, "I wonder what our Roman friends would think of this man's claim to be our King?"

I closed my eyes and saw that cross rear up, black against a blood-red sky. The pain that drove into my gut then was itself a kind of scream.

I whirled, caught Shimeon Kepha by his massive arm.

"Come, Kepha, Rock of Faith, let's get out of here! Don't just sit there, blockhead, dome of solid granite! We've things to do! You hear me, great tender fool? Dry your tears and come!" I said.

Chapter XXVIII

IT WAS very late in the day of Nisan thirteenth by then. All over Jerusalem, the heads of families were beginning the evening prayers. In the Temple, the priests had commenced the Korban Tamid sacrifices, marking the close of the day with all due and accustomed solemnity. But I, Nathan bar Yehudah, was racing like a frenzied ant all over a private map of Sheol, reeling, pain-drunken and sick, through a landscape no other man has ever seen, since it was sculptured from the shale rock of a curiously personal desolation.

First I sent Shimeon bar Yonah to warn Yeshu'a's followers to hide themselves, and to offer in my name the house Claudia had given me, the same one where we had eaten that last supper as a place of refuge for the Twelve, telling them especially, who had been most closely associated with him, to stay there until further notice lest they become the victims of a general slaughter. Then I went to old Sarah's place and called on Shelomith.

Shelomith stood as I came in, and her hand flew to the base of her throat.

"Oh, Nathan!" she said, or rather, wailed. "You—you're sick! You're *very* sick! Here, lie down. I'll get you some—"

I said: "No. There's no time, Shelom. Listen to me carefully—I don't even have time to say it over twice. They—"

"But, Nathan, lover, lamb, you look like a dead man! Your face—"

"Shut up!" I howled. "I am dead. Only I haven't had time to stretch out and stiffen so they can bury me. Shelom, they've arrested Yeshu'a. Condemned him. Tomorrow, they'll turn him over to Pilatus—"

She didn't say anything. She just sat down. Abruptly. From her shining, clean, well-scrubbed face all her rich burnt bronze color fled. I thought she was going to cry. I had to prevent that. I simply hadn't left in my shredded gut what it took to hear Shelomith cry.

So I said very fast, pumping the words out like one of those little catapults the Romans used to launch a stream of arrows one after another so swiftly that you can hardly see them: "I'm going to Pilatus. I don't think he'll listen to me, but I'm going, anyhow. I won't lie to you, Shelom. I don't think there's a chance this side of Sheol. So— damn you! don't cry or faint or anything. Forget you're a woman. If Pilatus condemns him—as that Iberian swine most likely will—I'll get you word. You'll have to come to the place of execution. You'll have to look at him hanging there. It will be awful. But you saw it before. You saw me. And you saved me. Remember that if you lose your senses, he'll die. Only *you* can save him, Shelom. You haven't forgot how to mix that stuff, have you?"

"No—" she whispered.

"Don't mix it until I send you word. It must be fresh. Yosef of Arimathæa and I will do the rest. If it *has* to be done that way— which God forbid!—you spread the rumor that we're laying his body in my family's tomb. Or in Yosef's. They're quite close to each other anyhow, so that won't make any difference. Which tomb it is, I mean. You know Miriam of Migdal-Nunaya, don't you?"

"Yes," Shelomith said.

"Tell her that. She's not all there. She believes anything anybody tells her. And you can approach her. She's always so—so remote that she won't remember who you are or, more to the point, what you were. Is all that clear, Shelom?"

"Yes. Nathan—don't go yet. Please don't go!"

"Shelom, in God's Name! There's no time—"

"A minute. Hold me. Till I stop shaking on the inside. Till I tell you I *can* do it. No good for you to leave thinking it's all arranged and then have me muck it for you because my guts have come apart. And they have, Nathan! They have! So hold me—"

I took her in my arms. She melted into me, flowed into all my hollows. She was sweating. Her sweat was like ice. The feel of her body through her robe was singularly unpleasant. Her flesh was alive, but with an independent life of its own. It crawled over mine like a host of creeping things. Every vein she had made a pulse and beat; every nerve she owned vibrated like plucked lyre strings until mine were screaming along with them.

"Nathan," she quavered.

"Yes, Shelom?"

"Kiss me. It doesn't mean anything, but it'll help. Charity. Mercy. A blessing for the damned. Please, huh? Please?"

I kissed her. She clung her mouth to mine a little æon, a tiny age. Then she—what? What *is* the word?—shuddered, say. That's all wrong, but say it anyhow. It went on and on and on, that longslowmelting-quiver. Became sound. Became a groan that was a taste against my mouth. A wild taste. Tart. Feral.

She tore free. Looked at me. Her gaze committed idolatry upon my face. I wondered if she was confusing me with him again.

"Turn me loose, Nathan," she said.

I turned her loose.

She stood there, staring at me. Her eyes combined those absolute antitheses: night and luminosity. She wasn't trembling anymore. She was utterly relaxed. More than relaxed. Limp.

"You," she said, "you. Most men, all night—and nothing. It's been years since anybody could. Not since Antonius, to tell the truth. But you. Standing up. With all our clothes on. Just kissing. You. Oh, you."

"Shelom, for God's sake!" I said.

She smiled at me. She had tears in her eyes, but she was smiling.

"Go. Get out of here, Nathan. You don't need to worry anymore. I can do it now. For you. For Yeshu'a. For the Yeshu'a-Ba'al that you are, and the Yeshu'a-God, that he is. I can. Now I can," she said.

When Pilatus came down to Jerusalem for the Festivals, he stayed at Herod's palace. He had apartments in the Tower of Phasael, and below them there was a large room paved with stones that he used as his Prætorium or headquarters.

So I went there. The guards admitted me at once, for their decurion was one of the officers who had been with Pilatus on the day that Yeshu'a had made his "triumphal" entry into Jerusalem; and he—since Lucius Pontius confided in no one, not even his wife—was laboring under the illusion that the relationship between the Procurator and me was at least nominally friendly. He sent a legionary upstairs with my name. The soldier returned in minutes with the word that I was to go up, that the Epitropos would see me.

A manservant—one of those Greek-speaking Syrian swine with which all our major cities were infested since our country had been made a subdivision of the Roman province of Syria—ushered me into the sitting room of Pilatus' apartment, and bade me wait. But no sooner had I sat down, when a slave girl, a fetching Canaanitish slut who under other circumstances would not have escaped an appreciative pinch or two from me upon that nicely rounded portion of herself upon which she sat, came into the room, bent swiftly and whispered into my ear: "Follow me, my lord! My Lady Claudia Procula would have a word with you. . . ."

"But—but the Epitropos!" I protested. "I must—"

"The Epitropos is dining with some dignitaries from the court of the Governor of Syria," the wench said. "He'll see you presently. There's time. . . ."

I got up and followed that delightful little swish and sway. But my feet dragged, my gut ached. The last thing on earth I wanted was further traffic with women, now.

Claudia was reclining on one of those couches you Greeks use at your banquets. She was picking at a bowl of fruit. She gave one of her characteristic squeals of pleasure and ran to me. But one rod away she stopped. She was wearing a new kind of perfume. An exotic eastern scent. It was very strong. It made my head ache.

"Oh, Nathan!" she breathed. "How awful you look!"

I was so tired that I couldn't even think of a new thing to say, so I repeated my wry jest to Shelom.

"I'm dead; but since they can't bury me until the twenty-second, after the Festival is over, I have to keep walking around and try not to rot too fast. How are you, Claudia?"

"Dead, too," she said quietly, "or at least existing in a state of suspended animation since you left me. I've been told you married that little creature. The sister of that absolutely divine man who looks like you. Did you? No! Don't tell me, yet. Kiss me first, then tell me. . . ."

I took her in my arms. That new perfume rose around my head like a cloud. It was designed to have an aphrodisiacal effect, I suppose. But I was past that, now. It made me feel sick.

I kissed her. Her lips were warm and soft. They tasted salt. I opened my eyes and saw that she was crying.

"Did you?" she said.

"Yes," I said harshly. "And we're expecting a child. So I'm sinning against her now. I specifically promised her that I wouldn't visit you."

"She's jealous of me?" Claudia said. "That's a comfort. And, anyhow, you *didn't* visit me. I sent for you. Tell her that. Tell her I had you dragged kicking and screaming before me by a whole century of the Legion. . . ."

"I don't mean to tell her a damned thing," I said. "What she doesn't know, won't hurt her. Besides, I've more serious problems than the possibility of fighting with my wife. My brother-in-law, Yeshu'a ha Notzri, has been arrested by the Sanhedrin, tried, and condemned to death—"

"Oh, no!" Claudia said. "Not that beautiful, beautiful man!"

"That beautiful, beautiful man," I said dryly; "but, for various reasons it would take me until next Passover to explain, and that wouldn't interest you anyhow, the Zadokim don't dare put him to death. So they plan to shove that delightful little chore off on Pilatus. Why risk the people's blaming them, when they have the Romans to shift the onus to?"

"So," Claudia said, "you want me to—"

"Intercede? Yes. Will you?"

"No," Claudia said, "because that would be to condemn him, surely."

"Why?" I said.

"He looks like you. Too much. Pontius would think it was because of that."

"I didn't think he cared, really," I said.

"About me? Not a fig. But you wounded his self-love by possessing me. And he'll never forgive you that. By the way, you'd better go back to the sitting room. He'll probably be finished with Vitellius' spies by now . . ."

"Claudia!" I groaned. "Can't you—won't you—?"

She thought. Then her eyes cleared.

"I'll tell him I had a dream," she said. "He has a great fear of my dreams. They always seem to come true. The bad ones, anyhow. Now kiss me, and go!"

My luck was at its miserable worst that day. When it shouldn't have been, when I couldn't even afford a mischance. For, when I got back to the sitting room, Lucius Pontius Pilatus, Procurator of Judea, was already there.

Which was one of the many things your scribes couldn't put into your *Besorahim*, your Gospels. One of the many, many intangibles they didn't know. One of the damned, nonsensical ironies that can and do stand between a man's life and his death. But I can tell you that one, because I caused it: When I went to plead with Pilatus for your Lord Iesous' life, the effect I produced upon the Epitropos was not one to incline him toward mercy. You see, I entered that would-be Cæsar's presence, fairly reeking of his wife's perfume.

I saw his nose twitch. But the bland mockery of his smile never wavered.

"Chatting with dear Claudia?" he said.

"Yes," I said. Lying was stupid, and I knew it.

He leaned forward, sniffed noisily.

"Must have been quite a chat!" he said.

"Lucius Pontius—" I groaned.

"Forget it," he said. "I know how demonstrative Claudia is. What did you come to see me about?"

I told him. He didn't interrupt me even once. His eyes never left my face. They didn't so much as blink. When I had finished, he smiled.

"What an enchanting liar you are, Nathanaeus!" he said. "You do it so well. The truth—distorted just so little. Or—incomplete. You still insist that those bearded beggars at the Temple are using your poor idiotic devil of a brother-in-law to get me recalled?"

"Yes," I said.

"A pity. Because, if you're right, I'll have to let him go. And I do so love a *good* crucifixion. Don't you?"

"Don't be an utter swine, Lucius Pontius!" I said.

He laughed.

"The best one will be the day I receive conclusive evidence against *you*, dear Caius Nathanaeus!" he said. "Don't blanch—I'm only joking. I'll see what I can do for your Iesus Nazarathæus. Give him a beating, perhaps, and make him ride three times around Jerusalem on that undersized little ass of his. D'you think that would please the Sanhedrin?"

"Since when have you started worrying your head about the Sanhedrin, Lucius Pontius?" I said.

"Oh, quite recently. Today, in fact. My new policy—appeasing the Jews. I'll have to see how it works out. . . ."

I got up then without so much as a by-your-leave. It was hopeless and I knew it.

"*Vale*, Cæsar-to-be!" I said.

"Why, Nathanaeus; what a flattering thought!" he said. And even after I'd left the room, I could hear the sibilant hiss and rasp of his laughter.

After that, I went to see Yosef of Arimathæa. He didn't waste my time or his own discussing the nonexistent possibility of Pilatus' freeing Yeshu'a. He said crisply: "It must be done well. With precision. Any false moves and—"

I said: "I know."

He went on: "My burial place is in the new necropolis that the High Priest recently blessed. You know where it is, of course? It's quite near the Hill of the Stonings, where they—"

"Stage the crucifixions. I know that, Rab Yosef. My father has bought tombs for us there, too. We—except Mother—are a new family in Jerusalem, so we had no place in the Mount of Olive tombs. And we couldn't buy there. Those burial places under the hill have been in the hands of the same families for centuries, so—"

It was pure, damned, screaming nerves that was making me rattle on like that. Yosef saw that, so he ignored what I was saying, didn't comment. Instead, he said: "We may have to lay him in my tomb for a while to keep them from becoming suspicious. If he's not too far gone by then, the rest will help. Then, as soon as it's dark, I'll have a covered cart, drawn by fast mules, brought to the garden—"

"Don't wait till it's dark, Rab Yosef," I said. "Have it there, waiting—"

He said: "It's risky."

And I: "Delay's riskier. He's not strong. Put stones in it. Gardener's tools. Anything that will make them think—"

And he: "All right. The precaution's wise. Nathan—"

"Yes, Rab Yosef?" I said.

"What's he got? What is it that—that moves me so? I look at him and—"

"Love," I said. "A new kind, Judge of Arimathæa! The kind that passes understanding. Your blessing, Rabbi! I go. . . ."

I rode all the way to Khirbet Qumrân. That's a long way. A very long way. Then, after I'd got there and told my Essene friends what was happening, what they'd have to be ready to do, I turned around and rode back home again.

By the time I got to my father's house, light was sculpturing form out of darkness. Do you know how long it had been since I'd eaten or slept by then? I don't, either. I woke Hagar up, made her bring me food. It came up the instant it hit my belly's pit. I howled for her to come clean up the bloody mess, and bring me more. *That* stayed down. I went to bed, leaving word for my father's manservant to go stand by the booths and to come wake me as soon as they brought Yeshu'a out to march him to the Prætorium. Then I slept. Really slept. Not even my anguish-shredded gut was proof against my weariness.

So it was that I was at the Tower of Phasael when they got there. I saw the man who led them, and recognized him. He was one of the lay members of the Sanhedrin, a Sopher—lawyer in this in-

stance—just turned forty, the minimum age for admission to that
august body, and his skill at Roman law had already made him famous. It was to this speciality, in fact, that Yohannan ben Zakkai, for
such was his name, owed his early elevation to the Lesser Court.
We had more jurists than it was possible to count who could recite
the Torah from beginning to end; but few indeed who knew Roman
law, and no other who could quote the *lex Julia majestatis*, the *Ubi
de criminibus*, the *de Poenis*, down to the *De bonis damnatorium*
in the original Latin the way Yohannan ben Zakkai could. It was
obviously, giving due consideration to the sad fact that the heel under
which we currently groaned was Roman, a most useful accomplishment.

I saw the rolled-up scroll of the written indictment in his hand and
my gut hurt. They were forgetting nothing. Every formality of the
Roman code was being scrupulously obeyed.

I know, I know! I've read your Gospels. They, especially in the latter
part of their narratives, are the products of appalling ignorance
combined with equally appalling spite. No Roman judge—and the Procurators were always men trained in jurisprudence—would have entertained an oral presentation of a legal case for as long as it would have
taken the Prosecutor to utter it[1] and I give less than a damn in Tartarus what your Sacred Books say. Pilatus, the Pilatus whom I knew,
and not that feeble idiot your pious lunatics present, would have had
that noisy, stupid, disrespectful rabble, equally ignorant of Roman and
Jewish law, depicted in your inspired Christianoi Scriptures driven
from his presence with whips and staves by his Prætorian Guard!
But then, those scribes of yours who paint the scene of Yeshu'a before
Pilatus were not there to witness it, and I was.

With ben Zakkai were only the *segens*, the Levite porters or police,
and Yeshu'a, himself. Wait. It was now Preparation Day, Nisan
fourteenth, the Eve of Passover. So, despite your *Besorahim*, your
Gospels, there were no priests, high or otherwise, present. Nor any
elders of the nation, whatever your *Evangelionoi* mean by that, since,
to the best of my knowledge, we have no such office, nor title among
us at all.[2] No, there was only Yohannan ben Zakkai, a layman, who
had both the time and the qualifications to do that ugly but necessary task.

For, on Preparation Day, my dear Theophilos, Jewish priests are
far too busy sacrificing the hundreds and hundreds of paschal lambs
for the people's Pesach to do anything else. Nor would they have
bothered on any other day. To you, Yeshu'a ha Notzri, Iesous the
Nazarene, is the center of history; to us, he was a very minor Gali-

lean rab, who had made enough trouble to become a danger to
Israel. Therefore—regrettably—he had to be removed. How could we
know then that he was going to be far more trouble, far more dangerous, after his death than he'd ever been in his lifetime?

I looked at him, as he strode along in the crowd of Temple police,
followed by a hooting mob of Greek-speaking Syrians, a numerous
representation of your own race from the Decapolis, some Idumæans,
some Canaanite and Cushite slaves, and even an outcast Jew or two,
though my own race was the smallest component element among that
howling rabble, because on the Eve of Pesach, pious Jews were too
busy preparing the Seder to have either the time or the inclination to
form mobs.

They had, of course, fed him in prison. And, apparently, he'd slept
throughout that night during which his judges walked together in
sleepless pairs, and debated soberly with each other and their own
consciences over his fate as our Law requires; for, once his death was
upon him, he'd lost his fear, summoned up his faith, called upon
his absolute belief in himself, in his mission, and regained his serenity.

And with it, his beauty. Now, looking at him, as he caught my eye
and smiled consolingly at me, that beauty of his tore my heart, so
that my eyes went blind, my tears dripped into my beard. Don't ask me
to describe him. I can't. Physically, by Grecian standards, I suppose he
was rather ugly, for he looked just like me. You'd have seen a small,
black-bearded Jew, with a great beak of a nose, rather sensual lips—
although his were tender, not lecherous the way mine are—long, somewhat kinky hair, and huge black eyes. When we were apart, people
often mistook me for him; when we were together, nobody did. It
wasn't the fact that through exercise, training, and war, my body was
far better developed than his that made the difference, for our clothes
hid and negated that. It was that he was the most beautiful human
being, male or female, I have ever known; and that he made you—
even when you didn't want to—love him. Even the people who
thought they hated him, loved him. Even ish Kriyoth my Brother, who
betrayed him. Even the men who condemned him to death. Even his
executioners. They couldn't help it. Nobody could. But they fought
against it, against what they considered an unmanly weakness in
themselves; and hence their murderous rage.

I didn't fight. I surrendered to him, always.

Bear with me a moment longer. I've said that we—he and I—were
almost twins; and you've seen me. So how could he have been beautiful? Don't ask me. I don't know. He was, that's all. He was! You
saw a small, stooped, black-bearded Jew coming toward you, flapping

along in his fringed robe. Then he stopped, looked at you, and his eyes swallowed the sun, he reared up twenty mountains tall, and all the Seraphim in heaven chanted murmuring choruses through his voice. He smiled, and the world reeled, drunk with joy. He touched you, and your flesh quivered. He told you you weren't blind anymore, and, for as long as he was there, you saw, though the torturers had put the irons to your eyes the day before. He told you you could lift your withered arm, and lift it you did despite all the laws of probability. He forgave you your sins, and they were gone; you were a newborn babe suckling at your mother's breast. . . .

I rave. I loved him. When he was gone, the world was too empty. Too desolate. So they had to bring him back. They had to! And upon that act of love, all your faith is built. Which is enough, isn't it? Many a faith, a creed, has been erected upon far lesser things.

Anyhow, as soon as Yohannan, Yeshu'a, and such of his guards as the decurion before the door would allow, had gone into the Præ- torium, I rushed in behind them. Of course the guards crossed their spears to bar me; but the decurion growled:

"Let him pass, you donkeys! Can't you see it's Caius Nathanaeus, the Procurator's friend?"

So, once aagin that dubious distinction saved me. I entered the hall. Pilatus saw me at once and called out: "Nathanaeus! Good! You can serve me as interpreter!"

He had, even as he spoke, his official interpreter at his side.

I came forward, said: "*Ave,* Representative of Cæsar! And who, may I ask, is that so august functionary sitting there next to you?"

"My interpreter," Pilatus said. "But you see, my dear Caius Natha- naeus, he lies to me. So do you; but, since you and he don't see eye to eye on political matters, your lies will cancel one another out, and I shall get at the truth. Come, sit here at my left hand . . ."

I came, and sat.

Yohannan ben Zakkai came forward, bowed. He was proud of his Latin, which was very good indeed, as far as reading and writing it went. But his accent was awful, since he'd learned the language of our conquerors at home and through books. So now, after having heard me bantering away with the Procurator in that tongue, he had the prudence, the good sense, not to attempt to speak it.

"My Lord Epitropos, may I present the indictment against the Accused?" he said in Greek.

Pilatus took the scroll from his hand. Then, without glancing at it, he passed it over to me.

"Read it," he said. Then, after a deliberate little pause that was mockery's exquisite self, he added: "Aloud."

I read it. It stated that Yeshu'a ben Yosef, called ha Notzri, a native of Nazareth in Galilee, had been found guilty of perverting the people against their rulers, both Jewish and Roman, that he had stirred all the people up, starting in his native Galilee and continuing his preaching of sedition all the way to Jerusalem itself; and that he claimed to be the Jewish Mashiah, and hence a King.[3] It did *not* have the charge that one of your writers sets down, "We found him opposing the taxes to Cæsar . . ."[4] for the very simple reason that the rigid standards imposed upon candidates for membership in the Sanhedrin effectively barred from that august body all idiots, morons, and fools. If your writers had known anything at all about conditions in Jerusalem in my early manhood, they'd have been forced to the conclusion that to make such a charge to Pilatus, whose swarming spies had already reported to him its direct opposite, would have been the height, or rather the depth, of folly.

I finished it, handed it back to the Procurator. Whereupon that sardonic monster immediately passed it over to his official interpreter, and said to him exactly the same words in exactly the same tone with exactly the same pause:

"Read it. . . . Aloud."

The interpreter read it. Passed it back to Pilatus.

"Hmmmn," Pilatus said. "You agree with one another. Amazing. P'haps I'd better read it myself. . . ."

He bent his head and began to study the scroll. Since it was in Greek, anyhow, it presented no difficulties. But, before he could finish it, he was interrupted. The Syrian manservant who had admitted me to the Procurator's apartments came into the Prætorium with a little roll of papyrus on a silver tray. He bowed, and held the tray out to Pilatus. With a gesture of annoyance, the Procurator took the roll, broke the seal, opened it.

I could see his eyes dance over the lines. Then with a lupine, twisted smile, he handed it to me.

I took it, read: *Pontius: Have nothing to do with that innocent man; I was much troubled on his account in my dreams last night. Claudia P.*[5]

I looked at Pilatus.

"So you did *chat* with her," he said.

"Of course. I told you that. What did you think, Lucius Pontius?"

"Don't know. Wrestled, likely. There must be some way to account for all that scent. . . ." Then, without another word, he went back to reading the indictment. I let my breath out, slowly.

"Hmmmn," he said again. "So this monstrous, terrible species of a Maccabaeus I see before me is a Galilean? Very well, send him to Antipas, then.[6] Court's dismissed."

At once Yohannan ben Zakkai was on his feet and bowing.

"My Lord Epitropos," he said smoothly, "would it be presumptuous of your humble servant to point out to Cæsar's Representative that under Imperial Law, the jurisdiction of the Court is determined, according to Laws One and Two of the codex *Ubi de Criminibus,* by the place in which the arrest was made, or, in any case, by the place in which the *last* offense of the criminal was committed,[7] both, in this instance, Judea? Why then should my Lord Epitropos turn him over to the Tetrarch? His offenses in Galilee were long ago—and minor. What concerns us here—is treason, under the *lex Julia majestatis,* laid down by the great Cæsar Augustus, the Imperial Grandsire of my lord's gracious Lady, some eighty years ago. . . ."[8]

Pilatus looked at him. His mocking smile became more mocking still.

"A wonder, eh, Caius Nathanaeus?" he said to me. "A Jew who *knows* the Law! Dangerous fellow, what? Maybe I'd better crucify *him.*"

Yohannan turned white. His knees shook visibly beneath his robe. At the sight of that, the procurator laughed aloud.

"Don't worry, Rab ben Zakkai!" he said. "I jest—as usual. Do not your people call me jesting Pilatus? And, incidentally, I have no intention of remitting this case to that filthy Idumæan swine whose soul is as full of rot as his father's body was. I merely mean to send this huge and frightful criminal of yours to Herod Antipas for a preliminary investigation, which, once made, I shall totally disregard. You see, I need another day in order to receive sufficient information to bulwark my heart against the piteous and effective lies our good friend Caius Nathanaeus—I beg your pardon!—Nathan bar Yehudah, here, will presently tell me in defense of his brother-in-law. So, as I said before, Court is dismissed until tomorrow morning—at nine o'clock, say. And, by the way, my dear Nathanaeus, you're definitely to be here. You'll spare me the trouble of sending a decuria after you, won't you? Commanded by your so very good friend Telemarchos, who has such exquisite reasons to love you?"

I stared at him. Was there nothing this monster of evil and mockery didn't know?

I bowed until my forehead almost touched the floor. To Pilatus, who knew me, the very exaggeration of the bow conveyed the contempt with which it was laden.

"I hear and obey, O Representative of Cæsar!" I said.

I had no power or influence that would cause me to be admitted to Antipas' palace. On the contrary, if I afforded the murderer of Yohannan Baptistes this priceless opportunity to get his hands on one of the banim Matthya, I'd never leave his dungeons alive. Therefore, since Yeshu'a's faint and diminishing chances of emerging from his ordeal with breath still in him depended to a large extent upon me, I prudently stayed away.

That night, for the second time in the same week, I ate Passover, this time with my father and mother. I meant it as a gesture of reconciliation between us, and so my father understood it.

At the close of it, when he and I were alone, he said in a hushed, choked, shame-baffled voice: "I couldn't have saved him; you know that, don't you, Nathan?"

"Yes, Father," I said; "I do know it."

"And you don't hold it against me?" he whispered.

"No, I don't hold it against you," I said.

"One man—against Israel. One life—or thousands. One death—or many. You see that, don't you?"

"I see it. Only you're leaving something out, Father."

"Which is?" he said.

"Quality. Numbers are rather meaningless, aren't they?"

"I don't follow you!" my father said.

"Give me the names of one Egyptian among Pharaoh's hosts who drowned in the Red Sea, Father. Or the names of any citizen of Sodom and Gemorrah. How many times has our God destroyed whole nations to save—a few of quality—Noah and his family, say. Or even—one man —like David, the King?"

"Well—" my father said.

"How do you—or I—know that Yeshu'a doesn't outweigh us all in the scale of God? Outweigh all Israel? Outweigh—"

"Don't blaspheme, Nathan!" my father said.

"Not blasphemy, Father. It's closer to idolatry. To me, he's unique. There's no one else like him. There never will be—"

"Which is merely an opinion, son."

"I know. But what isn't an opinion is that you and the Sanhedrin have gone whoring after stranger gods. I started to say 'false,' but then Anagke isn't false, is she?"

"Anagke?" my father said.

"Necessity. She's Greek. At least her name is. She herself is universal. Even Zeus bows to her. Tell me, Father, does YHWH bow to her, too?"

"Nathan!" my father thundered.

"Or is it—only his followers who bend their necks to expediency? Perform judicial assassinations? Condemn the innocent to—"

"Nathan!" my father said again; but this time the pain in his voice broke through my anger.

I turned to him, put my arms about his neck, kissed his bearded cheek.

"Forgive me, my father," I said.

At nine o'clock that next morning, I was at the Prætorium. I had to call out to the Prætorium Guards for help in order to force my way through the dense crowds. As on yesterday, they were ninety-nine percent foreigners. One hundred percent, for the circumcised scum among them were no longer really Jews. Jews were at home, or at the Temple, celebrating Pesach.

Pilatus sat on his dais, reading a document his spies had brought him. Ben Zakkai had brought reenforcements. Despite the fact that today was both Passover and Shabbat Eve, he had two other lay lawyers with him.

I—had brought nothing but my wits. And my grief. My gut-destroying pain.

A smile played over Lucius Pontius Pilatus' dark Spanish face. He was enjoying himself hugely.

"Have the prisoner brought before me," he said.

The *segens* led Yeshu'a forward.

Pilatus looked at him. Yeshu'a stared back serenely.

"Are you the King of the Jews?" Pilatus said.

"You have said it," Yeshu'a said.

All this, of course, was through the interpreters. At times I translated, when Pilatus nodded to me; at others, the official interpreter.

"Hmmmn," Pilatus said. "Dangerous fellow, eh, ben Zakkai? Aren't you afraid he'll climb up on that tiny little ass of his and ride us all down? How fierce he is! Now, really, do you Jews mean to make sport of me? I've half a mind to turn him loose. . . ."

"If you do, you're scarcely Cæsar's friend," Yohannan ben Zakkai said ominously.

"An opinion my wife's adoptive father often shares," Pilatus quipped. "But then, Cæsar has no friends, for how can mere mortals frequent divinity? Look you, Wise Lawyers, this skinny little fellow is bar Yehudah's brother-in-law. And one could clip that 'in-law' off of it with much justice, to look at them. Do you really insist I should use all the weight of Empire to crush a bastard? A pitiful little pious bastard at that?"

"My lord," ben Zakkai began, but Pilatus raised his hand.

"Caius Nathanaeus wants his brother-in-law saved," he said; "and I'm inclined to indulge him. Couldn't you have found me a fiercer looking traitor? A more imposing King? Come to think of it, that gives me an idea, by Zeus! I've another Yeshu'a in my dungeons. A princely looking fellow. A brigand. Probably a Zealot though I can't prove that. What do you say we swap? This Iesus for that one?"

He stood up suddenly, strode to the window.

"Good citizens!" he called out. "Whom shall I release to you? Yeshu'a bar Amma or Yeshu'a bar Abbas?⁹ Iesus son of—his mother? Or Iesus son of his father? Bastards both; but then, aren't you all?"

"Bar Abbas!" the mob screamed; "Give us Yeshu'a bar Abbas!"

"And what shall I do with Yeshu'a bar Amma? Send him home to his little *scorta* of a mother?"

"Crucify him!" the crowd bellowed. "Crucify him!"

Pilatus shrugged, turned back to his dais.

"Bad-tempered beggars, aren't they?" he said. "I suppose I'll have to oblige them. . . ."

"Lucius Pontius!" I all but wept.

"But, my dear Caius Nathanaeus," he purred, "they're an angry mob, and I'm but one poor weak—"

I stood up then and said it clearly, slowly, and in his own tongue:

"Vanaes populi non sunt audiendae, necenim vocibus eorum credi oportet aut noxium crimine absolvi aut innocentum condemnari desidereant—"

"Law Number Twelve, *Codex De Poenis*, Paragraph Nine, Section Forty-seven," he said solemnly. "Let's see if you can put it into Greek for the benefit of these gentlemen, Nathanaeus—"

So I said it again:

"The vain clamors of the people are not to be heeded, seeing that it is in no wise necessary to pay attention to the cries of those desiring the acquittal of the guilty or the condemnation of the innocent."

"Now once again in Hebrew," Pilatus said.

I translated it into my native tongue.

Pilatus pointed to his official interpreter.

"Now, you. In Greek, Aramaic, and Hebrew—"

That took another half hour.

"Hmmmn," Pilatus said, "not bad. But aren't you a part of the people, Nathanaeus? Aren't you clamoring for me to acquit this huge and terrible King who'd overthrow Cæsar?"

I said in Latin: "Oh, Fæces, Lucius Pontius!"

He grinned at me, turned once more to Yeshu'a.

"Tell me, fellow, are you a King, then?"

Yeshu'a looked at him. His dark eyes were icy with contempt.

" 'King' is your word," he said almost gently. "My task is to bear witness to the truth. For this I was born; for this I came into the world, and all who are not deaf to truth listen to my voice."

It was then that Lucius Pontius Pilatus, sardonic monster, epitome of evil, asked, for the second time in my presence, the greatest of all possible questions, the query upon which all of civilization hangs. He said quietly, thoughtfully, his gaze turned inward:

"What is truth?"[10]

Then, he stood up, an expression of annoyance on his lean, dark, mocking face. As if his own question had cut too deep. As it had, it had!

He clapped his hands, hard. The centurion of the Prætorian Guard came up to the dais, and, drawing his sword, saluted the Procurator with it.

"Take this little Jew bastard out and crucify him," Lucius Pontius Pilatus said.

Chapter XXIX

I RAN all the way home. When I got there, I hadn't any breath to talk with, and my legs weighed twenty tons each, and a nest of vipers fought a pitched battle with a swarm of fire lizards inside my gut. But Anagke, Necessity, clawed her fingers into my hair and held me upright by its roots until I got up the stair.

The first person I saw when I entered the sitting room was Hagar, my mother's maidservant. She was thirty-five, beginning to fade, and nobody had tumbled her in a long time, which had soured her disposition.

"Hagar," I panted. "Go to old Sarah's place. Tell Shelom—"

She stared at me.

"You don't mean Shelomith the harlot, do you, young master?" she said.

"The same. Tell her—"

"No," Hagar said, "I won't. I'm a decent girl, master! I wouldn't be caught dead exchanging the time of day with the likes of her! Why—"

She couldn't have chosen a worse moment to defy me if she had tried. I hit her so hard that she went over backwards across a little table. She was a skinny wench, but there wasn't anything left of that table but splinters. She scrambled to her knees, her eyes amber saucers into which all the terror in this world had been poured.

"Get going, Hagar!" I howled. "Or, by YHWH, himself, I'll disembowel you! Tell Shelom she's to mix the potion. Now. To bring it to the Hill of the Stonings. You hear me, Hagar!"

She got to her feet.

"Oh, young Master Nathan, I'll be disgraced forever!" she wailed.

I started toward her quietly. I said: "If you aren't out that door in three seconds flat, you won't be disgraced, you'll be dead!"

I meant it. I meant it absolutely. She saw that, and flew down those stairs, squawking like a hen.

I went into my room, took a pitcher, poured water over my head. I picked up a wine flask, but I put it down again. Before I could get it to my mouth, I felt the sickness rising in me. Pouring down my throat what was only going to come up again was further waste of the time I didn't have. So I climbed up on a stool to take down my sword. But I didn't do that, either.

That something in me—instinct, or maybe even a kind of intelligence —that always asks me the right questions at the right time, went jeering through my head, whispering and sibilant like Pilatus' voice: "What are you going to do with a sword against a century of the Legion, you fool? Eat it?"

I left it there. But I took my dagger. If it came to that, as it damned well could, a self-inflicted dagger thrust wasn't the worst known way to die.

I went down the stairs, making loops of my raw, quivering, stark-naked nerves, to clamp all the places where my insides were coming apart back together again. I didn't run. I saved every breath as though it were a mist of gold dust. I husbanded, I guarded my strength. What there was left of it by then, I mean.

I was headed toward the place of executions, the ancient hill outside the city where blasphemers, enticers, idolaters, and adulterers were stoned. Or where they had been before the Romans took it away

from us to use it for the unspeakable obscenity of crucifixions. I
cannot answer your question as to whether it was the place your Gospels call Golgotha or not. I was born in Jerusalem, lived much of my
life there; but the two places your writers lay the most stress on, I
never heard of. Like Gethsemane, Golgotha is not a Hebrew or an
Aramaic word. I don't know what kind of word it is or what it means.
Your scribes say it means "Place of the Skull." But skull in Hebrew is
gulgolet, and in Aramaic it's *gulgalto.* So, at the very best, your Greek
transliteration would have to be something like Gol-gol-tha, which to
my ear is a nonsense word, that doesn't mean anything either. I don't
think there ever was any such place. I think they made it up, to make
their readers imagine a hill strewn with skulls and bones—impossible
under our Sacred Law.[1]

But, as I rounded a corner, I came upon a band of revellers. They
were all Jews, which was shocking. They shouldn't have been shouting
and singing and drinking the way they were. Not on Pesach. Not on
the First Day of Unleavened Bread. Then I saw the big man in their
midst. A Herakles. Roped all over with muscle. A black, short, squared-
off beard, which was a violation of our Law.[2] One earring in one ear.
The left, I think. Bar Abbas. Yeshu'a bar Abbas. Whose life had been
purchased at the highest price in history. They were celebrating his
release. By *they* I mean the Zealots, of course.

I started to go to him. Ask him to rally the Zealots, draw steel to save—
his opposite. He just might do it. Yeshu'a bar Abbas liked me, was, in
a curious way, my friend.

But then I stopped. That icy, sibilant voice inside my skull was whispering: "Why should he? Why should any man risk his hide for a Prophet who advised giving unto Cæsar Cæsar's coin? And the Zealots?
Ha! They'd kill him themselves for less—"

Besides, they couldn't. That was another thing. A handful of Zealot
brigands, no matter how brave, were as nothing against a century of
the Legion, and Pilatus had three whole cohorts in Jerusalem now.

So I flattened myself against a wall until they had whooped and
bellowed past me. Then I went on, toward the Hill of the Stonings.

But, long before I got there, I saw Yeshu'a. He had that cross on his
shoulder. He was bent under it. Have you ever seen an ant carrying
a dead wasp twenty times its size? Like that. I could count the veins
in his forehead. I could see the sweat beading under his hair. He had
a sort of wreath woven out of *akkabith,* Gundelia Tournefortis, the
flowering plant that you call "Jewish Thorn," on his head. But it didn't
make him bleed the way your pictures show it now. In the first place,
akkabith hasn't any thorns to speak of, only some tiny little spines that

make you itch, and, in the second place, Pilatus' soldiers had set it on his head at a jaunty angle in mockery, not rammed it down about his ears.[3] He wasn't bleeding anywhere anymore; but his robe was stuck to his back where the leaded whips, which were the Romans' parting salute to a man setting out on that particular journey, had taken all the skin off it. The flies were at him. His mouth was open. He was trying to drag air into it over a tongue already swollen and turning black. He'd bitten it through to keep from screaming while Pilatus' gentle servitors were caressing his naked back so tenderly.

It was at that moment, of course, when, according to one of your better chroniclers, he made his long, eloquent, moving address to the daughters of Jerusalem.[4] Which, of course, his Roman guards let him make. Which he had the breath left to pronounce. The strength. Tell me, my dear Theophilos, among you Goyim, does a man tortured almost to death indulge in oratory? If so, I salute you, for you are made of sterner stuff than we!

I saw he was going to fall, so I hammered my way to his side through the mob of villainous scum who were enjoying the spectacle. I used my fist, my feet. I forgot my torn gut. I forgot everything but him, his agony, his pain.

He was lying there on the pavement and the cross was on top of him. I threw myself down beside him, and wormed myself half under it. I could smell him. He stank. Of sweat. Of terror. Of blood. Of despair.

I reared up, forcing that cross up off him. It weighed tons. It had all the weight of human misery embedded in it. It was loaded with all the sorrow there ever was in this world. I put my back to it. I stiffened my knees. My gut pulled apart. Inside me all the damned souls in Sheol screamed.

I got it up. Then a Roman soldier gave me the butt end of his lance in my belly's pit. I went down again, lay there gurgling bile and blood.

When I could move again, I saw that somehow Yeshu'a had got up again and was moving off, bearing his cross. I lay there fighting the death in me and watching a true miracle: the human spirit dominating death, a cadaver moving, walking, tottering over ground, under that crushing weight, upheld by whatever it is that defines manhood, clawed up by nerve-naked will from his guts, his testicles—or, if you prefer, sent down from heaven, by his father, God.

It wasn't enough. He went down again. They beat him and beat him and beat him. I could hear the blows. Dull. Sodden. Wet. Muffled by purpling flesh. Splattering all the pavement with his blood.

I got up. Don't ask me how. I heard a voice screaming:

"Bastards! Bastards! Sons of whores! Dung eaters! Offsprings of castrates cuckolded by apes! Fellatio artists! Ball-less wonders, who—"

Then I felt the raw rasping inside my throat and knew that voice was my own.

He couldn't get up. He couldn't. In another moment, crucifying him was going to be an anticlimax. So they stopped it.

"Hades," their decurion said. "If we beat him to death there'll be no fun in it. Here, you! You black-skinned bastard. Pick up his cross for him. You heard me! Or do you want a taste of the knout?"

The man was a Cyrenian, and as dark as Cyrenians usually are. Afterward I found out his name was Shimeon and that he had two sons called Alexander and Rufus. Anyhow, he was as strong as a bull. He carried that cross easily enough.

By that time, it had come to me that if I wasted my breath cursing those absolutely legitimate sons of Sin and Satan, the Romans, or provoked them into putting a *gladius* through my gut, I wasn't going to be able to do Yeshu'a very much good. So I got a grip on myself. I stopped thinking. I didn't ask myself how, in the name of Sheol and Gehenna both, a man as near death as Yeshu'a already was could be expected to stay alive hanging from a cross with the ropes stopping the circulation of his blood and the flies at him and his organs sagging down into his belly sac from their own weight, long enough for Shelom to get there with the soporific much less for us to get him down from there and into a tomb and out again and all the way to Khirbet Qumrân by road. I didn't ask myself that. Murdering hope wouldn't help anything either.

By the time we got to the Hill of the Stonings, Yosef ha Arimathæa was already there, standing by his horse, waiting. I didn't look at him or give any indication that I'd ever seen him before in my life. Instead, all the time, I kept looking around for Shelom, but I didn't see her. There was a group of women standing some distance away, but she wasn't among them. I should have recognized her if she had been with them. I did recognize Miriam the Migdalene. I couldn't make out her face; but her gestures were enough. I don't know why. Their vagueness, maybe. Their languor. I didn't know who the other women were. I only know who they weren't. They weren't the mothers of the banim Zebediah,[5] nor of Yaakob the Younger and Yosef, whoever those unknown gentlemen were supposed to be,[6] for the very simple reason that the mothers of men more than thirty years of age are generally too old to walk or even ride a donkey from Galilee to Jerusalem under a Nisan sun. And they most certainly weren't Yeshu'a's mother, nor the aunt I never even heard that he had, any more than I ever knew a family with so little inventiveness that they named *two* of their daughters Miriam.[7]

Don't ask me why I'm so sure. Ask your wife. Ask her what a woman and a mother would do at being told her son's being crucified? Ask her what she'd think of a woman who would or could, or even wanted to *watch* it? Many years later, during the anti-Jewish outbreaks at Alexandria, I saw just such a case, except they *made* that poor bitch watch it. She was stark raving mad two hours before her son finally died, and dead herself two days later. She only stopped screaming when she hadn't any voice left, and moaning after her last breath was gone. But that statue of tempered steel Iohannos—that was really his name—invented to represent poor Yeshu'a's mother in your Fourth Gospel stood there and—Ha! My mother-in-law, Miriam ha Yosef, had her share of faults. Maybe more than her share. But she wasn't a monster.

I saw the soldiers swarming all over Yeshu'a now. I didn't want to see it.

So I turned my back—and saw a pair of Yeshu'a bar Abbas' brigands hanging from crosses on the brow of the hill. I tried to turn away from that, too. But I couldn't. I stood there with my eyes stretched so wide they hurt, staring at them. They must have been there for quite some time, overnight, surely, because they'd already lost control and befouled themselves. Green stinking human dung slid slowly down the crosses between their bent legs. Their bellies were swollen tight as drums. Tongues the color and texture of three-day-old calf liver protruded from their mouths. Their penises dripped bloody urine. Their testicles were grossly swollen and had turned purple. Their hands and feet, beyond the places where the ropes bit flesh, were blue blobs. The flies explored every aperture, every hollow of their bodies.

Oh yes, these were the same men who, according to your Gospels, either taunted Yeshu'a from their crosses,[8] or disputed with one another in long and ringing sentences over his righteousness, and had Gan Eden promised one of them by him.[9] Theophilos, tell me: In the Unutterable, Unspeakable, Unknowable Name of God, what kind of lunatics wrote those Sacred Books of yours?

I was still staring at them when I heard those blows. Hammer blows. Then Yeshu'a screamed. Yes, the Only Begotten Son of God, Born of the Virgin Maria, screamed. And His Father up in Heaven was lucky. If the Romans had got their hands on Him, they'd have made Him scream his lungs up, too.

I turned with that scream vibrating in my gut like a hard driven blade. I saw what they were doing. They were *nailing*[10] him to that cross. I went crazy, then. Stark raving mad. I drew my dagger and started toward them. I don't know what, in the name of everything unholy, I thought I was going to be able to do with a dagger against a decuria of armed and armored Roman legionaries. But I drew it anyhow, and lurched forward. I didn't get there. I didn't even get close. For Shelom, who had come up the other side of the hill on a long, slanting diagonal, so that I hadn't seen her, put down the vase of drugged wine she was carrying very, very carefully, even choosing the flattest stretch of ground she could find to set it on, before racing toward me and throwing herself upon me like a wild thing.

We fought like a pair of savage dogs. It was a wonder I didn't kill her with that dagger I had in my hands. I started to; but at the last moment her face and my mind came clear.

"Nathan!" she moaned. "Oh Nathan Nathan Nathan Nathan Nathan!"

Then I sheathed the dagger and we stood there holding each other and rocking back and forth, and I heard those ditch-delivered sons of filth grunting and cursing, and that cross was swaying up, rising up, black against the sky, shutting out all the light there'd ever been in the world.

A few mattock and spade blows and they had it fixed in place. Shelomith's nails bit my flesh until they brought blood. She was gripping me like that, digging her claws into me and moaning like a gutted coursing hound bitch, but she wasn't looking at me. She was looking up to where he swung from that cross with his two matchlessly tender hands knotted and convulsed around the heads of those spikes. He was stark naked. The loin cloth your artists put on him in concession to your Christianoi conception of modesty wasn't an idea that appealed to those sons of whores and abominations, the Romans. He was very slim and fine and well made and beautiful and, all things considered, he was dying very well indeed.

I put up my hands and broke Shelom's grip.

"Get busy, you bitch!" I howled at her.

She turned me loose. Stood there, shaking. Then she took a deep breath and sort of—gathered herself together. Collected the pieces of her that were scattered all over Sheol by then into a kind of—integrity. That wasn't false. That was, I swear it, real. She wiped the tears from her eyes, the mad-from-suffering, rabid-with-grief bitch's foam from her mouth. Straightened up, strolled over to the decurion in charge of the crucifixion squad. He knew her, of course. Among those lecherous Roman swine, who didn't? I saw her fall easily into the practiced pantomimes of an old whore. The laughs. The winks. The teasing gestures. The playful pats. It was magical to watch. Her acting was glorious. She did it so well it made my torn gut ache.

She was obeying my instructions to the letter. And it was killing me. You see, I'd told her we couldn't counterfeit his death too soon. Some strong men last four days on a cross. The average, one and a half, to two. Some weak souls give up and die—of pure anguished terror, I think—within the hour. Yosef ha Arimathæa and I had calculated that three hours was the minimum that Pilatus would believe.

So I endured that horror. I wept, sweated, vomited blood. I died sixty times a minute for each of those three hours. I lost my manhood utterly. I behaved like an effeminate, like a woman: I shook, quavered, quaked, raved, babbled, screamed, tore the earth with frenzied fingers.

Then he opened his eyes, shook the maddening cloud of little, ferociously stinging green flies from about his head, and cried out loudly, terribly:

"My God, my God, why have you murdered me?"[11]

Yes, that's what I heard; and not a semipious quotation from Psalms. Not *lamah asabtani*, "forsaken", but *lamah sabachthani*, "slaughtered."

I hung there hearing that great cry lancing heavenward like a thunderbolt to knock little grimacing posturing useless imaginary God forever off his throne.

Then Yeshu'a whispered: "I thirst—"

As always, that matchless voice of his carried, unblurred even by his grossly swollen tongue. The decurion nodded to one of the legionaries. The soldier took a sponge, and started to dip it into a jar of that vinegary wine they always drink.

But Shelomith called out to him: "Wait! Give me the sponge. I have better. With lots of frankincense[12] in it. It will make it easier for him, the poor devil . . ."

"Why?" the decurion said. "Was he one of your lovers, Shelom?"

Shelomith looked up at Yeshu'a hanging there with the green flies at him.

"The best," she whispered, "absolutely the best. . . ."

"Ho!" the decurion said. "In virtue of that peerless distinction, you may ease him, my girl!"

Shelom took the sponge, squeezed it dry, dipped it into that close-to-lethal mixture the Essenes had given me. Then she gave it back to the soldier. He pushed the point of his lance[13] into it and held it up to Yeshu'a blackened, blood-crusted, enormously swollen lips. Yeshu'a sucked at it greedily, noisily. The exact second that amazingly powerful concoction hit his stomach, I saw his eyes glaze over. His head fell forward on his chest. He said nothing. Absolutely nothing at all.

I saw Yosef ha Arimathæa's robes flap as he swung himself up on his white Arabian. Then, old as he was, he pounded away at a hard gallop, bending over his horse's neck, riding like a desert wind, going on. That darkness that your scribes say was over the whole land by then, didn't bother him in the least, nor did that terrible earthquake with its splitting rocks and opening graves, for, being, like me, a rational man, he didn't even see them. And if any dead and risen saints got in his way, they were surely pounded back into their tombs by those flying hooves. As for the ripped Temple veil—Sheol! Why waste your time and mine refuting obvious nonsense, Theophilos, my friend? None of the wonders your *Besorahim* relate[14] happened; that's all. Believe me; I was there.

By then, it was hard upon the hour for the Korban Tamid, the evening sacrifices, and I saw one of the minor priests coming up the Hill of the Stonings. For despite your *Besorahim*, your Gospels, there were no priests, chief or otherwise, there; today being Pesach, they were all at home, engaged in meditation, ritual, and prayer; nor were there any "Elders" by which you seem to mean the lay members of the Sanhedrin; for in compliance with the Law, after eating Passover at sunset of the day before, they had not touched food or drink, nor left their houses; for our Law commands the judges who have condemned a man to death to fast and pray and mourn their victim during the whole of the day the execution takes place.[15]

The only reason the young priest had come was because his errand was urgent. Tomorrow was Shabbat. To have the bodies hanging there after sunset would be to profane it, since one minute after sunset, that Shabbat would begin. So now, he came not directly from the Temple but from the Prætorium. He'd already seen Pilatus, and bore a written order from the Procurator.

The decurion took the order, unrolled it, read it. He looked up with a gesture of disgust.

"Break their legs," he said.[16]

Shelom caught him by the arm, clung to him.

"Not him!" she said. "Not my poor sweet little old Yesu. I don't want him all broken up. Besides, can't you see he's dead?"

The decurion shoved her away from him, hard.

"Have to make sure, Shelom," he growled, "or the centurion will have the hide off my hairy ass in stripes. Here!" he said to a soldier. "Give me your *pilum*—"

He spoke to the soldier in Latin, so Shelom didn't understand him. But when she saw the soldier handing over his javelin, she hurled herself upon the decurion like a wild thing. He gave her the javelin shaft across the face so hard that she measured her length in the dirt beneath the cross. Then coolly, calmly, he plunged that javelin into Yeshu'a's side; and the last hope I had drained out of me like the blood and water that gushed from his side.

They broke those other two poor bastards' legs with sledgehammers, which caused them to swing with all their weight from arms. It was enough. Long before sunset, they were both dead.

But I wasn't there to see that by then. There was, of course, one more absolutely insupportable delay: the centurion of the Prætorian Guards came—sent by Pilatus himself, because that wily Iberian swine, logically enough, didn't believe that a man who had only been on a cross three hours was really dead[17]—to investigate the matter. One glance at that still, greenish-white, fly-infested body hanging there and the centurion snorted, went away to make his report. Shortly after that, Yosef came with his cart, bringing the winding sheet.

We—Yosef, his manservant, and I—took Yeshu'a down. I pulled those terrible spikes out of his hands and feet myself with pincers the Romans lent me. As we eased him down, my hand slid over his sweaty, blood-slimed flesh and I felt his heart.

It beat. Feebly, erratically, with many a pause; but it beat. It beat! Yosef saw the joy leaping and flaming in my eyes.

"Careful, son Nathan!" he said.

So, in order not to give the whole thing away, I endured the utter Sheol of having to drive those mules with funeral slowness to Yosef's burial place. Shelomith didn't come with us. She tried to, but the decurion yanked her back as she started toward the cart.

"Tonight you're mine, Shelom!" he said.

So she'd stood there beside him with a controlled grief, a suppressed despair in her eyes, more anguished, hurtful, bitter than any cry. She thought Yeshu'a was dead. And I couldn't tell her he wasn't. The decurion was from the *Cohors Sebastenorum,* which meant he was a Samaritan, and therefore Aramaic was his native language. To make it worse, all legionaries are forced to learn a rough sort of Greek in order to understand their officers who are usually Romans, Greek being the universal language then, as now. And Shelom's command of Latin was slight. So there was no way for me to tell her, no way at all.

Besides, the essential matter at that moment, it seemed to me, was keeping the flickering flame in Yeshu'a's poor broken body alight, not gladdening Shelom's heart. I was wrong. If, by sign or gesture, a quick squeeze of her hand, I had told her, I might have saved her life. But I didn't know that then.

I didn't know.

Chapter XXX

"SON NATHAN," Yosef ha Arimathæa said, "if you keep on beating the mules like that, they'll drop in their tracks long before we get to Qumrân. That is, if you don't overturn the cart first. Or start him bleeding again from all the jolting. Or—"

I pulled the mules up.

"Is he—?" I breathed.

"Alive? Yes," Yosef said; "just barely; but—yes."

I drove more slowly after that. We had left the manservant in the garden by the tomb. We wouldn't need him at Qumrân, and leaving him behind considerably reduced the load the mules had to draw. That was one thing. Another was that his not being there gave us the space to stretch Yeshu'a out full length, to make him more comfortable.

There was some hope. Not much, but some. You see, we'd been delayed again at the tombs, but that delay had proved an accidental blessing. For when we'd got to Yosef's garden tomb, we'd seen the women—Miriam of Migdal-Nunaya, Yohannah, the wife of Chuza, Antipas' steward, who had come up to Jerusalem with the Tetrarch's household to the Festival, the other Miriam, who your *Besorahim* say was the mother of Yaakob the Younger and Yosef, personages of whom I have no knowledge, and a certain Galilean woman called Shelomith, like my beloved—racing up the road after us, having followed us at a dead run all the way from the Hill of the Stonings to the garden.

So we'd had to take him into the tomb, and wait there with him until they'd left. Or else they'd have betrayed us, not out of malice, but out of the simple feminine inability to keep their mouths shut. Once we were inside the tomb with him, however, the venerable counselor produced the salves and medicines which, with wise foresight, he had already hidden in the tomb, and anointed and bandaged Yeshu'a's wounded side, and his nail-pierced hands and feet. The salves were Essene products, too. They seemed greatly to ease him, especially when, after washing my filthy hands, I gently rubbed his whip-torn back with them.

We followed the Jericho Road to the place where it forks, one branch of it looping north toward that populous town, and the other swinging south toward the Dead Sea. But we took neither. Instead we entered the Wady, the dried-up riverbed that leads straight down to Khirbet Qumrân. Then, as we were jolting over its stones, I heard him moan: "Tell them—tell them—"

I yanked back on the reins so hard that the mules almost reared. When they'd stopped prancing, I scrambled back over the seat to where Yosef already knelt by Yeshu'a's side.

"Yes, Yeshu'a, my son?" he was saying quietly.

Yeshu'a's voice subsided into a mumble. Then it rose again; came clear.

"Don't be afraid. Go take word to—to my—brothers—to go back to—Galilee. They'll see me there. I'll go. . . ."[1]

"Yeshu'a!" I groaned.

"Tell them—" he murmured; "tell them—"

"What?" Yosef said.

"To stay—to stay—in Jerusalem—until they are armed—with the power from above . . ."[2]

He was raving. I touched his forehead. It was like touching a brazier of live coals.

He caught my wrists with his poor, torn, hugely swollen, thickly bandaged hands, dragged himself half up. I don't know how he could have borne touching anything with them, much less closing them around my wrists, but he did it. His eyes bored into mine, blazing. But there was no mind behind them now, none at all.

"Shimeon bar Yonah," he grated, "do you love me more than all else?"

That hurt. That he didn't even know me, confused me with Kepha, I mean. I who had loved him with the only pure emotion I've ever felt in all my life, a feeling passing my love for women, hadn't meant enough to him for him to recognize me now. I swallowed the sick vileness rising in me, and answered him.

"Yes, Lord; you know I love you."

He smiled at me—a smile of pure, haunting, lyrical madness.

"Then feed my lambs," he whispered.

Yosef ha Arimathæa nodded to me meaningfully, scrambled forward, took the reins. We moved off.

Yeshu'a was silent; but he didn't let go of my wrists. Then he said it again, his voice soft and clear: "Shimeon bar Yonah; do you love me?"

I couldn't get it out. My tears were strangling me. But—for my want of faith, my failure of belief, at least—I had to. I owed him this act of abnegation, of love.

"Yes, Lord; you know I love you . . ." I said.

The light in his eyes was fading fast; I had to bend my ear to his mouth to hear his words.

"Then tend my sheep," he murmured. But almost immediately, a wave of strength surged through him; the last leap of the dying flame.

"Shimeon bar Yonah!" he cried out. "Do you love me?"

It wasn't to be borne. The pain, the grief inside me were themselves a kind of death.

"Master," I said, "you know everything. You know I love you."

He smiled. It was the most beatific smile I've ever seen.

"Feed—my—sheep," he said.

He lay there, breathing peacefully.

I am only human; he was clearly dying; I had to know what, if anything, I had meant to him. So I said: "And—Nathan, Rabbi? What of him?"

He opened his eyes, glared at me; said: "If it should be my will that he should wait until I come again, what's it to you, Kepha? Follow me!"[3]

Men say that's why I've lived so long, four score years now and more, with my wits undimmed. Some swear I shall never die. I hope they're wrong; I've seen too much of life to cling to it. Besides, I await him not; men don't return from death, that I know. But it was I, Nathan bar Yehudah, who was his Beloved Disciple, not that megalomaniacal fool who wrote the wildest of your *Besorahim*. I, who never followed him, who didn't even believe. Which is my justification and my glory. My hold on the only kind of immortality there is. For as long as men shall live, and memory have its seat in them, my name, for good or ill, will be forever linked with his.

He closed his eyes. His breathing slowed. I saw it—stop.

I screamed "Yeshu'a!" blazing his name across the sky in a high white splintering of pain; a wail of utter grief: "Yeshu'a!"

He opened his eyes, but not upon my face. He was gazing out upon —eternity, I suppose. He said, in a voice halfway between a whisper, and a sigh: "It is finished."[4]

And then, very quietly, he died.

We buried him in the cemetery of the Essenes at Khirbet Qumrân. Again their holy madness about the calendar served us well, for, to them, this was not the Shabbat, so they could bury him, perform some rarely moving rites, sing their weird and wondrous hymns above his grave. I stripped off my bloody, dust-covered clothing and put on an Essene robe of white in order to honor him. Afterward, I forgot to take it off and wore it back to Jerusalem. Which was why Miriam the Migdalene thought—but I go too fast. That can wait. Throughout the burial service, Yosef ha Arimathæa wept softly the kind of healing tears that are a balm to grief.

But I—I stood there dry-eyed, my heart a stone in me, and could not weep.

When it was over, and we started toward the cart to begin the long drive back to Jerusalem, Yosef saw how it was with me, and caught me by the arms.

"Cry, Nathan!" he said. "It's better for you. Go on—cry!"

But I couldn't. I simply couldn't.

He was an old man, but he shook me till my teeth rattled.

"Cry!" he said. "You hear me, Nathan! Cry!"

I moved my head from left to right very slowly in the gesture of denial. By then I couldn't even speak.

He hit me then, open-palmed across the mouth. Again. Again. A blinding unbroken linked chain of blows, jerking my head from side to side upon my neck until at last the tears exploded, jetted from my eyes. They watered the earth. And saved my mind, my life.

Then I was kneeling before Rab Yosef, embracing his bony knees, my face buried in the rich stuff of his fringed robe, and crying in a way I hadn't cried since I was a child, weeping with all of me, eyes, body, spirit, heart, and voice.

He raised me up, took me in his arms. I clung to him as though he were my father—no! as though he were my Uncle Hezron—and poured out my bottomless, abysmal, utterly inconsolable grief.

He had to drive. I only stopped crying when my eyes were scalded blind; when I could squeeze out not one more single tear.

By then, Jerusalem was in sight; and it was the dusk of that Shabbat Day.

I wouldn't let him take me home; he was too old, too exhausted by then. In me, strangely, some strength remained, or had returned during that long ride back from Qumrân to the Holy City. I got out at his door, and walked the rest of the way home.

I've told you, I think, that to reach my father's house coming from Yosef ha Arimathæa's, I had to cross one of the worst districts in the Holy City. Above three quarters of all the serious crimes of Jerusalem were committed there. A stranger, even dressed as I was, in the white priestly Essene robe I'd forgot to take off, risked his life by merely passing through.

But I was not thinking about the peril that I ran. I didn't even see those streets. I wasn't aware of the rats as big as puppies that scurried, squealing between my feet as I passed. I didn't even smell the quarter's habitual odor: a stench vile enough to turn the stomach of a goat. Instead I reeled through those tortuous cobblestoned alleys, slipping on their rich compost of mud and human dung, keeping my direction by sheer instinct, until a man came out of the shadows and took my arm.

I tried to pull free of him, but he held me in an iron grip. So I dropped my other hand toward the hilt of my dagger—or rather, toward where my dagger would have been if I hadn't forgot and left it at Khirbet Qumrân with my normal robes. But he couldn't see whether I wore a blade or not; and, anyhow, even if I had his voice would have stopped me. The anguish in it. The pain past human bearing. The intolerable grief.

He said quietly. "Later, Nathan. That is, if I don't save you the trouble. But now, you've another thing to do. More important than killing me."

I raised my eyes to his face. I didn't scream at him, call him traitor, filthy swine, bring up my two hands and make my fingers bite into his throat until I'd strangled him. Instead, I said, with a calm that matched his own, that was, like his, compounded of utter weariness, total grief: "What would you have me do, my brother?"

"You call me that still?" Yehudah ish Kriyoth said.

"Yes. All the damned are brothers, Yehudah. You, because you betrayed him; I, because I failed him. So tell me, Brother Bastard, Brother Swine, Brother Cain, what thing?"

He said: "It's Shelom, Nathan. We've got to save her. She's killed a Roman."

It wasn't very far. A house, like all the others in that quarter, shabby, filthy, nondescript. We came up to the door. It was half opened. Ish Kriyoth looked down, and a trembling got into him. He shook all over like a tamarisk caught in a rising gale. I could see his face clearly in the lamplight that came through the half-opened door. I have never seen anything more terrible or more pitiful in this world.

I said: "What in black Samaël's name—"

And stopped. The trembling had got into me, too. For a solid sheet of blood was flowing like a black scarlet river out that door. I stepped into it, splashing it about my ankles, as I had to, in order to get into that room. Stopped, just inside that door, doubled in half, added a libation of my own to that sanguine inundation, poured out from my grief-shredded gut, in a thick, hot, vile-tasting rush, a little more of my life. Then, half turning—to get out of there, I think, to run like a rat, to flee—I saw Yehudah's lips tear open, his head arch back, and I whirled upon him, clamping my hands over his mouth in time to stifle the scream that would have ruined everything, that would have brought the City Guards pounding down upon us to demand explanations which never in this life would they have believed.

It was that, I'm sure, which saved me. The necessity for action, I mean. A man seldom loses his mind while he's doing something. To go crazy, you have to have time to contemplate what's beyond bearing or even belief; you have to be still long enough for it to enter you, to shred your mind along the screaming network of your nerves. Fortunately for me, for what was left of my sanity by then, I had no time. Not even that required for going stark raving mad.

The decurion's armor lay in that mess on the floor. His cloak and tunic were tossed across a chair. He, or rather his cadaver, lay on the bed. The blood on the floor hadn't come from him. Shelomith had killed him with a single, wonderfully expert thrust to the base of his throat that hadn't even bled much. After he'd got what he'd paid for, to judge from the semen stains on the sheets.

Shelom, herself, was sitting in a chair, facing me. She was stark naked, so I could see it. The Zealots' punishment. What they do to our women who lie with Romans. Only she'd done it herself. Or tried to. She'd pushed that knife into her navel, and then hacked and sawed downward until—

I can't. There's no way to say it. And I wouldn't, if I could.

She was still shoving feebly against the handle of the knife. Do you know what that took? Or what it meant? Think about it. About what life, fate, necessity, even your eyeless, faceless, blind, three-headed son-sacrificing cannibalistic monster of a god had done to her by then that she should hate herself, loathe her glorious body so.

I yanked that sheet from under the decurion's corpse. Pulled Shelom's hands away from the knife, drew it out, dropped it to the floor, stuffed half that sheet—semen stains and all—into her, into the rent that she had made. I wrapped the rest of it around her. It and the other one and the decurion's cloak. Picked her up, walked out of there.

Shelom was a big girl. I staggered under her weight. Ish Kriyoth touched my arm.

"Give me her feet," he said.

We walked with her like that, through the sleeping city. With Yeshu'a, himself, leading the way, guiding and protecting us, surely.

There is no other explanation. How else could two men have carried a dying woman across half Jerusalem without meeting a single soul? It was night, of course. But that doesn't explain it. Nothing does.

Before she died, she spoke to me. She said: "Nathan—"

And I: "Shelom—"

"I'm—cold—Nathan . . . I'm so—awful—cold—"

I said: "Shelom, I love you. I always have. I always will. Nobody else—ever—no other woman in this world—ever—not even—"

I stopped, listened. Heard only the echoes of my insane, futile—truths.

"Stop trying to comfort her," Yehudah said harshly. "Can't you see she's dead?"

"But why, Yehudah?" I screamed at him. "In God's Name, why?"

He shook his head, said slowly, softly: "There aren't any whys, Nathan. We're creatures of blind accidentality, born of a mother named Absurdity, who lay down for a chance passerby called Confusion while she was drunk. We were delivered in a stinking ditch by a midwife known as Folly. And we die from God's boredom with us, from His forgetfulness that we exist, that is, if He ever knew, which I doubt, by the neglect of heaven—how would I know? Shelom was—beautiful and all men loved her except the man she loved, and him she couldn't have. So now I'm glad I got rid of that pious bastard so he couldn't go on wrecking—"

"Not that!" I cried. "Why did she—that is, if you even know—why did she—"

"Lie with the decurion? Or kill him, which?" Yehudah said.

"Both," I whispered. "Do you know why, Yehudah?"

"Of course I know! She told me. She opened her glorious thighs to that armored lump of filth because it didn't seem to matter. Nothing did. Not even the preservation of the renewed virtue—I was going to say *virginity*, but that's too much, isn't it?—that Yeshu'a had bestowed upon her seemed to matter with him gone. And she killed the decurion, slew that peerless representative of Imperial Glory because the bastard boasted about poking his lance into poor Yeshu'a. Said to her, 'You and your friends thought you'd get him down alive, didn't you? Filled him up with that dream juice to make us think he'd had his, and then—'"

"And then?" I whispered.

"She killed him. That's when I found her. Just after she'd stuck the uncircumcised swine. He was already dead, but she hadn't done anything to herself, yet. Hadn't split—"

"Yehudah!" I shrieked; but he went on imperturbably.

"—her poor little tripes out of her belly like a butchered she-goat. Not then. I tried to get her to come away with me. I swore by my mother's honor I wouldn't touch her, that all I wanted to do was to get her the Sheol away from Jerusalem before the Romans found out. But she said, 'I wouldn't puke on you now, you treacherous bastard!' and pulled that knife out of his neck and started for me with it. So I got out of there. I was going to your house to look for you because I figured that if any man living could talk some sense into her it was you, but you saved me the trouble by passing by. So now—"

"Now?" I said to him. "What do you plan to do, Yehudah? With all the rest of your life, I mean?"

"Live it," he said. "Can you think of anything worse, my brother?"

I couldn't, so we moved off, carrying that dead thing that didn't even look like it had been Shelom anymore, down that silent street, through that quiet night.

We laid her in the tomb that my father had had carved out for me. Yehudah and I pushed the stone door shut. Then I stood there looking at him. At the Betrayer. And my brother even in that. For, had I not betrayed Helvetia, Lydia, Claudia Procula, Pilatus, Shelomith, my religion, and my race? What man alive has no black treason in his heart? Whose hands are clean enough to lift the avenging stone? But I didn't say anything to him; nor he, to me. Not even goodbye.

I stood there, watching him lope away like a red-bearded, shaggy wolf. I never saw him again after that hour; but I believe in my heart of hearts that Yeshu'a forgave him. Because, afterward, his fortunes changed vastly for the better. A year or two later, he married Martha bath Bœzer, who had both become a widow and retained her inexplicable fondness for him. His father-in-law took him back into the counting house, and he became one of the wealthiest men in Jerusalem. Martha gave him many sons. I think he and his whole family perished during the siege of the Holy City by Titus. But I don't know that. I, Yohannah, and our brood had left Judea long before then.

Oh yes, I know your Gospels say he died by his own hand, hanged himself[5] after having returned the thirty pieces of silver I never even heard of, which your scribes derived from the two places in the Holy Writ where thirty shekels are laid down as the price of a slave.[6] But then, another of your Sacred Writings says he bought a field with the thirty shekels, and fell into it so hard that his belly burst open and his guts spilled out onto the earth, which is why they named that field Aceldamah, "Bloody Acre."[7] It takes no special cleverness to see that they didn't *know* what happened to Yehudah ish Kriyoth, to my Brother in Sorrow, that what they have set down is what they hoped would happen to him, their sick, impotent desire of vengeance, fleshed out in empty words. The other two writers of your *Besorahim,* your Gospels, have been, in this case, more honest; for you will note they have kept silent, thus clearly admitting their ignorance.[8]

No. Yehudah ish Kriyoth lived out his days, for which I pity him. I should not like to have had to go to bed at night, rise up in the morning, live and have my being day in day out through many years with what he must have had in his mind, his heart. Have none of you lived enough to know that it is death that is merciful, not life?

I sat there beside my own tomb-become-Shelomith's the rest of the night. I didn't pray. What could I have said to God except to reproach Him for His abysmal indifference, his abominable cruelty?

Then I got up and started home. I've told you, I think, that the tombs my father had had carved out for us were very near that of Yosef ha Arimathæa, for the simple reason that the old necropolis under the Hill of Olives[9] no longer had space for newcomers. Dumb with weariness, numb with grief, I started out, and, quite by accident, passed by the tomb in which we'd laid Yeshu'a's bleeding body for an hour.

And it was then and there that I saw Miriam of Migdal-Nunaya, whom you call the Magdalene.

I started to go on by her; because the horror and the grief in me were a kind of death, the weariness, a stone; but then I saw her face, heard the terrible way she cried. So, fool that I am, I stopped and said to her: "Don't weep so, child. What will weeping serve for now?"

She turned her madwoman's eyes upon me, and howled: "They've taken my Lord away, and I don't know where they have laid him!"

"Dear child—" I began softly.

"You!" she screamed. "You stole him, hid him away! Tell me where you've laid him so that I—"

Then she saw that white Essene robe I'd forgot I still had on, and raised her eyes to my face. Her whole expression changed. Her eyes caught the rising sun and threw all its light back in a reflected glow that was both a wonder and a glory. She sank to her knees, clasped her hands together in the attitude of prayer.

"Miriam!" I said.

"Rabbi!"[10] she whispered; and hurled herself upon me, clasping my knees.

"Turn me loose!" I shouted. "You crazy fool, don't cling to me like that!"

She obeyed me at once. She got up, stared at me, her beautiful eyes swimming with mad devotion, madder faith.

"You have—risen," she said quietly. Then she whirled and ran, screaming: "He has risen! Our Lord has risen! Come see! Here he is— my Master and my God!"

I wasn't going to wait around to see madness compounded into folly. I slipped away on a diagonal, away from the road that led to the tombs. As I did so I saw Shimeon Kepha and that young Pharisee priest—who had surrendered his heart to Yeshu'a in the Temple courts that same day his colder fellows had destroyed your Lord with that question about Cæsar's taxes, had become a devoted follower, and afterwards wrote the few short simple pages that the madman you call Iohannos has expanded, and changed into the most insane of your *Besorahim*— racing toward the tomb. But it never occurred to me what the result of an insane woman's hysteria was going to be. It didn't occur to me at all.

I went home, bathed myself, called for some fruit, a little wine. I ate the fruit, drank the wine. After that, I sent my manservant to the house Claudia had given me to warn those eleven pious idiots not to stir out of doors until Nisan Twenty-Second, when they could mingle with the crowds of pilgrims who would then be going home from the Festival, and thus escape the City without too great danger. Kepha's folly at letting himself be seen by daylight because crazy Miriam had screamed out nonsense was what reminded me to send my man to tell them that.

All that week, I rested. It surprised me that I could. But, in a way, Shelom's death, terrible as it was, had lifted a burden from my heart. She had suffered all her adult life, suffered abominably; even at the end she had chosen to die in an obscenely hideous excess of pain. But she was beyond all suffering now, beyond the boredom, tedium, the mindless, meaningless, ugly process we call life, in which one studies to make one's head ache, packs one's gut to defecate, drinks to urinate, copulates to beget continuity of one's private madness, to prolong human misery another thirty years in time. My glorious Shelomith, whom I had never really possessed in the flesh, and because I hadn't would keep forever unsullied in my heart, was dead. Dead and, presumably, at peace. At least I no longer had to worry what would become of her, or picture her grown old, her beauty gone, palsied and diseased, begging a crust of strangers at the Temple gate. Cruel as it indisputably was, her death remains—a mercy. I wonder if death isn't always the only true sign of compassion we ever get from that incorporeal absentee landlord that we call God. . . .

Twice during that week, I dreamed of Yeshu'a. Each time in my dreams, in some strange, gentle, wordless way, he comforted me. The difference between me and your Holy Apostles was that I knew I was dreaming. Even so, it helped. The agony in my gut quieted. The little I managed to eat, stayed down.

On the night before the morning they were to leave for Galilee, the Eleven sent Toma—called Didymus, the Twin, because he had had a brother born the same hour as he who hadn't lived[11]—to invite me to sup with them in fellowship. Now it so happened that I had already decided to go back to Galilee with them, for even my mother agreed that it was far safer for me to go back to Uncle Hezron's place for a year or two, what with the Romans turning the whole thieves and harlots' quarter upside down in their efforts to find out who had murdered the decurion and his paramour—for so they logically enough interpreted all the plentiful evidence Yehudah and I had left behind—and what had become of her body, and whether the whole bloody business were not a Zealot conspiracy. Besides, I was longing to see Yohannah, and dreading to, at one and the same time. Longing to, because I loved her; but dreading our meeting, because even the thought of having to put what had happened to Yeshu'a into words was enough to make me ill unto death. But I hadn't told the Eleven I was going back with them, so I should have joined them that night, anyhow, even if they hadn't sent Didymus.

Seeing him there in the doorway, instead of safely in hiding as he should have been, I cursed him, roundly.

"You fool!" I roared: "Don't you realize that if the Romans—"

"They won't take me, master," he said solemnly. "I am under the protection of Our Risen Lord—"

"Risen!" I said. "What kind of tomfool—" Then I remembered. "Miriam—Miriam Migdalene. That's it, isn't it, Toma?"

He shrugged his shoulders in the wry, doubtful way he had, and said: "She's crazy. Always has been, always will be. I'd never believe her—"

"Then who do you believe, Toma?" I said.

"Kleopah, sort of," Toma said. Then he launched into a long tale about how Kleopah, one of Yeshu'a's disciples, not, of course one of the Eleven, but one of the two-hundred-odd disciples, men and women, who had followed your Lord up from Galilee, had gone to the village of Emmaus with another of that band—for unlike the Eleven Apostles, these people couldn't be identified so easily and hence were in no great danger—and had encountered a stranger who had spent the whole day in their company, and part of the evening, too; but when they sat down to sup, they finally recognized him as Yeshu'a risen from the grave.[12]

"Now Miriam didn't have anything to do with *that*," Toma said; "and Kleopah is a sober man who—"

"Has been under the same nerve-racking strain as all of us," I said quietly, "and is nowise proof against contagious galloping hysteria, Toma. Besides he'd walked sixty stadia that day, according to you. A long way for a man his age. So he and his friend spent the whole day with this stranger, and *only* after they'd sat down to supper, and had taken a cup of wine or two or three or four, did they recognize the Lord they'd been following about for months. Come now, Toma! You, at least, I didn't think were so big a fool . . ."

Toma stared at me. A thoughtful frown tightened his forehead.

"You're right, master," he said; "I didn't believe it. I don't yet, I suppose. I told them that. I swore I wouldn't believe it until I touched the nail holes in his hands and feet, thrust my fingers into the lance wound in his side,[13] but they jawed at me so much that I said I did, but—"

"But come on, Toma. Time's awasting, Twin to Folly," I said.

We got to the house. Nathaniel bar Talmay let us in, and locked the door behind us. The others crowded around. Yaakob and Yohannan bar Zebediah, the Boane Ragsha, and Shimeon Kepha embraced me. Then as the others filed by one by one, took my arm, kissed my cheek, I saw that I had become something very special to them; the only man they knew and could talk to, who had witnessed their Lord's death upon the cross. It was intensely moving; too much so. Therefore when they began, "Tell us, Nathan, our beloved brother, how the Lord—" I waved them off.

"Later, after we have supped," I said.

But, when we entered that room where last we'd all broke bread with him on the night of his betrayal by ish Kriyoth, our memories were a weight, a felt presence, almost palpable upon the quiet air. They fell silent, dreaming. Then Shimeon Kepha leaped up from his chair, overturning it in his haste, and fell to his knees, tears streaming from his eyes.

"Master!" he sobbed and stretched out his arms toward—vacancy, toward nothing.

The others stared at him with troubled eyes, then one by one, Kepha's, Petros', madness, self-induced illusion, faith, mind-destroying love—call it what you will—communicated itself to them. I could hear the sodden thump of knees striking the floor, smell the sudden stench of armpit sweat as they stretched out their arms toward—that phantom, that fantasy created out of their love, their loss—until only Toma-Didymus and I remained on our feet, amid that kneeling, bobbing, weeping herd.

Then it happened. Toma's face went white. I saw him stumble forward, crash to his knees, put out his hands and run his fingers with aching tenderness, with a delicacy beyond that of women even, over the thin insubstantial air, thrust one forefinger forward, trembling, trembling to plunge it into—emptiness. His voice was the pure soprano of a bride experiencing orgasm as he gasped, wailed, shrieked: "My Lord and my God!"

I started to shout at them: "You fools! You hysterical pack of bearded women! I saw him die! I helped bury him with these two hands! He's not in that tomb because Yosef ha Arimathæa and I bore him away! The man that your Miriam with seventy-times-seven devils in her addled head saw was me! I tell you—"

But I didn't. It was too—beautiful. I realized I was in the presence of a miracle. The miracle of a love so strong that nothing could overcome it. Certainly not dull truth, plain, unlovely fact. The world without him was too empty, too desolate. So they—who loved him more than life—brought him back. And, as I told you once before, I think, upon that matchless act of love all your Faith is built.

But I—I could not join them, find him again. He had fled me much too far. The ugly details of his death were etched forever on the backs of my eyes by the acid of my tears. I had seen his bluish, greenish, so terribly dead body laid in the earth. And, like Yehudah ish Kriyoth, my brother, I am a Judean. I lack your Galilean's divinely muddled head.

I envied them. But my envy had no malice in it. I couldn't spoil their miracle for them. I took the key off the cupboard, went down the hall, unlocked the door, stole out into the warm and starry night.

Over my head a meteor blazed, trailing white fire across the dark. Far to the north it seemed to pause, to hang motionless on the sky before it flared up, burned out, disappeared. To the north. Over Galilee.

Perhaps, I thought, it's a sign. Perhaps now the Mashiah will come at last. Perhaps that little lump of Gehenna's fire I squeezed off into Yohannah will be—

I tried to smile at the thought. But my mouth hurt, having lost the use of it. I didn't know the feel of smiling anymore. I'd forgot how.

I tried and tried, but it wouldn't come. It was, I realized, much too soon. I'll learn to again, I thought. To manage smiling. To achieve laughter. To recover that dimly remembered thing called joy. But for now, to go on—upon my own resources. Upon my shredded gut. Without Mashiahs who never come. Without a father god who's never there.

So thinking, I mounted Bedu, and moved off slowly through the soft and flowering night. Northward toward Galilee where Yohannah waited with my son quickening inside her womb by now. My son. My continuation in time. My feeble grasp upon immortality. My little Yeshu'a. For I was going to call him by that lovely and awful name as was fitting, right, and just.

Thus set I out, following my star to begin—another legend.

Notes

GENERAL TERMINOLOGY

THE WRITER uses B.C.E. and C.E. to mean Before the Common Era and the Common Era, respectively. The conventional symbols B.C. and A.D. seem to him a bit presumptuous. Yeshu'a ha Notzri is not the Christ to millions of quite civilized people, nor Our Lord to uncounted millions more. Besides, the expression "Common Era's" clear implication that Christianity's unceasing efforts to commit patricide upon the faith that spawned it have so far failed, pleases him!

Bible sources: In general the source of New Testament quotations is *The New English Bible New Testament* (abbreviated NEB), Oxford and Cambridge University Presses, 1961. For Old Testament quotations, the Roman Catholic *Jerusalem Bible* (abbreviated JB), 1966, is the prevailing source; in a very few cases, where the beauty of the language takes precedence over the accuracy of the translation, the *King James Version* (KJV) is used. The reasoning behind this general preference is that, while both the NEB and the JB have excellent translations of the New Testament, the JB, in occasional verses, introductory sections, and footnotes, reveals the unscholarly influence of church dogma: It asserts that Yohannan ben Zebediah (John, the son of Zebedee), an illiterate Galilean fisherman, wrote the stately and majestic language of the Gospel According to St. John; that Mattathiah the Publican wrote the Gospel of Matthew as we now have it; and that Loukas the Physician wrote the Gospel According to St. Luke, instead of—as is far more probable—its having been written by younger disciples of his, from his notes.

In the frequent references to Josephus (*The Jewish Antiquities, The Jewish War*), Roman numerals stand for books or volumes, and Arabic numerals for sections or paragraphs, not pages.*

---

* Josephus, *The Jewish Antiquities, The Jewish War,* Loeb Classical Library, Cambridge: Harvard Univ. Press, 1955.

NOTES

CHAPTER I

1. The Mediterranean Sea.
2. Since the 9th century c.e., this has been replaced by the *Simchat Torah*.
3. That is, in 161 b.c.e. See Emil Schürer, *A History of the Jewish People in the Time of Jesus* (New York: Schocken Books, 1961), p. 41.
4. Schürer, *op. cit.*, pp. 34–35, describes how Shimeon ben Mattathiah, one of the five Maccabees, led all the Jews out of Galilee in the summer of 163 b.c.e., after having won many victories there, thus leaving that province completely Gentile.
5. Aristoboulos was the grandson of Shimeon ben Mattathiah (one of the original five Maccabees) and the son of Yohannan, known to us as John Hyrcanus I (135–105 b.c.e.). Aristoboulos' forcible conversion of the Gentiles of Galilee to Judaism in 105-104 is perhaps the reason for the Galileans' outrageously bad Aramaic (see Matt. 26:73–74) and for the suspicion with which the people from that province were regarded by other Jews.

CHAPTER II

1. The writer permits himself to wonder *what* name: Yosef ben Yaakob, as in Matt. 1:16, or Yosef ben Heli, as in Luke 3:27?
2. April. We do not know when Yeshu'a ha Notzri (Jesus of Nazareth) was born. Will Durant, in his monumental *Caesar and Christ* (New York: Simon and Schuster, 1944), pp. 557–558, has the best concise discussion of the difficulties confronting the general reader. The year is impossible to arrive at: Matt. 2:1 and Luke 1:5 both say he was born in the days when Herod was King of Judea, that is, before 4 b.c.e., as Herod the Great died that year. They are indirectly supported in this by John 8:57, which implies that Yeshu'a was in his forties at the time of his crucifixion, as he'd have to be if he were born during Herod's reign. But then St. Luke contradicts himself by saying that Yeshu'a was about thirty years old when Yohannan bar Zachariah, called Baptistes (John the Baptist), baptized him in the fifteenth year of the reign of Tiberius, which we know from Roman historians was 28–29 c.e., thus making his birthdate 2 b.c.e. And St. Luke goes on to compound confusion by linking his birth to the census decreed by Augustus when Quirinius was Governor of Syria. But we know from the Roman historians and from Flavius Josephus (*The Jewish Antiquities,** XVII:355, XVIII:1–2, and notably XVIII:26, in which Josephus clearly states that the census took place thirty-seven years after Caesar defeated Antony at Actium, on September 2, 31 b.c.e.) that Publius Sulpicius Quirinius was sent out to Syria in 6–7 c.e.
   The problem of the month is similar. Clement of Alexandra, writing *circa* 200 c.e. (see Durant, *loc. cit.*), quotes chronologists of his own times as giving April 19 and May 20; Clement himself gives November 17, 3 b.c.e. But that Yeshu'a was not born on December 25 is absolutely certain. This festival, the celebration of the winter solstice (actually December 23, the ancient calculations being two days in error) was borrowed, as were nearly all Christianity's festivals, from paganism; in this case, specifically from Mithraism, in which it was the *natalis invicti solis*, the "birthday of the unconquered sun."
3. This Herod, by allowing his brother Antipas to steal his wife Herodias, was the indirect cause of Yohannan Baptistes' execution.
4. See Josephus, *Antiquities*, XIV:158–160, for an account of the arrest of the Zealot Hezekiah, and XIV:168–180 for the description of Herod before the Sanhedrin.

* Hereafter referred to as *Antiquities*.

5. Josephus, *Antiquities*, XVII:174–179, gives the story of Herod's order to his sister and his brother-in-law to murder the prominent prisoners; and XVII:193–194 tells of their disregarding the order after his death. The list of Herod's crimes is also from Josephus, both *Antiquities* and *Jewish War*.

6. The best account of these events is to be found in Schürer, *op. cit.*, pp. 176–177.

7. In *Antiquities*, XVIII:26, Josephus says that Quirinius deposed Joazar ben Bœthus from the high priesthood. But in *Antiquities* XVII:339, he states that Archelaus deposed Joazar. It is impossible to reconcile the two statements.

CHAPTER III

1. Josephus, *Antiquities*, XVIII:35–38.

2. The month of Tishri in the Jewish lunar calendar is usually, but not always, our October. To give three recent examples, which the reader can easily check for himself:

In the Jewish Perfect Year 5709 (1948–1949 C.E.), Tishri began October 4 and ended November 2; hence we might say that in that year, Tishri was October. In the Jewish Regular Year 5718 (1957–1958 C.E.), Tishri began September 26 and ended October 25, so again we might call it largely October, although it had four days of September and lacked six days of October. However, in the Jewish Leap Year 5717 (1956–1957 C.E.), Tishri began September 6 and ended October 5, so in that year Tishri was September. The same variation, of course, can occur with any Jewish month in relation to the Occidental calendar. For leap years, because the Jewish calendar adds a thirteenth month, Ve-Adar, of twenty-nine days, between Adar and Nisan, the months which follow Adar vary even more widely, though this is somewhat compensated for by the fact that leap years usually begin from two weeks to a month earlier than normal ones.

CHAPTER IV

1. The Capernaum of the Gospels.
2. Ps. 137:5–6.
3. Exod. 20:3–5.
4. The other two were Puteoli and Portus.
5. Drama festivals, under the Caesars, held fifty-five times a year.
6. Tiberius expelled the Jews in the year 19 C.E. Later, about 31 C.E., convinced that he had been misled by Sejanus, he called them back and granted them religious freedom.

CHAPTER VII

1. There is a long passage in Josephus, *Antiquities*, XVIII:90–95, from which Schürer, *op. cit.*, p. 202, deduces—correctly, this writer thinks—that the High Priest's role had been in Roman custody since the year 6 C.E.

2. Joseph Klausner, *Jesus of Nazareth* (New York: Macmillan, 1925), p. 81, quotes both Karl Friedric Bahrdt (1741–1792), *Ausführung des Plans und Zwecks Jesu*, and Karl Heinrich Venturini (1758–1849), *Natürliche Geschichte des Grossen Propheten von Nazareth*, as being of the opinion that Joseph of Arimathæa was an Essene. Since the Essenes were famous for their medical skill, the two German scholars saw in Joseph the essential link upon which their theory of a natural explication of the Resurrection could be built.

3. For an explanation of the origin of the term "Sons of Zadok," the reader is referred to II Sam. 8:17 and Ezek. 40:46.

4. Pliny the Elder, *Historia naturalis*, Book V, Chapter 17, says in part: ". . . for there flock to them [the Essenes] from afar many who, wearied of battling with the rough seas of life, drift into their system . . ." And Josephus,

Jewish War, II:136: "They [the Essenes] display an extraordinary interest in the writings of the ancients, singling out in particular those which make for the welfare of the soul and body; with the help of these and with a view to the treatment of disease, they make investigations into medicinal roots and the properties of stones."

CHAPTER VIII

1. Josephus tells us, with an excess of detail that proves the custom unusual, that the Essenes were required to defecate into a trench they dug into the earth with their little mattocks, at the same time wrapping their mantles about them "so as not to offend the rays of the deity [the sun?]." Afterwards, they covered their individual latrines with earth and washed themselves, this last being an especial cause of wonder to Josephus! (*Jewish War*, II:145–149.)

2. Ps. 8:3–4.

3. Let the reader amuse himself finding these verses in Psalms.

4. The interpretation of Essene terms is impossibly difficult; there is conflict between recognized and authoritative Hebraists over their meanings, and we are unsure if they all denote separate offices or were sometimes combined under one man. Therefore the writer has chosen from among the various conflicting translations those which seem to him logical. He cannot vouch for the accuracy of his choice.

5. *Mebaqqer* is the Hebrew word usually rendered in Greek as *opiskopos*, and in English as *bishop*. But an Essene *Mebaqqer* was not a bishop in our terms. He was the head of the *Edah*, "assembly," *qahal*, "party," *esah*, "council," *yahad*, "community," all of which may or may not mean the same group, and might even represent various subdivisions thereof. G. Vermes, *The Dead Sea Scrolls in English* (Harmsworth, Middlesex, England: Penguin Books Ltd., 1962) renders *Mebaqqer* as "guardian." But there was also a *Mebaqqer al melekheth ha rabbin*, literally, "overseer of the works of the congregation," who also may or may not have been the same official. Vermes, who thinks this was a second official, translates it, not without humor, as "bursar." Again, the *Paqid*, "inspector," may also have been the same man as the *Mebaqqer*.

6. For a concise but clear account of the esoteric lore of the Essenes, see John Allegro, *The Dead Sea Scrolls, A Reappraisal* (Harmsworth, Middlesex, England: Penguin Books Ltd., 1966), pp. 126–127.

7. The Dead Sea is far below sea level, which accounts for the intense heat found there all year round.

8. In the complex Jewish lunar calendar, Shebat and Adar correspond usually but not always to January and February, while Ab and Elul in most years are roughly July and August.

9. *Melis* appears to mean "interpreter," presumably of the fine points of the Law, which makes this office difficult to distinguish from *Doresh ha Torah*, "Expositor of the Law." *Maskîl* should mean "master" or "teacher," but Theodore H. Gaster, *The Dead Sea Scriptures in English Translation* (New York: Doubleday, Anchor Books, 1956), p. 44, says: "It is not quite certain what the Hebrew word *Maskîl* means in these contexts." Again (see Nos. 4 and 5), it is impossible to determine these meanings with accuracy.

10. Gaster, *op. cit.*, pp. 169–170.

11. Vermes, *op. cit.*, p. 184.

12. Tacitus, *Historia*, Vol. 6: ". . . *fugit cruorem vestemque infectam sanguine quo feminae per menses exsolvuntur.*" See also Josephus, *Jewish War*, IV:476–480.

13. *Antiquities*, XVIII:55–62.

14. "Procurator" in Greek, which was what the people of Judea, who rarely had any knowledge of Latin, called the Roman official.

15. Deut. 32:41–43.

16. Such is the description of Pilate attributed to Agrippa I by Philo. See *De Legatione ad Caium*, Sec. 38, ii:590.

17. This version of Pilate's career is taken from Giovani Rosadi, *The Trial of Jesus*, Chapter XVI, as quoted by Hyman E. Goldin, in *The Case of the Nazarene Reopened* (New York: Exposition Press, 1948), p. 696.

18. *Cf.* ". . . he [Yaakob/James] used to enter alone into the Temple, and to be found kneeling and praying for the forgiveness of the people so that his knees grew hard like a camel's because of his constant worship of God, kneeling and asking forgiveness of the sins of the people." Hegesippus, 180 C.E., as quoted in Eusebius, *Historia Ecclesiastica*, Vol. II, 23, pp. 165–68. Yaakob, whom we know as James the Just, afterward became first Bishop of the Church at Jerusalem.

19. This is a pure hypothesis on the part of the present writer. It cannot be sustained historically. But it does have one great virtue: If Yeshu'a followed the Essene/Jubilees calendar, the conflict between the Synoptic Gospels and John over the day of the Last Supper and the Trial and Crucifixion disappears. Allegro, *op. cit.*, points this out very convincingly on p. 128 and pp. 165–166.

20. "They occupy no one city, but settle in large numbers in every town." Josephus, *Jewish War*, II:124.

21. "There are some among them who profess to tell the future, being versed from their early years in holy books, various forms of purification, and apophthegma of prophets; and seldom, if ever, do they err in their predictions." Josephus, *Jewish War*, II:159. See also *Jewish War*, I:78; II:113; and *Antiquities*, XIII:311 for examples of successful Essene prophecies. The Essenes' interest in, and possession of, a body of esoteric lore dealing with the art of prophecy has been fully confirmed by the Qumrân discoveries. See Allegro, *op. cit.*, pp. 126–127.

22. *Rab* means "Master." *Rab + oti* = "Rabbi," "My Master." *Rabban* = "Our Master." *Rabboni*, or *Rabbuni* (as found in some Gospels) is a grammatical impossibility.

23. The Protestant reader is referred to Matt. 13:53–58, Mark 6:3, and Rom. 8:29–30. The Catholic reader who is constrained by dogma to believe in the perpetual virginity of Miriam (Mary) is respectfully reminded that no modern linguist holds that ἀδελφοὶ means anything else but "brothers" in the literal sense.

24. Hegesippus (2nd century C.E.) is quoted by Eusebius, *Hist. Eccl.*, III:19–20, as saying that the grandsons of Yeshu'a's brother Yehudah (Judah) were persecuted by the Emperor Domitian.

25. The Bethlehem Story, the Wise Men, the Miraculous Conception and Birth, the Slaughter of the Innocents, the Flight into Egypt, etc., are part of the mythology of Christianity, being added to the simple Logos or Sayings of Yeshu'a after the new religion had left Israel and moved out into the pagan world. As Durant, *op. cit.*, says, "The mature mind will not resent this folk poetry."

26. Should the reader wonder, this is history. What is not history is the portrait of the mild, compassionate Pilate found in the Gospels. This scene is drawn from Josephus, *Jewish War*, II:169–174. The reader to whom Josephus may not be available is referred to Schürer, *op. cit.*, pp. 198–202, for a full account of the almost incredible cruelty and harshness of Lucius Pontius Pilatus.

CHAPTER IX

1. Schürer, *op. cit.*, p. 134, reports that in 31 B.C.E. more than 30,000 people perished in this great catastrophe.

2. April.

3. July and August in most years, August and September in others.

4. About a thousand ounces of silver; its present-day value is impossible to com-

pute, though some authorities give $6000 as the equivalent figure—in this writer's opinion, much too low.

5. In Greek, the Aramaic word *kepha*, "stone" or "rock," becomes *petros*, which is why we call this Apostle "Simon Peter."

6. Klausner, *op. cit.*, p. 260, suggests that Andrew must have been called Netzer, which is roughly equivalent to the Greek *Andrai*, since it would have been strange for a simple Galilean fisherman to have a Greek name.

7. And not "of thunder," as is usually given.

8. The writer hopes the reader has recognized poor Judas Iscariot by now under the name he actually bore in life.

9. June.

10. We do not know the names of Yeshu'a's sisters, if he had more than two, or of their husbands. The Gospels' use of the plural in Matt. 13:53–58 and Mark 6:3 indicates that he had at least two, and the expression "and do not his sisters dwell here among us?" would suggest that they were married; but beyond that, we know nothing. The writer asks your pardon for having profited from this gap in sacred history for the benefit of his plot.

CHAPTER X

1. "I see and approve the better; I follow the worse." Ovid.

2. Roman slang for *lupanarus*, brothel keeper.

3. Matt. 10:2–4; Mark 3:13–19. In the NEB, this disciple is identified as "Simon, a member of the Zealot Party." Luke 6:15 says, "Simon, who was called the Zealot." In the KJV, in both Matthew and Mark, Simon is called "the Canaanite," while in Luke an accurate translation of the Aramaic slips through: "Simon Zealotes." The reasons for these discrepancies are clear. The Gospels are believed to have been written in Greek on the basis of the Aramaic Logos attributed to Matthew, and perhaps from other sources now lost, long after the death of Yeshu'a, when the Christians 1) had split away from the Nazarene Sect at Jerusalem, which was headed by Yeshu'a's brother Yaakob (James) and had remained what Yeshu'a intended his entire following to be: a sect of Reformed Judaism; and 2) had given up their efforts to convert the Jews, who had refused to accept Yeshu'a as the Mashiah. The Christians therefore turned their efforts toward the Hellenic/Roman world, and in doing so suppressed or softened some of the facts about Yeshu'a. It was hardly wise to let it be known that he had welcomed into his movement violent, bloody revolutionaries against Roman rule, such as the Zealots. (The writer's somewhat antic sense of humor does not permit him to resist asking the reader to imagine a Parousia—Reappearance of the Nazarene in St. Patrick's Cathedral on Easter Sunday, in which He upsets the collection plates and lays about Him lustily with His whip of cords. One wonders how long it would take Him to get out of Bellevue, that is, if He ever arrived there with His head uncracked by a pious policeman's club!) To this same tendency of appeasement, of course, belongs the whitewashing of Pilate—an unmitigated scoundrel if there ever was one. Good public relations and the remaking of images were not unknown to the Church Fathers. See Klausner, *op. cit.*, pp. 206 and 284.

4. From *sica*, a dagger. The *sicarii*, dagger men, were the executioners of the Zealots. Their usual practice was to meet their intended victim in a crowd, stab him, and lose themselves among the throngs. See Josephus, *Jewish War*, II:254: 257.

5. *The Talmud*, Persahim, 57a, T. Menaroth XIII:21. As quoted by Klausner, *op. cit.*, p. 337.

6. Exactly as our "Johnny" from John.

CHAPTER XI

1. These four incidents are history, unlike the Gospel accounts of Pilate, which were written long after the events at a time when Christianity unfortunately already had acquired its strong anti-Semitic bias. The interested reader is referred to Josephus (*Jewish War*, II:169–174, and *Antiquities*, XVIII:55–59) for the first incident. For the second, *Jewish War*, II:175–177; *Antiquities*, XVIII:60–62.

For the third, there is no historical record; the references to Yeshu'a in Josephus, our chief source for the period, are held by nearly every respectable scholar to be pious frauds, interpolations by Christian copyists at a later date, or, at best, alterations so flagrant as to make the existing text worthless (which is what Schürer terms the so-called reference to Yeshu'a in Josephus). For it, since no other ancient writer seems to ever even have heard of Yeshu'a ha Notzri, we have to depend upon the Gospels, which (to put it as mildly as possible for readers brought up [as this writer also was] on such expressions as "That's Gospel truth!") simply are not history at all in any objective, disciplined sense, and very often are not true either. To help the pious reader adjust his thinking a little, he is referred to the following quotation from the new, and generally excellent, translation of the Scriptures known as *The Jerusalem Bible* [Roman Catholic], as found in the "Introduction to the Synoptic Gospels," p. 9: "Neither the apostles themselves, however, nor any of the preachers of the gospel message, and tellers of the gospel story ever aimed at writing or teaching history in the modern, technical sense of that word; their concern was sacred and theological: they preached to convert and edify, to infuse faith, to enlighten it and defend it against its opponents."

The fourth incident, Pilate's criminal massacre of the unarmed and defenseless Samaritan pilgrims on the way to their holy shrine, a feat of a magnitude of which the Nazi S.S. might well be proud, is found in *Antiquities*, XVIII:85–89. The reader who studies them will see the patent impossibility of reconciling the Pilate of history with the mild and compassionate Pilate of the Gospels.

2. Unlike the Sadducees, the P'rushim, or Pharisees, believed in a life after death and the immortality of the soul.

CHAPTER XII

1. Schürer, *op. cit.*, gives the various estimates of the length of this aqueduct, indisputably built by Pilate, as found in Josephus and Eusebius. He concludes, however, that if due consideration be given to its windings, it is all of 400 stadia long. When the present writer visited Jerusalem in November, 1966 (as well as every other major locale in this novel) he was struck with how little Roman it looks, how different from the aqueduct at Segovia and the ones near Rome. Upon his return to Rome this impression was strengthened; and upon reaching Madrid, a reading of Schürer confirmed that impression, making the probability that Pilate's engineer in this case was not a Roman Army man but a local builder all but overwhelming. Says Schürer, p. 366: "Many, however, owing to the absence of any trace of the characteristics of Roman building, hold it to have been still older than the time of Pilate, and suppose that Pilate only restored it. But this theory is in direct opposition to the words of Josephus."

2. Mic. 5:2.

3. Klausner, *op. cit.*, p. 164, quotes in a footnote this Mishna: "Waterways and city walls and towers and all municipal needs are to be supplied from the Temple Funds" (Ske. IV:2). Therefore Dr. Klausner concludes that the Qorban was a special fund.

4. See Josephus, *Jewish War*, II:175–177, or Schürer, *op. cit.*, pp. 192–200; or Klausner, *op. cit.*, p. 164, for an account of this one of the several massacres ordered by the man who, according to the Gospels, was so tenderhearted, so com-

passionate, and so just, that he had to be forced to crucify one Galilean prophet.

5. And not "Jesus," which is the Latin translation of his name.

6. Matt. 27:15–18. The NEB gives the name of Barabbas (i.e., bar, "son of" —Abba, "the father") as also being Yeshu'a. The JB unfortunately relegates this information to a footnote, and attributes it to an apocryphal tradition. For further explanation of the suppression of this otherwise harmless fact, see Chap. 28 and Note 9 for that chapter.

7. "Clean" meaning an edible variety. Klausner, *op. cit.*, in a footnote, p. 243, tells how the Bedouins still eat locusts to this day. See Matt. 3:4–5 for the reference to John the Baptist's use of this insect as a food.

CHAPTER XIII

1. We know surprisingly little about the organization of the Roman Army. A decuria was, of course, a platoon of ten men, led by a decurion, roughly equivalent to a corporal. A century was one hundred men, led by a centurion (roughly, a captain). A cohort (infantry) or an ala (cavalry) was from five hundred to one thousand men, and usually led by a dux, or a general.

2. Robert Graves, *The Greek Myths* (Baltimore: Penguin Books, Inc., 1955), Vol. II, p. 95, writes: "Greek and Roman archers drew the bowstring back to the chest, as children shoot, and their effective range was so short that the javelin remained the chief missile weapon of the Roman armies until the Sixth Century A.D., when Belisarius armed his Kataphracts [missile troops, usually archers and slingers] with heavy bows, and taught them to draw the string back to the ear, in Scythian fashion."

3. A talent was a little short of one thousand ounces, usually 912, or 57 pounds, or 25.9 kilograms.

CHAPTER XIV

1. By which contemptuous remark, the Dux Malvidius means the River Jordan.

2. Luke 3:10–14.

3. Dan. 7:13–14.

4. This ancestor of Cleopatra's reigned from 285–246 B.C.E. During this Ptolemy's reign, the great translation of the Old Testament into Greek known as the Septuagint was made, the exact dates being unknown.

5. Isa. 53:1–5.

6. Isa. 53:8.

7. II Sam. 18:33 (KJV).

CHAPTER XV

1. Says Will Durant, *op. cit.*, p. 559: "The tales later circulated by Celsus and others about Mary and a Roman soldier are, by critical consent, 'clumsy fabrications.'" Klausner, *op. cit.*, pp. 23–24, advances the workable theory that the Jews, hearing Yeshu'a constantly referred to by the Greek-speaking, Gentile *Christianoi* as *uios Parthenos*, "son of the Virgin," invented, as a joke, the word-play *Yeshu'a ben ha Pantera*, "Jesus, son of the Panther"; and later generations, not knowing the mocking origin of the term, took the whole thing seriously. However, this writer believes that there was some question about Yeshu'a's birth, even in his own times. Else the word-play of Pilate at the trial—which the translators have labored so long to hide by suppressing the fact that the Nazarene and bar Abbas were both named Yeshu'a—becomes pointless. And Pontius Pilate was never pointless; clearly he had heard something. This writer believes it possible that Miriam—a warm, normal, loving, and lovable woman, with blood in her veins —might well have given Yosef some slight, not very serious grounds for jealousy that, in a small town like Nazareth, quickly became wildly exaggerated. To the

devout, he cannot emphasize too strongly that here he is discussing Miriam, wife of Yosef the Carpenter, mother of his sons Yeshu'a, Yaakob, Shimeon, Yehudah, and Yose, and of his at least two daughters, and not by any stretch of the imagination "the Virgin Mary." By temperament, inclination, and intellect, this writer is not qualified to deal with semantic irrelevancies, nor is mythology his field.

2. It may not have been called Beth Anya. Some ancient manuscripts call it Beth Abara, others Beth Araba, which last, with its meaning of "House of Arabs," considering its location, seems to this writer the most probable of all. Klausner, *op. cit.*, p. 243, gives these variants and the probable location of the ford.

3. Luke 7:33–34 indicates that Yohannan Baptistes was thought mad.

4. Luke 3:7–14.

5. Which is what the Aramaic expression is. "To untie his shoes" is a Greek substitution for, rather than a translation of, what the Baptist must have said.

6. Luke 3:15–17.

7. The totally routine nature of the baptism of Yeshu'a is clear from Luke 3:21 and Mark 1:9–11. Matt. 3:13–14 and John 1:29–37 are theology, written much later to explain such theologically troublesome questions as: Why did the sinless son of God need baptism? and: How could he accept it at hands of one less than he?

8. Matt. 11:2–4. This has the uninflated simplicity of the truth.

9. Samaël was the personal name of Satan. The other names of angels and devils are taken from Klausner, *op. cit.*, p. 198.

10. Luke 4:1–13; Matthew 4:1–11.

11. "Oil they consider defiling, and anyone who accidentally comes in contact with it scours his person; for they make a point of keeping a dry skin." Josephus, *Jewish War*, II:123.

12. This interpretation of the forty days is based on the writer's personal experience of walking through that wilderness on foot.

13. Luke 15:8–9.

14. Luke 6:37.

15. Mark 10:2.

16. Luke 16:18.

17. Mark 16:9. None of the Gospels tell how or when the Seven Devils were driven out. When we meet Miriam of Migdal-Nunaya, this marvelous event has already happened.

CHAPTER XVI

1. A shekel, the Jewish coin that had to be used for religious purposes since it bore no graven image (hence the money changers in the Temple, as the Greek and Roman coins bore likenesses of the Emperors or Kings), was equivalent to the Greek tetradrachma, a coin equal in value to four ordinary drachmas, the drachma being used in the East instead of its Roman equivalent, the denarius. The shekel, like the tetradrachma, weighed not quite half an ounce of silver. Therefore four minae, 400 drachmas, would be the same as 100 tetradrachmas, or 100 shekels.

2. The *l'qutoth* were the hired laborers of whom Yeshu'a speaks so often in his parables. They were exclusively farm workers, and not to be confused with the *po'el*, who were artisans working for hire, among whom he himself (until he became a *rab*) and his brothers would be numbered.

3. This word is the foundation of sand upon which theology has erected one of its more imposing mountains of nonsense. In Isaiah 7:14, we find the prophecy which is held to be the cornerstone of the Messianic pretensions of Christianity:

> The Lord himself, therefore,
> will give you a sign.

It is this: the *almah* is with child
and soon will give birth to a son
Whom she will call Immanuel.

Says the JB in a footnote in reference to this verse: "The Greek version reads
'the Virgin,' being more explicit than the Hebrew, which uses *almah*, meaning
either a young girl or a young recently married woman." The writer suggests that
neither *parthenos*, which appears in this verse in the Septuagint, nor *almah* implies
virginity; both mean girl, usually an unmarried girl; and in no instance can it
be demonstrated that the ancient Hebrews who wrote the Old Testament, as well
as those who translated it into Greek, intended anything else. Harry M. Orlin-
sky, in his review of the JB (*Saturday Review*, December 3, 1966), points out:
"It was only subsequently when Christian theology developed that *parthenos*
acquired the meaning 'virgin' retroactively." Being realists, the Old Testament
writers used *almah* not only in its primary meaning of "girl," its secondary one of
"handmaiden" or female servant, but quite often in its third sense of "concubine,"
which proves how very far they were from associating it with virginity. The
reader and the Priestly Fathers, if they can be interested in uncomfortable
truth, are referred to *A Hebrew and English Lexicon of the Old Testament* (E.
Robinson and F. Brown, London: Oxford University Press, 1962), p. 51, which
lists, among others, as examples for this usage for *almah*, Gen. 20:17; 21:12;
and Exod. 23:12. The writer sincerely regrets to have to point out to the devout
that one of the cornerstones of their faith is based upon a mistranslation of Isaiah.

4. The correct, Judean, Hebrew spelling of this rather commonplace woman's
name is Yohannah. The Galileans, however, softened this to *Yuanna*, a dialectical,
probably Aramaic variant. Here, Nathan is flirtatiously playing with the Galilean
sound of it. Other variants are *Yunni*, a diminutive, pet name, and *Yuannah*, with
the hard terminal *a*, closer to the Hebrew.

5. Incest was the legally required method of propagating the Egyptian royal
family, not even cousins being considered regal enough. When the Macedonian
Greek Ptolemies came to power in Egypt, they adopted the custom. Cleopatra, like
all her ancestors, was the product of a brother-sister marriage, and was herself
married to her brother before Julius Caesar and Mark Antony *et al.* appeared
on the scene.

6. Mark 3:21, KVJ: "And when his friends heard of it, they went out to lay
hold on him; for they said, He is beside himself." JB: "When his relatives heard
of this, they set out to take charge of him, convinced he was out of his mind."
NEB: "When his family heard of this, they set out to take charge of him, for
people were saying that he was out of his mind." Among the three versions, the
JB translation (despite its shock-absorbing use of "relatives") is the most faithful to
the original.

7. "Galilean itinerant" is a literal translation of the phrase usually applied to
these wandering preachers by the educated classes of Israel, who held them in
contempt.

8. The writer is unable to use direct quotations here because Mark 3, Matt.
12, and Luke 8, all of which relate this scene with fair agreement, contradict
each other completely as to what Yeshu'a said.

9. Known to us as Mary Magdalene. This composite list of the female followers
of Yeshu'a is taken from Luke 8:1–3, 24:10; Mark 15:40; and Matt. 27:55–56.
The Miriams (Marys) are exceedingly confusing. John adds one more: Miriam,
wife of Klopah, whom he says was Yeshu'a's aunt, sister of his mother. But, apart
from the fact that the Gospel According to John must be used with extreme caution (it contradicts the other three in every major detail), the likelihood of one
family naming two of its daughters Mary seems a bit remote.

10. A *zereth* was a "span," 8.8 inches or 22 centimeters. A *tofah* was a "palm,"
3 inches or 7.2 centimeters. (From the tables in the back pages of the JB.)

11. Klausner, *op. cit.,* p. 266.

12. The account of the revolts which took place after Herod the Great's death is best found in Schürer, *op. cit.,* pp. 160–164.

13. Mark 3:31–35; Matt. 12:46; and Luke 8:19. Mariolatry was an invention of the Middle Ages. It can be demonstrated by the Gospels themselves that Yeshu'a never saw or spoke to his mother again after his disastrous attempt to preach and work miracles in Nazareth itself.

CHAPTER XVII

1. John 2:4–5.

2. In a footnote in reference to this verse, the JB says: "Unusual address from son to mother; the term is used again in 19:26, where there may be a reference to Genesis 3:15, 20. Mary is the Second Eve, 'The Mother of the Living.'" In the writer's opinion, this is nonsense; Yehu'a, for reasons unknown, did not like his mother.

3. Bartholomew. This disciple of Yeshu'a's is known only by his family name, or rather by the Greek corruption of it. Since in Aramaic, *bar* always means "son of," this cannot be a given name. The Aramaic spelling is bar Talmay. However, the JB suggests in a footnote that the Nathanael listed in John 1:44–51 and 21:1–3 (and nowhere else) as one of the disciples is probably bar Talmay. For this, there is not one iota of evidence; but the writer has adopted the suggestion for want of a better one.

4. This is an assumption, but almost certainly valid. All the English texts give "steward," in Greek *Epitropos* (which is why the Palestinians called the Procurators that, *i.e.,* "Stewards of Caesar"), but the text demands *Symposiarch* (Toastmaster, Banquet Master, Chosen Leader of the Revels, Master of Ceremonies) because, as this scene is depicted in John 2:1–11, the man does not fit the role of steward. If the Greek text does not read *Symposiarch* here, it is almost surely defective.

5. John 2:10.

6. A *ketoneth* was some sort of undergarment. All we know of it is that it was reserved exclusively for women. In a manuscript found in the Fourth Cave at Khirbet Qumrân, one passage reads ". . . but let him not wear a woman's Ketoneth under tunic." Allegro, *op. cit.,* p. 118.

7. Matt. 7:6.

CHAPTER XVIII

1. John 7:40–43. Beth means "House," le, "of," and Hem, "bread."

2. Here we are confronted with one of the major difficulties in scriptural studies: determining the names of all twelve. The Synoptic Gospels all list the following names: 1) Shimeon Kepha bar Yonah (Simon Peter, son of Jonas); 2) Netzer, or Andrai (Andrew), his brother; 3) Yaakob and 4) Yohannan bar Zebediah (James and John, sons of Zebedee), called the *Boane Ragsha* (not *Boanerges*), "Sons of Fury"; 5) Philip (strangely enough, a Greek name); 6) Bar Talmay (Bartholomew, i.e., son of Talmay); 7) Toma (Thomas, also called Didymus, "The Twin"—but twin of whom?); 8) Mattathiyahu—or Mattathiah in Hebrew, Matthya in Aramaic—a tax collector (Matthew the Publican); 9)———— ————(the Unknown Apostle, whose name gives most of the trouble, as we shall presently see); 10) Yaakob ben Halphai (James, son of Alphaeus); 11) Shimeon Zealotes (Simon the Zealot); 12) Yehuda ish Kriyoth, or Kerioth—a town in Judea (Judas Iscariot). These lists are from Matt. 10:2–5; Mark 3:15–19; Luke 6:14–16; and Acts 1:13. But as to the name of the Apostle which should be listed in the ninth place, thus completing the Twelve, only Luke and Acts, both probably written by a disciple of Loukas the Physician, are in agreement. In Matthew, he is called Lebbaeus; in Mark, Thaddaeus; in Luke and Acts, Yehudah bar Yaakob (Judas, son of James).

This Thaddaeus/Lebbaeus/Yehudah bar Yaakob controversy does have a rational solution, however. The writer accepts Dr. Klausner's theory (*op. cit.*, p. 284): In Aramaic, Thaddaeus is ben Thaddai, "son of the beast," too disrespectfully close in meaning to our modern "son of a bitch" for the first copyist to stomach. So they changed it to Lebbaeus, ben Lebbai, "son of the heart," which sounded better. And, as Dr. Klausner also points out, there is a strong possibility that these outlandish and/or outrageous names might well have been applied to Yehudah bar Yaakob (Judas, son of James) as nicknames, because of certain personal characteristics of his—impulsiveness, say—just as the banim Zebediah were called "Sons of Fury."

Nor, unfortunately, does the matter end here. We have no assurance that Matthew the Publican actually was named Matthew. Matt. 9:9 tells the story of Yeshu'a's (Jesus') summoning Matthew from his seat in the customhouse and indicates that Yeshu'a called him by that name. Nowhere in this Gospel is it indicated that he and Yaakob ben Halphai (Levi, son of Alphaeus) were brothers; Mark 2:14 tells the identical story in identical words, but now the Publican is called Levi bar Halphai (Levi, son of Alphaeus, and hence brother of James!). Again, Luke 5:27 tells the same story, but calls the tax gatherer Levi, without saying who his father was. Therefore, it has always been assumed that Levi bar Halphai and Matthew were the same man. But were they? Could there not have been more than one publican among the disciples? Is it not strange that none of the lists, all of which identify brothers as such, indicates that Matthew was the brother of James, son of Alphaeus?

This writer believes that Levi and Matthew were two different men. The Gospel According to John—which this writer is convinced contains a valuable primitive core overlaid later with much theological nonsense by a man who obviously had never set foot in Palestine in his life*—states (6:66), "From that time on, many of his disciples withdrew and no longer went about with him." At this time, could not Levi ben Halphai, Yaakob's brother, have left the company, never actually having—since Yeshu'a had many disciples, as opposed to only twelve Apostles—been numbered among the Twelve?

And, finally, to these lists, John 1:44–51 adds one other name, *i.e.*, Nathanael. The JB suggests in a footnote that this Nathanael was probably the given name of Bar Talmay (Bartholomew). He is mentioned again in John 21:1–3. In no other Gospel does he appear. (See Chap. 17, Note 3.)

3. Mark 4:35–41; Matt. 8:23–27; Luke 8:22–25.

4. Klausner, *op. cit.*, p. 269, describes how just this same freak of weather occurred to him personally while sailing on the Sea of Galilee in the spring of 1912. He adds: "Yet, for the Galilean fishermen, with their craving for marvels, it was a miracle that Jesus had performed."

5. Literally, in Hebrew and Greek, respectively, "Good News." The Old English word "Gospel" is a literal translation of the Greek.

6. The Apostle Paul, the actual founder of Christianity.

7. A. Powell Davies, *The Meaning of the Dead Sea Scrolls* (New York: New American Library, Signet Edition, 1956), p. 88. See also James Hasting, *Dictionary of the Bible* (New York: Scribner's, 1927), Vol. III, pp. 203ff. for the specific reference to the Magii visiting Nero, not Yeshu'a.

8. Matt. 1:1–17.

9. Luke 3:21–38.

10. Mic. 5:1–2.

---

* The sequences in John would require at least an automobile speed of 60 mph or more, considering the distances involved, *i.e.*, Cana and the Wilderness, where John the Baptist taught, are 270 miles apart, and yet John makes the Wedding at Cana seemingly occur the next day, after the Baptism. The author of John did *not* know Palestine.

11. So Luke 3:23. Matthew doesn't say.

12. See Vol. IX of the Loeb Library Josephus, pp. 2–3, the footnotes, in reference to the mention of Quirinius, in *Antiquities*, XVIII:1. Quirinius was sent out to Syria in 6 c.e., at which time, if we take Luke's word for it, Yeshu'a was eight years old. Pious scholars (and the dubiousness of the scholarship seems, unfortunately, to increase in geometric progression with the degree of piety), as the footnote also indicates, have tried to reread Luke as saying: "This census was the first before that held under the prefectureship of Quirinius in Syria." To support this theory, they cite a report in Tertullian, Adv. Marcion IV. 19, which lists a previous census held under Saturnius, Legate in Syria 8–7 b.c.e.

There are several things against this theory, to this writer's mind: 1) Luke specifically states that this registration was the first of its kind (Luke 2:2). 2) Josephus, whose coverage of Herod the Great's reign extends to minutiae, mentions the supposed census under Saturnius not at all. 3) To the ancient Jews, any census whatsoever would have been considered an acknowledgment that Caesar's power was above God's, and hence a blasphemy. They would have revolted against Saturnius as they did against Quirinius; yet Josephus, who described the attempted revolt against Quirinius' census in such detail (*Antiquities*, XVIII:1–10) said nothing of an earlier uproar. In this writer's view, it did not occur. He believes that the census was first proposed under Saturnius, and not carried out until the legateship of Quirinius. He also believes that the writers of the Gospels were propagandists, not historians, that they sought to prove that Yeshu'a was of the House of David—an utter impossibility which he, himself, specifically denied —and that they had to get Yosef and Miriam down to Beth le Hem somehow, in order to fulfill that prophecy, just as they had to invent genealogies to prove that a Galilean carpenter was a Judean prince.

13. Here Num. 23:22; Hos. 11:1; and Jer. 31:15.

14. See Chap. 2, Note 2. Note also that Josephus, who loathed Herod the Great and listed all his crimes at great length, does not mention "The Slaughter of the Innocents," as he would have been delighted to do, had it occurred. One fact is certain: We know absolutely nothing about Jesus the Nazarene before he was thirty years of age; and precious little about him after. Writes Allegro, *op. cit.*, p. 175, "As far as details in the New Testament record of Jesus' life are concerned, I would suggest that the scrolls give added grounds for believing that many incidents are merely projections into Jesus' own history of what was expected of the Messiah." Incidentally, the JB's footnotes on this section of Matthew are a marvel. They reinforce the writer's belief that theology is a mild form of insanity.

CHAPTER XIX

1. *Qana* is Aramaic for "Zealot."

2. One of the problems with trying to find the real man behind the myths that have totally obscured Yeshu'a ha Notzri is that the immense weight of our religio-cultural heritage is too strong for even the most rational of scholars. It seems to this writer that much of the Nazarene's behavior was neurotic, and some of it bordered on the psychotic; yet the only two scholars, O. Holtzman, *War Jesus Erstatiker?* (Türbingen, 1903), and Binet-Sanglé, *La Folie de Jésus* (3rd edition, 4 vols., Paris, 1911–1914), who have dared treat of this aspect of his personality have either been ignored or savagely attacked by the critics.

3. Dan. 7:13–14.

4. Matt. 14:22–33; Mark 6:47–51; John 6:16–21. Luke has no account of this "miracle."

5. Says Klausner, *op. cit.*, p. 293, in a footnote: "Theodor Reinach, *Revue des Études Juives*, XLVII, 177, holds that the name 'Legion' given to the unclean Spirits, and the swine into which the unclean spirits entered, arose from an ignorant

confusion with the Tenth Legion, stationed in Palestine 70–135 [c.e.], on whose standard was depicted a wild boar. This then would be a late accretion."

6. Matt. 8:28–35; Mark 5:1–20; Luke 8:26–39. The reader will note that Matthew has two madmen, Mark and Luke but one. The story is ridiculous upon the face of it. Wanton destructiveness of other people's property (even swine) was not one of Yeshu'a's characteristics.

7. See Matt. 12:43–45. The writer agrees with Dr. Klausner, op. cit., p. 271, that most of Yeshu'a's cures of neurasthenics and psychotics were probably only temporary. (While working in the Ethnic Group, Writers Projects, WPA, Chicago, 1938, the writer witnessed the performances of several quite remarkable cures by a faith healer. However, within two to six hours thereafter, the healed were in worse condition than before.)

8. Luke 7:11–17.

9. Matt. 9:20–21; Mark 5:25–34; Luke 8:43–48. This woman was cured of hemorrhages, probably vaginal, which, of course, Nathan could not see.

10. Matt. 9:18–26; Mark 5:21–43 (the best account); and Luke 8:49–56.

11. Cf. John 7:5–6: "For not even his brothers were believers in him."

CHAPTER XX

1. Unless the topography of Nazareth has changed over the centuries, there is no actual precipice in that town. Luke 4:29–30, reads "brow of the hill" and "edge," which suggest a cliff. But the writer has visited Nazareth twice, in 1951 and in 1966, and on neither occasion did he see anything like a precipice there. However, Klausner, op. cit., p. 230, states categorically: "The present Nazareth does not stand on the precise site of ancient Nazareth, which was destroyed at an early date, and, in the 12th or 13th century, rebuilt on a site below the old town."

2. Which is what Isaiah 61:1–2 actually says, as opposed to the defective version given in Luke 4:17–19. We know, from the Isaiah scroll found at Qumrân, that both the Greek Septuagint translation and the existing Hebrew versions of Isaiah are unexpectedly accurate; so, since the Isaiah scroll dates to within Yeshu'a's own time, there is no reason for him to have misquoted Isaiah, as Luke makes him do.

3. Let the reader study Matt. 13:53–58 and Mark 6:1–6 and see if this is not precisely the sense of what is written there. The fuller account in Luke, which this writer has followed as far as he was able (Luke trips all over himself in his efforts to make even the people who didn't—i.e., the overwhelming majority of Yeshu'a's fellow Jews—glorify his Lord), has the advantage of revealing what the Gospels try so hard to conceal: how deep the opposition to Yeshu'a was, from the very beginning.

4. Luke 4:14–30. See especially verse 30: "But he walked straight through them all, and went away."

5. Klausner, op. cit., p. 282: "He left Nazareth in despair, never to return." Says Harry Emerson Fosdick, The Man From Nazareth (New York: Pocket Books, 1953), p. 117: "Certainly this break between Jesus and his family was part of the tradition of the Church, for John's Gospel says, 'even his brothers did not believe in him,' and that it was a constant factor in Jesus' own thinking seems evident."

6. Klausner, op. cit., p. 272. "This dislike of publicity (so strongly emphasized in Mark and undoubtedly historical) is, by the majority of Christian scholars, accounted for by Jesus' unwillingness to be looked upon as a mere 'wonder-worker,' whose works counted for more than his teaching and ethical injunctions. But a simpler explanation is possible: His miracles were not always successful and he was afraid to attempt them too often; he even disliked publicity for the successful miracles lest the people insist on more."

CHAPTER XXI

1. March.
2. Ps. 100:1.
3. Matt. 5:38; Luke 6:29.
4. Matt. 16:13–20; Mark 8:27–29; Luke 9:18–21.
5. Gen. 22:1–14.
6. *Cf.* Luke 9:50 and 11:23.
7. Matt. 5:17–18; Luke 16:17.
8. Luke 5:37–39; Mark 2:21–22.
9. *In re* failure to wash hands: Matt. 15:1–2; Mark 7:1–8; Luke 11:37–41. *In re* plucking wheat on Shabbat: Matt. 12:1–8; Mark 2:23–26; Luke 6:1–5.
10. Mark 2:27.
11. Luke 13:31–33.
12. Matt. 23:13–36; Mark 12:38–39; Luke 11:37–52.
13. Lev. 13:45–46; II Kings 7:3. Charitably this writer attributes the Gospel accounts of the cure of lepers to their writers' total ignorance of Palestine and of age-old Jewish Law. For if their stories of lepers wandering about all over the landscape without let or hindrance for Yeshu'a to cure miraculously are not the products of overheated pious imaginations, they are something worse, plain unmitigated lies. Lepers were never permitted to wander around Palestine or live at Beth Anya.
14. Matt. 15:24; Mark 7:27.

CHAPTER XXII

1. Luke 10:1.
2. Luke 9:51–56.
3. Klausner, *op. cit.*, p. 306, describes the forest through which Yeshu'a and his followers passed on the way up to Jerusalem as being the Arabic "Zur," known as the "Pride of the Jordan" because of the luxurious growth of white poplars, tamarisks, large castors, licorice, and mallow trees.
4. Matt. 8:20; Luke 9:59.
5. Which is what Shimeon probably was. And not "the Leper," as the Gospels have it. Since the townspeople called the Essenes "the Lowly," the copyist's error is very comprehensible; the two words in Hebrew differ in only one letter: *ha zonua* (the lowly) and *ha zorua* (the leper). This is the theory of H. P. Chaps, given in his *Markus Studien*, pp. 74–75, as quoted by Klausner, *op. cit.*, p. 312. See also Chap. 21, Note 13, regarding the Law's restriction of lepers.
6. John 11:1–44 to the contrary, Miriam (Mary) and Martha probably had no brother at all. It is very clear that the raising of Eleazer (Lazarus) is derived from Luke 16:19–31. The reader is asked to consider why no other Gospel except John recounts this amazing tale. Or why Luke, who in 10:38–42, a simple and entirely convincing narrative, confirms the existence of Miriam and Martha, fails to even mention that they had a brother.
7. Zech. 9:9–10.
8. The writer has already pointed out that this theory, advanced by John Allegro, *op. cit.*, solves a great many difficulties, including how so much could have happened in an impossibly short space of time.
9. Wisd. 2:12–20 (*cf.* Douay Bible, JB, or the Protestant Apocrypha).
10. See Hyman E. Goldin, *The Case of the Nazarene Reopened*, pp. 424–436, for a full and careful discussion proving that Yeshu'a was actually guilty of this crime.
11. Luke 3:22. This is the Codex D version. (The JB, as usual, relegates it to a footnote and softens it into "This day I have become your father.") This version echoes Ps. 2:7, and is very probably what the original verse in Luke actually said.

12. Mark 9:1.

13. Pesachim 49 a.

14. Many modern scholars hold that Joseph of Arimathæa is an entirely mythical figure, invented by the Gospel writers for the purpose of furthering their mystical tale. Hugh J. Schonfield, *The Passover Plot* (New York: Bernard Geis Associates, 1965), p. 164, states the possibility—strong enough in this writer's opinion to be considered a probability—that Luke ransacked Josephus for details that had simply been lost after the great rebellion of 71 C.E. and the fall of Jerusalem. Now in the Greek text of Josephus we find "Joseph begot Matthias" (*i.e.*, the father of Flavius Josephus), which in Greek is Josepou Matthias. In the Greek of Mark, Joseph of Arimathæa is Joseph apo Arimathias," similar enough to trouble a hurried copyist. Further, as Dr. Schonfield points out, there is in Josephus, *Life* 420, this remarkable passage:

Once more, when I was sent by Titus Caesar with Cerealius and a thousand horse to a village called Tekoa [N.B. The birthplace of Amos, some twelve miles south of Jerusalem] to prospect whether it was a suitable camp, and, on my return, saw many prisoners who had been crucified, and recognized three of my acquaintances among them, I was cut to the heart, and came and told Titus with tears what I had seen. He gave orders immediately that they should be taken down and receive the most careful treatment. Two of them died in the physicians' hands; the third survived.

Now we know from Papias that the Apostle Mattithiah set down the sayings (logos) of Yeshu'a, but not his deeds. For the doings of Yeshu'a we have to depend upon a word-of-mouth tradition as set down by Iohannos Markos (St. Mark), who wrote down "what he could remember" of what Shimeon Kepha (St. Peter) told him. Therefore, it is highly probable that after the overwhelming catastrophe of the Jewish War with Rome, and the fall of Jerusalem, nothing remained of Yeshu'a ha Notzri in history but such high points in his career as would stick in the memories of aged and broken men. So the Gospels that we have are largely fictional, with a tremendous amount of imaginative materials added, which were taken from other sources. These scholars contend that the story of Yeshu'a disputing with the learned doctors at age twelve, the Crucifixion, and the Resurrection are all taken from Josephus' *Life;* and that Joseph of Arimathæa is none other than Flavius Josephus, himself, introduced into the Gospels to fill the gaps. Moreover, as pointed out by Goldin, *op. cit.*, p. 345, there is no record of a place called Arimathæa in the Old Testament, Torah, Talmud, or anywhere else except in the Gospels. Dr. Goldin states categorically that Joseph of Arimathæa is an invented figure.

Even so, he is useful to this writer's plot, as he was to the plots of Loukas, Mattithiah, Markos, and Yohannan—good novelists all!

CHAPTER XXIII

1. Here John 18:40, which states simply that bar Abbas was a bandit, and, possibly, Matt. 27:15-16, which does not list the specific charges against the prisoner, must be followed. Mark 15:6-15, and Luke 23:19-20 are obvious nonsense. Under Roman law, a prisoner charged with treason, insurrection, or any overt attack upon the Imperator's power, could be freed only by Caesar himself. Had Pilate released a man so charged, he would have made himself liable to arrest on at least suspicion of treason, which, once the case were brought before a man as paranoiacally distrustful of his own subordinates as Tiberius Caesar, would have been tantamount to suicide on Pilatus' part.

2. Says Klausner, *op. cit.*, p. 346: "When Pilate came to Jerusalem to be present during the time of Passover, he did not live in the Citadel of Antonia, but, according to the evidence of Josephus, in the Palace of Herod [one of the three towers, one of which survives under the title of 'Tower of David,' though it is really the 'Tower of Phasael'] where there was a garrison or large barracks."

3. Saints. This is the word from which our term Essenes, having been filtered through the Greek, is derived.

4. Luke 19:28–35; Mark 11:1–7; Matt. 21:1–4; John 12:14–15. It is interesting to note that the writer or editor of Matthew understood the text of Zechariah so badly that he thought it referred to two animals, not realizing that the "foal of an ass" is only an appositive modifier! The writer's nightshade sense of humor causes him to picture Yeshu'a solemnly riding into Jerusalem like a circus mountebank, one foot on the ass, the other on her foal. That would have been a triumphal entry indeed!

5. Matt. 20:29–34 (Matthew makes it two blind men!); Mark 10:46–52 (which gives the name of the blind man, Bartimaeus, *i.e.*, bar Timai); Luke 18:35–43. John has no mention of this miracle.

6. II Kings 9:13.

7. Thus Mark 11:9–10, the oldest and probably the most accurate account.

8. Matt. 21:9.

9. Luke 19:39–40.

10. *Ibid.*

11. Mark 11:11: "He entered Jerusalem and went into the Temple where he looked at the whole scene; but, as it was now late, he went out to Bethany with the Twelve." Despite the fact that all the other Gospels (except John, of course, who has him performing this feat three years earlier) claim that he drove out the money changers that same day, it is most unlikely that he did.

12. And very likely not a Pharisee as the Gospels have it. The P'rushim (Pharisees) were extremely lenient about capital punishment, framing their laws so that it was practically impossible to hand down the death sentence. On the other hand, the Sadducees were particularly harsh and cruel, as Josephus, *Antiquities* XX:199, tells us. But since the Sadducees were favorable to the Romans, the pro-Gentile tendencies that the early church was forced into by the Jews' (including the Nazareans, Yeshu'a's Jewish followers) logical rejection of the new paganistic religion with its three-headed corporation—God, adulterous Holy Ghost, earth mother/vegetation myth, matriarch virgin goddess, and Ba'al-like Supreme Being who sacrificed his only begotten son to himself to appease his own wrath at mankind's sins, a most godly piece of illogic if there ever was one!—forced them to whitewash the Zadokim in order to appease the Romans, just as they deodorized Pontius Pilate for the same reason.

13. This incident, which was left out of most of the early Bibles for fear of encouraging female immorality, has no fixed place in the Gospels. Usually it is placed in John 7:53–8:11. Other ancient manuscripts have it after Luke 21:38, still others after John 7:36, or 7:52, or 21:24. Since it does nothing to support either John's or Luke's theologies, it is very probably historical.

CHAPTER XXIV

1. The miracle of Yeshu'a's cursing the fig tree—what a bad-tempered and unreasonable creature the Gospels make of him, drowning pigs, killing trees, engaging in slanging matches with the Pharisees!—is obviously unhistorical, and probably derived from the name of this village. Mark, 6:34–44 and 7:1–9, clearly states that it was not the time for figs. Matt. 21:18–28, does not; but since this was before Passover, when figs are never ripe in Palestine, as Yeshu'a, as a native of that country, surely knew, the whole story becomes pointless, and but another example of the Gospel writers' monumental bad taste, and even more monumental ignorance of the country of their Lord. Luke, 13:6–9, gives the parable that the Hellenistic, pagan minds of the Evangelists transformed into another miracle.

2. This is distinctly debatable. Our authority for it is John 18:31, but, as should be clear by now, John is scarcely a reliable enough authority to justify anything. Beyond the fact that he is directly contradicted by the account of the stoning of

St. Stephen in Acts 7:58, the matter is still in dispute by recognized authorities. Klausner, *op. cit.*, p. 334, confirms that Jews were not permitted to try capital cases at this time, and quotes a Baraita to support this view. But Goldin, *op. cit.*, pp. 337–342, in an excellent and closely reasoned discussion of the mutually contradictory quotations from Talmudic authorities, concludes that the Jews did have the right to try capital cases and even to hand down the death sentence. Even so, it is clear that in the case of Yeshu'a, they had excellent reasons for passing the blame onto the Romans.

3. Exod. 20:4–5.

4. All the Gospels, *i.e.*, Matt. 21:12–13, Mark 10:15–19, Luke 19:45–48, and John 2:12–22, give the incident of the cleansing of the Temple. Typically, John places it at the beginning of Yeshu'a's mission, an impossibility, as Yeshu'a would never have remained alive even a week after committing such an outrage (as according to the Synoptics, he did not), much less than the three full years that "John" makes his mission last. But then "St. John's" ignorance of Palestinian conditions in the Second Temple Period is appalling. The writer believes that anyone who studies this incident, not reverently but with his critical faculties alert, must come to the conclusion that Yeshu'a's death was very close to suicide.

CHAPTER XXV

1. See Mark 13:3–27 for the apocalyptical, eschatological nature of Yeshu'a's teachings. The writer believes with the late, great Albert Schweitzer that Yeshu'a was an Oriental mystic of two thousand years ago, whose most profound concepts, contained especially in these passages, have little or no relevance for modern man. For Dr. Schweitzer's demonstration of his theory see *The Quest for the Historical Jesus* (New York: Macmillan, 10th edition, 1966), pp. 398–403.

2. Luke 7:36–39.

3. Matt. 26:6–13; Mark 14:3–9. John 12:1–8 makes it Miriam, the sister of Martha (and of the mythical Lazarus) who performs this matchlessly beautiful and tender act. The writer asks: Where would a woman too poor to afford a serving girl (as Luke 10:38–42 shows us) have got the money to buy so costly a perfume?

4. Goldin, *op. cit.*, pp. 422ff., discusses in brilliant detail the impossibility of condemning Yeshu'a for blasphemy, and the ease with which under the Jewish Law of his own times he could have been condemned to death by stoning for three religious crimes of which he was indisputably guilty: 1) *mesith,* or inducing the people to worship other gods than YHWH; 2) violating the Shabbat; 3) false prophecy.

5. Luke 13:31–32.

6. Luke 7:36 and 11:37.

7. Matt. 22:41–46; Mark 12:35–36; Luke 20:41–44; Ps. 110. That Yeshu'a here specifically denied being of Davidian descent cannot be negated. Says Dr. Klausner, *op. cit.*, p. 320, of this incident: "What, however, arouses surprise is that while Mark quotes the exposition as proof that Jesus need not be of the House of David, Matthew and Luke also quoted it, although they adduce the genealogy of Jesus, tracing his descent from the House of David through his father Joseph, who was not his father at all, since, according to them, he was born of the Holy Spirit. Thus naïve were the ancients in their traditions. Modern students can hardly trust their writings for the same accuracy and consistency called for in modern historical writings."

8. See Chap. 18, Note 12.

9. Matt. 22:15–22; Mark 12:13–17; Luke 20:20–26.

10. See Matt. 23:1–38.

11. Matt. 24:1–2; Mark 13:1–2; Luke 21:5–6.

1. Says Allegro, *op. cit.*, pp. 128f.: "At Qumrân, the Community was observing a different calendar from that in use in Jerusalem. Thus, in their eyes, all Temple ritual there was being observed on the wrong days, and its efficacy thus hopelessly impaired." The Essene calendar, according to Allegro, consisted of twelve months of thirty days each, with one day intercalated for each of the seasons, making 364 in all and exactly fifty-two weeks. Thus, festivals will recur on exactly the same day each week of the year, as ordained in "The Heavenly Tablets." This calendar is the main preoccupation of the book of Jubilees, a great favorite of the Essenes of Qumrân, as we know from the no fewer than ten fragmentary copies of it found in the Fourth Cave. Adds Allegro: "Furthermore, scholars have recently discovered that this old Jubilees calendar has a history going right back to the Exile, being used probably by Ezekiel, the priestly redactor of the Pentateuch, the Chronicler to whom we owe the book of Chronicles, Ezra, and Nehemiah."

2. Gen. 1:14–19.

3. See Allegro, *op. cit.*, pp. 132–133, for an interesting discussion of Mlle. Jaubert's proof that the Essenes began the year on a Wednesday, celebrated Passover on that day, and considered it the Shabbat.

4. *Cf.* Mark 14:1–2: "Now the Festival of Passover and Unleavened Bread was only two days off; and the chief priests and the doctors of the law were trying to devise some cunning plot to seize him and put him to death. 'It must not be during the festival,' they said, 'or we should have rioting among the people.'"

5. Goldin, *op. cit.*, p. 374, comments on the attempts to reconcile the conflict between John and the Synoptics, in which, according to John 13:29, 18:28, and 19:31, Yeshu'a and his disciples ate the Last Supper on Nisan 13th, instead of the night of Nisan 14th (already Nisan 15th by Jewish reckoning, since the day ends at sunset). These "harmonizers" have tried to prove that the Last Supper as described by John was actually Passover (as the Synoptics state it was), despite the fact that John says (13:29 and 18:28) it was not, and declares in so many words (19:31) that the Crucifixion took place on the Eve of Passover. Commenting on these efforts to make John say what he actually doesn't, Goldin writes: "The commentators and apologists have, of course, been at a loss to overcome the objection raised by many scholars that the priests at the Temple would have refused to offer the paschal lamb a day ahead of the prescribed time."

6. Writes Schonfield, *op. cit.*, p. 127: "Gallant and ingenious efforts have been made to reconcile the conflicting statements [*i.e.*, that the Last Supper was P'sach and eaten on the 14th/15th Nisan as per Matthew, Mark, and Luke; or an ordinary evening meal eaten on the 13th, as per John], one of the more recent suggestions being that while Jesus was crucified on Friday, Passover eve according to the official lunar calendar, he and his disciples kept the Passover on Tuesday evening in conformity with the Qumrân solar calendar."

Despite Dr. Schonfield's condescending tone, this writer is convinced that for the Sanhedrin to carry out its normal procedure in such cases (as opposed to the utterly impossible violation of every known Jewish and Roman law depicted in the Gospels), Yeshu'a and his disciples had to sit down to their Passover just before sunset on Tuesday, Nisan 12th; remain seated until after sunset, thus making it, according to Jewish custom, the beginning of Wednesday, Nisan 13th; go up to the Mount of Olives and be arrested on Nisan 13th. Or else there simply wouldn't have been time to try Yeshu'a at all before Nisan 22nd, since trials on the Eves of Festivals and during the Festivals themselves were forbidden by sacred Jewish Law. To contend that the Pharisees, at least, in the Sanhedrin who were outraged by Yeshu'a's repeated violations of the Shabbat (for which they could have stoned him twenty times over, if they hadn't been both forbearing and merciful) would have violated in the most serious fashion that same Sacred Law in order to do away with him, is to talk nonsense, or worse, to fall into the anti-Semitic prejudices of the surely Gentile authors of our present Gospels. This writer, as at least a nominal Christian, contends that it is high time that the Church stop teaching nonsense and actively promoting this sort of unhistorical immorality.

Says Allegro, *op. cit.*, p. 165: "If Jesus and his followers had been following this sectarian practice [*i.e.*, to celebrate Passover as the Essenes did] they, too, would have been partaking of their meal on Tuesday night. There would thus have been ample time for the arrest and trial before the day of Preparation, Friday, according to the official calendar which John would seem to be using for his account of the events. This is certainly an attractive suggestion for a way out of the chronological difficulties, and is not without its support in ancient Judeo-Christian tradition."

The most recent, at least partial, confirmation of this belief comes from the JB, footnote p. 59, Gospel According to St. Matthew: "Note: The Dead Sea Scrolls have recently revealed a community which, following a solar calendar, always celebrated the Passover supper on a Tuesday evening. It is possible that Jesus did the same. If so, the Synoptics have fitted into a few hours juridical process which in fact took days."

7. Writes Allegro, *op. cit.*, p. 129: "One of the most hated innovations of the Hellenistic movement was the introduction of the Greek lunar calendar. Naturally . . . day to day intercourse [*i.e.*, with the Hellenistic world] made standardization of the calendar absolutely essential, but the Sect [the Essenes] *and other conservative bodies* [this writer's italics] saw this as just one more step in the abandonment of the faith of their forefathers and fiercely resisted it." To this writer, it seems indisputable that one of the conservative bodies would be the Pharisees, from whom the Essenes differed only in degree in their teachings, while the Sadducees, who disbelieved in a life after death, and cooperated with the Romans, would go along with the lunar calendar as they did with most Hellenistic innovations.

8. The writer freely admits that this turn of his plot is more than a little doubtful; it is based on his conviction that the Last Supper took place on Tuesday, before which someone surely sacrificed the lamb.

9. Lev. 16:5–10.

10. Lev. 16:20–22.

11. Thus, at least, he is called in John 13:2–3.

12. Matt. 26:26–29; Mark 14:22–25; Luke 22:17–18. Since John contends that this was an ordinary supper, eaten on a different day, three years later, he has no record of these commands at all.

13. Says Dr. Klausner, *op. cit.*, p. 329: "But it is quite impossible to admit that Jesus would have said to his disciples that they should eat of his body and drink of his blood, 'the blood of the new covenant which was shed for many.' The drinking of blood, even if it was meant symbolically, could only have aroused horror in the minds of such simple Galilean Jews; and had he expected to die within a short time, he would not have been so disturbed when death proved imminent."

14. Writes Goldin, *op. cit.*, pp. 540–541: "This time they understood their Master perfectly, that one of their group would betray him into the hands of men, to be killed. This contention is proved by the testimony of this witness (Luke XXII:23) that the disciples nonchalantly inquired among themselves, 'Which of them it was that should do this thing?' Yet this witness asks you to believe that these saintly men, chosen by Jesus himself to be his Apostles, were neither grieved nor angered, nor did they make an attempt to find the scoundrel, but disregarding their Master's words, they began to quarrel among themselves as to who would be considered worthy of succeeding him!"

The present writer finds it perfectly clear that all such evidences of Yeshu'a's omniscience, even the story of Shimeon Kepha's triple denial, are later additions to the Gospel story, therein placed to still the Christianoi's wonder at how the Son of God could have been so painfully, pitifully ignorant of all the things he should have known. The story of the disciples neither lifting a finger nor voicing a rebuke against ish Kriyoth after Yeshu'a had revealed that the Judean disciple was going to betray him is beyond the credulity of any rational man. But then, this writer suspects that rational men are very seldom religious.

15. Deut. 16:7–8.

16. See Klausner, *op. cit.*, pp. 330–333; and Goldin, *op. cit.*, p. 331, for their convincing demonstrations of the impossibility of there ever having been a garden called Gethsemane.

17. Luke 22:35–38, says they had brought two swords. To defend "the Prince of Peace"? To turn the other cheek with? Or for lopping off ears, like any other band of revolutionaries?

18. Luke 22:43–44.

19. Luke 22:52–53.

20. Mark 14:51–52.

21. Says the Talmud (Rosh Ha-Sh. 31 a, Shab. 15 a, Ab. Zar. 8 b): "Forty years before the Destruction the Sanhedrin left the Chamber of the Hewn Stone and took its abode in the Booths." That is, in Yeshu'a's own lifetime.

22. John's contention (18:16–17) that the woman was guarding the door herself is worse than ridiculous under such circumstances.

23. Babli, Shabbat 10 a; Maimonides, *Hilkot Sanhedrin*, III:1.

24. A Baraita, quoted in Babli, Sanhedrin 88 b. See Sanhedrin I, Halakah 4.

25. Luke 22:66.

26. Here the writer feels that the account in John 18:12–18 makes much sense. Something like this must have happened for Simon Peter to be admitted into the courtyard.

27. Luke 22:63–65; Mark 14:65; Matt. 26:67–68.

28. Mishnah, Baba Kamma VII:7.

29. As in Mishnah, Yona 1:8, for example.

30. Says Klausner, *op. cit.*, pp. 340–341: "But the Sadducees themselves would not have conducted even a simple judicial enquiry either on the night of Passover, or on the first day of Passover (the feast of unleavened bread); the Mishnah lays it down that capital cases may not be judged on the eve of a Sabbath or on the eve of a festival to avoid delay should the case not be finished that day, since all trials were forbidden on a Sabbath or a Festival." To support this view, Dr. Klausner quotes from no less than five Talmudic texts.

31. Mishnah, Sanhedrin V:5; Maimonides, *Hilkot Sanhedrin*, XII:3. While these rules were put into writing long after Yeshu'a's time, they were certainly in force orally at the time of the Second Temple.

CHAPTER XXVII

1. Matt. 26:60 and Mark 14:56 both state that "many" came forward to testify against him. Both add, however, that the testimonies offered were "false" and "did not agree." While these assertions may be very comforting and even useful to the theology of whoever the authors of these two Gospels were, the fact remains that if it were really the intention of the lesser Sanhedrin to put Yeshu'a to death, they could have called (and probably did) hundreds of witnesses to testify to his repeated violations of Sacred Law on points clearly punishable by death. It is difficult to accept the view that the leaders of the Jewish Nation tried to convict a man upon clumsy, trumped-up charges, none of which, as described in the Gospels, was even actionable under Jewish Law, when, as is also attested to by those same Gospels, they had so many real ones for which he could have been executed.

2. Mishnah, Sanhedrin IV:5; Maimonides, *Hilkot Sanhedrin*, XII:3. The reader may legitimately object that these rules had not been codified in the time of the Nazarene; but to that, Goldin, *op. cit.*, p. 411, has an overwhelmingly convinc-

ing answer: "It would be well to bear in mind that the rules of law and procedure contained in the Mishnah compiled by Rabbi Judah ha Nasi, which forms the basic digest of the *lex non scripta*, were not proclaimed by an executive or legislative body. The entire system of jurisprudence had been in the process of development, orally transmitted, through the centuries long before the time of the Nazarene. Any student of jurisprudence knows that no system of law and procedure, especially one as elaborate as that of the Mishnah, can be worked out in such minute detail overnight. It is evolved by a natural, slow process, at times painfully gradual, extending over many years."

3. Mishnah, Sanhedrin VII:5.

4. Mark 14:58; Matt. 26:61–62. Neither Luke nor John mentions these charges. John, in fact, has no account of a trial by the Sanhedrin, but only of a questioning of Yeshu'a by Annas ben Seth, Doyen of the Priesthood.

5. This latter, stricter view is found in the Mishnah, Shebout IV:13, as a Baraita quoted in Babli, Sanhedrin 56 a. According to Rashi (and Sanhedrin 56 a, s.v. *al shem hammeyuhad*), the *Shem Hammeyuhad*, the real and unutterable Name of God, consists solely of the unpronounceable YHWH; but Maimonides extends the term—and hence the possibility of blasphemy—to the four letters ADNY, which are generally pronounced "Adonai" and are always substituted for YHWH orally. See Maimonides, *Hilkot Abodah Zarah*, II:7. The Christian reader may find it difficult to believe, but the name Yahweh or Jehovah found in Christian editions of the Bible is a nonsense word formed by arbitrarily adding random vowels to YHWH, which has not, and has never had, any oral pronunciation at all.

6. For instance Luke 4:41, 8:28; and Matt. 14:33. The clearest example of the crime of *mesith* is Matt. 16:13–19. Other references to Yeshu'a's assuming the powers of a deity (also *mesith* under the Law) are innumerable: forgiving sins, Matt. 9:2–6; Mark 2:5–7; Luke 5:20–21; saying that he could control the angels, Matt. 13:41–42, 24:31; Mark 13:26–27; Luke 12:8–9; giving Peter the keys to the Kingdom of Heaven, Matt. 16:19. These examples should suffice to explain to the thoughtful reader the actual charge that may have been made against Yeshu'a, which the Gospels, written by foreigners, perhaps innocently assumed to be blasphemy.

7. Matt. 12:1–8; Mark 2:23–28; Luke 6:1–5.

8. Matt. 12:9–14; Mark 3:1–6; Luke 6:6–11.

9. Who later defended the Apostles before the Sanhedrin. See Acts 5:33–42.

10. Matt. 15:11–12; Mark 7:14–19; Luke 11:37–41.

11. Matt. 5:31–32; Mark 10:2–12; Luke 16:16–18.

12. See Note 8 above.

13. John 9:1–6, 14.

14. Deut. 18:20–22.

15. Maimonides, *Hilkot Sanhedrin*, XV:13; Mishnah, Sanhedrin XI:1.

16. Deut. 13:1.

17. Exod. 20:8–11.

18. John 18:14.

19. See Deut. 13:2–6 and 18:20–22.

20. Babli, Sanhedrin 9 b, 25 a; Ketubot 18 b; Yebamot 25 b.

21. Babli, Baba Kamma 90 b; and Maimonides, *Hilkot Edut*, V:8; both emphasize this essential and humane precaution against injustice.

22. Thus Mark 14:61. The accounts in Matthew 26:63–66 and in Luke 22:66–71 are impossible. Matthew has the High Priest commit what is tantamount to blasphemy in open court by demanding that the prisoner swear by God, and asking him if he is the Messiah, the Son of God, a concept inconceivable to a Jewish jurist of the Second Temple Period. Both Matthew and Luke (as well as Mark) have him rend his garments at hearing what under Jewish Law was no blasphemy at all, and then state that no further witnesses need be called as Yeshu'a's own words have convicted him, a total impossibility under Talmudic

Law. The writers of the Gospels were both ignorant and prejudiced, a terrible combination, as all of subsequent history has proved.

NB. In this chapter, the writer has accepted the traditional view that Yosef ben Kaiapha (the Caiaphas of the Gospels) was the Nasi, or President, of the Sanhedrin in the time of Yeshu'a. But he feels it only fair to add that many Jewish scholars, supported by a strong Talmudic tradition (Babli, Shabbat 15 a, quoting a Baraita), hold that Gamaliel, the great and liberal grandson of Hillel the Elder, was President of the Sanhedrin which tried the Nazarene. Their arguments—including the fact that Gamaliel was the first to be called *Rabban*, "Our Master," a title which was reserved only for the Presidents of the Sanhedrin—are very persuasive, especially when the doubtful historicity of the Gospels is taken into consideration.

CHAPTER XXVIII

1. See Goldin, *op. cit.*, pp. 462ff., on this point.

2. There is further evidence that the authors and/or editors of the Gospels were all Gentiles, and probably Greeks. Since they had *Gerontes* (elders) in their *Gerousiae* (senates), they assumed the Jews had them, too. Actually, men of extremely advanced age were forbidden to sit in either of the two Sanhedrins lest their senility affect the justice of the Court. (Babli, Sanhedrin 17 a; Maimonides, *Hilkot Sanhedrin* II:3). Moreover, the Hebrew word *Zeken* (elder) was never a title, but a distinguishing appositive modifier, to avoid confusion between two men having the same name, just as we say John Jones, Senior, and John Jones, Junior.

3. Luke 23:2 and 23:5. Matt. 27:12 merely says "—and to the charges laid against him by the chief priests and the elders, he made no reply." The charges themselves are left unstated. Mark 15:4 states: "And the chief priests brought many charges against him." And puts in the mouth of Pilate the words: "Have you nothing to say in your defense? You see how many charges they are bringing against you." Again the nature of the charges is not stated. John 18:28 through 19:1–16, in a scene that is pure *Alice in Wonderland,* has Pilate ask the Jews what charges they have brought against Yeshu'a, to which they make the reply: "If he weren't a criminal, we wouldn't have brought him before you"—a piece of insolent nonsense for which the real Pilate would have had the lot of them flogged. Then, apparently being clairvoyant or telepathic, Pilate, who up until that moment had heard not one accusation whatsoever against the Nazarene, asks the accused: "Are you the King of the Jews?" To which Yeshu'a answers: "Is that your own idea or did somebody tell you this?"—enough to make a man like Pilate crucify him forty times over. But then the writer of the Gospel According to John often shows clear symptoms of paranoia, so let us leave his absolutely impossible version of these events and return to Luke. We have to as far as the trial is concerned. There simply isn't any other version that makes the remotest sense.

4. Luke 23:2.

5. Matt. 27:19.

6. Luke 23:6–12. Most scholars have doubted the possibility of this, considering the time element involved. If we follow the Synoptics' timetable, it is clearly impossible. Luke makes the Sanhedrin meet at dawn, try Yeshu'a, take him to Pilate, who tries him again, acquits him, sends him to Herod Antipas in another part of the city, who questions him at length, sends him back to Pilate, who tries him again, acquits him again, proposes to let him off with a whipping, gives way to the mob (the Pilate who had already slaughtered hundreds of people, and was to slaughter hundreds more, giving way to a weaponless mob, as if he did not have three whole cohorts of the Legion at his side!), and then sends Yeshu'a out to be crucified—all this before noon, which oddly resembles the speeded-up movements of an early motion picture.

But, if we follow the new hypothesis that Yeshu'a and his disciples used the Essene/Jubilees calendar, some such delay becomes essential rather than superfluous. For if, as it seems to this writer he must have been, Yeshu'a were brought before Pilate on Nisan 14th, the Eve of Passover, then, unless a day's delay ensued, John's date for the Crucifixion, Passover Eve, Friday, Nisan 14th, 33 c.e., is correct, rather than the Synoptics' Passover, Friday, Nisan 15th, 30 c.e.

Since all Gospels agree that the Crucifixion took place on a Friday, the difference of three years between John and the Synoptics is due to the fact that John states that this Friday was Passover Eve, and the Synoptics that it was Passover. So great is the fascination that the Nazarene has exercised upon Western man that several first-class astronomers—notably Schram, Ginzel, and Westberg—have devoted careful study to the question, calculating the day of the week, of the month, and even the hour of the day that the moon became full in the years during which the Crucifixion could have occurred. In 30 c.e., the full moon occurred on Thursday, April 6, at 10:30 p.m., which, since April 6 is not the vernal equinox, made it necessary for the Jews under Sacred Law to celebrate Passover the next night, Friday, April 7, which became for them Nisan 15th, and Passover. But in 33 c.e., the full moon fell on Friday, April 3, at 5:13 p.m., which, since it wasn't the vernal equinox either, made Passover fall on the next day, Saturday, April 4, the Shabbat. So, for John to be right, Yeshu'a had to be crucified three years later than the Synoptics say he was. John's text bears this out; the numerous comings and goings up and down the country fill three years.

This writer's objection to John's timetable is the historical impossibility of a man's doing what the author of this Gospel—surely a Greek, and possibly John the Elder, certainly not Yohannan bar Zebediah—makes Yeshu'a do and stay alive under the political conditions then extant in Palestine for as long as six months, much less the three full years that John makes his mission last.

Yet, if we follow Allegro's (and others') Essene/Jubilees calendar theory and have Yeshu'a brought before Pilate on Nisan 14th, we are confronted with the major difficulty that, if we accept the Synoptics' timetable, that day was a Thursday. Now there is no question but that Yeshu'a was executed on a Friday. How then to account for the days' delay? To this writer, Luke's tale of Pilate sending Yeshu'a to Antipas provides the solution. Of course it was illegal for Pilate to send Yeshu'a to Herod Antipas. But it was also illegal for him to beat the brains out of the people who protested his seizure of the sacred Temple Fund to build his aqueduct, illegal to bring the Signa of the Legions into Jerusalem, and to slaughter four thousand Samaritans on their Holy Mountain—all of which Lucius Pontius Pilatus did. What this writer is seeking in this work is truth—not Gospel.

7. See Goldin, op. cit., p. 470, for a masterly discussion of this point.

8. In 48 b.c.e.

9. This is in all probability exactly what Pilate said. See Klausner, op. cit., p. 113, for a discussion of this bitterly ironic word-play. See also Matt. 27:15-16, NEB. This text, despite the JB, should read: "There was then in custody a man of some notoriety called Jesus bar Abbas. When they assembled, Pilate said to them, 'Which would you like me to release to you—Jesus bar Abbas, or Jesus called the Messiah?'" The care with which this version has been suppressed in the later manuscripts leads one to suspect that there was more to it than the relatively harmless "Jesus, Son of the Father," and "Jesus, called the Christ." As Klausner points out, the popular scandal surrounding Yeshu'a's birth was widely believed, if not actually confirmed.

10. John 18:36-38. This is, of course, literature, not history. But it is magnificent literature, as so much of John is. Which is why this writer could not resist including it.

NB. The portrait of Lucius Pontius Pilatus, Procurator of Judea, as presented in this work, is so widely at variance with the picture of the thoughtful and compassionate man presented in the Gospels, that the writer is aware that devout readers will have difficulty accepting it. Therefore the writer offers them two quotations:

Luke 13:1–2: "At that very time there were some people present who told him about the Galileans whose blood Pilate had mingled with their sacrifices. He answered them: 'Do you imagine that, because these Galileans suffered this fate, they must have been greater sinners than anyone else in Galilee?'"

A letter from King Agrippa I to Caligula, as quoted by Philo, *De Legatione ad Caium*, Sec. 38—"He [Pilate] feared lest they might in reality go on an embassy to the Emperor, and might impeach him with respect to other particulars of his government, in respect to his corruption, and his acts of insolence, and his rapine, and his habit of insulting people, and his cruelty, and his continual murder of persons untried and uncondemned, and his never-ending, and gratuitous, and most grievous inhumanity."

CHAPTER XXIX

1. See Goldin, *op. cit.*, pp. 343–344.
2. See Lev. 21:5 and 19:27–28.
3. Klausner, *op. cit.*, p. 350, has an erudite discussion of what plant the "Crown of Thorns" was woven from.
4. Luke 23:28–31.
5. Matt. 27:55–56.
6. Mark 15:40–41; Luke 24:10.
7. All the Gospels disagree as to what female followers of Yeshu'a were present at the Crucifixion. All four agree that Miriam of Migdal-Nunaya (Mary Magdalene) was. The Synoptics all agree that a certain Miriam, mother of Yaakob and Yosef (Mary, Mother of James [in some versions called "the Younger"] and Joseph), was also there. None gives any clue as to whom these personages were, and Luke does not even list this Joseph, calling this woman simply, "Mary, Mother of James." To this list, so far common to all the Synoptics, Matt. 27:55–56 adds "the Mother of the banim Zebediah" ("the Mother of the sons of Zebedee"), without giving her name. Mark 15:40–41 does not list the Mother of Zebedee's sons, but does list a certain Shelomith (Salome). The JB assumes that this Shelomith is the Mother of the Boane Ragsha, Zebedee's sons, but there is not one shred of evidence for this assumption. Luke 24:10–11 lists neither the Mother of the Boane Ragsha nor Shelomith but replaces them (her?) by a certain Yohannah (Joanna), presumably the same Yohannah previously identified as the wife of Antipas' steward, Chuza.

Only John 19:25–27 contends that Yeshu'a's mother was present, and adds to the list her sister (Yeshu'a's Aunt Miriam, wife of Klopah ["Mary, wife of Clopas"]). In other words, John asks us to believe that in one single family there were two sisters bearing the same name. Further forgetting the fact that Miriam had four living sons and at least two daughters (theology had not yet invented either the Virgin Birth or the Dogma of the Perpetual Virginity of the Holy Mother), John turns her over to "the Beloved Disciple" as though she were left homeless by Yeshu'a's death. And—as this writer has attempted to indicate in the text of this chapter—John's lack of knowledge of how female, maternal human nature normally reacts to tragedy is appalling!

8. Matt. 27:44; Mark 15:32.
9. Luke 23:39–43.
10. Extremely doubtful. Only John 20:24–25 specifically states that Yeshu'a was nailed to the cross, though by stretching implication to its limits Luke 24:39 might be held to sustain him. Crucified victims were usually bound to the cross with ropes.
11. And not "My God, My God, why have You forsaken me?" If Yeshu'a knew the Bible at all—as clearly he did—he knew it in Hebrew, for in his times no Aramaic translation of it had yet been made. Psalm 22, which scholars have always assumed he quoted here, begins, "Eli, Eli, lamah asabtani," which does mean,

"My God, My God, why have You forsaken me?" It is difficult to believe that a man dying on a cross would indulge in translation; but if he did, the correct Aramaic translation of "Eli, Eli, lamah asabtani" is "Elahi, Elahi, metul mah shebaktani." Or possibly, "Elahi, Elahi, lema shebaktani . . ." which is closer to the Hebrew.

But according to the Gospels, he said neither. Matt. 27:46 has: "Eli, Eli, lama sabachthani." And Mark 15:34 has: "Eloi, Eloi, lama sabachthani." Both differ markedly from the Hebrew verse in Psalms, and even from its Aramaic translation.

Hence, asks Goldin, *op. cit.*, p. 508, why assume he was quoting at all? Suppose rather that he was voicing a terribly human and heart-rending protest against a God so monstrous that He could sacrifice His own Son to Himself to appease His own wrath, which is after all what Christian theology claims he did. For *sabachthani* is not Aramaic, as scholars have blithely assumed: It is Hebrew, a combination of *sabachtha* (to sacrifice, to slaughter, to kill) and the pronominal suffix *oti*, "me." The conclusion is inescapable: Yeshu'a was not quoting Psalms, and he died in despair.

To these passages this writer also assigns importance in another connection: as proof that the crowds at the trials and the Crucifixion were largely non-Jews. Beyond the fact that no Jew would have cried out "Crucify him!" since that death was considered an abomination, no Jew would have confused the word *Eli*, God (Hebrew), or even *Elahi*, God (Aramaic), with *Eliyahu* (the name "Elijah" in both languages), as the spectators do in Matt. 27:49 and Mark 15:35–36.

12. Whether the myrrh was offered before or after Yeshu'a was on the cross is irrelevant. What is relevant is the fact that myrrh, a strong stimulant, would have increased his sufferings. We know from other sources that the offering of drugged wine was a merciful gesture, like blindfolding the eyes of prisoners before the firing squad today.

13. Here, for once, John 19:29 makes more sense. To have a bystander run and fetch a sponge (from where?), hold it to Yeshu'a's lips on a cane (where would he have got the cane?), as Matt. 27:48 and Mark 15:36 have him do, strains credulity. But the Roman soldiers normally had javelins or lances or spears with them, and they were accustomed to quench their victim's thirst with sour wine held to his mouth by a sponge fixed on spear point—not out of mercy, but so that he would live and suffer more.

14. Matt. 27:50–54; Mark 15:33 and 38; Luke 23:44–45.

15. Semahot II:9; Sanhedrin 63 a; Moed Katan 14 b; and Maimonides, *Hilkot Sanhedrin*, 13:4.

16. John 19:31–35. Here John must be followed. His details are irresistibly persuasive. The only trouble is that he's just as persuasive when he is writing provable nonsense, and plain damned lies.

17. Mark 15:44.

CHAPTER XXX

1. Matt. 28:10.

2. Luke 24:49, which is a flat contradiction of the command given in Matt. 28:10 above.

3. John 21:15–23.

4. John 19:30.

5. Matt. 27:3–5.

6. Exod. 21:22; Zech. 11:12–13.

7. Acts 1:18–20.

8. Or the other three, if we grant the strong possibility that Acts was written by a disciple of Loukas rather than by the Physician himself. For neither Mark, Luke, nor John has any account of Judas Iscariot's subsequent fate. The conflicting accounts in Matthew and Acts (Notes 5 and 7 above) are clearly fruits of a wish-fulfillment psychosis.

9. Some of the tombs there have recently been excavated and can be seen by visitors to Jerusalem.

10. And not Rabboni or Rabbuni, as John 20:16 has her say. The title is *Rab*, "Master." Adding the pronominal suffix *oti* to it gives us *Rabbi*, "My Master." But *Rabban* means "Our Master." So adding *oti* to it, as John does here, would give us "My Our Master," which is nonsense. The writer/editor of John knew no Hebrew at all.

11. This is an assumption. The writer has been unable to find any explanation of why Toma was called "the Twin."

12. Luke 24:13–32 and probably also Mark 16:12–13. Mark is the earliest Gospel; John the latest. The unbemused reader can see how the tale grew and grew from Mark's stark and simple account to John's majestic theology.

13. John 2:25.

The writer hopes that, in one way or another, you have enjoyed this book.

The Author

Frank Yerby, who was born in Augusta, Georgia, in 1916, now lives in Spain. He was educated at Haines Institute, Paine College, Fisk University, and the University of Chicago. In 1947, the publication of his first book, THE FOXES OF HARROW, brought him instant recognition and he has since published nineteen other best-selling novels, several of which have been made into films. JUDAS, MY BROTHER, his twenty-first book, is the product of thirty years of intensive research.